D0936793

The
Reluctant
First Lady

The
Reluctant
First Lady

Venita Ellick

BROWN BOOKS
PUBLISHING GROUP

Hillside Public Library

© 2013 Venita Ellick

All rights reserved. No part of this book may be used or reproduced
in any manner without written permission except in the case of brief
quotations embodied in critical articles or reviews.

This is a work of fiction, which is neither endorsed nor connected
to any persons, businesses, or organizations. Names, characters,
businesses, organizations, places, events, and incidents either are
the product of the author's imagination or are used fictitiously. Any
resemblance to actual persons, living or dead, events, or locales, save
those allowed by law, is entirely coincidental.

The Reluctant First Lady

Brown Books Publishing Group
16250 Knoll Trail Drive, Suite 205
Dallas, Texas 75248
www.BrownBooks.com
(972) 381-0009

A New Era in Publishing™

ISBN 978-1-61254-113-6
LCCN 2013939405

Printed in the United States
10 9 8 7 6 5 4 3 2 1

For more information or to contact the author, please go to
www.VenitaEllick.com

This book is dedicated to the four men who
have enriched my life beyond measure:
my husband, David, and our sons,
Eric, Michael, and Sean

Author's Note

In this book, I have used real newscasters and comedians to report on completely fabricated news and situations that occur in the book. The conversations and jokes expressed by them are purely fictional. This story has no direct or indirect connection to them in any way.

Prologue

amn it, Ashley, be reasonable." Michael raked his hand through his hair.

"Reasonable? You've got to be kidding. I've never lied to you. From the beginning, I've made it abundantly clear I'm not interested in being involved in your political life. Why do you refuse to believe me?" Ashley shook her head in despair.

"I agreed to campaign on your behalf because I believe in you, Michael. I know if you're elected, you'll be a great president. But not once have I said I would give up my job and follow you to Washington. It's not like I'm going to change my mind at the final hour. I've said it from the beginning, and you and your campaign team need to deal with it. The public should know that I'm not part of the package. I feel dishonest every time I appear on stage with you. When are you going to let everyone know the truth?"

Ashley watched Michael's jaw stiffen. After more than two decades of marriage, she knew the signs of his anger every bit as well as he knew hers. She could read his facial expressions and body language like a road map. He didn't vocalize his displeasure or anger to the public or those he worked with; it wasn't his nature. Usually only his family saw his emotional side.

"You realize your decision could harm me politically and could hinder my ability to be an effective president. I'm not asking you to give up your career. I'm just asking you to put it on hold while I'm in office. I know that's asking a lot. I know how dedicated you are to your career and how you love the museum. Other First Ladies have had careers they loved, but when their husbands entered politics or were elected, they stepped up to serve their country right alongside them."

"Michael, this isn't about duty to my country. I never offered to serve; you did. I've never liked politics; you do. I love you and I want this for you because I know you'll be an amazing president. But all this is your dream, not mine." Ashley touched his arm, trying to bridge the gap growing between them. "Please, tell your team the truth. The longer you wait, the more likely someone will find out, and the press will have a field day."

"I can't believe you aren't going to change your mind. We've reached crossroads before where we've held differing opinions, but you've always compromised for the good of our marriage and our family's sake. If I'm elected, maybe you'll see things in a different light."

Ashley shook her head. "Not this time. You're making a mistake if you think I will."

Michael sighed and tried to smile at his beautiful but very stubborn wife. "We should get back out there. The results should be announced anytime. Otherwise they may begin to suspect we've been in our room for more than a break," he teased.

"Before we go, I want you to know, if this country is as smart as I think they are, you will be the next president of the United States. I'm so proud of you. I wish I could be what you want me to be, but I just can't. I've said it repeatedly throughout the years—politics is a dirty field of play, and I want nothing to do with it.

"Now, let's go see if things are still going in your favor." Ashley stopped him before he opened the door to the outer suite. "Honey, I really do want you to win. I am and have always been your biggest supporter."

1

huck, sorry to interrupt," Brian Williams cut in, "but NBC has just called the race in favor of Senator Michael Taylor. California has put Senator Taylor over the top, giving him the two hundred and seventy electoral votes required to win the presidency. To repeat, NBC has just called the presidential race in favor of Senator Michael Taylor. He will become the forty-fifth president of the United States."

Ashley watched as pandemonium erupted in the hotel suite. Her family and Michael's campaign team cheered, clapped, and exchanged hugs. They were overcome with the kind of exhilaration and elation that follows a long, hard-fought campaign. For the last eighteen months, they'd worked tirelessly because they believed the best candidate, the best man for the country's highest leadership position, was the intelligent and ethical man who'd just been elected.

Despite her earnest and impassioned exchange with Michael earlier, Ashley was the first to reach him. She put her arms around her husband's neck. "Mr. President, let me be the first to congratulate you." She hugged him tight and kissed him while she whispered in his ear, "I never doubted you for a moment. Now, the real work begins, eh?"

Jeremy, who was as tall as his father and just as good-looking, said, "My turn," as he jostled his mother aside and hugged his father. "It's nice to know our system of government works. The best man ruled the day after all. Yea for democracy." Jeremy, who was as exhausted as everyone else, even for a healthy twenty-one year old, started chanting a silly "Go Dad, Go Dad, Go Dad" in a syncopated rhythm imitating a geeky dance move that involved circling his fists in front of his body.

Juliette, Jeremy's twin, kissed her father's cheek. "I'm so proud of you, Daddy. Now, the country will know what we've always known—what an incredible man you are. I'm sorry I bitched about all the hard work and the fact that you were never at home. Have you given any thought as to how you're going to deal with Mom's decision?"

"Not yet, but don't worry, we'll figure it out." Less than five minutes had passed since the presidential race had been called, since his elation had soared, since the euphoria in the room had carried him into a warm embrace and, with lightning speed, dumped him back in reality.

He looked over at Ashley and wondered what he could say that would change her mind. Throughout their twenty-four years of marriage, they'd had many discussions about their goals and professions. Their love for one another was rooted deeply, and despite their differences, they were each other's best friend and confidant. They'd always supported one another's passions. For Michael, it was politics; for Ashley, it was art and being the director of a prestigious museum. How could they, or anyone, have known when they were starting out just how far each of them would go in their respective professions?

Champagne was served to everyone in the room. Ed Branton, Michael's campaign manager and future chief of staff, announced a toast. Ed raised his glass, "To the next president of the United States. May he learn, despite his work ethic, that there really are only twenty-four hours in a day. To you, Mr. President."

Everyone raised a glass to salute the newly elected president and then downed the cold, bubbly beverage. The adrenaline in the room was running at a fevered high, and the excitement and exuberance began to energize even the most exhausted in their midst.

Jack Sutton, the campaign's communication director and future press secretary, announced, "Michael, President Nelson is on the line. He'd like to speak to you."

Everyone present knew what the phone call meant. Concession. Michael walked over to Jack and took the receiver.

"Hello, Mr. President. Yes, I just heard the news. Thank you." Michael listened to President Nelson, knowing everybody wished he would put the call on speakerphone.

"I appreciate that," Michael responded. "I'll be looking forward to working with you during the transition. I wish you and your family nothing but the best. Thanks again. I'll see you tomorrow."

Michael turned to the room full of expectant faces. "President Nelson has offered us full cooperation as we transition into the White House, so we can hit the ground running.

"Now, if you'll excuse me, I'd like to look over my acceptance speech one last time."

He wasn't normally nervous before a speech, but the seed of reality his daughter had planted in his mind about Ashley kept nagging at him, and he wanted some time alone. He wondered, now that he'd been elected, what Ashley was thinking.

Ashley had been wonderful on the campaign trail. She had taken time away from her busy schedule at the museum to go on the road to support him. She had been magnificent, and he appreciated all of the time she'd given him. There had been several times she was unable to appear with him, but fortunately her absences hadn't been that obvious. It was imperative that the two of them sit down as soon as possible and hash this out.

With his speech polished to his satisfaction, they headed down to the ballroom.

Ashley had the twins in tow—although at their height and age, it looked more like they were pulling her along. Ed and Jack were organizing the rest of the presidential party that would appear on stage after he'd given his acceptance speech. Everything had been choreographed for Michael's appearance before the crowd gathered in the ballroom and for viewers watching at home.

As the elevator descended to the ballroom floor, Michael could see Ashley was deep in thought. He wished he had time to take her aside and find out what was going through that lovely head of hers. The expression on her face was extremely readable to him. She didn't like acting a part, and the mere fact that she was appearing with him on stage was most likely the cause for her pensive expression.

Just give me tonight, he silently prayed. Then, we'll have a chance to talk and try and work through our differences.

2

*B*ehind the curtain, Michael waited with his family for their stage cue. The heavy brocade curtains did little to suppress the noise generated by his loyal supporters. The throng of people, so exuberant in its display of emotions, began to cheer and chant "Taylor, Taylor, Taylor."

The First Family stepped onto the stage to thunderous applause. The sound of camera lenses snapping and lights flashing from thousands of cameras gave the stage a surreal quality reminiscent of a sixties psychedelic light show. Television crews and reporters inched forward to capture the moment for the majority of the voters who were at home watching the proceedings on television.

The next First Family worked the stage, walking first to one side and then the other. The networks used the time to continue their commentary about the president-elect and Mrs. Taylor.

NBC's Brian Williams began. "The wait is over. Here we have our next president of the United States, Senator Michael Taylor, and his lovely wife, Ashley, accompanied by their twins, Jeremy and Juliette.

"President-elect Taylor so far has a 52 percent lead over President Nelson's 48 percent, which is far outside the margin predicted by the polls."

Tom Brokaw cut in. "Some interesting background about President-elect Taylor. Many of you may know he did his undergraduate work at the University of California at Davis, receiving degrees in both political science and sociology. He went on to the University of California at Berkeley's Law School, Boalt Hall, where he graduated at the top of his class. He was promptly recruited by the San Francisco district attorney's office.

"He's had a meteoric rise in politics. After working for the district attorney's office for four years, he ran for Congress and won. He served three terms as a congressman from California and would probably have been re-elected if Senator Jim Burke hadn't died. With Burke's Senate seat available, Governor Feinman selected Representative Taylor to serve as Burke's replacement. He readily won the special election to fill the senator's seat, then ran for another term, and won again."

Savannah Guthrie added, "Mrs. Taylor is also very accomplished. She attended UC Berkeley and has a bachelor's degree in art history and a master's degree in museum studies. She's worked for the Cameron Museum of Art's chain since she was in graduate school while also giving birth to their twins. That took a lot of juggling. I'd say she's one dedicated woman when she wants something. It's rare to see two such high-powered careers in one family. I'd like to know their secret for keeping everything in balance."

Brokaw added, "The twins are twenty-one. Their son, Jeremy, is in his fourth year at Berkeley. He's majoring in criminology while Juliette attends Stanford and is an environmental studies major. I wouldn't relish being in their home during any football games between the two rival schools. One can only imagine the competitive atmosphere that occurs during those times. Maybe that's how President-elect Taylor became such a gifted politician. He's had to run interference between his children all these years."

As the president-elect kissed his wife and hugged his children before they left the stage, Fox News weighed in.

Sean Hannity announced, "President-elect Taylor comes into office with very little political experience. He's the third youngest president to be elected. He has no executive background or foreign policy experience. This leaves our country vulnerable on many levels, despite picking a senior and experienced senator as his running mate."

Bret Baier added, "I'm sure it was Senator Hughes's overall experience, and specifically his leadership on the foreign relations and appropriations committees, that made him the top choice for the vice-president slot. Still, it amazes me that President-elect Taylor got elected with such little political experience. Although it's hard to deny his charisma. I don't think anyone would argue with that."

Bill O'Reilly smiled and shook his head. "He's eye candy. He got the women's vote because of his looks. The Democratic Party is always trying to revive the Kennedy legacy of Camelot. With President-elect Taylor and his beautiful wife, Ashley, they've come as close to achieving that goal as possible."

Hannity nodded in agreement. "I think it should also be noted that the newly elected president is the first president to have graduated from Berkeley's Boalt Law School. Coming from Berkeley, does that tell us anything about the direction the future president might try to take this country?"

O'Reilly said, "Look, coming from Berkeley, which is well known for being very left of liberal, I think pretty much guarantees us that President-elect Taylor will have a strong liberal, socialist agenda."

As Ashley and the twins left the stage, Michael approached the podium. As the newly elected president stood waiting to speak before the jubilant assembly, he reflected on the steady and deliberate path that had brought him to this particular moment in time. He'd campaigned hard on his unwavering belief in the American people and the democratic system of government. He hoped he'd conveyed his integrity each time he spoke, no matter the size or composition of his audience. He believed the timing for his place in the roll call of presidents was perfect.

The handsome president-elect smiled at the exuberant crowd and spoke his first words,

"I want to thank you all . . ."

3

Backstage, Ashley was tormented with guilt for the part she was playing in what she believed was an elaborate ruse. She hated that she'd been put in this position, hated that she was going to throw a monkey wrench into her husband's new administration, and mostly hated that she'd allowed this deception to go on for so long.

She walked over to where Ed and Jack were standing. "I know you don't want to deal with the position I'm taking in regards to being the First Lady, but there's got to be some way to break it to the public. Michael convinced you if he was elected, I would change my mind. That's not going to happen. I went along with all of you during the campaign, but now Michael's been elected, and I really believe it's time to let the public know."

Ashley noted the expressions on Ed's and Jack's faces. They looked as if Ashley were a cobra ready to strike. It wasn't funny. Nothing about this situation was funny, but for some reason, their facial expressions reminded her of the words from a nursery rhyme she used to read to her kids. "Run, run, as fast as you can; you can't catch me, I'm the gingerbread man, I am, I am." Michael had run and had won; there would be no more running.

Ashley was aware that Jeremy and Juliette had flanked her sides. They were determined to weigh in on anything their mother had to say. Good grief, you teach them to talk when they're little, and when they grow up, they argue and become opinionated and never shut up.

"Mom," Juliette said, "please, think about what you're doing. Won't you change your mind? How often does your husband get elected president? Can't you give up your career just for a little while?"

"Do you know what you're asking, Juliette?" Ashley said. "Would you expect your dad to give up his political career for my job? Probably not. I hope if I've taught you anything, it's that as a woman you have the right to choose your own path. You don't have to follow in a man's footsteps. Just because I'm a woman, the first thing people assume is I should give up my career. That's completely unfair to me. I've worked every bit as hard to get where I am today as your dad has worked in his career."

Juliette tried again, "But, Mom . . ."

"No, Sis, Mom's right." Jeremy jumped into the fray. "Mom's never lied. The reason this is all so convoluted is because she's the first one to take this position. I agree with her. Just because something has always been done a certain way doesn't mean it's right or wrong, or good or bad; it's just that no one's ever challenged the status quo before."

Ed leveled a less-than-pleased look at Ashley. "You realize that your husband was just elected president, and before he's even sworn into office, you want the people who voted for him to deal with your news. Ashley, please reconsider. You're not being fair to Michael."

"I know that's what you believe, Ed. It's in the mind-set you grew up with. I understand where you're coming from. I don't want to hurt him or his administration, but this should have been dealt with from the start. Then maybe it wouldn't be such a huge elephant in the room. Will it really be so shocking for America to hear that even the president and his wife are a two-career family? I don't think you're giving the American people enough credit. Unfortunately now it's bound to become a bigger story than it needs to be. Did you all think I was going to change my mind?

"I just walked out on stage in front of most of America and acted as if we were all one big happy family; here we are, folks, the next First Family. When the news breaks regarding my decision, it's going to make me look like a liar and a traitor to my husband. Neither of those scenarios sits well with me. We should have been up-front from the beginning.

"I don't want to ruin this night for Michael. But, please, start trying to figure out how to deal with this. I'll be heading back to New York in a day or two, and people are going to want to know what's going on. I feel like we're already behind the eight ball."

Applause and pandemonium broke out on the other side of the curtain, indicating Michael had reached the end of his speech.

A stage manager nodded and, with Ashley and the twins leading the way, followed by the vice president-elect, his wife, and family, she stepped onto the stage and into the bright lights. The noise from the crowd grew in intensity as each of them came into view. They all walked forward to stand beside Michael, Ashley and the twins to his left; Robert Hughes, Catherine, and their children to his right.

The chaos and elation vibrating through the crowd was intoxicating. Cheers from a wildly exuberant audience and music blocked out what individuals were saying, but the camaraderie of those on the stage was evidenced by their smiles, hugs, and claps on the back. Before the world, she and Michael looked like the perfect couple. Michael pulled his family, plus Richard and his family, toward him while photographers snapped pictures of this historic event.

Amid the excitement, it almost went unnoticed that a reporter shouted a question at Ashley. She ignored him, hoping he would go away.

The reporter repeated his question. "Mrs. Taylor, what causes do you intend to champion during the next four years in the White House?"

Ashley winced inwardly, but no outward expression marred her serene expression. She had a choice. She could tell the truth or continue to go along with the lie. Damn it. She'd been dodging questions like this for months about what special causes she intended to champion if her husband were elected. In fact, she'd become a master of evasion, not something she was proud of. Unquestionably the smartest thing to do would be to give the same canned response she'd been giving throughout the campaign. It would be a lie, all of it. But then she wouldn't be accused of rocking the boat, a boat, she might add, that she knew was taking on a lot of water.

She was tired of being evasive. She was sick to death of lying by omission. Michael's managers had convinced her that he wouldn't be elected if she declared her intentions. But, Michael had been elected. Was it possible that she was making more of this than necessary?

She leaned toward the reporter and his microphone and began speaking in a quiet, clear voice.

"First, I'd like to thank everyone here and at home for their incredible support throughout the campaign. I'm extremely proud of Michael and have always believed he'd be a great leader and a great president. The American people have chosen wisely and well this day. As for me, with the election over, I'll be returning to my job as director of the Cameron Museum of Art in New York. It's never been my intention to serve as the First Lady. Over half of the families in our country are two-career families. Our family isn't any different. In fact . . ."

Ashley felt Michael's hand on her elbow. "Ashley, just smile and wave. We're getting off of the stage now."

Michael turned to the audience and waved as cheers and applause continued to ripple through the gathered body of well-wishers.

As soon as they were backstage, Michael turned to Ashley. "What the hell were you thinking, answering that reporter's question?"

Ashley was quiet for a moment. She felt like she was having an out-of-body experience. Had she really chosen to answer? She let out a pent-up breath. "I guess I was thinking you've been elected and it was okay to be honest. I've lived up to my part of the bargain. But, no more. I'm tired of living a lie. I just can't do it anymore. You strategized every aspect of your campaign, but never once did you discuss how to convey to the public that I wasn't part of the package. We've been over this more times than I can count. Did you think I was kidding?"

"I hoped that by being on the campaign trail with me, you'd see all the wonderful things you could accomplish and have a change of heart. Now, instead of enjoying my victory, I'll have to start dealing with damage control."

Everyone standing around backstage wasn't sure what to say. Finally Jeremy broke the silence. "Mom, Dad, we're gonna head up to our rooms." Jeremy stepped forward and hugged his mother while his sister simultaneously hugged their father. "We'll see you both in the morning."

Jeremy's reaction to his parents jump-started the rest of the group into action.

Richard Hughes turned to Michael. "We'll need to discuss this as soon as possible."

Ed Branton agreed. "We need to meet tonight, right now. I'm quite sure that piece of footage of Ashley talking to the reporter is already all over the airwaves. Station managers and newspaper editors are going to be having wet dreams. We need to devise a strategy for damage control now."

Michael nodded. "Let's meet in my suite in about thirty minutes. I want to react swiftly and with confidence. Ed, you and Jack get the campaign advisory team together and meet me upstairs."

"Will do," Ed responded.

Ashley was well aware that Michael was furious. She wondered how long she'd have to wait before the explosion came. She'd always been truthful. She'd never misled him or offered false promises. Still she felt guilty and hated that she did. Why did life and relationships have to be so complicated? She'd never wanted her husband to define who she was, and she'd be damned if she was going to allow that to happen now.

4

As they rode the elevator up to their penthouse suite surrounded by the secret service, Ashley felt cramped. It was probably more mental than physical discomfort. This was yet another thing she'd have to get used to. The secret service had been assigned to them during the campaign, but she supposed she thought of them as temporary. Now that Michael had been elected president, the Secret Service would become a permanent fixture in their lives. Michael would always be surrounded by an entourage of Secret Service and staff except when they were in their private rooms. God, how she hated that thought and wished for the bazillionth time that Michael had a normal job like everyone else.

Michael was in disbelief. He couldn't believe Ashley had responded to the reporter. He tilted his head back, resting it on the wall of the elevator, and closed his eyes. He was exhausted. He'd spent the last eighteen months crisscrossing the country multiple times delivering his message of hope to the American people. He wondered if her recent revelation was going to change his ability to carry out his goals.

Once they were safely ensconced in their suite and it was just the two of them, Michael released the explosive breath he'd been holding since Ashley had made her declaration to the reporter. He reminded himself to breathe: inhale, exhale, inhale, exhale. He walked over to the mini-bar and took out a cold beer and with great and deliberate care opened and poured the amber liquid into a glass. He was trying to focus on this simple task while his brain was attempting to put some sort of order to the cumulus clouds of thoughts forming in his mind.

His emotions were raging, an experience with which he was fairly unfamiliar. He was a man who prided himself on maintaining control during times of crisis and dealing with problems that arose in a reasonable and thoughtful manner. He was successful in this endeavor, except when it came to dealing with his wife. His public image was that of a very even-tempered, thoughtful politician, but no one could push his buttons like Ashley. She was the only person who saw the other side of his nature—Ashley and, occasionally, the twins. Tonight he felt as though he were navigating his way through a minefield.

He'd reluctantly succumbed to her refusal to be part of his political life from the beginning. After all, he couldn't hog-tie her and throw her over his shoulder and make her do what he wanted although the thought was tempting. However, in all of their conversations, in all of the years of her refusing to be part of his political life, they'd never factored into the equation just how far he might go in politics—or how far she would go in her profession.

He looked over at Ashley, who appeared to have found a safe haven at the end of an overstuffed sofa. Her eyes were closed, and her head was resting on the back of the sofa. She looked relaxed, but he would bet good money her brain was running like a high-speed Internet connection.

He was gradually calming down and regaining control over his emotions. He thought he could have a reasonable conversation with her now without trying to strangle her. "Ashley, why did you choose tonight to answer the reporter? You've been dodging questions like that for months. What were you thinking? You realize the consequences are going to be catastrophic for me. I can't believe you'd be so thoughtless."

Ashley knew it was pointless to respond. She knew exactly where this conversation was heading, and it wasn't going to be even remotely civil. In an exhausted voice, she answered, "I didn't plan on undermining your election night. My response wasn't premeditated. I'm just sick of all the deception. For months, I've been dodging the same question. I guess tonight I'd reached the end of my rope, and I wasn't interested in tying a knot and trying to hang on. The election is over, you've been elected, and I suppose I thought just maybe the public won't care if I become First Lady or not. We're not living in the dark ages, you know. Millions of families have two working spouses."

Michael interrupted her response. "What you fail to realize, what you've always failed to realize, is that politicians and their families are held to a different standard than other people. We're expected to portray the perfect family."

"Give me a break. I know you believe everything you're saying, and it may, in fact, be true. But did you ever stop to think that it *will* always stay that way unless someone challenges these ridiculous beliefs?"

"I'll be the first to admit how unreasonable the perception is, but that's the way it is. Your mini-rebellion isn't going to change it. You, and most assuredly I, are going to be crucified tomorrow. Every newscaster and blogger will be weighing in.

"Ed, Jack, Richard, and my team will be here in a few minutes. We need to figure out how to handle the crisis you've created. I can't believe . . ."

He watched as his wife closed her eyes and laid her head back on the sofa. She was shutting down.

She was a beautiful woman and at forty-four, she looked younger. He'd overheard his son's friends refer to her as a MILF often enough, which he didn't appreciate one bit. She radiated light. Her silvery-blonde hair and translucent skin glowed with vitality. She wore her hair shoulder length with wispy bangs that accentuated blue-green eyes that didn't miss much.

She looked delicate, but others, who weren't as close to Ashley, didn't realize how adept she was at using that luscious mouth of hers to whittle you down to size if necessary. She had no patience for pretense or pseudo-intellectuals. She had a genius intellect and an uncanny ability to reveal fakes and liars. She would say her crap detector was fully functional. Heaven help those at whom she decided to take aim. Michael was always intrigued that her deadly wit was so deceptively packaged within such a beautiful exterior. It was one of the traits that had drawn him to her from the beginning of their relationship way back in high school.

A knock at the door and the simultaneous ring of Ashley's cell phone interrupted Michael's train of thought. He wished he had more time to reason with his wife before he had to meet with everyone, but clearly that was out of the question now. He headed to the door to greet his team of advisors while Ashley yelled over her shoulder while disappearing toward their bedroom, "I'll take it in here."

Michael acknowledged his advisors as they entered the suite. He led them to the dining room, which boasted a banquet-size black glass dining room table. The team sat down, selecting their positions at the table as strategically as chess wizards deciding their next move. Michael offered them drinks, but all declined. Their purpose for being there didn't lend itself to the tinkling of ice cubes.

"Sorry to be the bearer of bad news, but here, you're going to want to see this," Ed began as he slid his laptop toward Michael and hit the play button. A clip of Ashley's exchange with the reporter was already on the network. "We're already behind on this story. But I think in order to reclaim the lead position, we need to hold a press conference as soon as possible. You've always been honest with the American people, and now's a good time to show them you meant it when you talked about complete transparency in your administration. Plus, maybe we can get Ashley to soften her position slightly."

Michael walked to the window and looked outside. The streets were well lit and surprisingly empty of pedestrian traffic. He identified with the emptiness he saw below. He felt empty inside and wondered how that could be when he'd just been elected president of the United States. He could never have imagined this day ending as it had. He wanted to give back to the country that had given him so much, but right this moment people were depending on him. He didn't have the luxury of trying to figure out where it all went wrong.

Decision time. He strode back to the group, smiled the half smile he was so famous for, and directed, "Schedule a press conference for first thing tomorrow morning. I've just been elected, and we're already in crisis mode. We need a plan of action immediately. The media is obviously already having a field day, and the GOP undoubtedly think manna has just landed in their lap. Let's take it away from them."

"We have to change Ashley's mind," Ed said with conviction.

"Unfortunately I don't think that's going to happen. We've discussed this ever since I first threw my hat into the ring. She's repeatedly said she wants no part of the White House or politics. It's really my fault. I should have dealt with this a long time ago. I foolhardily believed that if I were elected, she'd change her mind. And if I couldn't change her mind, I thought she'd more or less quietly slip away, back to New York and her career. Since that's no longer an option, the public needs to hear the truth from us."

No one spoke.

Finally Ed asked, "Has Ashley gone to bed, or is she available?"

"She's on the phone," Michael responded. "I'll see how much longer she'll be."

He stepped into the bedroom and interrupted his wife's conversation. "The advisory team is here, and they'd like to speak with you. Will you be much longer?"

Ashley didn't bother to cover the receiver with her hand. "It's Sienna. She says congratulations. Give me a few minutes, and then I'll be out."

Michael nodded and left the room. He could have predicted the call was from her cousin. They seemed to have an almost cosmic connection when it came to sensing when the other one needed something. Two sisters couldn't be any closer.

Sienna had introduced Ashley to him when they were in high school. Michael went to school with Sienna in Sacramento while Ashley grew up and went to school in Berkeley. He loved to tease Sienna about how she saddled him with an albatross, but she always countered with her own form of warfare. She'd married Michael's best friend, Jim, so was quick to point out that he'd done his fair share of damage to her life.

Ashley anticipated that Michael's special group of advisors would want to talk to her. She wasn't looking forward to what most likely would be a confrontation, but she wouldn't back down from it either. She turned her attention to Sienna.

"Well, the headhunters have come in search of blood and a human sacrifice. I should probably get off the phone. The more time I give them to think, the more deadly they may become."

Sienna's radar zeroed in on Ashley's voice. She could always tell Ashley's state of mind by just listening to her voice. It was like a windsock. "Go on; pick up where you left off," Sienna demanded. "I've already been on the phone with half the family. Most of them think you've lost your mind."

"Oh, I'm sure that's true; sometimes I think I've lost my mind. I also know some of our relatives probably didn't even vote for Michael. What's to say that I haven't already said a hundred times before? I don't understand why it's so hard for people to accept change. I know it's highly possible that I just started the debate of the century although that wasn't my intention. I didn't anticipate speaking to the reporter. I walked out on the stage and just snapped. It all seemed so stupid. I should have given the same stock answer I've been giving for months, but I also think this is an issue that's reached its time."

Sienna responded, "Whether it was intentional or not, you've just challenged the status quo, and it's a slap in the face of tradition. There's no way to predict how the public will respond to your being honest with them. However, if I were you, I'd pack my suitcase, grab your passport, and get out of Dodge."

Ashley agreed. "Probably excellent advice. Really, we're all speculating about how everyone's going to react, but I'm preparing for the worst. When Michael first entered politics, I told him I wasn't interested in being a politician's wife. At the time, we honestly believed we could manage everything—his career, mine, the kids. We thought we could find compromises so we could both continue to do the things we love. Neither of us wanted to stop the other from following our passions. But, God, this is a mess. I can't believe how naïve I've been. Michael has never accepted my decision not to join him in the White House. He never intended for us to work through this situation because he's been banking on me changing my mind."

Sienna cut in. "I don't envy either of you. The next days, weeks, and months are probably going to be pretty rough. Remember, I'm here if you need a safe place to land. Don't misunderstand. I do support you and your decision; I always have. But, I'm sympathetic to Michael and what he'll be dealing with too."

Ashley stood up. "I need to run. Thanks for calling. It was good to hear a friendly voice, but I might as well hit this subject head-on with Michael and his team. I've been waiting to have this conversation for a long time, so I certainly don't intend to back down now. Love you. I'll be in touch."

Ashley looked in the mirror. She braced her arms on the top of the dresser and leaned in closer to view her reflection. What was she made of? Sugar and spice? No, not anymore. She was ready to go into battle for her beliefs. She'd never wanted to be a politician's wife, but her judgment had been faulty. She thought she could have it all. She thought she could balance everything without anyone being neglected or getting hurt. Now the question was what price would she have to pay to stand up for her beliefs?

In all of the years they'd been married, she'd never stopped loving Michael. She remembered the first time she saw him. He took her breath away, although she would have died before admitting that to anyone, including Sienna. He was tall with golden brown hair and sky blue eyes and the cockiest walk she'd ever seen. He exuded masculinity from every pore of his body, but it was his exceptional intellect and hilarious sense of humor that were the pièce de résistance.

She'd also learned early in their relationship that Michael didn't have to say a word to cut her down to size. He had the ability to stop her dead in her tracks with just a look. In the early years of their marriage, she'd been severely wounded by his particular nonverbal form of warfare, but she had learned. While he fought silently, her retaliation in words made him think twice before leveling his deadly looks at her. They were evenly matched, both mindful of the effect they had on one another.

There had always been only one man for her. But how many times in their marriage had she sacrificed what she wanted in order to keep Michael happy and keep the peace? Sometimes she resented him for the times her love for him had been the impetus causing her to back down from her own goals. Time and maturity had been superior teachers. Now, more often than not, they found a way to compromise so they could both achieve their goals—until now.

5

*A*shley took a deep breath and walked into the dining room. The conversation stopped as each member of the team began assessing her in a new light. Before now, they'd always found Ashley charming and gracious. Now they viewed her as selfish and the creator of a bitch of a problem. She faced the speechless team ready for all their arguments.

She sat at the only empty chair at the table and said, "I'm guessing—just a wild guess, mind you—that you're here to make me see the error of my ways. I suppose the sooner we have this delightful conversation, the sooner we can all go to bed."

Ed took her statement as an opening. "Ashley, I don't know where to begin. You're throwing an American tradition out the window and into the faces of the very people who voted for your husband."

Ashley spoke softly. "I know that's what you all believe, but it's not what I believe. I know there's no precedent for the issue I'm forcing. I believe only fools follow tradition blindly. I'm choosing—emphasis on *choosing*—not to be the First Lady. I'm not interested in having a role thrust upon me merely because my husband has been elected president.

"I don't happen to believe it should be an expectation; it should be a choice. Each woman, or possibly one day a man, should choose what to do, not just have the role thrust upon her because that's the way it's always been done. I think the American people, when they hear my story, will possibly identify with me and not be as outraged as you think. It's not going to affect them personally, and it won't affect the president's policies.

"Wouldn't a more pertinent discussion be how to present my decision to the public without damaging Michael? Have any of you come up with a plan for defusing the situation?"

Jack answered. "We have a couple of ideas, but first let me ask you, would you be willing to postpone returning to New York? If you stay put for a while, you might help calm things down."

"How long would I need to stay? A month? Six months? A year? No matter how long I stay, when I go back to New York, this whole conversation is going to resurface. I don't think that's the solution. Michael, you need to hit this head-on, take control of the story. You're the only one who has exclusive access to me and what I'm thinking. That's an advantage. Tell the public you'll be presenting a plan to compensate for my decision during the transition process. It won't stop the pundits or the opposition party from coming after you, but it will put you a little more in the driver's seat."

"That's one solution we discussed before you joined us," Michael said. "We're holding a press conference tomorrow morning, and I'd like for you to be there."

Everyone in the room was trying to find a place to put their eyes. They hadn't expected Ashley to be so vehement. When they entered the suite, they thought they were dealing with a wrinkle that needed to be ironed out. It was clear, now, that they needed to create a whole new wardrobe.

Ed cleared his throat. "I think I'll have that drink. I didn't realize how badly I was going to need it."

Michael knew what they were up against; he had hoped someone else might be able to reason with Ashley. God knows, he hadn't had any luck. He wished they could agree on a compromise but doubted very much that they would reach one tonight, if ever. All of the diplomatic experience he had wasn't enough to prepare him for dealing with the likes of his wife.

Ed asked Ashley, "Do you see the possibility for any sort of compromise?

"That's a fair question, and I wish I were brilliant enough to find one. I've thought about this until my head feels like it's going to explode. I'm not interested in giving up my career, and I'm not remotely interested in politics. Plus, personally, I don't believe the First Lady position is a necessity. I've seen highly intelligent, educated, capable women enter the White House to become international hostesses. Important work, but not my work. Michael doesn't agree with me, but he isn't the one making the decision."

Ashley deliberately made eye contact with each person at the table. "All of you are here to support my husband, to see that he was elected, and you did an amazing job. I've seen how hard you've worked, and I congratulate you on a job well done, but my constituents are the patrons and public who visit the Cameron Museum of Art. It has one of the finest art collections in the world, and I love my job just as much as Michael loves his. So everyone here can quit hoping I'm going to see the error of my ways and change my mind. That's not going to happen. My advice is to schedule the press conference and let's get this three-ring circus underway."

Jack announced, "I'll contact the press immediately and schedule a press conference for tomorrow morning at nine. After what they heard tonight, everyone is going to be chomping at the bit to hear what you have to say officially. I also think it would be a good idea to have your son and daughter present to show family solidarity. It'll give the public and the media a chance to see that you aren't at odds over the decision within your family."

Ashley almost choked out her words. "That's not true. Of course, we're at odds over my decision. You know Michael wishes I'd fall in line. And, as for our kids, they have their own opinions."

Michael watched his wife lock horns with his communication director. "Look, there's no point in prolonging this discussion. Ashley and I will be at the press conference tomorrow, but as for the kids, I don't know. They aren't children. It'll be up to them."

Ashley added, "I'll call them and let them know they're invited, but it's their decision. I don't really see how having them there will help. I always hate it when a politician is in trouble, caught having an affair or misappropriating funds, and his handlers haul out the wife and kids to stand there looking as if they support him. It's a pathetic attempt to try to make everything look normal when nothing is."

"Thank you, Ashley," Ed said. "I appreciate you asking them. Before we go, would you like to walk through what you want to say at the press conference? Or would you prefer to work with one of our speechwriters to prepare a statement you can read?"

"Neither, thank you. I don't want what I have to say to feel rehearsed. I'd rather speak from my heart."

"I understand, but I don't think you realize how aggressive the press can be."

"There you go again, Ed, underestimating me. I didn't just come off the farm, or have you forgotten I deal with the press all the time at the museum? Granted, it's usually not over something so controversial, and the press has never been hostile to me, but I can handle it. Plus, isn't it Jack's job to control the press conference if things start to get out of control? I'll say what I have to say, and if I think a question is inflammatory or stupid, I'll refuse to answer it. I look at this press conference as a good thing. I realize none of you feels the same way, but for me, it's long overdue."

Jack stood up. "If there's nothing else to discuss, I need to get started notifying the media to set up tomorrow morning's press conference."

Michael nodded. "I think we've all had enough for one day. I'll walk you to the door."

As the leadership team left the suite, they were as congenial as ever to Michael but avoided making eye contact with Ashley. She was amused by this rather than annoyed and not surprised at all. It was so typical of politicians. You were either with them or against them. There never seemed to be any middle ground.

Ashley hoped Michael wouldn't continue the conversation they had been having prior to the team's arrival. There was no point. She needed a distraction.

"I'll call the kids and tell them about the press conference. Do you want to talk to them?"

"Only if they want to talk to me."

Ashley called Jeremy on her cell. "Hi, kiddo, it's me. How are you?"

"I'm not going to lie to you, Mom. I'm pretty depressed. I haven't come up with a foolproof way to break you out of jail—yet. I'd like to be prepared for any possibility. It'd be nice to have a plan in place."

Ignoring her son's outrageous sense of humor, Ashley asked, "And, your sister? How's she doing?"

"Ah, you know Juliette. She's a major drama queen. She's already got you and Dad divorced over this. What's up?"

"First, Dad and I would love to have breakfast with the two of you tomorrow. It would be nice to have a little family time. How about meeting us here at seven?"

"Sure, I'll tell Juliette. I know she's anxious to talk to you both."

"Good. Second, a press conference is being scheduled for nine in the morning. I'm finally going to get a chance to speak specifically about my position on the whole First Lady thing. Ed and Jack asked that you and your sister be there. Your dad and I told them the decision was yours. What do you think?"

"Yeah. I'm in, but you'll have to talk to Juliette. Hold on." Ashley could hear the mouthpiece of the phone being smothered by Jeremy's hand. He was only off for a moment. "Juliette says she's in too. How's Dad doing?"

"Here, you can talk to him yourself."

Ashley handed the phone to Michael.

"I'm here, Jeremy."

"Hi, Dad. How you holdin' up?"

"About as good as can be expected after taking a nosedive from total elation after winning the election to your mother's answering the reporter's question. It was a huge emotional shift by anyone's standards."

"Dad, I'm really proud of you. You'll be a great president. The only thing Juliette and I are worried about is how all this is going to affect you and Mom."

"Try not to worry about your mom and me. Somehow, it'll all work out. Listen, Jeremy, I'm about to drop where I'm standing. Let's continue our conversation at breakfast tomorrow."

"Sure, Dad. Goodnight."

Once Michael was off the phone, he turned to look at Ashley. She was removing her jewelry as she headed toward the bedroom. She was unaware that he was watching her. As she moved around the bedroom undressing and hanging up her clothes, he marveled at the desire she could still evoke in him.

Michael and Ashley prepared for bed in silence, deep in their own thoughts and unaware they had begun to distance themselves from one another. So much was at stake, far more than they'd ever believed possible.

Ashley sat down in a chair next to the window. She parted the curtains and looked outside at the darkness beyond. All she could see was her own reflection superimposed over the inky gloominess. It was a perfect visual analogy for her despairing mood.

Breaking the numbing silence, Ashley said, "Examining just the facts, the future does look dismal. I've never wanted to hold you back from anything you wanted to do. Likewise, I don't want to be pressured into doing something I'd despise. You've always known I dislike politics. I hate the microscopic lens directed toward politicians and their families. I simply cannot, will not, live under a microscope. I don't want people debating what I say or do or wear. People need to accept there's a difference between their right to know about their elected officials and the privacy of the elected official's family."

"You just don't get it," Michael argued. "I've just been elected president. No matter what you do, your actions, what you say, and yes, even what you wear, are going to be scrutinized, dissected, and discussed. Rejecting the official title isn't going to change that."

"I won't be a puppet on a string for you or the country. Granted, there will be a huge focus on my actions for a while, but I think as time passes, the interest in me will begin to wane and the media will move on to juicier and more relevant issues.

"I hope you know that if I did go along with you, it would kill me. My body would keep moving and I'd still smile and respond, but I'd be dead inside. I'd be like a Stepford First Lady."

Michael let the silence hang in the air. It didn't seem to matter what he said; he and Ashley didn't want the same thing. He sighed. "Your decision has the potential to cripple me in being able to effect real and positive change. Plus, you've just given the opposition a weapon to use against us. Isn't any kind of compromise possible?"

"That's the million-dollar question, isn't it? Being the director of the Cameron Museum of Art is as important to me as becoming president is to you. It's a huge responsibility, and I love every minute of it. I don't want to leave my work. We each have jobs we love—granted yours is a whopper—but at the end of the day, I'd still like us to find a way to remain a family."

Michael wanted that too, but for the time being, they were talked out. What else was there left to say?

6

Ashley was being pursued by a dozen men on horseback. She could hear the horses' hooves pounding on the solid, bone-dry earth, an indication they were getting closer. If they found her . . . She could hear the church bells beckoning from a distance. She ran toward the sound, hoping to make it to the unseen sanctuary before being captured. She didn't want to die.

She felt a hand on her shoulder gently shaking her, "Ashley, turn off the alarm."

"Hmm . . . um . . . 'kay."

As her dream world receded, reality began to take shape more clearly. She wasn't a morning person, period. She always needed awhile to shake off her somnolent state. She didn't want to talk to anyone, let alone get up and walk around. Her first word in the morning was almost always "coffee."

Michael shook her again. "Come on, sleepyhead. Up and at 'em. You'll go back to sleep if you don't get up now. It's a beautiful day."

Michael was the definitive morning person, the kind you wanted to hate but would feel small for doing so. He awoke rested and ready for what the day had to offer. Ashley thought it was unholy to wake up so cheerful, only because her internal clock swung in another direction.

She rolled onto her side, pushed herself up into a sitting position, swept her hair out of her eyes, and looked down at the floor and her legs. Again, she wondered what crazed person had set the barbaric, yet generally accepted, work day hours. She looked over at Michael, who was already dressed. He looked like every woman's idea of the perfect man, strikingly handsome while exuding a powerful masculinity. He was everything she'd ever wanted, the love of her life.

Ashley finally stood and dressed for a day that would most definitely leave its mark on her, Michael, and history. She chose a rich teal silk pantsuit with a mandarin collar and large black frog closures down the front of the jacket. The rich color was bound to improve her mood. She'd always loved unusual, vintage, and distinctive clothing. The artful designs in the items she chose never failed to boost her spirits.

A knock at the door indicated the twins had arrived. Ashley opened the door with a dramatic bow as Jeremy sauntered past with Juliette bringing up the rear. Jeremy pretended he didn't see his mother until he turned and grabbed her, lifting her off her feet while giving her a bear hug. Juliette waited until Jeremy was through with his antics to give her mother a peck on the cheek.

Jeremy was a force to be reckoned with. He had his father's good looks but his mother's coloring, fair skin and ash-blond hair, with the exception of his aquamarine eyes. He was often compared to a younger Brad Pitt. He had a devil-may-care attitude yet could slash you with his words if he so chose. He was fairly immune to the whole political scene, having cut his baby teeth on it. He admired his father and was proud of him; still, politics would be the last profession he'd choose for himself.

Juliette was more like her dad in personality. She loved to tease but took things far more seriously than her brother did. Ashley once found her at age four giving a speech to all of her dolls about the seriousness of driving without wearing seat belts. While both of their children were sensitive, Juliette tended to wear her heart on her sleeve while Jeremy either used sarcasm or took action to deal with his emotions.

They were close and communicated with one another as only twins can. They instinctively knew what the other needed and often called the other based on a "hunch." They had a strong sense of commitment and devotion to their parents and their family. They didn't want to choose sides.

Jeremy flopped down on the sofa while Juliette perched on the arm of one of the side chairs. "Do you feel like a condemned woman about to eat her last meal?" Jeremy asked.

"Not exactly, although it's so sweet of you to make that analogy." Ashley smiled at her son as she reached for the phone to call room service. "Do you know what you want for breakfast?"

Michael walked into the room. "I want pancakes and eggs and a pot of coffee strong enough to part my hair."

Ashley zeroed in on Michael's mood. Not good, not good at all. She sent a silent prayer heavenward. *Please, God, help me get through the next couple of hours.*

Michael asked, "Anyone here want to cancel on this morning's press conference?"

"Dad, I know you and Mom are going to be under fire this morning, and I'm sorry about that, but I'm glad Mom will have the chance to share her position. I think it's a good thing for America to know that even the president and his family disagree on issues. The idea that politicians have this perfect Norman Rockwell family is ridiculous," Jeremy said.

"It may be ridiculous to you. Unfortunately it's what's expected for the president and his family and for anyone with a political career," his father said..

Jeremy sighed. "We know you were born for this job, but Mom shouldn't have to do something she hates. Maybe this will turn out to be a good thing. It's just possible some people will relate to her. Maybe the time is right. But I wouldn't rule out the fact that she could end up on the FBI's Most Wanted list."

"And, if that were to happen, I'd expect you to figure out a way to keep me one step ahead of the law," Ashley grinned.

"I hate the fact that my decision is causing such chaos, and I'm truly sorry for any negativity it's generated toward you, Michael. I know what I said last night came as a shock to those who heard it. Hopefully I'll have the chance to explain my position with more clarity this morning. I'd be lying if I said I wasn't nervous about today and the future, but I have to have faith that somehow everything will work out."

Juliette shook her head. "I agree with Dad on this. Sorry, Mom. I know how much you love your job and the museum, but I don't see why you can't put that on hold while Dad is in office. It doesn't get any bigger or more significant than being the wife of the president of the United States. I don't think anything is more important than supporting him right now."

At times like this, Ashley wished she hadn't encouraged her children to speak their minds. She knew she had only herself to blame for their opinionated responses. Jeremy was heavily involved in social justice while Juliette was more traditional like her dad. Therefore, conversations around the kitchen table were full of passionate opinions and arguing. Nature versus nurture theorists would have a field day analyzing their family dynamics.

Breakfast arrived. For a while they were just an ordinary family sharing a meal and catching up on the news about their lives. Ashley loved having the kids around. They never failed to cheer her up with their banter on every topic from politics to movie trivia. Their conversation was a welcome relief from the turbulent political waters swirling around them.

An unwelcome knock on the door interrupted their small, momentary family oasis. Ed rushed in carrying a couple of newspapers. Anticipation and dread followed him into the room and chased normalcy out, kicking the door shut behind it.

Ed began, "It's pretty much what we expected. The headlines read, 'Taylor Wins! Mrs. Taylor Declines!' The other papers have some version of the same headline. Fox News is crucifying you and Ashley. MSNBC isn't damning you, but their opinion varies depending on whom you're watching, and network news is fact-checking like mad to understand what's happening. At the press conference this morning, you both need to lay it out for the American people how this decision came to be, how you're going to handle it, Michael, etcetera." Ed shook his head as he looked down at the headline again.

"Dad, what are you thinking?" Juliette asked.

Michael shook his head and pressed his lips firmly together. "I'm thinking what a mess this is. I'm thinking how I wish your mom wanted to serve as the First Lady, and I'm naturally wondering how all of this is going to affect my presidency. The newspaper's headlines only confirm what I already knew. The country isn't ready for your mom's position, and they may never be. They want a First Lady, and she's throwing the role and tradition in their faces. No one is going to take this lightly."

Jeremy jumped in before his mother could say anything that would escalate the animosity that was growing in the room. "We all agree. The headlines and newscasts only confirm what we suspected. I don't think anyone here thought the press was going to praise Mom for her decision. Won't a more accurate assessment of public opinion come after Mom's had a chance to speak her piece at the news conference this morning?"

No one spoke.

Ashley broke the silence by addressing her children. "Maybe you should reconsider attending. There's no reason to have you mixed up in this mess.'"

"I'm going," insisted Jeremy.

"Me, too," echoed Juliette.

Ashley realized Michael was watching her, or rather she felt as though he were dissecting her. She could see nothing in his face or body language that indicated a positive attitude.

She knew she was to blame for this crisis, but she also knew she had to ride out the storm without capitulating at the first sign of criticism.

She'd always known the path she'd chosen wasn't going to be easy, and she knew it would become a lot worse. Her stubborn streak was already getting rod stiff and unyielding. She was upset and frustrated but knew heightened emotions right now would serve no purpose. Staying calm and resolute for the press conference was imperative.

As if he were immune to all of the family dynamics, Ed announced, "It's time to go down to the ballroom. Ashley, you have just enough time to change your clothes, if you hurry."

Jeremy started laughing, which temporarily broke the tension in the room. He was waiting to see what his mother was going to say.

Ashley smiled and cocked her head to the right. "Is there something wrong with what I'm wearing, Ed? Perhaps a Nancy Reagan red suit or Barbara Bush pearls would be more to your liking?"

"Of course not. What you're wearing looks beautiful. Although, truthfully, I'm used to seeing First Ladies dressed more traditionally."

"Whoa on the whole First Lady thing. Instead of worrying about how I'm dressed, don't you think we should get going?"

Michael stood. "Ashley, may I see you in the bedroom for a minute before we go?"

Without waiting for her response, he began walking toward the back room.

"Everybody breathe. He's not going to murder me while you're here. Too many witnesses. We'll be out in a minute."

Once Ashley closed the door to the bedroom, she turned and looked at Michael. She could feel the fury radiating off of his body in waves.

"There's still time for you to change your mind. There's no shame in having a change of heart. No real harm has been done, yet. Just a lot of rumors flying around."

Ashley shook her head. "I'm not going to change my mind, Michael. I wish I could spare you the pain and embarrassment I'm causing you, but I can't live in your world. I love you. It's politics I can't stand."

Michael didn't respond to his wife's declaration. Whether she realized it or not, they were adversaries. Without another word, he turned and left the room.

"Well, that went well," Ashley said out loud.

Part of her wanted to run to Michael and fix things. It would be so much easier to give in to the pressure and do what everyone wanted her to do. Unquestionably, if she did what was expected, she'd be operating on remote control and would only be going through the motions of having a real life. That seemed okay with everyone else as long as she didn't rock the boat. If she did what they wanted, they might as well put her on Prozac now.

She walked out of the bedroom with her head held high. "Everyone try to relax. No matter how pushy or belligerent the press may get, I can deal with it. We'd better head down to the ballroom and get this party started."

7

As Michael and Ashley approached the ballroom, a secret service agent stepped forward to open the door. The media stood and began applauding. Ashley was aware that the twins had stepped behind and were following them to the platform. Her heart was pounding so hard she could hear her pulse in her ears. So much was at stake. What she said next and how well she could convey her sincerity to the public were crucial.

Other emotions were warring inside her too. She felt a good deal of righteous indignation over being in the middle of this controversy. Was she truly the first president's wife to have these thoughts? Perhaps others had, but she was the first to act on them. As Michael and the twins took their seats on the dais, Ashley stepped into place next to Jack at the podium.

Jack spoke briefly, setting the tone for the press conference, and then introduced her. Ashley looked at the reporters who were waiting for her to begin. She got the fleeting impression of an impending feeding frenzy when chum is thrown into water full of sharks, only in this instance, she was the chum.

"Good morning, everyone. Thank you for coming to a quickly scheduled news conference. I'm thrilled my husband was elected president. I truly believe he's the best man for the job. I love him and always want to offer him my support. I treasure my role as his wife and the mother of our children. But what you've most likely heard is true. I don't intend to assume the role of First Lady, which is the reason we've scheduled this conference. We wanted you all to hear the truth about the situation and be able to ask the many questions we assume you have."

A low, continuous sound arose from the reporters as they shifted in their seats, whispered to the reporter sitting next to them, and leaned forward a bit more to hear Mrs. Taylor better. Their eyes shifted quickly from Ashley's face to President-elect Taylor's in an attempt to gauge his reaction to her statement. There was none.

"My decision was not made lightly or on a whim. While I've never been interested in politics, I strongly believe Michael will be a great president, which is one of the reasons I campaigned for him so vigorously over the last year. It's never been a secret that I don't enjoy politics or being in the political arena.

"My passion is art and, as many of you know, I'm the director of the Cameron Museum of Art in Manhattan. I love my job, and I don't believe I should have to give up what I love any more than I would expect my husband to give up his interests for me. Now that Michael has been elected, I'll be returning to New York.

"Isn't it time to ask the question: Is the First Lady role a necessity or merely a byproduct of being the wife of the elected president? I believe that each woman, and someday man, should have the choice of whether or not they want to be part of their spouse's political life. I don't believe it should be a foregone conclusion.

"Previous First Ladies have considered it an honor to work alongside their husbands and have championed many important causes while their husbands were in office. We've been very fortunate to have First Ladies who were so passionate and dedicated to their work, and I salute them.

"Except for tradition, why does this have to be so complicated, so shocking? We're already a nation of two-career families. That's not new. We already have commuter marriages where husbands and wives live in different cities due to their jobs. That's not new. Isn't it time for current family dynamics and traditions to intersect with past, established customs? Or in other words, isn't this an issue whose time has come?

"I hope in the days and weeks to come, you'll begin to recognize my decision isn't so implausible but actually has merit. Thank you for your time. If you have any questions, I'll be happy to answer them."

Jack stepped forward to handle the avalanche of questions. He pointed to a reporter. "Chuck, your question?"

"Mrs. Taylor, do you think it was fair to the American public to withhold this information prior to the election?"

Ashley adjusted the microphone. "I don't think it was a matter of fairness. It wasn't pertinent, in my opinion. The public was electing a president, not a First Lady."

Jack pointed to another reporter. "Stan, your question?"

"Mrs. Taylor, other educated, professional women have been in your shoes, yet they chose to become the First Lady and work alongside their husbands. Why can't you do the same?"

"Again, I believe that whether or not the spouse of the president steps into that role should be a choice, not a foregone conclusion."

Stan pushed for another question before Jack could call on someone else. "If art is your passion, wouldn't you have more impact working on a national level than working at the Manhattan museum of art?"

Ashley leveled a determined look at the reporter. "I think it comes down to how you want to interact with your passion. As the director of the museum, I deal firsthand with all the details associated with art collections: procuring, exhibiting, storing valuable art, exchanges with other museums, over-seeing research projects and educational programs, fund-raising, and writing grant proposals and journal articles. Plus our museums promotes art internationally, not just here at home. I like the hands-on aspect of my job. I'm not interested in being a figurehead. I'd rather be in the thick of things."

Jack called on another reporter.

"Mrs. Taylor, do you realize the negative impact your decision could have on your husband's presidency?"

Ashley smiled. "Did you vote for my husband? No, don't tell me; that was a hypothetical question. I don't think you're giving Michael as much credit as he deserves. He's very smart and resourceful and an excellent problem solver. Why should my decision have a negative impact? I believe that's faulty thinking. My husband's decisions on key issues have nothing to do with whether or not I'm living in the White House. My choice becomes an issue only when others make it an issue."

"Sherry, your question," Jack indicated with a nod of his head.

A female reporter stood. "Forgive me for being blunt, Mrs. Taylor, but is there a problem in your marriage?"

Jack stepped forward to take over, but Ashley stopped him from commandeering the microphone.

Ashley stared the woman down. "That's exactly the kind of assumption I expected.

"Michael and I do not have a problem in our marriage. We don't agree on the position I'm taking, but I'll let him tell you that himself. The bigger concern I have is that you immediately jumped to that conclusion. I fully expect when I return to New York that rumors will begin to circulate about our marriage. They won't be true, but that won't stop the rumor mill. I love my husband and he loves me. People can agree to disagree and still love one another."

Jack covered the microphone with his hand and turned his back to the audience of reporters. "I think I should stop the questions and let Michael talk."

Ashley whispered, "I'd rather my portion of the press conference not end with that question. I'd like to answer one more question."

Jack nodded. He turned, announced there was time for one more question and called on another reporter.

"Mrs. Taylor, would you be more specific about what you plan to do or not do regarding the role of First Lady?"

"First, I don't think of myself as the First Lady. I'm not going to live in the White House except when I come to visit my husband. I have an apartment in New York, and like many other commuter marriages, Michael and I will live in two cities. I will commute back and forth between the two residences, just as I have while he was in Congress.

"When I'm here, I'd rather spend time with Michael away from all of the political and social influences. However, I'll definitely be at the inauguration and all of the activities surrounding it. Plus, it's possible I might attend some formal dinners when I'm here after that. I'm sure circumstances will arise that I can't anticipate at the moment. I feel confident that as new situations come up, Michael and I will find ways to work through them. My time is up. Thank you for listening."

Ashley turned and sat down next to her husband and children.

Jack introduced Michael. "Now, President-elect Taylor would like to say a few words."

Michael stood and went forward to the microphone. "Good morning. I hope you got a better night's sleep than I did."

The reporters laughed and shook their heads.

Michael continued. "I'm sure you're all wondering what I think about Ashley's decision." He looked out at the sea of reporters, and they were nodding their heads.

"First, I'd like to address a question that was directed to my wife regarding whether this information was deliberately withheld from the public during my campaign. The answer is no.

"While I knew Ashley wasn't interested in politics, she campaigned for me ardently. She worked as hard as anyone to help get me elected. I had hoped through her involvement in the campaign that she would want to join me in the

White House. Not until after the election did she make her intentions finally clear.

"I believe previous First Ladies have been tremendous assets to their husbands' administrations and we, as a nation, have benefited from their work. My wife wants something different, and I'm trying to honor her decision. I can't exactly drag her by the hair to the White House, now, can I?"

Laughter broke out again among the reporters.

"I recognize what a surprise this must be to the American people because this is the first time the wife of a president has declined to be involved in her husband's presidency. But, in actuality, whether she likes the label or not, she is and will be the First Lady as long as I'm president. Her rejection is aimed only at the traditional role past First Ladies have filled; however, I have great faith in my administration. Certainly it'll take some getting used to, but in the end, we'll reorganize certain responsibilities that past First Ladies have handled. The days ahead will bring greater clarity as to what type of needs exist and how best to fill them."

Jack called on another reporter.

"Congratulations on your overwhelming victory last night. Would you clarify your position on Afghanistan?"

Jack immediately stepped in. "This isn't the time for questions regarding policy issues. Additional press conferences will be scheduled at a later date to discuss other topics. Thank you all for coming."

Michael, Ashley, and the twins exited the ballroom. When they were out of sight and earshot of the reporters, Jack asked Michael, "Would you like to meet now to debrief the press conference, or would you prefer to do it later?"

Michael's face was like a steel mask except for the flexing

of his jaw muscle. "Schedule a meeting for later, say in an hour back at our headquarters. I want to escort Ashley back to our suite. I'll see you in an hour."

In another part of Washington, Ted Hoffman, Speaker of the House and a member of the opposition party, turned off the television and smiled at the other men in the room. "A huge gift has just landed in our lap. It's time to hold a press conference of our own."

8

*T*he reaction to the early morning press conference was swift and varied as network news, cable news channels, special interest groups, and even late-night comedians weighed in with their opinions. Within minutes of the press conference, a media frenzy had begun and a national debate was underway.

NBC News
"President-elect Michael Taylor and Mrs. Ashley Taylor just concluded a press conference in which it was confirmed that Mrs. Taylor does not intend to uphold the duties of the First Lady. Mrs. Taylor stated she'll be returning to her job as the director of the Cameron Museum of Art in Manhattan, one of the most prestigious museums in the nation. At the press conference this morning, one day after Taylor was elected by a significant majority, Mrs. Taylor had this to say."

The tape rolled as millions of viewers watched Ashley give the speech she'd delivered earlier outlining the reasons for her decision to return to work in New York.

Brian Williams noted, "This is a completely unprecedented situation that raises many questions and observations." Williams turned to address Tom Brokaw. "I really don't know what to say. It's such surprising news. I'm sure as we receive additional information, we'll see how the White House intends to respond."

Brokaw concurred. "It's very unorthodox. First Ladies have served alongside their husbands since the founding of the presidency in 1789. The only exception was when James Buchanan was president. He wasn't married and asked his niece to fill in as hostess for the White House. Most First Ladies have tended to champion causes they were interested in that were relevant to their times. Mrs. Taylor will be the first president's wife who has refused to accept the traditional role."

Matt Lauer weighed in. "It makes one wonder if there isn't more to the story than we're hearing. This news seems to have come out of nowhere. Surely there must have been some understanding between President-elect and Mrs. Taylor."

Brokaw added, "I think it's too soon to speculate about anything at this point. What we do know is that past First Ladies have worked alongside their husbands while they were in the White House and sponsored many noble causes such as ending childhood obesity, literacy, human rights, and healthcare reform. The list of causes goes on and on.

"In Mrs. Taylor's case, she says she enjoys a more hands-on approach in regards to the arts and finds that infinitely more rewarding than heading up any type of national program."

Williams spoke again. "To wrap things up, we were just informed that Mrs. Ashley Taylor, the wife of President-elect Taylor, does not intend to assume the role of the First Lady. She will be returning to New York and her job as the director of the Cameron Museum of Art. Stay tuned for additional news regarding this unparalleled turn of events. Back to you, Matt and Savannah."

Fox News

"I'm still shocked that Mrs. Taylor is rejecting her role as America's First Lady. She's thumbing her nose at a tradition that's over two hundred years old."

Sean Hannity continued. "You have to wonder why President-elect Taylor even bothered to run for office knowing his wife's position. And don't think for one minute he didn't know. They may try to tell us that, but don't you believe it. He knew."

Bill O'Reilly interjected, "I wonder what's wrong with her. There's got to be something wrong with a woman who blatantly throws a position of honor that has been bestowed on her back into the very faces of the good American people who voted for her husband.

"Here's the first example of what electing a Berkeley-educated, bleeding-heart liberal into the White House looks like. Now he and his wife are showing their true colors. Their behavior is clearly outside the mainstream values. Who does she think she is?" O'Reilly asked.

"Maybe she's doing it to bring publicity to the museum of art she's so fired up about. I mean, anything's possible with a woman who would do something like this. Maybe we should have another election. I wonder who'd win if we had a 'do-over' election now that this has been made public," Hannity joked.

O'Reilly added, "I'd like to point out how Mrs. Taylor was dressed for today's press conference. I mean she practically had on a kimono. She's untraditional in every sense of the word. Maybe it's a good thing she's refusing to become the First Lady. What kind of role model will she be for our children?"

MSNBC

"Yowza," Rachel Maddow cheered. "It's about time someone brought this issue into the forefront. Personally, as a woman, I'm proud of her. I think she's setting a wonderful example for other women and young girls.

"Data from the Department of Labor shows us that out of the one hundred and twenty-two million women ages sixteen and over, seventy-two million women, or 59.2 percent, were labor-force participants in the United States with 74 percent of those working full-time.

"Mrs. Taylor's decision is important on two fronts. First two working partners is the norm in most American families today. She's showing that's also true in the White House. Second she's a shining example that a woman can choose what she wants to do. You don't have to go along with tradition or what's always been done. Progress is what this is all about. We should be continuing to evolve as a nation, and Mrs. Taylor's decision shows us we are, in fact, still evolving.

"I applaud her. I don't know if I'd make the same decision if I were in her shoes, but that's one of the points she's making. Just because her husband got elected to the presidency doesn't mean she should automatically have to give up her job. Just looking at the facts, the position of the First Lady doesn't affect foreign policy or legislation. The job is mainly ceremonial. So, why is this so alarming? This is clearly an issue whose time has come. If a woman were elected president, would our nation expect her husband to be the official White House host? Good for her. Finally, a woman who thinks for herself and is willing to stand up for her beliefs."

Opposition Party Headquarters

Speaker of the House Ted Hoffman squinted against the glaring lights focused on him as news reporters aimed their cameras and microphones so as not to miss his reaction to the President-elect and Mrs. Taylor's press conference.

"I think I speak for the majority of Americans when I say this is a travesty directed at an American tradition. If President-elect Taylor can't influence his wife to accept her role as the First Lady, what are his chances of influencing others to pass needed legislation? Our country was founded on family values, and Mrs. Taylor is casting stones at those very values.

"One wonders how we will be viewed around the world. Our good name may diminish due to Mrs. Taylor's rash decision and President-elect Taylor's inability to reason with his wife.

"Who will welcome foreign dignitaries and their wives to the White House? With Mrs. Taylor turning her back on the job, we have no First Lady to act as a national hostess.

"Personally I believe President-elect Taylor should consider whether or not he can serve effectively as the leader of our great nation. This turn of events clearly indicates he's not ready to govern our country."

National Organization for Women (NOW)

The president of the National Organization for Women, Patricia Donaldson, faced the cameras. "I just have a short statement to make regarding Mrs. Ashley Taylor's decision to return to work in lieu of assuming the role of the First Lady.

"Personally I'm glad I've lived long enough to see this day come. I agree with Mrs. Taylor: becoming the First Lady should be a choice, not an expectation. There is no right or wrong in this decision.

"I would also like to congratulate President-elect Taylor. While he doesn't agree with his wife's decision and would obviously prefer for her to join him in the White House, he recognizes her right to make her own choice. I know how hard it must be for him to be under such immediate controversy so soon after the election. I admire him greatly for accepting his wife's decision."

Later that night, the late-night talk shows joined the national debate.

The Daily Show with Jon Stewart

"I think we all know the top story of the day is Mrs. Taylor's rejection of the First Lady position. I say, shame on you, Mrs. Taylor, shame on you." Jon smiled his sweet, sarcastic smile while shaking his finger at the camera.

"Who wouldn't want to have such a wonderful job? Let's see, just examining the facts, previous First Ladies have come into office as intelligent, educated women and are turned into fashion icons, trendsetters, and hostesses. I'm sure every father is happy to pay the tuition for a good college education to see his daughter turned into a hostess at Applebee's.

Oops." Stewart covered his mouth with his hand and giggled. "I meant to say First Lady."

Stewart swiveled in his chair and looked earnestly into a different camera. "We all know how much Jacqueline Kennedy was loved and admired. Here is some old news footage we found of her after being in the role of the First Lady for just one week."

An old NBC News Time Capsule interview of First Lady Jacqueline Kennedy showing off the White House to the press begins running. Her voice is light and whispery.

Stewart continued with straight-faced sincerity, "I'm not accusing Mrs. Kennedy of being on any mind-altering drugs—that would be libelous. I'm sure she was just very relaxed with all of the lights, cameras, newspeople, and millions of viewers focusing on her every word. Wouldn't you be? But, after only one week of being the First Lady, they turned an intelligent, articulate woman into a tour guide."

Late Show with David Letterman

David Letterman stood before his audience with his hands in his pockets. "Did you hear today that Mrs. Taylor, the wife of our new president, says she doesn't want to be the official First Lady or live in the White House? I find that interesting. Don't you, Paul?"

Paul Shaffer began playing "Hail to the Chief" and let the strains dwindle into silence. "Yes, I find that very interesting."

Letterman continued. "Well, we got to thinking. Why wouldn't you want to live in the White House? I mean it's a national monument, for God's sake. Here are some reasons Mrs. Taylor may have decided to forego living in a national monument.

- Everything in your house is a hand-me-down.
- Tours come through your house daily.
- Trying to get a good parking spot is a bitch.

"I'll bet you can never get a good parking spot at the White House." Letterman grinned. "I'd hate that. Next.

- You can't run around in your pajamas.
- You can't paint your house any color you want.

"Here again, don't you hate it when you live in a neighborhood and there's some kind of organized rules saying what color you can paint your house? If I want to paint my house lime green, it's my business.

- Creepy secret service guys are always around talking into their wrists

"And finally,

- Your favorite take-out restaurant won't deliver to your address."

Michael's advisors turned off the bank of television sets with the prerecorded newscasts they'd been watching. Each of the networks, the cable news channels, and the special interest groups were all true to form in their opinions and responses. It was going to take some quick thinking, a lot of tact, and a little luck to put the unleashed monster back in its cage, if that were even possible.

9

After the press conference, Michael and Ashley were unusually quiet as they returned to their suite. Maintaining their public persona of togetherness and support was taking its toll on both of them. Once behind closed doors, they were free to release their pent-up emotions and remove their public cloaks.

Ashley sat down on the sofa and waited for Michael to join her. Instead he sat on the arm of a chair across the room, distancing himself from her. "It's almost impossible to express how angry and disappointed I am. I've probably experienced every other emotion where you're concerned, but never this heartrending disappointment. You've taken the focus off of my election and the work I hope to accomplish."

Ashley stood up, kinetic energy surging through her body. "I'm sorry, I truly am. I've lost count of the number of times I tried to get you to discuss this with me before the election.

Or how many times I've urged you to brainstorm possible solutions. What you said at the press conference evidently isn't true. You don't respect my right to make my own decision. You want me to succumb to your way of thinking.

"You keep talking about how my decision is going to affect you and your presidency. I recognize that's a huge focus for you; how could it not be? The presidency is as big as it gets. But what I don't hear you saying is that you're going to miss me, just me. I'm disappointed in you too."

"Then it appears we're at a stalemate, and we have nothing else to say to one another," Michael shot back.

"Not true. I have something to say. I'm out of here. I'm leaving immediately for New York. I've given you all of the time I can afford. I've been gone off and on from my job for over a year to help campaign for you. No matter what I do, it's never enough.

"When you first ran for Congress, we agreed to try to make things work for both of us. We said we'd always put our family first. You followed your dreams, and I supported you. I've never done anything to give you the impression that I wanted to live in your shadow, so acting like my decision is something new is disingenuous."

Ashley was furious. At times like this, she felt like calling off their marriage. Before things escalated, she left the room and headed to the bedroom to start packing. If only she didn't love the thick-headed dope, it would make things a lot easier. Now all she wanted was just to get away, from Washington, from politics, and from him. Maybe absence would make their hearts grow fonder.

She wondered if Michael would follow her into the bedroom and try to ease the tension between them before she left. A soft click of the outer suite's door dispelled any hope of that.

So, that was it? He left without saying a word. Ashley's heart plummeted. Where were they headed? She didn't want to think about it. She needed to get away from all of this turmoil.

Despite everything she'd said, the urge to give in, to run to him and make things better was overwhelming. The stress was a tangible force to reckon with. Well, standing here feeling sorry for herself wasn't going to change anything. She needed to move. She needed to get back to New York and to as normal a life as possible, given the fact that her husband had just been elected president.

Ashley picked up the phone and dialed Jeremy's and Juliette's extension. "Hi, it's Mom. Can you come up for a minute? I'm leaving for New York sooner than I expected, and I want to say goodbye."

"We'll be right there," Jeremy answered.

A few moments later, they were all sitting around the suite's living room, strain showing on all of their faces.

"This isn't easy to talk about, but I want you to know what's going on. Your dad and I need some time away from one another. We're not splitting up; nothing like that has ever been discussed. We simply need a break from one another for a while. He has his work, and I need to get back to mine. I want you to prepare yourself for the possibility of some nasty rumors that the media may create. They'll undoubtedly be vicious and hurtful. You know you can call your dad or me and ask us the truth if you're really concerned about something.

"The sooner I get back to work, and the sooner your dad can start putting his transition plans into action, the better it will be for all of us. So I'm leaving for New York this afternoon as soon as I'm packed.

"I think the next few days and weeks are going to be crucial as to how all of this gets hammered out. I'm planning on taking it one day at a time, and hoping . . ."

"Mom, we know," Juliette interrupted. "We knew this was going to be messy. You and Dad want different things right now. We know how high the stakes are."

Ashley nodded. "I'd change things if I could, but I can't commit to something I'd hate."

Jeremy stressed, "We're not kids anymore, Mom. We'll handle what comes our way. I don't like some of the changes that will happen in my life, but the last thing you need to do is worry about us."

"Wouldn't it be great if I could say I wouldn't worry about you and really mean it? Fat chance. Worrying 101 is a special class we had to take during parent training or they wouldn't let us take you home from the hospital.

"I'll give you a call when I get back to New York and get settled in, and please call me when you get back to school. I love you guys. Now, give me a hug and off you go."

As Ashley watched her children walk down the hall to the elevator, she noticed the Secret Service agents following them and the ones stationed outside the door. Addressing them, she said, "I'm flying back to New York immediately. Would you make any necessary changes that are needed for my departure? I'll be ready to go as soon as I write my husband a note."

Ashley sat down at the dining room table to compose a note to Michael. What could she say that hadn't already been said? Still, she didn't want to leave without saying something.

It was bad enough that they weren't saying their goodbyes in person, but she couldn't stomach any more of Michael's disapproving looks. How she could convey some hope in her words?

Dear Michael,

I can't think of anything else to say for now, only that I love you. There's no point in rehashing this over and over; we've done enough of that already. We're just going in circles, so I'm returning to work.

I know you're going to be extremely busy in the coming days, but please find time to stay in touch and I'll do the same. Maybe given some time and space, we'll both be blessed with new insights that our emotions are presently hiding.

I love you,
Ashley

10

While Ashley was en route to New York, Michael was trying to remove the railroad spike his wife had hammered into his heart. He was ready to drop from exhaustion. He'd spent the entire afternoon and into the early night with his advisory team trying to decide the best strategy for dealing with an absentee First Lady. There were other important issues he needed to tackle, but the tyranny of the urgent put the absence of the First Lady at the top of his list.

Michael reviewed the various options he and his team had discussed about the best way to proceed. Every recommendation seemed rife with its own set of complications. His team had debated the pros and cons of not replacing Ashley as First Lady. But Michael felt strongly that if they didn't replace her or create a position to handle the duties that had been assumed by past First Ladies, they would be sending the message that the First Lady's role was unimportant. He definitely didn't want to set that precedent.

Richard had suggested his wife stand in for the First Lady. While Michael appreciated the offer, he knew Catherine had a full schedule at Georgetown University, where she taught master classes in molecular and cellular biology. He wasn't comfortable with that idea or any of the other suggestions that included using other politicians' wives. He didn't want to feel obligated to or to be perceived as being influenced by anyone who might step into the role.

As the discussion continued throughout the afternoon, Michael had become increasingly convinced that the best course of action was to create a new position, a White House director of protocol, a social director, so to speak. Once that decision was made, he and his team began hammering out the parameters and advantages of the new position. The director of protocol would assume the responsibility of being the official White House hostess. Other duties would be added to the job description as needs became known.

While Michael hated having officially to exclude Ashley from the role that was rightfully hers, it was necessary. Expediency was paramount in order to prove to the American people that regardless of his wife's decision, his administration would go forth unencumbered and with confidence. The new director of protocol would simply be another job in his administration, nothing more. His job would be to sell the press and the public on the merits of his decision.

His staff was working on the job description to include language allowing for unanticipated responsibilities. They were aware of the need to coordinate with other positions in Michael's administration where there might be some overlap of responsibilities. The next step would be to find the right candidate. Michael had someone in mind who might be perfect for the job, but he had been too tired to continue the discussion.

Michael headed back to the hotel suite, dreading any further confrontations with Ashley. When he closed the door, he was enveloped in silence. There was no sign to indicate the presence of his wife. He did a quick check around the suite and found it empty of her belongings. She'd obviously meant what she said about returning to New York. It was just as well. He'd hit a wall. Any additional battles with Ashley held the potential for disaster.

His need to unwind superseded every other thought. After taking off his jacket and tie and opening a cold beer, he fell into the cushions of the sofa. He didn't want to compromise with or accommodate anyone, especially his wife. Then he noticed an envelope on the coffee table. His name was written on the outside in Ashley's calligraphic handwriting. Just picking up the envelope put a knot in his stomach. He read the note, twice. What did he feel? Angry? Wounded? Indignant? Relieved? Honestly he was too tired to feel much of anything. She was right. There wasn't anything left to be said between the two of them, at least for now. He was furious with her and was glad she wasn't there.

He couldn't remember a time when he'd been this exhausted. What he'd been told by past presidents was true. After the surge of euphoria and adrenaline rush on election night, there came a tremendous emotional crash. He simply hadn't anticipated it being so dramatic, but then he'd never factored Ashley's untimely declaration to the world into the equation either.

Surely tomorrow would bring more optimism back into his life. He wasn't prone to moodiness. This blip on the wavelength of his emotions was strictly an anomaly. He fell asleep on the sofa, acknowledging somewhere in his brain he should get up, pack, and check out of the hotel.

He awoke with a start. He jumped up and banged his shin on the coffee table, causing him to fall as he grabbed his leg. The next thing he knew his Secret Service agents, who had heard the crash, were standing over him, some guarding him, others swinging their flashlights and guns around the darkened room to assess the situation.

"Are you okay, sir?" One of the agents asked, switching on a table lamp.

"I'm fine. I fell asleep on the sofa, woke up with a start, and bumped into the coffee table. About the only thing hurt is my pride. I don't usually get so disoriented coming out of a deep sleep. Thanks for checking, but it's definitely a false alarm."

"No problem, sir. Is there anything we can get for you?"

"No, but thanks."

"Then we'll be right outside if you need us."

Michael checked his watch; it was 5:00 a.m. He couldn't believe he'd slept straight through the night on the sofa. It was a little earlier than he normally started his day, but he might as well get to work.

He knew Ed would be up and eager to show him the latest headlines and any feedback from yesterday's press conference. He hoped today's news would be more encouraging, but he didn't harbor any unrealistic expectations. Ashley was completely misguided in her belief that she could step away from the spotlight. She would be more famous, more sought-after now than ever, but her attitude was always the same: "Maybe, but at least I'll be working at something I love."

Some of the traits that had attracted Michael to Ashley were her wit and humor and how tenacious and strong-willed she was. Now some of those same characteristics were causing him immeasurable harm. He'd never cared for clinging-vine females. Too much upkeep. No, he preferred someone who could carry her own weight. However, this time, Ashley had carried things too far. Despite the trouble and controversy her decision was causing him, he didn't want her with him if she didn't want to be there. He wanted her to want to share the White House experience with him. But if this is the way she wanted it, then fine. He'd manage without her, once he got past all of the fallout and put the director of protocol position in place.

Michael glanced at his watch as he called Ed's cell. "Good morning. Sorry for the early call. I got up earlier than normal. I'm still at the hotel; I didn't make it to my apartment. I fell asleep where I dropped last night. I need to check out, and then I'd like to meet with you and Jack around nine at the office. I'd like to hear the feedback from yesterday's press conference, and I want to get moving on the director of protocol position."

"Great. I'll get in touch with Jack, and we'll see you there." Ed hung up.

At nine o'clock, Jack handed a copy to both Michael and Ed of the synopsis he'd put together of the media's reaction to yesterday's press conference.

"As you might expect, everyone is still in shock over Ashley's position. There's a lot of division among the various factions. Most of the newspaper editorials are pretty predictable. The older, more established conservative publications are outraged. They're crucifying Ashley for walking away from her responsibilities. The more liberal publications are debating the merits of the First Lady role and are giving Ashley a lot of leeway. Have you seen any television coverage?"

"I saw a little bit of *Morning Joe.* Joe and Mika were arguing about Ashley's decision. Other than that, I haven't seen any other broadcasts."

"You probably know enough to realize Ashley is the top story, if not the only story, being covered today. As one might expect, the more conservative stations and broadcasters are ready to string her up and are casting serious aspersions on you, your judgment, and your ability to lead.

"The more liberal broadcasters are asking if the First Lady position really does matter. Rachel Maddow is doing a good job of representing the heart of the issue. She sees the role of the First Lady as representing tradition, which in her opinion is an important one. And, she sees Ashley's particular choice as something she has a right to make.

"Fox News is showing Ashley no mercy. They equate her decision to being a traitor She's being asked to serve her country, and she's turning her back on her civic duty.

"The opposition party is taking full advantage of the situation, which we expected. They're saying Ashley should be ashamed of herself for discrediting the role of the First Lady. They haven't come out in so many words and said a woman's place is in the home—they'd lose too many women voters if they did that—but short of that, they're saying Ashley's place is to stand beside you. Naturally, they're pointing out this indicates your inability to make good decisions, influence the opinion of others, portray the correct family values, and anything else they can throw into the mix."

Michael nodded. "Anything else?"

Jack knew he couldn't keep anything from Michael. "There have been a couple death threats against Ashley. We've contacted all the appropriate organizations, and they're checking into them. The Secret Service agents assigned to Ashley have been notified, so they're all over this. You know, we take every threat seriously, regardless of who the intended target is, but likely it's nothing more than someone venting."

Michael frowned. "I want additional security assigned to her, and I want to know immediately about any additional threats."

"Absolutely. Switching gears, I think the sooner we tell the public about the director of protocol position, the better it will be. Hopefully, things may begin to settle down somewhat after that," Ed said.

"I agree, but we need to be careful about how we play this thing out. We don't want to seem as though we had someone waiting in the wings. On the other hand, we want to make sure the public understands that Ashley's decision isn't going to cripple my administration. It's a high-wire act. I've been giving a lot of thought to the kind of person who would be a good fit for the director position. Do you remember Paula Foulon from California?"

Ed and Jack nodded.

"She's been active in all of my campaigns as far back as I can remember. As I'm sure you remember, she's from an old, established blue-chip family with a lot of political clout. She's hosted numerous fund-raising events for me throughout the years. What do you think about her for the job?"

"She's always impressed me as very charming, capable, a gifted organizer, and an extremely gracious hostess," Ed said.

"Precisely. She's someone who stays calm and gracious under fire. I once saw her defuse a fight between two contributors who'd had too much to drink, and they were like putty in her hands. I think she may just fit the bill. I'd want to have a serious discussion with her to make it very clear how I'd like to see this position shaped. It's such an unusual situation, and whoever takes the job must understand completely and exactly what the parameters are. Everyone will be watching and judging how this arrangement works."

"Obviously we'll need to vet her," Jack pointed out. "We need to know all about her background. Is there anything that could be embarrassing to us or be used to compromise her? Any arrests, any protesting for a wrong cause? We need to know everything. I don't need to tell you how important it is that we get this appointment right. We don't need a member of the administration going sideways on us. I'll start the process right away."

"I'd like to announce the decision to establish a director of protocol position at our next press conference. Let's schedule it for one week from today. That'll give us time to get started and make some inroads on the transition process. Also I'll be publicly naming you, Ed, as my chief of staff, and you, Jack, as my White House press secretary, even though everyone already knows you're in those roles. We'll make an official announcement at the conference. Plus, I could use the time to get in touch with Paula about the job, and I'll want to talk to Ashley about it before she hears it on the news.

"Let's adjourn for now and meet again this afternoon with the whole advisory team." Michael stood.

Jack and Ed headed for the door, ready to put the plans they'd discussed into motion. Ed turned to Michael before he left. "I know how hard this has been on you, particularly where Ashley's concerned. But, for what it's worth, I think you've made a very wise decision."

"I appreciate that, Ed. I'll see you this afternoon."

11

Commercial flights were a thing of the past for Ashley, at least for now. This was yet another adjustment she'd have to make now that Michael had been elected president. She understood from a security point of view why it was necessary, but she wished it weren't so. It felt like an unnecessary luxury to have a plane at her disposal, and at a great cost to the government. However, of all the things she had to worry about right now, this one, for the time being, could be put on hold.

The flight between Washington, DC, and New York was a little over an hour. Usually she used her travel time to shift gears from one aspect of her life to another. Unfortunately the shift didn't occur during this flight. She kept replaying in her head conversations she had with Michael or wished she'd had. Her brain was tired from working the problem, trying to come up with some sort of a compromise that would work for both of them.

Regardless of their differences, she hated leaving Michael without saying goodbye in person and, worse, leaving with so much animosity between them. They'd fought before; what couple hadn't? But this was the first time they'd been unable to find some sort of halfway solution on which they could both agree.

Ashley laid her head back on the headrest of the black SUV that was transporting her from the airport to her apartment in the Upper East Side of Manhattan. This, too, was something she resented. How in the hell could she live her life and conduct her business with the Secret Service always in the way? She barely tolerated their presence during the campaign, and now they were going to be a permanent fixture in her life. Swell, just swell.

Thinking about her lack of freedom made her want to scream. She was used to coming and going as she pleased, but the Secret Service made clear that she no longer had that option. She was expected to give them a daily itinerary listing where she would be going and with whom she'd be meeting so they could secure the areas where she'd appear. Ashley felt depressed thinking about the impact the Secret Service was going to have on her life.

She obviously needed to have a serious talk with the agents assigned to her. She knew they were under orders, that their job was to protect her, and that most likely they weren't any more fond of being assigned to her than she was of having them around. Maybe a compromise could be made. She would not live like a prisoner.

The SUV stopped in front of her apartment building, and she noticed two other agents talking to her doorman. Great. Agents seemed to be multiplying like cockroaches. She reached for the door handle to exit, but before she could open the door, an agent opened the door and offered her his hand. She knew he was being polite, but she couldn't stand being treated like a delicate flower. Childishly she ignored his hand, grabbed her briefcase and purse, and got out of the van without making eye contact. She was embarrassing herself. It wasn't like her to be so ungracious. She needed an attitude adjustment.

"Hi, Gordon," Ashley said to her doorman. "Are these two guys causing you trouble?" Ashley asked in a teasing voice, trying to make light of the situation.

"Not at all, Mrs. Taylor. They were explaining to me some of the additional precautions that we'll need to take now that you're the First Lady. Congratulations, by the way, on Senator Taylor's, I mean, President Taylor's victory. I voted for him, you know." Gordon beamed and stood a little taller, indicating his importance was greater now that the president's wife lived in his building.

A bright flash made Ashley turn in the direction from where it had come. Agents immediately surrounded her as other agents went after a scruffy-looking man with a camera hanging around his neck.

"Hey, let go of me. I'm protected under the Constitution. This is still America, and I have the right to walk on this street and take pictures of what I want." The photographer continued to rant. "You can't stop me from taking pictures. There's no harm in that. I can sue you for assault."

The agent released him and said something softly to him that Ashley couldn't hear. The man smiled and saluted him, turned, and bowed to Ashley before saying, "It was nice to see you again, Mrs. Taylor. Do you have any comments for the press?"

"I have a lot of comments, but none of them are printable. Stay away from me," Ashley said as she turned and walked into the building.

Ashley could have kicked herself. Ed and Jack had told her repeatedly not to respond to the press, to say simply "No comment." She just proved she couldn't even handle that. Unfortunately it wasn't in her DNA. Her response had been automatic. Surely what she'd said would appear in the newspaper tomorrow morning, adding more fuel to the media blaze.

Once she was in the foyer of her building, she turned to the agents who evidently planned to accompany her to her apartment. "Where does this end? You're not staying in my apartment with me, and I don't want you at the museum. Just how is all of this security going to work? I know that sounds ungracious, and I'm sorry, but can you imagine how you would feel if this were to happen to you and you hadn't signed on for any of it?" Ashley asked.

The taller of the two agents spoke to her calmly. "We understand that this feels like an invasion of your privacy. Anyone would feel the same way. However, that doesn't change the fact that you need to be protected, and it's our job to see that you are. We'll try to accommodate you as best we can."

"What's your name?"

"Agent Campton, ma'am."

"Dear God, did you just call me ma'am?" Ashley shook her head. "Please, no more. Call me Ashley. Ma'am is for some old lady down the block. I'm only forty-four. I think I have a few years to go before I'll be in the ma'am category." Ashley shook her head. "Oh, and the hits just keep on coming. What's your first name, Agent Campton?"

"Matt."

"Then, may I call you Matt?" Not waiting for his answer, she turned to the other agent, "And, you? What's your name?"

"Agent Felts, I mean, Dave."

"Okay, Matt and Dave, I will try to keep you informed of where I'm going to be and any appointments I may have. And I'd appreciate your presence at the museum to be indiscernible. I have a business to run. The Cameron Museum of Art is like the Guggenheim. It's a huge, beautiful, and distinctive architectural building on the outside and filled with world-renowned art treasures. It's one of the few privately owned chains of museums in the world. I don't know how agents in your position managed other people they have protected, but I'd appreciate it if you'd stay in the background and keep a low profile.

"Now, I'd like to go up to my apartment and relax. I'm going in to work tomorrow, and I'll be working there until I feel I'm somewhat caught up. Is there anything else we need to discuss before I go?"

"Mrs. Taylor, we'll be accompanying you up to your apartment. There will always be at least two agents outside of your apartment day or night. We've already made sure your apartment is safe," Matt said.

"What does that mean?"

"While you were in Washington, New York field agents went through your apartment and made sure it was safe. We made a few alterations here and there to make the apartment more secure."

Ashley looked up, shaking her head and searching the heavens for the right words for her indignation. She knew their job was to protect her and they were only doing their job, but each additional adjustment seemed like another affront to her privacy. She teased, "Have you bugged my apartment? Did you install hidden cameras? Am I not to have any privacy?"

Agent Campton answered. "Your apartment isn't bugged, nor are there any hidden cameras. We needed to assess the risk of someone gaining access to your apartment other than by the front door. We made a few adjustments, all for your protection and your safety. It's nothing invasive at all."

Matt pressed the elevator button. What he'd heard about Mrs. Taylor was true. They were told she wouldn't be an easy assignment. That was an understatement. He and Dave and the other agents were going to have their hands full. She was just the kind of woman who might try to give them the slip. Truthfully, he thought, she was capable of anything. What kind of woman would make the decision not to be the First Lady?

When the elevator arrived, Ashley and the two agents stepped into its compartment. Ashley leaned over to press the button for her floor, only to be stopped by Agent Felts.

"Excuse me, ma'am, I mean Mrs. Taylor. One of the adjustments we made to your living situation was to program the elevator to stop only on your floor when a key is inserted here." Dave pointed to the circular keyhole next to the button for her floor. "Here's your key. We have our keys, and we have additional keys for your children and the president. It's just another precaution. Would you like me to use my key, or would you prefer to use yours?"

Ashley pursed her lips and shook her head, speechless for a nanosecond. She swallowed. "This is not being invasive? What's next? Secret panels in the walls of my apartment?

Damn it! Go ahead; use your key. I'm sure you're getting a kick out of this."

Agent Felts stepped forward and inserted his key while Agent Campton answered Ashley's accusation. "No, Mrs. Taylor, we aren't getting a kick out of this."

Ashley said under her breath, "Like hell you aren't."

Agent Campton asked, "What's that? I apologize; I didn't hear what you said."

"Oh, nothing." Ashley clamped her mouth shut.

When the elevator stopped, she rushed to get out of the confined space. Her outer foyer had been changed or rather modified. An additional table had been added, plus two more chairs. There was a clipboard on the table, and a telephone had been installed that was obviously a landline. Two other agents immediately arose from the chairs and walked toward her.

Agent Campton made the introductions. She had to keep reminding herself: none of this was their fault. They were only carrying out the duties assigned to them.

All Ashley wanted to do was to get into her apartment and be alone. She took out the key for her door and inserted it in the lock. Before going in, she turned to look at the agents. "Goodnight. I'll be going to work around seven in the morning." She gave what may have passed for a smile and went in and shut the door, leaning against the other side of it.

She let out a long breath. She wanted to cry but wouldn't. She knew that was only her initial reaction. She depended on her sense of righteous indignation to come riding in to save her. She was in this prison despite everything she'd done to avoid it. At least she wasn't living in Washington, DC, and hadn't been sequestered in a world she despised. She needed to focus on her work and that's what she'd do. Tomorrow would be a new day, and with any luck, the public would tire of her as a worthy news item. God, she hoped so.

She shook her head to clear it. How could she have ever imagined when she first met Michael and fell in love where it would take them? They were both from working-class families. Both of her parents worked. Her father worked in construction, and her mother was a pharmacy assistant. Michael's father was a pastor, and his mother was a housewife. The most she and Michael had hoped for was a college education and working in careers they loved. Never in their wildest dreams could they have imagined the future in which they now lived.

12

Ashley awoke the following morning feeling anxious, feeling as though she'd spent the entire night dreaming of the summer when she and Michael met. It was a vivid reminder of how tenuous their relationship had been at another time in their lives, but the fragility of a teenage crush couldn't compare to the strength and power of their love now or their current situation. Her unconscious mind was obviously working overtime, picking and pulling at the issue dividing her and Michael. Even in sleep, she found no respite from the pressure of living in a fishbowl.

She wished she had time to get away from all of the chaos swirling around her. She needed time to think objectively about possible compromises, but the day-to-day pressure was like a rabid dog waiting just outside her door ready to nip at her heels. Today was no better. She was meeting Steve, a friend and event planner, for breakfast. She wanted to run through her ideas again for this year's annual Black Tie Dinner for the museum.

Running late, she breezed through the door of the City Bakery, well known for its sinfully delicious food. The mouthwatering smells made her stomach growl. She hadn't allowed time for more than a cup of coffee, set on her vanity as a companion, while she dressed for the day.

She scanned the restaurant. Steve waved from the second floor. He'd apparently commandeered a private spot upstairs where there would be less people traffic.

He kissed her on her cheek and whispered, "My, my, your secret service agents blend in about as well as a pair of horses in the middle of the lingerie department at Saks."

"I know. Don't remind me." Chuckling, Ashley sat down. The silky chords of jazz playing quietly in the background released the stiffness already building between her shoulders and neck.

"So, what's your pleasure this morning?" Steve asked. "My treat."

"How about a hot chocolate and a croissant."

"Will do. I'll be back in a minute, and we can get down to business."

While Steve was getting their food, Ashley leaned back into the soft beige cushions and closed her eyes. She had this brief moment to herself before the day began its steady and relentless climb to pandemonium. Michael popped into her wandering mind. She vowed she would call him as soon as she got to her office. The standoff had gone on long enough. It was time to de-escalate the situation and get things back on a more normal footing, if that were possible.

The days and nights were beginning to blend into one continuous stream, and she knew it was probably worse for Michael. She was the one who left without saying goodbye in person, so she should be the one to bring this stalemate to a close.

"Earth to Ashley." Steve's voice broke through her trance.

"Sorry. I was trying to block out the world for a few minutes. Other than my apartment, it's hard to find a place where I can unwind without being followed and photographed."

"I know how much you hate the press, but you are rather the 'It Girl' at the moment."

"What did you think would happen after you announced to the world you wanted nothing to do with the White House? Did you think someone was going to rush forward with a bouquet of roses?" Steve shook his head and continued.

"If you ever decide you absolutely need to get away, I have a cabin in Ludlow, Vermont. It's fairly isolated. You're always welcome to use it. I consider it my lifeline to sanity and try to get up there as often as I can. A nice retired couple maintains it for me and keeps it well stocked with food. It's available anytime you need it."

"Thanks. It sounds wonderful. Don't be surprised if I take you up on it someday. At the moment, I have too much to do for the fund-raiser and Michael's inauguration, but after that, who knows?

"Speaking of the fund-raiser, I'm anxious to go over my ideas again. I hope anything I've changed is still within my budget."

Steve took out his pad and started making notes as he and Ashley discussed this year's black tie fund-raiser. They worked together for the next couple of hours, bouncing ideas off one another, completely engaged in their conversation.

Ashley looked at her watch. "My God, I didn't realize the time. If I don't get to the office soon, I might as well go back home. Can you come to the museum and see where I want things to go?"

"I can't right now, but I could be there around four, if that will work for you?"

Ashley said, "I'll make it work. Unless you hear from me, I'll see you at four."

"I need to run or I'd see you out, but then the black-suited goons might think I'm invading their territory and vying for their jobs. Poor babies. You know they've got to love their job." Steve grinned.

"I'm sure they hate being assigned to me. It's not very glamorous guarding the future president's wife. And there's nothing poor about them. They're quite self-sufficient. See you this afternoon."

Ashley had the overwhelming desire to throw in the towel for the day. How incredible it would be to have a day entirely to herself without any agenda. Where time was concerned, it was either feast or famine.

As she collected her things, she reminded herself once again that as soon as she got to the office, she would call Michael. However, once at the museum, an avalanche of issues was waiting to bury her. Ashley plunged headfirst into her day.

13

Ashley had been back at work for two days, and she'd yet to return all of the calls received in her absence. Her mantra: *I'll just handle one more phone call, one more piece of mail, one more thing, and then I'll go home.*

She was stalling. She still hadn't called Michael, which she'd promised herself she would do. They'd always talked to each other at least every other night when they were separated. It made being apart more bearable. This time, however, Michael seemed to be managing just fine without her.

Undoubtedly he'd seen her picture and the comment she'd made to the photographer in the newspaper. She was sure he wasn't any happier about it than she was. The reporter had caught her off guard outside her apartment, and instead of replying, "No, comment," she'd flung sarcasm over her shoulder. The reporter used her comment to further tarnish her and worse had dubbed her the "Reluctant First Lady." Even Ed and Jack hadn't contacted her to remind her, once again, she was to say "No comment" when reporters approached her. It was a small thing to ask of her, and she'd blown it.

Getting back to work had helped to distract her from all of the animosity that had grown between them. However, there were moments when the magnitude of the situation came crashing down around her. It took her breath away. Yes, she'd stood up for her beliefs, but at what price? Her marriage?

Ashley looked through the phone messages she'd yet to return, which were mostly from the media. Everyone wanted an interview; everyone wanted a piece of her. She debated the merits of giving no interviews or doing just one with a journalist she felt she could trust. Thankfully she didn't have to decide anything right now.

There was one message that was a no-brainer. It was from her cousin Sienna. Talking to family was just the panacea she needed right now. Sienna picked up the phone on the third ring.

"Hi, it's your disgraceful cousin. I'm thinking of going into exile in another country. Wanna come?"

"Absolutely. When do we leave, and may I suggest Verona, Italy?" Sienna answered.

"We should have left yesterday. Actually I wanted to bounce a couple of ideas off you. Do you have a minute?"

"Yeah, Jim's having dinner with some potential investors for his latest documentary project, and Samantha's at a rehearsal for her high school play."

"How is my niece? Is she still going to make me proud by attending the New School in New York after she graduates?"

"That's the plan. I swear she seems more like your daughter than mine. Do you know she actually showed up in her biology class wearing a frog costume? She was protesting the dissection of frogs and other creatures. I got called to the school, and it's lucky they decided not to suspend her. Although she has been assigned to community service around the school. And her attitude about it—well, it was worth it, of course. Now who does that sound like?"

"Could you give me a hint?" Ashley laughed. "I hope after you get over your indignation, you'll appreciate the spirited and conscientious daughter you have."

"Hmm . . . actually, it reminded me of when you wore a gorilla costume to a dinner for the district attorneys."

"Michael deserved that. He ordered me to be there like I was some trained monkey who did things on command. Besides, underneath that excellent costume, I was wearing a beautiful cocktail dress. Everyone enjoyed the joke, including Michael."

Well, Jim thinks you've had entirely too much influence on her."

"God, I hope so. Who'd have thought he'd turn into such a Neanderthal after you two married? She's a natural actress; why not promote her talent?"

"I'm sure you didn't call to discuss Samantha's future when yours is so shaky. I've been listening to replays of your press conference. Some stations are staying a little more neutral than before, but overall the country is still in the middle of a national debate. I'm glad I'm not in your shoes.

You've always kicked tradition in the face, but you may have gone too far this time. What's up?" Sienna asked.

"First of all, I'm returning your call. In the huge pile of phone messages on my desk, yours seemed the friendliest. Second I needed to talk to someone who loves me. I'm not very popular right now, particularly with Michael and his crowd, so lucky you. You get to hear my ramblings."

"Ramble on," Sienna encouraged.

"Things are about as bad as they can get between Michael and me, short of a divorce. We haven't talked in a several days, and we're both too proud to call and break the ice. It seemed pointless for me to stay in Washington any longer. We kept going over the same old ground, so I left. Worse, I left without saying goodbye in person. I'm being hounded by the press for interviews, the secret service is driving me crazy, and I'm about to start wearing disguises."

Sienna laughed, "What else is new? You never stopped wearing costumes and disguises. Just look at the way you dress."

"What do you think about me giving one exclusive interview just to get the press off my back? I'm sick of avoiding them, and maybe they'd lighten up a bit if I agreed to an interview. Plus, Mavis and Kathy came to the door of my office today insisting they be released from having to be courteous and diplomatic to everyone who calls. As gracious as they are, I smell mutiny afoot."

Sienna commented, "It must be bad if your saintly secretaries are fed up. I don't think there's anything you can do to get the press off your back. This is your new normal. I'm sorry. I wish I had more encouraging words, but this is just part and parcel of being married to Michael.

"Whether you stay at the White House or not, you're news. You've done something totally unexpected, and the media and the public want to know what makes you tick. I don't think you're ever going to be rid of the media. Jackie O was in the news her entire life. As sorry as I am to say this, the media is in your life to stay, no matter what you do."

"And, to think I called you to cheer me up. Gee, thanks. You're doing such a great job. I know what you're saying is true. I hate it, but it is the new normal for me, and I need to try and find a way to accept that. At least, I'm not living in Washington and watching all the political posturing. I swear politicians make actors look like amateurs.

"Change of subject, sort of. Designers are already contacting me with their designs for outfits and ball gowns to wear during the inauguration ceremonies. Want me to send them to you so you can pick out something you'd like?"

"Don't drag me into this mess. What did you expect, Ashley? Have you given any thought about what you're going to wear? Or have you decided out of spite to wear a burlap bag with a designer label sewn into it, like Gold Medal Flour or C&H Sugar?"

"I've actually decided to wear only the labels since that's all it seems anyone cares about. Maybe you'd like to design something for me?"

"What did I ever do to you?" Sienna teased.

"Well, there was that time we went fishing when we were about eight. Remember, when you hooked my knee while you were casting your line?"

"Accident, Ash, accident. I was more horrified than you about the hook in your knee."

"I know, but I can still make you feel guilty after all these years. Listen, thanks for putting up with my complaining. You might not think you did anything, but I already feel better."

"Ashley, call me anytime you need to talk. I mean it."

"Hmm . . . I suppose if I get too lonely, I can always engage the secret service agents in a conversation. They're not exactly the friendly type, and I'm sure they think I'm a pain in the butt, but don't you worry, I'll wear them down. I better get going. Thanks again. Say hi to Sam and Jim for me. I'll talk to you soon. I love you."

Talking to Sienna had definitely improved her mood. Talking to family always helped to keep things in perspective.

Ashley walked to her office door and looked outside. There they were, the two wonder boys, Matt and Dave, keeping vigil right outside her door. The other agents were undoubtedly not far away.

"I'll be ready to leave in a few minutes. If you'd like to go on ahead without me, please feel free to do so. I can assure you, I know how to get home by myself."

Agent Campton and Agent Felts let Ashley's teasing roll right off of them. They were used to difficult assignments. They stood at their post and waited for her to gather her things so they could escort her home.

The first thing Ashley did was check her phone to see if the message light was on. It was. Keeping her fingers crossed, she quickly went through a myriad of calls only to be disappointed. None of them was from Michael. She wished not hearing from him didn't hurt so much.

At bedtime she missed him most. She and Michael had always had a ravenous appetite for one another. She missed having him next to her. When they were separated, she missed their nightly calls. They'd always joked they were only one phone call away. Before she fell asleep, she vowed she would swallow the very large pill of pride and call him tomorrow.

14

Michael reached for the phone to call Ashley and then stopped. He was used to sharing his days with her, and the temptation to call her was overwhelming. Still, she was the one who had distanced herself from him and to hell with the consequences. Thank you very much, Ashley.

He knew to a certain extent he was being unfair. She'd never lied to him. She'd always been open about her feelings regarding politics. She stood up for her beliefs and hadn't budged even in the face of great adversity. He didn't know why he'd been so optimistic about her changing her mind. He'd been a fool, and that didn't sit well with him.

There really was no point in dwelling on his miscalculation any longer. He was determined to manage the situation without her and turn a disaster into a success to whatever extent was possible. It was time to move on his decision to create the director of protocol position.

He dialed Paula Foulon's number, and a very sleepy voice answered. "Is this Paula?"

"Yes, who's this?" an annoyed voice asked.

"It's Michael Taylor. I'm sorry. Did I wake you? I can call back another time." He looked at his watch. It was close to midnight on the West Coast. What had he been thinking?

"No, wait. Let me turn on the light. You must have called about something important if you're calling this late," Paula said, as she sat up, turned on the light, and finger-combed her hair. "By the way, congratulations on your big win, Mr. President—but then I always believed you'd win."

"Again, I apologize for calling so late. I was working and wasn't paying attention to the time. I can call back tomorrow."

"It's already tomorrow where you are. Why are you calling?" Paula asked.

"I'll get right to the point. I'd like to meet with you tomorrow if you're free to fly out to Washington. There's a position in my administration I'd like to discuss with you."

Paula was absolutely thrilled. "Yes, I'll catch the first plane out tomorrow morning." She'd move heaven and earth to get to Washington, DC.

"Great. Do you think you can get here for a five o'clock meeting?"

"I'll be there. Are you still in your old office?" Paula asked.

"Yes. I'll be here until the inauguration. Go back to sleep; I'll see you tomorrow, and let me apologize again for calling so late."

"Wait, can't you tell me more?" Paula pleaded.

"I'd rather not. I'd like to talk to you in person. Tell Connor he's welcome to come, too. I'll see you tomorrow."

Michael hung up before Paula could ask any more questions. He sat for a moment reflecting on what he just possibly set into motion. He wished like hell he hadn't been forced to make this choice, but he might as well move forward. The sooner he offered the public a solution to Ashley's absence, the sooner things might begin to calm down.

The next day, true to her word, Paula arrived on time for their five o'clock meeting.

Georgia, Michael's secretary, ushered her into his office. Michael stood and extended his hand. "Thank you for coming on such short notice."

"No problem. I'm anxious to hear what initiated your late-night call and invitation."

While Georgia was getting coffee for Paula and engaging her in small talk, Michael did a quick mental review of Paula's qualifications. She was smart and savvy, had a lot of connections through both her family and her husband, had led a privileged and cultured life among the very rich, and was the ultimate hostess in California.

She was tall and slender, had glossy black hair, which she wore in a chin-length bob. He imagined she probably hadn't been denied much in her life. Her father and her husband, Connor, absolutely adored and doted on her, and among the San Francisco elite, she was its reigning queen. She came from old money, and her entire family had supported and contributed a great deal of money to his campaigns throughout the years.

Once Paula was settled with a cup of coffee, Michael began. "I'm sure you've heard that Ashley intends to continue working at the museum and isn't planning on assuming the First Lady role."

Paula nodded. "It's never been a secret to those of us who know the two of you that she's never been interested in politics. Although I was rather surprised she was so forthcoming with the press."

Michael didn't want to discuss the press conference or Ashley. "After Ashley's announcement, my transition team and I discussed a variety of ways to proceed without a First Lady. I decided to create a new position, the director of protocol, which would encompass previous First Lady responsibilities. That's where you come in. I'd like you to consider filling the new position. I'm being totally honest when I say we're not too sure how the public is going to react to this. The controversy Ashley has raised is still raw and festering."

Paula didn't have to think about her answer; this was the opportunity of a lifetime. She'd always thought Michael and Ashley weren't a good match in any way. She would have been a much better partner for Michael. Working closely with Michael would have numerous benefits. Michael had impressed her from their first meeting, which she remembered vividly. She even remembered what he'd been wearing.

"First I'm flattered you thought about me to fill this new position, and second the answer is yes. I'd be honored to have the opportunity to work in your administration."

"I'm glad to hear you're so willing to step into a position that's still so undeveloped. I'll have to add 'adventurer' to your list of qualifications. However, you should probably sleep on your decision and talk it over with Connor and your family before you say yes so quickly.

"I'm going to be very adamant about the parameters for the director position. It's being designed specifically to fill the responsibilities a First Lady would normally have as the White House hostess, without any personal or emotional aspects associated with being the wife of the president. Ashley is the First Lady, whether she acknowledges the title or not. I need someone to fulfill the social obligations of previous First Ladies without overstepping the boundaries into privileges that are normally afforded the wife of a president.

"I'm confident you have the qualifications to do the job. I've watched you organize and finesse enough people at fund-raisers and parties to be keenly aware of your abilities as a hostess. But you really may want to give this more thought. Are you sure you want to jump into uncharted waters? There's no way to know how many sharks will be circling, ready to take a bite."

Paula smiled at Michael. "I'm absolutely sure I want the job, and I'm not going to change my mind. I feel quite certain we'll work very well together. And, as far as keeping the personal and professional aspects of the job separate, I understand exactly what you're trying to achieve."

"Do you think you can walk that tightrope?"

"Yes, I believe I can. Getting started and articulating the parameters of the position to the media will be the most difficult. I'm bound to make some blunders along the way, but I'm willing to help establish the right balance and tone you want."

Michael was relieved. He'd been very direct about wanting Ashley to maintain the social status that came with being his wife. Paula hadn't flinched from the distinction between the job and Ashley's rightful position.

"I was hoping you'd understand and still be willing to tackle the unknown. Are you sure you don't want to give Connor a call and see how he feels about it? This will impact your lives in a variety of ways."

"I realize my husband will be affected by my decision, but I'm equally sure he'd want me to accept your position and that I'll have his complete support. I appreciate your sensitivity where he's concerned."

During the next hour, Michael and Paula discussed various aspects of the director of protocol job. "I'm planning to announce the creation of the position at my next press conference,"

"Do you want me to be there?"

"I'm meeting with my transition team later tonight to discuss a variety of issues. Someone will call you tomorrow morning to tell you what we decide. I'd appreciate it if you'd talk only to Connor about this for now. I don't want any information leaked to the press before the official announcement. You'll learn keeping information from the media is harder than you think."

Paula agreed. "Of course, I recognize that this is a highly sensitive situation. I'm sorry Ashley chose to continue working at the museum. I honestly believed she'd change her mind once you were elected."

Michael had no intention of discussing Ashley with anyone. He was beginning to hope there might be a chance of adequately coping with Ashley's abdication. True, he was establishing a new position, which would set a precedent for future First Ladies. But once his decision was announced and explained, maybe some of the pressure would lessen.

"I feel confident that we can move forward on a positive note. Thanks again for coming on such short notice."

Paula got the hint; she was being dismissed. She got up and extended her hand to shake Michael's. "Thank you. Your trust means a great deal to me. I'm looking forward to working with you, more than you know."

"I hope you still feel that way once you're officially the director and the media starts hammering away at you."

"I'm not easily deterred from a goal once I set my mind to it. I'll talk to you later."

Paula seemed almost to float out of his office.

Michael turned to his desk. He hoped to God he was making the right decision. Out of all of the possibilities he and his staff had discussed to compensate for Ashley's absence, this solution seemed the least likely to be troublesome.

Almost a week had passed since he'd last talked to Ashley, and that spoke volumes. He needed to call her. He'd meant to call her before now, but he honestly didn't know what to say to her. Now at least he had something to tell her. He'd give her a call tonight and make arrangements for them to spend a weekend together.

Michael picked up the phone and dialed Ed. "Hey, I just finished meeting with Paula, and I wanted to confirm our seven o'clock meeting this evening. I'd like to give you my impressions."

"How did it go? Did you decide anything?"

"As a matter of fact, I did. I offered her the job, and I didn't sugarcoat it. I was quite clear about the boundaries I want established right from the start. I'll have to say, she didn't even flinch. At the meeting tonight, I'd like to discuss the best way of presenting this appointment to the press."

"I'll see that it gets added to the agenda. Have you said anything to Ashley about the decisions you've made?"

"Not yet. I'll give her a call tonight and give her a heads-up. See you at the meeting."

15

Ashley felt it was now or never. She needed to call Michael. She felt responsible for the distance that had grown between them and putting if off any longer would only make matters worse. She dialed his number, and as soon as she heard his secretary's voice, the acid began to bubble in her stomach.

"Hi, Georgia; it's Ashley. Is Michael available?"

"He's in a meeting, but I'll see if he can break free to take your call. Please hold the line."

Ashley heard the difference in the sound of the connection as she was placed on hold. It was going to take a whole bottle of antacids to get through this. She was just plain dumb to feel this nervous about talking to her own husband. Of course, it was guilt. Guilt over her decision to return to work, guilt over leaving Michael the way she had, and guilt over not calling for almost a week.

Georgia came back on the line. "Hold on, Ashley. I'm putting the call through to his office."

"Thanks, Georgia."

Ashley heard Michael pick up. "Hello, stranger."

She felt as though the nerve endings in her body were totally exposed. She could even feel her pulse accelerating. Damn it. Well, the best course of action was a good opening line.

"Hi, Michael. Think we can have a civilized discussion? Or is banishing me to a Third World country still on the table? I'm really sorry I've let so much time go by without contacting you."

Typical Ashley. One thing she didn't do was mince words. She aimed her arrow and let it fly. "I could have called you, too. I've been absolutely swamped," Michael confessed. The excuse sounded lame even to him although it was true. "I was going to call you after my meeting, as a matter of fact, and catch you up on what's been going on here. Plus, I wanted to hear how things are going in New York."

"You go first," Ashley insisted. "I'm sure my news isn't nearly as exciting as yours."

"As you might expect, it's been nonstop meetings and decisions regarding the transition and appointments I'll be making. There are so many things to do during this time of transferring from one administration to the next; it's mind-boggling. We've all been pretty much living on caffeine, but we've made good progress in a number of areas. We made a decision about how to deal with your absence from the First Lady position. Do you want to hear about it?"

"Absolutely. I'd love to hear what you've decided, and I mean that sincerely."

"Well, after much deliberation, we've created a position we're calling the director of protocol. We've designed it to be flexible yet one that will assume some of the responsibilities of past First Ladies and leave room for what we haven't anticipated. We brainstormed a variety of ideas, and this one seemed the most pragmatic."

"Good for you. I had every confidence that you would come up with a good alternative. I know it's not what you wanted, but it sounds like an excellent solution. In fact, you'll be setting a precedent for future presidents and their spouses. I think that's brilliant. When do you plan to fill the position?"

"I've already offered the position to someone."

"In less than a week, you've created a new position *and* filled it? My, you have been busy, but then I've always had faith in you and knew once you started working seriously on the issue, you'd come up with an effective solution. Who's the lucky person?"

"Paula Foulon."

There was silence on Ashley's end of the phone. She was trying to get over the jealousy that just stabbed her heart.

Ashley repeated, "Paula Foulon?"

"Yes, as a matter of fact, we met today to discuss the position, and she didn't hesitate to accept it. She understands the parameters I'm trying to establish, and I think she'll do a good job. She enjoys the political scene and seems to be excited to work in my administration."

I'll just bet she is. Paula had never impressed Ashley. She'd witnessed how manipulative Paula was with both her husband and her father, the kind of manipulation that men didn't often recognize. She threw her money, her family, and her social status in other people's faces. She'd once heard her put another politician's wife down because of her background, which made Ashley wonder what Paula was saying behind her back. Maybe other people didn't recognize a barracuda when they saw one, but Ashley did. Paula would kill to get her hooks into Michael and the whole White House scene. She was quite sure Paula would do her best to insinuate herself into Michael's life.

Ashley had met several women like her at political functions and the museum's Black Tie Dinner. They were pampered, spoiled, and rich. It didn't bother them in the least that their status had been achieved through their husband's or their family's work or good name. Her type felt privilege was an entitlement.

"Sounds like a match made in heaven. It seems your problem has been solved and all the wringing of hands was over nothing."

"You know damn well I didn't want to have to do this. I'm sorry if you're not happy with the choice I've made, but I needed to move quickly. I wanted you to hear about it before I announce it at a press conference. I didn't want the information to come out of left field for you."

"Thank you. That was very considerate. I know this is a touchy subject for us, and I have no right to feel anything about the decisions you've made. I'm glad you found a solution, and I truly hope it works out. Really, honey, congratulations to you and your team for finding an alternative to an extremely delicate and explosive situation. I hope the press and public accept it and you can move on."

"I hope so, too. Are you being hounded by the press?"

"Constantly. I get dozens of calls every day from someone wanting an interview. I even got an anonymous letter threatening me. It seems some Neanderthal out there feels strongly that I'm not doing my wifely duty by you."

"It sounds as though you're not taking the threat seriously. That would be a mistake," Michael warned.

"Give me a break. Someone is just letting off steam."

"Ashley, this could be serious, or it could be nothing at all. I know you think it's a crackpot, but I want you to give the letter to your Secret Service agents so we can have it analyzed. There are a lot of screwballs out there, and you could be one of their targets. Promise me you'll give the letter to your agents."

"I can't. I threw it away."

"You threw a letter away that was evidence of your being threatened?"

"Michael, please. I told you what I was thinking: Crackpot. If any more threatening letters are delivered, I'll hand them over to my agents," Ashley promised.

"You need to understand: you're fair game for people who are disgruntled, or worse, over your decision. It doesn't matter where you live—here, in New York, or Timbuktu—you're still a possible target."

"Okay, okay. I don't like it, but I get it. The Secret Service will scan not only my packages but everything that comes to the museum before they turn it over to us. That should calm you down somewhat."

"Good. I've also notified Homeland Security and let them know about the threat."

"How could you have already notified Homeland Security when I just told you about the threatening letter I received? Wait . . . you already knew about the threat to me, didn't you?

"Yes and no. The day after our press conference, Ed and Jack informed me of a threat made against you. We put everything into motion then to find out what we could and placed the necessary protection around you that we deemed prudent. I didn't know you'd personally received a threat until you mentioned the letter to me just now. Just promise me you'll keep the agents around you informed of anything suspicious or any further threats," Michael pleaded.

"I will, but you realize how crazy this is? Right? You've been in politics for years, and I went completely unnoticed. Now, I'm shark bait." Ashley sighed. "It's inconceivable to me that someone would care so passionately about what I do or don't do. Michael, what about Jeremy and Juliette? Has anyone threatened them?" Ashley held her breath waiting for his answer.

"No. Don't worry; they're fine. Have you talked to them recently?"

"Yes. I called them both when I got back to New York. They're glad to be back at college. Juliette is dealing with security better than Jeremy, which was predictable. I'm assuming campus security at both Stanford and Berkeley are working in conjunction with the Secret Service?"

"Everything is being done to keep us all safe. The Secret Service is good at their job. Trust them and quit giving them a bad time," Michael ordered.

"Hey, I resent that. All I do is tease them. But you . . . you have to deal with them all the time. It's hard to imagine why anyone would want to be president. It seems the negative aspects far outweigh the positive. How do you cope with all of the negativity, the lies, the manipulation, and the life-and-death decisions?"

"For me, it will be a matter of keeping a clear focus on what's good for the country and in the best interests of the American people."

"I understand the rewards of public service. Helping people is in my blood too. I just enjoy working at it on a much smaller scale than you. I like working in the trenches with people. Any kind of public service is a good thing.

"Change of subject. How would you feel if I gave one in-depth interview? The press is not letting up, and I thought if I chose someone I felt I could trust . . ."

"No matter what you do, you'll never be able to satisfy the public. You've made yourself more of a media target by rejecting the role of the First Lady than if you hadn't. People want to know all about you. I wish them luck. I've been married to you for over two decades, and I'm still surprised when you do the unexpected. Unfortunately, Ashley, the media is going to be part of your life from now on whether you like it or not. They're completely fascinated with you. I know you hate it, but surely you recognize the truth in what I'm saying."

Michael's comments were met with silence. Ashley knew he was right. She wished to God he wasn't; she'd never asked for any of it.

Michael continued, "But if you do decide to give an interview, I'd appreciate it if you'd wait until after the inauguration. Dealing with the media is tricky, and I'd like to see if there's any chance that some of the hoopla over your decision will die down, especially in light of the new position I've created."

"Fair enough. If I decide to give an interview, I'll wait until after the inauguration, and I'll let you know about it well in advance. Another change of topic, are you planning on attending the Black Tie Dinner this year? As you might expect, I've been spending the majority of my time since I came back to New York working on the event."

"Honey, I don't think it's a good idea. You're asking for far more headaches than you know. In the past when I've been there, it's been as your husband. When I was a senator, it was no big deal. Now that I've been elected president, the amount of security that would need to be in place for me to be there, not to mention all the screening and security checks your guests would have to endure, would make the hassle not worth it for you and them. I want to attend—I do—but my coming will change the focus of the evening. Do you understand?"

"Yes, unfortunately. I know you don't like hearing this, and it's unfair for me to say it, but I wish you'd never gone into politics. We didn't have a clue how much our lives would be affected when you decided to run for public office. The media spotlight, the constant scrutiny, and being followed around by the secret service—it wasn't anything we could ever have anticipated when we were younger. And I hate what it's doing to us."

"I wish you wanted to be the First Lady. I wish you wanted to share this experience with me. I hate the fact that your life and our kids' lives are being affected by my career decisions. I wish I could take all of the attention off of you, but let's focus on what we can control. Is there any way you can come for a visit?"

"How about this weekend? Can you fit me in?"

"I'll make sure my schedule is cleared to the extent I can. I've really missed you."

"I've missed you, too, Michael, so much. Okay, we have a date for this coming weekend. You won't forget, will you?"

"Forget you? Not likely. I'm glad you called although I was planning to call you tonight after my meeting. After the inauguration, I hope I'll be able to establish a little more of a normal work schedule, which should make it easier for us to plan times to be together."

"I'd love that. I'd welcome some consistency in our life even though you have taken on the biggest job in the United States. Did you have to aim so high? I'd like to remind you again—I love you; it's politics I hate."

"Right back at you on the 'love you' part although I still wish I could get you to change your mind. What happened to the good old days when women did what they were told?"

Ashley laughed. "Those would be the good old days for whom? Please, I beg you, don't launch into your barbaric days of yore. I might ask, what happened to the Prince Edwards of the world? When he had to choose between the crown and Mrs. Simpson, he chose love. Ah, now those were the good old days.

"Honey, I need to get back to work regardless of how much fun it is to sit here and exchange barbs with you over how women were once considered chattel and how long it took for women to get the vote. Congratulations again on finding a workable solution to the problem I created. I'll see you Friday."

After hanging up, Ashley felt the knot in her stomach relax. Michael was the best medicine in the world for what ailed her. He'd always been. They were never at their best when they were at odds with one another or apart for very long.

16

Michael was relieved and pleased that Ashley had called. Their stalemate had come to an end, at least partially. He was still hurt and disappointed that she didn't want to share his experience in the White House. He wondered if he'd ever get over how deeply she was hurting him. Even if he could eventually forgive her, hurt seemed to have a memory and a life all its own, a way of springing forth and setting itself free when you least expected it.

Time to get back to work. He knew the meeting had come to a halt in his absence. No decisions could be made without his stamp of approval. When Georgia interrupted his meeting saying Ashley was on the phone, he had wanted to talk to her and was glad she had called. She was reaching out to him, trying to repair the gaping hole in their relationship.

He hoped this coming weekend they could steer clear of the many land mines scattered between them. He missed the closeness they had shared before the election got in the way. Besides being his wife, Ashley was his best friend. That hadn't changed, and he missed his best friend.

Michael opened the door to the conference room, and eight pairs of eyes assessed his mood as he made his way to his chair. They knew it was Ashley who'd called, and they were waiting for the other shoe to drop.

"Sorry for the interruption," Michael said. "Where were we?"

Ed resumed the conversation. "We were just about to discuss the current opinion polls about Ashley. The numbers still show the majority of the nation disagreeing with her, but she's gaining supporters with women in the eighteen to forty-five age group. Plus, there's been a shift in the undecided category. She's gained 3 percent in that group. A greater concern is the correspondence we're receiving from other heads of state.

Michael said, "It's too early to gauge reactions. It's been only about a week since Ashley's decision became public knowledge. All we're getting now is a read on knee-jerk reactions. It's natural for there to be an adjustment period. I think we'll have a far more accurate picture in a couple of months."

"True," Ed agreed, "but we'll continue to monitor the polls to see if there's any shift in public opinion. At any rate, I think it's time to move forward with your plan for the director of protocol."

Michael nodded. "I'll announce the position tomorrow morning at the press conference. However, I'd like your feedback. Should we announce the position and introduce Paula at the same time? Or just announce the position and introduce Paula later?"

"Personally," Jack responded, "I think you should announce only the creation of the position tomorrow. If you introduce Paula too soon, it will look like you're moving too fast to replace your wife, like we had someone waiting in the wings."

"I agree. That was my take. So, we'll announce the new position as part of transitioning from one administration to the other."

Ed added, "One of the key points we need to convey is that your administration is capable of handling anything that comes your way and not to act as if this has immobilized us."

Michael agreed. "I'll have Georgia call Paula and let her know she won't be needed at the meeting tomorrow. He stood up and stretched. "Let's meet again first thing in the morning. We've got a lot to accomplish before the inauguration."

Everyone was keenly aware of the workload that lay ahead, but every member of Michael's advisory team was still operating on an adrenaline high from winning the election. They had complete confidence in Michael's ability to lead and be a great president. They felt fortunate to be part of such a historic event.

Back at his apartment, Michael kicked off his shoes and raided the refrigerator. He plopped down on the sofa and covered his eyes with his forearm. Nothing had really gone as he'd expected this past week. Ashley's announcement had dwarfed almost everything else. Michael was thankful he'd found a workable solution to the dilemma. He hoped he'd made the right choice in filling the void Ashley's absence had created. He felt cautiously optimistic about the possibilities.

17

Some reporters talked among themselves while others recorded introductions for tapes that would be completed and aired after the press conference. There was an air of expectancy. They hadn't been told ahead of time what would be discussed, so there was a great deal of speculation about what the newly elected president might be covering. With all of the drama of the past week, the reporters were ready for just about anything.

President-elect Taylor was prompt. He walked into the room accompanied by Vice President-elect Hughes. Both were smiling and seemed in good humor. Ed Branton and Jack Sutton followed behind them closely.

The president-elect stepped up to the microphone. "Good morning, everyone. We've had a busy week, but I'm happy to report we're making good progress toward transitioning from one administration to another. I'd like to thank President Nelson for all of his cooperation this past week. He's to be commended for his generosity, and I'd like to thank him for his assistance during this period of transition.

"Two appointments you're already familiar with. Ed Branton is now my chief of staff, and Jack Sutton is my new press secretary. You've seen both of these men in action during my campaign, so you know how capable they are. If it weren't for them, I probably wouldn't be here. I'm extremely grateful to both and happy they are joining my White House staff.

"As you all know, last week my wife, Ashley, announced she didn't intend to fulfill the role of the First Lady. I know that came as a shock, and as I shared at the press conference a week ago, I would have preferred for her to assume the traditional role as past First Ladies have. However, she has chosen to continue her work and has returned to Manhattan.

"This is an unprecedented situation, which called for an unprecedented solution. I believe past First Ladies have accomplished remarkable achievements during their husbands' time in office, and equally important, they've served as official hostess for the White House.

"To preserve that tradition, I've created a new administrative position entitled the director of protocol. The number one responsibility for this new director will be to function as the official White House hostess. Other duties will be added to this position as the days unfold.

"I'm confident that this will enable the White House to continue to greet foreign dignitaries and their wives as they always have with the exception that the hostess duties are now separated from the responsibility of the wife of the president.

"In major corporations, the responsibility for entertaining, decorum, and formalities is generally assumed by a staff member of that corporation. In the military, there are officers in charge of protocol. So this isn't such a giant leap for this administration to take.

"As soon as I fill the director of protocol position, Jack will announce it at one of his daily briefings. Now, if you have any questions, I have time to answer a few."

Jack stepped forward to assume the responsibility for the remainder of the press conference. He pointed at a reporter. "Your question, Chuck."

"Mr. President, what other options did you consider before deciding to create the director of protocol job?

Michael listed the other possibilities that had been discussed for dealing with the absence of the First Lady and the possible ramifications of the other choices.

Jack called on another reporter.

"Mr. President, I'm assuming you believed creating a new administrative position was the best solution. Are you anticipating any problems in filling the position?"

"No. I already have a short list of people under consideration for the position, but as you know, before I can decide, each potential candidate has to be vetted."

Jack pointed to another reporter. "Last question."

Todd Conway stood. "Have you told your wife about the direction you're taking, and if so, what was her reaction?"

"Yes, I did tell Ashley as soon as I made the decision. She's very glad that we were able to reach such a workable solution and wished us well."

Jack intervened. "Thank you all for coming. We'll have further announcements regarding President-elect Taylor's selections for his national security team coming shortly, in addition to other key cabinet positions. Remember, until the inauguration, I'll be holding daily briefings here at ten in the morning. See you all tomorrow."

18

NBC – Breaking News – Brian Williams

"In another unprecedented decision, President-elect Taylor has announced the creation of a new position within his administration. He's calling it the director of protocol. His purpose is to have the new position assume the hosting responsibilities for the absentee First Lady, Ashley Taylor.

"Since election night, Mrs. Taylor has made it clear she does not want to assume the traditional role of the First Lady but rather intends to continue in her job as the director of the Cameron Museum of Art.

"This is the first time the wife of a president has declined to serve in the capacity of the First Lady, and she's received harsh criticism from both sides of the aisle as has President-elect Taylor. However, Mrs. Taylor doesn't appear to be reversing her decision even with what I'm sure is a great deal of pressure from many sources.

"It will be interesting to see how this solution will work. We'll be sure to keep you informed as this story unfolds."

MSNBC – Rachel Maddow

"The President-elect, Michael Taylor, announced today he's creating a new position, the director of protocol, to assume the duties traditionally held by the First Lady.

"It will be interesting to see who is appointed to the job. I can't imagine stepping into a role that is relatively undefined. None of us really knows what the First Lady does besides acting as the hostess for the White House and generally adopting some additional cause to champion while her husband is in the White House.

"And what happens when Mrs. Taylor visits her husband and there's a state dinner? Who's the head hostess then? I'm glad I don't have to figure it out.

"We tried to reach Ashley Taylor for comment, but so far she hasn't returned our calls.

"I agree with Mrs. Taylor's original position, which is the spouse of an elected president should have the right to choose whether or not he or she wants to be part of his or her spouse's political life. To date, this is the first time this issue has been called into question. What do the rest of you think? You can log onto Rachel Maddow.com to give us your opinion.

Fox News – Bill O'Reilly

"Do you remember when I told you voting a president into office who comes from Berkeley had the potential of being bad for our country? Well, here's further proof.

"President-elect Taylor has created a position to replace his wife; he calls it the director of protocol.

"There's nothing about this decision that is good or right or moral for our country. Do you know what the word is for betraying one's country? It's treason. Most men would be ashamed of their wives for this almost treasonous behavior, and they would have the dignity to step down from the office.

"Mrs. Taylor is being unpatriotic and, I'd have to add, selfish. The example she's setting for the young women of America isn't to be tolerated. I'm calling on all of the citizens of our country to let their voices be heard. Call your congressman and weigh in on this very important issue."

Late Night with Jimmy Fallon

Jimmy deadpans to his audience, "Did you hear President-elect Taylor is going to appoint a director of proto-call girl? That would be proto-call girl." He pronounces "protocol" again with the emphasis on "call girl." The audience laughs.

"What?" He places his hand to his ear as though he's listening to a message in a nonexistent earpiece.

"I'm sorry. I meant to say, he's appointing a director of protocol to handle the duties of his wife." Jimmy raises his eyebrows and makes a suggestive face. The audience laughs again.

"What?" He listens again to a supposed earpiece.

"Let me try this one more time. Today, President-elect Taylor announced he's creating a new position in his administration called the director of protocol. This position will assume many of the responsibilities of past First Ladies, and it will be under him."

The audience laughs as Jimmy shakes his head and grins. "Listen, this is serious business. I'm just trying to report the news here."

19

Two weeks had passed since Michael had announced the director of protocol position, and the media was rabid to get a direct response from Ashley. Reporters and paparazzi followed her everywhere, constantly bombarding her with questions.

"What was your first reaction when President-elect Taylor told you about his solution for filling the First Lady position?"

"Are you and President-elect Taylor separating?"

"Are you getting a divorce?"

That's it; she'd had it. It was easier said than done to keep repeating "No comment." Ashley threw caution to the wind. Her patience had been stretched to the point of snapping, and her fuse was short. After hearing the next ridiculous question—"Is there another woman in President-elect Taylor's life?"—Ashley stopped and turned to face the reporters.

"I'm only going to say this once. The president and I are not separating or getting a divorce, nor is my husband fooling around with another woman. But it doesn't really matter what I say, does it? Because you'll edit and splice my comments until you come up with a sound bite that suits the inflammatory story you want to tell."

Ashley had the childish urge to give the crowd of reporters the finger, but she knew that would only make matters worse. She flashed on the picture that would appear on the front page of every newspaper if she gave in to her impulse. Of course, she'd be doing exactly what they wanted her to do. She sucked it up and entered the museum. At times like these, she was extremely grateful to have the Secret Service running interference for her. They couldn't shield her entirely, but it was a lot better than it would be if they weren't around.

To their credit, they did a great job of keeping the media out of the museum and from blocking its entrance. The number of visitors had almost doubled due partly to all of the notoriety surrounding her. Ashley hoped that, given time, some other juicy news story would come along and the press would find a new target for their focus.

Ashley sat back and looked at the stack of work accumulating on her desk. She glanced at her watch; it was only nine thirty, and she already felt as if she'd put in a full day of work. The weeks and days before the museum's Black Tie Dinner were hell. No matter how much advance planning went into the affair, a million details had to be handled at the last minute.

Every year she wondered why she agreed to host the event. She worried over every detail of the glittering black tie affair. Yet, not once in the years since she'd been in charge of planning the event had there been even the slightest glitch in the scheme of things.

Even her boss and friend, Robert Cameron, the owner of the famous Cameron Museum of Art chain, was confident that under Ashley's supervision, the Black Tie Dinner would be a stellar event. Robert was lavish with his praise about the way she handled things. And, if the increases in her annual salary were any indication of his sincerity, he meant every single word. She was currently making about the same amount of money that Michael would be making as president. It was a far cry from where she had started life, living in a one-bedroom apartment with her mother. Despite her achievements and rise in social status, she was still filled with doubts, and her doubts had a voice: if only she worked harder; if only she worked longer hours, if only she worked smarter if only she worked more efficiently. If, if, if.

Her relationship with Robert and his museums went back almost two decades. He hired her right out of college, and she quickly made her mark on the San Francisco museum with her fresh perspectives. She was well liked by her coworkers, popular among the patrons, and sought out by new artists looking to place their work. She negotiated important exhibition exchanges with other museums and galleries.

She loved her job. She was thrilled to be working while Michael was in law school. It never occurred to her to think of herself as the breadwinner. She and Michael were a team. What each did was for their future together. However, after law school when Michael began working for the district attorney's office in San Francisco, he wanted and expected Ashley to quit her job. Ashley felt as if, having served her purpose, she was being put out to pasture. Her job became a constant source of irritation between them right up to the day she gave birth to the twins, Jeremy and Juliette.

Michael maintained she should stay at home while the children were little, a completely unnecessary demand for him to make as far as Ashley was concerned. She didn't want her children raised by someone else. She wanted to be there for all of their "firsts." She had no intention of working until they started school, but just the fact that Michael was trying to tell her what to do infuriated her. Once the twins started kindergarten, she made it clear to Michael she planned to go back to work. Michael didn't want his wife to work. His mother had been a housewife while Ashley's mother had always worked. It never occurred to her that she wouldn't do the same thing. She wanted to work, and she loved her job.

Against her husband's advice and wishes, Ashley returned to work. She called Robert Cameron to see if there was a job available in his organization. He didn't hesitate to rehire her. She'd been an outstanding employee. Not only did she have a passion for the arts and the museum, but she also was an astute businesswoman.

Her ruminations had put Ashley in a sentimental mood this morning. This would be the first Black Tie Dinner that Michael would miss since she'd begun hosting them. Lord knows, she didn't have time to daydream, but she felt like indulging herself anyway. She smiled just thinking about the weekend she and Michael had shared just a week ago.

It began with awkward silences and polite responses. They'd made a pact to leave their disagreements at the door. However, thrashing out their positions again might have been better than trying to act as if everything were just fine, which it obviously was not. Hurt feelings and nervous tension kept them from returning to the easy companionship they'd always shared.

Michael made a concerted effort to stock the kitchen with all of their favorite foods, hoping to avoid the need to go out. Their time together was a gift, and they both wanted desperately to put their relationship back on an even keel. They ached from their need for one another and hated how disagreements and separations had hindered their relationship and sex life. It was as though there were a barrier in the room they couldn't remove.

Ashley finally plunged in. "We've got to get past this, Michael, or our marriage will truly be over whether we stay together or not."

Michael didn't speak for a minute, which gave Ashley a doomed, sinking feeling in the pit of her stomach. Finally he let out a long sigh. "I don't know if I can get over you refusing to be the First Lady. I want to, and it doesn't have anything to do with the media or my image or appearances. I'm hurt that you don't want to be at my side during my presidency. We've always tried to be there for one another during key times in our lives, and this time you checked out.

"Plus, I can see what great things you could accomplish as the First Lady. You could promote art and the fine arts for the nation, not just for the museum. Doesn't that appeal to you on some level?"

Ashley couldn't think of anything to say to make it better. She would never be happy running a national campaign for the arts. She reached up and put her arms around her husband's neck and kissed him, first tentatively, then with increased passion. That was all it took to shatter the glass wall that had formed between them.

Making it to the bedroom was out of the question; their need for one another was too great. Michael began raining small kisses all over Ashley's face and neck, working his way down to the top of her breasts and back up again to her mouth. He kissed her with unchecked desire, separating her lips with his tongue as he sought the sweet cavern within her mouth.

All control was gone as they ripped buttons and seams in an effort to rid themselves of their clothes. Michael reached for Ashley's breasts and kneaded them as she reached for his rigid manhood that lay against her stomach. The groans they uttered only intensified their need for one another.

He entered her body swiftly with her hips rising to meet his thrusts as their bodies began a long dance of remembered lovemaking. Their abstinence had made their joining all the more fevered and sweet.

Michael slowed his movements as he covered Ashley's breasts with his hands. He teased her nipples with his thumbs, bringing them erect. He closed his mouth over one breast and laved it with his tongue and pulled at it slightly with his lips as Ashley ran her fingers through his thick hair. They were overripe for one another's bodies. Each movement sent lust pulsating through their nervous system. Their climaxes came fast and strong, leaving them dazed and breathless.

Ashley leaned forward and rested her head on her husband's shoulder. "I've missed us."

Michael stroked the hills and the valleys of his wife's body, all so familiar, and yet he would never grow tired of touching her. She was the woman he'd love until the day he died, despite the fact that she was a real pain in the ass sometimes.

Ashley stood to gather her clothes, but Michael captured her hand. "You mean, that's it? That's all you've got?" he said, teasing and taunting her.

"I need to be fed, now," Ashley insisted. "And I'll take the biggest glass of water that you have."

With their arms wrapped around each other's waists, they went in search of food.

Over cold chicken and potato salad, Michael asked, "Do you think there's any chance you could transfer to the Cameron Museum here in Washington?"

Despite the laziness that had overtaken her body, Ashley's radar went up immediately. "Of course, I could probably make it happen, but that's not being fair to Ted, who runs the Washington, DC, gallery. I won't use my influence, or yours, to get reassigned to Washington. That's not playing fair, Michael."

"Is it fair or acceptable that the two of us remain apart? Is it fair that the wife of the president lives in another state?" Michael asked.

Ashley spoke quietly as she rebutted her husband's remarks. "It didn't seem to bother you when you were a congressman or a senator. We lived apart then, and you never pressured me to live in Washington. Just because you're going to be the president doesn't mean we should be stepping on other people's toes. Don't you dare intervene."

That was the last conversation they'd had on the topic. For the rest of the weekend, they were like teenagers. The only time they got out of bed was to eat, bathe, and seek out other imaginative places to make love.

On the plane ride back to New York, she'd already begun to feel the emptiness inside her that only Michael could fill. Why were relationships so hard? You'd think finding the one man you'd love forever would be good enough to carry you through life. But no, it seemed fate had a sense of humor. It seemed to say, let's see what happens if we throw these obstacles at them. Well, fine. A plan was beginning to form in her mind, and after the fund-raiser and the inaugural celebration, she would give it her full attention.

20

shley picked up her office phone on the second ring. "Ashley Taylor speaking."

"Hi, Ashley, it's Steve. Have I caught you at a bad time?"

"Describe bad. Bad as in having a paper cut, or bad like I'm in one of those Indiana Jones movies trapped in a room with the walls slowly closing in on me? Please, no Indiana Jones bad news; my heart can't take it."

"Oh, honey, you *are* close to the edge. I'm not sure 9-1-1 responds to neurosis attacks. I was thinking of coming over. I thought we could go over any last-minute details or changes that you may want to make. I could be there in about thirty minutes. Will you be free?"

"Free? I used to know what that was; now it's a vague concept. Yes, I'll be here, and I'd love for you to come over. I can't believe it's all going to be over day after tomorrow."

"It does sound as though you could use a distraction, but then you get crazy every year around this time worrying about how it's all going to turn out."

"The decorations and the ambience of the whole fundraiser are pretty important, don't you think? After all, this is a museum of art, and most of the people who attend are used to luxurious surroundings. Coming up with ideas that will dazzle everyone year after year isn't so easy, you know."

"Well, so far, you've done a damn good job; you're the reigning queen. I'll see you in half an hour, and you can let your neurosis hang out all over me. See you soon."

Ashley was looking forward to going over everything again. You could never check too many times if your goal was perfection, and it reassured her to check and double-check the ideas she'd developed for the event.

This year's theme was "In a Galaxy Far, Far Away." Twelve walls, scattered throughout the four floors of the museum would be completely covered in tiny white lights. Each wall would depict one of the twelve constellations of the zodiac using tiny red bulbs among the white lights to form the constellations. A brass plaque would identify the sign of the zodiac. Likewise all of the ceilings would be covered in tiny white lights, giving the illusion of a starlit night.

She worked with Steve and a floral designer to create artful flower arrangements made entirely from white gardenias and silver beaded twigs wound with tiny white lights. More than sixty-five arrangements would be placed on dinner tables and lighted pedestals throughout the four floors. Ashley wanted the scent of gardenias to be embedded in her guests' minds when they remembered their night at the museum.

On a serving table in the center of the main hall would stand an enormous ice sculpture of Rockefeller Center's golden god, Prometheus, surrounded by his ring depicting the twelve signs of the zodiac. Around the base of the ice sculpture, twelve silver baskets, one for each astrological sign, were arranged. Each basket would hold a paper scroll tied with silver ribbons heralding the upcoming year's astrological predictions for the sign it represented. These were offered as yet another whimsical token for the museum's guests in memory of the evening.

Ashley picked up the invitation to the fund-raiser and looked at it once again with critical eyes, knowing full well there was nothing she could do now to change it since they'd already been sent out. The invitation was printed on white marbled vellum backed by gold-flecked black card stock. The Cameron Museum of Art emblem was embossed in silver wax at the top of the invitation joining the vellum to the card stock. The message was simple: support the arts by enjoying an evening of fine food and drinks from the gods, accompanied by music and dancing.

Over three hundred invitations had been sent to members, patrons, board members, and friends of the museum. At twenty thousand dollars a plate, only the rich and elite made up the final guest list. With close to seven hundred thousand millionaires in Manhattan, the competition was fierce for support from donors among the museums, galleries, and performing arts centers. And this year for the first time, close to one hundred additional requests were received for tickets to the event. Ashley was well aware that the upswing in popularity of the fund-raiser had more to do with people hoping to rub elbows with her husband than a burning desire to support the arts. She asked Mavis, her secretary and close friend, to call everyone who had requested tickets and tell them the president-elect would not be attending the affair this year. But, in spite of that, people were still choosing to attend, most likely to get a look at the woman behind all of the controversy.

The fund-raiser was very lucrative for the museum. Last year, over five million dollars had been raised from the reservation fees alone. Ashley hoped after all of the reservation fees and donations were tabulated this year, the museum would surpass last year's goal.

The annual event had become quite famous for its unusual themes and décor. She knew New Yorkers. They loved to dress up and be seen and photographed. Top magazines and newspapers vied for coverage of the event, and with the guest list reading like a Who's Who in New York, most patrons saved a spot in their busy holiday schedules for the event. The fund-raiser was well attended, hugely successful, and had to date received excellent coverage by the media.

Mavis buzzed Ashley to announce Steve had arrived. When she opened the door to welcome him, she saw Matt and Dave camped outside her office. The Secret Service was completely in charge of security for the fund-raiser this year, and she'd already witnessed the difference in the level of intensity from the year before. Ashley felt they were going way beyond what was necessary, but she had little say in the matter.

She turned to Steve. "Hey, there. I'm so glad you're here. No matter how many times I run through all the arrangements for tomorrow night, I'm sure I've forgotten something."

Steve felt her forehead. "Prognosis, total neurosis, but I'm here to put your fears to rest. Where do you want to start?"

"Let's start in the conference room so we can spread out the floor plans on the table. That'll give us a visual to look at as we discuss the progress we've made and what's left to do."

When they had the plans rolled out and secured on each corner by a tape dispenser, stapler, and paperweights, Steve explained, "The ceiling lights are completed here, here, and here. We still have this area to complete, and then we'll be finished with the ceiling lights. I didn't want to start the walls until you close tonight. I'm assuming the museum will be closed tomorrow as usual on the day of the fund-raiser."

"Yes, workmen will be setting up all over the place. I'd like to have everything ready by late afternoon so I can go home and relax a little before I have to be back here to greet my guests."

"Is your husband coming?"

"No. We talked about it, but he felt dealing with the additional security necessary for him to attend wasn't worth it. I wish . . . oh, never mind. Just ignore me. Thanks again for your help in creating such a magical environment. I really appreciate how you never flinch when I come up with my crazy schemes. You're amazing."

"I simply breathe life into your visions. And, Ashley, if you ever decide to change professions, you can come and work for me."

"Thanks. Are you planning on attending?"

"I wouldn't miss it for the world. In fact, since your husband isn't coming, why don't I swing by your place and pick you up? That way we'll both be here to see that everything's ready."

"What about Craig? Isn't he coming with you? You two haven't parted ways, have you?"

"No, he has a theater dinner to attend. He said if it finishes early, he'll try and scoot over here. And, even if he were coming, picking you up isn't a problem."

"Then I'll take you up on your offer. I want to get here ahead of everyone else to walk through the museum one last time, and I'd appreciate your company and a second opinion. Don't plan to take me home, though. I'll be staying until the bitter end, and you undoubtedly will have better things to do."

"Then, I'll see you at five thirty tomorrow."

"That's perfect. Steve, thanks again for all of your help."

21

Showtime! Ashley looked at her image in the mirror and saw an elegant, composed woman. How could that be when butterflies had invaded her stomach and her knees had turned to Jell-O? She concentrated on taking deep, cleansing breaths, exhaling slowly, and created a visual image of the tension flowing out of her body and away from her. Please let this evening be a success.

The doorman rang her apartment to announce Steve had arrived and was waiting downstairs. The mantel clock indicated the witching hour had arrived. Picking up her cloak, she glanced one last time at the mirror to assure herself she hadn't turned into a pumpkin.

She and her Secret Service agents rode the elevator down to the lobby. When she stepped out of the elevator, Steve was there waiting, looking extremely calm and handsome. He was wearing a black Versace tuxedo with a shawl collar, which was trimmed in black bugle beads.

Ashley laughed as she held her arms away from her body to model her dress for Steve. She, too, was wearing black, a strapless dress entirely covered in bugle beads. It was a complete departure from her normal style; however, she'd fallen in love with the simplicity of the dress. She wore her hair down, flowing smoothly over her bare shoulders, one side pulled back and secured with a diamond clasp. The only other jewelry she wore was a pair of diamond earrings.

"Well, aren't we a couple of bookends?" Ashley smiled. "You look great. No one will believe we didn't coordinate our outfits ahead of time."

Always confident and generally sarcastic, Steve replied, "I work only with people who have superb taste. Time to get Cinderella to the ball." He held the door open for her, and they walked out into the freezing night air.

A sleek, black limousine waited at the curb to whisk them away to the fund-raiser.

Agent Campton stepped forward. "Excuse me, Mrs. Taylor. You failed to tell us you were being picked up. I'm sorry for the inconvenience, but we'll need to drive you. Turning to Steve, he said, "You're welcome to ride with us, sir."

Ashley was annoyed with herself for forgetting and inconveniencing Steve.

"I'm sorry, Steve. It's my fault. Would you consider dismissing the limousine and riding with me?"

"Sure, give me a second." Steve walked over to speak to the driver of the limousine. Ashley noticed he gave him some money before joining her in the back seat of the car.

"Let me reimburse you. I know you paid the driver something for his time," Ashley offered.

"Not to worry. I use Charlie's service all the time, and he was very understanding. I'm just glad we have a little time together before the night begins."

Tonight would be her first appearance socially since she'd rejected the First Lady position. She expected to be treated differently; it would be naïve to hope that she wouldn't be, but she prayed that her guests would be civil and that their good manners would keep their opinions and most critical thoughts in check.

She and Steve were the first of the staff to arrive at the museum although security was already there in full force. Each person attending would be searched before being admitted. Agents would be stationed both inside and outside the gallery. Ashley had pleaded with them to wear formal attire and, to her surprise, they had. At least now they would blend in instead of screaming "Secret Service."

After putting her belongings away in her office, Ashley conducted a quick tour of the museum. True to his word, Steve's merry band of magicians had completed all of the tasks they'd discussed; her vision was now a reality. The Cameron Museum of Art's lighting had been dimmed to accent the decorations, creating a luminescence that set just the right ambience.

Ashley looked up. The museum ceiling had been transformed to a starlit night with twinkling lights. The walls dedicated to the zodiac constellations glowed with a festive and whimsical flair. The sweet smell of gardenias wafted throughout the museum, and the diffused lighting and lit pedestals showcased the snow-white blossoms and silver beaded twig arrangements strategically placed around the four floors of galleries.

The small orchestra was in the process of setting up for the evening's performance. Ashley met with the leader briefly to double-check if he'd received the updated list of music she'd requested. She'd worked with this group before and knew they were top-notch musicians whose tranquil music would contribute to the evening's mood.

Steve checked the buffet table to make sure the hors d'oeuvres were artfully arranged on tables draped with silver lace tablecloths. The ice sculpture would be set in place just before the doors opened. Feeding over three-hundred-and-fifty people was an enormous task. The majority of the waitstaff had worked for the museum before and were excellent at serving and clearing promptly. The dance floor gleamed and reflected the starlit ceiling above giving the illusion that one would truly be dancing among the stars.

Ashley didn't hear Steve come up behind her. "Are you satisfied with everything?"

She turned around and kissed him on the cheek. "Everything looks beautiful, just like I imagined it would. Thank you for putting up with me and my craziness year after year."

"It's my pleasure although I wish you could learn to relax more about this event. I suspect even now you're about to jump out of your skin, judging by the way you flinched when I approached. Would you like me to get you a glass of champagne?" Steve asked.

"No, thanks. We're about to open the doors, and I want my hands free to greet my guests. You know, tonight's the first time I've been in a social situation since Michael was elected. I guess I'm a little nervous about how people are going to treat me or what they might say." Ashley shook her head. "I need to get past caring about things like that."

"Don't expect too much from yourself. You're bound to be nervous under the circumstances. But I'm betting people are going to be so thrilled to be around the wife of the next president that they'll be on their best behavior with you."

"From your mouth to God's ears. Anyway, I hope you have a good time tonight. You deserve a night on the town. See you later."

Ashley moved toward the front entrance of the museum. Time to get things started.

Robert Cameron suddenly appeared to stand beside her. She greeted him warmly with a hug. "I hope everything meets with your approval." Ashley smiled up at him.

Robert nodded. "How could it not? Each year you up the ante on your creative genius. The museum looks spectacular. Thank you for all of the effort you put in to making this annual event so special. Is Michael coming?"

"No, unfortunately. Dealing with the security necessary for him to attend would have been a nightmare. As it is, I'm not thrilled about all the security that's necessary just for me. I hope you're not upset about it."

"On the contrary, I believe it's quite necessary. Are you forgetting you're married to the next president of the United States and your safety must be guarded? Remember, Ashley, my museums are getting a lot of free publicity because of you right now. We're reaping the benefits of your notoriety. By the way, I'd like to speak to you later about a sensitive matter when you have time. Why don't you give me a call tomorrow, and we'll see if we can find a good time to meet?"

"Will do. Right now my only concern is assuring the success of this evening, but I'll call you first thing in the morning. Now I believe it's time to get things started." She nodded to one of the museum employees and indicated with a turn of her wrist to unlock the front doors.

As the guests entered, Ashley greeted each one individually, always remembering some personal tidbit of information.

"Mr. and Mrs. Nystrom, I'm so glad you could make it. How's Carmine faring at Vassar?"

"Mr. and Mrs. Binkman, it's such a pleasure to see you again. Did you finally get away to Barbados? Last time I saw you, you were looking forward to the trip."

Ashley was fortunate to have a photographic memory, so it wasn't hard to recall some piece of personal information from her index of thoughts. However, she didn't rely on her memory completely; she also kept a journal with personal information about the various patrons of the museum.

Soon the museum was filled with a low buzzing sound from the hundreds of conversations taking place. Old friends reconnected and were introduced to new acquaintances. Throughout dinner, conversations grew louder, aided by alcohol and the clattering of tableware. The New York elite took great pleasure in a meal well prepared and presented. They felt privilege was their due and loved hobnobbing in the company of the woman married to the future president of the United States.

After dessert was served, Ashley made her way to the orchestra and makeshift dance floor. She stepped up to the microphone. "Welcome and good evening. I'm sorry for the interruption. I hope you've all enjoyed your dinner. And, for those of you still eating, I promise I'll be brief." She waited while her guests quieted and refocused on the woman they were all curious about.

"First, welcome to the Cameron Museum of Art and 'A Galaxy Far, Far Away.' Thank you all for coming to our extravaganza tonight and for your continued support of the museum. The support you give so willingly allows us to continue to offer outstanding programs and events for all ages. My experience has shown me that New Yorkers are among the most generous people on earth. I hope you have a wonderful time this evening, and if there's anything you need, don't hesitate to ask for it. Thank you for coming." She finished by applauding the group of people around the main room.

As Ashley finished her welcoming speech, Robert approached the microphone and extended his hand to her. As was their tradition, she and Robert began the evening's dancing with the first dance. The orchestra played 'Starry, Starry Night' as she and Robert glided across the floor under the star-studded sky.

"Another successful opening. I'm surprised you're not interested in assuming the role of the First Lady. You're a natural hostess."

Ashley stiffened.

Robert added, "Now, don't get your dander up. It's a natural comment to make. I've known you too many years to measure my words. What I said is true. However, I respect your decision to keep working. After all, as I said earlier, my museums are getting a lot of free publicity because of you."

"I'm sorry, Robert. I'm extremely touchy about the whole subject. The decision I made was never about my feeling I couldn't handle the responsibilities of being the First Lady.

It's just a job I don't want. I've never wanted to be part of the political arena. Michael hasn't been sworn in yet, and I'm being hounded by the press until I'm about ready to scream. My privacy is nonexistent, and I'm going to have to live with this for at least four more years and who knows how many years after that. There's no question I was naïve to believe I could simply walk away unscathed. But I'm hoping in time people will accept my position and there won't be as much of an uproar about it."

"Maybe they will eventually. Stranger things have happened."

"You don't believe that, do you?" Ashley looked up at her boss.

"I think you've got the whole nation debating the issue, and perhaps it's time to re-evaluate the necessity of the First Lady role and entertain the possibility that a woman should get to choose. But I'd be lying if I said I didn't sympathize with Michael."

"I know. I imagine all men, and many women, do," Ashley said. "Thanks for the dance. Now it's time for me to get back to work. If I don't get another chance to talk to you tonight, I'll give you a call first thing tomorrow morning so we can set up a time to meet."

Ashley turned and headed toward the food service area where the waitstaff and caterers were working. She worked her way through the crowd, stopping to speak to several groups of people she encountered on the way. She listened intently to what they had to say and laughed easily at the various anecdotes. She was the ultimate hostess.

Geoffrey Carruthers watched her as she moved with ease from one group of people to another. She looked exquisite tonight. Their paths had crossed many times before at various fund-raisers and charity events. They weren't strangers, but something was different tonight. He felt drawn to her like a moth to a flame.

Ashley sensed she was being watched and turned to scan the room of familiar faces. Her eyes stopped when she recognized Mr. Carruthers, billionaire, land developer, and international playboy. He was staring at her intently. He lifted his champagne glass to her in a mock salute. How odd. She nodded slightly to acknowledge his presence before turning her attention back to the conversation at hand. She knew she'd have an opportunity to greet him before the night was over.

It was well known that Mr. Carruthers was a ruthless and cunning businessman, and his wealth was an obvious testimony to that truth. He enjoyed the hunt and challenge that his various enterprises and holdings brought him. He was like a panther on the prowl, ready to spring into action and consume any unsuspecting or wounded business he encountered.

His reputation with women was unparalleled. Rumors portrayed him as a gifted womanizer, capable of making any woman feel as if she were the most important thing in his life. He was also an unabashed flirt. He seemed to take great pride in outmaneuvering his prey. The women who were the targets of his relentless pursuits blossomed under his steady and deliberate attention, unaware they were about to be eaten alive.

Geoffrey had been keeping track of Ashley's movements since he first arrived at the museum. He'd always thought she was beautiful but definitely off-limits due to her unapproachable demeanor where men were concerned.

Now, with her recent announcement rejecting the role of the First Lady, he suspected all was not well within the Taylor household. What kind of woman would turn down being the First Lady? He certainly intended to find out. He had to admit, she intrigued him. She was a surprise, and he was rarely, if ever, surprised anymore. There was far more depth to her than he'd previously imagined, and he was determined to find out a great deal more about her.

He drifted over to an area that Ashley would have to pass when she left the catering area. He wanted a few minutes of her time. Without an awareness of where his mind was drifting, he was already fabricating a reason to meet with her outside the museum.

Ashley stepped away from the banquet table and turned to rejoin her guests. As she headed toward one of their more generous benefactors, she felt a warm hand encircle her arm. She turned to see who was delaying her and came face to face with not only Geoffrey Carruthers but also her Secret Service agents.

"Mr. Carruthers, please remove your hand from Mrs. Taylor's arm."

Ashley looked at Matt and Dave. "You don't need to worry that I'll be whisked away by Mr. Carruthers; he's an old acquaintance."

Matt and Dave were unimpressed. They were tired of babysitting her. They were tired of trying to convince her that anyone, *anyone*, could be a potential threat. And if anyone could get to her, anyone would have the leverage they needed to get to the president.

Geoffrey dropped his hand from Ashley's arm and spoke to the agents. "I apologize for alarming you, especially since you're carrying those big guns," he joked. "I just wanted a quick word with Mrs. Taylor. I can assure you, she's perfectly safe with me." He almost choked on his words.

Ashley was embarrassed to have Mr. Carruthers spoken to as if he were a threat. After all, he was a guest of the museum. She addressed Matt and Dave. "Why don't the two of you get something to drink? There are several nonalcoholic beverages being offered. I assure you I have no intention of leaving this room, so you'll have no problem keeping me under surveillance."

That seemed to satisfy the two agents because they moved away from Ashley back to their original position, completely ignoring the offer of refreshments. From their vantage point, they continued to monitor the exchange between Ashley and Mr. Carruthers. They knew him by reputation only, but there was something about him that bothered them, and they had learned to trust their instincts. He behaved like a man on the prowl.

Ashley turned and said, "Hello, Mr. Carruthers. I'm sorry for the confrontational display of security although I'm sure a man like you is keenly aware of the pitfalls of dealing with security and bodyguards. I'm glad you stopped me; I haven't had a chance to welcome you to tonight's affair. I'm glad you were able to make it. I hope you're enjoying yourself."

"I am although I'll have to admit that many of the events I attend bore me. Congratulations on another well-executed gala. You've created a very otherworldly atmosphere. Quite charming. Everyone I've talked to appreciates your ability to create such original and entertaining themes."

"Thank you. Your presence always makes things extra special."

"I don't know about that. I think New Yorkers, more than most, enjoy good artistic expression in whatever form it takes. I suspect after attending one of your fund-raisers, most people would keep their calendars open for any of your future events. Your artistic sense of beauty is truly quite extraordinary. Have you ever thought of leaving the museum to pursue other lines of work?"

Ashley laughed. "Actually, I recently received a job offer, which I turned down." Why did she say that? She hardly knew Mr. Carruthers. "I love my work. I love being around such beautiful and timeless pieces of art and feel extremely lucky to work for the museum."

"You must love your work to reject being the First Lady. Most women would have jumped at the chance."

"Maybe it's never occurred to others to refuse the position," Ashley countered.

"I have to say, I feel sorry for your husband," Geoffrey pushed.

"Do you feel equally sorry for me?"

"Now you've put me on the spot. It's natural for me to identify more with your husband than with you. Yet I do understand your passion for your work, but even though I understand the reasons you made the choice you did, I don't agree with it. I guess I'm old-fashioned."

Ashley reminded herself, as the director of the museum, she must be pleasant to all of her guests, no matter how badly she might be provoked. As far as Geoffrey Carruthers being old-fashioned—*what a crock.*

"I suppose I should get used to hearing people say they don't agree with my decision. It may be too much to hope that those who are more cosmopolitan, like you, might come to understand and accept the stand I've taken."

"You've overlooked the fact that the more money people generally have, the more entrenched they are in maintaining the status quo and tradition. You're very naïve. I don't mean that as an insult; in fact, I find it rather charming."

Oh, no insult taken, buster. I love philandering playboy billionaires thinking of me as naïve. Ashley was surprised that Mr. Carruthers was being so bold and outspoken with her. He'd hardly spoken to her before tonight, and their previous exchanges were never more than a polite greeting. She was annoyed that she couldn't tell him exactly where to go with his opinions.

"Everyone is entitled to his own opinion. Now, if you'll excuse me."

"Wait, I didn't mean to make you mad."

Of course you didn't. You just wanted to share your opinions, whether they offended me or not. "Whatever makes you think I'm mad?" Ashley smiled. "My responsibilities include seeing to all of my guests, and it's time I do that, so please excuse me. I hope the rest of your evening is enjoyable. Thank you for coming."

"Wait. Before you go, would you do me the honor of a dance?"

"Persistent, aren't you?" Ashley said charmingly. "Is that how you win so many of your acquisitions, by wearing your opponents down?"

"I hope you don't think of yourself as an opponent. Nothing could be further from the truth. I highly admire you. Now, how about that dance?"

Ashley noted Geoffrey's relaxed posture. He always appeared cool and controlled. She wondered if that were true. He was very good-looking and could be quite charming. He loved women and seemed to collect them easily. The press followed him around like royalty, and they loved the juicy stories he seemed to create in his wake.

She knew it would be bad form to turn down his offer to dance, and so did he. He was one of the museum's biggest financial supporters and had recently inquired about a board position. Plus, it would be rude, and she couldn't allow her personal feelings to interfere with her business sense. "Shall we?" Ashley turned toward the dance floor.

Geoffrey knew he'd cornered her. Good manners and being the head of the museum demanded she accept his offer to dance. He didn't care how he managed it; he wanted her in his arms. He wanted to smell her and feel her body next to his. He wanted a lot more from Ashley, but he was willing to wait. She stimulated him in a way other women didn't. She argued and challenged him. He was used to being catered to and agreed with by other women. He'd made his fortune by using cool logic and taking calculated risks, but for what he had in mind for Ashley, he needed to act as nonchalant as possible. He wasn't too sure how easily she spooked or what might make her treat him like a piranha.

The orchestra began playing a slow song as Geoffrey led Ashley out onto the dance floor. He took her into his arms and held her closer than she obviously wanted because she adjusted the distance between them immediately. Easy, just take it easy. He kept saying it like a mantra. He intended to see her again, and there would be other opportunities to find out just how deep her passions went. For now, he needed to win her trust and friendship.

"I apologize if I offended you. I know the decision you made must have been very hard for you. I'm sure you felt pulled in a million different directions. It takes a lot of courage to do what you did. I admire courage even though I don't share your opinion. I'm sure it would have been a lot easier to just give in to your husband's wishes."

Maybe she underestimated Geoffrey. He seemed to grasp the difficulty of the dilemma she had faced. "It was literally the hardest decision of my life."

A flash and a soft whirring sound interrupted their conversation. A photographer from one of the New York papers—actually the same photographer who had been outside her apartment building—had just captured two of the country's most well-known personalities dancing together. The photographer's mind was already racing with ideas about a caption for the picture. He was sure the paper would run it—a notorious playboy and the Reluctant First Lady dancing without a husband or a girlfriend in sight. Well, well.

As the song came to an end, Ashley stepped back. "Thank you for the dance."

"Thank you. Good luck surviving the storm of publicity."

"I think I'm going to need more than luck although I appreciate the thought. Again, thank you for coming. I hope you enjoy the rest of your evening." Ashley smiled.

Leaning toward Ashley and speaking in a conspirator's tone, he whispered, "I think the best part of my evening just ended. It's bound to be all downhill from here, I'm afraid."

He watched her as she walked away from him. He thought he could get very used to watching her walk toward him. He thought about their conversation, how her temper flared and her attempt to keep it under control, how direct she was in regards to her current publicity nightmare. There was no doubt he would see her again. An idea was already taking shape like molded clay.

He knew the cost of pursuing her openly. They were both extremely high-profile personalities; anything he did would be noticed and recorded by the media. Plus, she was married to the next president of the United States. He was playing with fire; he knew that. It only made the chase that much more exhilarating. Was it worth it? He wouldn't know for sure until he got a little closer.

22

The next morning, Ashley awoke begrudgingly. She sighed, wishing she didn't have to get up. She lay in bed trying to chase away her vivid dreams, which she'd rather enjoyed, but it was time to face another day with its new set of challenges. It wasn't that she didn't enjoy the day once she got up; it was the getting up part that was so hard, especially when the warmth of the bed was so inviting.

Once she was vertical, her thoughts turned immediately to the events of the previous night. The fund-raiser had been a success, another bullet dodged. The money received from the reservation fees alone had totaled over six and a half million dollars. That pleased her; however, the actual amount donated from the event wouldn't truly be known until the individual donations from all of the patrons had been collected. She knew many of the museum's benefactors would send checks before the end of the year to be sure they could claim their donation as a tax write-off. It wouldn't be until after the first of the year that she would have an accurate picture of the true success of last night's affair.

Ashley stretched one last time as she made her way into the kitchen. First the essentials: hot coffee, an English muffin, and the morning paper. She still wanted to read an actual newspaper in the morning although the rest of the time she read the news on her laptop. She mused about how anyone could function without a morning cup of coffee. Didn't they need a champion to chase away the urge to crawl back into bed? That first sip of hot, fragrant coffee comforted her soul. She swore the feeling of warmth that flowed through her body and loosened her neck and shoulder muscles was one of the closest parallels to a spa treatment a person could have.

As she waited for her coffee to finish brewing, she went to retrieve the morning paper. Sitting down with her coffee and English muffin, she separated the society section from the rest of the paper. Staring back at her on the front page of the society section was a picture of her and Geoffrey Carruthers dancing. The picture captured what appeared to be a very intimate moment, which it most definitely was not. The worst part was the caption underneath the photograph: "America's playboy, Geoffrey Carruthers, and the Reluctant First Lady, Mrs. Ashley Taylor, dance among the stars." The article that followed did an excellent job of covering last night's event. It was good publicity for the museum. What galled her was the caption under the picture; it was so misleading.

Damn. She felt a sense of dread. Certainly Michael's press secretary and his staff would be monitoring the major newspapers around the country and, in particular, the New York papers. There wasn't a doubt in her mind that if this picture of her dancing with Geoffrey wasn't in Michael's hands already, it soon would be. Great. One more thing to worry about.

Unfortunately she knew this type of thing was only the beginning. How did one adjust to being relatively unknown one day and a high-priority news item the next? The rehabilitation centers and graveyards were filled with those to whom success and celebrity came suddenly, like a flash flood, and who were unable to cope. It would be so easy to lose one's way, especially if there were no lighthouse or homing beacon, in whatever form, to keep one grounded and safely off the rocks.

By the time Ashley arrived at the museum, all traces of last night's affair had been removed. All the planning, the work, the worries, and execution had been stripped away and discarded after one shining evening of success. She always felt the same each year the day after the fund-raiser. Peggy Lee's old song "Is That All There Is?" came to mind. She had to be careful not to be overly dramatic. It seemed as though with most of life's big events, there was a huge emotional buildup, the excitement of the event, then just a whimper afterwards. *Jeez, Ash, get a grip.*

She asked Mavis and Kathy at the same time, "Okay, on a scale of one to ten, how's the day going so far?"

Without looking up from her work, Mavis said, "We've been pretty busy, but we're very glad the Grand Old Fund-Raiser is behind us."

"Me, too. Maybe now we can get back to our regular work routine that has been slip-slidin' away." Ashley broke into song for the past part of her declaration.

At her desk, Ashley took out her iPhone and pulled up her calendar while calling Robert to schedule the meeting he mentioned the night before. Now she had time to be curious about why he wanted to meet with her.

Robert's secretary answered the phone. "Hey, Pamela, it's Ashley. Is Robert available? He asked me to call."

"I'll check. Heard everything went well last night, yeah? I wouldn't have you upsetting him." This was said in a very stern voice and a lovely Irish accent.

"Who, me? Upset Robert? Really, Pamela, you should be worried about him upsetting me. Whatever would make you think I'm a troublemaker?" Ashley laughed.

"Don't be putting me on; I read the newspaper, don't you know. Hang on and I'll get him for you." Pamela put her on hold.

Robert's deep voice came on the line immediately. "How's my favorite muse this morning? You did it again. I've already received half a dozen calls complimenting you on last night's affair."

"Glad you're pleased. Even though it's an irritating cliché, you know it takes a village, blah, blah, blah."

"Well, every village needs its muse, and you're mine."

"I promised I'd call so we could set up that meeting. How urgent is it?"

"Nothing terribly urgent but definitely something I want to talk to you about."

"You want to give me a hint?"

"I'd rather talk about it in person. I know with Christmas coming up and then the inauguration on the horizon, you're undoubtedly swamped right now. Why don't we set up a meeting for some time at the end of January or the first of February?"

"If it can wait that long, it'd be a big help. I'm trying to wrap up things here at the museum. I'm planning to leave for Washington the week before Christmas, and I won't be returning until after the inauguration. Max will be in charge during my absence. You know, he's a curator worth his weight in gold. I would not have been able to take off so much time during Michael's campaign without having Max to back me up. How's the first week in February look for you?"

"Right now, it looks fine. How about February seventh at ten in the morning?" Robert asked.

"I'm making a notation on my calendar as we speak."

"I'm doing the same. Listen, Ashley, I hope you're able to put the museum out of your mind while you're in Washington."

"I intend to try and do just that. I trust Max completely. He's one you should keep your eye on. I'm excited and looking forward to the swearing-in ceremony. It's such a historic and momentous occasion for Michael, our family, and the country. I'm so proud of him; he'll be a wonderful president. I don't think people truly realize what a great man he is. He's everything this country needs. Just wait until you see him in action."

"I know how proud you are of Michael, and I think you're right—he's exactly what this country needs right now."

"Oh, I almost forgot to tell you the good news, Robert. We've already taken in over six and half million dollars from the Black Tie Dinner. When I get back, I'll have a more accurate picture of the money raised from last night's event.

"Are you and Audrey getting out of the city for the holidays?" Ashley asked.

"Yes, we're planning to spend the holidays at our home in Vermont. All of the kids and grandkids are coming home for Christmas, and we always look forward to being with all of them. How about your family? Will you be together at Christmas this year?"

"That's the plan. Jeremy and Juliette are coming to Washington for Christmas; then of course, they'll be back for the inauguration."

"I'll be watching with the rest of the country and the world, so behave yourself," Robert joked.

"I'll do my best. See you in February."

That night, when Ashley was back in her apartment and nestled into her comfy chair, she punched in Michael's private number. She was hoping for a nice, long chat with her husband. Unfortunately his message machine came on.

"Hi, honey. I just wanted to touch base with you about my arrangements to return to Washington. I have about a month off. I was planning to come next week and stay until after the inauguration. I'm looking forward to spending time with you even though I know you'll be extremely busy.

"The fund-raiser went off without a hitch, thank goodness. The only thing missing was you, and I'm not saying that to make you feel guilty; I just miss you. Call me if you get a chance. I hope you're holding up under all the pressure. I can't imagine all the meetings and briefings you must be having. Hope to talk to you soon. I love you."

23

Michael listened to Ashley's voice on his message machine after the phone rang, but he was in no mood to deal with her so didn't pick up. Instead he sat in his favorite chair looking at the press clipping of his wife dancing in the arms of none other than Geoffrey Carruthers. He didn't trust himself to keep the anger out of his voice. Where Ashley was concerned, he knew he lost his ability to be reasonable. He was far too jealous where she was concerned, but he'd always tried to hide it. To no one, he said, "Yeah, I'll just bet she missed me. It sure didn't look like it from the picture in the newspaper. You and Geoffrey looked way too cozy."

He'd been working in his office when Jack dropped the press clipping on his desk. He appeared unaffected in front of Jack; in fact, he was furious and seething inside. Not only was his wife not with him, she was on the front page of the society section dancing with one of the world's best-known playboys, and the caption underneath the picture was irresponsible journalism at its best. The caption insinuated something was going on between his wife and Geoffrey Carruthers, which he knew in his heart was not the case. To make matters worse, the reporter had used a moniker, "the Reluctant First Lady"; the nickname was bound to stick and be picked up by other newspapers and the media.

He knew he was being unfair. Ashley was most certainly performing her duties as the director of the museum; it was part of her job. He couldn't fault her for that. It was this crazy world where the media started rumors deliberately to sell their product without assuming any of the responsibility to the people they slandered. They didn't care what potential damage and pain they might cause with their innuendos and lies.

Still, it hurt. He wanted Ashley with him to share his presidency, not in another town living a separate life from him. Yet, to be fair, he knew he didn't have the right to insist she follow him when he was unwilling to do the same for her. She was right when she reminded him that they'd lived apart for years when he was in Congress and the Senate.

He was looking forward to having Ashley with him for a solid month. Maybe she'd see that living in Washington wasn't so bad. Maybe she'd realize how much they were missing by not being together on a daily basis; just maybe she would come to her senses. Yeah, right. That was a hell of a lot of maybes.

Now he felt guilty that he hadn't picked up the phone when she called. He needed to get a grip on his jealousy. It was unfair and unwarranted. He dialed her number and after one ring heard Ashley pick up.

"Hi, there. Sorry I missed your call. Sounds like the fundraiser went well. Are you feeling a letdown?"

"Absolutely not. I'm thankful it's over. It went well, and I'm pretty sure we topped last year's revenues. I'm exhausted, but it's a good exhausted if there is such a thing. I'm looking forward to my visit with you and having some time with our kids. Plus, there's this very special event I'm attending that's a tradition after a president has been elected. At least, I've been told it's special, but then my sources aren't all that reliable," Ashley teased. "I'm planning to fly to Washington on December fourteenth and will return a few days after the inauguration."

"Honey, that's great. I'm looking forward to having you here, if only for a few weeks. It's been hectic with all of the meetings and prep for the transition. Between meeting with potential cabinet members and dealing with the many issues of our country, there's never any time to relax, but then I knew that going into this job. Did you see the announcement about the director of protocol on television?"

"I did. It seemed to go well; it looked like your camp had all the contingencies under control. Have you had a lot of fallout from the announcement? You know I don't follow the polls; how did you fare?"

"The press is all over the map about my announcement. It's a new concept, a change from past practice, and it takes a lot of time for most people to adjust to change. The majority are still having trouble understanding why you rejected a role that every other president's wife has accepted. The politicians who are in my camp think creating the new position was a good idea, given your decision. The staunch conservatives will never understand the position you've taken and are pretty sure you're on a fast train to hell. Overall, the poll numbers don't look all that different.

"Honey, after the holidays I need to start organizing and packing my things for my move to the White House. Will you help me while you're here? I'd love for you to take a look at the residence and make it as homey as possible. It will be my home for the next four years, and like it or not, when you and the kids visit, it'll be your home too."

"Of course I'll help you. Plus, I'll be there to help organize things after the move. I know the residence is a lovely place. Mrs. Nelson was kind enough to send me pictures of the various rooms and floor plans. Although personally, I wouldn't want to live at the same place where I work. I'll try to make it a comfortable place for you to hang your hat even if it's usually a baseball cap. And, you're absolutely right, when the kids and I visit, we'll be staying there, too, so it needs to feel homey.

"As far as the White House being our home, the place that always feels the most like home to me is our California house. I look forward to the time when we both retire and move back there permanently."

Michael said, "Do you believe either of us will ever be able to retire? Somehow I find that hard to imagine."

"I don't think of it in terms of retirement as much as I think about us shifting gears and doing something different. I think whatever we do we'll always be involved in something. It's having the choice to be involved or not that appeals to me."

"Yeah, that appeals to me, too. And, we'll live in the same state and the same house at the same time. You don't think it will ruin our marriage, do you?" Michael teased.

"Oh, I think we'll be able to manage. We've managed so far."

"I'm really looking forward to you being here, far more than you know," Michael confessed.

"And, I'm looking forward to being there. Try not to work yourself into the ground. I'll see you in about a week. Goodnight, honey. I love you."

"I love you, too, Ash."

After hanging up, Ashley realized Michael hadn't said a word about the picture in the newspaper. She was sure he'd seen it. He was either still too furious to talk about it or had decided to chalk it up to being part of her job. She wished she felt more comfortable talking about things like the damn picture openly. They were both trying to act as normal as possible, but the strain was always there just under the surface.

24

*M*ichael stood before the Chief Justice with his hand placed on his father's Bible. The words he was about to speak had been spoken many times before, and he was quite certain that every man who had stood in this place before him and took the oath of office did so with pure and sincere intentions. He repeated the oath after the Chief Justice's words.

"I, Michael Taylor, do solemnly swear that I will faithfully execute the office of the president of the United States and will, to the best of my ability, preserve, protect, and defend the Constitution of the United States, so help me God."

It was such a short, simple statement yet one that would forever change his life and the history of a nation. He was humbled by the ceremony and fought against the emotions that swelled in his throat and threatened to choke him. He felt the weight for the leadership of the country shift from the current president to himself. The responsibility for the greatest nation on earth now lay in his hands.

His senses were heightened; he could smell Ashley's perfume; he could hear Jeremy and Juliette whispering. He knew his family was proud of him and had faith in his ability to carry the heavy charge just placed on his shoulders.

Michael shook hands with the Chief Justice and turned to kiss Ashley and hug each of the twins before he moved to stand before the podium to deliver his inaugural address.

"Vice President Hughes, Chief Justice Campbell, President Nelson, Vice President McClain, my family, distinguished guests, and all of our nation's citizens both here and abroad, you have just witnessed a ceremony that has been conducted for over two hundred years. Our nation is unparalleled in its ability to transfer successfully the seat of leadership from one leader to the next in a peaceful fashion, and as such we share a tradition of continuity.

"We live in the greatest nation on earth. No other nation can claim the ethnic diversity we enjoy in the United States. Our very differences give us our strength. We are a country composed of people from every other country on earth, yet we stand as a testimony to the world that people from diverse backgrounds, religions, and philosophies can live together in peace, prosperity, and hard times and still have the capacity to achieve great things. Dr. Martin Luther King saw this vision, this rainbow coalition, and knew it for what it was and could be. Our differences bind rather than divide us.

"A great nation such as ours demands the highest standards for its government. We must shine our light brightly into the night sky so our message of unity can stand as a witness for others. We are a civilization who will not be broken by hardships that come our way, for it is when Americans are challenged that they show the strength of character they truly possess.

"Each of us has a choice every day to make a difference, whether at home, at work, in our community, or in the world. We can choose to extend kindness and civility to others, to reach out to those who need our help and support, and thereby to live in peace and harmony with our fellow man. I believe Americans will always choose the high road and extend a helping hand to those in need. We recognize the truth in the saying 'Except by the grace of God, there go I.'

"I have pledged to keep my promises. They were not empty rhetoric or campaign slogans to get your vote. I stand behind the words I've spoken. We will take care of our sick and elderly. Healthcare, ample food, and financial security are the rights of every American. The elderly should not have to worry about whether a system they have contributed to their entire lives will disappear. A wise society recognizes the treasure of information, advice, and wisdom that lie within our parents and grandparents and should act as advocates on their behalf.

"We will provide the best education system possible for our children, for they are our future citizens and leaders. Our job is see that all children, no matter their background, reach their full potential and to assist them in becoming seekers of knowledge. It's never as easy as saying the words, but the job can be done.

"I will fight lawlessness and misconduct wherever I find it, whether in the form of unethical business practices, senseless violence, drug warfare, or threats of terrorism. We will search out the perpetrators of hate crimes, and with every means available to us, we will hold the lawbreakers accountable for their actions. It must be clear that, while I seek peace, I will fiercely defend our freedoms and our way of life.

"A prosperous nation needs to be prosperous for all of its citizens, not just a few. We have much to do in the area of creating jobs and stimulating our economy. However, we will continue to labor until the job is done, and the people who want to work will be given that opportunity.

"Throughout my campaign, I referred to the silent majority and challenged them to stand up and be heard, and they didn't disappoint me. More people voted in this election than in any previous election in history. All ages and ethnic groups took up the challenge and decided to have a greater influence on their government and their country. Now, we must work together. We must be strong advocates for America. It is our job to assure the survival of freedom in this global community in which we all live.

"We are the keepers of our inalienable rights as passed down to us by the authors of the Declaration of Independence. Our job is to pass these freedoms and traditions on to our children. We must maintain their heritage so they can carry the torch after us. We hold their future in our hands, and we must gently carry it until we can lay it down for them to pick up. We are all part of history, and history will judge how well we did our job, how well we preserved our planet, society, and our children's heritage.

"God bless you, and God bless America."

There was no turning back from his role in history. Now it begins. Relatively few men in the history of the United States had been charged with similar duties and powers.

He turned and grasped Ashley's hand and, with fingers intertwined, raised their arms together as they stood before all of those gathered to witness history in the making. The applause was enthusiastic and heartfelt. Both he and Ashley turned to include Jeremy and Juliette. They wanted them to share in this moment. Their family had always been close, and Michael felt his victory belonged to them all.

Arm in arm, Michael and Ashley, accompanied by the Secret Service, walked up Pennsylvania Avenue to their new residence. Michael leaned over to Ashley and said, "I wish my dad could have lived to see this."

Ashley responded, "He did see it, Michael. He simply has a higher vantage point than most of us. He'd be as proud of you as the rest of us are."

He looked over at his wife; she was absolutely luminous. She radiated charm and grace. If only she'd recognize the good she could do if she took her rightful place as the First Lady.

Her energy, drive, and passion could achieve such impressive things.

It had been wonderful having her with him these past few weeks. She'd been terrific at handling all of the events associated with the transition and pre-inaugural activities. She'd accompanied him to all of the scheduled events and never complained about the hectic and demanding itinerary. She was charming to all she met, drawing them in with her winning smile and keen sense of humor. It was easy to forget that she didn't intend to stay by his side and share in his journey.

Many designers had approached her about designs for dresses for tonight's balls; she rejected each of them politely.

She summed them up to Michael: "Too fitted, too formal, too restricting." Ashley had found many new designers in SoHo she liked. Ultimately she had purchased a dress from one of their shops. It was a floor-length dress done in swirling shades of purple, with a fitted halter top that left her back fully exposed. She liked it; it was simple, and she felt comfortable in it.

Her picture was already appearing in fashion magazines, usually under negative titles for the clothes she chose to wear. She was heralded as eccentric. Fashion experts claimed she seemed to choose clothes as an expression of her moods, and she had a penchant for clothes and designs from various ethnic backgrounds. Michael realized he didn't really notice what she wore anymore; he was so used to her style. But the press, accustomed to seeing past First Ladies in very traditional dresses and suits, didn't quite know what to make of Ashley.

As the Taylor family entered the residence at the White House for the first time, there were no quips or trivial conversations. Reality had descended and left its mark on each member of their family. What they'd discussed for weeks in the abstract was now a reality. Glibness had been replaced with reverence as the historical aura of the rooms vibrated with the vital force of the previous generations that had stood there before them.

"Kind of a heady experience, regardless of where you stand politically, huh?" Jeremy interjected his thoughts into the silence.

"No kidding," Juliette agreed. "When you think of all the presidents and their families who've lived here, it really humbles you. I like the way you've made it seem like home,

Mom. I noticed you had Dad's old chair sent here from California. What's he going to sit on when he goes home? He'll roam the house like an old dog who can't find the bone he's buried."

Ashley laughed, "I'll have to go on a scouting trip to find an exact duplicate of the chair, complete with broken springs. Otherwise, it's true, he won't know where to light, or if he does, he'll complain.

"Are you two planning to attend any of the balls?" Ashley asked.

Jeremy responded, "Yes, we were planning to go to one or two. We want the full meal deal while we're here. Fortunately we don't have to attend them all like you do. We'll probably pick out a couple that appeal to us and spend the majority of our time there."

"Just a word of advice: Don't let your guard down for a minute. It's not just your father who's newsworthy. Everything you say and do is a potential story for the press, so don't give them any place to go." Ashley used her most imperious voice with her kids, not that it would do any good. She knew she had no control over their actions anymore, but she also knew they wouldn't deliberately embarrass their father.

"Don't get into any philosophical discussions where you end up backing someone into a corner and making them look like a fool. And Jeremy, no matter what may be said, stay calm. Your dad and I don't need to be protected; we can take care of ourselves. Do you understand me?" Ashley asked, her hands on her hips for emphasis.

Ashley looked at her beautiful children sitting on the sofa. They both delighted and tortured her. She knew a lecture on deportment was a waste of her time; they always followed their own path. She'd taught them that. They weren't her babies anymore, and her influence on them was minimal at best and nil most of the time.

Michael intervened. "I trust you both to conduct yourself appropriately."

"Dad, we won't do anything to cause you to worry," Juliette responded.

Ashley rolled her eyes.

25

*M*ichael, it isn't as bad as you think. The press and everyone else were totally out of earshot and unaware of what happened between Paula and me. What was said was between the two of us. The only reason you know is because I'm telling you. You didn't honestly expect me to stand there and take her sarcastic, superior attitude, did you?" Ashley was pacing back and forth in their bedroom as she talked. She felt if she kept moving, the air flowing over and around her body would cool her down from her current boiling point.

Michael looked over at the clock. They'd attended seven balls, and he was exhausted. "Honey, it's three in the morning. I can see that you're upset, but can't it wait until we get up?" Michael asked. He had to get some sleep.

"Not really. I think you should know what you're dealing with in the Paula department. I'll do my best to make this short."

From listening to Ashley, Paula had said or done something to really upset her. He was curious as to what that was. As tired as he was, in his heart he hoped the root cause of Ashley's fury was jealousy. He wondered if he'd had that in mind subconsciously when he appointed Paula.

Up until now, the day had gone well. He was proud to have his family all around him at the inaugural activities. The luncheon was relaxed, and the toasts were good natured and friendly. Their time back at the residence visiting with family was like an oasis he'd discovered in the middle of a parched desert. As much as he enjoyed all of the pomp and circumstance surrounding his inauguration, he welcomed the time he was able to spend with his loved ones. He was completely relaxed and thoroughly enjoyed all of the good-natured kidding and joking even when he was the target.

Everyone was excited about the balls. His schedule tentatively planned for him and Ashley to spend about thirty minutes at each one. Ashley and Sienna kept reminding Jeremy and Juliette to keep an eye on Samantha and act as her guardians.

Jeremy joked, "Mom, Aunt Sienna, don't worry about Sam. We'll take good care of her, and I'm sure we can get a good price for her. Sam, don't you need to add a little more makeup? We want you to look your best tonight."

Sam went along with everything her cousins said and did; they could do no wrong in her eyes. She idolized them as they did her.

Ashley and Sienna didn't respond to Jeremy's outlandish remarks and deliberate baiting. They both were keenly aware that Jeremy and Juliette would be as protective toward Samantha as either of them would be. If anyone so much as even looked at Sam the wrong way, her cousins would descend upon them like archangels.

The whirlwind of balls had been exhausting. Michael and Ashley tried to keep to their established timeline, and at each ball, after dancing with one another, they danced with a few others before moving on to the next ball. Photographers were everywhere and were having a field day taking pictures of the new president and his wife. They made such good copy. Not since the Kennedys had such a handsome couple sparked such interest by the entire country. They each had an abundance of charisma, so just a word or gesture of recognition was all that was needed to make those around them feel special and singled out.

Naturally there was a great deal of speculation about the possibility that Ashley had changed her mind regarding her role as the First Lady. She'd been in Washington for almost a month, so it was only natural that rumors began to erupt about her intentions. Unfortunately the media had picked up the phrase in the caption under the picture of Ashley and Geoffrey Carruthers in New York, and the Reluctant First Lady nickname stuck. Ashley had come to terms with it; Michael had not.

From what Ashley had told him so far, it wasn't until they were at their sixth ball that a problem arose between her and Paula. He'd noticed the two of them deep in conversation but assumed they were catching up on gossip from California. The battle of wills that was being played out never occurred to him.

After all of Michael's ruminations, he finally answered Ashley. "No, honey, I didn't realize there was a problem, and I certainly wouldn't expect you to ignore rudeness or sarcasm, if in fact that was what it truly was. I'll have to hand it to you; you did an excellent job of keeping your cool and not creating a scene or bringing any attention to the two of you, but are you sure Paula was being deliberately sarcastic?"

Ashley rolled her eyes heavenward, her body language screaming "Give me a break." "You mean, did I imagine it? Could it possibly be that Miss Holier-Than-Thou could be sarcastic to your wife when you so clearly believe that's *my* best trait? I didn't misunderstand her words or her intentions."

Michael thought, *Deep water; tread lightly.* "I know how keen your intuition is, but isn't it reasonable for me to ask if it might be a misunderstanding?"

"Possibly it's reasonable for you to ask," Ashley responded. "But you've been too busy these past weeks and days to notice her behavior, and you haven't witnessed her comments to me. She makes sure she gets her digs in when you're not around or you're out of earshot.

"I understand you've had a million things on your mind, so it doesn't surprise me that you're unaware of what's been going on under your very nose. But if you had noticed Paula, you might have begun by noticing what she was wearing today, both at the inauguration and at the balls. Now, don't start dismissing me before I'm finished. And don't deny you are. I can see it from the expression on your face.

"At the inauguration ceremony this morning, she wore a little red suit very reminiscent of Nancy Reagan. How very First Ladylike."

"Are you telling me you're upset over what she was wearing?" Michael asked, confused. This had to be a woman thing. "Did you want to wear a red suit?"

"Dear God, please give me the self-control not to hit my husband over the head with some sharp object. Of course I don't want to start wearing suits, red or any other color. I hate suits, but that's not the point. Just listen.

"At the balls, she wore a very traditional ball gown designed especially for the occasion. She looked more like the expected First Lady than I did. Still, I ignored her obvious attempts to replace me in your eyes. She was silently screaming to you, 'See how much better I would be as your First Lady.'"

"Let me get this straight," Michael interrupted. "You and Paula had words over what she was wearing and the fact that you felt she was trying to act like the First Lady, a job you've clearly indicated you have no wish to fill."

"Would you give me a little credit, Michael? It's not just what she was wearing although your last statement seems to indicate to me that you wouldn't care if she did start acting like the First Lady, but I'll come back to that. No, there's a little more to it than what she was wearing.

"Finally, at the last ball, Paula and I had a chance to talk in private for a few minutes. In the beginning, our conversation was mostly chitchat about San Francisco and home, but she had that aloof, superior attitude she always has dangling around her neck like the Hope Diamond. But, the kicker is, she said she just couldn't understand why I wouldn't want to serve with you in the White House. And you can insert here her very fake attempt to look naïve and innocent, fluttering eyelashes and all. She mentioned what a disappointment it was for you that I had declined to be the First Lady. Did she stop there? Oh, no. She went on to say what a joy it was to work in your administration and how she intended to make you proud that you hired her. Then again, she asked as sweetly as possible—insert another fake smile here—how could I pass up the opportunity to work alongside you?

"You're lucky I didn't throttle her on the spot. I explained patiently that I didn't care for politics. To which she countered, she couldn't understand why; it's so exciting. I stressed how much I loved my job. To that, she said she felt I was very misguided. Finally I told her not every woman wants access to power through a man and that some women actually prefer to make their own mark in the world through their own work. I pointed out not all women wanted to live their lives in the shadow of their husband's career, and as hard as it may be for her to understand, I love my job and see no reason to give it up. I asked her if I should expect you to give up your job to be with me.

"Of course, she just smiled that insincere smile of hers and said any woman would be proud to stand at your side and share in your presidency. To which I replied, 'Evidently not, since it's not what I chose to do.' I'm telling you, Michael, she's got her eyes set on you, and it's not for the role you've put her in. I think she's looking to replace me as your wife."

"Do you think you could be overreacting just a bit? Remember she's being paid to be the official White House hostess, and I'm sure she's wearing the wardrobe she sees fit to go with her position. Plus, she and Connor are happily married."

Ashley raised an eyebrow. "Oh, really? Did you ever see Paula with Connor? In fact, did you even see him tonight?"

"Not that I recall, but you know how it is at these events. There are so many people to see and talk to. It's easy to miss someone."

"That is so typical of you, Michael. You've never been able to tell when some female is hitting on you. Your radar has always been tuned in to who might be coming on to me instead. Well don't be surprised if one day you find her trying to put you in a compromising position from which she could benefit."

"Ashley, just because you don't like Paula doesn't mean she's set her sights on me or that she'd behave in an inappropriate manner."

"I wouldn't bet the farm on it. Women like Paula are used to getting what they want, and when they don't get it, they'd rather see it destroyed than just leave it alone."

Michael was tired of this conversation. Ashley had always had great instincts. He usually trusted them, but he wasn't sure she was right in this situation. He did know it wasn't good to have Paula and Ashley at odds with one another. He thought he'd made it perfectly clear to Paula what was expected of her, and she seemed to grasp the situation he'd laid out.

"Ash, I know you fully believe what you're saying is true, but there is absolutely no chance of anything happening between Paula and me. In case I haven't mentioned this to you before now, when I first discussed the position of director of protocol with Paula, I made it perfectly clear to her that the position would not—emphasis on 'would not'—be replacing your rightful place as First Lady. I spelled it all out for her. I told her I didn't want any position I created to take away your rightful place at my side and that I was only looking for someone to take over the responsibilities First Ladies typically have."

Ashley shook her head. "As smart as you are, sometimes you're terribly dumb when it comes to understanding women and their motives. I appreciate the fact that you tried to be very clear in spelling out the parameters for the position to Paula and that you were trying to be considerate to me. But remember, you're the one who's always told me it's not wise to be constantly in the company of a coworker of the opposite sex. That despite all of the good intentions of the parties involved, it could possibly set two people up for temptation."

"Sweetheart, you need to have more faith in me. There's never been anyone for me but you. Plus, just so you know, Paula and I are hardly around one another at all at work."

"It's not you I don't have faith in; you know that. Paula makes me crazy. I've never cared for her although I've always tried to be gracious to her because of all of the support her family has extended to you through the years, but I've always thought she was pampered and spoiled. In regards to Paula, the gloves are off, as far as I'm concerned, and I for one have no intention of putting them back on."

Ashley sat down in a chair opposite her husband and put her head in her hands. Michael heard an "Ah, shit" escape her lips.

He got up and stepped behind her chair and began massaging her shoulders trying to relieve some of her tension. She'd been such a trouper this past month, matching her pace to his, and he'd been so proud to have her at his side. If only he could make her want to stay.

He continued to massage the back of her neck and shoulders; he whispered in her ear, "There's more, isn't there? What aren't you saying? What are you thinking?"

"There's so much I want to talk to you about, but as you pointed out, it's after three in the morning, and we have an open house tomorrow. If we both don't want to look and act like zombies, I think we'd better turn in. But, before I leave to go back to New York, we need to find some time to talk."

"Works for me; I'm dead on my feet. I promise you we'll find time to talk through whatever's bothering you before you leave."

Michael reached out and took Ashley's hand and pulled her up into a standing position. "I'm afraid if I don't drag you into the bedroom with me, you'll fall asleep right where you sit."

"Wise man. Lead on."

At the end of another long and arduous day, Michael and Ashley had welcomed people to the White House, graciously extending goodwill to all. With so many events to fill their time, it was easy to forget what lay ahead. They hardly took notice of how quickly the day passed until they withdrew from their public personas and were faced with saying goodbye to their kids and Sienna's family. Goodbyes were never easy, and this occasion was no different.

Michael was now the president of the United States. Their lives had changed, and they'd all needed to adjust to their new reality. Although the personal price was high for being so closely related to the president, they wouldn't have changed a thing. Each would make the personal sacrifices and adjustments necessary for Michael's sake.

When Michael and Ashley returned to the residence, it seemed eerily quiet, at least compared to the day before when it was filled with so many loved ones and good cheer.

Ashley planned to return to New York the following day, and she knew she and Michael needed to talk before she left. She was hesitant to speak about what was on her mind, an unusual feeling for her. She didn't want the time they had left together to be marred by any unpleasantness.

"Well, now that all the celebrations are over, it's time to get down to the business of running the country." Michael broke the silence in the room.

"Ashley, it's been wonderful having you here this past month. It's going to be hard to adjust to not seeing you every day and not sleeping with you every night—and I'm not saying that to make you feel guilty. I've loved having you here, but I understand it was only temporary."

She couldn't have had a more perfect lead-in to the conversation she wanted to have. "Do you? Do you really understand what's happening between us, Michael? How could anyone really understand what we've chosen to do, including us? I'm scared, and I've never been scared about our relationship before now. This past month has been wonderful; it's reminded me of all of the reasons we married and have always stayed together. But the fact remains, the stakes are so much greater than we ever imagined, and so are the temptations when we're apart."

"Are you referring to Paula again?" Michael asked, while running his hand through his thick hair.

"No, it's not just Paula. She's just a symbol of the separate lives we're leading and all of the extraneous people we're surrounded by on a daily basis. It's hard to stay close when so much is pulling us apart. I know this is how we've fashioned our lives, but I keep wondering what the true price is going to be for all the decisions we've made along the way."

"Are you considering leaving your job at the museum and coming to live in Washington with me?" Michael held his breath waiting for her response.

Ashley shook her head. "I still detest politics; I think it's mostly unethical and self-serving. But I'm afraid the price for the decisions we've made throughout the years will be our relationship. Are you willing to sacrifice that?"

"You already know the answer to that. Besides, as bad as the next four years will be in regards to our finding time to spend together, at least we're on the same coast." Michael reached for Ashley's hand.

Ashley looked down at their joined hands. "I'm worried that won't be enough. Look, I don't have any new insights into solving our problem, but we've had a taste of being together again on a daily basis, and we're going to miss it. There's just got to be a middle ground. I can promise you I'll be giving my full attention to finding a possible solution."

Michael was deep in thought about what Ashley had said. He agreed the price for the two of them following their dreams might be too high, and like his wife, he didn't have a clue how to bring any resolution to their dilemma, yet.

26

As soon as Ashley closed the door to her apartment, she dropped into her favorite overstuffed chair. Next to their home in California, she loved this place best. The apartment had three bedrooms and was very spacious by New York standards.

She'd redone the apartment so almost every wall was covered in bookshelves filled with books, family treasures, photographs, and some of her own creations. In this place, her favorite things from the various fragments of her life mingled and blended together.

She ached to just sit where she was and relax, but she wouldn't allow herself the pleasure until she was unpacked. She grudgingly got up and crossed the room to the phone. The message light was blinking; she'd deal with that later. If it was anything important, she would have a received a call on her cell. Whatever messages there were could wait. Instead she picked up the receiver and called downstairs.

"Hi, Albert, it's Ashley. I should have picked up my mail when I passed through the lobby, but my hands were full. Is there a lot?"

"Quite a bit, Mrs. Taylor. I'll have it sent up. Or would you prefer to have one of your Secret Service agents come down and get it?"

"I'd appreciate it if you'd have it sent up. I'm sure Matt and Dave will be interested in going through it before I have a chance to see it. I'll let them know you're sending it up. Thanks for keeping an eye on things while I was gone."

"Just doing my job. If you need anything, let me know."

Ashley stuck her head outside the door to let her agents know that the mail was being sent up. They nodded. She'd made a slight dent in their rigid demeanor. She was sure it was the chocolate chip cookies she pushed on them one afternoon. It seemed strange to her that these two young men were so inflexible. She was used to teasing and bantering with her kids, and she'd allowed some of that teasing to carry over to these two. She could tell that Dave wanted to unbend a little, but Matt was very conscientious and was all business, all the time.

Ashley started unpacking and putting her things away, then stopped and sat on the bed. For just a moment she sat there and looked around. There was very little here that belonged to Michael. There were a couple of changes of clothes but no real personal belongings. Likewise, the rest of her apartment was devoid of Michael's books or even the little pile he always made where he laid his keys and wallet. This was further evidence of the separate lives they lived.

It would be the same thing for him in the White House; very few of Ashley's things could be found there. The only place where their belongings shared a roof like normal married couples was at their home in California, and for the past several years, they'd spent only a few weeks there together. What a very sad and tangible sign of their own personal state of the union.

Ashley had no intention of wallowing in self-pity. For the time being, this was her life; this was her reality. She finished unpacking and went to retrieve her mail from Matt and Dave. "Could I interest either of you in a cup of coffee or tea?"

"No, thanks, but we appreciate the offer. Here's your mail. Everything seems to be in order," Matt said.

"No bombs, no hate mail, nothing to interest you at all? How very disappointing for you. It would've been much more fun if there was something suspect, don't you think? Now don't go getting all uptight on me. I can see from the expression on your faces, my sarcasm irritates you. Believe me, it's nothing personal; it's a habit from being around my kids so recently. I appreciate your concern for my safety; I really do. See you guys in the morning. I'll be leaving for work a little earlier tomorrow since I've been away for so long. Goodnight."

Matt and Dave both said goodnight. "You know, I don't think she means to taunt us. I've heard her with her kids, and they're always joking around. I think she's sincere when she says it's nothing personal." Dave waited for Matt's response.

"I know. I really like her, but her safety is our job. We're here to protect her. It's not my dream job or, I suspect, yours, but what really concerns me is that she might use that charm or sense of humor to put us off our guard and then give us the slip." Matt rolled his head to release the tension in his neck and shoulders.

"Do you really think she'd do something like that?" Dave asked.

"What do you think? So far, she's rejected becoming the official First Lady, and she's rejected living in Washington, DC, with the president. She acts as if her life hasn't changed, and she continues to charge into the thick of things without any thought to potential threats to herself. I'm pretty sure she's capable of just about anything. That's why I think we need to keep our guard up regardless of how charming she is or how many chocolate chip cookies she gives us."

While Matt and Dave discussed the First Lady, Ashley was going through her mail. Upon seeing an envelope from Sienna, she walked over and sat down in her favorite chair. Using a gold-plated letter opener she received from Juliette for Christmas, Ashley slit open the envelope.

The single sheet of paper within was definitely *not* from Sienna. It was a message written using piecemeal letters cut from printed material. The note said, "*gIvE Up YorE jo B! BEcUM tHE 1st LaDy OR dIe!*"

Ashley was shocked to receive another threat. Emotions surged through her, but anger was at the top of the list. She looked again at the envelope and realized the handwriting was not Sienna's.

"This is outrageous," Ashley said out loud to no one; however, the dialogue continued in her head. Now the crazies are using my relatives to get to me.

Ashley debated throwing the threatening note away as she had the others she'd received. However, this time Sienna and her family's safety could be at stake.

She crossed her living room quickly and opened the door. Matt and Dave stood up immediately.

"This letter," Ashley raised the paper for them to see, "is another death threat." She rushed on. "Whoever it is knows I have a cousin, knows her address, and used her address to get the letter to me. What can be done to protect Sienna and her family?"

Matt reached in his pocket for a pair of latex gloves. After putting them on, he asked, "May I see the letter?"

Ashley handed him the note. "I'm sorry. Naturally, I've handled the letter . . ."

"We can isolate your fingerprints from any others, but for now we need to get this to our investigative unit to see what clues we can garner from it."

Dave already had a clear plastic bag in his hands. He held it open so Matt could place the evidence inside.

"Look," Ashley explained. "I don't think this is a serious threat to me. What does concern me, however, is that whoever's sending these letters knows that Sienna is my cousin and used her identity to get to me. I think her family needs some sort of protection."

Dave responded immediately. "We take every threat seriously. You never know what a person's intentions are who would write a letter like this. We will follow procedure to the letter. This is not something you should treat lightly."

Ashley knew that was true, and she especially wanted to get to the bottom of it since Sienna's name had been used. "I think I'll turn in. Would you please let me know the results of your investigation?"

"Of course, we'll keep you informed," Dave answered. "Maybe now you won't treat your security so lightly."

"You're right, but you'll forgive me if I don't see danger around every corner or behind every potted plant. I'll see you both in the morning, and thanks for your help with this."

Ashley closed the door before either Matt or Dave could respond. She didn't need any further lectures on security. She might as well go to bed and curl up with a good book. Tomorrow would be her first day back to work since before Christmas, and she was quite sure she was going to need all the energy she could muster.

She had just settled in for the night with her trusty novel when her cell's musical message interrupted the serenity of her bedroom. Ashley hated late-night calls. Late-night calls equaled bad news, an attitude that was a holdover from her children's teenage years when they were out at night and before they had safely returned home. So, with dread, she reached for her phone. Caller ID identified the caller as Michael. Really? Did he already know about the threatening note?

"Hi, honey. Missing me already?"

"Why didn't you call and tell me about the note?" Michael demanded.

Ashley looked at the clock. "Boy, that was fast. It's been less than an hour since I turned it over to the Secret Service. I was going to call you tomorrow."

She could hear Michael slowly exhale, most likely counting his breath, a relaxation habit he had picked up from a book Jeremy had given him, Clark Strand's *The Wooden Bowl.* "A quick call tonight would have sufficed. Ashley, I want to know immediately about anything that concerns you. I worry constantly about your safety; you know I do. And while I know the secret service is superior at keeping us all safe, I would feel better if we lived under the same roof. Just imagine for a moment you heard about a threat to either Jeremy or Juliette's safety secondhand. How would you feel?"

"Okay, I get your point, but it's most likely nothing, and the Secret Service are very good at their job; you just said so. I know how busy you are; I saw that every day while I was there. You don't need to worry about me just because I'm not in your sight."

"I repeat, think about how you would feel if it were Jeremy or Juliette."

He had her there. She would have been frantic, despite the fact that there was nothing she could do, and she would absolutely need to hear their voices to help calm her down.

She conceded his point. "You're right. I should have called. I'm sorry. You realize, though, whether I was there with you or you were here, there isn't any more that you could do than you're doing right now. Lighten up and see the humor in the situation. Granted there isn't much, but someone out there really believes the little woman should be taking care of her man, and they don't think I'm doing that. Pul-lease. Cue the Tammy Wynette music."

"Ashley, there's no place for jokes about a threat to the First Lady. Besides, you haven't been gone even a day, and I already miss you."

Ashley got serious. "I know. I miss you, too. Honey, I need to get some sleep. Tomorrow is my first day back to work after being gone for over a month, and I'm already dreading the mountain of work that I'm sure is waiting for me. So, until the next death threat, I need to say goodnight."

"You know, you're impossible, don't you? Okay, goodnight for now. I'll talk to you tomorrow night," Michael said as he hung up.

Ashley thought for a second before she turned out the light; they'd be very lucky if they could stay in touch on a daily basis. Both of their worlds were spinning faster and faster and seemed to be heading in completely opposite directions.

27

Ashley swept into the museum the next morning balancing a cardboard cup holder carrying three hot drinks. She grinned at her secretaries. "I bring you nectar from the gods. Anyone interested in a tall white chocolate latte or a hot chocolate with whipped cream? I come bearing gifts for the troops in the field."

Her secretaries, both good friends, began bowing, repeating, "We are not worthy; we are not worthy," as each reached for the drink of choice.

Ashley hugged both of her friends. "Please tell me that every problem that occurred in my absence has been tastefully and tactfully handled and I return to an office free of problems and turmoil."

"Well . . ." Mavis said thoughtfully, "it all depends on your personal standard of tasteful and tactful. If you're not overly fussy, I think you may be in luck."

"Hey, I missed you guys. You know the White House staff could really use a couple of sassy secretaries. It would jazz up an otherwise rather dreary place. But don't you dare think of defecting; I won't write you a letter of recommendation worth a damn. We're a team, and a team sticks together. Tell me, what'd you two do while I was gone to stay out of trouble?"

"We were dutiful secretaries, so we watched the inauguration, of course. We saw Michael, I mean President Taylor, get sworn in and you and the kids standing beside him. It was surreal to see you standing in the middle of our country's most important event. Even though we work with you and know pretty much what goes on in your life, it's still hard to believe that you're married to the president of the United States.

"The purple silk pantsuit looked great on television. Every time you moved, the beads that dangled from the hemline of the top and the cuffs of the sleeves moved and glistened—quite glitzy for daytime in Washington, DC. You were lucky the weather was unseasonably warm so you didn't have to wear a coat. Plus, it was fun to listen to the reaction from the press, who think your style is outrageous.

"We noticed that all the rest of the women were wearing tailored suits in a variety of somber colors, just as you said they would, and that Paula lady wore a red one. They looked like their clothes came off an assembly line. We're glad you didn't feel pressured to follow suit, no pun intended," Mavis snickered.

"I'll bet you didn't know about the clothing factory in Washington, DC. There's a conveyor belt that stamps out boring outfits specifically dedicated to the clothing for the wives of politicians and, naturally, our women legislators.

Each garment is stamped with a tag saying "Property of the United States Government." Shoot me if I ever start dressing like that. I mean, really, shoot me because I won't be me anymore. The invasion of the body snatchers will have taken over my body."

Kathy said, "Unfortunately there were plenty of comments about what you were or were not wearing and the fact that you don't want to be the First Lady. News reporters were having a field day at your expense, but I guess that was to be expected, especially during the inauguration. At any rate, you and Michael, or rather, you and the president, looked great. We're so proud of you."

"Yeah, it was a very emotional day for our family, too," Ashley admitted. "Almost like an out-of-body experience and a very intense one at that. I'm glad it's over, and I'm so proud of Michael. He'll be a great president.

"Well, enough about that. I'm relieved to be back at work. Would you please buzz Max and see if he can meet with me sometime this morning? Also I'm sure you've kept a list of things that need my attention. If you've got it, I'll swing into action."

Mavis responded, "It's already on your desk. I'll let Maxwell know you want to see him. Welcome back—and thanks for the liquid inspiration."

Ashley looked around at her perfectly tidy office. It was just as she'd left it with the exception of the stack of papers and messages on her desk. So much had happened since she'd last been here; she halfway expected to see some big changes in her office. And yet, in many ways, it seemed like she'd never been gone. She looked over the list that Mavis had prepared for her. She began prioritizing items in the order she intended to handle them. She noticed Geoffrey Carruthers had called. She wondered what he wanted. Before she could deal with any of the items on the list, she wanted to go over what had happened during her absence with Max.

Before she had a chance to make her first phone call, Max knocked on her open door and stuck his head in. "Welcome back, boss. Do I have to treat you differently now that you're related to the president of the United States?"

"Absolutely. You can start looking around for some sort of tiara to buy me to wear while I'm here in the office. I suggest you begin your search at Tiffany's."

Ashley was thankful she could maintain her normal playful attitude with her coworkers. She was glad everyone was acting the same and not treating her differently. How different things were in Washington. There everything was so serious.

"Come in; sit down. I'm anxious to get caught up on what I missed while I was gone."

"Actually, you're in luck. It was pretty slow over the holidays. I dealt with some of the new acquisitions that will be arriving, and I've been working with the San Francisco museum about the Black History Month exhibitions we're planning to exchange with them. I've put all of the information together for you in this memo. Here's a copy." Max leaned over and handed Ashley the sheet of paper containing the information.

Ashley briefly scanned the memo. "Thanks, Max. I'm glad you didn't have to deal with any catastrophes. It gave me tremendous peace of mind to know you were in charge while I was gone. Truthfully, with you in charge I didn't worry about the museum at all."

"Thank you. I appreciate your confidence in me. How did you feel being in the center of history?" Max asked.

"I loved having time with Michael. We rarely have that much time together anymore, so for me that was a real treat. But I can't stand politics. It all seems so contrived, but Michael believes he can work within the system. If anyone can make it more real and honest, my husband can. He's such an optimist and a diplomat. I hope he can make the difference he wants and not get hurt in the process.

"When you're around some politicians, I swear they puff up like roosters preening in a henhouse. It makes me sick. But there're some who are in Washington for the right reasons and want to do what's good for America. I just hope they outnumber all the glory seekers.

"Most of them are highly suspicious of me, which I suppose under the circumstances is to be expected. The fact that I don't want to give up my career and fall in line like a dutiful politician's wife makes a lot of the men uncomfortable. I think they're afraid I'm setting a bad example for their wives. Some of the women aren't much better. Some of them really don't care and that's refreshing, but for the most part, I think most of the politicians wore garlic necklaces hidden under their shirts and suits to ward off any evil spirits I may possess. Heaven forbid if a picture were to be taken of them talking to me. They probably think it would hurt their careers—guilt by association and all that rubbish."

"Ashley, I've tried to put myself in both your place and Michael's. When I do, I feel sympathy for each of you. This has got to be a tremendous strain on your marriage, and even though you're not asking my opinion or advice, I'd think very carefully about not only what you want for now but what you want in five, ten, and twenty years down the road. What do you want your life to look like then?"

"When did you get to be so wise? I appreciate the thought. It's very good advice. That's exactly what I intend to do; I intend to think about the future. I've been formulating a plan of sorts in my head, and when I get it all figured out, maybe there will be a solution. As for now, thank you for all of your support. Now we both better get back to work unless there's something else you think I should know."

"Nope. It's all in the memo. Welcome back and let me know if there's anything that needs more explaining, but I suspect with that quick brain of yours, there won't be. I'll see you later."

Max stood to leave and just as he got to the door, he tossed a remark over his shoulder. "And, thanks for thinking of me when you were bringing the dynamic duo their drinks."

"Max. Have you started drinking something to fortify you in the morning? I'd gladly get you something when I pick up our morning drinks."

"No. Just trying to pull your chain."

Ashley yelled, "Quick, you two, throw darts at the back of that man leaving my office."

Mavis and Kathy didn't even look up from their work. They were used to Ashley's humor and wisecracks. They just shook their heads and kept working. They'd missed her while she was gone; it was good to have her back and in such good spirits. Since the election and before the fund-raiser, Ashley had been beginning to show signs of the strain that was accumulating. While she never lost her sense of humor, the tension in the office had begun to build. And when she got crazy, she made them crazy.

28

uring Ashley's first week back at work, she was in a constant footrace trying to catch up on matters that had been left for her personal attention. The day-to-day operations were back on an even keel, and she was knee-deep in plans for the museum's next major exhibit.

As she worked through the list of phone calls she needed to return, she noticed there were several calls from patrons of the museum who wanted to donate additional money. This was exactly what her boss had referred to, the status and attention she would bring to the museum because she was married to the president.

Ashley realized it was inevitable; being annoyed about it served no purpose. The whole situation was thick with irony. She'd spent a lifetime establishing her own identity, and now the interest in her was primarily because Michael had become the president of the United States. There was no sidestepping the situation. She had no choice but to suck it up and move forward.

There were three phone calls in her pile of messages that held more interest for her than the rest. One was from her boss, another was from Geoffrey Carruthers, and the third was from Oprah Winfrey. She could guess that Robert's call was a reminder about the meeting they'd scheduled before she left for Washington, and she was pretty sure that Oprah wanted to schedule an interview with her, but she didn't have a clue why Geoffrey would be calling. Might as well get to them.

Robert answered on the first ring.

"So, you're answering your own phone now," Ashley chuckled. "What else has changed while I was gone? Where's Pamela? You know I'd steal her from you if I could."

"Welcome back, Madam . . . uh, never mind. Pamela had to run uptown for a birthday gift, and you know perfectly well I can answer my own phone. But I'm looking forward to talking to you. Are we still on for tomorrow?"

"Absolutely. I'll be there at ten. Are you sure you wouldn't like to give me a hint about our meeting?"

"You've waited this long. I'm sure you can wait another day. I'm also very excited to hear about your backstage view of the inauguration."

Ashley laughed. "Oh, I think I can give you a reasonably good account. I'll see you tomorrow."

The next call was to Geoffrey Carruthers.

"Mr. Carruthers's office. May I help you?"

"Yes, thank you. This is Ashley Taylor, and I'm returning Mr. Carruthers's call. Is he available?"

"No, I'm sorry, Mrs. Taylor. However, he left instructions for me in the event you called. He'd like to meet with you for lunch to discuss the possibility of becoming a board member and establishing an endowment fund for the museum. Could you meet him for lunch day after tomorrow at the Russian Tea Room at one o'clock?"

Ashley quickly checked her calendar. The time was open.

"Yes, that would work for me. Please tell him I'll see him there at one."

"I'll be sure to give Mr. Carruthers your answer. Thank you for calling back."

The third call was to Oprah. The press had been hounding Ashley nonstop since she'd renounced the role of First Lady, and there had been no letup since the inauguration. If possible, the press was getting even more aggressive. She was being pursued by all of the anchors of the major networks and cable TV stations. She'd given a great deal of thought about whom she felt she could trust if she were to give an interview. She'd narrowed it down to three: Barbara Walters, Brian Williams, and Oprah Winfrey. She respected all three of them tremendously.

She hoped she was making the right decision to give an interview. She didn't know Oprah personally, but she felt a kinship with her as she imagined did most of her viewers.

Ashley dialed Oprah's number.

"Good morning, Ms. Winfrey's office. May I help you?"

"Yes, this is Ashley Taylor calling, and I'm actually returning Ms. Winfrey's call. Is she available?"

"Please hold, and I'll check."

Ashley waited just a few minutes before she heard the voice that millions could identify.

"Hello, Mrs. Taylor. Thank you so much for returning my call."

"Please, call me Ashley."

"Okay, but only if you agree to call me Oprah."

"I don't think that will be hard at all since that's how I've referred to you for many years."

"I must say, Ashley, I was very impressed with President Taylor's campaign message and his inauguration speech. But, you must realize, as much as everyone wants to know about our new president, they're even more interested in you. Would you meet with me to discuss a possible interview?"

"I don't have to tell you how crazy my life has been since I made the choice I did. I've debated for several months about whether or not to give an interview and finally decided to do one, and I'd like it to be with you. So, the answer is yes."

"I'm so pleased to hear that. Could you meet with me next week? Say Wednesday or Thursday?"

"Hmm . . . I can meet with you on Thursday in the afternoon. Will that work for you?"

Yes, it will. I'm really looking forward to finally meeting you."

"I feel the same way. Could we meet here at my office? Would that be too inconvenient?"

"No, I can make that work."

"Well, fine then. I can meet with you on Thursday at one o'clock. And, Oprah, I want you to know I'm still very nervous about doing an interview. In all honesty, I hate interviews, but I'm willing to put my trust in you."

"I understand completely. I'll see you at your office next week."

After Ashley hung up, she mentally ticked through the phone calls she'd just made. Yes, she was definitely getting back into the swing of things. There were always things to deal with and fires to put out, but she was doing the work she loved and was trying to settle into an exaggerated life filled with all the trappings that went along with being the wife of the president. She hated the media attention; however, she acknowledged it would probably never get any better while Michael was in office and recognized it could get a whole lot worse.

The next day, she was exactly on time for her meeting with Robert. She held out her hand to greet him. "I'm so glad to see you. How have you been?"

Robert took her hand, then pulled her in for a hug. "I'm fine but anxious to hear about you."

"Hold on there. You've made me wait for over a month to hear what you wanted to talk about. Time's up. What gives? We can chitchat later."

"Typical Ashley. No small talk; cutting right to the chase. Would you like something to drink before we begin? Coffee, water, something stronger?"

"Why? Am I going to need it?"

"I'd say probably not although I'm not too sure about me. At any rate, it's good to see you. Audrey and I watched all the television coverage. It's pretty rare to see a man we know so well in the Oval Office. We expect great things from him. But more importantly, how did you fare with all the hype surrounding the inauguration?'

"I managed. I loved being with Michael for a whole month; the rest I tolerated. We had a little time with Jeremy and Juliette, but there's never enough time to be with the people you love, is there? Okay, I'd say you've stalled long enough. What is it you wanted to see me about?"

"There's something important I've been wanting to discuss with you; however, I want you to promise me you'll hear me out and you won't get all riled up."

"Any meeting that starts with a statement like that can't be good. The most I can promise is I'll listen."

"That's good enough. Ashley, you know how important you are to me and my organization. You're an invaluable part of our family business and a good friend, and I want to see you happy. I would like you to consider transferring to the Washington, DC, museum. Working in Washington just might meet more of your needs. You'd still be doing the work you love, but you could see Michael every day, or at least you'd have the possibility of seeing him."

Ashley stood up immediately, sat down, then stood up again. She didn't know how to deal with all of her pent-up frustrations. She knew Robert was making this offer not based on the quality of her work; on the contrary, he was trying to make things more workable for her and Michael.

"What are you thinking?" Robert interrupted her thoughts.

"I know I shouldn't be, but I'm frustrated that you're trying to iron out my life."

"I'm not insisting you transfer; I'm offering you a chance to move to Washington, continue to work at a job you love, and be closer to your husband, whom you just told me you missed. If you and Ted switch museums, it would make things a lot easier on you."

"Please tell me you haven't talked to Ted about this."

"I haven't. I wanted to discuss it with you first. I think it's a good solution to the dilemma you're in, and I don't think Ted would mind."

Ashley began pacing. "First I don't want anyone making accommodations for me because of whom I'm married to. Hasn't anybody been listening? Secondly Ted has been with you as long as I have, and he's always said how much he loves the Washington museum. Third, yes, working in Washington would give me a chance to be closer to Michael, but it would also force me to be around the political world I detest so much. And lastly, I love working and living in New York. You know how much I love this city.

"I understand what you're trying to do. I know you have my best interests at heart. Even so, I don't want other people inconvenienced or pressured on my behalf because of Michael. Please tell me that you haven't had any conversations with my husband and that the two of you didn't cook up this offer?"

"I haven't spoken to anyone about this idea. I know you love New York and would prefer working here rather than in Washington, but aren't you putting your love of New York before the love you have for Michael?"

"It's not that simple, Robert. Of course, I love Michael more than I do New York. Although the New York museum is the star of your organization, it's still not the reason I want to stay here. I hate politics; Washington equals politics. Missing Michael is huge for me; nonetheless, please give me the courtesy of finding a solution that best fits Michael and me.

"I'd appreciate it if you wouldn't say anything to Ted. It's not something I want him to worry about although, knowing Ted, I'm sure it's already crossed his mind. Please accept the fact that this is what I want for now. I love my work here and am proud of what I've accomplished.

"Think about it, Robert. What's really changed, except now Michael is the president? When he was in Congress and the Senate, we had the same living arrangements we do now. Why all of a sudden does everyone want me to live in Washington? Don't answer that; I already know the answer. We've managed our commuter marriage for years. We aren't crazy about it; still we accept that it's been a necessity," Ashley said, winding down.

Robert raised his hands in surrender. "All right, I give. However, I want you to know the door is always open for negotiations on this topic if you should change your mind."

"I appreciate that, and thank you for caring enough to make the suggestion. Now how about some good news that should make you fairly happy?"

"Shoot. I can always make room in my day for good news."

"To date, the Black Tie Dinner has brought in over eight and a half million dollars. Plus, Geoffrey Carruthers called and invited me to lunch tomorrow to discuss his becoming a board member, and he also wants to establish an endowment for the museum." Ashley smiled like the Cheshire Cat in *Alice in Wonderland.*

Robert gazed at the pleasure he saw on Ashley's face. She really did love her job and reveled in every accomplishment made on behalf of the museum.

"Nice going, although I never doubted for one moment the fund-raiser wouldn't be a huge success. I told you; you're my muse. It's interesting that Geoffrey wants to become a board member and set up an endowment. While he's always been a consistent and generous patron in the past, he's never shown as much interest in the museum as he's showing now. I'd be cautious, Ashley. Geoffrey usually has ulterior motives. He may be hoping to reach Michael through you somehow."

"I'm well aware that people may try to use me in ways they haven't before in hopes of scoring points with my husband. It's insulting but a reality I have to deal with. At any rate, I'll give you a call after lunch tomorrow and fill you in on the juicy details. I need to run for now. I'm meeting with one of our benefactors who's interested in donating a painting to the museum from her private collection.

"Robert, thanks for caring about me so much. I truly appreciate it. I'll be in touch." Ashley moved toward Robert's office door. As she opened it, she asked, "If Ted were to call you about transferring here, you'd let me know, wouldn't you?"

"Yes, I would. Ted is a great guy, and I think if he was thinking along those lines, he'd call you first. So if that happens, you'd let me know, wouldn't you?"

"Absolutely. Talk to you later."

At the end of her workday, Ashley was curled up before a fire with a book in her lap and a cup of aromatic tea sitting next to her on an end table. She gazed hypnotically into the fire searching for answers. There was always something comforting about a fire. She chalked it up to something genetically imprinted in humans that celebrated their thrill at mastering fire. While the flames danced, she thought about her day.

Contrary to what everyone seemed to think, she felt as if she and Michael were on the downside of the years of separation. They had already lived apart for a great portion of each year for almost two decades. It didn't seem so far in the future anymore that the day would come when they could live together permanently. Wouldn't it be ironic if they had more trouble living together than living apart?

29

Ashley was running late for her meeting with Geoffrey Carruthers, and she suspected that a man like him was not used to waiting. She also thought being late probably diminished a person's esteem in his eyes. Further, she truthfully didn't have even a semblance of a good reason for being late. Time had simply gotten away from her again, and even taking into account the Secret Service escort, the city traffic was simply not in favor of her reaching her destination on time.

She didn't have Geoffrey's cell number with her, so she called the restaurant and asked to speak with Mr. Carruthers, that is, if he was still there.

He came on the line almost immediately. "Hello, Carruthers here."

"Hi, Geoffrey; it's Ashley. I'm running late. I'm sorry for the inconvenience. Would you prefer to reschedule for another day?"

"Where are you now?"

Ashley described her current location. "I should be there in another fifteen minutes."

"No problem. I'll have some appetizers and wine ready for you when you arrive so you can catch your breath."

"Thanks. I'll see you in a few minutes."

After hanging up, Ashley noted she was getting the full and quite focused attention Mr. Carruthers was so famous for with the ladies. Why would he bother turning on the charm for her? Probably something to do with Michael although it was quite possible that those characteristics were so ingrained in his personality, he didn't even realize he was doing it.

Geoffrey was thinking along quite different lines. He suspected a woman like Ashley would feel certain indebtedness to him for having arrived late. He would almost bet she was a very organized and precise person when it came to her work. This perceived inconvenience to him could work to his advantage.

Suddenly she was walking toward him. She looked ravishing, which led him to imagine what she would look like in his bed in the morning after a full night of lovemaking. The only thing marring her beauty was the Secret Service, who placed themselves around the room in order to keep an eye on her and the entrance and exits to the restaurant.

She was wearing a white lacy blouse tucked into a long, dark-green velvet skirt. It was accentuated by a large gold-coin belt worn slightly askew, which accentuated her slim hips and figure. Quite unconventional compared to the wardrobes of the majority of working women with whom he was acquainted. Her blonde hair was loose and windblown, but she looked absolutely stunning.

He arose as she approached their table and took her hand in his. He wanted to place a kiss on the back of it, but that would have been inappropriate at this stage. He felt satisfied to have her hand in his. He gently squeezed it, acknowledging her greeting. He could smell her distinctive perfume, which he guessed might be Dior's Poison, a fragrance he very much appreciated. He wished he had the privilege of watching her apply it. With luck, one day he might.

"I'm so sorry I'm late. I have no excuse. I wish I did so I wouldn't feel so guilty."

"No need to worry. I was able to make good use of the extra time you gave me. With iPhones and iPads, a person can run a business from almost anywhere. Ah, here are our appetizers and some wine. I thought you could use a little time to catch your breath before we order lunch and get down to business."

"I don't mean to be rude, but wouldn't it be better if we just got down to business? After all, I've already wasted enough of your time," Ashley remarked.

"Ashley, relax. It's obvious you've been rushing around all morning. Take a moment to catch your breath. Enjoy the appetizers and wine. We'll get to our business over lunch. Tell me, how did you enjoy all of the inaugural activities? Naturally I saw it on television; even so, I'd love to hear your firsthand account."

Ashley's first thought was *Aha, he's looking to make a connection to me because of Michael.* Her second thought was how tired she was of recounting the inauguration for others, but not to respond would be rude. "The experience was both exhausting and very sobering. I would have preferred to put my head under a pillow and ignore it all. Unfortunately that wasn't an option. Also, being in the thick of things felt very surreal, almost like watching a movie. I kept wanting to say, 'Cut' and 'Scene.' I wish I could protect Michael from all the turmoil and stress that comes with the office, but I recognize how unrealistic that is."

"You'd think with that attitude, you'd want to live in Washington and cause him less stress by stepping into the role of First Lady. Instead you've become, as the newspapers have now dubbed you, the Reluctant First Lady."

"Quite frankly, I'm sick to death of discussing the inauguration and politics. I understand everyone's curiosity; still, couldn't we talk about something else?"

Geoffrey smiled, "You're pretty direct, aren't you? I like that; however, are there situations where you'd do something you truly disliked?"

"Possibly, depending on the circumstances, but for the most part I try to steer clear of situations I don't enjoy. Sometimes that causes problems for the people I love. I generally don't do things I dislike, yet I try to be reasonable about it.

"Once Michael became a United States congressman and I was working full time and raising the children, I began to get more selfish about how I spent any free time I had. That was when I began to make conscious choices about what I'd do or wouldn't do.

"I'm sure that's far more than you really want to know. I don't normally drink, and the wine is going straight to my head. Would you mind if we ordered lunch now? I need to get some food in me; otherwise, there's no telling what I might say."

As a matter of fact, he did mind, but he signaled the waiter. He'd love to see what Ashley was like when she let loose and didn't care what she said or did. How very interesting that might be. Previously in all of the conversations they'd had, which weren't that many, she always seemed aloof and reserved.

"What about you?" Ashley asked. "Haven't you ever wanted to settle down? The press may have labeled me the Reluctant First Lady, but your reputation as an international playboy is notorious the world over. Oops. Again, I apologize. It's the wine. You don't have to answer that if you don't want to; it's really none of my business."

"I don't mind answering. My life is much too interesting without all the trappings of marriage. I can go wherever I want, whenever I want. I've never enjoyed being limited to one field of play. That's also been true where my business ventures are concerned."

"That sounds pretty self-absorbed. Don't you ever get lonely?"

Geoffrey raised an eyebrow and cocked his head slightly, indicating how absurd he found her question. He was never without female companionship when he wanted it, and he didn't have to deal with anyone when he wasn't in the mood.

Ashley assured him, "When the right woman comes along, you'll change your tune. Of course, even if you're lucky enough to find the love of your life, there are always compromises to be made."

"Now, you're thinking of you and your husband."

"Yes, I am. Unfortunately I've rambled on far too long about my personal life. Why don't we discuss the purpose for our meeting? You said you're interested in becoming a board member and establishing an endowment for the museum."

"Direct and straightforward, two qualities I admire. To answer your question about the purpose of our meeting, I'm afraid I haven't been entirely honest with you. Yes, I'm interested in becoming a board member, and I'd like to establish an endowment for the museum, but I'd also like to do something to help you. I'd like to host a dinner party at my residence to raise more money for your museum."

"Why would you want to help me, and what makes you think I need your help? You barely know me. The businesswoman in me graciously accepts the endowment; conversely, I'm wary of your reasons for wanting to host a money-raising event for the museum. What's behind your grand gesture?"

"Let's just say, hosting a money-raising event for the museum provides many advantages for me."

"Would one of them be expecting something in return from my husband? I'm sorry I have to ask; however, I find it necessary."

"I can assure you my gesture has absolutely nothing whatsoever to do with your husband."

"And there are no strings attached in any way?"

"None."

"To be honest, Geoffrey, I realize I should be extremely grateful for your offer, and as I said, I do accept the endowment on behalf of the museum. That's very generous of you. As far as becoming a board member, there are no vacancies at the moment; however, I'll keep your offer in mind if something opens up. In regards to hosting a fund-raiser, humor me. How do you benefit from making such a magnanimous gesture on my behalf?"

Geoffrey laughed. "I didn't think trying to do something for you and your museum was going to be so difficult."

"I'm sorry. I know I'm handling this badly, and I've completely crossed over the line between the business-patron relationship; still, I need my curiosity appeased."

"Very well. The most obvious reason, of course, is my donation to the museum provides an excellent tax write-off for me. Also, I truly am a patron of the arts. I appreciate beautiful and unique things more than you know. And lastly, I want to help you raise money for the museum because I think your dedication to your profession should be rewarded."

"The first two reasons I understand and believe. But why your interest in me, all of a sudden?"

Geoffrey was pensive. Several answers came to mind. A lot was riding on how well he answered this question. It was paramount to his overall plan to play this game precisely right. He wanted her to begin thinking of him as a friend in order to develop a sense of trust between them. He had a gut feeling that Ashley let very few people into her inner circle.

"Honestly, you fascinate me. I'm like the rest of the citizens of this country. I'm totally intrigued with the woman who rejected the role of the First Lady. Shocked would be more truthful. Most women love the prestige they gain from being married to or associated with a man with so much power. They don't mind how they get the clout; they just want it, whatever the terms may be. You're different. You walked away from it all.

"I've met you on several occasions throughout the years, and you always struck me as unique but never stubborn. What I heard and saw on the night of your husband's acceptance speech and during the next day's news conference was a woman speaking up for her rights, a woman determined to do things in her own way and to hell with tradition. I hope I'm not offending you because that's not my intention. I'm trying to pay you a compliment.

"I believe you're just as ambitious as your husband, and you don't want to follow in his shadow. You want to cut your own path in this world. I admire that, and as it happens, I'm in a position to help you."

Ashley stared at Geoffrey. "Again, I don't mean to be ungrateful, but what's the difference if I use my husband's power to get where I want to go or accept your help? Either way, I wouldn't be achieving my goals through my efforts or skill."

"I disagree. I might give an endowment to the museum; however, I'd never go as far as inviting my colleagues into my home unless I recognized and believed in your talent and abilities as head of the museum. Ashley, you could be running your own museum or gallery instead of someone else's. Think about it for a minute. If I were Robert, you'd think of my attempt to help you as a way of promoting you. It all goes back to your abilities, your talent."

Ashley thought about what Geoffrey said. It was true when Robert promoted her talent, she didn't give it a second thought. She felt she'd earned it.

"I don't know what to say, partly because this has come as such a surprise, partly because I hardly know you, and partly because I've had entirely too much to drink. I appreciate your desire to establish an endowment for the museum, and I'm grateful to you for wanting to host a dinner party to raise more money for us. Thank you for your generosity. We'll be in your debt for your kindness."

These last words were exactly what Geoffrey had been waiting to hear. She was grateful to him and was trying to find a way to thank him appropriately. A woman like Ashley didn't like to feel in debt to someone. He wished he could tell her exactly how she could thank him.

In the beginning, the fact that she was married to the president of the United States was the biggest obstacle. How do you seduce a president's wife? The answer was like the punch line to a bad joke; one did it very carefully or not at all. If Ashley suspected for one second she was his goal, she would refuse to meet with him. This afternoon's meeting was extremely enlightening. She had shown more of herself today than in all of the years he had known her.

Now, unfortunately for him, there was a sudden shift in the cosmos. He truly liked and respected her; she was unique and utterly charming. He felt uncomfortable about where his feelings about her were taking him. He had never met a woman quite like Ashley; hell, he really did admire her spunk and courage. He wondered what it would be like to have her in his life permanently.

As they were leaving the restaurant, Geoffrey mentioned he'd call her the next day to go over possible dates for the dinner party he intended to host. He also mentioned he'd have his attorney contact the museum's attorney to establish the endowment fund.

Ashley was still reeling slightly from the wine and said, "I know I'm being redundant, but thank you again for your generosity."

"I think you know I can afford the money," Geoffrey commented. "Let me give you a lift back to the museum. My limousine and driver are available."

"Thanks, but these days I only travel via the Secret Service."

As Geoffrey's limousine pulled up to the curb, he assisted Ashley with her coat and was about to say goodbye when someone called their names. They both looked up simultaneously in the direction of the voice.

The same photographer who had been at the fundraiser and outside of Ashley's apartment building snapped their picture. He had received an anonymous tip regarding their whereabouts and had waited outside for over two hours hoping to get the two of them coming out of the restaurant together. His wait paid off. He was rewarded with another photo splashed on the front of the newspaper's society section.

The Reluctant First Lady and the most eligible bachelor in town were together again; this time, completely alone. This was hot news. It was the second time these two particular people had been seen together. It was his job to keep the public informed, and this was the kind of news that paid big money. He began thinking of the possible caption that he could put under their picture. None of them were going to make the two parties involved very happy, but then that wasn't his problem.

30

Since the inauguration, Michael had spent his days in a continuous stream of meetings. His daily schedule was jam-packed from morning until late in the evening. As the president, he was more aware than ever the true motivations of those around him. It rankled him how politicians always seemed to vie for all they could get personally out of every agreement. Too often, it was all about getting re-elected and staying in power at all cost. He wasn't green behind the ears. He'd witnessed this same mind-set as a congressman and senator; nevertheless, it sickened him to think how much time went into political posturing rather than talking about good legislation that could help those they were elected to represent. If the average citizen could eavesdrop on many of these behind-the-scenes meetings, they'd see the political process at work but most definitely not at its best.

At almost every meeting, negotiations included politicians trying to gain something for themselves or their party. Why wasn't the focus on the advantages to the people and the country? He certainly intended to do his best to adjust the thinking of those who were around him. Ethics. It was all about ethics and doing what was right for the American people. Michael was very sure many legislators had forgotten the reason they'd run for office in the first place. The classic scenario of "you scratch my back, and I'll scratch yours" was still part and parcel of the good-old-boy system. Politics was dirty and mean-spirited, just like Ashley always said it was; nevertheless, he still had hope that the system could change under good leadership.

There was nothing in his past that could come back to bite him. There were no dirty deals, no womanizing, no under-the-table bribes that his opponents could feed upon. He'd never done anything dishonest, and he'd been completely faithful to his wife. The only blot on his career to date was Ashley's refusal to be the First Lady.

Georgia buzzed him on the intercom. "Mr. President, Jack is here and says he needs to speak to you immediately. Shall I have him come back, or do you want to see him now?"

Michael had left instructions with his secretary not to disturb him unless it was an emergency. He was sure Georgia had conveyed that message to Jack, and yet Jack was insistent about seeing him, so it must be important.

"Please send him in, Georgia."

Within seconds, the door opened and Jack hurried in with several newspapers in his hands. Seeing the expression on Jack's face, Michael joked, "It's only nine o'clock in the morning; surely, it's too early for that expression."

Jack didn't answer. He simply walked over to Michael and laid the society section of the *New York Post* on his desk.

Michael looked down at the front page of the society section and saw a picture of Geoffrey Carruthers assisting Ashley with her coat. The caption read, "The Reluctant First Lady and Geoffrey Carruthers, Together Again." He didn't bother to read the short article adjacent to the picture.

The newspaper faded as did Michael's desk and for that matter the room. He didn't hear Jack speaking to him; there was just the blinding color red. Rage, so encompassing it interfered with his breathing, flooding his senses. He could smell and taste it. His only thought was getting to Ashley.

"Jack, would you tell Georgia and Ed to clear my schedule? I want everything ready for me to leave for New York as soon as possible. I'll be spending the night with Ashley and returning tomorrow, so if there's something that needs immediate attention, see that you give it to me before I leave.

"Mr. President, shouldn't we talk about this? Do you think it's a good idea to take off for New York right now when you're so upset? Why don't you just call Ashley? I'm sure there's a good reason that she was with Carruthers. Part of her job is to meet with supporters and patrons of the museum, and she's bound to meet people outside of her office. You do."

Michael was so angry he didn't trust himself to speak. Jack didn't understand. How could he? It wasn't Ashley he didn't trust. He knew Carruthers, and more importantly, he knew his reputation. To date, there had been two pictures of them in the newspaper together. He'd deliberately chosen not to mention the first picture to Ashley. He'd chalked it up to her involvement with the Black Tie Dinner. But twice?

That was more than a coincidence. He wanted some answers, now.

"Jack, please do as I asked. I need to see Ashley and discuss this. Other than the Secret Service, I won't need anyone else to go with me. I'll be staying at Ashley's apartment in New York, and I'll be back tomorrow. The Secret Service will make all the necessary arrangements for security. Please get moving on this; I want to be at Ashley's apartment when she gets home from work."

"Wouldn't you like to talk about any political ramifications these pictures might have before you take off?" Jack asked.

"No. We'll discuss what needs to be done about the picture from a political point of view, if anything, tomorrow when I return. Right now, I want to see my wife."

Jack took Michael's remarks as his dismissal. He immediately went to see Ed and explained what happened. Ed was almost as upset as the president. They were both convinced it was a simple matter of Ashley executing her responsibilities as the director of the Cameron Museum of Art. Still, the last thing they needed was for the picture to get legs and take off.

During Michael's trip to New York, he made the decision to meet with Geoffrey Carruthers first before he met with Ashley. Michael notified the Secret Service of his intention so they could make the necessary arrangements for his visit. In addition, he asked Georgia to call his wife and let her know he was coming to New York and would see her later today. He wanted to give Ashley the chance to clear her schedule for this evening.

Michael realized his visit to Carruthers's office wouldn't go unnoticed; all the same, who was to say they weren't discussing business affairs? He was well aware it might not be the most prudent thing to do, especially given the picture in the newspaper, but he also knew no one would know the true reason for his visit. He was relatively sure the conversation he would be having with Carruthers would be kept between the two of them; however, even if it wasn't, it was a conversation he intended to have. He perceived a threat to his wife and that wasn't to be tolerated.

As he exited his vehicle, he glanced up at Carruthers Tower, one of many skyscrapers owned by him in New York City. Michael had called ahead to be sure Carruthers was in town and to let him know he was on his way to see him. He took several deep, calming breaths, composing himself for the little chat he intended to have with the land-developing tycoon. He didn't want to lose his temper; he had a feeling Geoffrey would like that very much. Where his wife was concerned, he had very little patience with interference from others.

With the Secret Service in tow, Michael made his way through the lobby and took the elevator to the top floor. He'd already instructed the agents that he wanted to speak to Mr. Carruthers privately and expected them to wait in the outer office.

When they reached the top floor, the elevator doors opened to an enormous and quite lavishly decorated foyer. The receptionist behind a circular desk stepped forward and welcomed the president and his entourage. Without hesitating, she ushered the president into Mr. Carruthers's office.

Once his office doors were closed and they were alone, Geoffrey walked over to the bar in his office. "I was surprised to hear from you and am interested in the reason for your visit. Congratulations on winning the election. I was quite sure you would. Can I interest you in something to drink?"

Michael refused. He wasn't interested in small talk. Rather, he immediately zeroed in on his purpose for coming. "Why have two pictures of you and my wife made the national papers in the last two months?"

Geoffrey wasn't surprised by the question as much as he was surprised that the president didn't intend to engage in any small talk. He knew he had to be very careful with his response. Michael wasn't a fool, and he knew not to underestimate him.

"Those were unfortunate pictures in the New York papers."

"Unfortunate? Why? Because you were caught with my wife in both of them?"

"Yesterday's picture was taken after Ashley and I had lunch. We met to discuss my establishing an endowment fund for the museum. I was helping her with her coat when a photographer snapped our picture. It was all perfectly innocent, I can assure you."

"Oh, I know it was innocent on Ashley's part. And what about the other picture at the fund-raiser? Also perfectly innocent?"

"Absolutely. I was an invited guest, and your wife was merely performing her duties as the museum's director."

"It's not my wife I'm concerned about. I trust her implicitly. It's your intentions I'm curious about. Your reputation is well known, and all of a sudden, within a relatively short amount of time, you've managed to have your picture taken with my wife twice. That makes me highly suspicious about your motives."

"I don't know if I should be insulted or flattered, Mr. President. I have no grand designs on your wife. There are plenty of other women available—ones who aren't as newsworthy as your wife and who aren't married to the president of the United States. I'm sorry you felt you needed to have this conversation."

"I don't trust you, Carruthers. I can sense you're up to something. I'm warning you to be very careful. My wife is off-limits. Any business you have to conduct with her can be done at the museum. I hope I'm making myself perfectly clear."

"I don't particularly like your assumptions or your ultimatum."

"I don't care what you like or don't like. I highly suspect you're manipulating situations where Ashley is concerned. For what purpose, I don't know yet, but I'm warning you, stay away from my wife."

31

Ashley came whistling through her apartment door. She was so excited to see Michael. She couldn't believe that he'd actually made the trip to New York to see her on the spur of the moment. She felt lucky to be married to the kind of man who would put such an important job on hold to come to see his wife in the middle of the week. Her fears about his becoming the president and never having time for her may have been unfounded, for here he was.

"Hi, honey. I'm so glad you're here. I've missed you so . . ." Ashley stopped dead in her tracks. The look on Michael's face meant only one thing. Something was very wrong.

"Michael, has something happened? Are Jeremy and Juliette all right? Please, what is it? What's wrong?"

Michael had been sitting in his wife's apartment waiting for her to come home. He'd been doing deep breathing exercises and had been practicing other relaxation techniques in an attempt to stay calm and not attack Ashley the minute she walked through the door. He knew his wife well enough to know it was best not to put her on the defensive.

He thought back to another time. It was after he and Ashley were married when he was in law school and Ashley was working late at the Berkeley museum one night. The phone rang, and when he answered it, a man asked to speak to Ashley. When he explained that Ashley wasn't at home and offered to take a message, the caller replied, "Tell her Howard called, and I was wondering if she would like to go out for coffee?"

Michael nearly lost it, but he patiently pointed out to the man that Ashley wouldn't be going out with anybody; she was married to him. To which Howard answered, "Well, now, that's really not your decision to make, is it?"

After threatening old Howard with every law he could think of if he ever tried to contact his wife again, he waited for Ashley to come home from work. He worked up a scenario in his mind where Ashley had met someone at the museum and given him their home number. By the time she got home, he was rip-roaring drunk and ready to nail her to the wall.

Ashley couldn't figure out for the life of her what Michael was talking about. He was drunk as a skunk, was threatening her, and was making all sorts of crazy accusations. What she did know was that she didn't deserve the treatment she was receiving. She'd been charged guilty without the benefit of a trial.

After piecing together some of Michael's crazy statements, she gathered some man called asking for her, which threw Michael into a jealous frenzy. She tried to reason with him and explain that she didn't know any Howard, but no amount of reasoning had any effect on his drunken rage. Finally Ashley made a few threats of her own, including leaving him. That sobered him up long enough to have the good sense to take a cold shower and then sit down and discuss the whole situation more reasonably. He learned that night that if you pushed Ashley too far, she came out swinging.

He always remembered the lesson he learned that night. Now photographs of his wife with Carruthers had been thrust in his face twice, and whatever else he did, he needed to discuss them calmly with her without causing their tempers to escalate.

"The kids are fine; I needed to see you. Josh brought me the picture of you and Carruthers that was in the society section of the *New York Post* this morning. Have you seen it?"

"As a matter of fact, I haven't. I've been so busy today, I haven't had a chance to do anything but deal with other museums about the exhibits we're exchanging."

Michael walked over and handed her the paper with her and Carruthers's picture in it. He watched her expression. First it was one of surprise, then frustration, followed by disgust, and finally anger. He was waiting for her to say something.

Instead, she walked over and sat down on the sofa. "You didn't come here to see me because you missed me, did you? You came because of this picture in the newspaper." Her voice was soft and sounded disheartened.

"I think an explanation is a reasonable thing to ask," Michael said quietly.

"Excuse me; let me see if I get this right. You saw this picture in the newspaper and decided to pay your wife a little visit, which leads me to believe you think there's something behind the picture. How close am I?"

"I've never accused you of being slow. This is the second picture of you and that man together in as many months. What's going on?"

"Are you asking as my husband, or are you asking as a president who feels his wife's behavior may affect him politically?"

"Don't push me, Ashley. I don't care how this looks to anyone else. I want to know what's going on with you and the biggest playboy in the western hemisphere."

Ashley was furious. "Yes, I guess the cat is out of the bag. So sorry you had to find out about it like this." Before it even registered with her what she was doing, she rolled up a magazine and threw it at her husband. "You idiot."

Michael managed to dodge the magazine, but his temper was quickly catching up with Ashley's. "This is not the time for sarcasm; tell me about the pictures."

"Not a chance. If you don't have more faith in me than what you are so obviously demonstrating, you don't deserve an answer. By the way, how's our lovely Paula? Has she made any advances yet?"

In one stride, Michael crossed the room and stood directly in front of his wife. "Ashley, you damn well know there's nothing going on between Paula and me, and that was a cheap shot. I wonder how you'd feel if you saw a couple of cozy pictures in the newspaper of Paula and me. So far, the only time we've been in a photo together, we've been at the opposite ends of a receiving line."

Ashley's pent-up breath released like an overinflated balloon. He was right; she would have wondered what was going on although she would've probably assumed it was job-related. Why couldn't they be like everyone else? The super-powered microscope lens was focused on their every move. She hated the way they were living their lives.

"I don't like anything about the way you've handled this situation, but the pictures, while annoying, are completely innocent. The first one was taken at the annual fund-raiser—let me insert here, part of my job. The second one was taken yesterday after Mr. Carruthers and I had lunch while we discussed a very generous endowment he's establishing for the museum. Again, part of my job. I had no knowledge that either picture was being taken until I saw them in the newspaper. Surely you know there's nothing going on between us."

"What I know is that Geoffrey Carruthers has popped up twice in connection with you in the newspaper in the last few weeks. I don't know if the pictures are being planned by him ahead of time or if it's merely a coincidence, but I suspect he's got something up his sleeve where you're concerned although he denies it. I trust you; it's him I don't trust."

"What do you mean, he denies it? Michael Taylor, don't you dare tell me you've talked to him about all of this."

"As a matter of fact, I have. I wanted him to know that I'm aware of the games he plays with the feminine population, and he better stay the hell away from you."

Ashley was almost speechless. "I can't believe you'd do something so stupid. Did you challenge him to a duel? How dare you interfere in my professional life? You don't see me sashaying into your office deciding to make a few decisions here and there for the country. What if he decides not to go through with the endowment? And, as bad as it may be for the museum, don't you see how demeaning what you've done is to you?"

"It's not me I'm concerned about," Michael reasserted. "I don't think you fully understand. You're not playing in the kiddie pool when it comes to Geoffrey Carruthers. I repeat, he's dangerous and he's up to something. You once accused me of not recognizing that Paula was scheming to replace you; well, you need to take a good, long look in the mirror, honey, because you're being pursued big time."

Ashley stood up and began pacing the room. She needed to think, and she thought best when she was moving. Could Michael be right? Could there be more behind Geoffrey's generosity than altruism? If Michael was right, that made Geoffrey far more than a scoundrel who preyed on women. His actions would have been calculated and part of his chase.

"Let's assume for a minute you're right about Geoffrey and he has ulterior motives although I can't imagine what they might be. I want you to know that nothing has happened between us, and the things you're suggesting never occurred to me. In all my dealings with him, the museum has been the main focus. He's been the very essence of a gentleman and never given even the slightest hint that he's coming on to me."

Michael walked over to his wife, wrapped his arms around her, and kissed her on the forehead. Ashley, who always had a sassy response for everyone, didn't realize the power and the ruthless character behind a man like Carruthers, nor did she realize how desirable she was. She always liked to think she was capable of handling anything that came her way, but she hadn't been exposed to the seamier side of life, and while he was glad she hadn't been, it made her more vulnerable than he liked.

The last two decades of dealing with politicians, lobbyists, and the underbelly of big business had taught him more than he ever wanted to know. People like Geoffrey Carruthers assumed they could get away with anything. They thought they were smarter than others, and that's generally how you could catch them. Their overconfidence made them vulnerable.

"Michael, I'm not sure if you're right about Geoffrey, but I'll be very careful where he's concerned. It's exactly this kind of thing I was talking about before I left Washington. We can't foresee the people who'll be entering our lives. Therefore we can't predict the potential problems that could come our way. I love you, and whatever I might do, it will always be for us. Remember that, will you?"

Michael raised Ashley's chin and looked into her eyes. She had been his Ashley since they were seventeen years old. He kissed her on the forehead, her nose, then settled his mouth on her ripe, luscious lips. They were made for kissing.

"Could I interest you in America's favorite pastime?" Michael asked.

"What, you want to play baseball now?" Ashley batted her eyelashes at him.

"I was thinking more of this pastime." Michael picked up his wife and carried her into the bedroom. Words were unnecessary. Their movements were as old as time. A caress here, a stroke there, each motion intended to bring pleasure and satisfaction to the other. The whole night lay ahead of them, and the promise of two satiated lovers was assured.

32

A week had gone by since Michael's trip to New York. Ashley got goose pimples thinking about all of the things they did to one another that night. Sex had always been incredible between them, but it seemed that night they'd reached new heights.

Unfortunately Ashley and Michael had spent a good part of their married life apart; nevertheless, their separations never got easier. She could still see the cocky boy who had won her heart in the man she was married to today. He was still her one and only love though she sometimes felt that life had its own plan for them and it consisted of the two of them never really being together. Well, life, look out. I have some plans of my own and intend for them to become my reality.

Mavis buzzed her on the intercom. "Ms. Winfrey is here for her appointment."

"Please send her right in." As soon as Ashley hung up the phone, she headed toward the door to her office. Ashley smiled at Oprah and held out her hand. "Welcome. I'm glad we're finally getting a chance to meet. Naturally I've seen you on television, so I feel like I already know you. I'll bet you hear that all the time."

Oprah smiled as she took Ashley's hand. There seemed to be an automatic kinship between the two women. That was undoubtedly one of the reasons Oprah was so successful in her career. She was a natural at putting people at ease. Oprah responded, "I've been looking forward to meeting you, and yes, you're right, I hear that a lot. Thank you for agreeing to meet with me to discuss the possibility of an interview."

Ashley led Oprah over to a couple of chairs. "Is there anything I can get for you? A cup of coffee, tea, a soft drink, some water?"

"No, thanks. I'm fine for now; maybe later."

Ashley began, "I'm not trying to be coy or naïve, but it's still hard for me to believe that anyone would be interested in hearing anything more about me. The newspapers seem to be filled with made-up articles about me. I realize I don't fit the image of what a woman married to the president should be like, but you'd think people would be sick of hearing about me by now."

"You couldn't be more wrong. Because of who you are and the decision you've made, you're the hottest ticket in town, and I'm sorry to say, you most likely will be for the rest of your life. The very fact that you didn't fall in line and do what all of the other presidents' wives have done before you is exactly why they want to know what makes you tick. You're an anomaly to them."

"I wish everyone would just let it go. I've debated whether giving an interview is the wisest things to do. It seems like anything I say will be redundant, and I'm not thrilled about being in the public eye. How wrong I've been about that aspect of my life. My son predicted my rejecting the role of the First Lady would create more curiosity about me than ever. No matter what I say or do or wear or where I go, the media wants to comment on it."

"I know a little bit about that myself. It takes a long time to get used to all of the attention. To this day, I keep saying to myself, 'Why all the hoopla?' I'm afraid those of us in the middle of the storm aren't always the most perceptive when it comes to ourselves. I know you're hesitant about giving any interviews, which is why I'm here. I wanted to talk to you about it in person. Giving an interview isn't going to make the media go away, and an interview isn't going to satisfy the public's curiosity about you. They'll always want more; it's the nature of the beast. But what it will do is give you a chance to talk about other things besides your decision not to become the First Lady. It would provide viewers an opportunity to understand a little more about who Ashley Taylor really is."

"You live in the public eye. Don't you ever get tired of it?"

"Yes, I do. I have to cope with the media just like you. They always want more. It does get annoying, and yet I recognize as long as I'm in the position I'm in people are going to be curious about my life. So I try to give them a little bit of myself on my terms. That way it doesn't feel so intrusive."

"That's quite a tightrope you're on. Since I've decided to do this interview, could it be somewhere private, with just the two of us and a cameraman?"

"That won't be a problem. In fact, if it would make you more comfortable, we could do the interview here in your office."

"What about the questions? Could we discuss the parameters of the questions before the interview?"

"Yes. I'm not trying to blindside you; however, sometimes a question does come to me on the spur of the moment. Or an idea occurs to me because of something you say. Just because a question is asked, it doesn't mean you have to answer it. I was thinking we could talk about where you grew up, your background, how you met the president, your first date, your children, your job, and lead up to the reason you made the decision you did, that kind of thing." Oprah waited for a response.

"I'd be lying if I said I was excited about doing an interview. Still, since I'm going to do one, I'm glad it will be with you."

"I'm glad you feel that way because I'd very much like to interview you. When would be the best time for you, Mrs. Taylor?"

"Let me check." Ashley brought up the calendar on her computer. She wrote down several dates and times on a sheet of paper. "Here are some available times I have now. Why don't you look at your schedule and get back to me with a date that will work for you?"

"I'll call you when I get back to my office. Thank you for agreeing to do the interview. I promise to make you as comfortable as I can."

Ashley leaned forward and hugged Oprah on the spur of the moment. "I don't know why I feel like thanking you, but I do. Maybe we could have lunch together sometime, and you could give me more insight on how you've learned to handle the public and the press. I'm sure you could teach me a great deal. I'll wait to hear from you."

Once Oprah left, Ashley picked up her phone to call Michael. He was unavailable, so she left a message with Georgia. She hoped she'd made a wise decision. She felt if she could trust anyone, it was Oprah. Ashley believed she would try and make the experience as painless as possible.

33

"Welcome back." Oprah smiled into the camera after coming off a commercial break. "In case you're just joining us, I have the distinct pleasure of having Mrs. Ashley Taylor as my guest. We were discussing how she and President Taylor met. Ashley, why don't you pick up your story from where you left off?" Oprah encouraged Ashley to continue.

"Sure. We both grew up in California, me in Berkeley and Michael in Sacramento. My parents were divorced, and my dad lived in Sacramento where most of my relatives still live. I lived in Berkeley with my mom, but I spent all of my vacation and free time with my dad, aunts and uncles, and my cousins in Sacramento.

"As I've said before, Michael and I both came from working-class families. The biggest difference in our upbringing was my mother worked outside the home, and

Michael's mother was a stay-at-home mom, which I know from experience is every bit as much work.

"I actually met Michael through my cousin, Sienna, who went to high school with him. Michael and I met at a drive-in movie during the summer between our junior and senior year of high school."

Oprah said, "Ah, high school sweethearts. Was it love at first sight?"

Ashley laughed. "Hardly. We were both a little standoffish at first. In fact, we weren't sure we even liked one another. About a week later, we'd become inseparable. You can always get a good family argument going over who made the first move."

Oprah began, "We've talked about your background, your family, and your job. I'm sure you're aware that everyone is interested in the woman who doesn't want to be the First Lady. Ashley, would you explain why you made that decision? I mean it's a huge departure from tradition."

"There's not one simple answer. Actually, the easiest thing to do would have been just to go along with the program and do what everyone wanted me to do. But as I've repeatedly said, I've never liked politics. I'm not wild about being in the public eye or for that matter having my every move tracked by the media. My passion has always been and remains the arts. I love my job and don't see why I should have to give that up because my husband is very good at what he does.

"Plus—and your audience has heard this before—why should the spouse of the president be expected to assume a role simply because her husband—or someday wife—is elected? One wonders if the same set of expectations would be applied to a First Husband. I think probably not. When our first president, George Washington, was elected, they had to scramble to figure out what to call his wife. History tells us as our new nation was being formed, the politicians of the time were very careful not to use any language associated with royalty. At that time, women were expected to be good hostesses. I think the whole role grew out of an extension of being a housewife."

"Do you still think you made the right decision?"

"Yes, I do, for me. I'm not cut out for political life. I believe the wife of the president should really want to be there. It's a grueling schedule, and many demands are made on the First Lady's time. We've had some amazing First Ladies, whose popularity was actually greater than their husbands. I believe you either step into the position one hundred percent or should consider not doing it at all, as I have.

"You know, when you're young and in love, it never occurs to you that one day your future husband might become the president of the United States. It's just not how most of us think. You aren't prepared for all of the twists and turns your life will take together. But, through it all, Michael and I have tried to respect what the other one has wanted to do and have tried to be supportive of one another."

"Do you ever see yourself changing your mind about assuming the role of the First Lady?"

Ashley smiled. "I learned a long time ago to be very careful about using the words 'never' and 'always'; however, I can't imagine it right now."

"What would you say has been the biggest adjustment you've had to make since your husband became the president?"

"That's easy. The loss of privacy. The media is constantly around. Also, dealing with security. You never feel like you're alone or have any privacy. It amazes me that the family of the president is considered fair game for the media and the public. We really are just an ordinary family that's ended up in extraordinary circumstances. It seems the public wants us to be this perfect family, but we're no different from other families. We have good days and bad; we argue; we worry, just like everyone else. Yet the media analyzes and talks about every sniffle, glance, or expression."

Oprah added, "Not everybody's husband is the president of the United States, so that does make you different. There isn't a celebrity out there who can't identify with what you're saying about your privacy, but you and they live lives that most people only dream about."

"That may be true, still I wonder if your audience would truly want to give up their privacy, have expectations heaped on them, and be expected to participate in something in which they weren't interested. It's a hard pill to swallow."

"Last question. What do you think of the nickname you've been given, the Reluctant First Lady?"

"I just ignore it. Still, the sentiment is true."

"Before we close, I want to thank you for giving me and my viewers a chance to get to know you a little better. You certainly are one of a kind. Thank you so much for sharing yourself with us."

Ashley smiled. "Thank you, Oprah, for making this interview as painless as possible. I appreciate your kindness more than I can say. It really didn't hurt as much as I thought it would."

Oprah and Ashley smiled and continued talking quietly until someone behind the camera yelled, "That's a wrap."

34

Ashley turned the television off and turned toward her secretaries. "Okay, what did you think? Intelligent conversation, mediocre chattering, or dead woman talking? Don't forget; I can tell when you're lying."

Mavis and Kathy laughed. "What did you think, Kathy?" Mavis asked.

"I'd give it a ten on a scale of one to ten. I thought it was great. Your opinion, Mavis?"

"Is 'great' going to be satisfactory enough for you?" Mavis asked Ashley.

"Define 'great,'" Ashley shot back.

"Well, Miss Neurotic, you need to remember there was nothing new for Kathy and me. We've worked with you for a long time," Mavis said.

"Humph . . . you're just covering because you think I bombed, right?"

Kathy shook her head.

"What I want to know is how you think I came across to people who don't know me?"

"It was a wonderful interview. You looked relaxed, and you and Oprah had good rapport. You had a chance in a more casual setting to say what was on your mind. What more did you want? If you wanted everyone all of sudden to understand and accept your decision not to step into the role of the First Lady, I think you aimed too high," Mavis responded.

Behind them, phones began ringing.

Before turning to answer the phone, Kathy said, "I think you accomplished what you meant to do. I think you struck just the right note."

Mavis interrupted, "Sienna is on line one. Shall I tell her you're too busy to talk right now because you're having a nervous breakdown?"

Ashley squinted and shot Mavis an appraising look. Then she said jokingly, "You do remember I'm the one who does your evaluations, don't you? Yes, for Pete's sake, put her through to my office. And, thanks, you guys. I don't know what I'd do without your overwhelming verbal assessments."

Ashley picked up her office phone. "Hi there."

"I know you're sitting at work fretting about how you thought the interview went and are probably driving Mavis and Kathy crazy with your questions. Admit it. You're analyzing every little detail of your conversation with Oprah. So I called to put your fears to rest. It was wonderful. It was exactly right."

"I thought it went pretty well when we taped it, but I guess I was hoping all of America would say, 'Gee, now I understand why that poor woman made the decision she did, and if I were in her shoes, I'd do the same thing.' I suppose you think that's a little too much to hope for?"

"What? You, unrealistic? Absolutely not. Never you. Give me a break. I've been watching the polls; little by little people are beginning to see it really doesn't make any difference that you're not officially in the role of the First Lady. What more could you want?"

"I suppose I should be satisfied with that. I think eventually people will see that the role of the First Lady isn't a necessity but that its true value lies in its tradition. Some presidents' wives will want to be part of that tradition and others won't.

"How are all of you? It looks like California is already getting some warm weather."

"We're so used to it being nice, we hardly notice the weather. Unless, of course, it turns nasty; then we wonder what we did to offend the gods. We're going rafting this weekend."

"Michael will be envious when he hears that. I wonder how that would work with all of the security around him. Listen, I'll need to call you back later to catch up. We're being inundated with calls, and Kathy just put a note on my desk saying Michael's on another line. I'll give you a call in the next couple of days. We need to talk about when we can get together again."

"I agree. Tell Michael hi for me."

"Will do. Love you."

Ashley immediately punched the button for another line. "Good morning, Mr. President, and to what do I owe the honor of this call?'

"Hi, honey. A few of us just watched your interview, and I wanted to tell you how well we thought it went. Congratulations. If you continue to come across so charmingly, you're going to win over the entire nation."

"Fat chance, but I'm glad you thought it went well. How are things in your neck of the woods? I'm sure you have more important things to do than watch me on television."

"Oh, I don't know; the programming was pretty interesting today. However, to answer your question, I'm booked solid with meetings as usual; I hardly have time to breathe. I wish you were here. By the way, this coming Saturday there's a state dinner at the French Embassy. Any chance you can make it?"

"I'm sorry, Michael, I wish I could. This weekend is the New York Council for the Arts function. I've already said I'd attend. Robert can't go, and we both felt strongly that the museum should be represented. Maybe I can make it to something else in the future. Why don't you have Georgia send me a copy of some of the dates of your upcoming events, and I'll see what I might be able to attend in the future."

"I'll do that, but you realize Paula will be going. I'm only mentioning it because it could make the news, and she'll be attending as the official White House hostess. I don't want you to get upset or make more of it than it is. Remember, these kinds of events are part of her job. I'd much rather have you there; you know that, don't you?"

"I'll try to keep that in mind while I'm seething. I know this is the reason you created the director of protocol position, but I still think Paula is out for a position much higher on the ladder, like becoming your wife. Be careful. Whether you recognize it or not, she's as dangerous to you as you claim Geoffrey Carruthers is to me. Please try and trust my instincts about this."

"Warning noted. Again, I wish you could be there."

"Me too. I'd love to come for a visit. Check to see how next weekend looks. I could make a trip to Washington, if you're not too busy."

"I'll do that. I need to go; I'm already running behind schedule. Just wanted to touch base and let you know I thought the interview went very well. I'll be in touch. Love you."

"Love you too."

Ashley felt lonely the minute she got off the phone. Mavis, who was on another line, held up a finger indicating to wait before leaving the area. After hanging up, she said, "We're being swamped by calls. Between the two of us, we have about thirty or so."

"Just put the messages on my desk. I want to walk around the museum and when I get back, I'll start returning calls. Sorry for the telephone overload. I know it's cutting into your workday. If there's anything else I can do to give you some relief, let me know."

"That would be two lattes, a raise, and three months off in the summer. Is there anything you can think of, Kathy?" Mavis asked.

"Nope, that pretty much sums it up. Oh, yeah, and we'd like secretaries of our own."

Ashley laughed as she left the office and went about her day. She made a mental note to order flowers for her secretaries when she got back to the office.

One of her favorite things to do as she started her day was to walk around the museum to see how visitors responded to the various art collections. As she passed from one corridor and gallery to another, she reflected on her interview with Oprah. It was true what she'd said; life comes at you in unexpected ways. Ashley reflected on her and Michael's early beginnings and how their one true beacon had always been their love for one another and their family. Yet, here they were, all living in separate cities, sort of an umbrella of love with the spokes all pointing in different directions.

Ashley knew what she had to do, but it would take some planning, some manipulation, and a good bit of luck. She needed some time to think and plan, and unfortunately that might involve putting stress on others she loved temporarily.

Once she returned to her office, she couldn't believe the pile of messages that had accumulated on her desk. It was going to take days to return all of these calls. She separated the messages into two piles—ones she would handle personally, and another pile for Max to answer. Unfortunately her stack of messages was twice as big as his.

Ashley spent the rest of the morning returning phone calls and doing the necessary follow-up. So far, she'd avoided returning Geoffrey's call; still, she knew she couldn't ignore it forever. The man had just established a sizable endowment for the museum. That put him in the unique position of getting preferential treatment.

She didn't know why she kept avoiding calling him back except she was more wary of him now ever since Michael had made such a big deal out of his behavior. She still heard Michael's warnings in her head, and he'd planted a seed of doubt where Geoffrey was concerned. Could she really be that blind to a man's intentions? He'd never been inappropriate around her. She knew Michael could be blindsided by the female population, but could she be equally naïve about men? She just prayed the conversation between Michael and Geoffrey wouldn't come up.

She dialed Geoffrey's number. His secretary answered. "Good morning, Mr. Carruthers's office."

"Hi, Mrs. Peters. It's Ashley Taylor. I'm returning a call from Mr. Carruthers. Is he available?"

"He's in a meeting right now, Mrs. Taylor. Even so, let me tell him you're on the line. "Would you hold for a moment, please?"

"No problem," Ashley responded. What she really hoped was that Geoffrey was too busy to take the call. She'd rather avoid having to speak with him directly. It would be enough for him to know she had returned his call.

Ashley heard the line click. "Thank you for waiting, Mrs. Taylor. Mr. Carruthers asked if you could hold for just a moment while he wraps up his meeting. Will you please hold?"

"I can hold for a couple of minutes, but then I have to go. Please let Mr. Carruthers know that, in case our call is disconnected."

"I most certainly will. I'm sure he'll be with you as fast as he can."

Ashley decided to hold for three minutes, no longer. She was already behind in her work. At least she'd made an attempt to return his phone call. Just about the time she was ready to hang up, Geoffrey came on the line.

"Glad you called. I saw your interview with Oprah this morning; it was terrific. You're determined to whittle away at public opinion, aren't you?"

"Oprah made things easy for me, so any congratulations need to go to her. I doubt seriously if I'll have any effect on public opinion. At any rate, I'm sure you didn't call to comment on my interview. What can I do for you?"

"You're always all business, nose to the grindstone and all that. Okay, then I'll get right to it. In addition to congratulating you on the interview, I was calling about business. When you and I had lunch, I mentioned hosting an open house to raise additional funding for the museum. Are you still in favor of the idea?"

How could she possibly say no? It was her job to secure financial support for the museum, and Geoffrey was dropping a rare opportunity right into her lap. She had to accept his gracious offer. To refuse would be folly.

"Of course, I am. What did you have in mind?"

"I thought perhaps to kick off the summer in high style, we could have an open house at my home in the Hamptons. Some of my most valuable pieces of art are there; I'd love to show them to you. I'll send out invitations making clear the purpose of the event. You should reap a significant return to the museum."

"Geoffrey, it's not that I don't appreciate the offer. I do. Even so, I'm still unclear as to why you would do this for me."

"I thought we went over this ground at the luncheon. Don't tell me the wine affected your memory?"

Irritated, Ashley responded, "Of course, it didn't. I recall what you said. Just the same, for some reason your being such a good Samaritan doesn't really match the bad-boy image you portray so well in public."

"Bad-boy image? Certainly, you of all people don't believe everything you read in the press? As I said, I like to encourage talent where I see it. Ashley, as much as you hate to admit it, you draw people to you simply because you're married to the president and because you rejected the position of the First Lady. I realize you don't like hearing that, and I can almost hear your feathers ruffling. Even so, you know what I'm saying is true."

Annoyed but determined to hide it, Ashley responded, "Yes, I suppose you're right sans the ruffling feathers. Robert and I will both try to attend the event together. In fact, I'll call him and make arrangements for the two of us to be there. Have you selected a date?"

Geoffrey hadn't expected her to go to such lengths to avoid being alone with him; he'd underestimated her. That wouldn't happen again.

"How's June twelfth?"

"I'll call Robert right now and see if that works for him. He'll get back to you with a confirmation. On behalf of the Cameron Museum of Art, I want to thank you. We greatly appreciate your efforts on our behalf."

"I wouldn't do it if I didn't want to. I think you know that. I'll be in touch."

After they hung up, Geoffrey leaned back in his chair and put his hands behind his head to think. He had to play this just right. On one hand, she was a strong-willed and determined businesswoman, but on the other hand, she was rather skittish. She was definitely an enigma.

No one had interested him this much in a long time. In spite of that, he knew he was playing with fire. The president had already paid a visit warning him to stay away from his wife. He didn't like being told what to do, and he never passed up a challenge. Yes, this was definitely a dangerous undertaking.

Ashley immediately called Robert. She was anxious to let him know what Geoffrey Carruthers was planning and hoped he would be able to make it to the open house.

Ashley started humming a Lady Gaga tune that was stuck in her brain while she waited for Robert to come on the line. She didn't want to attend the open house without him. She would have her Secret Service agents with her; still, she wanted Robert as a further barrier between her and Mr. Carruthers. With the money for the museum at stake, it was her job to be the gracious recipient of goodwill and to finesse sloppy drunks and frisky benefactors.

Robert's voice suddenly boomed in her ear. "I was just about to call you. I thought your interview went extremely well. Congratulations. But I had another reason for calling. Have you heard about Ted, by any chance?"

Ashley didn't like the sound of Robert's voice. "No. Is something wrong?"

"He was in a bad car accident this morning. He was hit broadside by a semi that ran a red light. He's alive, but barely. He hasn't regained consciousness. The doctors don't know the extent of his injuries, so they're running tests and keeping him under observation in the ICU. I'm going to see him this afternoon."

"Have you talked to his wife?"

"Just briefly. She called to let me know about the accident."

"Oh, Robert, this is just horrible. Poor Ted—and Cynthia. It makes me sick. Would you please call me after you've seen him? I'd like to send something to the hospital to let them know I'm thinking of and praying for him."

"Will do. I'll call as soon as I know more," Robert said

"Thanks. I'm sorry we have to deal with business right now, but I just got off the phone with Geoffrey Carruthers, and true to his word, he's planning to host an open house to promote further donations to the museum. He's decided to hold it at his house in the Hamptons rather than at his apartment in New York, and he's set the date for June twelfth.

"Remember how you wanted me to be careful around Geoffrey? Well, Michael feels the same way. So I was hoping you'd go with me to the open house. I told Geoffrey I'd talk to you, and I thought it would be a good idea for us both to attend. How about it? Will you go with me?"

"Hang on; I'll check my calendar. Did you say the twelfth of June? If you did, I'm free and you can let your mind rest. We'll go as a united front."

"That's great. I would have attended without you, but Michael would have my head on a platter. I'm so glad you'll be able to make it. I'll be a lot more comfortable with you and my security agents close at hand. I have another favor. Would you please call Mr. Carruthers and confirm the date and that we'll both be there?"

"Of course, but Geoffrey hasn't said or done anything unseemly, has he?" Robert asked.

"No. But I can sense his mind working overtime when I'm around him, and he watches me as if he's constantly assessing me against some sort of standard and deciding if I pass muster. It unnerves me, but I'd die before I'd admit it to him. Plus, I get the impression he wouldn't be opposed to some sort of dalliance. He's stepping around the issue very carefully. Then there's always the chance I'm imagining it all."

"Personally, I'd go with your instincts. Rest assured, I'll be with you at the open house."

"Thanks. Please call me later about Ted. You won't forget?"

"No. I promise I'll call as soon as I know something."

Ashley hung up. Once again, she was aware of how fragile life is, and that no matter how much you planned, the future was completely capricious.

35

Ashley had promised to call Michael after she'd talked to Juliette and Jeremy, and even though it was late, she knew he'd still be up. His workload had quadrupled since he took office. For that matter, his work hours were 24/7. He was always on duty. He was always the president.

His voice came on the line. "I'm so glad you called."

"I promised I'd call and let you know how the kids were, so I'm reporting in. I hope I didn't wake you."

"I wish. That would mean my day had actually ended, but no such luck," Michael said.

Michael sounded exhausted. "I hope you're taking care of yourself and getting some exercise. I was recently thinking about how much the presidency always ages the person in office. I'd prefer for that not to happen to you. Are you taking your vitamins?"

Michael ignored her comment about the vitamins. "So, were you able to talk to both of the kids?"

"I was, and after talking to them, I realized again how much I miss them. I wish we all lived on the same coast. And sometimes, I wish I could turn the clock back and make them little again."

"You're in a sentimental mood today. Have you forgotten how they drove you crazy when they were growing up? Do you remember when they hid the tape recorder under the sofa to record our conversations? Or when Jeremy was about three and he got his hands on a screwdriver and unscrewed every screw in the house he could reach?"

"No. I don't remember any of those things. I remember holding them in my arms before they went to sleep, wishing I could stop time because those moments were so perfect."

"Typical mom. The kids grow up and they become saints. So, how are the saints?"

"They sound great. I'm glad they're both working toward degrees in something they're passionate about. They're healthy and seem to be having minimal problems in the boyfriend and girlfriend department although I think Juliette is getting serious about Eric. Other than that, things are pretty much status quo for them."

"What makes you think Juliette is getting serious?"

"Instinct. She's like you; it's not so much what she says as what she doesn't say that you need to listen for. Anyway, they're both fine."

"I'm glad to hear that. I need to give them a call too. I'll do that in the next couple of days. I miss them too."

"Michael, there's a couple of other things I need to tell you." Ashley relayed the news about Ted. "Now for this next part, please stay calm until you hear me out. Do you think you can do that?"

"No promises with an intro like that. What's up?"

"Geoffrey Carruthers is . . ."

"Damn it, Ashley. I told you to stay away from him."

"Do you want to hear what I have to say or continue to yell at me?"

"Go on."

"Anyway, Geoffrey Carruthers is hosting an open house at his house in the Hamptons to raise money for the museum. I need to go; however, Robert will be going with me as well as the Secret Service. So there's really nothing for you to worry about."

"I could send an entire division of marines to guard you, and I still wouldn't feel comfortable having you around him. That man is up to something, and I don't want you anywhere near him."

"Then perhaps you'd like to go instead of me because part of my job is doing everything I can to drum up additional funds for the museum, and what you're telling me is to not do my job."

"Just let Robert attend the damn thing."

"Robert and I talked about that; however, we know that having me there will attract more potential contributors. I don't like being used in this way; still, it's for the sake of the museum. You know, you could go with me."

"When is this lovely little affair?"

"June twelfth. Would you consider going? I'd love to have you there."

'Unfortunately I'll still be in Europe. Otherwise I'd make every effort to go."

"Honey, please understand; this is something I have to do for my job. Also, I'm not asking your permission. I'm explaining to you what's going to happen. I don't like it any better than I liked you going to the state dinner with Paula, but it's the kind of thing we both have to do."

"You're right. In spite of that, I want you to be extremely careful and make sure you're never alone with that creep. He's not to be trusted. I can feel it."

"I'll do my very best, I promise. With Robert—and Dave and Matt—around, I'll be perfectly safe."

"Tell me more about Ted."

"He still hasn't regained consciousness, and that's a bad sign. The longer he's out, the more danger there is of his not regaining consciousness. Robert visited him the other day, and so far the doctors aren't very encouraging. Naturally we're all hoping for a complete recovery."

"Please let me know if there's anything you'd like me to do at this end, Ash. I know you're very fond of Ted."

"Yes, I am, and I appreciate the offer. He's a good man and great director for the museum. It would be a senseless tragedy if he makes less than a complete recovery. There's also something I've been mulling over I'd like to share with you. I've been giving our situation a lot of thought, and there are some things nagging at the edges of my brain. I need some time to put it all together, but when I do, I'd really appreciate some time with you to discuss what I've yet to figure out."

"That's about as clear as mud, Ashley. I think I'm following you although at this time of night nothing makes much sense. When you're ready to talk, I'll be ready to listen."

"Thanks. Listen, I'd better let you go. Please keep in touch when you can. I worry about you. With our schedules, time seems to have a way of evaporating. Goodnight, sweetheart."

36

Ashley found it hard to believe almost six months had passed since the inauguration. The passing months were almost a blur, so much had happened. However, a quick scan of her calendar revealed each overbooked and grueling day.

The plan she'd been working on for the past several months was taking shape. She'd secured the necessary essentials to implement her scheme if and when the appropriate occasion arose, assuming that the right set of circumstances ever occurred. She was keenly aware of what was at stake if she followed through with her plan and that if it wasn't executed with care, people she loved could be hurt by her actions. Unfortunately her loved ones were bound to be upset even if she took the utmost care in turning her thoughts into actions.

She missed Michael. He'd been gone for over a week on his trip to Europe, and communication between them had been scarce. Between the time difference and their schedules, finding a good time to talk was a challenge. She tracked his movements through the media. Fortunately the press he was getting from his trip was better than she'd expected. A sharp pain stabbed her insides every time she saw a picture of Michael, especially if Paula was in it too. He felt so far away. They'd been separated by continents before in their parallel yet separate lives, but this time for some reason, Ashley was having a more difficult time coping.

Ashley had wanted to accompany him on his first trip to Europe as president, yet she knew she couldn't take any more time off after all the time at Christmas and for the inauguration. Plus, she had the open house at Geoffrey's this coming weekend. She was thankful for his generous support, and in all honesty, she didn't perceive him as a threat to her. Although she didn't enjoy the cocktail party circuit, her job requirements demanded she attend.

On the afternoon of the open house, Ashley and her Secret Service agents arrived at Robert's apartment to pick up him and his wife, Audrey. Riding together only made sense.

The event wasn't formal, but the late afternoon gathering demanded something a little dressier than beach clothes, a certain casual chic style.

Ashley chose to wear a bright crimson and gold sari, its neckline and sleeves trimmed in three inches of gold banding. She thought East Indian women had the right idea about their style of dress. They chose absolutely beautiful fabrics, colorful and comfortable to boot.

She wore her hair down in loose waves, which looked as though she'd spent the day at a fashionable salon to get the very coveted windblown look but was just what her thick hair did naturally. She was happy with her choice of comfortable clothes.

Ashley felt as if she had everything under control where Geoffrey was concerned although she knew Michael's feelings were quite different. Where other men were concerned, Michael had always been extremely jealous. He should know by now that she wasn't as open and trusting as he believed. She let very few people get past the barriers she erected.

The black SUV pulled up in front of Robert's apartment building, and Dave got out to wait for him in the lobby. The wait was longer than Ashley had expected. She reminded Robert earlier that day what time they'd be by to pick him up, and he was generally a very punctual man. She was surprised he was taking so long. She, on the other hand, was habitually late, always thinking she had enough time to cram one more thing into her schedule before she had to leave for an appointment.

A few more minutes passed before Dave came back to the car. "I've got some upsetting news. Robert won't be able to attend the open house with you. He and his wife just received news that their son, Rick, has had a heart attack. They're leaving immediately for the hospital where he's been taken."

"Oh my God. Rick isn't that old. Maybe I should go see if there's anything I can do to help."

"I don't think there is, Mrs. Taylor. They're leaving immediately."

"Well, at least I can give them my love and let them know I'll be praying for Rick. Hang on for a second while I run in and talk to Robert."

Ashley got out of the car and headed toward the building. Dave scrambled out of the car to keep up with her. Just as she reached the front door to the apartment building, Robert and Audrey were coming out. A cab pulled up behind the SUV and gave a short honk.

Ashley reached out to Robert and Audrey, hugging one and then the other. "I won't keep you. I'm so sorry to hear about Rick. I'll be praying for him. I'll call later to check on his progress."

"Thanks, Ashley." Robert and his wife headed toward the cab. He turned back to address Ashley. "I'm sorry I won't be able to go with you to the open house."

"Nonsense. That's the last thing that should be on your mind. I'll handle everything. Just remember, you're taking my love and prayers with you. Now go."

Ashley got back into the SUV, clearly shaken. She voiced her fears to Matt and Dave. "I can't believe it. Rick's about the same age as Michael. I only hope everything will be all right. I won't allow myself to think any other way. Anyhow, it'll just be us for tonight."

Ashley was thinking of her kids and of Michael. First she had been jolted by Ted's car accident and the fact that life was so precarious and now Rick. This was further proof that she couldn't take anything for granted. You never know how much time you have left with the ones you love. Each day should be cherished. Again, she thought of her plan. Were these tragedies a sign she should continue?

37

The open house was in full swing by the time Ashley arrived. Valet parking was being provided, but Matt flashed his credentials to the young man parking cars, indicating his services would not be needed.

Matt stopped the SUV in front of the house, and Dave got out and opened the car door for Ashley. They'd wait in front of the house for Matt to park the car and return. Only then would Ashley enter Mr. Carruthers's home.

Geoffrey must have been alerted that she'd arrived because he walked out onto the front porch where Ashley and Dave were waiting. "Welcome. Are you sure you're Mrs. Taylor and not someone hired to entertain my guests?"

"Ah, a nice way to greet your guest, by criticizing her choice of dress. Smooth, really smooth," Ashley replied.

"Maybe you're here to tell their fortunes."

"I seriously doubt anything needs to be foretold here tonight. Your guests already have riches beyond most people's imaginations, or they wouldn't have been invited to this affair."

"You'd be amazed at how the rich are continually looking for ways to make more money.

And, regarding your appearance, you look exactly as you should, very unique. I don't see Robert. Wasn't he able to make it, or is he with one of your agents?"

"Robert isn't coming. Just before we were ready to leave, he and Audrey received word that their son had suffered a heart attack. They left for the hospital immediately. In fact, I'd like to go someplace quiet so I can call them on my cell. I'd like to check on him."

"Of course, follow me. I'll show you a private area where you can use your phone."

"Thank you."

Dave started to stop Ashley from leaving before Matt returned, but he could see Matt walking toward them. He quickly filled him in on Ashley's wishes to contact Robert about his son. Geoffrey led Ashley and her two agents around to the side of the house and through a side door where they entered what appeared to be an office. Geoffrey asked, "Would you like me to wait?"

Matt spoke up before Ashley could respond. "That won't be necessary, Mr. Carruthers. As soon as Mrs. Taylor is finished, we'll bring her around to the front door."

Ashley was about to say the same thing and was rather annoyed that Matt had answered for her. He was getting awfully proprietary where she was concerned. When they got back to New York this evening, she intended to speak to him about this matter. Typical male behavior—taking over whether he was asked to or not.

Geoffrey nodded. "All right. I'll see you in a few minutes. Ashley, please convey my best wishes to Robert and his wife. I hope you find all is well."

Ashley first called information to get the number of the hospital where Rick had been taken. She began searching for a scrap of paper and a pen. Dave stepped forward and handed her what she needed.

She called the hospital and spoke quietly to the receptionist. She was connected to the nurse's station outside of the intensive care unit. She explained to the nurse why she was calling and asked if Robert was available. The nurse said he was presently at his son's bedside. Ashley, not wanting to disturb him, asked how Rick was doing. The prognosis was positive although he wasn't completely out of the woods. Ashley asked the nurse to tell Robert that she'd called and that she'd call again later in the evening.

She turned to Matt and Dave. "It sounds like he's holding his own. They'll be monitoring him and making decisions as the doctors receive more information from the tests they've run. Now I suppose it's showtime for me, but before we go into the party, there's something I want to say.

"I know your assignment to protect me isn't exactly the job you were hoping for, and I'm sorry about that. I haven't been quiet about my displeasure that the Secret Service is assigned to me either. I don't like it, but then I don't imagine many people in my position do. I'm used to doing things in my own way and not having interference from others. I guess what I'm trying to say is none of us is thrilled about the situation we're in and we're all trying to make the best of it. However, I don't need to have you two hovering over me while I'm at this party. You were given the guest list ahead of time per your request, and you've had plenty of time to do background checks on everyone in that room, so please give me some space."

Matt and Dave looked nonplussed at Mrs. Taylor; then Matt spoke. "We understand your feelings. However, we will do the job we've been assigned to do."

Ashley sighed. "I understand your assignment; still, this isn't the time or place for overkill."

As they escorted Ashley back to the front entrance of the house, Matt and Dave were thinking pretty much the same thing. They would protect her, even against herself.

Geoffrey stood waiting to greet Ashley as she stepped into the foyer. He took her hand and secured it in the crook of his arm as he escorted her into the main room. He whispered, "I hope everything is well with Robert's son."

"Rick is holding his own. The doctors will know more later this evening."

"I'm glad to hear that. For now, I'll let you mingle. After all, the event is for the museum. Enjoy yourself." He released her hand and headed into the throng of people.

For the next couple of hours, Ashley exchanged pleasantries with all of the invited guests. Most asked the same questions about the museum. They made the kind of small talk they thought was necessary for as long as they thought was polite before launching into their real interest—politics and questions about Michael. They commented on his trip abroad, how they thought it was going, and how lucky they felt to have such a brilliant man in office.

Ashley felt a headache coming, so she stopped a waiter going by and asked if he would mind getting her a couple of aspirin. Shortly she felt a tap on her shoulder. She turned around to see Geoffrey standing with two aspirin in one hand and a glass of ice water in the other.

"At your service."

Ashley laughed at how ridiculous he looked. "Geoffrey, you made the right decision to be rich. Playing the dutiful servant, while appreciated, doesn't remotely fit your demeanor. Why in the world would one of your waitstaff tell you I requested some aspirin?"

"You still don't get it, do you? Your every whim could be fulfilled with just a snap of your fingers, and yet you refuse to believe that you're anything more than an ordinary woman."

"I am an ordinary woman, who just happens to be married to someone from whom everyone wants something. I never asked for any of it."

"Why don't you take a break from all the goodwill circulating around you? I keep some of my most treasured art pieces in my den. I'd love to show them to you and give the aspirin a chance to begin working."

"That doesn't sound like a bad idea. A small break might be more beneficial than the aspirin; however, I need to speak to my security agents first."

Ashley walked over to where Matt and Dave were watching the proceedings and assessing any potential threats to their charge. "I'm leaving the main room for a few minutes. Geoffrey's going to show me some of the art pieces he keeps in his den. You don't need to worry; I'll be perfectly safe and I'll be back in a minute. Stay here; there's no need for you to follow us."

As Ashley and Geoffrey headed to the den, Matt and Dave communicated without a word. They moved to follow Mrs. Taylor discreetly so she wouldn't get upset.

Ashley commented, "This is a very beautiful house. How long have you owned it?"

"I had it built about fifteen years ago. I have a husband-and-wife team that lives here on the grounds who keep it up for me."

"You certainly don't lack for much in your life, do you?"

"I wouldn't say my life is without wanting. Not everything has a price." He opened the doors to his favorite room and stood back to let Ashley enter first.

The room was lovely and inviting. Dark cherrywood covered the walls, creating a cozy and intimate room despite its size. Priceless paintings were interspersed among the bookshelves and alcoves, which displayed original and costly sculptures.

The river-rock fireplace commanded Ashley's attention when she first entered the room, but as she adjusted to its majesty, her eyes began to wander around the room to the many exquisite pieces of art perfectly and tastefully lit to show each to its best advantage. Even though it was a warm evening, a fire had been lit. Its light danced along reflective surfaces. The sofa and chairs were covered in soft, fawn-colored suede. Ashley let her fingers slide along the back of one of the chairs. The sensation reminded her of one of the softest pairs of suede gloves she owned. This room was designed for comfort and indulgence and to create a sense of serenity that might elude one in the outside world.

"May I have a closer look at your paintings?" Ashley asked.

"That's why I brought you here. I wanted you to see this room and part of my art collection."

Ashley stepped closer to a Renoir, which had been beautifully framed and perfectly lit.

Silently she moved to the next painting and the next, all superbly showcased. Geoffrey's art collection was quite eclectic. He also had an exquisite collection of handcrafted glasswork and Fabergé eggs. But what surprised her most was the Matisse, a painter she considered rather whimsical when it came to his use of color. Most of Geoffrey's art collection was more elegant and refined in its beauty.

As she stood before the painting, studying its composition, she wasn't aware that her host was beside her, just a breath away. She was so deep in thought, she jumped when he spoke.

"I can think of only one thing to add to this room to make it complete."

"Your collection is extraordinary. What more could you want?"

"I want you." Without waiting for Ashley to respond, he grabbed her and claimed her mouth. At first, his kiss was gentle, but it quickly grew demanding.

Ashley was shocked. Was this really happening? She pushed Geoffrey away, furious with him for putting the two of them in this situation and furious with herself for not being more aware of him after Michael had warned her.

"How dare you? What the hell are you thinking?"

"I think what I'm thinking is fairly obvious."

"Knock it off. I'm not one of those silly women you pursue who stand around panting and waiting for your attention."

"I know that. I'm keenly aware of who you are. Don't tell me that you aren't the least bit curious about me, or rather us, and how we might be together."

Ashley doubled up her fist and punched him as hard as she could. "You are certifiable." Ashley turned toward the door while shaking her hand from the pain in her knuckles after delivering a well-deserved blow.

Geoffrey was surprised that Ashley had slugged him like a man rather than slap him as most women might do. He grabbed her wrist, firmly enough to keep her from going anyplace. "If you're so uninterested, why didn't you stop the kiss immediately?"

"Shock . . . I can't believe you. Let go of me immediately. Do you realize my husband could kill you for this?" Ashley wrenched her arm away and moved to put some furniture between the two of them.

"You're living in a fantasy world, Geoffrey. I'm not available, and if you touch me again, you'll be missing one or more of your body parts."

Geoffrey threw back his head and laughed. "You're magnificent. You're threatening me?"

"You bet I am. I don't need my husband or anyone else to fight my battles for me." Ashley walked toward an expensive vase. "How much did this little beauty cost you?"

"Oh, now you're going to pretend as though nothing happened."

"On the contrary. I'll never forget what happened and what a fool I've been. How much did you say this cost?"

"I paid fifty thousand dollars for that piece."

"I wish it had been more," Ashley responded, deliberately knocking it off its pedestal. A loud crash and the sound of shattered glass resounded in the room. She quickly moved toward another beautiful glass sculpture.

"And, this one?"

Geoffrey said nothing as the door flew open and Matt and Dave came through the portal, guns drawn.

"Are you all right, Mrs. Taylor?" Matt asked.

Geoffrey promptly spoke up. "There's just been a little accident. No problem."

"Is that right?" Dave asked, watching Ashley's face.

Ashley responded, "Actually there was an accident, and there's about to be another one."

She quickly picked up another glass sculpture, took aim at the river-rock fireplace, and threw it as hard as she could. It hit the rocks and broke apart and fell to the floor.

"Now, if you'll excuse me, Mr. Carruthers, we're leaving." She walked over to her Secret Service agents and said, "Time to go."

When they were outside, heading toward the car, Matt asked, "Is there anything we should know, Mrs. Taylor?"

"No, not at all. What happened in that room is between Mr. Carruthers and me, and it's going to stay that way. And I'd appreciate it if you never mention that you saw me destroy a beautiful piece of art." Ashley smiled at herself.

On one hand, she'd never felt such satisfaction from an action. On the other hand, she'd destroyed a miniature masterpiece. Sometimes the price one paid for one's mistakes was costly. It was a lesson that both she and her host had just learned.

During the drive back to Manhattan, she constantly wrestled with her conscience. Had she done something to encourage Geoffrey's behavior? Clearly he had intended to add another trophy to his already long list of female conquests.

Ashley believed everything happened for a reason. Starting with Ted's devastating car accident, Rick's heart attack, and Geoffrey's incredible ego and horrendous bad judgment, she realized she must reassess her priorities and put her plan in action. She rested her head on the back of the seat. She felt confident that what she was about to do was necessary although she was aware there would be consequences. Nevertheless, she believed the price was worth it.

Geoffrey knew he needed to return to his guests. He couldn't leave them alone much longer, or they'd begin to question where he and Ashley were; tongues would start to wag, and rumors would be born. Naturally he would need to explain Ashley's sudden departure. That would be easy enough. He would cite Robert's son's heart attack as the reason; everybody knew how close Robert and Ashley were.

He wanted to analyze what had happened and where his plan had failed. Most probably, he'd made his advance too fast. He should have given her more time and planned a few more get-togethers to win her trust before pursuing her more overtly.

God, she'd been incredible. He smiled, thinking about her hitting him on the jaw, destroying the hand-blown glass vase, and throwing his glass sculpture at the fireplace. In that moment, he had seen both a siren and an Amazon warrior. His financial sacrifice was minimal. He would gladly wager that it hurt Ashley far more than him to destroy his precious artwork.

What he needed to decide was how best to proceed. She most likely would be indignant and shun or ignore him. Proof, in his opinion, that he had successfully scaled the walls she had so carefully built around herself.

There was always the money collected from this weekend's event to use as bait to meet with her again. It would be necessary to contact her to arrange for the transfer of funds to the museum. He bet that Ashley wouldn't back down from another meeting with him, if for no other reason than to prove to him that what had occurred between them had no effect on her in any way.

Ah, a proud woman was usually a good target, especially one who prided herself on being able to handle everything that came her way. Ashley's traits would work to his advantage. Yes, the next phase of this very tricky undertaking should be both interesting and entertaining.

38

As soon as Ashley said goodnight to Matt and Dave, she turned her attention to executing the escape strategy she'd been working on for months. It was time to get away and do some uninterrupted thinking. She needed to be alone, completely alone with no pressure and no one else trying to influence her or distract her.

She'd gone over and over her plan for months to see where she might get tripped up if she decided to activate her scheme. She knew ditching Matt and Dave would be far more difficult than getting away from the agents assigned to her at night. Matt and Dave seemed to be continually suspicious of her.

She also had given a great deal of thought about how to let her loved ones know she was okay and safe after she left. She knew they'd be worried initially, but she hoped her plan would minimize the amount of stress they would have due to her actions.

In the bedroom, she packed a black canvas backpack with two changes of clothes and the necessary toiletries. She changed into a pair of jeans, a T-shirt, walking shoes, and a hooded sweatshirt, all in black. She needed to blend into the night.

She'd been putting aside small amounts of cash for months so she wouldn't have to use her credit cards. She knew she could be traced through those. She'd probably seen too many spy movies. Still, it was better to be paranoid than to be blasé.

She'd lived for months with the Secret Service always being one room away, but during that time, she'd been able to study their patterns and habits. It was helpful information as she began formulating her scheme; it led her to the time that would most likely be the best window of opportunity for her getaway.

Ashley sat down on the bed and called Mavis's direct line at the museum. Since it was after hours and Mavis had gone home, her voice mail would pick up. She left specific instructions for Mavis, explaining what she was doing and letting her know who to contact and what to tell them. She wondered again if she'd thought of everyone who needed to be reached: Michael, Robert, her kids, and Sienna.

They must know she was leaving town of her own free will and would be gone about three days to an undisclosed destination. She promised she would be safe and asked Mavis to ask Michael to try to keep her absence a secret. No good could possibly come from the media getting wind of her departure. She promised she would be in touch soon. She also asked that Michael talk to the head of Homeland Security to run interference for the Secret Service agents who were on duty when she left. She didn't want them blamed for her actions.

Probably very few people could understand her need to be completely alone. She'd thought of every possible scenario before settling on this drastic measure. Every other solution she'd entertained brought with it some kind of interruption. How could she possibly make a good decision if she didn't take the necessary time and space to make it?

She called Robert next. She wanted to hear how Rick was doing before she left. The hospital receptionist came on the line immediately, and Ashley relayed her request to speak to Robert.

While she waited, she tried to imagine how completely helpless she would feel if one of her kids was in the ICU under similar circumstances. It was every parent's nightmare. You just didn't expect anything to happen to your children, especially for them to die before you did. It just wasn't the natural order of things.

"Hello, this is Robert."

"Hi, it's Ashley. How's Rick?"

"As good as can be expected. The cardiologist will be taking him into surgery soon. There was some damage, but they tell us they'll be able to repair it. They'll also be doing a double bypass on him. We're all scared to death."

"How could you not be? Robert, I'm so sorry about Rick. It's further proof that none of us can take anything for granted. How are you and Audrey holding up?"

"As well as can be expected under the circumstances. Rick's wife is here and all of the other kids, too, so we're all supporting one another."

"I'm glad you're all together. I'll let you go. I know you need to get back. Please give my love to Rick and Audrey and all the rest of your family."

"I will. Before you go, how was the open house?"

"There were a lot of people there, so I think we can expect a healthy chunk of change from the event; however, we won't know until Mr. Carruthers calls and transfers the money over to the museum."

"It was certainly generous of him to do this for us. I hope you realize it was your influence that triggered this whole affair."

"I've argued that point with you before, but now I know that's true."

"I'm glad you've quit being so modest about your influence on him."

"I need to run for now, Robert. I'll check back with you later about Rick's condition."

"Ashley, thanks for calling."

"I'll talk to you soon."

Ashley had covered everything she could think of before she took off. Only two more things to do: put on her disguise and deactivate her cell phone. She opened the drawer where she'd been hiding a black wig and a pair of black horn-rimmed glasses. She quickly put them on, and when she looked in the mirror, she saw a studious-looking woman with a short black bob. She didn't look anything like herself. She smiled to see if it made a difference. Yes, smiling made her look a little more like herself, so she needed to remember not to smile.

Now for her phone. It could lead them to her, but she wanted access. She removed the battery and quickly stored it in one of the zippered pockets in her backpack.

Time to leave. Ashley walked through the apartment, turning off lights and making the usual sounds she made before going to bed. The next part was the hard part. She needed to disarm her security alarm in order to open the bedroom window through which she intended to escape.

She put on the backpack so she'd be ready for action once she deactivated the alarm. She didn't know how long it would be before the agents noticed the alarm was off. They were sharp, but she didn't need a lot of time, just a few minutes. She pressed the necessary buttons to disarm the security system and then took off toward the bedroom as quietly as she could.

She opened the window she'd been oiling for weeks to assure it would glide easily and silently and climbed out onto the fire escape. She didn't hesitate for even a second. The minute she was on the metal platform, she started her descent down the ladders as silently as possible. So far, so good.

When she reached the bottom, she knew she'd have to drop to the ground. The drop was farther than she liked risking, but there was simply no other way. She hung from the bottom rung of the metal ladder and tried to balance her body so that when she landed, her weight would be evenly distributed on her knees, ankles, and feet to absorb the shock. She didn't need a twisted or sprained ankle right now.

She took a deep breath, let it out slowly, and then let go. When she landed, the impact on her ankles and knees caused a shudder to run through her body. She took another breath and assessed the strength of her ankles. Not bad. Her heart was beating like a war drum—or was the sound she heard the footsteps of the Secret Service coming her way?

She concentrated on bringing her breathing under control while she shifted her position from under the fire escape to the wall of the building. Breathe in, breathe out slowly; that's all the time she had. She began walking away from her building through the alley to the next street over. She walked for about ten blocks before she flagged a cab and asked to be taken to the Port Authority bus terminal.

All the time she'd been walking, she expected to hear sirens or footsteps pounding on the pavement. She hadn't heard anything to suggest they were aware she'd given them the slip, but surely by now not only were the agents aware she was gone, but so was the head of Homeland Security and her husband.

She knew the anger Michael would be feeling and his sense of helplessness. She hoped he wouldn't make a connection between her disappearance and the open house she'd attended at Geoffrey's home. He would be furious and crazed though very soon he would hear the real reason for her disappearance.

When she returned home, she'd try to calm everyone and make each one understand the necessity of her actions. Still, she wasn't free and clear yet. The taxi pulled up in front of the bus terminal, and she paid her fare. Fortunately the driver was completely unaware of who his passenger was. Luck was with her so far; she hoped it would hold. She hated feeling like a fugitive, but unfortunately that was what she was for now.

39

When the Secret Service agents noticed the alarm was off in Ashley's apartment, they took immediate action. They knocked on the door and, after receiving no response, drew their weapons, barged through the door, and yelled her name. They did a thorough search of the apartment and found it empty with one bedroom window open—the one leading to the fire escape.

One agent climbed down the fire escape; the other one rechecked the apartment. Both came up short; Mrs. Taylor was nowhere to be found. There was no sign of a struggle, just an open bedroom window.

They knew time was of the essence, so although they'd rather take a beating than make a call to their boss, they called him and explained what happened. Their boss, in turn, called the president, who was due to return from Europe the next day.

After hearing the details of his wife's disappearance, Michael knew Ashley had deliberately taken off on her own. Still, he worried that someone was trying to make it look as though she'd skipped out. The first person he thought of was Geoffrey Carruthers, but even he wasn't brazen enough or stupid enough to pull off something like this.

Michael's first call was to Robert Cameron. He and Ashley were supposed to attend the open house in the Hamptons tonight. Maybe Robert could shed some light on Ashley's disappearance. No answer. Hmmm . . . It seemed like it was late enough for the two of them to have returned to New York, but maybe not.

His next call was to Geoffrey Carruthers.

"Mr. Carruthers's residence."

"Hello, this is President Taylor. I'd like to speak to Mr. Carruthers immediately."

"Of course, Mr. President. I'll get him for you. Please hold."

Michael was impatient for Geoffrey to pick up the line. Fortunately he didn't have long to wait.

"Hello, Mr. President. To what do I owe the honor of this call?"

"I need some information. Wasn't tonight the night of your open house?"

"Yes. Tonight was the open house, and it was quite successful. I was sorry Robert was unable to attend; however, given the circumstances, who would have expected him to?"

"What are you talking about?"

"Oh, I assumed you had talked to your wife; I guess you haven't. Robert was unable to attend the festivities tonight because his son Rick had a heart attack and was rushed to one of the New York hospitals."

"So, Ashley came to the open house without Robert?"

"Yes, naturally.

"I hope you remembered the conversation we had in relationship to my wife."

"Absolutely. Business is business. Is there a reason you're calling?"

"Just wanted to speak to my wife, and since Ashley and Robert weren't home yet, I thought they might still be at your place. Goodnight." Michael hung up before Carruthers could ask any more questions. Ashley had gone alone to the open house. He wondered if she intended to tell him about that little turn of events.

It was a long shot, but maybe Robert could shed some light on Ashley's disappearance. Since his earlier call to Robert hadn't been answered, either he didn't have his cell with him or had turned it off while he was in the hospital. Michael instructed his secretary to call all of the hospitals in Manhattan and find the one where Rick had been taken. Once she had Robert on the line, she transferred the call to Michael.

"Hi, Robert. It's Michael Taylor. I heard about your son; how is he?"

"Oh, did Ashley tell you about Rick? Bless her heart. He's in surgery right now. Thank you for caring enough to call."

"I do care about your son, and I did know about him having a heart attack, but it was Geoffrey Carruthers who told me. Robert, Ashley's missing. I'm sorry to add that to your troubles."

"Missing? What do you mean missing? I just talked to her."

"It looks as though she's deliberately ditched her Secret Service detail."

"I don't know what to say. Ashley called me after she got home to check on Rick. Have you thought of calling her secretary?"

"No, I hadn't, but that's a very good idea. Thank you, Robert, and my prayers are with you and Audrey, and of course, Rick. By the way, please don't mention this to anyone. I'll get back to you when I know more."

"You can count on me to be discreet. I know you must be worried. You know how she is regarding the Secret Service. If she wanted to get lost for a while, she's capable of master-minding an escape. Michael, I'm sure Ashley's safe."

"God, I hope so. Goodnight, and I'll be in touch."

The next call was to Ashley's secretary. "Hi, Mavis. It's Michael Taylor. Sorry for the late phone call, but I need your help. Ashley's missing. In fact, it appears she's deliberately ditched her Secret Service agents, and I'm trying to locate her. By any chance, would you know where she is or where she might have gone?"

"I know she was going to Mr. Carruthers's tonight, but she didn't tell me about any other plans. Knowing Ashley, if she decided to take off and she wanted some lead time, she wouldn't have told me because she knows I would have tried to talk her out of it. I'll bet she left a voice mail on my machine at work so when I went back to work, I'd get the message."

"Good thinking. Would you please check your voice mail and get back to me? I'll transfer you to Georgia, and she'll give you the number where I can be reached."

"I'll check right now, and I'll call you right back."

"Thanks. I'd appreciate that."

After Mavis hung up, she said out loud, "For God's sake, Ashley, what have you done now?"

Michael was thankful for Mavis's quick thinking. She and Ashley were close, and Mavis was right; if Ashley wanted a head start, she just might have left a message that she knew would be picked up later.

Michael was handed an intelligence report. Ashley had not been located, but her fingerprints were all over the windowsill and the fire escape ladder. Michael swore. That woman was going to be the death of him yet. He'd always loved how unpredictable she was, but she'd gone too far this time. He was going to kill her for this stunt, and then his next thoughts were *please God, keep her safe.*

True to her word, Mavis checked her messages at work. She skipped through them quickly, hoping she'd been right about Ashley leaving a message for her to find. Just when she was beginning to think she hadn't, Ashley's voice came on the line.

"Hi, Mavis; it's me. By the time you get this message, hopefully I'll be long gone. I just can't take it anymore. I need to get away by myself to think things through. After Ted's horrible accident and not knowing if he's going to recover, and then tonight Robert's son had a heart attack, it got me to thinking even more about my family and my priorities. I've talked to Robert, and it looks like Rick is going to be okay, but would you call the hospital and check on his progress for me?

"Anyway, I need to take an honest look at my life and re-evaluate my goals, and for that I need to be completely alone. Actually I've been planning on how to get away from the Secret Service for some time. When I get off the phone, I'm taking off. Wish me luck even if you don't want to.

"Please call Michael, Robert, the kids, and Sienna and tell them you've heard from me, and I'm okay. I'll be gone for about three days, I think. No one has forced me to do this; I'm totally responsible for leaving on my own.

"Tell Michael I'm sorry I had to go to such drastic measures to get a little time to myself and ask him not to send the troops after me. I'll be fine, really. Also, ask him to try to keep this from the media and defend the poor agents who were guarding me. I don't want them to get into trouble because of me.

"Well, that pretty much sums it up. I can already hear you talking to me in my head. Don't worry; I've got a good plan, and I'll share everything with you when I get back. Gotta go."

Mavis shook her head. Ashley had never come to terms with being the wife of a politician, much less the president. She still thought of herself as someone who could lead a normal life. She honestly didn't believe she should have to change her life in any way, and because she refused to accept who she was and her position, she made herself vulnerable.

She hated calling Michael back. She knew the stress he was under, and this little stunt of Ashley's wasn't going to help.

When Michael came on the line, Mavis relayed Ashley's message.

Michael asked, "Did she sound like herself?"

"Yes, she did. Are you worried that someone might have forced her to leave a message?"

"It's a possibility I can't rule out."

"Of course, you're right, but she sounded like herself to me. I'm not an expert, but she sounded like she always does, especially when she's up to something. Honestly I could picture the expression on her face."

"I'm sure you know there's nothing about this situation I find amusing. I'd like a copy of the message on your phone. We'll want to see if we can pick up any additional clues from it. What's your password for accessing your voice mail?"

Mavis recited her code.

"Mavis, thanks for your help."

"I'm glad there was something I could do. If I remember anything I think can help, I'll call you."

"I'd appreciate that. I'll call the kids and Sienna and let them know what's going on. Would you give Robert a call? I talked to him earlier this evening, and he knows Ashley's missing. He will want to know about her message. Thanks again, Mavis."

Michael was unaware of the movement around him. He was staring into space, trying to think like Ashley. What an effort in futility. If Ashley could pull off something like this, there's no telling what she was thinking. When she was completely safe and back in his arms, they were going to have a showdown.

40

Ashley tried to assume the body posture of a distracted student weighed down with too many books and thoughts. Her bus would be leaving in fifteen minutes. Her nerves were shot. Her palms were sweaty, and she expected to be surrounded by either the police or the Secret Service at any moment. For God's sake, she wasn't a criminal although she needed to think like one for now.

She glanced up occasionally to check for anything that seemed out of the ordinary. She tried to blend into her surroundings. She was almost home free and could hardly wait to be on her way. Thank goodness, she had Steve's help.

Months ago, she'd gone to him and told him about what she'd been thinking. She swore him to secrecy, which was no great accomplishment. He loved challenging the system. In fact, he helped her with her entire plan, including lending her his vacation cabin in Ludlow, Vermont. He offered to call his part-time housekeeper and ask her to freshen up the cabin and stock it with food so Ashley wouldn't have to venture out until she decided to return to New York.

Steve bought the wig and helped her with the disguise. If by chance her disappearance did become public knowledge, some salesperson might remember her buying a black wig. She probably could have managed without Steve's help, but having it made everything a lot easier.

She didn't think many people, if anyone, would make a connection between the two of them. No one knew what good friends they'd become. They were kindred spirits; both enjoyed the creative process, the beauty that surrounded them, and the unexpected. If the Secret Service decided to question Steve, she was confident he wouldn't say a word.

Her thoughts were interrupted by an announcement over the public address system. She checked her watch; it was time to board the bus. Her goal was just within her reach.

She was well aware of the consequences of her actions. She knew her disappearance would throw everyone into a panic, and they'd be searching for her. She was truly sorry for any pain and fear she was causing her loved ones. She hoped the message she left Mavis would be found quickly and that it would help calm everyone somewhat although she knew nothing would calm Michael down. She felt guilty about the manpower that would be wasted trying to find her. In the end, however, if she could find a workable solution to their problem, it would be worth it.

As the bus lurched forward, Ashley reached for the seat in front of her to steady herself. She could still hear her heart beating in her ears, but with each mile traveled away from Manhattan, she became more convinced she was not being followed.

41

Michael was glad to be back in the United States. His trip to Europe had been successful. His goal had been to meet and get to know the heads of the European countries. He was very glad that Ashley hadn't pulled this stunt during the middle of his time abroad. He would've been hard-pressed to stay put in Europe knowing Ashley had disappeared. His heart would have wanted to lead him home. Yet he knew that what he wanted to do and what he could do were decidedly different now that he was the president. He couldn't just walk away from encouraging better diplomatic relations because his wife decided to ditch her Secret Service agents and take off.

Michael asked his secretary to set up a conference call with Jeremy and Juliette. So far he had been able to keep Ashley's disappearance out of the newspapers; however, if by some chance the news leaked, they needed to know their mother was okay and had pulled off this latest means of trying to drive him crazy all by herself. Further news of her disregard for authority would stir up the whole First Lady controversy again, and that he didn't need.

Michael had already met with the head of Homeland Security to decide whether they should have the Secret Service pursue her disappearance. From the evidence they had gathered thus far, it appeared that Ashley had acted alone. Michael wondered what exactly had pushed her far enough to decide disappearing like this was worth it. He didn't believe for one minute that it was a coincidence that she took off on the night she attended Geoffrey Carruthers's open house. Somehow there was a link; somehow there was a connection.

His fear was that her disappearance was staged. Although all forensic evidence indicated no one else was involved, Michael still considered it a possibility. It was decided to keep her disappearance on a "need to know" basis. Only the agents normally assigned to guard her would investigate her whereabouts. They didn't want to give anyone in the media a heads-up regarding Ashley's apparent escape.

Even though the incident didn't happen on Matt's and Dave's watch, they were ticked off. When they heard what Ashley had done, it only confirmed what they had always suspected about her. She was unpredictable and capable of anything. They were determined to find her and knew they had their work cut out for them. They would be discreet, but nothing would stand in the way of tracking her down; the image of them catching her during her little hiatus was a sweet, sweet thought.

Georgia indicated that the conference call was set up and that Michael's children were waiting for him to pick up.

"Hi, kids, sorry for keeping you waiting. I hope I haven't alarmed you with this conference call."

Jeremy spoke up. "Dad, something must be pretty serious if you felt the need to get Juliette and me on the phone at the same time."

"Well, I wanted to fill you in on a situation that's come up."

Juliette asked, "What's that?"

"It has to do with your mother. She's not hurt; she's okay, but I wanted you to know what's going on."

Jeremy barely let his father get the words out of his mouth before he asked, "What's wrong? Is Mom okay?"

"Yes, she's fine; at least I think she is. Listen, let me get this all out, and then you can ask questions."

Silence from his two children indicated they intended to do just that.

"All right, here's the situation. Sometime after a fundraiser your mother attended on Saturday evening, she gave the Secret Service agents the slip, and she's taken off for God knows where."

Jeremy interrupted, "Cool. Way to go, Mom."

Michael responded, "No, not so cool. She's got everyone upset, particularly me. It happened the night before I returned from Europe. She left a message for us on Mavis's voice mail. She said she wanted to get away for a couple of days to think and that she was okay. She also mentioned she didn't want any of us to worry. She asked Mavis to call all of us."

Juliette asked, "How did she manage to get away?"

"She slipped out at night after they thought she had gone to bed. They noticed the security alarm system to her apartment was off. When they knocked on the door, there was no answer. They went in and found her missing and one of the bedroom windows open. She evidently climbed down the fire escape."

"All right, Mom. Score one for the Taylor family," Jeremy cheered.

Michael voiced his displeasure over his son's reaction. "Jeremy, there is nothing about this that's cool, and I don't appreciate your thinking there is."

Jeremy fell silent.

"How do you know the whole thing wasn't staged to look like Mom skipped out?" Juliette asked.

"That was one of my concerns as well, but everything, including the message she left, indicates she's behind the whole thing. We've had the Secret Service go through Mom's apartment, and we've analyzed the message. All the evidence points to it being planned and executed by just your mom."

"So, what now?" Juliette asked.

"Good question. We've assigned the agents who normally guard your mom to the case. They're the most familiar with her daily movements. The two she's had the most interaction with are furious and determined to find her. I have a sneaking hunch if she's decided to get lost, no one is going to find her until she's ready to be found.

"I'm sorry to have to give you such scary news and then run, but I wanted you to know what had happened. If you hear anything from your mother, I want you to call me immediately, and I'll do the same for you."

"Dad," Jeremy stopped him before he could hang up. "Has anyone tried to call her cell phone? I know it's a pretty obvious thing to do, but I was just wondering. I know how worried you are about Mom, and so are we, but I really think she's going to be okay."

"Yes, we've tried to call her cell phone, but she's either ditched it or deactivated it somehow. I wish reaching her was that easy. But, in my heart I want to believe you're right; still, I'm terrified that she might not be all right. Knowing your mom, she'll probably pop back up just like she disappeared. I hope none of you mind if I strangle her when she does."

With an equal amount of emotion in their voices, they responded in one fashion or another. "Be our guest. Just don't hurt her badly; we're kind of attached to her."

"I'll try to keep that in mind. Remember, this is between you and me. We're trying to keep your mom's disappearance from the media."

"Okay. Call us if you hear anything," Jeremy said.

After hanging up, Michael called Sienna. He went through the same information with her as he had the kids. Sienna took it rather well, not acting in the least bit surprised.

"Sienna, did you already know about this? Did Ashley talk to you about her plans?"

"No, but it doesn't surprise me. In fact, I'm surprised she's waited as long as she has. Michael, there's one thing about which I'm absolutely certain: Ashley has done this for a very good reason. She wouldn't put the people she loves through this if it weren't for something extremely important. I think Ashley's on the verge of making a life-changing decision, and she needed to get away to think. When we were kids and she would visit, occasionally she'd disappear. She usually climbed up high into a tree. She would say she needed to be alone to think. She obviously wanted time away from everyone and everything so she could think through something very serious."

"I hope you're right. You've always understood her better than I do. I swear you two have a psychic connection. After all these years, she still baffles me. Anyway, I'm going to trust that you really don't know anything."

"I can assure you, I don't. If she calls me, I'll try to find out where she is and encourage her to call you. Michael, promise me you won't have our phones tapped."

"You've been reading way too many novels. No, no phone-tapping. Please keep in touch, and I'll do the same. Tell Jim hi for me and remind him he's the lucky one. I don't think I can ever remember your pulling any crazy stunts like this unless your cousin dragged you into them."

"I'll be sure to tell him you called. Let me know if you hear from her."

Michael was completely exhausted, and his day was just beginning.

42

Ashley felt like an escaped convict. She tried to be as inconspicuous as possible. During the bus trip, she kept her eyes glued to a book she pretended to read. If threatened with bodily harm, she wouldn't be able to tell you the title of the book or anything else written on the pages she continued to turn at a steady rate.

When Ashley finally reached the safe harbor of Ludlow, Vermont, she began to feel the tension in her body ease. Steve's cabin was all he claimed it to be, a safe haven where she could find refuge and a place to reflect and contemplate the current status of her life. True to his word, the cabin was fully stocked with food and everything else he thought she might need. She wouldn't need to leave the cabin for anything. There was comfort in knowing she could just *be*. She closed her eyes and breathed. She'd made it this far. That was a start.

The two-bedroom cedar log cabin was charming. It smelled wonderfully woodsy, an ancient smell so familiar it seeped into her pores and spoke to her primitive brain of a comfort once received in another time and place. The lower level housed the living room, dining room, kitchen, and one bathroom. The upper level had a narrow balcony that wrapped around the second floor with doors leading to two huge bedrooms and another bathroom that boasted a deep soaking Jacuzzi tub. The whole cabin was beautifully and artfully decorated. Rustic and antique furniture were combined with splashes of bright colors and whimsical accents insisting that its occupants not take life too seriously.

Ashley thought of Michael and the headache her leaving was undoubtedly creating for him. Michael was strong; he would be all right. Besides being furious about her ditching her security, his main concern would be for her safety. She would need to do a lot of explaining and repair work when she returned. She knew no matter what she would say to assure him she'd been safe, he would be convinced she'd put herself in harm's way.

She had promised him early in their marriage she would never place herself deliberately in an unsafe or dangerous situation, and he would most assuredly view this as a breach of that promise. Ashley was very sure that Michael, while concerned about her safety, would also be mad as hell. There was nothing she could do about that now; she had known how he'd react before she left, and yet she still felt she must leave. Sometimes it was necessary to fly through the turbulence of clouds to get to the smooth sky above.

Michael would view her call and message to Mavis's voice mail as throwing him a bone. He knew her well enough to know she must have been planning to leave for some time. That, in itself, would infuriate him. She was very sure that he would see absolutely no reason why she needed to have time to herself. Still, after all their years of marriage, he didn't understand her need to be completely alone at times.

Ashley stood up and stretched. She was physically drained from her ordeal; she definitely needed a nap. She hadn't slept a wink during her entire four-hour bus trip. Who could have? She needed to re-energize her body so she could begin thinking about what had brought her here in the first place.

She made her way up the staircase and immediately started undressing. The cool sheets felt like a soothing balm to her bunched-up muscles. When she woke, if she ever did, she'd begin to address the purpose of her exodus. She was determined to find a resolution to the quagmire in which she and Michael were stuck. She drifted off to sleep, determined not to leave this cabin until she found a solution.

Ashley awoke abruptly but was immediately aware of where she was. She listened to see if some sound had disturbed her, but she heard nothing. She stretched and looked out the window opposite the bed. It was daytime. She reached for her watch to check the time; it was two in the afternoon. She'd been gone over twelve hours. She needed to boost her blood cells with a stimulant. She needed caffeine.

When she finally had her coffee and toast in front of her, she smiled thinking about what a creature of habit she was and how easy it was to please her. With the very first swallow of the aromatic blend, every nerve ending and electrical current in her body bowed down to the supremacy of the magical elixir. She let out a deep sigh and released the last remnants of nervous energy left over from making her escape from New York.

She retrieved a tablet of paper from her backpack. She intended to attack this problem logically. At least she hoped she could bypass her emotions long enough to let the logical side of her brain operate for a while. She drew a line down the center of the paper and wrote at the top "pro" on one side of the line and "con" on the other. Now to begin the truly difficult part: total honesty.

Before she began, she poured herself another cup of coffee. She leaned against the counter, thinking about all of the times in her married life she'd sought to bring some kind of harmony to a situation or to find some resolution to a problem between her and Michael. They'd always had their differences but never of the magnitude of what they were dealing with now. She felt like she'd been doing this same thing throughout most of their married life. With both of them being such strong-willed people and with each dedicated to careers, disharmony was practically a way of life.

Yet, through all of the years, they'd stayed together and not for the sake of their children. Beneath all of their differences, they were truly in love with one another, deeply and forever. One would think love would bring comfort rather than so much discord. It would have been easier if they didn't love each other so much. They would have separated a long time ago, and all of the friction arising from their love could easily have been handled with a couple of good attorneys.

Ashley went to work on her pro-and-con list. A couple of quotes from an old Kevin Costner movie popped into her head. He had referred to a defining moment. His character said, "When a defining moment comes along, either you define the moment or the moment defines you." In her opinion, this was a defining moment.

The other quote was "Greatness courts failure." Michael had been willing to take enormous risks to achieve his goals. He'd risked failure in his quest for the presidency. Now it was time for her to take a risk of her own in an attempt to balance their lives.

Ashley looked at the list she'd created. Almost every item listed, regardless of which side it was on, carried with it an almost equal consequence on the opposite side. Each side painted a possible picture of the future. The path she would choose had to be for the sake of her marriage and her family and still allow her the career she'd worked so hard to achieve.

New circumstances had been introduced into the equation that allowed for new solutions to be considered. As always, she had a lot to think about, but even with a snapshot of possible futures for her and Michael, the consequences of the decision she might make needed to be weighed and measured carefully.

If she were to follow the path that could bring more harmony between her and Michael, she had a list of conditions that he'd need to meet too. Before she could decide anything for sure, there were other people she needed to talk to. If her plan broke down anywhere along the way, she'd have to scrap the whole idea and try to hammer out another way of achieving balance in their lives.

Ashley wanted to spend what was left of the day relaxing. She picked up her book and headed for the bedroom. It was already dark, and even though she'd taken a nap, she knew she would sleep well tonight because she'd finally had some uninterrupted time to think things through and outline some fresh possibilities.

When she awoke the next morning, Ashley looked over her notes from the previous day and decided there was nothing she'd written down that she would change. Basically, once she'd gotten away from all the stress, confusion, and demands, she was able to figure out what she thought might be the best course of action. She acknowledged to herself that she'd been consciously and unconsciously working on the problem for months but that what she desperately had needed was some time away from the fishbowl existence she'd been living.

Life shouldn't be taken for granted, and she felt as though she and Michael had been taking one another and their love for granted for far too long. Ashley didn't want to have any regrets when she lay dying. She'd always grabbed life with open arms and embraced it firmly and with purpose. But had she been doing that lately?

She decided to spend her second day soaking up nature. There was always something purifying about getting away from the city where noise and crowds constantly bombarded the senses. She dressed warmly and went for a long walk. It was a beautiful day, and the sound of the trees rustling soothed her. She breathed in the fresh country air and let the last of her pent-up stress release itself into the wind.

When she returned to the cabin, she decided to rest outside on the deck. Steve had outdone himself in creating a beautiful, serene environment. With its abundant potted plants and flowers and its fashionable outdoor furniture arranged for comfort and conversation, it was perfect. She eyed what looked like a very comfortable chaise longue. She didn't have to go anywhere or talk to anyone, and no one was expecting anything from her, praise be. How often did that happen anymore?

Ashley carried a radio outside and turned it to a channel that played jazz. She watched the clouds drift by for a while and imagined all sorts of creatures in their billowy shapes. She read and she rested. She closed her eyes and breathed in the fragrant air. She let her mind wander until the sounds of footsteps interrupted her thoughts—soft ones, but definitely footsteps. She sat up and looked back toward the house. Nothing.

When she turned back around, she saw a man walking toward her on the deck. Not just any man, but the photographer who had been at her apartment, at the fund-raiser, and outside the Russian Tea Room. The one who had taken the controversial pictures of her and Geoffrey. Only this time, she didn't see a camera.

The expression on his face alarmed her. He looked predatory.

Ashley jumped up and took off for the door. Just as she reached the kitchen door, a hand clamped down on her shoulder.

"What? You don't have something to say to me this time, Mrs. Taylor?" The photographer, if he was a photographer, said in a very contemptuous voice.

In that moment, adrenaline surged through her body, and she was unafraid. She turned toward the man. "Take your hands off of me." The look on her face must have made him rethink what he was doing because he removed his hand from her shoulder and took a step back.

Ashley continued her offensive. "What are you doing here? How did you find me? Is it more pictures you want? You've let your paparazzi mentality affect your judgment."

His surprise at her reaction only slowed him down a second, "Listen, Miss High-and-Mighty, you may have other people fooled but not me. You were easy to find. You may have the Secret Service's panties all in a wad, but I recognize what you really are. You think you're too good for the rest of us. Someone needs to teach you a lesson."

He reached forward to lift the hem of her T-shirt and touched bare skin. The feel of his hand grazing her flesh set off war drums in her head. Ashley slapped his hand away and let out a bloodcurdling scream.

He hadn't expected her to act so aggressively, first with words and now bodily. He thought he could intimidate her easily. Her screaming could possibly bring unnecessary attention. Attention that he, and most certainly his employer, didn't want.

He turned to leave. "This isn't over. I can get to you anytime I want. My employer is very interested in you. So, until next time . . ." He grabbed her hand and kissed the back of it.

Ashley stumbled into the cabin and locked the door. She looked out the kitchen window to see if he was still around, but there was nothing to see. Her breathing was coming in ragged breaths. Now that she could no longer see the interloper, her brave front crumbled. It was time to get out of here even though she'd originally planned to stay another day.

She ran upstairs and threw her things into her backpack and headed to the front door. When she opened it, she stifled another scream; Matt and Dave were standing on the front porch. Neither looked as though he was in the mood for any nonsense. The expression on their faces indicated they were furious.

Dave responded sarcastically, "What? You don't look glad to see us?"

Ashley grabbed each of them by an arm. "Quick. There was a man on the back deck." She pointed in the direction of the deck. "He threatened me."

Dave stayed with Ashley while Matt went through the kitchen and out the back door. He returned shortly and shook his head at Dave. "We need to call in our investigative unit and see what we can find."

"I know who it was. In fact, so do you. Remember the photographer who took my picture outside my apartment when I first returned from the inauguration? It was him. He came up to me on the deck and said I was easy to find, like he'd been following me. I ran toward the house, but he grabbed me. He said he could get to me anytime he wanted and someone needed to teach me a lesson. Then he . . ." Ashley stammered, finally realizing the danger she had truly been in. "Then he tried to lift my T-shirt. That's when I screamed."

"We didn't hear any scream," Matt said.

Ashley said, almost absentmindedly, "I did scream . . . as loud as I could. You must not have been close enough to the house."

Dave and Matt exchanged a look. This was precisely the kind of situation they had tried to protect Mrs. Taylor from. What transpired here would be thoroughly investigated, but at least they had a face, and soon a name, to start their inquiry.

"On our trip back to New York, we'd like you to go over what happened and what was said. It's important to remember even the smallest detail. It looked like you were leaving when you opened the door. Do you have everything?" Matt asked.

The threat from the man on the deck had completely erased any thoughts she previously had, but now she realized Dave and Matt had actually found her. "How did you find me?"

Dave answered, "I don't think that's important. What's really more to the point is why we had to find you at all."

"I wasn't trying to cause any trouble, and that's the truth. But I needed to get away to think. It's not natural to have people watching your every move; surely you recognize that. I felt like I couldn't breathe. I needed to think, so I took off. I don't think a federal case needs to be made out of it although I'm sure it already has. Again, how did you find me?"

Dave and Matt said nothing.

"Fine. Have it your way. I'd planned to stay another day, but after what's happened, I'm ready to go back. And the two of you don't need to look so smug. Eventually I'll figure out how you found me."

Dave coughed into his fisted hand. "Bullshit."

"What did you say?"

"Absolutely nothing. I was simply clearing my throat." Dave looked completely innocent.

Ashley looked at Dave suspiciously, "Uh-huh, I'm sure. Jeremy often coughs to clear his throat in exactly the same way. At any rate, I'm ready to go. I need to get back to New York, and truthfully I'm a little shaken by the encounter with that man. I'm glad you showed up when you did. "

Matt interjected, "I think you should know, we're under orders from the president. He told us to find you and bring you back, and that's what we're going to do. If you have a problem with that, feel free to call him and . . ." Matt stopped what he was saying as another government- issued SUV pulled up in front of Steve's cabin. Two men stepped out and walked toward them.

The agents all nodded to one another. Dave brought the other agents up to speed on what had happened. Then, three of them went inside the cabin where Ashley could no longer hear them. She supposed the new agents would thoroughly investigate the scene and see if they could find any clues.

Dave returned and spoke to Matt. "It's time we get Mrs. Taylor back to New York." To which Matt replied, "I completely agree."

43

During the drive back to New York, the atmosphere in the SUV was strained. Matt and Dave asked Ashley to recount exactly what happened at the cabin, which she was glad to do while it was fresh in her mind. While she repeated the story, they were both struck with how unafraid Ashley had been during the incident. She was angry more than anything else. Still, she had escaped what could have been a very nasty situation, all of which could've have been avoided if she hadn't ditched her Secret Service agents.

They didn't need to lecture her. President Taylor would handle his wife.

Their preference would have been to put her on the closest plane heading back to New York, but with strict orders to keep Ashley's disappearance quiet and out of the media, it was probably smarter to drive her there. That way, no one would be wiser.

Ashley was physically and emotionally drained from her unnerving experience on the deck. With each hour that passed and with each mile they drove away from Steve's Vermont retreat, the more she realized the bullet she had dodged. Now that it was over and she was safe, she felt like a deflated balloon.

Still, she wondered what the man could possibly have wanted . . . and he'd mentioned something about having an employer, which meant he was working for someone else, and she suspected he wasn't referring to a newspaper. Whoever it was had evidently had her followed, but for what purpose? Why would someone deliberately try to scare her? Plus, the man hadn't covered his face with a mask. In the movies and books, that was generally a sign that the attacker intended to kill his victim. Why didn't he wear a mask? Certainly he knew she would recognize him. The more questions she asked, the more confusing his motive seemed. The whole situation was like a crazy dream.

She shook her head as if by doing so, she could shake off the whole incident. It was time to get to work. Ashley picked up her cell phone to call Robert.

Robert looked at his caller ID as he answered. "Where are you, young lady?"

"I'm on my way back to New York, and I'd like to talk to you this afternoon. Do you have any free time?"

"I'll make some. Do you have any idea how much you've upset your husband, not to mention the rest of us."

"Robert," Ashley said in a low, soft voice, "how's Rick?"

"Not so quick, Ashley. What you did was childish and inconsiderate. I really didn't think you'd put your loved ones through such an ordeal."

"I believe I had very good reasons, which I'll tell you when I see you this afternoon. You can lecture me when I get there, but for now, please tell me, how is Rick?"

"Before I tell you about Rick, I want you to know this conversation is definitely not over. And you can be certain that when you get here, it will continue. As for Rick, we were lucky. The damage to his heart wasn't as severe as they first thought. The doctors performed the double bypass. He's still in the hospital, but we hope he can go home in a few days."

"I'm so relieved. I asked Mavis to call and check on his progress daily so she could bring me up-to-date when I returned."

All of a sudden, something occurred to Robert. "Where are you exactly?"

"I'm in the backseat of a car with two of my Secret Service agents." She spoke a little louder so her fellow travelers would be sure to hear her. "They're being very unfriendly and uncommunicative right now. Nevertheless, I'm on my way back to the city, and I want to explain to you why I left and discuss a possible solution to the situation I created by not taking on the role of the First Lady."

"I'll be interested to hear what exactly drove you to take such drastic actions. What time should I expect you?"

"I don't know—in a few hours."

"Okay, I'll see you then."

"Goodbye, Robert, and simmer down. Nothing happened to me."

"There are so many things wrong with that statement, but my comments will have to wait until I see you."

As soon as Ashley clicked off her cell, it rang again. The number on the call waiting indicated it was Michael. *Oh boy, here we go.*

"Hello, Michael."

"What the hell were you thinking?" Michael was in no mood for any niceties.

"Listen . . ."

"Ashley, you scared the living daylights out of me, your kids, your cousin, and your boss, and you made the Secret Service agents guarding you look like they're completely incompetent, and you want me to listen?"

"Yes, I want a chance to explain. I left a message with Mavis so you wouldn't worry. I told her I'd be gone for about three days and that I needed time alone to think. I've done that now, and I've made some decisions I'd like to share with you, but first I need to talk to a couple of people, and then I'll come to Washington."

"No. You're coming to Washington now. You can talk to whomever you want to talk to from here. What you did is irresponsible and completely unacceptable."

"Michael, I realize you can't see the situation from my point of view, but what I did, I did for us."

"Really?" Michael said, his voice dripping with sarcasm. "As if there's a reasonable explanation for your actions. Go ahead, explain your absolutely reckless behavior."

"I'd rather explain it all to you in person. You know communications on the phone or e-mail can be misinterpreted; you can't see a person's body language. I need to see Robert, and after that I'll come to Washington." Ashley promptly disconnected the call before her husband could say anything else.

Almost instantaneously, Matt's phone rang. "Agent Campton speaking."

Whoever had called him, Matt was listening intently. He responded, "Yes, sir, I understand. Yes, sir, I'll bring her to Washington immediately." Again, silence on Matt's part. "Thank you, sir. We appreciate that, Mr. President. We should be in Washington this afternoon."

After Matt hung up, he spoke to Dave. "Change of plans. President Taylor wants us to drive Mrs. Taylor directly to Washington. He also thanked us both for finding her."

Ashley spoke from the back seat. "Do not take me to Washington. I need to speak with my boss first. We can go to Washington after that."

"The president has directed us to bring you straight to Washington. I think you know whose orders we'll be following. If what you have to say to your boss is so important, I suggest you call him back and have the conversation you wanted to have while we're en route."

Ashley was furious. She had known when she left he'd be angry, but she thought he'd be a little more reasonable when she explained her reasons for leaving. She also knew it would do no good to argue with Matt and Dave. They would do exactly as the president had ordered. She picked up her phone again. At least, she could use the time to talk to Robert about her proposal.

44

"Robert, it's Ashley again. I won't be coming to New York after all. Michael is insisting that I come directly to Washington, and he's not taking no for an answer."

"Good for him. I'm sure he needs to see that you're all right, and no amount of calming his fears can possibly take the place of seeing you in person. It's what I'd do if I were him."

Ashley let out an exasperated sigh. "Of course, you would. Anyway, instead of getting to talk to you in person as I wanted, I have to settle with having the conversation over the phone. Can you put aside your support of Michael long enough to listen to why I felt I needed to get away from everyone and everything? I think I may have found a way to make things work for Michael and me, but I'll need your help to carry through with my plan."

"Of course I'll listen; I'd love to know what drove you to do something so crazy."

"Remember when you talked to me after the inauguration about possibly moving to the Washington museum? I'm assuming the door is still open for that discussion."

"Of course it is. Have you changed your mind?"

"It depends. A lot has changed since we had that conversation. Since Ted's wreck, I've been hoping and praying for a full recovery, but it looks as though he's got at least a year of rehabilitation ahead of him if he's ever able to return to work. I don't know what you've been thinking about in regards to replacing him, but I'd like to make a suggestion. I could head up both museums. I'd commute between the two, either dividing each week or spending one week at one museum and the next week at the other. Max could cover for me when I'm not in New York, and Elise could cover for me while I'm not in Washington. I know she's excellent, and she and Ted work together very much as Max and I do. Both Max and Elise are top-notch curators. This would leave Ted's job open for him to come back to if he's physically able. Plus, it would give me a chance to be with Michael about half of each month, and I could get an idea of how working in Washington would feel without making a lasting commitment. It allows me to have a foot in the door but doesn't close the door. What do you think?"

Robert said almost immediately, "I think it's a brilliant solution. You're right. It would help Ted, and I think it'll be an extra incentive for him to work harder to get well since I know he'd feel it was an imposition on you. Just as you said, it allows you to try on the Washington museum to see how it fits. It's really a good idea, Ashley. I agree Max and Elise can carry the load in your absence. When would you want to start?"

"Can I get back to you on that? I'd like to start right away, but I need to talk to Michael to see what he thinks although I can probably predict fairly accurately that he'll be in favor of my solution. Realistically I would think we could activate our plan within the next two weeks. How does that sound?"

"I'll support whatever works for you. I don't agree with what you did or how you did it, but I must say this is a well-thought-out plan. I hope you know I wish you well."

"I do. Thank you."

Robert added, "Before I let you go, Mr. Carruthers called your office several times asking for you. Your secretaries covered for you and told him you were in meetings. Finally, they referred him to me. He was calling to let you know how much was raised in donations from the open house."

"How much?"

"Almost two million dollars. Not bad for a night's work."

"No, not bad, but I'd appreciate it if you'd handle everything involving Geoffrey from now on. Would you let him know that his association with me has been terminated—naturally, after the money has been transferred into the museum's account? Oh, and find a better word than 'terminated.' That sounds so ominous. Still, the bottom line is I won't be dealing with him anymore."

"Did something happen between you two?"

"Yes. He's a user. He doesn't do anything unless there's something in it for him."

"Sounds like your opinion of Geoffrey has hit the skids; however, now that you're going to be dividing your time between the New York and Washington museums, you can easily hand off your dealings with him to Max."

"I'm counting on that. I need to call Mavis now. I'll be in touch later to discuss the specifics regarding a timeline. Thanks for giving me the latitude to make this change. I think it will be beneficial to Ted and for me."

"Shoot, Ashley, if you recall, your working at the Washington museum was my idea in the first place. Call me after you talk to your husband."

Ashley called Mavis next. "Hi. I'm back."

"Great. Leave us all hanging and wondering how you are, and then just call and act as though you've just stepped out of the office for a moment. Where are you?"

"I'm on my way to Washington. Michael's acting all 'Me Tarzan, you Jane' on me. I'll be gone tomorrow for sure although I expect to be back in the office the day after that. I'll let you know what's going on after I see Michael; he's almost foaming at the mouth, he's so mad."

"Can you blame him after the stunt you pulled?"

"Thanks. It's nice to know one of my closest friends is in my corner. Been consorting with the enemy, have you?"

"Ashley, your husband has been half crazy worrying about your safety. If you had talked to him, you'd feel sorry for him too."

"You have compassion for Michael. What about me? Remember, I didn't take off on a whim. There were some pretty heady issues I needed to think through. I've made some decisions, and I'm anxious to talk to you and Kathy about them. I need to go for now, but I'll call you as soon as I can."

"You're not just going to leave me hanging?" Mavis protested in disbelief.

"Just for another day; I promise. I'll talk to you soon."

45

As she and the agents raced toward Washington, DC, Ashley reflected on her conversation with Robert. She finally felt she was making progress in finding a working solution for the situation she and Michael were in. Sure, it was only temporary—a year, hopefully, at the most—but it would give her a chance to see how she liked the Washington museum and, more importantly, whether or not she could stomach living in the White House and being so close to the center of politics without giving up her job in New York and her autonomy.

Her next phone call was to Georgia, Michael's secretary. "Hey, Georgia, it's Ashley. Would you let Michael know I'll be arriving at the White House around dinnertime? If he doesn't have any plans for this evening, maybe we could have dinner together."

Georgia said she would pass along the message, but she thought the president already had dinner plans.

Matt and Dave were still stonewalling her, but they couldn't have been happier than to be delivering their charge to the White House. When they arrived at the private entrance to the family residence, they opened the car door for her and picked up her backpack.

"You don't have to go any further. I can manage from here," Ashley said.

"Thank you for your consideration. We'll see you to the door of the residence. The other agents can take over from there," Matt replied.

"For goodness' sake, you'd think I was a criminal. I'm not going to try to escape. Now you're just being silly."

"All the same," David answered, "we'll see that you make it all the way to your destination."

Matt and Dave dropped her off at the entrance to the family residence. Other agents were close by, so they evidently felt they could leave her without her bolting again. It was going to take a lot of time trying to re-establish some sort of a relationship with the two of them. Who was she kidding? They would never completely trust her again, and in all truth they probably never had.

When Ashley walked into the second floor residence, she stood completely still and listened. The apartment was silent. Could she honestly make this place her home? What choice did she have?

The final stage of her plan had to do with Michael. He needed to agree to the terms of her arrangement. She hoped he'd be willing to meet her halfway. Otherwise, she wouldn't follow through with her proposal.

The phone on the end table rang. She hoped it was Michael.

"Hello."

"Good evening, Mrs. Taylor. The president asked me to call and let you know he already had dinner plans and after that he has another meeting. He said he'll see you later this evening, probably around ten or ten thirty."

"Thanks for the call, Georgia. I'll have something sent up for me to eat."

"I can do that for you."

"No, thank you. It's way past your workday. Go home and unwind. I'll give the kitchen a call. Thanks for offering, though."

As soon as Ashley got off the phone, she called the kitchen and asked if she could have a sandwich sent up. While she was waiting for it to be delivered, she unpacked her backpack and took a little tour around the rooms to see what she might do to make it more personal for her. She didn't like the idea of living in the White House, but at least she didn't have to work here.

She had long ago accepted that even though she considered Michael and herself equal partners, she was still the one who made the majority of the compromises when necessary. Only after Jeremy and Juliette left for college had she really started holding her ground. She knew what a huge blow it was for Michael when she refused to follow him to the White House. He'd bounced back with a great idea for filling the void despite having hired the hypocritical Paula. If only Michael understood, like many other women who knew Paula, she'd throw Connor down the mine shaft in a hot second if she thought she had a chance with Michael.

Ashley answered the knock on the door. Food. She was hungrier than she thought. She realized now that she hadn't eaten anything since breakfast early this morning. Sitting in the apartment was comparable to sitting in a tomb; she wished Michael were here with her. She was anxious to get their initial meeting over and all of the emotional accusations and repercussions out of the way so they could have a conversation about the solution she thought might work.

While waiting for Michael to return, Ashley decided to call Jeremy and Juliette. She picked up the phone and pressed a button. She asked the person who answered how to make a conference call. She might as well talk to them both at the same time. Otherwise, she'd just be repeating herself.

The person who assisted her was eager to set up the call for her. Ashley knew she should be thankful for how helpful everyone was trying to be, and she was. She realized the entire White House staff wanted to make her feel welcome, but she didn't want everything done for her. She'd never liked being waited on. Here at the White House, there was a whole staff just waiting to do things for the First Family. That wasn't a habit she wanted to get used to.

The phone rang, breaking the silence in the room. Ashley scooted quickly into a comfortable chair before she picked up the receiver. "Hello."

"Hi, Mom. So you decided to turn yourself in?" Jeremy asked.

"Hi to both of you. How are you?"

"Mom," Juliette said quietly, "why don't you tell us why you felt the need to take off and how Dad's doing now that you're back?"

Whatever made her think she could control a conversation with her kids? "Fair enough. First I needed to get away completely alone for a few days to think through some things regarding your dad and me. I needed some quiet, uninterrupted time. It wasn't the smartest thing I've ever done, so don't try to follow in my footsteps. I hope you're listening, Jeremy. The good news is I was able to find a possible solution to the situation between your dad and me."

She told them all about Ted's accident and how he was doing.

"While Ted is recovering, I could work at both the New York and the Washington museums. That way I'd be holding Ted's job open for him to return to, and it would allow me to be in Washington about half of every month. Max and Elise could help run the museums when I'm not in New York or Washington. I'm still not interested in taking over any responsibilities of the First Lady, but at least your dad and I would live together and be in the same town for about half the month.

"I'm sitting here waiting to talk to your father to let him know I think I've found a solution for us, at least, temporarily. Unfortunately he's still in meetings."

"It sounds like a good solution, Mom. However, the Washington museum can't be as exciting as the one in New York," Jeremy commented.

"All museums can be exciting. It's what you do to promote them that's important. However, the most important thing to me is our family, and I don't want to continue being at odds with your dad. Plus, I'm not giving up my career. Be happy for your dad and me. I think I've hit on a solution that will make things a lot easier on us."

"We are happy for you, Mom. All the same, aren't you worried that you'll get dragged into the whole political thing by just living there?" Juliette asked.

"I won't allow anyone to drag me anywhere. Nothing is going to change except my work routine. Trust me; I have no intentions of doing anything political."

"Then we wish you luck," Juliette said.

"Yeah, we do, but we hope you aren't going to need any. Do you feel like you've got the situation under control?" Jeremy wanted to know.

"I'd like to think so. I've talked to Robert, and he's completely supportive. About the only thing I still need to do is see your dad for the first time since I took off. I'm not exactly looking forward to that, but I'll deal with it. I just wanted to touch base with both of you to let you know I'm back, why I took off, and of course, the decision I've made. I really need to go. I'm expecting your dad before long, and I don't think it would be healthy for you to hear your father trying to murder your mother over the phone. It would be bad for your development. I'll call again soon. I love you."

"We love you, too, Mom," they responded in unison.

She missed her kids the minute she got off the phone. It was getting harder and harder to keep up with everything going on in their lives. They were both living on their own, and even though that was the natural order of things, she didn't have to like it. Letting go and trusting that you'd taught your children everything they needed to know to live safe, happy, healthy, and productive lives was one of the hardest things a parent had to do.

Ashley moved into the bedroom. She changed into her nightgown and grabbed the book she was currently reading. She must've dozed off because she heard a steely, calm voice say, "Ashley, wake up." Her heart was pounding, and all she wanted to do was get out of the room where the cold, emotionless voice spoke to her.

She sat up and turned on the light next to the bed. She saw Michael immediately. He was sitting in a chair right across from her, watching her as if she were some oddity to be figured out, and he looked as though he were contemplating murder. She needed to get the upper hand, fast.

"Michael, you're finally here. I'm so glad."

"Don't act as if nothing is wrong. You're not stupid, and you have an excellent ability to assess people and their moods. So I'm guessing you've assessed mine and think the best thing to do is act nonchalant. That would definitely be the wrong approach."

Ashley got out of bed and headed to the closet for a robe. Before she reached the closet, she felt her arm caught in a viselike grip. "You're not going anywhere. Sit down."

"I don't like the way you're talking to me."

"No? Too bad. I didn't like the way you took off leaving me to wonder if you were all right or if you'd been kidnapped or if you were dead. Sit down."

"Watch it, Michael. You're overplaying the angry husband role and beginning to make me mad."

"Am I really? Well I'm just worried sick about that. Sit down."

"You're behaving like a barbarian, and after I've come here to tell you about a solution I think I've found that will help us be together more. Don't create more of a problem than there is."

"My biggest problem is you, and don't think you can manipulate me into forgetting about your most recent escapade by trying to throw me off with another subject.

You're going to tell me exactly when you cooked up your little scheme to ditch your agents and why the hell you thought it was necessary. I'd like to know how your mind works and under what conditions you thought it might be okay to put yourself in danger. And, yes, I've heard all about the man who attacked you at the cabin."

Ashley looked down. "I wouldn't call it an attack exactly. It was more of a surprise really. Let go of my arm and sit down like the reasonable man the people of this country think they elected, or I'll scream down this whole damn place."

Michael never cared for threats, and most specifically, he didn't care for this one. He had no intention of letting Ashley get away with her show of defiance. Her domineering attitude threw many people off, but he knew her and she wasn't going to dissuade him from getting the answers to every one of his questions.

"Nice try. I'll let go when I'm damned good and ready. Start talking."

"Then, perhaps tomorrow I'll wear a sleeveless blouse to highlight the lovely bruises I'll be sporting from your death grip."

He didn't realize how tightly he'd been holding her arm. He loosened his grip and led her over to the chair he'd been sitting in and sat her down. "Don't you dare think about moving from that spot."

"How dare you talk to me like that?" Ashley stood up. "Damn you for being so blasted arrogant."

"But, my dear, isn't that one of the very traits you so admired in me when we first met?"

"You're being unreasonable. I came here of my own free will."

"I'd hardly call me giving specific instructions to bring you directly to Washington coming here of your free will. Sit down and start talking."

"I was deluded into thinking I'd found a possible solution for the two of us. I don't want to be around you for another second, let alone try to live here with you. I'm leaving."

Michael heard what she'd said; she was talking about living here with him. He factored her words into how he would proceed. "Ashley, I'm warning you. I've repeatedly asked you to sit down. You're on my turf now, and if I so choose, I could see to it that you don't leave until I'm good and ready for you to leave. Remember, here in the White House, people actually want to please me."

"You're behaving like a barbarian. All this power has gone to your head. Believe me, I could get out of here if I wanted. There's no way in hell you can keep me here against my will."

An arm snaked around her waist and pulled her back, lifting her off her feet.

"I told you to sit down, and if I have to, I'll sit on you. Quit struggling and decide how you'd like the rest of our conversation to go. I think you'd find it a lot easier to talk if I weren't sitting on you."

Damn his stubborn hide. If he actually sat on her or held her down, there'd be no chance of escape. She needed to act like she was being somewhat reasonable. "All right, I'll sit, but don't think I'm going to forget your brutish behavior."

"That just worries me to death, Ash. I didn't like you taking off in the dead of night for God knows where either or your being accosted at your cabin getaway. Do you know how scared I was? To think some man actually touched you and threatened you. How would you feel if the same thing happened to Juliette? Or imagine, if you can, that Jeremy decided to ditch his Secret Service agents, and you were left wringing your hands about where he was, wondering whether he was safe or not or if someone had masterminded his disappearance and he was in the hands of someone who could harm or kill him. Can you imagine that? Just think about how you would react."

Michael couldn't have painted a stronger picture or a better example than using their children to make her see what she'd put him through. Her children meant everything to her. She'd always feared if anything were to happen to one of them she might never recover. When Ashley loved, she loved completely and forever.

Michael watched his wife. She was calming down a bit. Mentioning the kids had affected her like a sedative, replacing her fury with reflection.

"Now maybe you understand some of what I've been going through. I want to know exactly what happened, why you felt you needed to do what you did. I don't think that's unreasonable. Now start from the beginning." Michael leaned back in his chair to appear more relaxed, but he was ready to grab his wife at the slightest indication that she was going to bolt again.

Ashley let out a long sigh and began speaking in a monotone. Michael didn't care how deflated she was behaving; she needed to understand the consequences of her actions. Plus, with Ashley, her behavior could be an act to make him let his guard down.

"During your campaign for the presidency, I constantly tried to figure out if you were elected how we could solve the dilemma of us living in different cities. It never seemed as though there was a viable solution to our problem, at least not one I felt I could live with. Then, when Ted had his accident and it looked like he might not recover, I realized I couldn't step into his shoes at the Washington museum; I would always feel like I'd used his tragedy for my gain. However, as Ted has fought so hard to regain mobility and his speech, I realized he could, with time, make close to a full recovery. I tried to think about how I could help him. I knew that in order to get some time for myself, I would have to get away from everyone and everything. I needed time to just sit and think. I mean really alone. No bodyguards, no job demands, nobody around me, just me and my brain working through a problem to find a solution. So, I talked to a friend who I knew had a cabin in Ludlow, Vermont. This friend . . ."

"You don't have to protect Steve. We know it was his cabin. After all, the Secret Service agents did find you there."

"I'd like to know how they found me."

"I don't think they'll ever tell you. They were furious that you gave the slip to the night watch. They took the whole ordeal very personally. You're their responsibility, and even if they don't show it, I have firsthand knowledge that they're both quite attached to you. Go on. Go back to your story."

"Anyway, I talked to Steve about using his cabin and why I wanted to get away. He could see how distressed I was about the situation between the two of us and the situation with Ted, so he was glad he could help. He didn't have anything to do with the escape plan; that was all my doing. I wasn't sure when, or if, I might actually do it, but I prepared everything for the possibility.

"Then on the night of the open house, Robert's son had a heart attack, and I realized life is too short not to be with the people you love. No job was as important as my family. I decided after the open house I'd put my plan into action, and you pretty well know the rest."

"Actually, I don't. Were you planning to tell me you went to Carruthers's house alone?"

"I didn't go alone. My Secret Service agents were with me."

"Right, and you never left their sight?"

"Not that I can think of," Ashley lied.

"I think you should tell me what happened at the open house. I know about the scene in the den." Ashley was trying to figure out what to say about that. Matt and Dave had only seen the incident involving one glass sculpture. They didn't know anything about what had happened between her and Geoffrey before they entered the room. If she told Michael the whole truth, he would better understand how the two events, Robert's son having a heart attack and the awful scene with Geoffrey, had contributed to her need to get away and think though a solution to their living arrangements. But if she told him about Geoffrey kissing her, God only knew what he might do. A half-truth would suffice.

"There was a scene in the den. I was there with Mr. Carruthers because I was nursing a headache and wanted to get away from the crowd of people. He offered to show me some of his more valuable art collection, which he houses in his den."

"Didn't his suggestion reek of the old come-on line, 'Come up to my place and I'll show you my etchings'?"

"No, it didn't. I was already at the party. The place was full of people, including the Secret Service. I had a headache, and

I didn't think there would be any harm in stepping into the next room. Once I did, it wasn't long before I figured out Mr. Carruthers thought there was more between us than business dealings. I was insulted that he was so presumptuous, so to put him in his place, I threw the sculpture at his fireplace and it broke. That's what Matt and Dave saw."

"You destroyed a piece of art because you thought Geoffrey might be assuming there was more between you than just business?"

"Yes."

"And he didn't make a pass at you?"

"None that I couldn't handle."

Michael was furious. He would deal with Geoffrey Carruthers in his own way. "You wouldn't have had to handle anything if you had listened to me. I told you to stay away from him."

"The open house was a commitment and responsibility for my job, and I take my responsibilities very seriously. I would have preferred to have had Robert with me; unfortunately that wasn't possible.

"When I thought about Robert's son, Ted's accident, and the incident with Carruthers, I realized everything I was worried about regarding us being apart seemed to be coming to fruition. I decided right then to put my plan into action."

"Humor me. Tell me how you managed the whole escape thing, if you don't mind."

Ashley began speaking again, telling him of her plan, the escape, each step that led her to Vermont, but this time there was a little more life in her voice, like she enjoyed telling this part of the story.

Michael watched his wife wind down from telling the story. What she'd just told him seemed completely reasonable to her. She wasn't aware of the hell she'd put him through.

"Ashley, you do know I was still in Europe the night you took off?"

"Yes, and I knew you'd be flying home the next day. I knew I wouldn't upset your trip."

"Were you aware for a few hours we all thought that your disappearance might have been staged to look like you planned it but in fact you'd been kidnapped?"

"But I left a message with Mavis."

"Which we didn't get for several hours after you were reported missing. Thank God it occurred to Mavis to check her voice mail."

"Michael, I'm sorry I scared you."

"You're sorry you scared me? That's it? Must I remind you again how you'd feel if one of the kids had pulled this stunt instead of you?"

"I don't know what else to say. I wasn't trying to be thoughtless or mean. I felt the end justified the means."

"And do you also realize the man that attacked you today . . ."

"Michael, I wouldn't exactly call it an attack."

"What would you call it? You told the agents he grabbed you and wouldn't let go when you tried to enter the house and that he threatened you."

"I can't begin to know what he was thinking, but I recognized him as the photographer who has snapped my picture a couple of times. I guess I thought the paparazzi had gone too far. It wasn't until he grabbed me and said he could get to me any time he wanted that I begin to worry. Although, at the time, I was damn good and mad and wanted to rip him apart."

Michael stood up and pulled Ashley out of her chair. He hugged her and held her close, smelling her perfumed hair. Thank God nothing more had happened to her. What she had done was reckless and selfish and wrong in every way, but he doubted very much she would ever completely see it that way.

Michael didn't say anything. He looked at his wife, taking in her beauty and the sincerity on her face. As smart as she was, sometimes she didn't have a clue. She'd explained how she'd managed the whole affair; still, she hadn't said what it was she'd figured out at the cabin, although he had to admit, he hadn't been ready to hear anything except an explanation for her behavior until now.

"Was scaring me to death worth it?"

"That all depends. I think I came up with a pretty good solution for our current dilemma."

When Michael didn't say anything, she presumed he was waiting for her to go on.

"As I said, I've been trying to figure out a way for us to be together without either one of us losing. When I was at the cabin, I made a list of possible solutions, and I have an idea I think might work."

"I'm all ears."

"The solution only has to do with our living arrangements. I'm still not interested in being involved in politics in any way. I've already talked to Robert, and I have his complete support. I suggested that while Ted is recuperating I run both the New York and Washington museums with the help of Max and Elise. Elise is Max's counterpart at the Washington museum. Each can act on my behalf when I'm at the other museum. I could alternate my work locations weekly. With all of the technology available now, it's easy to conduct business from almost anywhere."

Michael was thrilled, but he was still angry at Ashley's blatant disregard for her safety. He needed to think. "I need a drink. Would you like something?"

"Just a glass of water, please."

Michael walked into the kitchen and got out a beer and poured a glass of water for Ashley. She'd put him through hell, but now she was willing to take the lead at both the New York and the Washington museums, at least while Ted recuperated. That meant she was willing to live in Washington with him part time. A person could get whiplash from her contradictory moves. He walked back into the bedroom and handed Ashley her water before he sat down.

"Is that all of it?"

"Well, there are a few more contingencies."

"Uh-huh, somehow I thought there might be."

"I want you to know up-front that I mean it when I say I'm not going to have anything to do with politics. I'm not interested in being the First Lady. As much as I can't stand Paula personally, the job seems to be working fine although I do intend to have lunch or coffee with her and let her know she'd better keep her eyes glued to her own husband and off mine. If I have to, I'll have a talk with Connor too. Bet she'd hate that. Anyway, don't you think for one minute that you're going to talk me out of that little conversation.

"I mean it. No politics. I don't want to attend state dinners or fly overseas with you unless it's a vacation. I still expect Paula to fulfill the duties she was hired for. I'm merely dividing my time between New York and Washington to be with you. I don't want you to think you can ease me into some of your political activities. You can't. I won't get involved in that world. In fact, if you start hammering away at me to get involved, I'll move out and get my own place here in Washington."

"Wouldn't that be another terrific media circus? Is there anything else?" Michael asked, raising an eyebrow.

"Sort of. I'd like someplace around here to fix up as my home office, and I don't want an office in the White House. I want something private in our own apartment. Do you think you can agree to all of that?"

"First I never thought I'd see the day when you'd willingly give working at the Washington museum a chance, but then none of us could have anticipated Ted's horrible accident. That in itself is beyond tragic; I'm glad to hear there's hope for his future. Plus, I know you. You're trying to encourage Robert to keep Ted's job available for him until the doctors can predict with more accuracy whether he'll be able to return to work. That's very admirable.

"And while I still haven't forgiven you for scaring me to death, I'm trying to understand why you thought you had to go to such extremes to make this decision. But I accept your terms and love you for caring so much about Ted's situation and our relationship to take on such an enormous workload. It's going to be rough, Ashley.

"As for not being involved in politics, I'll try not to insinuate things from my political life onto you. There may be times I slip up, but I'm quite sure you'll put me in my place if I do.

"Regarding finding you a spot for your office, I'm sure we can manage to find somewhere in this enormous residence that will fit your needs. I'd gladly give up any room in the place if that's what it takes for you to move in here and live with me."

"Honey, I've always told you, I love you. It's politics I can't stand. I'm looking forward to us actually living in the same city, same house for a change. I miss you, and since you were elected president, finding time to be together has become a nightmare. Now why don't you kiss me so we don't have to worry about 'will we or won't we' end the night with a kiss."

Michael laughed. She was still his wicked little witch. As unpredictable as she was, and including all of the grief she caused him, he would never want anyone else. He picked up his wife and carried her to the bedroom.

"I think I can do a little better than a kiss, but I have just one more comment. There's only one point in your story that just doesn't ring true."

"And what would that be?" Ashley asked, unbuttoning Michael's shirt. She thought he might still be inclined to pursue his line of questioning regarding Geoffrey Carruthers.

Michael chuckled, "You seriously bought and used a backpack? I can't believe you bought a backpack. You've never really been known as the outdoor type."

Relieved that he'd accepted her story, she proceeded unbuttoning his shirt and placed little kisses on the bare skin she could reach. "Don't you have something better to do than tease me about the blasted backpack?"

"I believe I do, Mrs. Taylor," he answered as he pulled her nightgown up over her head. "Yes, I believe I most definitely do."

Acknowledgments

My profound thanks goes to my family, who continually surround me with their love, support, and encouragement. I love you all and feel blessed to have each of you in my life. Thank you to my three sons, who never take it easy on me and are always there to push me further. Thank you to the first readers of my manuscript, David Ellick and Shirlene Lansdon. I value your opinions so much. Thank you to Susan Wiggs for her graciousness and time spent teaching me so much about the world of publishing throughout the years and who once said, "There are many roads to the Land of Oz."

Also, I would like to express my gratitude to Milli Brown of Brown Books Publishing Group and her entire team of magicians. Thank you, Janet Harris, for your wisdom, discernment, and editorial advice about how to improve my manuscript and also for allowing me to share my insecurities. Thank you, Cathy Williams and Cindy Birne, for getting behind the idea of this book, for thinking everyone needs to read it, and for working tirelessly to make that happen. And thank you to all of you at Brown Books, including Omar Mediano, Kathy Penny, Lucia Retta, Beth Robinson, and Danny Whitworth, who worked diligently to bring this book to life; I'd like to express my deepest appreciation.

About the Author

*V*enita Ellick was fated to be a writer. She was named for a character in a book her mother was reading at the time of the birth. As a young girl, she spent so much time in libraries that librarians would save books for her almost daily visits. She began writing stories in the first grade, which her mother patiently read. The intervention of a career as an educator and raising three sons delayed her focus on writing, but she has now completed three novels. *The Reluctant First Lady* is her fourth.

Mistress of Mellyn by Victoria Holt and *Pride and Prejudice* by Jane Austen captivated her as a teenager. The power and imagery of the printed word made her wonder what each heroine was thinking and feeling. She wanted to be the woman with the cape and hood standing on the edge of the cliff with the wind whipping around her. The mysteries that could be found in stories fascinated her and are echoed in *The Reluctant First Lady.*

Ellick draws on her experiences as a wife, mother, teacher, and principal to create her characters. Her sense of humor and recognition of the absurd and often whimsical nature of life have allowed her to capture her characters' lives with authenticity and emotional resonance.

Venita and her husband David have experience as a two-career couple. They live on an island in the state of Washington.

RECEIVED

HILLSIDE PUBLIC LIBRARY

3 6642 00226 5061

5/
14

RECEIVED
8/28/13

To
Peggy Baker
for her continued understanding and encouragement

Robert A. Baker is affiliated with the National Research Program, Water Resources Division of the U.S. Geological Survey. He holds a BChE from North Carolina State University, MChE and MS from Villanova University, and a D.Sc. from the Graduate School of Public Health, University of Pittsburgh. Dr. Baker's professional career has involved research, consultation, and management related to environmental science and engineering problems. He is active in professional societies and has authored over 70 books, patents, and papers.

Preface

Water resources managers, regulators, and researchers require definitive information that describes the highly correlated, interdisciplinary factors that influence fate and transport of water contaminants. Not unexpectedly, evolving questions stay ahead of advances in scientific and engineering developments. One of the most important and significant aspects currently being intensely investigated is the role of particulates and sediments in contaminant behavior. This three-volume compilation documents the proceedings of a symposium dedicated to the subject of organic substances and sediments in water. Stress was placed on the organic substances because so many of the anthropogenic contaminants which pose potential problems at all trophic levels are organic in nature.

The symposium program from which the proceedings derive included critical reviews which describe the state-of-the-science, and often identify major needs. This should be especially valuable to the reader, regardless of individual interest. As in any symposium proceedings, topics are treated with varying depth. However, coverage over the interdisciplinary subject is reasonably complete.

The first volume delves into the roles of humic substances and soils-sediments in the sorption and mobility of contaminants. Both regimes are introduced by comprehensive review papers, and both reviews are followed by papers that treat specific topics in depth.

The second volume combines papers that summarize various processes involved in contaminant fate and transport as well as analytical developments. The processes section has been divided into aquatic particle-organic chemical interaction (characterization and contaminant geochemistry); fate and transport; and interfacial and organic-inorganic processes. The processes and analytical sections present theoretical as well as case study developments.

The third volume is devoted to biological processes. It begins with a state-of-the-science summary which incorporates references to the other papers deriving from the symposium. The papers are divided under subheadings: integrating chemistry and toxicology of sediment-water interactions; uptake and accumulation (bioavailability and bioaccumulation); biodegradation (aerobic dechlorinations and co-metabolism).

This compilation extends over the broad interdisciplinary subject of organic substances and sediments in water. It should prove valuable to experienced scientists as well as those making initial inquiries.

Acknowledgments

An American Chemical Society symposium on the subject "Contaminants and Sediments" was held in Honolulu, April 1–6, 1979. A two-volume publication of the same title was published by Ann Arbor Science in 1980. These publications have frequently been cited in the literature. Several years ago colleagues suggested that the writer consider organization of another symposium to foster technology transfer and to update the proceedings of the previous state-of-the-science summary. This led to the symposium "Organic Substances and Sediments in Water" held at the American Chemical Society Meeting in Boston, April 22–27, 1990. The symposium emphasized organic substances and the complex processes effecting their fate and transport, particularly as these occur at the interface of suspended and fixed surfaces. Interdisciplinary contributions were solicited and development of topical sessions shared with recognized experts. These were: V. D. Adams, Tennessee Technical University; D. Armstrong, University of Wisconsin; S.A. Boyd, Michigan State University; C.T. Chiou, U.S. Geological Survey; B. Dempsey, Pennsylvania State University; B.J. Eadie, Great Lakes Environmental Research Laboratories; S.J. Eisenreich, University of Minnesota; P.F. Landrum, Great Lakes Environmental Research Laboratory; J. Leenheer, U.S. Geological Survey; R.L. Malcolm, U.S. Geological Survey; J.F. McCarthy, Oak Ridge National Laboratory; A.V. Palumbo, Oak Ridge National Laboratory; and A. Stone, Johns Hopkins University. Their dedication and cooperation was of the finest from onset through final manuscript peer review.

In addition to North American participants, scientists and engineers from other continents contributed. Five invited European scientists were: Jacques Buffle, University of Geneva, Switzerland; Hans Borén, Linköping University, Sweden; Egil Gjessing, Norwegian Institute for Water Research, Oslo, Norway; Jussi Kukkonen, University of Joensuu, Finland; and Paolo Sequi, Istituto D. Chimica Agraria, Bologna, Italy. Their perceptions and comments were as valuable as their technical contributions. A grant from the U.S. Environmental Protection Agency provided travel support for the invited speakers. Louis Swaby, Office of Exploratory Research, Washington, DC, and Wayne Garrison, Environmental Research Laboratory, Athens, Georgia provided program development assistance and liaison.

Chemical sciences are often an integral aspect of scientific and engineering processes perceived as nonchemical in nature. To improve knowledge of such situations and to facilitate communication among interdisciplinary contributions, the American Chemical Society, through its Committee on Science, has established a Pedagogical Symposium program. These tutorial symposia typically offer overview and research presentations by acknowledged experts in related fields. A competitive proposal to conduct a pedagogical symposium on the same subject as the research symposium was awarded by the Committee on Science. The tutorial was held on April 24, 1990. The lecturers were: E.J. Bouwer, Johns Hopkins University; D.M.D. Toro, Manhattan College; J.W. Farrington, University of Massachusetts; I. Knight, University of Maryland; J.R. Pratt, Pennsylvania State University; R.E. Speece, Vanderbilt University; and J.A. Symons, University of Houston. Their presentations dramatically demonstrated the interdependence of various scientific and engineering processes as well as the benefits of interdisciplinary technology transfer. Drs. Pratt, Speece, and Knight contributed papers to these proceedings.

Financial support for the pedagogical symposium was from the Committee on Science and from the Environmental Chemistry Division of the American Chemical Society. The research symposium and the pedagogical symposium were held under the auspices of the Environmental Chemistry Division. Encouragement and support of the officers and members of these organizational units is gratefully acknowledged.

The endeavor would have been of no avail without the contribution of the scientists and engineers whose manuscripts are contained in these proceedings. The editor appreciates their willingness to share knowledge.

Contents

PART IV. BIODEGRADATION

A. Anaerobic Dechlorinations

B. Cometabolism

PART I

INTRODUCTION

CHAPTER 1

Organic Contaminants in Sediments: Biological Processes

John F. McCarthy, Peter F. Landrum, and Anthony V. Palumbo

INTRODUCTION

A wide variety of organic contaminants enter the environment through myriad sources, including inputs from industrial or municipal effluents, ocean dumping of wastes, terrestrial runoff, and atmospheric deposition. Many aspects of the physical and chemical processes affecting the transport and fate of contaminants within sediment are addressed in other chapters of this book on organic substances and sediments in water. This chapter focuses on the role of biological processes in sediments, either in the uptake of toxic chemicals by biota, the redistribution of sediments and sediment-bound contaminants by burrowing organisms, or microbial metabolism as a mechanism for remediating existing pollution. Biological processes are, of course, central to issues of environmental contamination. Our concern about toxic chemicals in the environment stems not from a mere academic interest in their chemistry, but rather a more anthropocentric concern for the adverse health and ecological effects of these compounds. In this volume, Pratt provides a pedagogical review of environmental toxicology, describing the current approaches to evaluating the effect of hazardous chemicals on ecological processes.[1]

Two major biological processes relevant to the toxic effects of sediment-associated contaminants are: bioaccumulation of contaminants from sediments (including the role of bioturbation in redistribution of contaminants to the bioactive zone), and biodegradation of toxic compounds within aquatic and aquifer sediments. In this chapter, we provide an overview of current understanding and major research directions being pursued in these areas. In this overview, the contributions of authors of subsequent chapters are highlighted.

BIOAVAILABILITY OF SEDIMENT-ASSOCIATED CONTAMINANTS

Many of the contaminants of ecological interest are compounds possessing characteristics that make them resistant to degradation and cause them to sorb strongly to particles. The movement of these particles to the sediments is the main route for the clearance of these persistent contaminants from the water column. These particles are subsequently transported to depositional areas in the particular water body by the existing current regime. Such movement results in the concentration of the contaminants primarily in the low-energy depositional regions of water bodies. These deposits can result in extremely high concentrations of contaminants in localized regions. Some of the more common areas for such concentration include harbors, which are generally areas of historic industrial contaminant discharge as well as areas of deposition. Further, by their construction or natural features, harbors are low-energy environments and often have very high rates of deposition. Such harbor areas have the highest levels of sediment-associated contaminants. In addition to their high levels of contamination, harbors are also areas requiring frequent dredging for navigational purposes. This dredging can result in the resuspension of buried contaminants.

In the context of dredging, the issue of contaminated sediments has been recognized for many years, and regulations have been established to prohibit the open-water disposal of contaminated materials dredged from harbors because of their potential impact on the biological community.[2] The significance of in-place or sediment-associated contaminants as sources of problems outside the dredging arena has been slower to be recognized. However, with the improvements of water quality through controls on discharges, these in-place contaminants are currently recognized as important contaminant sources equal to nonpoint runoff and atmospheric deposition.

In addition to harbor areas, natural depositional basins may also collect sufficient contaminant concentrations to result in alteration of benthic communities, as has been observed in the Great Lakes.[3] While most of the observed effects of contaminated sediments have been found in harbors and near shore areas, even the open-water depositional basins of the Great Lakes show sufficient contaminant concentrations to elicit effects on oligochaetes in laboratory bioassays.[4] From a regulatory perspective, it is often important to be able to determine the contribution of different sources of anthropogenic pollutants to bioaccumulation. In this volume, Sherblom and Eganhouse evaluate the use of source-specific marker compounds detected in biota to document and characterize the impact of municipal wastewaters on tissue burdens of specific contaminants.[5]

In addition to recognizing the impact of contaminated sediments on particular benthic species, sediment-associated contaminants have also been recognized as a potentially significant food chain contaminant source. This general recognition of the importance of contaminated sediments has highlighted the need to establish sediment quality criteria. These criteria must protect both the indigenous benthic species that are directly exposed to sediment-associated contaminants and account for the accumulation of the contaminants through the food chain. Development of such criteria requires a fundamental understanding of the bioavailability of sediment-associated contaminants and the factors that control this bioavailability.

In order to understand bioavailability, a definition and a measure must be available so that comparisons can be made. Bioavailability of sediment-associated contaminants can be defined as "the fraction of the total contaminant in the interstitial water and on the sediment particles that is available for bioaccumulation,"[6] where *bioaccumulation* is the accumulation of a contaminant via all routes available to the organism. Chemical measures of contaminant concentration in sediment do not always reflect the bioavailable fraction of the sediment-associated contaminants;[7,8] therefore, a simple measurement of sediment residue is insufficient to describe the contaminant concentration to which biota are truly exposed. Two approaches have been described in the literature to describe the bioavailability of sediment-associated contaminants: (1) a comparison of the contaminant concentration in the organism and the sediment at steady state,[9-13] and (2) measurement of the uptake clearance of sediment-associated contaminants.[7,14-19] In spite of having two biological approaches available, no chemical approach is available to define the bioavailable fraction of sediment-bound residues. Thus, better approaches for describing the bioavailable fraction of sediments are needed.

The main factors that appear to affect bioavailability can be divided into two major areas: factors that alter the partitioning of contaminants to sediments, and biological factors that alter the exposure and accumulation of the contaminants.[20-23] In all cases, the physicochemical characteristics of the organic contaminant, primarily the compound's water solubility and hydrophobicity, are the major factors for determining its bioavailability. A complicating factor in any physicochemical assessment of bioavailability is the role of natural "dissolved" (or colloidal) organic matter (DOM) in sorbing hydrophobic organic contaminants and metals.[24] In general, organic contaminants sorbed to DOM are unavailable for uptake by biota.[14,25-27] However, predictions of the fraction of truly dissolved (i.e., bioavailable) pollutant in bulk or interstitial water is hampered by poorly understood variability in the contaminant binding capacity of DOM from different natural waters.[28-29] In this volume, Evans demonstrates that the DOM present in water from one Canadian lake has little effect on bioaccumulation of a polychlorinated biphenyl (PCB).[30] In contrast, Kukkonen et al. (also in this volume) examine a range of natural waters and demonstrate that the chemical and physical properties of DOM influence the extent of binding of polycyclic aromatic hydrocarbon (PAH) versus PCBs, but that the reduction in bioavailability remains correlated with physicochemical association of the contaminant with the natural organic macromolecule.[31] Södergren (also this volume) proposes an innovative monitoring tool to empirically estimate the bioavailable fraction of a contaminant in a natural system; the approach is based on the use of solvent-filled dialysis bags to mimic bioaccumulation of organic contaminants by lipid pools of aquatic organisms.[32]

Accurate estimation of physicochemical partitioning of contaminants is not, by itself, sufficient to predict accumulation of environmental contaminants. Bioavailability of the sediment-associated contaminants needs to be understood as a complex interaction between physical, chemical, and biological characteristics that change with site, compound, and species of interest, thus making it difficult to understand and predict the bioavailability without detailed, site-specific information. Lee (this volume) illustrates this point by demonstrating the complicating influences of feeding behavior, burrowing characteristics, contact time of pollutants with sediment, and nonequilibrium sorption processes on bioaccumulation of organic contaminants in benthic invertebrates.[19]

An important, but poorly understood, aspect of contaminant accumulation from sediment is the relative role of water versus sediment particles as the source of exposure. The uptake of contaminants by sediment-associated organisms has generally been reported as primarily via the interstitial water; however, more recent studies suggest that ingestion of contaminated particles may play as large a role—or even a larger role—in bioaccumulation of sediment-associated contaminants.[7,33] Establishing which of the routes of accumulation are most important for these contaminants—both for specific benthos and for organisms strongly coupled to the benthos through food chain transport—will dictate the approach required for establishing sediment quality criteria. There are currently several approaches for the establishment of sediment quality criteria, including, but not limited to, sediment quality triad, apparent effects threshold, screening level concentration, equilibrium partitioning approach, and spiked sediment bioassays. In terms of effects on the benthos, several of the approaches give very similar estimates of the level of sediment-associated contaminants producing effects.[34] In spite of the similarity of the results from the above comparison, the science is not sufficiently established that one method for establishing criteria can be selected over another. Given the weaknesses in our current understanding, the use and comparison of several of the available methods may be the best approach for making decisions about the extent and significance of sediment contamination.

Even with several methods available for estimating an effects level for specific contaminants, there are limitations to the types of situations that can be addressed. There is no method that can establish the appropriate level of contaminants where the exposure occurs in mixtures, the usual situation in sediment exposures. Further, most of the bioassays currently in use for contaminated sediments address acute and, in some cases, subacute end points. There is, in general, an absence of bioassays available for measuring chronic effects. Finally, none of the criteria approaches consider the effects of food chain transfer and its impact on higher trophic level species.

An alternate approach to evaluating the significance of sediment exposures is the measurement of biological markers in macroinvertebrates and fish collected from contaminated areas. In this approach, it is the biochemical or physiological expression of contaminant exposure and effect (e.g., genotoxic damage, induction of detoxication systems, or histological lesions) that is assayed, rather than the level of individual contaminants in either the sediment or the organism.[35] Biomarkers have the advantage that the complexities of physicochemical partitioning, bioaccumulation, and pharmacodynamics are bypassed, and the end points of most direct concern to animal health are probed explicitly. Long and Buchman have compared and found reasonable agreement between the results of biomarker-based biomonitoring of San Francisco Bay with several more traditional end points such as toxicity tests and concentrations of chemicals in sediments.[36] While biomarker responses measured in organisms from sites with contaminated sediments offer the promise of providing an integrated assessment of the biological significance of exposure, the approach is still under development and requires more research before it can be used as a reliable indicator of sediment quality.

In the above discussion, the concentrations of contaminants in the sediment were assumed to be constant. However, both physical and biological processes can affect the amount of a chemical in the sediment. One of the major factors (in addition to the biological and partitioning factors considered above) that will modify exposure is alteration of the sediment concentration through removal of contaminated sediments from the bioactive layer. The influx of fresh sediment will bury and, to some extent, dilute the contaminated sediment in the bioactive layer, particularly if remedial changes have reduced the concentration on incoming particles. This burial can, however, be modified through bioturbation by benthos that feed in a conveyor-belt fashion. Such bioturbation processes will result in the transport of contaminant-laden particles to the top of the bioactive zone.[37,38] These bioturbing processes extend the duration of exposure of benthic organisms to incoming particle-associated contaminants. Such actions, in conjunction with changes in the depositional regimes, may actually result in the reappearance of contaminants into the bioactive layers of sediments.

A productive approach to integrating the range of physical, chemical, and biological processes that can affect bioaccumulation from sediments involves mathematical modeling of multiply-interacting processes. Mackay et al. (this volume) illustrate the useful insights that can be obtained with "environmental video games" based on a mass balance model of pollutant fate, transport, and bioaccumulation.[39] Young et al. (also this volume) provide an example of field observations of DDE and PCB accumulation from marine sediments that are encouragingly consistent with the fugacity models.[40]

The principal objective of this portion of the symposium is to highlight and illustrate the complex interactions that dictate the total exposure of the biota to sediment-associated contaminants and to indicate gaps in our understanding that limit capabilities to predict the results of such exposures. Even with the number of papers on the interaction of biota with sediment-associated contaminants increasing rapidly, this field is very young and of such complexity that a complete understanding will require many years of effort. As a result, complete understanding of this field will not occur rapidly and interim approaches will be required for assessing and controlling contaminated sediments.

BIODEGRADATION OF SEDIMENT-ASSOCIATED CONTAMINANTS

While our focus on contaminants in sediments may be motivated by our concern about their toxic effects on biological systems, it is one of the symmetries of nature that biological processes also act to alleviate these concerns by catalyzing the degradation of contaminants. While the degradative capabilities of microorganisms have long been recognized, they have more recently become the focal point for environmental initiatives aimed at restoring contaminated areas. Attempts to remove or isolate contamination through physical and chemical techniques are expensive and often ineffective. It has become clear that in situ bioremediation offers the best practical hope for removing contaminants in natural systems.

Although many organic contaminants that associate with sediments have proven to be highly resistant to aerobic biodegradation, new approaches and understandings are promising increased potential for the biodegradation of many of these contaminants. The purpose of this section is not to extensively review biodegradation of sediment-associated contaminants, but rather to highlight productive and promising research areas associated with biodegradation and to place the papers in this section in the context of current research. Increasing attention to anaerobic degradation, particularly anaerobic dechlorinations,[41,42] and cometabolism has led to a greater appreciation of the degradability of organic compounds by mechanisms not commonly examined. Also, a wider range of compounds have also proven to be degradable by aerobic mechanisms (e.g., PCBs). Often the expression of these degradative capabilities in nature is limited, but genetic engineering offers the potential for increasing the expression of degradative genes and for providing tools for the examination of biodegradation in sediments. Knight and Colwell (in this volume) provide an overview of both the theory and practice of molecular genetics and recombinant DNA technology.[43]

The search for understanding of the degradation of sediment-associated organic compounds has been pursued in many types of sedimentary environments. Exciting research on degradation of PCBs in aquatic sediments has been complemented by new ideas and approaches being developed in examinations of aquifer sediments and in unsaturated terrestrial sediments. The most significant work on biodegradation through anaerobic dechlorination has focused on the fate of PCBs in aquatic sediments, most of which are anaerobic. On the other hand, many of the interesting new findings related to both traditional aerobic degradation and to cometabolic mechanisms come from work on unsaturated terrestrial sediments or on oxygenated aquifer sediment and groundwater.

Traditionally, many types of contaminants that have been considered to be resistant to biodegradation—ranging from relatively simple chlorinated ethenes (such as trichloroethylene), to much larger, more complex chlorinated compounds (such as PCBs), and large, complex nonchlorinated organic compounds (such as the PAHs). Different classes of these compounds are likely to be found in different sediment settings, and this influences the type of degradative processes that are important in the fate of these compounds. The higher-molecular-weight, nonpolar classes are relatively insoluble in water. Thus, they can be found in aquatic sediments which are likely to be anaerobic, in unsaturated soils where they are likely to be exposed to aerobic conditions, and in groundwater sediments where the conditions may either be aerobic or anaerobic. The lower-molecular-weight, polar compounds are likely only to be found in the terrestrial systems, such as the surface soils, aquifer sediment, and groundwater environments. These compounds would probably not become associated with aquatic sediments due to their relatively high aqueous solubility. However, they may be found in detectable quantities in aquifer sediments due to limited water flow through these sediments. The examination of these varied environments is leading to new approaches to biodegradation, including the linking of anaerobic-aerobic systems for degradation of chlorinated compounds.[44]

There are both broad similarities in the degradation of compounds in terrestrial and aquatic sediments and significant differences. One similarity is the issue of the bioavailability of the high-molecular-weight, nonpolar compounds. In aquatic sediments, unsaturated terrestrial sediments, and aquifer sediments, these compounds will tend to be strongly sorbed to particles. In this state they are likely to more resistant to biological degradation simply due to the inability of the bacteria to access this material. Due to the similarities among the sediment systems, comparisons of processes and rates of bacterial activity in aquatic and aquifer sediments can be useful in obtaining insights into microbial function in these environments.[45] A significant difference between the aquatic sediments and aquifer sediments is the presence of macroinvertebrates and other fauna in the aquatic sediments. Bioturbation and other effects can increase biodegradation rates of organic contaminants on sediments.[46,47] Also, the presence of exotic natural compounds, such as halophenols, may stimulate populations able to degrade similar organic contaminants, thus serving as a source of bacteria for biodegradation of a much broader array of contaminants.[48]

Anaerobic Dechlorinations

Intense research on the reductive dechlorinations of PCBs was prompted by the observation of dechlorination of PCBs in aquatic sediments.[42,49,50] Analysis of other sediments by Lake et al. (this volume) has expanded the range of sediments in which dechlorinations of PCBs have been observed.[51] Laboratory demonstrations of dechlorination of PCBs soon followed.[52] Questen et al. have found that *meta* and *para* chlorines were removed during dechlorination and that dechlorination was slower and less effective with increasing chlorination.[44] They also found that sediment samples from different sites contained microorganisms with different specificities for PCB dechlorination.

Chlorinated ethylenes (CEs) are also degraded via anaerobic dechlorination. Bouwer et al. have observed anaerobic degradation of perchloroethylene (PCE), trichloroethylene (TCE), and dichloroethylene (DCE) by dechlorination mechanisms and concluded that methanogenesis was the principal biochemical reaction responsible for transforming TCE and PCE.[53,54] Fathepure et al. have demonstrated that a pure methanogenic culture (*Methanosarcina* sp. DCM) degraded TCE and PCE and proposed that PCE was reduced by the same electron carrier that would normally reduce carbon dioxide to methane.[55,56] Freedman and Gossett have shown that numerous chlorinated ethenes may be dechlorinated by a mixed methanogenic culture.[57] Although anaerobic dechlorination is a slow process, it is the only known mechanism for PCE degradation. Unfortunately, PCE or TCE dechlorination often yields vinyl chloride, which is considered to be one of the most carcinogenic compounds.[58]

Dechlorinations of other compounds, such as chloroaromatic compounds, pesticides, and herbicides, have also been a recent focus of study,[41] and much of that work indicates that dehalogenation does not occur with sulfate as an elector acceptor.[59] Dehalogenation may be inhibited in groundwater aquifer sediments by the presence of sulfate,[60] and similar results have been reported for aquatic sediments.[61] Suflita et al. (this volume) examine both the conditions promoting anaerobic biotransformation of herbicides (finding dehalogenation under methanogenic conditions) and the pathways for the degradation.[62] The relationship between sediment/water properties and the reductive dechlorination of various other compounds is addressed by Hale et al. (also in this volume), who have related reductive dechlorination of dichlorophenols to characteristics such as pH, nitrate and sulfate concentrations, and redox potential.[63]

Cometabolism

The terms *cometabolism, fortuitous metabolism,* and *cooxidation* are often used to describe the same process, and much debate is centered on the use of these terms. In aerobic degradation, the bacteria obtain carbon and energy from oxidation of the contaminants, whereas with cometabolism this benefit to the bacteria does not occur. Dalton and Stirling define cometabolism as having four features:[64]

1. A cometabolite does not support growth.
2. The products accumulate stoichiometrically.

3. Transformation is associated with increased oxygen uptake.
4. Cometabolism entails adventitious utilization of existing enzyme systems.

Most cometabolic metabolism has been associated with the activity of various mono- and dioxygenase enzymes. Some of the primary groups of organisms associated with cometabolic metabolism are methane oxidizers, toluene degraders, and ammonia oxidizers. Mono- and dioxygenase enzymes in other types of bacteria have also been implicated in the cometabolic degradation.

The key to cometabolism is the broad substrate specificity of the oxygenase enzymes. Perhaps the best-studied enzyme involved in cometabolism is methane monooxygenase (MMO). The interest in MMO was largely prompted by the work of Wilson and Wilson on TCE degradation.[65] Since then, all CEs except PCE have been reported to be degraded by methanotrophic mixed cultures.[66-70] This MMO enzyme catalyzes the transformation of methane to methanol in the presence of nicotinamide-adenine-dinucleotide (NADH) and oxygen. MMO has been found to have a broad substrate range, which in addition to methane and the CEs includes benzene, bicyclohexyl, butadiene, chlorophenol, cresol, ethylbenzene, phenol, ethene, propene, pyridine, styrene, toluene, and xylene,[71] as well as carbon monoxide[72,73] and ammonia.[74] The details of the pathways and kinetics, as well as the effect of groundwater chemistry on CE degradation, have been examined in a number of studies using pure cultures.[75-77] Palumbo et al. (in this volume) describe the inhibitory effect of ammonia as well as the effect of other groundwater components on TCE degradation by the methanotrophs.[78]

The utility of methanotrophs for in situ degradation of CEs in aquifer sediments has been examined in simulated and actual aquifer systems. Moore et al. spiked a methane-stimulated aquifer with *trans*-1,2-DCE (1 mg/L) and found that 80% of the *trans*-1,2-DCE was degraded after 200 hours.[79] In field studies, Semprini et al. found that *trans*-DCE was degraded to a greater degree than either *cis*-1,2-DCE or TCE but was not degraded as fast as vinyl chloride.[80] Laboratory studies by Grbic-Galic et al. (in this volume) indicate that formate may increase TCE degradation in aquifer sediments by providing an alterative source of reducing power that is not a competitive inhibitor of TCE degradation.[81]

Mono- and dioxygenases from other types of bacteria have also been implicated in oxidation of organic contaminants. The ammonia monooxygenase (AMO) enzyme from nitrifying bacteria, *Nitrosomonas europaea,* has also been shown to have the ability to degrade numerous contaminants including aliphatic, cyclic, and halogenated hydrocarbons.[82-84] AMO is structurally similar to MMO,[85] and the mechanisms of degradation may be similar too because the AMO is capable of oxidizing methane and most other MMO substrates. Similarly, the toluene dioxygenase from *Pseudomonas putida* is able to oxidize TCE and related compounds.[86-89]

Aerobic Degradation

Perhaps the best examples of aerobic mechanisms for the degradation of recalcitrant compounds is the current work on PCBs and PAHs. Degradation of the PCBs with few chlorines was described in the 1970s and early 1980s.[90-93] Since then the range of congeners that have been demonstrated to be degraded has expanded and now includes congeners up to hexachlorobiphenyls.[94,95] In a hazard assessment of PCBs, Hooper et al. describe the many problems remaining in the understanding of PCB degradation.[96]

In addition to their role in cometabolic degradation of numerous substrates, mono- and dioxygenase enzymes have also been implicated in the aerobic degradation of PAH by Cerniglia (in this volume).[97] A *Mycobacterium* species capable of growth on phenanthrene has been isolated from estuarine sediment.[98] PAH degradation has been examined in marine sediments, and the rates of degradation have been related to preexposure to related compounds.[99,100]

The importance of acclimation of bacterial to contaminants in both aerobic and anaerobic environments is receiving increasing attention.[101-103] PAH oxidation in marine sediments has been shown to be positively related to oxygen content and to acclimation to high concentrations of PAH for 1 to 2 weeks.[102] In anaerobic lake sediments, the existence of a lag period and subsequent acclimation for degradation of halobenzoates has been noted[104] and characterized.[103] The acclimation effect has also been noted for other compounds in water samples.[105] Schermerhorn and Ventullo (in this volume) have devised a method for examination of acclimation of periphyton communities to organic chemicals.[106] They found that exposure to linear alkylbenzene sulfonate decreased lag times and increased rate constants for degradation.

Genetic Engineering and Molecular Techniques

Potential applications of genetic engineering to degradation of sediment-associated contaminants include changing the regulatory control of degradative genes and providing tools for examination of degradation. The regulatory control of degradative enzymes can be changed to enable production of degradative enzymes without the presence of an inducer (which may compete with the contaminant for sites on the enzyme) or to shift the expression of the enzyme to a nongrowth stage of the bacterial cell growth cycle. Genetic engineering can be also used to provide tools for the examination of the degradative process through the use of "reporter" constructs.

One example of using genetic engineering to alter regulatory control of biodegradative enzymes comes from work with the control of oxygenase expression for degradation of TCE. Typically, degradation of contaminants at low concentrations is difficult due a variety of factors, including, in the case of oxygenase enzymes, competitive inhibition by the enzyme's preferred substrate, which needs to be present to promote production of the enzyme. A change in regulatory control of the enzyme expression can reduce this problem. The toluene-degrading (C1C2BADE) genes from *Pseudomonas putida* were introduced into *E. coli* JM109.[107] The construct degraded TCE at a constant rate, whereas *Pseudomonas putida* degraded TCE at a faster rate initially but at a slower rate at the end of the experiment. Winter et al. cloned the toluene monooxygenase genes into *E. coli* and were able to degrade TCE from 16 ppm to 2 ppb, a level that it is difficult to achieve with nonengineered bacteria.[108]

The use of "reporter" constructs and other molecular techniques may enable researchers to better understand the function of degradative bacteria in sediments. Detection of catabolic genotypes in sediments can give indications of the capacity of the microbial community for degradation of organic contaminants. Tracing of microbial populations capable of chlorinated biphenyl degradation has been demonstrated both in aquatic systems and in terrestrial sediments,[109-111] and the use of DNA probes for detection of metal resistance in soils and aquatic environments has been demonstrated.[112,113] Molecular probes hybridizing with 16S RNA have been developed for the detection of methylotrophic organisms.[114] Sayler et al. (in this volume) describe the use of bioluminescence technology for measuring activity of degradative genes in sediments and also review the information on the occurrence of specific degradative genes in subsurface communities.[115] As pointed out by Knight and Colwell,[43] molecular technology is a rapidly evolving frontier that offers great promise in remediation of environmental contamination.

SUMMARY

This volume will examine key concepts and processes related to biological processes affecting organic contaminants in sediments. We begin with integrative overviews of the physicochemical, biological, and toxicological processes that need to be understood in order to evaluate the fate and effects of hazardous chemicals in sediment-water systems, as well as an overview of new molecular techniques offering great promise for enhancing our capabilities to remediate environmental contamination. Innovative approaches to assessing higher-level ecological responses to contaminants are being developed, and modeling of sediment-water interactions provide valuable insights into the distribution of contaminants on a macroscopic scale; however, it is clear that we have an incomplete understanding of key biological processes controlling the dose of contaminant to which organisms are exposed. The concepts and processes associated with uptake and accumulation of sediment-associated contaminants are divided into two sections focusing on aspects of bioavailability of contaminants, and observations of bioaccumulation of contaminants in natural sediments.

Part IV of this volume is devoted to discussion of biological processes that offer the promise of ameliorating existing problems through biological degradation of sediment-associated contaminants. Chapters are divided into sections focusing on processes of anaerobic dechlorinations and cometabolism of contaminants. The final chapter illustrates an application of molecular techniques in bacteria to better understand the functioning of degradative bacteria in sediments.

ACKNOWLEDGMENTS

This work was sponsored in part by the Oak Ridge Y-12 Plant, Department of Environmental Management, Health, Safety, Environment, and Accountability Division and by the Subsurface Science Program of the Ecological Research Division, Office of Health and Environmental Research, U.S. Department of Energy. The Oak Ridge Y-12 Plant and the Oak Ridge National Laboratory are managed by Martin Marietta Energy Systems, Inc., under contract DE-AC05-84OR21400 with the U.S. Department of Energy. Publication no. 3706 of the Environmental Sciences Division, Oak Ridge National Laboratory. Contribution No. 739 of the Great Lakes Environmental Research Laboratory of the National Oceanic and Atmospheric Administration.

REFERENCES

1. Pratt, J. R. "Making the Transition from Toxicology to Ecotoxicology," Chapter 2, this volume.
2. Engler, R. M. "Prediction of Pollution Potential through Geochemical and Biological Procedures: Development of Regulation Guidelines and Criteria for the Discharge of Dredged and Fill Material," in *Contaminants and Sediments, Volume 1, Fate and Transport, Case Studies, Modeling, Toxicity*, R. A. Baker, Ed. (Ann Arbor, MI: Ann Arbor Science, 1980), Chapter 7, pp. 143–170.
3. Nalepa, T. F., and P. F. Landrum. "Benthic Invertebrates and Contaminant Levels in the Great Lakes: Effects, Fates and Role in Cycling," in *Toxic Contaminants and Ecosystem Health: A Great Lakes Focus*, M. S. Evans, Ed. (New York: John Wiley and Sons, 1988), pp. 77–102.
4. Keilty, T. J., and P. F. Landrum. "Population-Specific Responses by the Freshwater Oligochaete, *Stylodrilius heringianus,* in Natural Lake Michigan Sediment," *Environ. Toxicol. Chem.* 9:1147–1154 (1990).
5. Sherblom, P. M., and R. P. Eganhouse. "Bioaccumulation of Molecular Markers for Municipal Wastes by *Mytilus edulis,*" Chapter 9, this volume.
6. Landrum, P. F., and J. A. Robbins. "Bioavailability of Sediment-Associated Contaminants to Benthic Invertebrates," in *Sediments: Chemistry and Toxicity of In-Place Pollutants*, R. Baudo, J. P. Giesy, and H. Muntau, Eds. (Chelsea, MI: Lewis Publishers, 1990), Chapter 8, pp. 237–263.
7. Landrum, P. F. "Bioavailability and Toxicokinetics of Polycyclic Aromatic Hydrocarbons Sorbed to Sediments for the Amphipod, *Pontoporeia hoyi,*" *Environ. Sci. Tech.* 23:588–595 (1989).
8. Landrum, P. F., W. R. Faust, and B. J. Eadie. "Bioavailability and Toxicity of a

Mixture of Sediment-Associated Chlorinated Hydrocarbons to the Amphipod *Pontoporeia hoyi*," in *Aquatic Toxicology and Hazard Assessment: 12th Volume, ASTM STP 1027*, U. M. Cowgill and L. R. Williams, Eds. (Philadelphia: American Society for Testing and Materials, 1989), pp. 315–329.

9. McFarland, V. A. "Activity-Based Evaluation of Potential Bioaccumulation for Sediments," in *Dredging and Dredged Material Disposal*, Vol. 1, R. L. Montgomery and J. W. Leach, Eds. (New York: American Society of Civil Engineers, 1984), pp. 461–467.

10. Lake, J. L., N. Rubinstein, and S. Pavigano. "Predicting Bioaccumulation: Development of a Simple Partitioning Model for Use as a Screening Tool for Regulating Ocean Disposal Wastes," in *Fate and Effects of Sediment-Bound Chemicals in Aquatic Systems*, K. L. Dickson, A. W. Maki, and W. A. Brungs, Eds. (New York: Pergamon Press, 1987), Chapter 12, pp. 151–166.

11. Foster, G. D., and D. A. Wright. "Unsubstituted Polynuclear Aromatic Hydrocarbons in Sediments, Clams, and Clam Worms for Chesapeake Bay," *Mar. Pollut. Bull.* 19:790–792 (1988).

12. McElroy, A. E., and J. C. Means. "Factors Affecting the Bioavailability of Hexachlorobiphenyls to Benthic Organisms," in *Aquatic Toxicology and Hazard Assessment: 10th Volume, ASTM STP 971*, W. J. Adams, G. A. Chapman, and W. G. Landis, Eds. (Philadelphia: American Society for Testing and Materials, 1988), pp. 149–158.

13. Pereira, W. E., C. E. Rostad, C. T. Chiou, T. I. Briton, L. B. Barber, D. K. Demcheck, and C. R. Demas. "Contamination of Estuarine Water, Biota, and Sediment by Halogenated Organic Compounds: A Field Study," *Environ. Sci. Tech.* 22:772–778 (1988).

14. Landrum, P. F., B. J. Eadie, W. R. Faust, N. R. Morehead, and M. J. McCormick. "Role of Sediment in the Bioaccumulation of Benzo(a)pyrene by the Amphipod, *Pontoporeia hoyi*," in *Polynuclear Aromatic Hydrocarbons: Eighth International Symposium on Mechanisms, Methods, and Metabolism*, M. W. Cooke and A. J. Dennis, Eds. (Columbus, OH: Battelle Press, 1985), pp. 799–812.

15. Tatem, H. E. "Bioaccumulation of Polychlorinated Biphenyls and Metals from Contaminated Sediment by Freshwater Prawns, *Macrobrachium rosenbergii*, and Clams, *Corbicula fluminea*," *Arch. Environ. Contam. Toxicol.* 15:171–183 (1986).

16. Foster, G. D., S. M. Baksi, and J. C. Means. "Bioaccumulation of Trace Organic Contaminants from Sediment by Baltic Clams (*Macoma balthica*) and Soft-Shelled Clams (*Mya arenaria*)," *Environ. Toxicol. Chem.* 6:969–976 (1987).

17. Shaw, G. R., and D. W. Connell. "Comparative Kinetics for Bioaccumulation of Polychlorinated Biphenyls by the Polychaete (*Capitella capitata*) and Fish (*Mugil cephalus*)," *Ecotox. Environ. Safety* 13:84–91 (1987).

18. Landrum, P. F., and R. Poore. "Toxicokinetics of Selected Xenobiotics in *Hexagenia limbata*," *J. Great Lakes Res.* 14:427–437 (1988).

19. Lee, H. "A Clam's-Eye View of the Bioavailability of Sediment-Associated Pollutants," Chapter 5, this volume.

20. Reynoldson, T. B. "Interactions between Sediment Contaminants and Benthic Organisms," *Hydrobiologia* 149:53–66 (1987).

21. Knezovitch, J. P., F. L. Harrison, and R. G. Wilhelm. "The Bioavailability of

Sediment-Sorbed Organic Chemicals: A Review," *Water Air Soil Pollut.* 32:233–245 (1987).

22. Neff, J. "Bioaccumulation of Organic Micropollutants from Sediments and Suspended Particulates by Aquatic Animals," *Fres. Z. Anal. Chem.* 319:132–136 (1984).

23. Adams, W. J., R. A. Kimerle, and R. G. Mosher. "Aquatic Safety Assessment of Chemicals Sorbed to Sediments," in *Aquatic Toxicology and Hazard Assessment: Seventh Symposium. ASTM STP 854,* R. D. Cardwell, R. Purdy, and R. C. Bahner, Eds. (Philadelphia: American Society for Testing and Materials, 1985), pp. 429–453.

24. McCarthy, J. F. "Bioavailability and Toxicity of Metals and Hydrophobic Organic Contaminants," in *Influence of Aquatic Humic Substances on the Fate and Treatment of Pollutants,* Advances in Chemistry Series No. 219, I. H. Suffet and P. MacCarthy, Eds. (Washington, DC: American Chemical Society, 1989), pp. 263–280.

25. McCarthy, J. F., B. D. Jimenez, and T. Barbee. "Effect of Dissolved Humic Material on Accumulation of Polycyclic Aromatic Hydrocarbons: Structure-Activity Relationships," *Aquat. Toxicol.* 7:15–24 (1985).

26. Black, M. C., and J. F. McCarthy. "Dissolved Organic Matter Reduces the Uptake of Hydrophobic Organic Contaminants by Gills of the Rainbow Trout, *Salmo gairdneri*," *Environ. Toxicol. Chem.* 7:593–600 (1988).

27. Kukkonen, J., J. F. McCarthy, and A. Oikari. "Effects of XAD-8 Fractions of Dissolved Organic Carbon on the Sorption and Bioavailability of Organic Micropollutants," *Arch. Environ. Contam. Toxicol.* 19:551–557 (1990).

28. Morehead, N. R., B. J. Eadie, B. Lake, P. F. Landrum, and D. Berner. "The Sorption of PAN onto Dissolved Organic Matter in Lake Michigan Waters," *Chemosphere* 15:403–412 (1986).

29. McCarthy, J. F., L. E. Roberson, and L. E. Burris. "Association of Benzo(a)pyrene with Dissolved Organic Matter: Prediction of K_{dom} from Structural and Chemical Properties of the Organic Matter," *Chemosphere* 19:1911–1920 (1989).

30. Evans, H. E. "The Influence of Water Column DOC on the Uptake of 2,2′,4,4′,5,5′-Hexachlorobiphenyl (PCB 153) by *Daphnia magna*," Chapter 6, this volume.

31. Kukkonen, J., J. F. McCarthy, and A. Oikari. "Binding and Bioavailability of Organic Micropollutants in Natural Waters: Effects of the Quality and the Quantity of Dissolved Organic Material," Chapter 7, this volume.

32. Södergren, A. "Solvent-Filled Dialysis Membranes Mimic Bioaccumulation of Pollutants in Aquatic Environments," Chapter 8, this volume.

33. Boese, B. L., H. Lee, D. T. Specht, R. C. Randall, and M. Windsor. "Comparison of Aqueous and Solid Phase Uptake for Hexachlorobenzene in the Tellinid Clam, *Macoma nasuta* (Conrad): A Mass Balance Approach," *Environ. Toxicol. Chem.* 9:221–231 (1990).

34. Chapman, P. M., R. C. Barrick, J. M. Neff, and R. C. Swartz. "Four Independent Approaches to Developing Sediment Quality Criteria Yield Similar Values for Model Contaminants," *Environ. Toxicol. Chem.* 6:723–725 (1987).

35. McCarthy, J. F., and L. R. Shugart, Eds. *Biomarkers of Environmental Contamination* (Chelsea, MI: Lewis Publishers, 1990).

36. Long, L. R., and M. F. Buchman. "A Comparative Evaluation of Selected Measures of Biological Effects of Exposure of Marine Organisms to Toxic Chemi-

cals," in *Biomarkers of Environmental Contamination*, J. F. McCarthy and L. R. Shugart, Eds. (Chelsea, MI: Lewis Publishers, 1990), pp. 355–418.

37. Keilty, T. J., D. S. White, and P. F. Landrum. "Sublethal Responses to Endrin in Sediment by *Stylodrilius heringianus* (Lumbriculidae) as Measured by a [137]Cesium Marker Layer Technique," *Aquat. Toxicol.* 13:251–270 (1988).

38. Keilty, T. J., D. S. White, and P. F. Landrum. "Sublethal Responses to Endrin in Sediment by *Limnodrilius hoffmeisteri* (Tubificidae), and in mixed culture with *Stylodrilius heringianus* (Lumbriculidae)," *Aquat. Toxicol.* 13:227–250 (1988).

39. Mackay, D., M. Diamond, and W. Stiver. "The Case for Modeling Sediment-Water Interactions in Aquatic and Marine Systems," Chapter 3, this volume.

40. Young, D. R., A. J. Mearns, and R. W. Gossett. "Bioaccumulation of *p,p'*-DDE and PCB 1254 by a Flatfish Bioindicator from Highly Contaminated Marine Sediments of Southern California," Chapter 10, this volume.

41. Suflita, J. M., A. Horowitz, D. R. Shelton, and J. M. Tiedje. "Dehalogenation: A Novel Pathway for the Anaerobic Biodegradation of Haloaromatic Compounds," *Science* 218:1115–1116 (1982).

42. Brown, J. F., D. L. Bedard, M. J. Brennan, J. C. Carnahan, H. Feng, and R. E. Wagner. "Polychlorinated Biphenyl Dechlorination in Aquatic Sediments," *Science* 236:709–712 (1987).

43. Knight, I. T., and R. R. Colwell. "Application of Biotechnology to Water Quality Monitoring," Chapter 4, this volume.

44. Questen, J. F., III, S. A. Boyd, and J. M. Tiedje. "Dechlorination of Four Commercial Polychlorinated Biphenyl Mixtures (Aroclors) by Anaerobic Microorganisms from Sediments," *Appl. Environ. Microbiol.* 56:2360–2369 (1990).

45. Chapelle, F. H., and D. R. Lovley. "Rates of Microbial Metabolism in Deep Coastal Plain Aquifers," *Appl. Environ. Microbiol.* 56:1865–1874 (1990).

46. Koerting-Walker, C., and J. D. Buck. "The Effect of Bacteria and Bioturbation by *Clymenelala torquata* on Oil Removal from Sediment," *Water Air Soil Pollut.* 43:413–424 (1989).

47. Bauer, J. E., and D. G. Capone. "Effects of Co-Occurring Aromatic Hydrocarbons on the Degradation of Individual Polycyclic Aromatic Hydrocarbons in Marine Sediment Slurries," *Appl. Environ. Microbiol.* 54:1649–1655 (1988).

48. King, G. W. "Dehalogenation in Marine Sediments Containing Natural Sources of Halophenols," *Appl. Environ. Microbiol.* 54(12):3079–3085 (1988).

49. Brown, J. F., R. E. Wagner, H. Feng, D. L. Bedard, M. J. Brennan, J. C. Carnahan, and R. J. May. "Environmental Dechlorination of PCBs," *Environ. Toxicol. Chem.* 6:579–593 (1987).

50. Brown, J. F., R. E. Wagner, D. L. Bedard, M. J. Brennan, J. C. Carnahan, R. J. May, and T. J. Tofflemire. "PCB Transformations in Upper Hudson Sediments," *Northeastern Environ. Sci.* 3:167–179 (1984).

51. Lake, J. L., R. J. Pruell, and F. A. Osterman. "Dechlorinations of PCBs in Sediments of New Bedford Harbor," Chapter 11, this volume.

52. Questen, J. F., III, J. M. Tiedje, and S. A. Boyd. "Reductive Dechlorination of Polychlorinated Biphenyls by Anaerobic Microorganisms from Sediments," *Appl. Environ. Microbiol. Science* 242:752–754 (1988).

53. Bouwer, E. J., and P. L. McCarty. "Transformations of 1-and 2-Carbon Halogenated Aliphatic Organic Compounds under Methanogenic Conditions," *Appl. Environ. Microbiol.* 45:1286–1294 (1983).

54. Bouwer, E. J., B. E. Rittmann, and P. L. McCarty. "Anaerobic Degradation of

Halogenated 1- and 2-Carbon Organic Compounds," *Environ. Sci. Technol.* 15:596–599 (1981).

55. Fathepure, B. Z., and S. A Boyd. "Dependence of Tetrachloroethylene Dechlorination on Methanogenic Substrate Consumption by *Methanosarcina* sp. Strain DCM," *Appl. Environ. Microbiol.* 54:2976–2980 (1988).

56. Fathepure, B. Z., J. P. Nengu, and S. A. Boyd. "Anaerobic Bacteria That Dechlorinate Perchloroethene," *Appl. Environ. Microbiol.* 53:2671–2674 (1987).

57. Freedman, D. L., and J. M. Gossett. "Biological Reductive Dechlorination of Tetrachloroethylene and Trichloroethylene to Ethylene under Methanogenic Conditions," *Appl. Environ. Microbiol.* 55:2144–2151 (1989).

58. Vogel, T. M., and P. L. McCarty. "Biotransformation of Tetrachloroethylene to Trichloroethylene, Dichloroethylene, Vinyl Chloride, and Carbon Dioxide under Methanogenic Conditions," *Appl. Environ. Microbiol.* 49:1080–1083 (1985).

59. Gibson, S. A., and J. M. Suflita. "Extrapolation of Biodegradation Results to Groundwater Aquifers: Reductive Dehalogenation of Aromatic Compounds," *Appl. Environ. Microbiol.* 52:681–688 (1986).

60. Gibson, S. A., and J. M. Suflita. "Anaerobic Biodegradation of 2,4,5-Trichloropheoxyacetic Acid in Samples from a Methanogenic Aquifer: Stimulation by Short-Chain Organic Acids and Alcohols," *Appl. Environ. Microbiol.* 56:1825–1832 (1990).

61. Genthner, B. R. S., W. A. Price II, and P. H. Pritchard. "Anaerobic Degradation of Chloroaromatic Compounds in Aquatic Sediments under a Variety of Enrichment Conditions," *Appl. Environ. Microbiol.* 55:1466–1471 (1989).

62. Suflita, J. M., K. Ramanand, and N. Adrian. "Anaerobic Biotransformation of Halogenated Pesticides in Aquifer Slurries," Chapter 12, this volume.

63. Hale, D. D., J. E. Rogers, and J. Wiegel. "Reductive Dechlorination of Dichlorophenols in Anaerobic Pond Sediments," Chapter 13, this volume.

64. Dalton, H., and D. I. Stirling. "Co-Metabolism," *Phosil. Trans. R. Soc. London Ser. B.* 297:481–496 (1982).

65. Wilson, J. T., and B. H. Wilson. "Biotransformation of Trichloroethylene in Soil," *Appl. Environ. Microbiol.* 49:242–243 (1985).

66. Fogel, M. M., A. R. Taddeo, and S. Fogel. "Biodegradation of Chlorinated Ethenes by a Methane-Utilizing Mixed Culture," *Appl. Environ. Microbiol.* 51:720–724 (1986).

67. Strandberg, G. W., T. L. Donaldson, and L. L. Farr. "Degradation of Trichloroethylene and *trans*-1,2-Dichloroethylene by a Methanotrophic Consortium in a Fixed-Film, Packed Bed Bioreactor," *Environ. Sci. Technol.* 23:1422–1425 (1989).

68. Henson, J. M., M. Y. Yates, and J. W. Cochran. "Metabolism of Chlorinated Methanes, Ethanes and Ethylenes by a Mixed Bacterial Culture Growing on Methane," *J. Ind. Microbiol.* 4:29–35 (1989).

69. Garland, S. B., A. V. Palumbo, G. W. Strandberg, T. L. Donaldson, L. L. Farr, W. Eng, and C. D. Little. "The Use of Methanotrophic Bacteria for the Treatment of Groundwater Contaminated with Trichloroethylene at the U.S. Department of Energy Kansas City Plant," ORNL/TM-11084, Oak Ridge National Laboratory, Oak Ridge, Tennessee (1989).

70. Uchiyama, H., T. Nakajima, and O. Yagi. "Aerobic Degradation of Trichloroethylene at High Concentration by a Methane-Utilizing Mixed Culture," *Agric. Biol. Chem.* 53:1019–1024 (1989).

71. Higgins, I. J., R. C. Hammond, F. S. Sariaslani, D. Best, M. M. Davies, S. E. Tryhorn, and F. Taylor. "Biotransformation of Hydrocarbons and Related Compounds by Whole Cell Suspensions," *Biochem. Biophys. Res. Commun.* 89:671–677 (1979).

72. Hubley, J. H., J. R. Mitton, and J. F. Wilkinson. "The Oxidation of Carbon Monoxide by Methane-Oxidizing Bacteria," *Arch. Microbiol.* 95:365–368 (1971).

73. Ferenci, T., T. Strom, and J. R. Quayle. "Oxidation of Carbon Monoxide and Methane by *Pseudomonas methanica*," *J. Gen. Microbiol.* 91:79–91 (1975).

74. O'Neill, J. G., and J. F. Wilkinson. "Oxidation of Ammonia by Methane-Oxidizing Bacteria and the Effects of Ammonia on Methane Oxidization," *J. Gen. Microbiol.* 100:407–412 (1977).

75. Janssen, D. B., G. Grobben, R. Hoekstra, R. Oldenhuis, and B. Witholt. "Degradation of *trans*-1,2-Dichloroethene by Mixed and Pure Cultures of Methanotrophic Bacteria," *Appl. Microbiol. Biotechnol.* 29:392–399 (1988).

76. Tsien, H., G. A. Brusseau, R. S. Hanson, and L. P. Wackett. "Biodegradation of Trichloroethylene by *Methylosinus trichosporium* OB3b," *Appl. Environ. Microbiol.* 55:3155–3161 (1989).

77. Oldenhuis, R., R. L. J. M. Vink, D. B. Janssen, and B. Witholt. "Degradation of Chlorinated Aliphatic Hydrocarbons by *Methylosinus trichosporium* OB3b Expressing Soluble Methane Monooxygenase," *Appl. Environ. Microbiol.* 55:2819–2826 (1989).

78. Palumbo, A. V., W. Eng, and G. W. Strandberg. "The Effects of Groundwater Chemistry on Cometabolism of Chlorinated Solvents by Methanotrophic Bacteria," Chapter 14, this volume.

79. Moore, A. T., A. Vira, and S. Fogel. "Biodegradation of *trans*-1,2-Dichloroethylene by Methane-Utilizing Bacteria in an Aquifer Simulator," *Environ. Sci. Technol.* 23:403–406 (1989).

80. Semprini, L., P. V. Roberts, G. D. Hopkins, and P. L. McCarty. "A Field Evaluation of In-Situ Biodegradation of Chlorinated Ethenes: Part 2, Results of Biostimulation and Biotransformation Experiments" 28(5):715–727 (1990).

81. Grbic-Galic, D., S. M. Henry, E. M. Godsy, E. Edwards, and K. P. Mayer. "Anaerobic Degradation of Aromatic Hydrocarbons and Aerobic Degradation of Trichloroethylene by Subsurface Microorganisms," Chapter 15, this volume.

82. Arciero, D., T. Vannelli, M. Logan, and A. B. Hooper. "Degradation of Trichloroethylene by the Ammonia-Oxidizing Bacterium *Nitrosomonas europaea*," *Biochem. Biophys. Res. Commun.* 159:640–643 (1989).

83. Hyman, M. R., I. B. Murton, and D. J. Arp. "Interaction of Ammonia Monooxygenase from *Nitrosomonas europaea* with Alkanes, Alkenes, and Alkynes," *Appl. Environ. Microbiol.* 54:3187–3190 (1988).

84. Rasche, M. E., M. R. Hyman, and D. J. Arp. "Biodegradation of Halogenated Hydrocarbon Fumigants by Nitrifying Bacteria," *Appl. Environ. Microbiol.* 56:2568–2571 (1990).

85. Bedard, C., and R. Knowles. "Physiology, Biochemistry, and Specific Inhibitors of CH_4, NH_4^+, and CO Oxidation by Methanotrophs and Nitrifiers," *Microbiol. Rev.* 53:68–84 (1989).

86. Nelson, M. J. K., S. O. Montgomery, W. R. Mahaffey, and P. H. Pritchard. "Biodegradation of Trichloroethylene and Involvement of an Aromatic Biodegradative Pathway," *Appl. Environ. Microbiol.* 53:949–954 (1987).

87. Nelson, M. J. K., S. O. Montgomery, E. J. O'Neill, and P. H. Pritchard. "Aero-

bic Metabolism of Trichloroethylene by a Bacterial Isolate," *Appl. Environ. Microbiol.* 52:383–384 (1986).

88. Nelson, M. J. K., S. O. Montgomery, and P. H. Pritchard. "Trichloroethylene Metabolism by Microorganisms That Degrade Aromatic Compounds," *Appl. Environ. Microbiol.* 54:604–606 (1988).

89. Wackett, L. P., and D. T. Gibson. "Degradation of Trichloroethylene by Toluene Dioxygenase in Whole-Cell Studies with *Pseudomonas putida* F1," *Appl. Environ. Microbiol.* 54:1703–1708 (1988).

90. Ahmed, M., and D. D. Focht. "Degradation of Polychlorinated Biphenyls by Two Species of *Achromobacter*," *Can. J. Microbiol.* 19:48–52 (1973).

91. Sayler, G. S., M. Shon, and R. R. Colwell. "Growth of an Estuarine *Pseudomonas* sp. on Polychlorinated Biphenyls," *Microbial Ecol.* 3:241–255 (1977).

92. Klages, U., and F. Lingens. "Degradation of 4-Chlorobenzoic Acid by a *Pseudomonas* sp.," *Zentralbl. Bakterio. Mirobiol. Hyg. l Abt. Orig.* C 1:215–223 (1980).

93. Shiaris, M. P., and G. S. Sayler. "Biotransformation of PCB by Natural Assemblages of Freshwater Microorganisms," *Environ. Sci. Technol.* 16:367–369 (1982).

94. Bedard, D. L., M. J. Brennan, R. E. Wagner, and J. F. Brown. "Extensive Degradation of Aroclors and Environmentally Transformed PCBs by *Alcaligenes eutrophus* H850," *Appl. Environ. Microbiol.* 53:1094–1102 (1987).

95. Kohler, H.-P. E., D. Kohler-Staub, and D. D. Focht. "Cometabolism of PCBs: Enhanced Transformation of Aroclor 1254 by Growing Cells," *Appl. Environ. Microbiol.* 54:1940–1945 (1988).

96. Hooper, S. W., C. A. Pettigrew, and G. S. Sayler. "Ecological Fate, Effects and Prospects for the Elimination of Environmental Polychlorinated Biphenyls (PCBs)," *Environ. Toxicol. Chem.* 9:655–667 (1990).

97. Cerneglia, C. E. "Biodegradation of Organic Contaminants in Sediments: Overview and Examples with Polycyclic Aromatic Hydrocarbons," Chapter 16, this volume.

98. Lee, R. F., and C. Ryan. "Microbial and Photochemical Degradation of Polycyclic Aromatic Hydrocarbons in Estuarine Waters and Sediments," *Can. J. Fish. Aquat. Sci.* 40(Suppl. 2):86–94 (1983).

99. Bauer, J. E., and D. G. Capone. "Effects of Co-Occurring Aromatic Hydrocarbons on Degradation of Individual Polycyclic Aromatic Hydrocarbons in Marine Sediment Slurries," *Appl. Environ. Microbiol.* 54(7):1649–1655 (1988).

100. Heitkamp, M. A., and C. E. Cerniglia. "Effects of Chemical Structure and Exposure on the Microbial Degradation of Polycyclic Aromatic Hydrocarbons in Freshwater and Estuarine Ecosystems," *Environ. Toxicol. Chem.* 6:535–546 (1987).

101. Larson, R. J., and D. H. Davidson. "Acclimation to and Biodegradation of Nitrilotriacetic Acid at Trace Concentrations in Natural Waters," *Water Res.* 16:1597–1604 (1982).

102. Bauer, J. E., and D. G. Capone. "Degradation and Mineralization of Polycyclic Aromatic Hydrocarbons Anthracene Naphthalene in Intertidal Marine Sediments," *Appl. Environ. Microbiol.* 50:81–90 (1985).

103. Linkfield, T. G., J. M. Suflita, and J. M. Tiedje. "Characterization of the Acclimation Period before Anaerobic Dehalogenation of Halobenzoates," *Appl. Environ. Microbiol.* 55(11):2773–2778 (1989).

104. Horowitz, A., J. M. Suflita, and J. M. Tiedje. "Reductive Dehalogenations of

Halobenzoates by Anaerobic Lake Sediment Microorganisms," *Appl. Environ. Microbiol.* 45(5):1459–1465 (1983).

105. Ventullo, R. M., and R. J. Larson. "Adaptation of Aquatic Microbial Communities to Quaternary Ammonium Compounds," *Appl. Environ. Microbiol.* 51:356–361 (1986).

106. Schermerhorn, S. D., G. Abbate, and R. M. Ventullo. "The Use of Chemical Diffusing Substrata to Monitor the Response of Periphyton to Synthetic Organic Chemicals," Chapter 17, this volume.

107. Zylstra, G. J., L. P. Wackett, and D. T. Gibson. "Trichloroethylene Degradation by *Escherichia coli* Containing the Cloned *Pseudomonas putida* F1 Toluene Dioxygenase Genes," *Appl. Environ. Microbiol.* 55:3162–3166 (1989).

108. Winter, R. B., K. Yen, and B. D. Ensley. "Efficient Degradation of Trichloroethylene by a Recombinant *Escherichia coli*," *Bio/Technology* 7:282–285 (1989).

109. Steffan, R. J., A. Breen, R. M. Atlas, and G. S. Sayler. "Monitoring Genetically Engineered Microorganisms in Freshwater Microcosms," *J. Ind. Microbiol.* 4:441–446 (1989).

110. Packard, J., A. Breen, G. S. Sayler, and A. V. Palumbo. "Monitoring Population of 4-Chlorobiphenyl-Degrading Bacteria in Soil and Lake Water Microcosms Using Colony Hybridization," in *Biotreatment: Proceedings of the 2nd National Conference,* (Silver Spring, MD: Hazardous Materials Control Research Institute, 1989), pp. 119–126.

111. Walia, S., A. Khan, and N. Fosenthal. "Construction and Applications of DNA Probes for Detection of Polychlorinated Biphenyl-Degrading Genotypes in Toxic Organic-Contaminated Soil Environments," *Appl. Environ. Microbiol.* 56:254–259 (1990).

112. Barkay, T., D. L. Fouts, and B. H. Olson. "Preparation of a DNA Gene Probe for Detection of Mercury Resistance Genes in Gram-Negative Bacteria Communities," *Appl. Environ. Microbiol.* 49:686–692 (1985).

113. Diels, L., and M. Mergeay. "DNA Probe-Mediated Detection of Resistant Bacteria from Soils Highly Polluted by Heavy Metals," *Appl. Environ. Microbiol.* 56:1481–1491 (1990).

114. Tsien, H. C., B. J. Bratina, K. Tsuji, and R. S. Hanson. "Use of Oligodeoxynucleotide Signature Probes for Identification of Physiological Groups of Methylotrophic Bacteria," *Appl. Environ. Microbiol.* 56(9):2858–2865 (1990).

115. Sayler, G. S., J. M. H. King, R. Burlage, and F. Larimer. "Molecular Analysis of Biodegradative Bacterial Populations: Application of Bioluminescence Technology," Chapter 18, this volume.

PART II

INTEGRATING CHEMISTRY AND TOXICOLOGY OF SEDIMENT-WATER INTERACTIONS

CHAPTER 2

Making the Transition from Toxicology to Ecotoxicology

James R. Pratt

INTRODUCTION

The sciences of toxicology and ecology are at a crossroads. Toxicological methods have served as quick, convenient, and pragmatic ways of estimating the effects of chemical stressors and mixtures on aquatic life. Ecological risk assessment as practiced by regulatory agencies is, however, nothing more than a series of increasingly sensitive toxicity tests linked together in a tiered or sequential fashion.[1] While these tests examine effects on species of different ecological positions, different life histories, and different longevities, present risk assessment practices in no way evaluate any ecologically meaningful interactions.

Field ecologists have played a major role in assessing environmental damage through biological surveys of the presence, absence, and abundance of a variety of taxa ranging from microorganisms to fish. Concurrent with the "toxicological era" of environmental regulation, a great deal has been learned about the important structures and processes in aquatic ecosystems. The flow of energy through stream ecosystems has been estimated, and the functional role of a variety of taxa within the ecosystems that normally receive our wastes is increasingly better understood.[2] Additionally, our concept of ecosystems has changed to include the importance of energy and nutrient flow and cycling, so that the traditional focus on indicator species[3] holds very little relevance for most ecosystem ecologists.

My purpose is not to review toxicology and applied ecology. Rather, my purpose is to provide a pedagogical review of environmental toxicology as practiced and applied in the regulatory framework, to compare toxicological responses with ecological responses to toxic chemicals, to examine the applicability of ecotoxicological testing, and to make recommendations for adapting and adopting ecological toxicity testing.

A number of professionals like to be known as ecotoxicologists, but the number of practicing ecotoxicologists is small. In fact, it may be a set with no members. An ecotoxicologist applies ecological principles, measures, and information in the evaluation of chemical hazards and risks.[4] I define *hazard* according to a dose-response relationship in which the relative hazard of toxicants is ranked by the dose required to produce a significant, adverse response. A *risk* is defined by hazard and by the probability of exposure of organisms to hazardous concentrations. In protecting aquatic life, ecotoxicological information is not being used. Because of the reliance on sensitive, surrogate species, some chemicals are overregulated with respect to their ecological hazards and risks and some chemicals are underregulated; that is, the best scientific information is not being used to regulate chemicals. This brief chapter in no way summarizes the vast toxicological literature, or even the debate on the appropriateness of tests for regulation. The interested reader is referred to texts that can put these fields in some scientific perspective.[5-7]

TOXICITY AND BIOASSAYS

Toxicity is usually defined as the inherent property of a chemical to produce adverse biological effects. These effects usually are conceived of ranging from acute responses (occurring over a small part of an organism's life cycle), such as mortality or behavioral responses, to chronic effects (occurring over a long period of an organism's life cycle), such as impaired reproduction or reduced growth. The definition of toxicity is critical in the regulatory framework since the general intent, based on the Clean Water Act, has been to eliminate toxic chemicals in toxic amounts from our surface waters. With respect to aquatic life, a chemical is not of concern if it does not appear in the environment or if it appears in such a low concentration that its biological effects are not measurable. Clearly, the definition of toxicity and the means by which it is measured are crucial in environmental protection. If toxicity were defined only as acute toxicity, then allowed environmental concentrations of chemicals would be much higher than if toxicity is defined over a chronic exposure. The ratio of the concentration of chemical that produces acute toxicity to the concentration that produces chronic effects can vary from almost one to several orders of magnitude. A variety of now standard procedures for assessing the toxicity of a chemical has been developed. These procedures—bioassays—use biological material to assess the potential for a chemical to cause damage. The specific mode(s) of action of most toxic chemicals is not known, and so healthy, sensitive organisms must be used to assess biological effects.

Over the years a small group of organisms has been used to assess toxicity (Table 2.1). These organisms serve as surrogates for the larger assemblage of species in an ecosystem, the overwhelming majority of which can never be tested. The surrogates selected are expected to be broadly sensitive, well-studied, and commercially or ecologically important.[7] Ecosystems are quite diverse, and very few species are truly representative of a large number of

Table 2.1. Representative Standard Test Organisms Used to Assess Toxicity

Freshwater	Marine
Fish	Fish
Fathead minnow	Sheepshead minnow
Bluegill sunfish	Mummichog
Rainbow trout	Silverside
Invertebrates	Invertebrates
Daphnids (water fleas)	Grass shrimp
	Mysid shrimp
Algae	Algae
Selenastrum	*Skeletonema*

ecosystems. Perhaps more important criteria in the selection of test species beyond their sensitivity are their availability and ease of culture. This presents a fundamental conflict in toxicology. Test organisms that are sensitive may be fastidious and, therefore, difficult to rear in sufficient numbers for routine testing. The selected group of surrogates is really quite small when one considers that there are probably between 5 and 50 million species on earth and that several thousand of these occur in any ecosystem. Further, the selection of surrogates strongly favors familiar organisms such as fish over smaller, less familiar, but extremely abundant invertebrates and algae.

Two approaches to using bioassays might be envisioned. One would be to test indigenous or representative species from a particular ecosystem that might receive toxic chemicals. Such an approach could lead to regionally specific limits on the exposure of indigenous species to particular chemicals. A second approach, the one that is widely used in regulation today, is to use a fixed set of biological sensors (the standard test species) to test every chemical or chemical mixture. In this way, the biological material is a constant and the relative hazards of individual stressors can be evaluated. Since the procedures are standardized, there is a reasonable assumption of comparability among laboratories, although interlaboratory comparisons have been equivocal.

Deriving water quality criteria or standards is based on the assumption that the sensitivities of species are normally distributed (Figure 2.1) and that by testing species at the sensitive end of the distribution a relationship between dose and the cumulative effects on an array of species can be used to extrapolate to the larger assemblage of species found in ecosystems. While the assumptions might be acceptable if one examines the sensitivities of individual species, it lacks the ability to predict effects on ecological interactions. Further, many compounds must be regulated in the absence of sufficient information. For example, prior to 1980, water quality standards for chronic zinc discharges were based on the toxicity of zinc to rainbow trout because there were insufficient data to relate chronic responses and dose and because rainbow trout are recreationally (and therefore economically) important.[8] Because of the egalitarian nature of regulation, zinc standards were the same all over the country, meaning that even ecosystems that lacked rainbow trout were

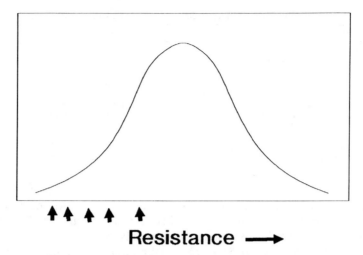

Resistance ⟶

Figure 2.1. Hypothetical distribution of sensitivities to a toxicant. *Arrows* denote the assumed relative sensitivities of common toxicity test species.

regulated at the same zinc concentrations as those that did contain rainbow trout. We now understand that zinc toxicity is affected by water hardness, and zinc criteria differ among soft and hard water streams.[9]

Bioassay information has been used in a standard fashion to develop water quality criteria for over 100 pollutants; however, 6500 chemicals are in common use and may commonly appear in the environment. The bioassay model has been extended to complex mixtures as a way of regulating effluent streams,[10] but because the chemical constituents of an effluent may vary or may not be known, the "dose" can only be expressed in terms of the relative dilution of the effluent by clean water. Nevertheless, the bioassay can differentiate between the relative toxicities evidenced by different compounds or mixtures. Bioassays do not, however, provide direct predictions of ecological effects.

Most toxicological evaluations focus on the responses of small laboratory populations of the surrogate species. While the laboratory populations might serve as surrogates of ecological populations, testing usually focuses on a sensitive life stage (typically juveniles) and so lacks much of the population realism that occurs in the field, where populations have variable age structures and growth is limited by the availability of food and other life requisites. If ecosystems are viewed hierarchically,[11] most of the important ecological processes are a result of interacting populations (Figure 2.2). For example, nutrients are cycled by decomposer food chains. Food chains link species together by predator-prey interactions. Species compete for resources, and those with superior competitive abilities under existing conditions typify certain environments. A large number of ecologists consider themselves to be community ecologists,[12] and although communities as interacting units in the biological

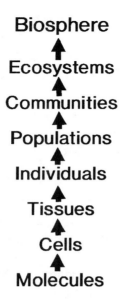

Figure 2.2.   The biological hierarchy. Each higher level is assumed to consist of several components from the next lower level.

hierarchy probably do not exist, communities do form understandable subsets of the larger ecosystem.

From a human perspective, ecosystems provide a variety of essential services ranging from biomass production (food and fiber) to waste assimilation. It has never been clearly demonstrated that chemical regulation and the regulation of discharges have resulted in the protection of these ecosystem services. In fact, ecosystems are providing mixed messages to environmental scientists because there are signs of both improvement and continued degradation in related systems. For example, body burdens of DDT and PCBs in lake trout have decreased in Lake Huron[13] but have either remained the same or increased in Lake Ontario over the past decade (Figure 2.3). Commercial fisheries landings show similar confounding responses: catches of some fish have improved, while catches of other fish have decreased significantly (Figure 2.4). It is well known that human influences on terrestrial ecosystems have decreased overall productivity,[14] so it is reasonable to assume that in certain heavily used aquatic ecosystems similar effects might be expected.

Bioassays have been criticized because they lack the ability to predict effects of chemicals at the community and ecosystem level.[5] While the responses of standard test species may vary considerably to a toxic challenge, it would be surprising if the responses of interacting groups of species differed widely from the responses of sensitive surrogate test organisms. In other words, there should be sufficient similarity in the biological machinery so that exposures toxic to standard test species would also be toxic to multispecies assemblages.

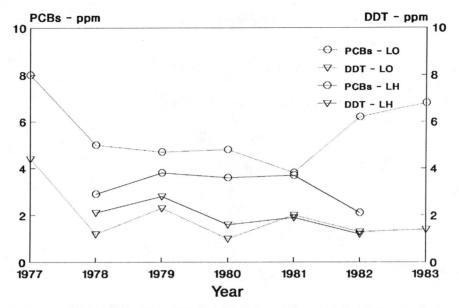

Figure 2.3. Changes in levels of contaminants in lake trout from the Great Lakes. *LO* = Lake Ontario; *LH* = Lake Huron. Adapted from *Environmental Trends*.[13]

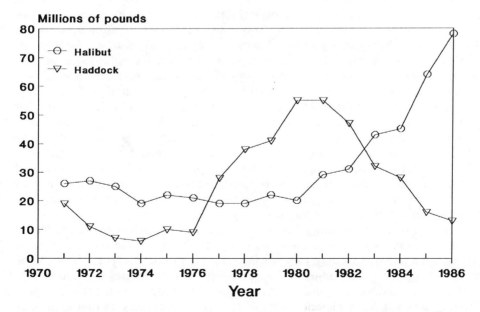

Figure 2.4. Changes in domestic fish landings. Adapted from *Environmental Trends*.[13]

From an evolutionary perspective, metabolic and physiological processes are remarkably constant across all living things. I believe the major point of contention lies not in the prediction of the *concentration* of a particular chemical that might be toxic, but rather prediction of the *magnitude* and *type* of effects that might be observed at the ecosystem level. Since most testing focuses on organisms representative of only a few functions in ecosystems, effects of toxicants on the typically untested species, such as bacteria, other microbes, and plants, are more problematic.

Both toxicologists and ecologists have been somewhat unwilling to accept the concept of laboratory-controlled, ecological test systems where species interactions and ecologically meaningful variables could be measured. Over the past decade it has become clear that laboratory manipulation of species assemblages is not only possible but achievable with sufficiently low variability that important ecological responses can be discerned, both in the investigation of basic questions of ecosystem structure and function and in the applied aspects of anthropogenic influences on ecological phenomena.[15] Ecological test systems should not be expected to be used in the routine way that bioassays are used in chemical regulation.[16] However, laboratory-scale ecosystems can provide important "quality control" checks on predictions from single-species bioassays and can also identify those properties of ecosystems that might be reasonable to measure both in the laboratory and field.

Ecosystems have both collective and emergent properties that result from the occurrence of species in the same place at the same time. *Collective properties* include measures that express the state of an ecological system at a particular time and include population, community, and ecosystem variables. *Emergent properties* are those properties that emerge from the interactions among species and include such processes as predator-prey interactions, nutrient cycling, competition, and succession. These emergent properties are typically measured as rate processes. In a general way, the collective properties of systems can be thought of as measures of the structure of the system, and the emergent properties can be considered measures of system function. In the next section, examples of ecological responses to stress are given and related to conceptual models of expected changes in ecosystems under stress.

ECOLOGICAL TOXICITY TESTING

The diversity of laboratory-scale systems that display ecological properties is quite amazing, ranging from sediment-water systems of only a few milliliters to large channels, tanks, or ponds of around one million liters.[15] Smaller systems have usually been termed microcosms, and larger systems are called mesocosms. The most intensively tested systems are usually a few liters and rarely include organisms as large as fish.[17] Mesocosms that are closer to field scale usually include fish and other large, long-lived organisms.[18] Typically, as the size and longevity of the component organisms increases, experiments must be run over a longer period of time and the cost increases significantly. Artificial pond mesocosms are currently being used to evaluate pesticides.[19]

The criteria for establishing a successful laboratory-scale ecosystem are generally considered to be demonstrations of several ecological properties. Artificial ecosystems should display energy and matter processing, nutrient cycling, and succession; that is, the system should be sustainable and should change with time. For purposes of experimental manipulation and interpretation of results, laboratory-scale systems must be replicable—meaning not that each system is an identical copy of the other, but that variability among systems is sufficiently low that measured properties can be considered similar in the replicates and that during experiments systems develop in approximately the same way.

Approaches to studying the effects of toxic materials on ecosystem structure and function in microcosms have ranged from completely synthetic systems to naturally derived communities. For example, the standard aquatic microcosm (SAM), developed by Taub et al.,[20] assembles an ecosystem from cultured components including protozoa, algae, and crustaceans. The assembled microcosms are dosed with toxic chemicals and are periodically reinoculated from the cultures. This system is nearly totally defined from the culture medium to the component taxa. A second approach, the mixed flask culture (MFC), originally developed by Leffler, assembles a test system from a cultured collection of pond or lake water in a defined medium. Only taxa capable of surviving in the defined medium are eventually apportioned to the microcosms for testing. In the SAM, population dynamics and nutrient pools are measured in response to the toxic dose. In the MFC, functional responses such as primary production and respiration are measured along with nondestructive measures of biomass.

A very different approach, which does not involve culturing, has been used by Giddings et al.,[21] who developed microcosms in large aquaria using sediment, plants, and water from a pond. In this microcosm, the amount of water and sediment are fixed, and a constant wet weight of plants added to each microcosm. No attempt is made to culture or select species; rather, the community is allowed to develop after the microcosm is assembled. By thoroughly mixing sediment and water, there is a good probability of equitable distribution of taxa among replicates. Following the addition of the toxic chemical, microcosms are studied for numbers and kinds of selected taxa, diurnal production and respiration, and major nutrient pools.

Each of the above microcosms uses a static test system. Typically, although not always, the toxic material is supplied in a single dose or a series of pulses. Our laboratory has taken an alternative approach using natural communities and incorporating a continuous input of the diluted toxic material.[22] Microcosms are developed by collecting natural communities and microorganisms on artificial substrata (polyurethane foam) at a reference or unimpacted site in a stream. These communities form the seed material for the replicate microcosms. The toxic chemical is added from a serial dilution device so that the 4-7

L contents of the microcosms are replaced at least five times per day. Communities from the artificial substrata are sampled by removing a substratum and squeezing it into a collecting container. Microcosms are evaluated for species richness of protista, community biomass (protein, chlorophyll) activity of nutrient-transporting enzymes, major nutrient pools, and diurnal production and respiration patterns.

Each microcosm design has unique advantages and disadvantages, and there is not general agreement among ecologists or toxicologists as to the biological significance of certain responses. However, it seems clear that microcosms play an important intermediate role between surrogate species testing and the release of chemicals in ecosystems. Examples of the effects of toxicants on microbial communities in microcosms follow.

Zinc

Zinc is a heavy metal ubiquitous in waste streams. It is known to be bioaccumulated by algae. The water quality criteria for zinc are hardness dependent, but for an intermediate water hardness of 100 mg/L, the chronic zinc criterion for freshwaters is approximately 100 μg/L.[9] Effects of zinc on microbial communities and microcosms showed that species numbers responded quickly and significantly to zinc inputs, resulting in significant depressions of the biota at zinc concentrations above about 90 μg/L (Figure 2.5). Concurrent with the loss of species, both protein and chlorophyll biomass decreased with zinc dose, with chlorophyll showing extremely high sensitivity to the zinc input (Figure 2.5). In other words, algal biomass was severely depressed by zinc addition over ambient. The rate of alkaline phosphatase activity, a measure of the ability of the microbiota to recover phosphorous from organic compounds, was enhanced as phosphate pools in the test systems dropped (Figure 2.6).

It is worth noting that most of the significant responses in the test systems occurred at zinc levels below current water quality criteria and that biomass responses were significant at levels of more than one order of magnitude lower than the current standard (Table 2.2). Summaries of previous research have shown that microcosm responses are comparatively sensitive when compared to the responses of surrogate species.

Atrazine

Atrazine is not a priority pollutant whose environmental levels are regulated as are many compounds discharged from point sources. Atrazine enters the environment primarily from agricultural and horticulture uses because it is a commonly used herbicide. Atrazine comprises a significant proportion (greater than 10%) of the annual poundage of pesticide used in the United States. It is widely used as a preemergence herbicide. Related triazine herbicides find diverse uses, from clearing rights of way to aquatic plant control.

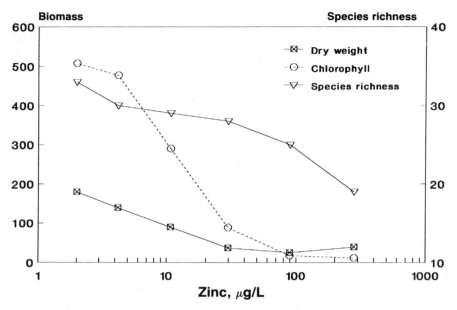

Figure 2.5. Effect of added zinc on community structure of laboratory microcosms. Species richness data are for protozoa. Dry weight units are μg/mL. Chlorophyll was measured as fluorometric units. Controls had 2 μg Zn/L but are plotted as 2 μg/L. Points are means of triplicates.

All of these herbicides are photosynthetic inhibitors affecting the Hill reaction and electron flow of photosystem II.

Our investigations of atrazine toxicity in microcosms showed unexpected patterns, including the stimulation of biomass production and increases in species number (Figure 2.7). At elevated doses of atrazine, alkaline phosphatase activity increased dramatically as phosphorus was lost from experimental systems (Figure 2.8). Although biomass was stimulated, the production of oxygen in experimental systems did not increase, suggesting that although more chlorophyll was present, no additional primary production was taking place. Presumably, the elaboration of chlorophyll biomass was a response to the inhibition of photosynthesis by the added atrazine. Increases in species richness can only be interpreted as indicative of the breakdown of normal control mechanisms in communities. Interestingly, these effects of atrazine occur at concentrations that have been measured in the field in areas where atrazine is widely used as an agricultural chemical.

These examples are not intended to show the superiority of a particular testing system, but demonstrate the potential for ecologically meaningful measures of complex interacting communities to be made under laboratory conditions using experimental designs similar to those used in surrogate species testing. Modeling the dose response of toxic chemicals is critical to conducting

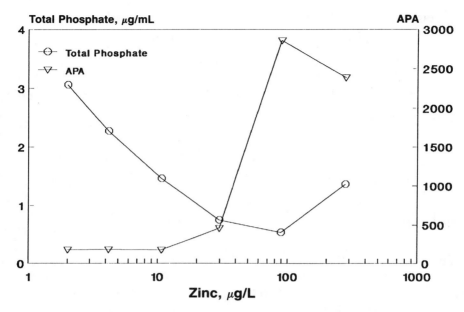

Figure 2.6. Effect of added zinc on nutrient cycling in laboratory microcosms. Units for alkaline phosphatase activity (APA) are nmoles *p*-nitrophenol/mg protein/hr. Controls had <2μg Zn/L but are plotted as 2μg/L.

quantitative risk assessments, and it is now clear that ecological measures can be used to differentiate adverse responses from normal variability in communities. Ecological responses are not as variable as had once been anticipated, assuming that adequate experimental design, sampling, and analysis are exercised to improve detection power.

Table 2.2. Summary of Zinc Toxicity in Naturally Derived Microcosms. [Table values are μg Zn/L. The chronic value (ChV) is the geometric mean of the lowest observable effect concentration (LOEC) and the no observable effect concentration (NOEC) determined by comparisons to controls. The EPA water quality criterion is shown for water hardness of 65 mg CaCO₃/L, the water hardness of the experimental systems. The NOEC could not be calculated when all responses differed from controls.]

Variable	NOEC	LOEC	ChV
Species richness	89.2	280	158
Dryweight	—	4.2	—
Chlorophyll *a*	4.2	10.7	6.7
Dissolved oxygen	—	4.2	—
Alkaline phosphatase activity	29.8	89.2	51.6
EPA criterion			73.6

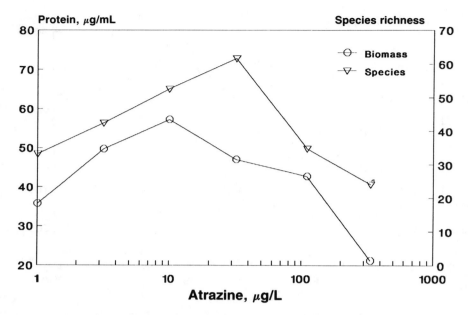

Figure 2.7.   Effect of atrazine on community structure of laboratory microcosms. Species richness data are for protozoa. Biomass data are total protein (μg/mL). Controls are plotted as 1 μg atrazine/L.

EXPECTED CHANGES IN STRESSED ECOSYSTEMS

If microcosms are valid test systems, their responses should be congruent with predictions and observations of ecosystem response to stress. This congruence does not validate the microcosm approach to evaluating ecological toxicity, but does show that microcosms can respond in a manner that might be anticipated by observers of larger systems. Several recent papers have reflected on the types of changes that might be anticipated in stressed systems, although not all of these anticipated changes are readily observed.[23-25]

Species richness

Species are usually considered to be normally distributed (Figure 2.9) in most communities.[26,27] Chemicals affecting communities usually reduce the abundance and diversity of taxa. Occasionally, species numbers are stimulated, and both effects result in a deviation from the nominal state, indicating adverse ecological effects.

Biomass

Toxic influences usually reduce standing crop, but stimulation is not unknown since resistant species or groups of species may be capable of exploiting stressed environments when normal competitive controls are released.

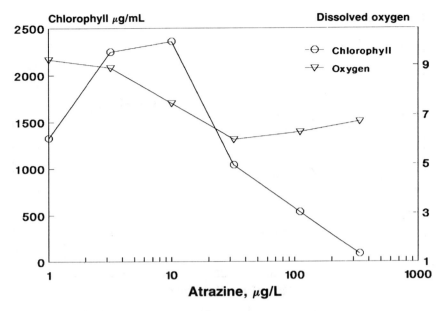

Figure 2.8. Effect of atrazine on chlorophyll biomass and midmorning dissolved oxygen levels in laboratory microcosms. Chlorophyll units are μg chlorophyll a/L. Dissolved oxygen units are mg/L. Controls are plotted as 1 μg atrazine/L.

Primary production

The photosynthetic machinery of most ecosystems is sensitive to the abundance of photosynthetic individuals and the availability of nutrients. Like biomass changes, productivity may be depressed by toxic chemicals or enhanced by the removal of competitors. While primary productivity responds to both nutrient enrichment and toxicity, primary production is usually limited by the availability of nutrients. In aquatic systems affected by toxicants, primary productivity may respond more to nutrient limitation than to toxicity. For example, in a stream that had 50 algal taxa whose primary productivity was limited by phosphate availability, the effect of a toxicant that removed all but 10 taxa but had no effect on the supply of phosphate might be observed to have no effect on production.

Productivity measures are further complicated by methodological limitations, so that only relatively gross changes can be detected. When biomass is low, radiotracer techniques may require relatively long incubation times to achieve detectable uptake of labeled compounds. The resulting measure of primary production often has a coefficient of variation as high as 100%. We have attempted to measure diurnal production and respiration patterns indirectly in microcosms using continuous measures of pH and have discovered

Number of Species

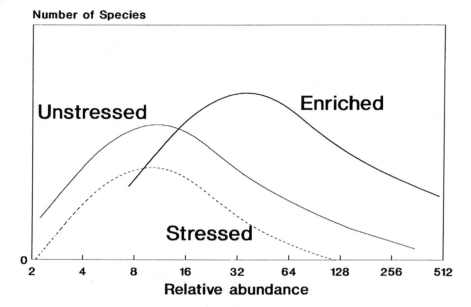

Figure 2.9.   Changes in relative abundance and numbers of species in communities under stress. Enriched communities often show large population sizes of insensitive species. Stressed communities show depressed population sizes and species richness when compared to unstressed reference communities. From Preston[26] and Patrick.[27]

that not only are production and respiration affected by toxic action, but the coupling of processes clearly decreases as toxicity increases.

Energy flow

As primary production is inhibited in ecosystems, there are increasing trends toward heterotrophy. In most stable ecosystems there is a balance between production and respiration. However, as toxicity depresses primary production, decomposer pathways can dominate.

Macronutrients

Ecosystems under stress commonly are unable to recover nutrients that are usually tightly cycled and the systems become "leaky" (e.g., Figure 2.6). Similarly, as systems shift from plant dominated (where potassium levels are high) to animal dominated or decomposer dominated, system pools of a variety of nutrients can shift.

Homeostasis

At the extremes of stress effects, systems are no longer able to compensate for small perturbations. The inability of systems to maintain structure and function under stress is simply the cumulative effect of all the responses listed above: changing species richness, changing standing crop, and changing productivity dynamics.

Unfortunately, ecosystem stress is widespread, and ecological studies have not characterized a sufficient diversity of ecosystems for us to understand the normal operating range of most ecosystems. Additionally, it must be remembered that the development of every ecosystem is a unique, historical process, and although ecosystems share many common structures and functions, the diversity of even neighboring ecosystems is a result of numerous processes that are not understood. Regional approaches to understanding the normal structures in terms of species composition of ecosystems may provide some baseline against which to compare future changes or current conditions, but it is unlikely that we will have good information on the range of processes and the normal community structure at a variety of taxonomic and trophic levels for very many ecosystems unless there is a significant change in the research interests of funding organizations.

To a cynical mind, this ignorance is blissful because we have considerable difficulty detecting when ecosystem changes have occurred. Evidence now clearly points to the importance of understanding the community and population dynamics of small, rapidly reproducing, poorly dispersing species as indicators of ecosystem change. Interestingly, the biology and ecology of these species has been wantonly ignored by all but a small number of professionals, so that the expertise is not available to assess many ecosystems. Further, taxonomic skill is rapidly disappearing in the biological sciences, so that our ability to monitor ecosystems by the species present is compromised. Even if we were to suddenly return to the biological survey as a way of evaluating ecosystem conditions, it would be difficult to identify many taxa since work on their systematic position, identity, tolerances, and distribution essentially stopped 20 years ago.

SUMMARY AND CONCLUSIONS

The single-species bioassay remains the workhorse of environmental toxicology. Surrogate species are used to rank the relative hazards of chemicals in both acute and chronic exposures. Such standard assays, when coupled with information about the environmental fate of chemicals, are a useful first step for establishing standards for allowable environmental concentrations of potentially toxic materials. However, ecological information is increasingly needed both in sensing the condition of the environment and in checking the accuracy of predictions based on surrogate species testing. Surrogate species cannot be used to predict the kinds of ecological changes that might occur from the exposure of complex ecosystems to toxic materials, even though there is some consistency in the innate biological machinery of all living organisms. Some toxic materials may be bioaccumulated and bioconcentrated and produce harmful effects that cannot be predicted from short-term laboratory tests. Other chemicals may be relatively harmless in the environment because they may be rapidly metabolized or in other ways sequestered in the environment. Ecological toxicity testing can serve as an intermediate step between surrogate species testing and environmental release. Laboratory-scale ecosystems are used to evaluate ecological responses in ecosystem-like settings. For conservative chemicals, such as heavy metals or organic materials with long environmental persistence, ecological testing can serve as a necessary quality control step in standard setting. For nonconservative pollutants, ecological testing can reveal the degree to which toxicity can be ameliorated by ecosystem processes such that presumptions of hazard may be reduced.

At the present time, ecological testing is sufficiently well developed to be used in site-specific cases or in cases where additional, ecologically meaningful information is needed to evaluate environmental effects of chemicals. However, considerably more study is needed to understand the relative vulnerability of differing ecosystems so that standards may vary regionally based on ecological characteristics rather than simple measures such as water hardness. The factors that influence ecosystem variability are not well understood, but ecological toxicity testing using natural communities could certainly unravel these problems. Additional work is needed to understand the natural variability of ecosystems so that ecologists and environmental scientists can distinguish between anthropogenic changes and natural oscillations in the ecosystems. Despite the ability to measure a variety of biochemical changes in systems, the identities of component species continue to be important, and failure to adequately characterize the taxonomic composition of ecosystems will result in poor detection power for scientists endeavoring to protect ecosystem structure and function.

ACKNOWLEDGEMENTS

This work was supported in part by grants from the Air Force Office of Scientific Research (AFOSR085-0324), the U.S. Environmental Protection Agency (R-812813-01-0), and the U.S. Army Biomedical Research and Development Laboratory (DAMD17-88-C-8068), and an award from the Air Force Office of Scientific Research and the Society of Environmental Toxicology and Chemistry. Opinions, interpretations, conclusions, and recommendations are those of the author and are not necessarily endorsed by the granting agencies. The assistance of N. J. Bowers is gratefully acknowledged.

REFERENCES

1. Urban, D. J., and N. J. Cook. "Hazard Evaluation Division Standard Evaluation Procedure Ecological Risk Assessment," U.S. EPA Report-540/9-85-001 (1986).

2. Vannote, R., G. W. Minshall, K. W. Cummings, J. R. Sedell, and C. E. Cushing. "The River Continuum Concept," *Can. J. Fish. Aquat. Sci.* 37:130–137 (1980).

3. Metcalfe, J. "Biological Water Quality Assessment of Running Waters Based on Macroinvertebrate Communities: History and Present Status in Europe," *Environ. Pollut.* 60:101–139 (1989).

4. Cairns, J. "Will the Real Ecotoxicologist Please Stand Up," *Environ. Toxicol. Chem.* 7:843–844 (1989).

5. *Testing for Effects of Chemicals on Ecosystems* (Washington, DC: National Academy Press, 1981), p. 103.

6. Moriarty, F. *Ecotoxicology, the Study of Pollutants in Ecosystems* (London: Academic Press, 1989), p. 289.

7. Rand, G., and S. Petrocelli. *Fundamentals of Aquatic Toxicology, Methods and Applications* (Washingon, DC: Hemisphere Publishing Corp., 1984), p. 666.

8. "Ambient Water Quality Criteria for Zinc," U.S. EPA Report-440/5-80-079 (1980).

9. "Quality Criteria for Water," U.S. EPA Report-440/5-86-001 (1986).

10. "Technical Support Document for Water Quality-Based Toxics Control," Office of Water, U.S. EPA (1974), p. 74.

11. Webster, J. R. "Hierarchical Organization of Ecosystems," in *Theoretical Systems Ecology*, A. Halfon, Ed. (New York: Academic Press, 1979), p. 119.

12. Travis, J. "Results of the Survey of the Membership of the Ecological Society of America: 1987–1988," *Bull. Ecol. Soc. Am.* 70:78–88 (1989).

13. *Environmental Trends* (Washington, DC: Council of Environmental Quality, 1989), p. 152.

14. Turner, M. G., E. P. Odum, R. Costanza, and T. M. Springer. "Market and Nonmarket Values of the Georgia Landscape," *Environ. Man.* 12:209–217 (1988).

15. Giesy, J., Ed. *Microcosms in Ecological Research* (Washington, DC: Technical Information Service, U.S. Department of Energy, 1980), p. 1110.

16. Harrass, M. C., and P. G. Sayre. "Use of Microcosm Data for Regulatory Decisions," in *Aquatic Toxicology and Hazard Assessment, 12th Volume*, U. M. Cowgill and L. R. Williams, Eds. (Philadelphia: American Society for Testing and Materials, 1989), p. 204.

17. Sheehan, P. J. "Statistical and Nonstatistical Considerations in Quantifying Pollutant-Induced Changes in Microcosms," in *Aquatic Toxicology and Hazard Assessment, 12th Volume*, U. M. Cowgill and L. R. Williams, Eds. (Philadelphia: American Society for Testing and Materials, 1989), p. 178.

18. deNoyelles, F., Jr. and W. D. Kettle. "Experimental Ponds for Evaluating Bioassay Predictions," in *Validation and Predictability of Laboratory Models for Assessing the Fate and Effects of Contaminants in Aquatic Ecosystems*, T. P. Boyle, Ed. (Philadelphia: American Society for Testing and Materials, 1985), p. 91.

19. Touart, L. "Simulated Aquatic Ecosystems to Support Pesticide Registrations," U.S. EPA Draft Report (1986), p. 18.

20. Taub, F. B., A. C. Kindig, and L. L. Conquest. "Preliminary Results of Interlaboratory Testing on a Standardized Aquatic Microcosm Protocol," in *Community Toxicity Testing*, J. Cairns, Jr., Ed. (Philadelphia: American Society for Testing and Materials, 1986), p. 158.

21. Giddings, J. M., and P. Franco. "Calibration of Laboratory Bioassays with Results from Microcosms and Ponds," in *Validation and Predictability of Laboratory Models for Assessing the Fate and Effects of Contaminants in Aquatic Eco-*

systems, T. P. Boyle, Ed. (Philadelphia: American Society for Testing and Materials, 1985), p. 104.

22. Pratt, J. R., and N. J. Bowers. "A Microcosm Procedure for Estimating Ecological Effects of Chemicals and Mixtures," *Toxicity Assess.* 5:189–205 (1990).

23. Odum, E. P. "Trends Expected in Stressed Ecosystems," *BioScience* 35:419–422 (1985).

24. Schindler, D. W. "Detecting Ecosystem Responses to Anthropogenic Stress," *Can. J. Fish. Aquat. Sci.* 44(Suppl. 1):6–25 (1987).

25. Schaeffer, D. J., E. E. Herricks, and H. W. Kerster. "Ecosystem Health. I. Measuring Ecosystem Health," *Environ. Man.* 12:445–455 (1988).

26. Preston, H. "The Commonness, and Rarity, of Species," *Ecology* 29:254–283 (1948).

27. Patrick, R. "The Effect of Invasion Rate, Species Pool, and Size of Area on the Structure of the Diatom Community," *Proc. Acad. Nat. Sci. (Phila.)* 58:335–342 (1967).

CHAPTER 3

The Case for Modeling Sediment-Water Interactions in Aquatic and Marine Systems

Donald Mackay, Miriam Diamond, and Warren Stiver

INTRODUCTION

There are numerous situations in which aquatic and marine sediments have become contaminated with metals and organic chemicals as a result of high levels of past chemical discharge. When discharges are reduced or eliminated, bottom sediments may cease to act as a net sink for contaminants and become in-place sources of contamination. Ecosystem recovery may then be retarded as chemical "bleeds" steadily from the sediments to the water column. In this chapter, we argue that when assessing the present condition of such systems, and especially when deciding on remedial measures, it is important to understand, as quantitatively as is possible, the dynamics of the contaminants in the system. This includes information on where the contaminant resides, which processes are responsible for transformation and transport between water, sediment, and biota living in both media, and, thus, how long it may take for the system to become restored naturally, in response to remedial interventions. Much of this information can, and usually is, obtained by monitoring programs, in which sediments, water, and biota are sampled and analyzed and the analytical results interpreted, but there are compelling arguments for proceeding to an even higher level of sophistication of data interpretation by compiling a mass balance model in which the rates of chemical transport and transformation are estimated. If a reliable model is available, it becomes possible to test various remedial strategies, and essentially play "environmental video games" on the computer. We believe that this procedure helps to obtain and transmit a higher level of understanding of the nature of the system and how it may respond to natural processes and to remedial measures. A comprehensive recent treatment of this issue can be found in the compilation of studies by Hites and Eisenreich.[1]

In essence, monitoring efforts yield information about concentrations that are a snapshot in time of a set of complex, dynamic, interacting processes. By assembling a model, we attempt to create a quantitative picture of the often unmeasurable and invisible dynamic processes of transport and transformation that result in these concentrations and ultimately cause ecologically adverse effects.

Our aim in this chapter is first to present a simple sediment-water interaction model, discuss various aspects and applications of the model, and explore some of its implications for probing the nature of sediment-water systems. We first assemble a relatively simple linear mass balance model in which chemical is exchanged between a well-mixed sediment layer, a well-mixed overlying water layer, and the atmosphere. We then apply the "linear additivity principle" of Stiver and Mackay[2] to this model as a method of discriminating between sources of contaminant in various components of the ecosystem, and especially the contribution of in-place pollution. We suggest that the primary incentive for efforts of this type is to gain an improved appreciation of the system for management and remediation purposes. The analysis highlights the importance of developing an improved capability of modeling sediment-water exchange processes, because it is these processes that usually control the remediation or recovery time of sediments. Accordingly, in the second part we examine in some detail a more narrowly focused model of sediment-water exchange and address questions such as:

- Which chemicals are of concern as potential in-place contaminants?
- What is the role of biomonitoring?
- Which are the most important transport and transformation processes?
- How can we best probe sediment-water dynamics and estimate process rates?

To accomplish this task, we use a simple evaluative model, similar in dimensions and properties to Lake Ontario. This enables us to draw on several recent studies of this system, notably that of Mackay.[3,4] We first examine the fate of a chemical similar to PCBs in the system and later examine the effect of changing chemical properties. Although an approximation to Lake Ontario is used as an example, it is believed that the principles presented here are applicable to other lakes, and even to near-shore and estuarine marine systems.

MODEL STRUCTURE

When assembling models of this type, we prefer to use the fugacity or aquivalence formalism as described in a series of papers by Mackay et al.,[5] Mackay and Paterson,[6] Mackay and Diamond,[7] Reuber et al.,[8] Diamond et al.,[9] and Mackay.[3,4] The fugacity approach has been described in these studies, and only a brief review of salient features is presented here. It should be emphasized that the same results can be obtained using conventional concentration-based models.

The partitioning of chemical between various phases is characterized by Z values, one Z value quantifying the capacity of each medium for each chemi-

Table 3.1. System Dimensions, Chemical Properties, Z and D Values for PCBs

System Dimensions

Lake area (m^2)	1.95×10^{10}
Water depth (m)	86
Sediment depth (m)	0.005
Water particles (g/m^3)	0.5
Sediment porosity	0.85
Particle OC content	0.2
Sediment OC content	0.0359
Solids density (kg/m^3)	2400

Chemical Properties

Molecular mass (g/mol)	326
Henry's law constant (Pa m^3/mol)	12.2
Log K_{ow}	6.6

Z Values (mol/m^3 Pa)

Z for air	0.0042
Z for water	0.0818
Z for water particles	64100
Z for sediment particles	11500
Z for biota	18900

D Values (mol/Pa hr $\times$ 10^{-6})

Burial (DB)	2.29
Sediment reaction (DS)	0.34
Sediment resuspension (DR)	2.26
Water-sediment diffusion (DT)	0.64
Sediment deposition (DD)	30.5
Water transformation (DW)	0.79
Air-water diffusion (DV)	5.43
Water inflow (DI)	1.98
Water particle inflow (DX)	15.2
Water outflow (DJ)	1.98
Water particle outflow (DY)	0.38
Rain dissolution (DM)	0.14
Wet particle deposition (DC)	14.7
Dry particle deposition (DQ)	6.1

cal. Z values, with dimensions of mol/Pa m^3, are proportionality constants that relate concentration (C, mol/m^3) to fugacity (f, Pa), i.e., C = Zf. They are deduced from the physico-chemical properties (especially the partition coefficients) of the chemical. The phases or media treated here are air, aerosols, water, suspended particulate matter, sediments and pore water, and biota in the water column and in the sediments. Z values can also be defined for bulk or mixed phases such as water containing suspended matter. The properties and Z values of a PCB-like chemical illustrated here are listed in Table 3.1, the values being essentially those suggested by Mackay.[3]

Transport and transformation rates (with units of mol/hr) are characterized by D values (with dimensions of mol/Pa hr); for example, the rate of each process is Df, the product of a D value and a fugacity. D values are calculated from quantities such as flow rates, mass transfer coefficients, and diffusivities as described earlier by Mackay.[3] The total quantity of chemical in a well-mixed medium is then VC (mol), where V is volume (m³). This amount is also VZf (mol).

In the interest of simplicity, it is assumed that air is in equilibrium with aerosol particles. water is in equilibrium with water column particles and biota, and the bottom sediment solids are in equilibrium with pore water and sediment biota. There are, thus, three fugacities in the system that characterize the concentrations throughout the system. A listing of the system dimensions, Z values, and D values, including definitions, is given in Table 3.1.

Mass balance differential equations can be written for the sediment and water compartments by equating the rate of inventory change of chemical in the system to the sum of the input rates less the sum of the output rates, resulting in Equations 3.1 and 3.2 below. The rate of direct discharge of chemical to the water is E (mol/hr), and the subscripts of fugacity f (Pa) refer to water W, inflowing water I, sediment S, air A, total water phase (including particles) WT, and total sediment phase of solids and pore water ST.

$$V_W Z_{WT} df_W/dt = f_I(DI + DX) + E + f_A(DV + DM + DC + DQ) + \\ f_S(DR + DT) - f_W(DJ + DY + DV + DW + DD + DT) \quad (3.1)$$

$$V_S Z_{ST} df_S/dt = f_W(DD + DT) - f_S(DR + DT + DS + DB) \quad (3.2)$$

Also of interest are the steady-state versions of these equations, which can be obtained by setting the derivatives equal to zero. This yields Equations 3.3 and 3.4 below, which can be solved to give Equation 3.5, in which the water fugacity, f_W, is a function of only the input parameters. The sediment fugacity, f_S, is calculated from Equation 3.4.

$$f_W = \frac{f_I(DI + DX) + E + f_A(DV + DM + DC + DQ) + f_S(DR + DT)}{DJ + DY + DV + DW + DD + DT} \quad (3.3)$$

$$f_S = \frac{f_W(DD + DT)}{(DR + DT + DS + DB)} \quad (3.4)$$

$$f_W = \frac{f_I(DI + DX) + E + f_A(DV + DM + DC + DQ)}{DJ + DY + DV + DW + \dfrac{(DD + DT)(DS + DB)}{(DR + DT + DS + DB)}} \quad (3.5)$$

$$f_W = \frac{f_I(DI + DX)}{DTOT} + \frac{E}{DTOT} + \frac{f_A(DV + DM + DC + DQ)}{DTOT} \quad (3.6)$$

where DTOT is the sum of the D terms in the denominator of Equation 3.5.

A noteworthy feature of these equations is the presence in the numerator of Equation 3.5 of the three input terms to the system as a simple linear addition, i.e., the inputs from water inflow to the system, direct discharges, and from the atmosphere. Equation 3.5 can thus be rewritten in the form of Equation

3.6 as the sum of three separate terms, each representing that part of the water fugacity attributable to the specific input term. Since the sediment fugacity and the sediment biota fugacities and concentrations are directly related to the water fugacity, it is clear that the concentrations in these compartments and the chemical masses attributable to the specific inputs can also be calculated individually and added to give the total. The model thus permits the total fugacities (and hence the concentrations) to be decoupled into contributions from each source, i.e., "blame" can be assigned quantitatively.

For illustrative purposes, concentrations can also be calculated in water column and sediment biota by assuming equi-fugacity and a lipid content of 5%, i.e., the bioconcentration factor is $0.05 \, K_{ow}$, where K_{ow} is the octanol-water partition coefficient. This attribution of concentrations to sources is only possible if all expressions in the model equations are linear.

APPLICATIONS OF THE WHOLE LAKE MODEL

Figure 3.1 and Table 3.2 give the results of the steady-state mass balance calculation (Equations 3.4 and 3.5) for assumed chemical inputs in air (as f_A or C_A), in water (as f_I or C_I), and by direct discharge (E). The important processes are clearly deposition, resuspension, volatilization, and burial. Quite different fate profiles would be obtained for other chemicals that are more volatile, or reactive, or less hydrophobic. Figure 3.1 contains a wealth of process information not available from perusal of concentration data alone.

Table 3.2 consists of rows corresponding to selected output quantities from the model, such as concentrations, masses, and fugacities. These quantities are regarded as being the key descriptors of the condition of the chemical within the system. The columns represent values obtained as a result of various calculations. The first column is observed or monitored data for the status of the chemical at a particular point in time, typical of data which would be obtained as a result of a conventional monitoring program. The values are similar to those reported for PCBs in Lake Ontario in the mid-1980s.[3] Column 2 and the data in Figure 3.1 are the result of steady-state calculation of the concentrations and fugacities assuming all three inputs to apply, i.e., using Equations 3.3 and 3.4. Column 3 gives the values obtained by assuming only inputs by direct discharge. Column 4 treats only input by advective inflow, and Column 5 has input only from the air. Essentially, columns 2, 3, 4, and 5 are the results of applying Equation 3.6, first in total, then term by term.

It is obvious by inspection of both the numbers and their algebraic origin that columns 3, 4, and 5 add to give column 2. It is thus possible to assert that the calculated steady-state concentration in the ecosystem as calculated in column 2 is attributable 86% to water inflow, 4% to direct discharges, and 10% to atmospheric sources.

Column 6 is obtained by subtracting column 2 from column 1. This set of quantities represents mathematically the unsteady-state contributions to the

Table 3.2. System Response to Various Inputs

	Col. 1 Observed Concentrations	Col. 2 3 Inputs	Col. 3 Discharge Only	Col. 4 Water Inflow Only	Col. 5 Air Concentration Only	Col. 6 Unsteady Contribution
Input Data						
Air concentration (ng/m^3)	—	0.512	0	0	0.512	
Water inflow concentration (ng/L)	—	10	0	10	0	
Discharges (kg/year)	—	100	100	0	0	
Air source (kg/year)	—	254	0	0	254	
Water source (kg/year)	—	2097	0	2097	0	
Water Column Data						
Concentration (ng/L)	1.5	1.14	0.04	0.97	0.12	0.36
Fugacity (nPa)	48	36.7	1.5	31.4	3.8	11
Mass of chemical (kg)	2500	1900	77	1626	197	600
Bottom Sediment Data						
Concentration (ng/g)	500	323	13	276	34	177
Fugacity (nPa)	320	207	8.4	177	21.4	113
Mass of chemical (kg)	17500	11310	461	9675	1174	6200
Biotic Data						
Water col. concentration (µg/g)	0.3	0.19	0.01	0.16	0.02	0.11
Sediment concentration (µg/g)	—	1.10	0.04	0.94	0.11	—
Percent of Col. 2	—	100	4.0	85.6	10.4	—
Percent of Col. 1 (Sediment concentration)	100	65	3	55	7	35

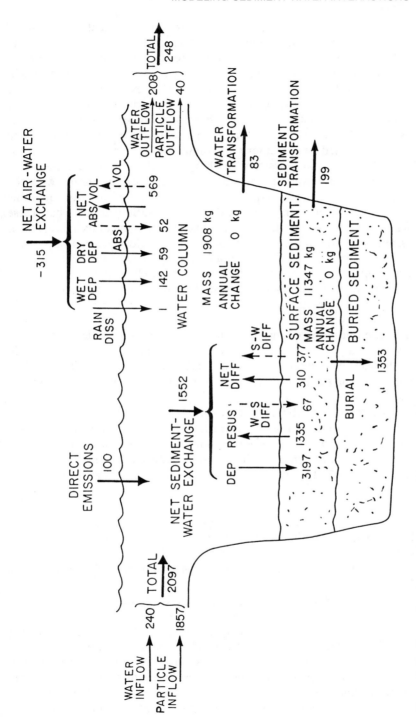

Figure 3.1.   Comprehensive steady-state mass balance with all rates in kg/year.

present condition. It also contains any error that may be present in the model; however, for purposes of this discussion we assume that the model is correct and that the difference is entirely attributable to the unsteady-state nature of the response of the system. The agreement between the water concentrations in columns 1 and 2 is fairly good and could be within experimental error, but there is obviously a severe discrepancy between the sediment concentrations. This is probably attributable to past discharges at higher-than-present levels that caused, at that time, higher water and sediment concentrations. The sediment has retained the memory of these higher discharge rates. For example, in this case it appears that discharges in the recent past may have been about twice the current estimated values, resulting in about twice the present calculated steady-state sediment concentration. Neither the equations nor the quantities in column 6 contain any information about when these discharges took place or their magnitudes. The amounts in column 6 represent an excess amount, now present, over values that would eventually prevail if current levels of input were to be maintained over time. In the event that air inflow and discharge rates were maintained indefinitely at the values used to deduce column 2, the system would adjust eventually to the values in column 2. The contribution in column 6 would gradually decay to zero, as depicted in Figure 3.2.

In practice, because there is error in the analyses and the model, and spatial variability in the aquatic ecosystem, it is more rigorous to present the data in columns 1 to 6 as best estimates with confidence intervals. This will help avoid over-interpreting the data and may show, for example, that certain column 6 quantities may be zero.

Of obvious interest is the time that will be required for decay of the unsteady-state component to take place; that is, will it be 1 year or 20 years? Determination of an accurate response time requires numerical integration. An approximate response time can, however, be deduced by mere inspection of Equations 3.1 and 3.2. These equations take the form of Equation 3.7 below:

$$VZ \, df/dt = I - f \, D_E \qquad (3.7)$$

where I is the sum of the input terms and D_E is the sum of the D values by which chemical can leave the compartment; that is, it is the total "exit" D value. Assuming I to be constant and integrating from initial fugacity f_O gives

$$f = I/D_E + (f_O - I/D_E) \exp(-D_E \, t/VZ) \qquad (3.8)$$

Clearly the rate constant is D_E/VZ. Its reciprocal, the characteristic time, that is, the time to approach to approximately 70% of equilibrium or steady state, is VZ/D_E. In this case the response times are 0.46 years for water and 3.5 years for sediment. In reality these are minimum response times since they contain the assumption that chemical that has left a compartment, such as sediment, will not return to that compartment. In practice, contaminant released from

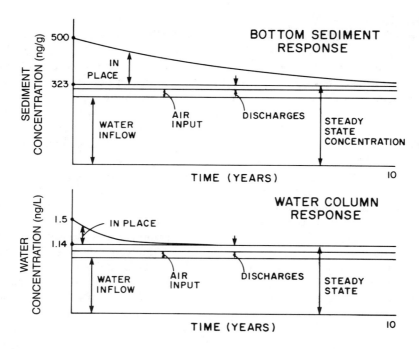

Figure 3.2.   Illustrative unsteady-state response of bottom sediment and water column to a new steady state, showing the relative proportions of the in-place water inflow (Niagara River), air inputs, and direct discharges. The more rapid water response is apparent.

the sediment to the water will return, at least to some extent, to the sediment to prolong the recovery time. A more realistic and longer recovery time can be estimated by multiplying the above time by a factor corresponding to the fraction of the material that, on leaving the compartment, will never return. If this is done it increases the sediment response time to 6 years. Obviously, the sediment response time is directly dependent on the sediment volume or depth selected, which in this case is only 5 mm. Increasing this by a factor of ten, to 5 cm, would cause a tenfold increase in response time; that is, clearance would take ten times longer. This depth is clearly a critically important parameter in controlling the recovery time.

The most reliable way of estimating these recovery times is to undertake a numerical integration of Equations 3.1 and 3.2, calculate the changing concentrations over time, and read off the response time from a plot similar to that in Figure 3.2. The value obtained should be similar in magnitude to the response times deduced approximately above. Analytical solution is also possible, but the resulting equations are too complex to be easily interpreted.

It is now possible to assert that the present sediment concentration as observed in column 1 can be broken down as follows: 55% is attributable to advective Niagara River inflow, 3% is attributable to current discharges, 7% is attributable to atmospheric sources at present concentration levels, and 35% is attributable to in-place contamination resulting from previous, higher-than-present loadings. Corresponding values can be obtained for water and biotic concentrations. It is believed that this calculation can be very useful from a management point of view because it indicates the extent to which recent and planned measures to reduce the sources of contamination will be sufficient to achieve (eventually) desired low levels. For example, if in-place contribution is 90% of the total, there is probably little justification for reducing present inputs further. If the in-place contribution is only 20%, then further reduction of inputs is obviously indicated. The model thus assists the regulator in assigning resources in the most effective way, i.e., to source reduction, or to attempts to remediate in-place contamination. There is little merit in remediating if the inputs are such that recontamination will occur.

Obviously of critical importance in this decision is the response time of the sediment, but in some cases it may also be important to assess the water column response time. The simplest method of assessing the relative contributions of the water and the sediment is to calculate the mass of contaminant in each compartment. In this case, the water contains 12% of the contaminant, and the sediment 88%; thus, it is clear that most of the contaminant is bound up in a slowly responding sediment compartment, and it is the rate at which this compartment can clear chemical that will control the system's recovery. It is on the detailed determinants of this rate of clearance or recovery that we focus next.

SEDIMENT-WATER EXCHANGE PROCESSES

In this section, we explore the mechanisms of transport of chemicals of varying hydrophobicity between the water column and the sediment. This analysis is similar to that of Diamond et al. for radio-isotopes with varying sorptive tendencies.[9] We apply the model developed earlier with the same parameters, but we allow the chemical's octanol-water partition coefficient (K_{ow}) to vary from 10^3 to 10^8, all other properties being identical. This has the effect of changing the D values for any process in which the chemical is partitioned, transported, or transformed in an organic phase, notably the bottom and suspended sediment and biotic phases. We assume that there is a constant total concentration in the water column in all cases of 1.14 ng/L of chemical, and we calculate the steady-state sediment fugacity and concentration from this water concentration using Equation 3.4. Biotic concentrations are also deduced by assuming equifugacity with the residing medium.

It is useful at this stage to examine the terms in Equation 3.2 in more detail. Transport from the water column to the sediment occurs by two mechanisms, diffusion in the water column (described by DT) and transport associated with settling organic matter (described by DD). Transport of chemical from water to sediment is thus accomplished in parallel in two distinct phases, in solution in water and in association with particulate organic carbon. The relative importance of these transfer routes depends on the organic carbon to water partition coefficient K_{oc}, which depends on K_{ow}, the octanol-water partition coefficient. When K_{oc} or K_{ow} is large, it is expected that most transfer will take place in association with particulate organic carbon. When K_{ow} is small, the transfer will be primarily in water solution. It is not, however, clear over which ranges of K_{ow} values one or the other mechanism will predominate. We do not treat any partitioning or transport influenced by dissolved or colloidal organic carbon.

Transport of contaminant from sediment to water also occurs by two parallel processes: in solution in water, described by DT, and in association with particulate organic matter, described by DR. The resuspension term DR includes material conveyed from the sediment layer back into the water column as a result of disturbances of a hydrodynamic or biological origin, and it could be modified to include diffusion of organic colloids containing absorbed chemical. DR is thus viewed as expressing the sum of all processes conveying chemical from sediment to water in association with organic matter, whether the organic matter be on sediment solids or in colloids. Again, as K_{ow} increases, it is expected that most chemical transport from sediment to water will be in association with these organic phases.

It is noteworthy that DD is about ten times DR; that is, deposition is potentially ten times faster than resuspension. There are two reasons. The mass of depositing material is greater, because some is buried and thus fails to be resuspended. More importantly, the organic carbon content of the settling material is 20%, compared with only 3.6% for the resuspended, partly mineralized material.[3] Hydrophobic chemicals are thus readily conveyed to the bottom but have difficulty returning to the water because of the lack of available organic carbon carrier. It is assumed that when the organic carbon is mineralized, the chemical is "freed" and partitions onto the remaining organic carbon, or remains in the pore water.

The other two chemical removal processes in the sediment, burial and reaction, apply to the bulk chemical in the sediment regardless of whether it is sorbed to solids or associated with the pore water. Generally, however, because of the relatively high solids concentration in the sediment of typically 10 to 30%, most chemical will be associated with solids and very little will be in dissolved form. This contrasts with the water column, in which generally most chemical will be in dissolved form, and only when K_{ow} is very large, will there be a significant fraction of the chemical associated with the particulate and colloidal phases.

The model was run for a series of chemicals of log K_{ow} ranging from 3 to 8, including PCBs. The results are summarized in Table 3.3 and are discussed in sequence below. In the interests of brevity, the chemicals are referred to as chemicals 3, 4, 5, etc., corresponding to their log K_{ow} values.

Table 3.3. Effect of Varying K_{ow} on Sediment-Water Exchange Processes

log K_{ow}	3	4	5	6	6.6 (PCB)	7	8
Concentration in water (g/m³)							
Total	1.14	1.14	1.14	1.14	1.14	1.14	1.14
Dissolved	1.14	1.14	1.13	1.09	0.98	0.81	0.22
Sorbed	0.0001	0.001	0.01	0.05	0.16	.33	0.92
Fugacity in water (nPa)	42.7	42.7	42.5	41.0	36.7	30.3	8.4
Fugacity in sediment (nPa)	43.1	46.9	78.5	182.5	20.7	181.1	52.0
Concentration in sediment μg/g	1.7×10^{-5}	1.8×10^{-4}	3×10^{-3}	7.1×10^{-2}	0.3	0.7	2.0
Ratio f_s/f_w	1.01	1.10	1.85	4.45	5.6	6.0	6.2
Biotic concentration (μg/g)							
In water	6×10^{-5}	6×10^{-4}	6×10^{-3}	0.05	0.19	0.4	1.12
In sediment	6×10^{-5}	6×10^{-4}	10×10^{-3}	0.24	1.10	2.4	6.94
Transfer rates (kg/year)							
Water-sediment transfer	78.7	87.0	170.4	971	3264	6678	18325
Deposition	0.9	9.3	93	897	3197	6623	18310
Diffusion	77.8	77.7	77.4	74	67	55	15
Sediment to water transfer	78.6	86.2	155.6	628	1712	3266	8525
Resuspension	.1	0.8	12.7	295	1335	2935	8430
Diffusion	78.5	85.4	142.9	332	377	330	95
Burial	.07	0.8	12.9	300	1353	2976	8546
Reaction	.01	0.1	1.9	44	199	436	1253
Mass in water (kg)	1908	1908	1908	1908	1908	1908	1908
Mass in sediment (kg)	0.7	7	108	2514	11347	25000	71680
Ratio s/w masses	0.0003	0.003	0.06	1.32	5.9	13.1	38
Residence times (years)							
Water	24	22	11	2	0.6	0.3	0.1
Sediment	0.01	0.1	0.6	2.6	3.5	3.7	3.9

Condition in the Water Column

The water column concentration of sorbing organic matter is assumed to be approximately 0.1 ppm; thus only when log K_{ow} exceeds 6 is there an appreciable fraction of the chemical sorbed to the suspended matter. Chemicals 3, 4, and 5 are almost entirely in solution, 6 is 5% sorbed, 7 is nearly equipartitioned, and chemical 8 is only 20% in solution. As a result, the water column fugacities of chemicals 3, 4, 5, and 6 are fairly constant, most chemical being in dissolved form and thus able to exert its full fugacity. The water column fugacity falls for 7, and more significantly for 8. The mass of chemical in the water column is a constant 1900 kg because of the imposed constant concentration.

The equilibrium concentration in water column biota (e.g., small fish) increases steadily and linearly with K_{ow} from negligible values for chemicals 3 and 4, to approximately 0.05 $\mu g/g$ for 6, 0.4 $\mu g/g$ for 7, and 1.1 $\mu g/g$ for 8. There is thus a tendency for this increase in concentration to level off. Although the organism-to-water partition coefficient is steadily increasing, the fraction of the chemical available or "bioavailable" in the water column to accomplish this partitioning is decreasing. The high bioaccumulation levels expected with very hydrophobic chemicals are therefore offset significantly by competitive partitioning into particulate (and also colloidal) organic matter in the water column. In reality, there may be a kinetic limitation to partitioning of chemicals 7 and 8; thus, lower concentrations may be encountered. Further, as discussed by Thomann,[10] the food chain effect becomes more important than water-to-lipid partitioning; thus, this simple calculation could be misleading. It does, however, show the nature of the basic dependence of bioconcentration on K_{ow}, and on bioavailability as controlled by the organic matter content of the water column.

Condition in the Sediment

The sediment fugacities increase relatively slowly for chemicals 3, 4, and 5, with values similar to, but somewhat exceeding, those in the water column. The ratio of sediment-to-water fugacity rises from about 1 to about 1.8 because decomposition or mineralization of the deposited organic carbon increases the concentration of chemical in the remaining organic carbon, and thus causes an increase in the chemical's fugacity. Essentially the "solvent" is partially removed. If there was no mineralization of the organic carbon, the fugacity in the sediment would be approximately equal to that of the water. If the chemical were to react significantly in the sediment, the fugacity would be reduced. When DT is large compared to DD and DR (i.e., the chemical is less hydrophobic), diffusion tends to restore equi-fugacity between sediment and water. This raises an interesting point: in monitoring programs it may be valuable to examine the equilibrium status of the sediment relative to that of the water. This has been attempted by Murphy,[11] who has undertaken air stripping experiments to show that in lake systems the sediment and water fugacities are similar in magnitude.

It would be interesting to examine a wide range of lake sediment and water column data, to test the assertion that the fugacities are similar in magnitude, and to explore if there is some systematic variation in their fugacity ratios with parameters such as K_{ow} and organic carbon fate.

The steady-state sediment concentrations rise from negligible values for chemical 3 approximately in proportion to K_{ow}, but with a tendency to level off for chemicals 7 and 8. The mass of chemical in the sediment rises correspondingly; thus, the ratio of the mass of chemical in the sediment to mass in water is very small for chemicals 3, 4, and 5, and about equal for chemical 6, while for 7 and 8, the mass in the sediment greatly exceeds that in the water. If there is an in-place contaminant problem, the contaminant will be in-place in the water for chemicals 3, 4, and 5, and in the sediment for 6, 7, and 8. Since water is usually advected from the system fairly rapidly, except in very large lakes such as Lake Superior, the in-place pollution problem generally lies (as is intuitively obvious) in the sediment.

Chemical concentrations in the benthos track the concentrations in the sediment generally with a constant ratio, because in both benthos and solids the contaminant is dissolved in an organic carbon or lipid matrix, which have generally similar properties. This relationship between benthic and sediment concentrations has been noted by Connor[12] and discussed by Reuber et al.[8] The biota concentrations in the water track the fugacity in the water column and are generally similar in magnitude to those of the sediments, but because the fugacity effect in the sediment tends to exceed that in the water, the benthos usually have a greater contaminant concentration than water column organisms.

The results suggest gathering and analyzing data on water column and sediment biotic concentrations, preferably normalized on a lipid basis. Indeed, biotic concentrations may be the most reliable indicators of fugacities in the system, at least for chemicals that are not metabolized. Detailed examination of these fugacities by Connolly has shown that, in practice, most benthic organisms are at a somewhat higher fugacity than the sediment,[13] perhaps due to the consumption of organic carbon, which increases the contaminant fugacity by a simple concentration mechanism.

Recently Ferraro et al. have undertaken a comprehensive test of such a fugacity-based model and, in addition to providing an excellent review of this growing literature, have shown that the fugacity, or "accumulation factor," model gives a satisfactory description of the basic relationship between levels of sediment and benthic biota contamination.[14]

Water-to-Sediment Transfer

The calculated water-to-sediment transfer process rates suggest that diffusion rates are relatively constant for chemicals 3 to 6, whereas particle deposition increases greatly with K_{ow}. As a result of the preferential partitioning of chemical into these particles, the deposition rate tends to reach a maximum when virtually all the chemical in the water column is sorbed and is subject to particle deposition. Although water-phase processes are most important for low K_{ow} chemicals, particle transport becomes most important at high K_{ow} values, as was suggested earlier.

In this series of calculations a constant water column concentration was arbitrarily imposed on the system. If a constant chemical input rate had been imposed, the water column concentrations would have been very low for the high K_{ow} chemicals because of the efficient removal. In practice, it would be difficult to sustain a large water column concentration of a very hydrophobic chemical without very large emission rates, which would be equivalent to the large calculated deposition rates.

If the amount in the water column (kg) is divided by the transfer rates (kg/year), a clearance time is obtained. This is the time necessary for the removal processes to substantially deplete the water column of chemical. As is shown in Table 3.3, this is very long for chemicals 3, 4, and 5, but it becomes fairly short for chemicals 6, 7, and 8. The implication is that hydrophobic chemicals present in the water column will be appreciably removed by deposition, while more hydrophilic chemicals will tend to remain in the water to be removed by other processes such as evaporation, water advection, diffusion, and biodegradation.

The very short water residence times for chemicals 7 and 8 are unrealistic because deposition will be limited by the velocity at which particles can settle, i.e., about 1 m per day, and by the seasonal fluctuations in particulate organic carbon content of the water column. The equations contain the inherent assumption that conditions are well-mixed and constant throughout the year; thus, residence times of a fraction of a year are possible. In reality the seasonal fluctuations invalidate this simple assumption. The key point is that the model shows that for very hydrophobic chemicals, deposition will be controlled by the particulate organic carbon budget, not by K_{ow}.

Sediment-to-Water Transfer and Sediment Losses

Considering the reverse processes contributing to loss of chemical from sediment, the total rate must, of course, equal the rate of transport from the water. Diffusion in solution from sediment to water generally exceeds that from water to sediment because of the higher sediment fugacity, but the diffusive rates are only significant for low K_{ow} chemicals — 3, 4, 5, and 6.

Transport of chemical to the water column in association with particulate organic carbon becomes more important as K_{ow} increases. This transport can occur either by direct resuspension of sediment solids or by diffusion of organic colloids containing the chemical. There is considerable uncertainty about these rates; however, it appears that they may be comparable in magnitude. Since both involve the same medium for transport, the ratio of resuspension-to-colloid diffusion rates should be fairly constant.

The burial and reaction terms generally involve the removal of chemical from a fixed proportion of the sediment volume per year. Thus, since most of the chemical is associated with the organic carbon, or at least with the solid phase, these rates increase in parallel with the resuspension rates. Here the ratio of rates are approximately resuspension, 8; burial, 8; reaction, 1; with diffusion being variable. It must be emphasized that, as discussed by Mackay,[3] the assumed reaction rate is purely illustrative, but it is believed to be reasonable in magnitude. Although constant reaction rates and burial rates are assumed here, the magnitude of the absolute rate (kg/year) increases significantly with K_{ow} because of the larger mass of chemical in the sediment that is susceptible to these processes. Thus, even very slow reactions, with half-lives measured in decades, can become very significant as removal processes for hydrophobic chemicals that are predominantly partitioned into the sediments, and remain there for periods of decades prior to burial.

Finally, the clearance time for chemical from sediment can be calculated as the ratio of the amount in the sediment to the transfer rate to, or from, the sediment. This time is very short for chemicals 3, 4, and 5 but increases to about 4 years for the more hydrophobic chemicals. This time is very sensitive to the assumed sediment depth. This reinforces the concept that sediment plays a relatively minor role for chemicals 3, 4, and 5 since its capacity for these chemicals is limited, and there is rapid transport of these chemicals back to the water column.

Some of these findings are consolidated in Figure 3.3, which shows the water-to-sediment and sediment loss processes. For chemicals 3, 4, and 5, which are primarily in a dissolved state, diffusion from water to sediment, and sediment to water, are the dominant exchange mechanisms, with most chemical remaining in the water column and the sediment playing a relatively minor role. For chemicals 6, 7, and 8, most chemical is transported in association with particulate organic carbon, and it is the solids' behavior that controls the chemicals' dynamics. Most chemical is associated with the sediment, and the water plays a relatively minor role. Processes in which the chemicals are transported in the water phase are unimportant. These deductions are, of course, sensitive to the ratio of water-to-sediment depths of the system (here 17200). It is when the sediment-water partition coefficient equals this number that the "switch" from hydrophilic water-dominated to hydrophobic sediment-solids-dominated behavior tends to occur. This ratio may be a useful descriptor of lake characteristics, varying from about 10^4 for deep lakes, to 10^2 for shallow lakes, and in the extreme to about 1.0 for wetlands or marshes. Resuspension, colloid diffusion, burial, and reaction each tends to contribute a constant proportion to the overall loss process. Throughout the range of chemical hydrophobicity, the fugacity of a conservative chemical in the sediment should be comparable to that in the water, and the biotic concentrations should show

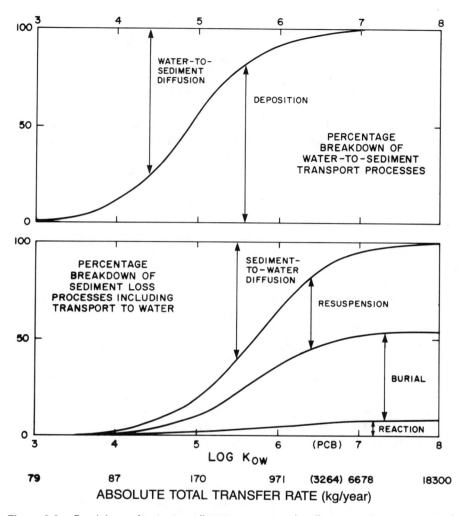

Figure 3.3. Breakdown of water-to-sediment transport and sediment-to-water transport and transformation processes at steady state under the conditions defined in Table 3.3.

similar behavior, with a biomagnification effect of uncertain magnitude tending to increase biotic fugacities.

DISCUSSION

This analysis has demonstrated what are believed to be the likely general behavior patterns of chemicals as they exchange between the water column and sediment as a function of K_{ow}, or the related particle-to-water partition coefficient. Obviously, when there are relatively fast removal processes in the water column—for example, evaporation, biodegradation, or water flow, as may occur in rivers—these simple relationships will break down.

The principal weakness in this discussion is the assumption of a well-mixed sediment layer. Greater fidelity to actual conditions could be obtained by invoking multiple layers and defining rates of transport of pore water, sediment solids, and colloids between these layers. However, as more layers are introduced, the model becomes more complex, and there is a corresponding need for more transport and transformation rate data as a function of depth in the sediment. Studies of multilayer transport have been most valuable when examining sediment chronology, i.e., the nature of sediment concentration profiles as a function of depth or time of chemical entry into the aquatic system, as has been discussed, for example, by Charles and Hites,[15] Christensen and Goetz,[16] and for Lake Ontario by Eisenreich et al.[17]

In many respects, the problem of calculating the behavior of chemicals in sediment is similar to that of calculating the behavior of chemicals in soils exposed to the atmosphere. Transfer to the atmosphere by evaporation is strongly dependent on the depth of chemical incorporation into the soil. This has been discussed by Stiver and Mackay,[2] who suggested a procedure, essentially the one originally presented by Christensen and Goetz,[16] that it should be possible to use linear mathematical models to calculate the fate of unit concentration of chemical in each layer. This is depicted schematically in Figure 3.4, in which hypothetical times are suggested. For example, after 5 years, of the amount of chemical initially in layer 3, 5% will return to the water column, 10% will move to layer 1, 15% will rise to layer 2, 20% will remain in layer 3, 10% will degrade, and the remaining 40% will be conveyed to greater depths in layers 4, 5, and 6, largely as a result of burial. It can thus be argued that after 5 years the water column will be exposed to 5% of the chemical now present in layer 3. This figure will ultimately rise to, say, 8%. A similar analysis may show that 25% of chemical in layer 2 will return to the water. Chemical presently deeper than layer 4 may be essentially permanently isolated from the water column. By examining observed sediment profiles with such mass balance statements in matrix form, it may be possible to estimate the amount of chemical in the sediment that is, or will become, accessible to the water column. If the estimated exposure is too large, remedial actions such as dredging or capping may be desirable. Regrettably, there is a tendency for much of the excellent work on sediment transport chronology to be under-utilized for practical purposes because of the complexity of the mathematics involved and the problem of translating the results into readily assimilable form. We suggest that by presenting the results of these mathematical models in terms of simple unit responses in matrix form, it should be possible to facilitate and encourage the use of these data in support of regulatory decisionmaking.

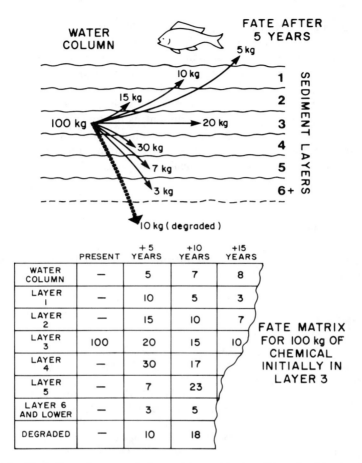

Figure 3.4. Illustration of a mass balance fate matrix describing the future behavior of chemical presently in a layer of contaminated sediment. Similar matrices could be compiled for other layers and for various time periods. It is thus possible to estimate the effective depth at which contaminant becomes essentially inaccessible to the water column.

CONCLUSIONS

In this chapter, we have first suggested that by having available a reliable, simple, linear model of an aquatic system, it may be possible to discriminate between sources of chemical contamination, such as atmospheric deposition, direct discharges, and advective inflow, and also to quantify the contribution from in-place pollution. It is believed that by using this approach, the regulatory decisionmaking process can be improved. Second, by exploring the fate of a range of chemicals in an evaluative lake, certain generalizations of contaminant behavior emerge. Most important is the assertion that for low K_{ow} chemicals, water-phase processes are most important; for high K_{ow} chemicals, the fate of particulate organic carbon is critical. An intermediate range exists in which both processes are important. It is suggested that examining the equilibrium status of chemicals (as a supplement to concentrations) present in water, sediment, and their biota has the potential to bring enhanced insights into chemical behavior in these important, and still inadequately understood, systems. Finally, there is an incentive to develop a deeper understanding of the fundamental chemical dynamics in sediment as a function of depth in order that the major weaknesses imposed by assuming a single well-mixed layer to apply can be remedied. These depths and dynamics ultimately control the capacity of sediment to retain chemicals or to return them to recontaminate the overlying aquatic ecosystem.

ACKNOWLEDGMENT

The authors are grateful to the Ontario Ministry of the Environment for financial support.

REFERENCES

1. Hites, R. A., and S. J. Eisenreich. *Sources and Fates of Aquatic Pollutants,* American Chemical Society Advances in Chemistry Series 216 (Washington, DC: American Chemical Society, 1987).
2. Stiver, W., and D. Mackay. "The Linear Additivity Principle in Environmental Modelling: Application to Chemical Behavior in Soil," *Chemosphere* 19:1187–1198 (1989).
3. Mackay, D. "Modeling the Long Term Behavior of an Organic Contaminant in a Large Lake: Application to PCBs in Lake Ontario," *J. Great Lakes Res.* 15(2):283–297 (1989).
4. Mackay, D. "Atmospheric Contributions to Contamination of Lake Ontario," in *Long Range Transport of Pesticides,* D. A. Kurtz, Ed. (Chelsea, MI: Lewis Publishers, 1990), Chapter 21, pp. 317–326.
5. Mackay, D., M. Joy, and S. Paterson. "A Quantitative Water, Air, Sediment Interaction (QWASI) Fugacity Model for Describing the Fate of Chemicals in Lakes," *Chemosphere* 12:981–997 (1983).
6. Mackay, D., and S. Paterson. "Fugacity Revisited," *Environ. Sci. Technol.* 16:654A-660A (1982).
7. Mackay, D., and M. L. Diamond. "Application of the QWASI (Quantitative Water Air Sediment Interaction) Model to the Dynamics of Organic and Inorganic Chemicals in Lakes," *Chemosphere* 18:1343–1365 (1989).
8. Reuber, B., D. Mackay, S. Paterson, and P. Stokes. "A Discussion of Chemical Equilibrium and Transport at the Sediment Water Interface," *Environ. Toxicol. Chem.* 6:731–739 (1987).
9. Diamond, M. L., D. Mackay, J. Cornett, and L. A. Chant. "A Model of Exchange of Inorganic Chemicals between Water and Sediments," *Environ. Sci. Technol.* 24:713–722 (1990).

10. Thomann, R. V. "Bioaccumulation Model of Organic Chemical Distribution in Aquatic Food Chains," *Environ. Sci. Technol.* 23:699–707 (1989).
11. Murphy, T. J., D. L. Galinis, and C. Arnold. "The Activity in PCBs in Sediment and Water from Lake Calumet and Waukegan Harbor," Report HWRICRRO39, Hazardous Waste Research and Information Center, Savoy, IL (1989).
12. Connor, M. S. "Fish/Sediment Concentration Ratios for Organic Compounds," *Environ. Sci. Technol.* 18:31–35 (1984).
13. Connolly, J. P., T. Parkerton, and R. V. Thomann. "Factors Controlling the Accumulation of Organic Chemicals from Sediments," paper presented at 33rd IAGLR Conference on Great Lakes Research, Windsor, Ontario, May 1990.
14. Ferraro, S. P., H. L. Lee, R. J. Ozretich, and D. T. Specht. "Predicting Bioconcentration Potential: A Test of a Fugacity Based Model," *Arch. Environ. Contam. Toxicol.* 19:386–394 (1990).
15. Charles, M. J., and R. A. Hites. "Sediments as Archives of Environmental Pollution Trends," in *Sources and Fates of Aquatic Pollutants,* American Chemical Society Advances in Chemistry Series 216, R. A. Hites and S. J. Eisenreich, Eds. (Washington, DC: American Chemical Society, 1987), Chapter 12, pp. 365–389.
16. Christensen, E. R. and R. H. Goetz. "Historical Fluxes of Particle-Bound Pollutants from Deconvoluted Sedimentary Records," *Environ. Sci. Technol.* 21:1088–1096 (1987).
17. Eisenreich, S. J., P. D. Copel, J. A. Robbins, and R. Bourbonniere. "Accumulation and Diagenesis of Chlorinated Hydrocarbons in Lacustrine Sediments," *Environ. Sci. Technol.* 23:1116–1129 (1989).

CHAPTER **4**

Application of Biotechnology to Water Quality Monitoring

Ivor T. Knight and Rita R. Colwell

INTRODUCTION

The fields of molecular genetics and, in particular, recombinant DNA technology have enabled the development of new approaches to environmental monitoring. One area of research is the use of DNA and RNA hybridization probes to identify contaminating microorganisms in water systems. Probes that are specific for selected indicator organisms or pathogens have already been produced and are being tested for use in determining the microbiological quality of drinking, fishing, and recreational waters. A second approach is the use of genetically engineered microorganisms as biosensors to indicate the concentration of toxic contaminants in a given environment more sensitively than can be done by traditional chemical methods and instrumentation. Both of these approaches employ the novel tools of molecular biology to improve both the specificity and sensitivity of water quality assays. This overview discusses both the theory and practice of these approaches and evaluates their application to future water quality monitoring methodology.

HYBRIDIZATION PROBES

The basis of the hybridization probe assay is the ability of complementary single strands of nucleic acid to form stable, double-stranded structures via base pairing. The reaction, commonly termed *renaturation* or *annealing,* can occur between two strands of DNA, two strands of RNA, or between a strand of RNA and a strand of DNA. Since renaturation results in hydrogen bonds between complementary bases in each strand, conditions that affect hydrogen bonding, such as temperature and ionic strength, can influence the specificity of the reaction. If, for example, hybridization is performed under conditions that approach those in which the hybrid is unstable, then only highly complimentary strands will form stable hybrids. These conditions are referred to as

65

high stringency conditions because they require that both strands be well matched for them to anneal. Low stringency hybridization conditions are achieved by lowering the temperature and raising the concentration of monovalent cations and result in formation of hybrids between strands which are not as well matched.

Nucleic acid probes are molecules of single-stranded DNA or RNA that have been labeled, either chemically or radioactively, so that they can be detected in a mixture of renatured nucleic acids. The probe is incubated with denatured test DNA or RNA (often total cellular DNA) and, under appropriate conditions, hybridizes with regions of the test nucleic acid that are complementary (target sequence). Excess, unhybridized probe is selectively removed and probe:target hybrids are detected using methods appropriate to the particular labeling strategy. If, for example, the probe is radioactively labeled, it can be detected by autoradiography or liquid scintillation counting. Nonradioactive labels are generally detected using a color development system.

The most common format for the probe hybridization assay is the mixed-phase or membrane hybridization assay, pioneered by Southern.[1] Test DNA or RNA is denatured and allowed to bind to nitrosylated cellulose membrane (nitrocellulose), a nylon-based membrane, or a membrane composed of a nylon-nitrocellulose mixture. These membranes bind single-stranded nucleic acids reversibly, but by heat treatment or by exposure to ultraviolet light the DNA can be linked covalently to the membrane, with the target sequence available for hybridization with probe nucleic acid. After incubation with the probe (hybridization), excess unhybridized probe is washed from the filter, and the filter is examined for presence and amount of hybridized probe. Discussion of the theory and practice of mixed-phase hybridization is provided by Meinkoth and Wahl.[2]

DNA and RNA hybridization probes offer a means of circumventing one of the acute problems encountered in the assessment of the microbiological quality of water, namely, determining the degree of contamination by pathogenic and indicator microorganisms which cannot be easily cultured in the laboratory. Since present microbiological analyses rely upon cultivation procedures before a determination is made,[3] organisms that grow poorly or cannot be cultured will be grossly underestimated. This is especially a problem for enumeration of viruses, but can also be a significant problem for bacteria, as well.

The efficacy of culturing methods for detection of bacterial pathogens from water samples is complicated by the nonculturable stage and "sublethal injury" phenomena, both of which have been described for many enteropathogenic bacteria found in the aquatic environment. The nonculturable stage is part of a survival strategy, described by Roszak and Colwell,[4] whereby bacteria, including many enteric organisms, respond to a transition from nutrient-rich, stable environments (such as an animal gut or a laboratory culture) to a less supportive environment (such as estuarine water) by entering a dormant stage. The response is observed as a state in which the organism is viable, as measured by substrate uptake assay, but fails to grow in culture.[4] This phenomenon has been observed for several waterborne pathogens, including *Salmonella enteriditis*,[5] enterotoxigenic *E. coli, Vibrio cholerae, Shigella* spp.,[6,7] and *Campylobacter jejuni*.[8] "Sublethal injury" of enteropathogenic bacteria has been described by Singh and McFeters as sublethal cellular lesions and alterations in physiology following exposure to aquatic stress factors which result in a temporary reduction or loss of virulence and reduced ability to grow on selective media.[9] Stressors, such as chlorine and copper ions, in water supply and distribution systems have been shown to induce sublethal injury in several enteropathogenic bacteria.[10]

The application of nucleic acid probes to the detection of enteropathogenic microorganisms in water offers a means of eliminating the necessity of isolating specific pathogens in culture, prior to identification and enumeration. Many pathogen-specific probes have already been constructed and are being tested for use in water quality analysis.

Assays that use hybridization probes vary in their sensitivity, depending upon the type of probe used and the labeling and detection system employed to measure the amount of probe which is hybridized to the target sequence. In general, however, the lowest amount of target DNA required is from 0.1 to 1 pg. If the target is present only once per organism, then the minimum number of organisms required for a positive signal may be as many as 10^6. Methods that increase target concentration are presently an active area of research.

Two approaches have proved successful thus far. The first is sample concentration prior to nucleic acid extraction, and the second is specific target amplification using an in vitro enzymatic method called the polymerase chain reaction (PCR). One example of the former approach is the method developed by Somerville et al., which uses a high capacity disposable membrane filtration unit to concentrate the microflora in aquatic samples for extraction of DNA and RNA.[11] The method is capable of extracting the microbial DNA and RNA from 10-L samples in an efficient, cost-effective manner. This method, developed in our laboratory, was used to recover DNA from estuarine samples for the application of a *Salmonella*-specific hybridization probe assay.[12]

PCR, described by Mullis and Faloona,[13] is a technique for amplifying discrete fragments of DNA from complex mixtures and has recently been improved by Saiki et al. to provide a simple method for increasing target DNA concentration over a billionfold.[14] The method is called polymerase chain reaction because DNA polymerase is used in conjunction with primers which flank the target sequence to synthesize nascent DNA between the primers. The nascent DNA then serves as a target for subsequent rounds of polymerization, resulting in a geometric increase in concentration of the target sequence. This technique has been incorporated into a DNA probe assay for detection of fecal coliform bacteria in drinking water[15] and for specific detection of enterotoxigenic bacteria.[16] Although PCR is a powerful method for enhancing the detection of rare targets in DNA samples, it has the disadvantage of making the probe assay qualitative rather than quantitative, since amplification does not proceed at a constant rate over the entire course of the reaction.

While the use of DNA and RNA probes for analysis of water quality is an active area of research, there are several hurdles that must be overcome before hybridization probes are used routinely in testing laboratories. The technology is more expensive than standard methods and employs more sophisticated techniques, and so requires a higher level of training in personnel. Also, radioactive labeling systems, with their attendant safety hazards, remain the method of choice for hybridization assays. Although nonradioactive labels are improving to the point where their sensitivity rivals that of radioactive labels, there are still problems of cross-reactivity arising from colormetric detection systems that must be solved before routine application of nonradioactive probes can be considered. Simplification of the probe assay to reduce the cost and training necessary to conduct them and the development of reliable nonradioactive detection systems are, however, areas of active research. Private firms, hoping to market probe-based detection kits, are especially active in resolving the problems and making probe assays accessible to testing laboratories. In the near future there will likely be reliable, nonradioactive probe-based detection kits on the market for determining the microbiological quality of water.

BIOSENSORS

Another area where recombinant DNA technology will impact on environmental testing is in the development of microorganisms that are genetically engineered to respond to specific toxicants by producing a response that can be measured by conventional instrumentation. These organisms are called *biosensors* and can be much more sensitive than conventional quantitative techniques.

The ability to construct such genetically engineered microorganisms (GEMs) is derived, in large part, from basic research into the molecular genetics of catabolic phenotypes in bacteria. Research on the genes controlling naphthalene degradation by bacteria has provided the basis for the most recent breakthrough in this field, the construction of a naphthalene biosensor that employs a bioluminescent reporter gene.[17] This biosensor was constructed by modifying a naturally occurring bacterium that degrades naphthalene. It was modified by inserting bacterial luciferase (*lux*) genes, which encodes light production, into a gene in the naphthalene catabolic pathway (*nahG*) in such a way that the expression of the *lux* gene is regulated by the same elements that control the *nahG* gene. Normally, when naphthalene-degrading bacteria are growing in the presence of naphthalene, the *nahG* gene produces salicylate hydrolase, an enzyme that breaks down an intermediate in the naphthalene catabolic pathway. In the modified bacterium, the same regulatory elements now control the *lux* genes, and light is produced in the presence of naphthalene. This light can be measured using a photomultiplier detection system. The developers of the naphthalene biosensor have demonstrated that the luminescent response to naphthalene in sediments is rapid and concentration-dependent, and they make the case that this technology could be applied to on-line monitoring of groundwater supplies.[17]

Bacterial degradation and transformation of toxic substances is an active area of research, and as the molecular genetics of these processes is elucidated, one can expect construction of more recombinant bacteria for use as biosensors.

REFERENCES

1. Southern, E. M. "Detection of Species Specific Sequences among DNA Fragments Separated by Gel Electrophoresis," *J. Mol. Biol.* 98:503–517 (1975).
2. Meinkoth, J., and G. Wahl. "Hybridization of Nucleic Acids Immobilized on Solid Supports," *Anal. Biochem.* 38:267–284 (1984).
3. *Standard Methods for the Examination of Water and Wastewater*, 17th ed. (Washington, DC: American Public Health Association, 1989), pp. 9.1–9.208.
4. Roszak, D. B., and R. R. Colwell. "Survival Strategies of Bacteria in the Natural Environment," *Microbiol. Rev.* 51:365–379 (1987).
5. Roszak, D. B., D. J. Grimes, and R. R. Colwell. "Viable but Nonrecoverable Stage of *Salmonella enteritidis* in Aquatic Systems," *Can. J. Microbiol.* 30:334–338 (1984).
6. Colwell, R. R., P. R. Brayton, D. J. Grimes, D. R. Roszak, S. A. Huq, and L. M. Palmer. "Viable, but Non-Culturable *Vibrio cholerae* and Related Pathogens in the Environment: Implications for Release of Genetically Engineered Microorganisms," *Bio/Technol.* 3:817–820 (1985).
7. Xu, H.-S., N. Roberts, F. L. Singleton, R. W. Attwell, D. J. Grimes, and R. R. Colwell. "Survival and Viability of Non-Culturable *Escherichia coli* and *Vibrio cholerae* in the Estuarine and Marine Environment," *Microb. Ecol.* 8:313–323 (1982).
8. Rollins, D. M., and R. R. Colwell. "Viable but Nonculturable Stage of *Campylobacter jejuni* and Its Role in Survival in the Natural Aquatic Environment," *Appl. Environ. Microbiol.* 52:531–538 (1986).
9. Singh, A., and G. A. McFeters. "Injury of Enteropathogenic Bacteria in Drinking Water," in *Drinking Water Microbiology: Progress and Recent Developments*, G. McFeters, Ed. (New York: Springer-Verlag, 1990), pp. 368–379.
10. LeChevallier, M. W., A. Singh, D. A. Shiemann, and G. A. McFeters. "Changes in Virulence of Waterborne Enteropathogens with Chlorine Injury," *Appl. Environ. Microbiol.* 50:412–419 (1985).
11. Somerville, C. C., I. T. Knight, W. L. Straube, and R. R. Colwell. "Simple, Rapid Method for Direct Isolation of Nucleic Acids from Aquatic Environments," *Appl. Environ. Microbiol.* 55:548–554 (1989).
12. Knight, I. T., S. Shults, C. W. Kaspar, and R. R. Colwell. "Direct Detection of *Salmonella* spp. in Estuaries by Using a DNA Probe," *Appl. Environ. Microbiol.* 56:1059–1066 (1990).
13. Mullis, K. B., and F. A. Faloona. "Specific Synthesis of DNA In Vitro via a Polymerase-Catalyzed Chain Reaction," *Methods Enzymol.* 155:335–351 (1987).

14. Saiki, R. K., D. H. Gelfand, S. Stoffel, S. J. Scharf, R. Higuchi, G. T. Horn, K. B. Mullis, and H. A. Erlich. "Primer-Directed Enzymatic Amplification of DNA with a Thermostable DNA Polymerase," *Science* 239:487–491 (1988).
15. Bej, A. K., R. J. Steffan, J. DiCesare, L. Haff, and R. Atlas. "Detection of Coliform Bacteria in Water by Polymerase Chain Reaction and Gene Probes," *Appl. Environ. Microbiol.* 56:307–314 (1990).
16. Knight, I. T., J. DiRuggiero, and R. R. Colwell. "Direct Detection of Enteropathogenic Bacteria in Estuarine Water Using Nucleic Acid Probes," *Water Sci. Technol.* 22 (in press).
17. King, J. M. H., P. M. DiGrazia, B. Applegate, R. Burlage, J. Sanseverino, P. Dunbar, F. Larimer, and G. S. Sayler. "Rapid, Sensitive Bioluminescent Reporter Technology for Naphthalene Exposure and Biodegradation," *Science* 249:778–781 (1990).

PART III

UPTAKE AND ACCUMULATION OF SEDIMENT—ASSOCIATED CONTAMINANTS
A. Bioavailability

CHAPTER 5

A Clam's Eye View
of the Bioavailability of
Sediment-Associated Pollutants

Henry Lee II

INTRODUCTION

Bioavailability of a pollutant is one of the key factors controlling its bioaccumulation and toxicity. For a truly dissolved pollutant, bioavailability can be considered as how readily an organism accumulates a pollutant from the surrounding water. The concept of bioavailability is more difficult to apply to sediment-associated pollutants, and the term is often used without an exact definition. This difficulty is related both to the presence of multiple sources of sediment-associated pollutants (e.g., interstitial water, particulates) and to the ability of sediment-dwelling organisms to modify their exposure by manipulating their local environment. However, without a rigorous definition it is difficult to assess the importance of the chemical and biological factors regulating sediment bioavailability or to quantitatively compare bioavailability among compounds, sediments, or organisms.

This chapter proposes a definition of bioavailability for sediment-associated pollutants and outlines the approaches to quantifying sediment bioavailability. The chapter then presents an overview of the ecological and physiological processes potentially affecting bioavailability. This overview draws heavily on our work with polychlorinated biphenyls (PCBs) and hexachlorobenzene (HCB) with the marine deposit-feeding clam *Macoma nasuta*. One of the main points is that standard measurements of sediment pollutant concentrations may not adequately represent an organism's exposure.

73

DEFINITION AND MEASUREMENT OF THE BIOAVAILABILITY OF SEDIMENT-ASSOCIATED POLLUTANTS

Definition of Sediment Bioavailability

In a general sense, a pollutant can be considered bioavailable if it is transferred from the sediment milieu into an infaunal organism. The greater the transfer, the greater the bioavailability. To avoid confounding effects, the measure of bioavailability should include only factors directly related to the transfer of the contaminant. At least four measures of sediment bioavailability have been used or implied in the literature: steady-state body burdens, toxicity, efficiency of pollutant uptake, and the rate of pollutant uptake.

Steady-state body burdens are a function of an organism's ability to depurate/metabolize the parent compound as well as the uptake of the parent compound. The rate of depuration and metabolism vary substantially among species and can vary with tissue residue (e.g., induction of enzymes). It is possible for two species to have similar uptake rates but substantially different steady-state body burdens because of differences in elimination rates. For this reason, steady-state body burdens are not a suitable absolute measure of bioavailability. However, steady-state tissue residues can be used as a comparative measure of the relative bioavailability if the elimination rate can be assumed to be equal, such as when the same species is exposed to different sediment types.

Similarly, sediment toxicity as a measure of bioavailability is confounded by a whole suite of physiological-biochemical processes. Because toxicity may vary with the rate of accumulation as well as with the amount accumulated and the physiological-biochemical process may vary among sediment types, toxicity should be used with caution even as a comparative measure of sediment bioavailability.

The third potential measure is how efficiently the organism extracts (or assimilates) the pollutant from the sediment. Such a measure would be analogous to the efficiency of gill uptake used to measure the relative bioavailability of dissolved pollutants in fish.[1,2] However, as opposed to dissolved pollutants, there are several potential sediment uptake routes with different sites of accumulation (e.g., interstitial water at gills, ingested sediment particles in gut) making it impossible to assign a single efficiency value to the entire sediment.

The last potential measure is the rate transfer of a pollutant from the sediment milieu to an organism. Defining bioavailability as the rate of transfer or uptake from the entire sediment integrates uptake from the various pollutant pools, thereby avoiding the problem associated with the efficiency measurements. At least to a first approximation, the rate of uptake is assumed to be independent of the tissue residue,[3,4] thereby avoiding or at least reducing the problem of confounding uptake and elimination processes. This rate needs to be normalized by organism weight and sediment pollutant concentration to account for differences in organism size and pollutant concentration, respectively. Therefore, sediment bioavailability becomes the weight-specific increase in tissue residues per unit time normalized to the sediment pollutant concentration:

$$\frac{dCt/dt}{C_s} = \frac{\mu g/(g \text{ tissue} \times \text{time})}{\mu g/(g \text{ sediment})} \tag{5.1}$$

or

$$K_s = (g \text{ sediment})/(g \text{ tissue} \times \text{time})$$

where C_t = tissue residue on weight-specific basis ($\mu g/g$ tissue)
   C_s = sediment pollutant concentration ($\mu g/g$ sediment)
   t = time
   K_s = sediment uptake rate coefficient, or uptake clearance

K_s can be referred to as the *sediment uptake rate coefficient*, or the *uptake clearance* as used in Landrum.[5] It is referred to as a "coefficient" rather than a "constant" because the value for a compound is not fixed but can vary with physical and biological factors. The term *uptake clearance* comes from pharmacokinetics and in this case represents the amount of sediment cleared (stripped) of pollutant per gram of tissue per unit time. Uptake clearance is not a concept used widely in aquatic toxicology, though the use of pharmacokinetic nomenclature would promote comparisons between toxicokinetic and clinical pharmacokinetic models.

If the grams are canceled in Equation 5.1, K_s collapses to 1/time, or the *uptake rate constant*, k_1. Uptake rate constants derived from water exposures are frequently used in predicting water uptake,[3,4,6] and the use of k_1's derived from sediment exposures have been suggested as a way to predict steady-state body burdens in infaunal organisms.[7] However, as has been pointed out (Stehly et al.[8] and P. Landrum, personal communication), the grams should not be canceled and the appropriate units are $g/(g \times \text{time})$ for sediment and $mL/(g \times \text{time})$ for water exposures. This does not change the numerical value but helps avoid confusing rates derived from a water exposure versus a sediment exposure. Maintaining the units also reveals that the value of K_s will vary depending on whether the tissue and sediment concentrations were in dry or wet weight units. K_s's derived from wet and dry weight concentrations can vary several fold, so it is important to define the units used. It is also important to emphasize that this definition of bioavailability does not imply that a K_s for a compound is necessarily constant either among sediments or species.

Measurement and Comparison of Sediment Bioavailability

The K_s for a particular sediment type for a particular species can be determined by dividing the slope of the rate of increase in tissue residues ($\mu g/g$

tissue × time) measured during the linear uptake phase by the sediment concentration (μg/g sediment) (Figure 5.1). A good fit to a linear regression indicates the uptake was in the linear uptake phase; a poor fit suggests that the exposure duration extended past the linear uptake phase. A K_s derived from a nonlinear uptake curve, where elimination is nontrivial, will underestimate the true K_s. Figure 5.1 shows the uptake of three PCB congeners over ten days by *Macoma* (work in progress). Both 2,2′,5,5′-tetrachlorobiphenyl (IUPAC #52) and 2,2′,4,4′,5,5′-hexachlorobiphenyl (IUPAC #153) showed a highly significant linear regression, and the K_s can be calculated from the slope. However, for 2,2′,5-trichlorobiphenyl (IUPAC #18) the regression is not significant, presumably because this lower K_{ow} compound approaches steady-state within a few days.

The rate of uptake can also be estimated from a single tissue residue as long as the single sampling period is within the linear uptake phase. For the 11 PCB congeners and HCB that fit the linear regression, the average difference between the K_s calculated from the linear regression and the K_s calculated from

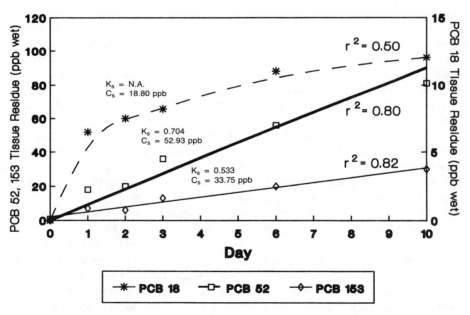

Figure 5.1. Calculation of K_s from the uptake rate measured in the linear uptake phase. K_s was calculated by dividing the slope of the linear regression of tissue residues versus time (μg/g tissue × day) by the sediment pollutant concentration (C_s = μg/g sediment). Both 2,2′,5,5′-tetrachlorobiphenyl (IUPAC #52) and 2,2′,4,4′,5,5′-hexachlorobiphenyl (IUPAC #153) showed a significant linear regression. 2,2′,5-Trichlorobiphenyl (IUPAC #18) had a nonlinear uptake curve over 10 days, so calculation by this method is not appropriate. All values are for *Macoma nasuta,* and the clams were not purged before chemical analysis. Sediment concentrations are in ppb dry weight, and the tissue residues were converted to dry weight before calculating K_s.

the 10-day tissue residue was only 3.3%. Use of the single point estimation approach allows calculation of K_s from published bioaccumulation tests that used a single exposure period, but the technique has to be applied with some knowledge of the elimination rate of the compound. K_s can also be calculated by fitting of nonlinear equations if the uptake is nonlinear (i.e., extends past linear uptake phase) or the sediment pollutant concentration varies.[5,8,9] However, the direct measurement of K_s during the linear uptake phase is favored because it avoids the possibility of nonexact solutions to the nonlinear equations and requires fitting only one parameter, which should generate a more accurate estimate for K_s.

Defining sediment bioavailability as K_s allows quantitative comparisons among studies. For example, Figure 5.2 shows the K_s's for 14 chlorinated compounds using *Macoma* (work in progress), the K_s's for several PAHs, and a PCB congener using the freshwater amphipod *Pontoporeia hoyi*,[5] and K_s's

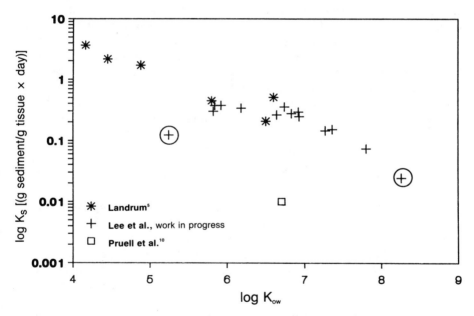

Figure 5.2. Log K_s as a function of log K_{ow}. Data from three different studies are plotted to show how expressing sediment bioavailability as K_s allows quantitative comparisons among studies. In all cases, the K_s's were calculated using dry sediment and tissue pollutant concentrations. Data from Lee et al. (work in progress) are for 13 PCB congeners and HCB using *Macoma nasuta*. The inclusion of PCB congeners 18 and 209 (⊕), which did not fit the linear uptake curve, is for illustrative purposes. TOC of the sediment was 1.3%. Data from Landrum are for 5 PAHs and a PCB using the freshwater amphipod *Pontoporeia hoyi*.[5] TOC of the sediment was 1.3%. Data from Pruell et al. are for 2,3,7,8-TCDD and total PCBs using *Nereis virens*, *Macoma nasuta*, and *Palaemonetes* sp.[10] All six TCDD and PCB values are represented by the single point. TOC of the sediment was 5.7%

for 2,3,7,8-TCDD and total PCBs for three estuarine species, including *Macoma*.[10] The values for *Pontoporeia* were derived using nonlinear equations, while the values for TCDD and total PCBs were calculated from the tissue residues at 10 days with residues at later sampling dates demonstrating that the organisms were still in the linear uptake phase. All values were converted to standard units (dry weight concentrations and day^{-1}). From Figure 5.2, it is possible to speculate that K_s declines with both log K_{ow} and TOC. A more detailed comparison is required before any specific conclusions can be drawn, and the main point of this comparison is to demonstrate that expressing bioavailability as K_s allows quantitative comparisons among studies using different sediments, organisms, and estimation techniques.

Toxicokinetic Representation of Sediment Bioavailability

K_s integrates uptake from all sediment phases and is a measure of the overall bioavailability of a compound in a particular sediment. While this is a required characteristic of a general measure of sediment bioavailability, K_s offers little insight into the routes of uptake. It is theoretically possible to have the same bioavailability from two sediments even though interstitial water was the dominant uptake route in one case and ingested sediment in the other. However, by using a bioenergetic-based toxicokinetic model,[11] it is possible to dissect this integrated measure into the actual processes regulating the pollutant transfer. Modifying the bioenergetic-based model for sediment uptake,[12] the rate of change in tissue residues in a sediment-dwelling organism can be modeled as

$$dC_t/dt = \Sigma(F_X C_{PX} E_{PX}) - E \tag{5.2}$$

where $\quad C_t =$ tissue residue on weight-specific basis ($\mu g/g$)
$\qquad t =$ time
$\qquad F_X =$ weight-specific flux of phase X through organism (g/g tissue × time)
$\qquad C_{PX} =$ pollutant concentration in phase X ($\mu g/g$)
$\qquad E_{PX} =$ extraction efficiency of pollutant in phase X (unitless)
$\qquad X =$ phase to which the organism is exposed ($W_o =$ overlying water; $W_i =$ interstitial water; S = sediment; F = food)
$\qquad E =$ elimination rate of pollutant due to depuration of parent compound and metabolic degradation ($\mu g/g$ tissue × time)

Normalizing for sediment concentration and assuming the uptake is in the linear uptake phase so that the elimination rate is trivial (i.e., E approaches 0), the equation becomes

$$\frac{dC_t/dt}{C_s} = \frac{\Sigma(F_x C_{px} E_{px})}{C_s} = K_s \tag{5.3}$$

This equation identifies the two general processes regulating sediment bioavailability. The first is the organism's exposure, the mass of pollutant actually coming into contact with the organism. In terms of Equations 5.2 and 5.3, an organism's exposure is the product of the flux of water, food, or sediment (F_X) times the concentration in the phase (C_{PX}). Exposure is used here only on the microhabitat scale, the scale at which organisms can affect the flux (F_X) or concentration (C_{PX}) of a pollutant. These processes are intrinsic characteristics of each species and, hence, of a species' propensity to bioaccumulate. Of the pollutant coming into contact with the organism, only a portion of it is transferred from the environment across the organism's membranes. Therefore, the second process regulating bioavailability is the fraction of the pollutant extracted (or assimilated) by the organism. These are the E_{PX} terms in Equations 5.2 and 5.3, with each route of uptake having its own efficiency term.

The remainder of the chapter will explore how organisms can potentially modify their exposure to sediment pollutants or the transfer of the pollutant from the environment to the organism.

EXPOSURE PROCESSES

By living in a solid matrix, infaunal organisms are able to modify their local environment, and hence their pollutant exposure, to a much greater extent than water column organisms. As a result, an infaunal organism may be exposed to substantially different interstitial water pollutant concentrations (C_{PWi}) or particle pollutant concentrations (C_{PS}) than measured by standard sampling and chemical procedures.

Exposure to Sorbed Pollutants

Ingested sediment particles are the dominant uptake route for several high K_{ow} organic pollutants for certain organisms.[5,12,13] Therefore, the effects of feeding behavior on the flux of sediment (F_S) or pollutant concentration of the ingested particles (C_{PS}) may substantially affect sediment bioavailability. One important behavior is the organism's feeding zone. Deposit feeders show a wide variety of feeding types.[14] At one extreme, surface deposit feeders such as *Macoma* feed primarily on the upper few millimeters of sediment. At the other extreme, "conveyor-belt" species, which are head down and anus up in the sediment, ingest particles as deep as 20–30 cm below the surface. In sediments with distinct sediment horizons, these organisms would be exposed to substantially different pollutant concentrations than surface feeders (Figure 5.3).

Although the depth distributions in Figure 5.3 are hypothetical, dramatic differences in pollutant concentrations have been documented within the potential feeding range of deposit feeders. For example, the concentration of DDT has been as much as an order-of-magnitude greater at 20-cm depth than

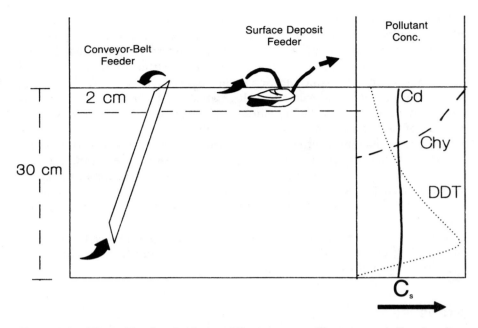

Figure 5.3.   Effect of feeding depth on pollutant exposure. The conveyor-belt and surface deposit feeding modes illustrate the range in feeding depth by deposit feeders. The "standard" sediment collection depth of 2 cm for pollutant analysis is illustrated by the dashed line. The variations in sediment concentrations (C_s) of Cd, DDT, and chrysene (Chy) with depth are hypothetical but within the ranges reported for various sites. In this scenario, the standard sediment collection techniques would not adequately represent the exposure regime of either feeding type.

in the surface sediment on the Palos Verdes Peninsula.[15] PCBs also tend to be two- to threefold higher in the deeper sediments off of Palos Verdes.[16] These higher concentrations in deep sediment reflect the historical discharges of these chemicals. In other sites where there is a recent pollutant input or where there is an input of a rapidly degraded pollutant, the higher concentrations may be in the surface sediments. In these cases, the standard technique of sampling the upper few centimeters of sediment for pollutant analysis could substantially underestimate or overestimate an organism's exposure.

An aspect of deposit-feeding behavior that has been largely ignored in terms of pollutant exposure is selective feeding. Most deposit feeders selectively ingest the finer, higher TOC particles while discarding the larger, low TOC particles. This behavior can concentrate the organic content of the ingested sediment by more than an order-of-magnitude over that of the parent sediment. Using the 23 measurements in Cammen,[17] organic enrichment in the gut compared to the sediment averaged about 5-fold. Excluding the 61-fold increase reported for a deposit-feeding crab reduced the mean to a 2.4-fold organic carbon enrichment.

Because the sorption of neutral organic pollutants is directly related to the carbon content of the solids,[18,19] the pollutant concentration on the high TOC ingested particles should be correspondingly greater than that of the parent sediment. This was found with *Macoma,* in which the HCB concentration and the TOC of the ingested sediment was about two- to fourfold greater than the parent sediment concentration.[20] The greatest relative increase in pollutant concentration in the ingested sediment should occur in sandier sediments, which offer a relatively greater opportunity for selection of high TOC particles, and with compounds with high organic carbon partitioning coefficients (K_{oc}). However, the effect is not limited to neutral organics, as indicated by the 1.2- to 1.7-fold enrichment in the metal concentrations in the feces of deposit feeders.[21]

As a consequence of selective feeding, the pollutant concentrations measured in the parent sediment underestimate the actual dose ingested by selective deposit feeders. In essence, the organisms are "seeing" a more polluted environment than measured by standard techniques. Normalization of sediment pollutant concentrations to an organic carbon basis will partially account for this selection. This normalization assumes the carbon measured chemically is the same as that enriched in the ingested particles. This assumption is likely to be incorrect at least for species that select particles on the basis of protein levels.[22] Also, carbon normalization would not account for any processes related to the total pollutant concentration rather than carbon concentrations nor for processes dependent upon the volume or the volumetric flow of food, such as uptake by the GI tract.[23] Nonetheless, expressing pollutant concentrations on an organic carbon basis helps correct for the biological enhancement of neutral organics.

Exposure to Interstitial Water

Pollutant concentrations in interstitial water are normally many times higher than those in the overlying water. With these relatively high concentrations, interstitial water has the potential of being an important uptake route; Adams suggests that interstitial water is the dominant uptake route for neutral organics with a log K_{ow} of less than about 5.[24] In support of this suggestion, several experimenters have concluded that interstitial water was the dominant uptake route for certain neutral organics and heavy metals.[25,26] As with the ingested solids, biological processes affecting either the flux of the interstitial water (F_{wi}) or the pollutant concentration in the interstitial water (C_{pwi}) can have a substantial impact on sediment bioavailability.

One of the key processes affecting exposure to interstitial water is the relative proportion ventilated compared to the amount of overlying water ventilated. The ventilation of interstitial water (F_{wi}) varies both with the feeding type and the burrowing behavior of the organism. Infaunal filter feeders, such as *Mercenaria* and *Mya,* feed by filtering particles from the overlying water and so ventilate little interstitial water. Likewise, surface deposit-feeding bivalves, such as *Macoma*, ventilate an insignificant amount of interstitial water.[27] For these organisms, the only significant exposure to interstitial water pollutants is by sorption of dissolved pollutants to the integument. Passive sorption does not appear to be a major uptake route, at least for *Macoma* exposed to HCB.[12] At the other extreme, free-burrowing amphipods and polychaetes ventilate interstitial water exclusively (at least while buried in the sediment). Assuming that interstitial water concentrations approach the equilibrium concentrations established by the compound's K_{oc} and the TOC of the sediment, interstitial water could be a major uptake route for these organisms.

Dilution of Interstitial Water Pollutants

The assumption of equilibrium pollutant concentrations in the ventilated interstitial water would overestimate exposure if pollutant concentrations in the microhabitat surrounding the free-burrowing species are reduced by organismal uptake and/or advection of overlying water. The importance of depletion by organism uptake can be approximated from the rate of aqueous phase uptake (i.e., $F_{Wi}C_{PWi}E_{PW}$). The depleted pollutants can be renewed by desorption, diffusion, movement of the organism, advection of interstitial water, and excretion of the parent compound. To take the simplest case, let's assume that desorption is the only renewal mechanism, so the desorption rate has to equal or exceed the rate of aqueous-phase uptake to maintain the equilibrium interstitial water pollutant concentrations.

Using *Macoma* as an example, it is possible to estimate the volume of interstitial water potentially depleted. The uptake rate for HCB averaged about 0.008 $\mu g/$(g wet tissue $\times$ day) for *Macoma* (work in progress). *Macoma* extracts about 65% of the dissolved HCB,[28] and HCB has a water solubility of about 6 $\mu g/L$. Applying these values to a free-burrowing species and making a worst case assumption that all the uptake is from interstitial water, a 1-g organism would totally deplete about 2 mL of interstitial water per day. This is a relatively small volume and presumably a moderate desorption rate would maintain the concentration close to the equilibrium concentration. For very low solubility compounds (e.g., 2,3,7,8-TCDD = 0.2 ppb), a proportionally greater amount of interstitial water would be depleted for the same uptake rate. Therefore, it appears possible that biological uptake could deplete interstitial water concentrations, but that such effects would be limited to very low solubility pollutants.

The potentially more important process is the advection of overlying water diluting interstitial water concentrations. The volume of overlying water advected into the surface oxic sediment layer can be estimated from the renewal of interstitial oxygen. With no connection to the surface, free-burrowing forms (e.g., *Rhepoxynius*) meet their oxygen requirements by ventilating interstitial water and therefore have to spend the majority of their time in the oxic sediment layer. As there is no significant within-sediment genera-

tion of oxygen, the amount of oxygen advected into the sediment equals the total community respiration rate (sum of macrofaunal and microbial respiration and chemical oxygen demand) under steady-state conditions. Figure 5.4 is a representation of the process and shows a simplified method of estimating the minimum number of turnovers of the interstitial water in the oxic layer required to maintain an equilibrium oxygen concentration. Based on the values in Figure 5.4, a minimum of about 84 turnovers of the interstitial water per day are required. At this rate of 3–4 turnovers per hour, dilution of the interstitial water with overlying water may exceed the desorption rate of many pollutants. Admittedly, these calculations are oversimplifications, but they raise the possibility that infaunal organisms in the oxic layer may be exposed to interstitial water concentrations substantially less than equilibrium concentrations. If dilution is important, predictions of toxicity or bioaccumulation from equilibrium interstitial water concentrations will be overestimated. Also, estimates of the importance of interstitial water as an uptake route by applying bioconcentration factors (BCFs) to interstitial water may be overestimated because the concentration of the interstitial water in the microhabitat is overestimated. By overestimating the interstitial water route, such calculations would underestimate the importance of uptake from ingested sediment. These suggestions need to be tested by carefully sampling the interstitial water in the sediment layer inhabited by the free-burrowing organisms.

Tubes and Burrows

Another behavior affecting exposure to interstitial water is tube or burrow construction. Tubes and well-defined burrows are common among polychaetes, amphipods, and many other infaunal taxa. Tube/burrows are constructed of a polysaccharide inner lining and an outer layer of sediment of modified mineralogy, often with a higher TOC (Figure 5.5).[29,30] There is no definitive difference between a tube and a burrow, but in general a tube has a more defined structure whereas a burrow is the modification of the surrounding sediment. For the purposes of this discussion they are treated together.

Tubes and burrows vary greatly in their size, shape, and amount of water fluxed through the tube/burrow (i.e., irrigation) (Figure 5.5). All these constructs serve to wall the organism off from the surrounding sediment and should reduce the organism's direct exposure to interstitial water. Also, the open channel to the surface facilitates the ventilation of overlying water. Consequently, tubicolous species ventilate relatively more overlying water than free-burrowing species without siphons extending into the overlying water.

Besides reducing contact with interstitial water, the differential permeability of tubes/burrows changes the chemical composition of water in the tube compared to the surrounding interstitial water. Aller's studies on small inorganic solutes suggests that tubes act as "molecular sieves" (Figure 5.6).[30,31] The passage of certain anions (Br$^-$) through the tube/burrow walls were hindered relative to cations (NH$_4^+$) because of negative charges on the inside of the tube.

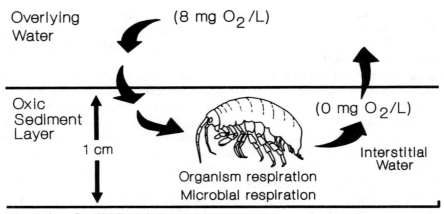

Figure 5.4. Calculation of turnovers of interstitial water required to maintain oxic sediment layer. Assuming equilibrium and no other source of oxygen input, the O_2 advected from the overlying water into the oxic sediment layer equals the O_2 respired by infauna and microbes (including chemical oxygen demand). Therefore, the number of turnovers of the interstitial water in the oxic layer can be estimated from the volume of overlying water required to supply the O_2 consumed by benthic respiration. It is assumed that all the O_2 consumption occurs in the oxic layer so areal measurements of benthic respiration (g/m^2 × day) can be expressed on basis of the volume of the oxic layer (g/m^2 × cm × day). Oxygen concentration in the overlying water is also expressed on a volume basis (g/m^2 cm). To calculate the volume of interstitial water, it is necessary to estimate the depth of the oxic layer and the percentage of the oxic layer consisting of interstitial water (i.e., porosity). The minimum number of turnovers required to meet the benthic oxygen demand can then be calculated from the oxygen concentration in the overlying water:

$$\text{Turnovers/day} = O_2 \text{ consumption}/(O_2 \text{ conc. OW} \times \%IW/100)$$

The turnovers can be calculated assuming the following:
- Depth of oxic layer = 1 cm.
- O_2 consumption rate = 3.38 g/(m^2 × cm × day). From Kemp and Boynton.[42]
- Interstitial water volume (%IW) = 50% of the oxic layer.
- O_2 conc. overlying water (OW) = 8 mg/L = 0.08 g/(m^2 × cm).
- 100% of the interstitial water is replaced each turnover.
- 100% of the oxygen is consumed each turnover.
- 100% of the oxygen consumption occurs in the oxic layer.

Using these values, a minimum of 84 turnovers of the interstitial water in the oxic layer are required to supply the respired oxygen. With this turnover rate, pollutants would need desorption rates on the order of hours to maintain equilibrium pollutant concentrations in the interstitial water.

Other solutes were restricted in their passage through the tubes due to consumptive reactions within the tube and by sorption on the tube.

Using Aller's work as a base, it is possible to postulate four different processes modifying the pollutant composition of tube/burrow water versus the

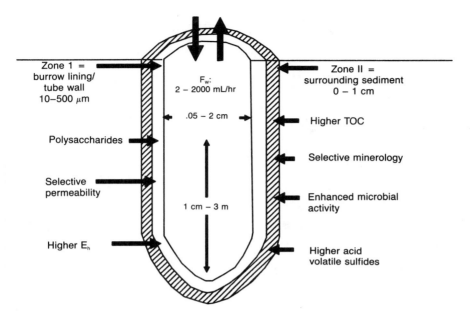

Figure 5.5. Properties of infaunal tubes and burrows. A generalized schematic to illustrate the structure and the range in the dimensions and flux of water (F_W or "irrigation") of tubes and burrows. The actual dimensions and shapes vary greatly among species. The irrigation rates are from Lee and Swartz.[14] The other characteristics are from Aller and Yingst,[29] Aller,[30] and Aller et al.[31]

surrounding interstitial water (Figure 5.6). First, higher K_{ow} neutral organics would bind to the organic matter of the tubes/burrow, hindering their diffusion into and through the tube.

Second, passage of large molecules may be hindered in their passage through tubes by steric effects, while polar molecules may be hindered by charge interactions. Dissolved organic matter (DOM) consists of a high percentage of large molecules so DOM concentration may be reduced as interstitial water passes through a tube/burrow wall. The reduction in DOM may enhance the relative proportion of truly dissolved pollutant to DOM-bound pollutant, resulting in an increase in the bioavailability of organic pollutants (see Landrum et al.[32] and Servos and Muir[33] for effects of DOM).

The third process relates to the presence of higher levels of acid volatile sulfides (AVS) in certain burrow walls.[29] AVS may "bind" free metals and thus control their bioavailability, as suggested by the relationship between cadmium toxicity and AVS levels in sediments.[34] With the higher AVS concentrations, the concentrations of free metals may decline as they diffuse through the burrow wall, reducing their bioavailability.

The last process is the enhanced microbial activity in tube/burrow walls,[29] which could result in enhanced microbial degradation of organic pollutants. However, it is unclear whether the degradation would be sufficiently rapid to

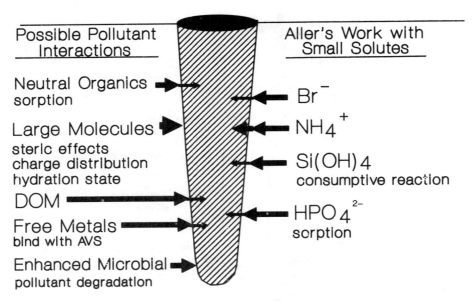

Figure 5.6. Tubes/burrows as molecular sieves and possible effects on interstitial water pollutants. Tube/burrow wall acted as molecular sieves with small inorganic solutes.[30] Tube/burrow walls affected diffusion of solutes by charge interactions (slower diffusion of Br^- compared to NH_4^+), consumptive reactions within the tube ($Si(OH)_4$), and sorption to the tube/burrow (HPO_4^{2-}). Similar reactions can be postulated for pollutants. In particular, diffusion of neutral organics may be hindered by sorption to the TOC of the wall or by steric effects. Free metals may bind with the acid-free sulfides (AVS) present in high concentrations in certain burrow walls.[29] Organic pollutants may be degraded more rapidly as a result of the enhanced microbial activity in tube/burrow walls.

affect the exposure of the tube/burrow inhabitant or whether the degradation would result in a more toxic intermediate breakdown product.

TRANSFER PROCESSES

Once an organism is exposed, the transfer of the pollutant from the water or sediment into the organism is primarily regulated by two processes. The first is the ease of "release" or "extraction" of the pollutant from the aqueous or particulate phase, and the second is the assimilation of the released pollutant by the gill, gut, or integument. Bioavailability is reduced if either process is rate limited. In the following discussion, it is assumed that interstitial water pollutants are accumulated only at the gill surface, whereas pollutants sorbed to solids are accumulated only in the gut.

Extraction and Assimilation of Interstitial Water Pollutants

Truly dissolved pollutants do not have to be "extracted" from the water per se, so the important processes are those occurring at the gill membrane. However, there is growing evidence that a substantial percentage of the aqueous-phase organic pollutants are bound to DOM and that these bound pollutants have a reduced bioavailability.[32,33] The size of the freely dissolved pool in interstitial water is thought to be small,[5] suggesting that the rate of desorption from the DOM-bound pool is one of the factors regulating the availability of organic pollutants (Figure 5.7). To gain a better understanding of the role of interstitial water, future studies should attempt to separate the free and bound pools, though as of yet it is not clear which of the several techniques (dialysis, ultrafiltration, photolysis, hydrolysis, gas purging, and reverse-phase separation) is most suitable.

The major role organisms have on the extractability of interstitial pollutants is by influencing DOM concentrations. Infaunal organisms and microbes can increase the concentration of DOM through excretion or by in situ decomposition. For example, decomposing marine diatoms released humic and fulvic acids, though none were found in the living cells.[35] Infaunal organisms can also reduce DOM by directly assimilating dissolved carbohydrates and amino

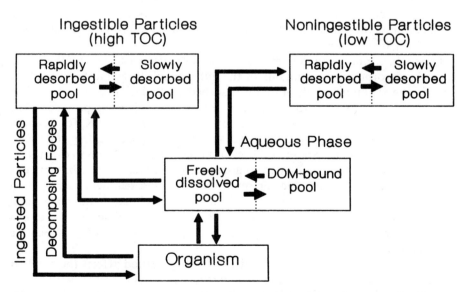

Figure 5.7. Conceptual model of sediment bioavailability. Conceptual model showing the aqueous- and solid-phase pollutant pools in sediments and the important transfers among the pools and infaunal organisms. *Ingestible particles* are the smaller, high TOC particles ingested by selective deposit feeders. *Noningestible particles* are the larger, lower TOC particles rejected or consumed only in small amounts by selective deposit feeders. Diagram modified from Landrum.[5]

acids, though it seems unlikely that infaunal organisms could substantially reduce interstitial water DOM concentrations.

Once a dissolved pollutant comes in contact with the gill surface, uptake is regulated by the physical/chemical properties of the pollutant and the characteristics of the membrane. With fish, the efficiency of gill uptake (E_{PW}) of dissolved organic pollutants initially increased from a log K_{ow} of 1, then plateaued from log K_{ow} of 3 to 6, and declined at higher K_{ow}'s.[1,36] There have been no comparable multiple compound studies with infaunal invertebrates, but the similarity of the gill uptake efficiency of HCB for *Macoma*[28] to that reported for fish[1] suggests a qualitatively similar pattern may occur.

Extraction and Assimilation of Sorbed Pollutants

One route of uptake from pollutants sorbed to solids is desorption in the gut and then assimilation of the dissolved pollutant across the gut membrane. Sorbed pollutants can be divided into a "rapidly reversible pool" and a "slowly reversible pool."[37] Pollutants in the rapidly reversible pool desorb within minutes to hours, whereas pollutants in the slowly reversible pool take days or months to desorb. Because most deposit feeders have a gut retention time on the order of hours, uptake from desorbed pollutants should be primarily from the rapidly reversible pool. This assumes the digestive processes do not greatly increase the release of the slowly desorbed pool compared to laboratory techniques to measure desorption. The validity of this assumption needs to be tested because the gut is a harsh environment evolved to promote the assimilation of organic molecules.

Other than modifying gut retention time, organisms can potentially influence the desorption of pollutants in the gut through three mechanisms. The first is the stripping of the rapidly desorbed pool during digestion with a subsequent reduction in the bioavailability of the defecated particles. The importance of this process is suggested by the reduction in the K_s for phenanthrene measured in sequential sets of *Pontoporeia* exposed to the same sediment.[5] In the sediment exposed to three sets of amphipods over 6 weeks, the K_s declined by about 60% compared to about a 34% reduction in sediment aged without organisms. In benthic communities with rapid sediment reprocessing rates,[14] biological stripping of the rapidly desorbed pool may result in a general decrease in bioavailability. Consequently, bioavailability of sorbed pollutants may vary with the density and types of organism comprising a benthic community.

The second factor is how an organism's feeding method affects the "age" of ingested sediment. The size of the rapidly reversible pool decreases with equilibration time,[37] so recently polluted sediments should have a higher bioavailability than older sediments, which have had more time to equilibrate. Therefore, a species feeding on the surface would ingest sediment with a higher bioavailability than a deep-feeding species. The evidence for decreases in bioavailability over short aging periods includes the approximate 34% reduction in the bioavailability of phenanthrene after storing the spiked sediment an extra 4 weeks.[5] To examine the effects of aging over years or decades, it is worth reanalyzing a study in which we measured the accumulation factors (AF = lipid-normalized tissue residue/sediment pollutant concentration on organic carbon basis) for PCBs, DDE, DDD, and five PAHs using surface (0–2 cm) and deeper sediments (4–8 cm or 8–12 cm) collected at three sites off the Los Angeles County sewage discharge.[16] The AFs were measured in the laboratory by exposing *Macoma* to the sediments for 28 days. Because AFs are measures of steady-state body burdens rather than the rate of uptake, AFs are used only as a comparative measure of bioavailability. Although the ages of the sediment at different strata are unknown, these data can be reinterpreted assuming that the deeper sediments are several years to decades older.[15]

The ratio of the AFs derived from the surface sediment to the AFs from the deeper sediment averaged 2.4 for the 29 site-chemical combinations ($p < 0.05$, paired t-test), and the higher AF occurred in the surface sediment in 20 cases ($p < 0.05$, chi square test). The higher AFs in the surface sediments suggest the pollutants sorbed to the younger surface sediments were more bioavailable. The apparent increase in bioavailability in surface sediment was not related to pollutant type, though it was related to site, with the greatest enhancement at the reference site. Of the nine compounds at the reference site, the ratio of the surface AF to deep AF was > 2 in 8 cases. In comparison, this ratio was < 2 in all 20 comparisons at the two polluted sites. The cause for this apparent trend is not known.

The third process potentially affecting the uptake of sorbed pollutants is the increase in pollutant fugacity and pollutant concentration in the gut as the volume of food decreases and lipids are hydrolyzed during digestion.[23] Digestion alters the thermodynamic gradient such that there is a net flux of pollutant from the gut contents into the gut. This digestive-driven change in gut fugacity should have the greatest affect on the tissue residues of slowly eliminated or metabolized compounds (e.g., PCBs). This process may explain why tissue residues of high K_{ow} compounds often exceed the concentrations predicted from thermodynamic partitioning with the external environment (e.g., Connolly and Pederson[38]).

Another process that could account for tissue residues in excess of that predicted by simple partitioning is facilitated or active uptake in which the organism expends energy to incorporate a compound. For example, ion pumps can carry charged solutes against a thermodynamic gradient. Phagocytosis, in which digestive cells engulf organic particles, could transport neutral organic pollutants sorbed to the engulfed particle into the gut membrane regardless of the thermodynamic gradient. Although these processes are known to occur, their exact role in the uptake of metals is unclear.[39] Based on our studies with the PCB congeners, their role in the uptake of neutral organics is also unclear. As discussed below, there was no apparent gut uptake of decachlorobiphenyl by *Macoma*. One interpretation is that the active uptake of neutral organics was trivial and lost in the noise. Alternatively, active uptake may have carried the decachlorobiphenyl into the gut membrane, but then the PCB congener was trapped in the membrane by steric or other effects. If the latter interpretation is true, then active uptake could still be an important uptake mechanism for compounds not subject to steric effects.

Understanding the importance of these gut processes and the magnitude of uptake from ingested sediment requires estimates of the efficiency of uptake from ingested sediment (E_{PSi}). To date, there are only two published measurements of the assimilation of organic pollutants from ingested sediment—a value of 24% for a hexachlorobiphenyl with oligochaetes by Klump et al.[40] and a value of 39–56% for HCB with *Macoma*.[20] One problem with the dual label approach used by Klump is the possibility of underestimating the efficiency of uptake if the organism selects for high TOC particles, as was discussed above. To avoid this problem, we derived a direct measurement approach,[20] using a "clambox" (see Specht and Lee[41]) that corrects for sediment selection by using TOC as a pollutant tracer.

Besides the measurement with HCB, we have measured E_{PSi} for 13 PCB congeners and HCB (work in progress). Based on the preliminary data, there is an indication that E_{PSi} declines with K_{ow}. Sediment uptake efficiencies declined from about 90% for 2,2′,5-trichlorobiphenyl (IUPAC #18) to 0% for decachlorobiphenyl (IUPAC #209) over a log K_{ow} range of 5.2 to 8.2. The small amount of accumulation of the decachlorobiphenyl over 10 days (Figure 5.2) is thought to be due to sorption to the integument and/or the gut wall rather than internal tissues. Qualitatively similar declines in efficiency at high K_{ow} have been reported in fish for both uptake of dissolved pollutants across the gills (E_{PW})[1] and for the uptake efficiencies of food in the gut (E_{PF}).[23] However, in these studies the decline in the efficiency terms began at a higher log K_{ow}: > 6.0 for gill uptake and > 6.5 for gut uptake.

CONCLUSIONS

The first purpose of this chapter was to propose K_s, the uptake rate coefficient, as the definition for sediment bioavailability. Standardization of terminology will help avoid confusion and assist in making quantitative comparisons among studies. Other measures, such as steady-state tissue residues, can generate insights into the processes regulating bioavailability but, as defined here, are not measures of sediment bioavailability per se. The second purpose was to identify potential processes by which organisms can alter their exposure regime and the efficiency of pollutant assimilation. Not all the processes discussed will be important for any single species, sediment type, or pollutant, and future studies may well demonstrate that some of the processes have a trivial effect on sediment bioavailability. However, there is sufficient data to warn us that, at least in some cases, standard sampling and chemical procedures can do a poor job of estimating an organism's exposure. The documentation of these biological processes should also warn of the danger of treating infaunal organisms as static players driven solely by thermodynamic partitioning with the external environment (see Figure 5.7).

ACKNOWLEDGMENTS

The good ideas in this chapter benefited from comments by Drs. B. Boese, W. Davis, P. Landrum, R. Ozretich, members of the Bioaccumulation Team, and an anonymous reviewer. They claim no connection with the bad ones. Martha Winsor helped in calculating the turnover of interstitial water. Judy Pelletier drew the figures. David Specht helped gather references. Tricia Lawson edited an earlier version of the manuscript. The contents of this chapter do not necessarily reflect the views and policies of the EPA, nor does mention of trade names or commercial products constitute endorsement or recommendation for use. Contribution number N-141 of the U.S. Environmental Protection Agency, Environmental Research Laboratory, Narragansett, RI.

REFERENCES

1. McKim, J., P. Schmieder, and G. Veith. "Absorption Dynamics of Organic Chemical Transport across Trout Gills as Related to Octanol-Water Partition Coefficient," *Toxicol. Appl. Pharm.* 77:1–10 (1985).
2. Boese, B. L. "Uptake Efficiency of the Gills of English Sole (*Parophrys vetulus*) for Four Phthalate Esters," *Can. J. Fish. Aquat. Sci.* 41:1713–1718 (1984).
3. Spacie, A., and J. L. Hamelink. "Alternate Models for Describing the Bioconcentration of Organics in Fish," *Environ. Toxicol. Chem.* 1:309–320 (1982).
4. Davies, R. P., and A. J. Dobbs. "The Prediction of Bioconcentration in Fish," *Water Res.* 18:1253–1262 (1984).
5. Landrum, P. "Bioavailability and Toxicokinetics of Polycyclic Aromatic Hydrocarbons Sorbed to Sediments for the Amphipod *Pontoporeia hoyi*," *Environ. Sci. Technol.* 23:588–595 (1989).
6. "Standard Practice for Conducting Bioconcentration Tests with Fishes and Saltwater Bivalve Molluscs," ASTM E 1022-84, Philadelphia, PA (1984).
7. Lee, H., II, B. L. Boese, J. Pelletier, M. Winsor, D. T. Specht, and R. C. Randall. "Guidance Manual: Bedded Sediment Bioaccumulation Tests," U.S. EPA Report, ERL-Narragansett Contribution No. N111 (1989).
8. Stehly, G. R., P. F. Landrum, M. G. Henry, and C. Klemm. "Toxicokinetics of PAHs in *Hexagenia*," *Environ. Toxicol. Chem.* 9:167–174 (1990).
9. Foster, G. D., S. M. Baski, and J. C. Means. "Bioaccumulation of Trace Organic Contaminants from Sediment by Baltic Clams (*Macoma balthica*) and Soft-Shell Clams (*Mya arenaria*)," *Environ. Toxicol. Chem.* 6:969–976 (1987).
10. Pruell, R. J., N. J. Rubinstein, B. K. Taplin, J. A. LiVosi, and C. B. Norwood. "2,3,7,8-TCDD, 2,3,7,8-TCDF, and PCBs in Marine Sediments and Biota: Laboratory and Field Studies," U.S. EPA, ERL-Narragansett, final report to Army Corps of Engineers, New York District (1990).
11. Norstrom, R. J., A. E. McKinnon, and A. S. deFreitas. "A Bioenergetic Based

Model for Pollutant Accumulation by Fish. Simulation of PCB and Methylmercury Residue Levels in Ottawa River," *J. Fish. Res. Bd. Can.* 33:248–267 (1976).

12. Boese, B. L., H. Lee II, D. T. Specht, R. C. Randall, and M. Winsor. "Comparison of Aqueous and Solid-Phase Uptake for Hexachlorobenzene in the Tellinid Clam, *Macoma nasuta* (Conrad): A Mass Balance Approach," *Environ. Toxicol. Chem.* 9:221–231 (1990).

13. Knezovich, J. P., F. L. Harrison, and R. G. Wilhelm. "The Bioavailability of Sediment-Sorbed Organic Chemicals," *Water Air Soil Pollut.* 32:233–245 (1987).

14. Lee, H., II, and R. Swartz. "Biological Processes Affecting the Distribution of Pollutants in Marine Sediments. Part II. Biodeposition and Bioturbation," in *Contaminants and Sediments,* Vol. 2, R. A. Baker, Ed. (Ann Arbor, MI: Ann Arbor Science, 1980), pp. 555–606.

15. Stull, J. K., R. B. Baird, and T. C. Heesen. "Marine Sediment Core Profiles of Trace Constituents Offshore of a Deep Wastewater Outfall," *J. Water Pollut. Control Fed.* 58:985–991 (1986).

16. Ferraro, S., H. Lee II, R. Ozretich, and D. Specht. "Predicting Bioaccumulation Potential: A Test of a Fugacity-Based Model," *Arch. Environ. Contamin. Toxicol.* 19:386–394 (1990).

17. Cammen, L. M. "Ingestion Rate: An Empirical Model for Aquatic Deposit Feeders and Detritivores," *Oecologia* 44:303–310 (1980).

18. Hassett, J. J., J. C. Means, W. L. Banwart, and S. G. Wood. "Sorption Properties of Sediments and Energy-Related Pollutants," U.S. EPA Report-600/3–80–041 (1980).

19. Karickhoff, S. W. "Organic Pollutant Sorption in Aquatic Systems," *J. Hydraul. Eng.* 110:707–735 (1984).

20. Lee, H., II, B. L. Boese, J. Pelletier, and R. C. Randall. "A Method to Estimate Gut Uptake Efficiencies for Hydrophobic Organic Pollutants," *Environ. Toxicol. Chem.* 9:215–219 (1990).

21. Brown, S. L. "Feces of Intertidal Benthic Invertebrates: Influence of Particle Selection in Feeding on Trace Element Concentration," *Mar. Ecol. Prog. Series* 28:219–231 (1986).

22. Tagon, G. L., and P. A. Jumars. "Variable Ingestion Rate and Its Role in Optimal Foraging Behavior of Marine Deposit-Feeders," *Ecology* 65:549–558 (1984).

23. Gobas, F., C. Derek, and D. MacKay. "Dynamics of Dietary Bioaccumulation and Fecal Elimination of Hydrophobic Organic Chemicals in Fish," *Chemosphere* 17:943–962 (1988).

24. Adams, W. J. "Bioavailability of Neutral Lipophilic Organic Chemicals Contained on Sediments: A Review," in *Fate And Effects Of Sediment-Bound Chemical In Aquatic Systems,* K. L. Dickson, A. W. Maki, and W. A. Brungs, Eds. (New York: Pergamon Press, 1987), pp. 219–244.

25. Adams, W. J., R. A. Kimerle, and R. G. Mosher. "Aquatic Safety Assessment of Chemicals Sorbed to Sediments," in *Aquatic Toxicology and Hazard Assessment: Seventh Symposium,* ASTM STP 854, R. D. Cardwell, R. Purdy, and R. C. Bahner, Eds. (Philadelphia: American Society for Testing and Materials, 1985), pp. 429–453.

26. Kemp, P. F., and R. C. Swartz. "Acute Toxicity of Interstitial and Particle-Bound Cadmium to a Marine Infaunal Amphipod," *Mar. Environ. Res.* 26:135–153 (1988).

27. Winsor, M., B. L. Boese, H. Lee II, R. C. Randall, and D. T. Specht. "Determina-

tion of the Ventilation Rate of Interstitial and Overlying Water by the Clam *Macoma nasuta*," *Environ. Toxicol. Chem.* 9:209–213 (1990).

28. Boese, B. L., H. Lee II, and D. T. Specht. "The Efficiency of Uptake of Hexachlorobenzene from Water by the Tellinid Clam *Macoma nasuta*," *Aquat. Toxicol.* 12:345–356 (1988).

29. Aller, R. C., and J. Y. Yingst. "Biogeochemistry of Tube-Dwellings: A Study of the Sedentary Polychaete *Amphitrite ornata* (Leidy)," *J. Mar. Res.* 36:201–254 (1978).

30. Aller, R. C. "The Importance of the Diffusive Permeability of Animal Burrow Linings in Determining Marine Sediment Chemistry," *J. Mar. Res.* 41:299–322 (1983).

31. Aller, R. C., J. Y. Yingst, and W. J. Ullman. "Comparative Biogeochemistry of Water in Intertidal *Onuphis* (Polychaeta) and *Upogebia* (Crustacea) Burrows: Temporal Patterns and Causes," *J. Mar. Res.* 41:571–604 (1983).

32. Landrum, P. F., S. R. Nihart, B. J. Eadie, and L. R. Herche. "Reduction in Bioavailability of Organic Contaminants to the Amphipod *Pontoporeia hoyi* by Dissolved Organic Matter of Sediment Interstitial Water," *Environ. Toxicol. Chem.* 6:11–20 (1987).

33. Servos, M. R., and D. C. G. Muir. "Effect of Dissolved Organic Matter from Canadian Shield Lakes on the Bioavailability of 1,3,6,8-Tetrachlorodibenzo-p-dioxin to the Amphipod *Crangonyx laurentianus*," *Environ. Toxicol. Chem.* 8:141–150 (1989).

34. DiToro, D. M., J. D. Mahony, D. J. Hansen, K. J. Scott, M. B. Hicks, S. M. Mayr, and M. S. Redmond. "Toxicity of Cadmium in Sediments: The Role of Acid Volatile Sulfide," *Environ. Toxicol. Chem.* 9:1489–1504 (1990).

35. Poutanen, E. L., and R. J. Morris. "A Study of the Formation of High Molecular Weight Compounds during Decomposition of a Field Diatom Population," *Estuar. Coast. Shelf Sci.* 17:189–196 (1983).

36. Erickson, R. J., and J. M. McKim. "A Simple Flow-Limited Model for Exchange of Organic Chemicals at Fish Gills," *Environ. Toxicol. Chem.* 9:159–165 (1990).

37. Karickhoff, S., and K. Morris. "Sorption Dynamics of Hydrophobic Pollutants in Sediment Suspensions," *Environ. Toxicol. Chem.* 4:469–479 (1985).

38. Connolly, J. P., and C. J. Pederson. "A Thermodynamic-Based Evaluation of Organic Chemical Accumulation in Aquatic Organisms," *Environ. Sci. Technol.* 22:99–103 (1988).

39. Simkiss, K., and A. Z. Mason. "Metal Ions: Metabolic and Toxic Effects," in *The Mollusca. Vol. 2. Environmental Biochemistry and Physiology*, P. W. Hochachka, Ed. (New York: Academic Press, 1983), pp. 101–164.

40. Klump, J. V., J. Krezoski, M. Smith, and J. Kaster. "Dual Tracer Studies of the Assimilation of an Organic Contaminant from Sediments by Deposit Feeding Oligochaetes," *Can. J. Fish. Aquat. Sci.* 44:1574–1583 (1987).

41. Specht, D. T., and H. Lee II. "Direct Measurement Technique for Determining Ventilation Rate in the Deposit-Feeding Clam *Macoma nasuta* (Bivalvia, Tellinacea)," *Mar. Biol.* 101:211–218 (1989).

42. Kemp, W. M., and W. Boynton. "External and Internal Factors Regulating Metabolic Rates of an Estuarine Benthic Community," *Oecologia* 51:19–27 (1981).

CHAPTER **6**

The Influence of Water Column Dissolved Organic Carbon on the Uptake of 2,2′,4,4′,5,5′-Hexachlorobiphenyl (PCB 153) by *Daphnia magna*

Hayla E. Evans

INTRODUCTION

In recent years, there have been a plethora of laboratory studies that have demonstrated that the bioavailability of many organic contaminants can be changed by the presence of humic acid (HA). For example, it has been shown that HA can reduce the uptake of dioxin, polychlorinated biphenyls (PCBs), and/or certain polycyclic aromatic hydrocarbons (PAH) by pelagic invertebrates such as *Daphnia magna*;[1,2] by benthic invertebrates such as *Pontoporeia hoyi*[3] and *Crangonyx laurentianus*;[4] and by fish such as *Lepomis macrochirus*,[5,6] *Salmo gairdneri*,[7,8] and *S. salar*.[9,10]

Similarly, the dissolved organic carbon (DOC) extracted from sediment interstitial waters has been shown to decrease the uptake rate constant of two PAHs (pyrene and benzo(a)pyrene) and a PCB (2,2′,4,4′-tetrachlorobiphenyl) by *P. hoyi*.[11] On the other hand, HA had no effect on *Daphnia* accumulation of several other PAHs, including anthracene, dibenzanthracene, dimethylbenzanthrazene, and naphthalene.[1,2] Naphthalene accumulation by sunfish was also unaffected by the presence of HA,[5] as was anthracene accumulation.[6] However, HA actually increased the accumulation of methylcholanthrene by *Daphnia*,[1] although these results were contradictory to those obtained later by McCarthy et al.[2]

Fewer bioavailability investigations have been carried out using "natural" or water column DOC, presumably because of the difficulty in obtaining a wide range of DOC concentrations in situ. This is unfortunate because it is becoming increasingly apparent that water column DOC may be considerably less effective than either HA or sediment interstitial DOC in the binding of hydrophobic organic contaminants in lakes.[12-15] Furthermore, in laboratory investigations in which invertebrates are used, the effect of lipid content (or condi-

Table 6.1. Chemical Composition of the Water Used for PCB 153 Uptake Experiments by D. Magna

	Composition (mg/L)							pH	Cond (μmhos/cm)	Color (Hazen Units)
	Ca	Mg	Na	K	Cl	SO$_4$	DOC			
SLW	2.50	0.65	0.90	0.56	0.74	3.15	<0.1	—	—	—
FLW										
4/11/89	2.45	0.63	1.03	0.70	1.24	6.9	7.7	—	36	69
5/9/89	2.75	0.66	1.31	0.52	1.50	6.6	7.5	—	33	70
6/14/89	2.90	0.62	1.49	0.83	1.51	6.4	8.7	—	—	—
1978–86[a]	2.64	0.62	0.84	0.55	0.74	7.2	8.5	5.6	29	110
2X-FLW										
+ 6/14/89	5.95	1.32	2.50	1.19	2.58	12.05	12.7	—	—	—

Note: SLW = simulated lake water, FLW = filtered Fawn lake water, 2X-FLW = concentrated filtered Fawn lake water (see text for explanation).
[a]1978–1986 whole-lake "ice-free" mean, n = 8 (from Reid and Girard).[32]

tion) of the experimental animals on contaminant uptake has been largely ignored. This practice also may be unwise because studies have shown that lipid content contributes to experimental variability[16] and to the ultimate concentration of pollutants such as PCBs in zooplankton.[17] Certainly for fish, it is widely accepted that the bioconcentration of hydrophobic organic contaminants is largely dependent on the animals' lipid fraction.[18,19]

Therefore, the purpose of this study was to investigate the uptake of 2,2′,4,4′,5,5′-hexachlorobiphenyl (PCB 153) by the freshwater cladoceran *Daphnia magna* using water column DOC at various concentrations. Also an attempt was made to examine and maintain a consistent lipid content in the animals.

MATERIALS AND METHODS

Collection and Preparation of the Water

Water for the uptake experiments was either DOC-free simulated lake water (SLW) or filtered lake water (FLW) collected from Fawn Lake, a small (0.858 km^2) brown-water lake located ~250 km north of Toronto, Ontario. The SLW was prepared by adding 7 mg/L MgSO$_4$ · 7H$_2$O, 2.5 mg/L Na$_2$SO$_4$, 1 mg/L KCl, 0.5 mg/L CaCl$_2$ · 2H$_2$O, and 8 mg/L CaCO$_3$ into distilled deionized water. The resulting chemical composition of the water (Table 6.1) is typical of soft-water lakes in south central Ontario.

Water was collected from the outflow of Fawn Lake in 4-L amber glass bottles on April 11, May 9, and June 14, 1989. Within 24 hr, the water was pumped through a 0.45-μm Gelman flow-through filtration system. The filtered water was refrigerated, in darkness, and used for the uptake experiments within 2 weeks of collection. The concentrations of Ca, Mg, Na, K, SO$_4$, Cl, and DOC in the lake on each sampling day, together with long-term data for

Fawn Lake are given in Table 6.1. All analyses were conducted by the Ontario Ministry of the Environment (OMOE).[20]

The FLW from the April 11th collection was not used directly for uptake experiments. Rather, it was evaporated at 50°C in a drying oven in order to reduce the volume of water by ~130 times. This concentrate was then added back into FLW that had been collected from the lake on June 14th, so that an increase in the ambient DOC concentration of the lake water could be achieved. The resulting ionic composition of this water (i.e., 2X-FLW) is given in Table 6.1. Thus, the DOC concentrations of the water used in the uptake experiments were 0, 7.5, and 12.7 mg C/L.

Culturing of Animals

Daphnia magna were obtained from a culture maintained at the University of Toronto; however, for these uptake experiments, a new culture was started by placing a single daphnid into SLW. The second (i.e., F_2) generation of offspring from this *Daphnia* were then distributed between two 4-L jars (one containing SLW and one containing autoclaved FLW) and fed ~1 mL of a *Chlamydomonas* culture daily. *Daphnia* for the uptake experiments were taken either from the jar containing SLW (for the SLW experiments) or the jar containing autoclaved FLW (for the experiments using FLW and 2X-FLW). SLW or autoclaved FLW was added to each jar as required.

Experimental Design

To begin each experiment, the amber glass bottles containing 4 L of SLW, FLW, or 2X-FLW were spiked with ~4 μL of ^{14}C-labeled PCB 153 (~4 μg PCB/L; specific activity = 9.4 μCi/μmol; Pathfinder Laboratories, St. Louis, MO) in hexane carrier. The bottles were capped and allowed to equilibrate for 17–70 hr. After equilibration, a 2-mL subsample of water was taken for the determination of total PCB concentration (i.e., C_T in dpm/mL). At the same time, the amount of PCB bound to the DOC (i.e., C_B in dpm/mL) was ascertained using Sep-Pak C_{18} cartridges (see Evans[14]). Briefly, a 5-mL glass syringe was used to rinse 2.5 mL of water through the column at a flow rate of ~10 mL/min, following which an additional 2.5 mL of water was passed through the column. A 2-mL sample of the eluant was then obtained and immediately placed into a glass vial containing 18 mL of aqueous counting scintillant (ACS, Amersham).

Next, 199 ± 1 mL of the ^{14}C-PCB 153 labeled water was weighed directly into twenty 250-mL Erlenmeyer flasks. Prior to the actual start of the experiment, *Daphnia* were examined microscopically and hand-selected to be of approximately similar size and lipid content (following the lipid index of Tessier and Goulden[21]). At time zero, a single *Daphnia* was added to each flask.

Five replicate flasks were sampled at 1-, 2-, 4-, and 8-hr time intervals. Total PCB concentration (C_T) was determined on 2-mL samples taken from each flask. The individual *Daphnia* were then removed from the water, put into 1–3 mL of clean water, blotted, and weighed immediately to determine wet weight. Each daphnid was then placed directly into a glass vial containing ACS.

Previous experiments that I had conducted had shown about a 5% decrease in the wet weight of a daphnid within the first minute after blotting. Consequently, the time between the blotting and weighing of the animals was kept as short and as constant as possible in order to minimize variation in *Daphnia* wet weights. For the 8-hr samples only, the *Daphnia* were quickly reexamined (prior to being weighed), and the lipid index was ascertained. In addition, the amount of PCB bound to DOC (C_B) was determined (as explained above) on a centrifuged (1000 rpm for a minimum of 10 min) subsample of water taken from one of the flasks.

In total, twelve uptake experiments were performed: five with the SLW ([DOC] = 0 mg/L), four with the FLW ([DOC] = 7.5 mg/L), and three with the 2X-FLW ([DOC] = 12.7 mg/L). To account for the extent of accumulation attributed to sorption to the carapace as well as to that occurring through passive diffusion, an uptake experiment was also conducted using dead *Daphnia* in SLW. The same procedure was applied except that the animals were heat-killed (50°C for 10 min) prior to the experiment.

Depuration of radiolabeled PCB by the *Daphnia* was measured in SLW. As with the uptake experiments, 4 L of water were spiked with ^{14}C-labeled PCB and allowed to equilibrate for 47 hr. Then the water was weighed into twenty Erlenmeyer flasks, and one *Daphnia* (hand-selected as before) was added to each flask. After a 4-hr exposure to the PCB, the *Daphnia* and the water in five of the flasks were sampled. Meanwhile, the remaining fifteen *Daphnia* were transferred to fifteen flasks, each containing 199 ± 1 mL of clean, nonradiolabeled SLW. These flasks were then sampled after 2, 4, and 8 hr (following the procedures outlined above).

All the samples (i.e., water and *Daphnia*) were counted for 10 or 20 min on a Beckman LS 7000 liquid scintillation counter. In order to calculate dpm, the samples were corrected for counting efficiency (92.5–95.5%) and background (44–55 dpm) using the H number method of quench monitoring (an external standardization technique).

Calculations

After exposure to a known concentration of contaminant in water, the uptake rate constant (K_u in mL/mg wet weight/hr) for PCB 153 by *Daphnia* can be determined from the conventional uptake-depuration equation for aquatic biota:

$$dC_D/dt = K_u C_T - K_d C_D \qquad (6.1)$$

where C_D = concentration of PCB in the *Daphnia* (dpm/mg)
         C_T = total concentration of PCB in the water (dpm/mL)

K_d = depuration rate constant (hr^{-1})
t = time (hr)

In these experiments, the total concentration of PCB 153 in the water changed approximately linearly through time according to the equation:

$$C_T = C_{T(0)}(1 + K_w t) \qquad (6.2)$$

where $C_{T(0)}$ = predicted concentration of PCB in the water at time zero (dpm/mL)
K_w = rate of loss/increase of PCB (hr^{-1}) in the water

Thus, for each uptake experiment, the data on the change in PCB concentration in the water through time were fitted to Equation 6.2, and the values for $C_{T(0)}$ and K_w were ascertained. Substituting Equation 6.2 into Equation 6.1 yields

$$dC_D/dt = K_u C_{T(0)}(1 + K_w t) - K_d C_D \qquad (6.3)$$

Equation 6.3 can be integrated using an integrating factor method. The result is, for $C_D = 0$ when $t = 0$,

$$C_D = (K_u/K_d)C_{T(0)}[(1 - e^{-K_d t}) + (K_w/K_d)(K_d t - 1 + e^{-K_d t})] \qquad (6.4)$$

Depuration of PCB 153 (K_d) was determined by placing contaminated *Daphnia* into clean water as described above. From Equation 6.1, the concentration of PCB 153 in the animals through time is given by

$$dC_D/dt = -K_d C_D \qquad (6.5)$$

which yields after integration

$$C_D = C_{D(0)}e^{-K_d t} \qquad (6.6)$$

or

$$\ln C_D = \ln C_{D(0)} - K_d t \qquad (6.7)$$

where $C_{D(0)}$ (dpm/mg) is the initial (i.e., contaminated) concentration of PCB 153 in the *Daphnia*. Consequently, a semilog plot of C_D versus time should give a straight line with slope = K_d. The K_d value, together with the values for K_w and $C_{T(0)}$ determined from Equation 6.2 and the C_D measurements made at each sampling period, were substituted into Equation 6.4, so that four estimates of the uptake rate constant, K_u, could be made (i.e., at 1, 2, 4, and 8 hr). The average of these estimates was used to test for differences in the K_u values among the various DOC concentrations using a one-way analysis of variance (ANOVA).

The association coefficient calculated on the basis of DOC (K_{DOC} in mL/g C) can be determined from

$$K_{DOC} = \frac{C_B/[DOC]}{C_T - C_B} \qquad (6.8)$$

where [DOC] is the DOC concentration in the water in g/L. The fraction of hydrophobic contaminant that passes through the Sep-Pak column in the absence of DOC was previously determined to be 5% for PCB 153,[14] and so a breakthrough factor (BF = 0.05 C_T, in dpm/mL) was subtracted from C_B prior to calculating K_{DOC} values.

RESULTS AND DISCUSSION

After equilibration of the water with the PCB, that is, at the beginning of each uptake experiment, and also at the 8-hr sampling interval, the amount of PCB bound to DOC was less than 5 dpm/mL in the FLW experiments (i.e., < 9% of the PCB 153 was bound to the DOC), and less than 14 dpm/mL in the 2X-FLW experiments (i.e., < 13% of the PCB was bound to the DOC). Since counting errors at these low levels are very high (i.e., $\pm\sqrt{N}/N \times 100\%$, where N is the total number of counts), K_{DOC} values were not determined in any of the FLW experiments nor were they determined at the beginning of the 2X-FLW experiments. However, at the 8-hr sampling period, the association coefficient ranged between 8.2×10^3 and 1.1×10^4 mL/g C. These K_{DOC} values are about one-third to one-half of the value of 2.6×10^4 mL/g C reported for the association of PCB 153 with the DOC in Lake Michigan ([DOC] = 0.83–5.8 mg C/L)[22] and also about one-third to one-half of the values previously reported for Fawn Lake.[14]

While the slightly lower K_{DOC} values calculated in this study are due most likely to natural variation, alternately some PCB could be associating with hexane carrier still remaining in the 4-L bottles after the equilibration period. This "hexane-bound" PCB would not pass through the Sep-Pak column and would result in an anomalously low K_{DOC} value. A change in the chemistry, and thus the binding capacity, of the water during the evaporation and subsequent dilution procedure is also a possibility, although a similar concentration procedure previously was found to have no effect on the molecular weight distribution of the DOC, < 5000 daltons in size, collected from this lake.[23]

The recovery (i.e., the total amount of isotope in the water + *Daphnia* at the end of the experiment divided by the total amount of isotope added at the start of the experiment) of PCB 153 measured in one SLW experiment was found to be 60% after the 8-hr uptake experiment (following 18-hr equilibration). This is comparable to the recovery obtained during other investigations where no *Daphnia* were present.[14] About 94% of the recovered isotope was in

Table 6.2. Linear Regressions of the Total PCB Concentration in the Water (C_T,dpm/mL) versus Time (hours) in each of the 12 Uptake Experiments

Experiment		p	K_w
4400–SLW	C_T = 89.2 − 2.58 (time)	0.086	−0.029
4700–SLW	C_T = 75.9 − 1.45 (time)	0.238	−0.019
4300–SLW	C_T = 75.7 − 2.86 (time)	0.001	−0.038
4200–SLW	C_T = 65.9 − 2.77 (time)	0.088	−0.042
4100–SLW	C_T = 59.3 − 2.26 (time)	0.004	−0.038
3800–FLW	C_T = 57.0 − 1.03 (time)	0.160	−0.018
3500–FLW	C_T = 15.5 + 0.357 (time)	0.035	0.023
3900–FLW	C_T = 86.3 − 1.99 (time)	0.000	−0.023
4000–FLW	C_T = 92.9 − 1.60 (time)	0.080	−0.017
5100–2X–FLW	C_T = 184 − 6.83 (time)	0.044	−0.037
4900–2X–FLW	C_T = 82.9 − 2.73 (time)	0.000	−0.033
5000–2X–FLW	C_T = 115 − 2.22 (time)	0.022	−0.019

Note: K_w = rate of loss/increase of PCB from the water (hr^{-1}) calculated according to Equation 6.2.

the water and 6% in the *Daphnia*. The 40% loss of isotope may have occurred as a result of coevaporation (with the hexane) during the equilibration period or when the radiolabeled water was being poured from the 4-L amber glass bottle into the Erlenmeyer flasks. Alternately, adsorption of the isotope onto the walls of the glassware may have occurred, especially in the absence of DOC.[24]

The results of the twelve linear regressions of the total PCB concentration in the water versus time according to Equation 6.2 are given in Table 6.2. In six of the twelve uptake experiments, there is a significant decrease in C_T through time ($p < 0.05$), and in one experiment, there is a significant increase in C_T through time. The corresponding values for K_w range between −0.019 and −0.042/hr in eleven of the uptake experiments, and 0.023/hr in one experiment.

The results of the depuration experiment are shown in Figure 6.1. In this figure, two data points (one at t = 0 and one at t = 8 hr), which were greater than three standard deviations from the mean of the other four points, were eliminated from the analysis. However, because biological variability is still large and elimination is very slow, the slope (K_d) of the semilog plot of C_D versus time is not significantly different from zero over the 8-hr depuration period ($p > 0.05$). Nonetheless, the K_d value of 0.0235/hr derived from these data was used as the best estimate of the depuration rate constant. Uptake of PCB 153 by direct sorption to the carapace of the *Daphnia* and by passive diffusion (ascertained using heat-killed *Daphnia*) was negligible (< 1 dpm/mg wet weight/hr, which was < 4% of the total PCB activity in the water).

Typical plots of C_D versus time are shown in Figure 6.2. It can be seen that generally C_D increases linearly through time, although in Figure 6.2c (5100–2X-FLW), the PCB concentrations in the *Daphnia* appear to plateau. This phenomenon was observed in other experiments in which there was a

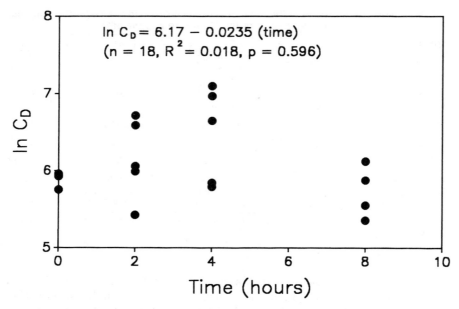

Figure 6.1 Depuration of PCB 153 by *Daphnia magna* following 4-hr exposure to the contaminant. C_D = concentration of PCB 153 in the *Daphnia* in dpm/mg wet weight.

significant decrease in C_T through time (see Table 6.2). Thus, the observed plateau in the data most likely is a reflection of decreasing water concentrations and not of steady state. An estimate of the amount of time required to reach steady state can be made from the depuration rate constant, K_d, since the half-life ($t_{1/2}$, in hours) of the PCB 153 in the *Daphnia* is given by

$$t_{1/2} = 0.693/K_d \qquad (6.9)$$

Assuming a K_d value of 0.0235/hr (Figure 6.1), the half-life of PCB 153 in the *Daphnia* is calculated to be about 29 hr. Since the uptake experiments lasted only 8 hr, it is unlikely that steady state was attained. The observation that the plots of C_D continue to increase linearly over the 8-hr experiment (see Figure 6.2), except where there are changes in C_T, would also support this conclusion.

The wet weights of the *Daphnia* used for each experiment are given in Table 6.3. While they vary about threefold within each experiment (average coefficient of variation in wet weights = 26.8% ± 5.9 for the 12 uptake experiments, n = 20 for each experiment), an ANOVA revealed that the average wet weight of the *Daphnia* was not significantly different among the three DOC concentrations (p = 0.756) with average values of 0.950 ± 0.194 (n = 5), 1.049 ± 0.180 (n = 4), and 0.993 ± 0.212 (n = 3) mg wet weight for the SLW, FLW, and 2X-FLW experiments, respectively.

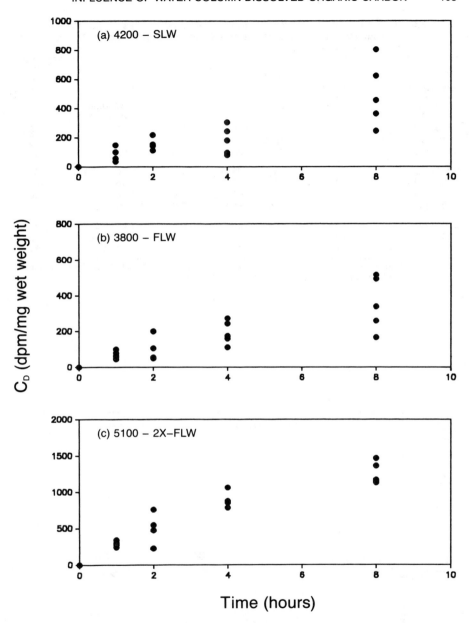

Figure 6.2   Uptake of PCB 153 by *Daphnia magna* through time in *(a)* SLW, *(b)* FLW, and *(c)* 2X-FLW. C_D = concentration of PCB 153 in the *Daphnia* in dpm/mg wet weight.

Table 6.3. DOC Concentrations, Wet Weights, and Lipid Indices of the *Daphnia*, and Average Uptake Rate Constants and Bioconcentration Factors for Each of the 12 Uptake Experiments

Experiment	[DOC] (mg C/L)	Wet Weight (mg)	Lipid Index	K_u (mL/ mg ww/hr)	BCF (mL/ mg ww)
4400–SLW	0	0.855 (0.298)	0.5	2.32 (0.94)	99
4700–SLW	0	0.682 (0.106)	0.5	1.81 (0.76)	77
4300–SLW	0	1.069 (0.259)	1.0	1.41 (1.17)	60
4200–SLW	0	1.184 (0.300)	1.5	1.16 (0.25)	49
4100–SLW	0	0.961 (0.332)	2.0	1.95 (1.73)	83
3800–FLW	7.5	1.293 (0.334)	1.0	1.06 (0.17)	45
3500–FLW	7.5	1.042 (0.261)	1.5	1.16 (0.30)	49
3900–FLW	7.5	0.995 (0.995)	2.0	1.56 (0.82)	66
4000–FLW	7.5	0.869 (0.869)	2.0	2.83 (0.85)	120
5100–2X–FLW	12.7	1.055 (0.280)	0.5	1.40 (0.22)	60
4900–2X–FLW	12.7	0.765 (0.211)	1.0	1.92 (0.46)	82
5000–2X–FLW	12.7	1.178 (0.414)	1.5	1.91 (0.33)	81

Notes: Average uptake rate constants (K_u) calculated from Equation 6.4. BCF calculated as K_u/K_d. Numbers in parentheses are one standard deviation.

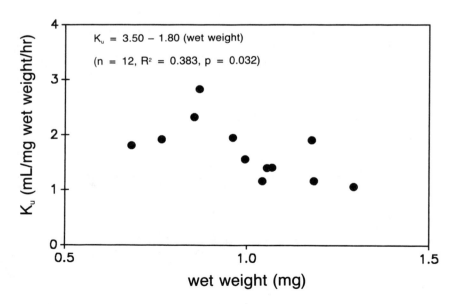

Figure 6.3 Relationship between the uptake rate constant, K_u (mL/mg wet weight/hr), for PCB 153 and the wet weight of the *Daphnia* (mg wet weight).

The average uptake rate constants, calculated according to Equation 6.4 are also given in Table 6.3. They range between 1.06 and 2.83 mL/mg wet weight/hr (mean = 1.71 ± 0.52, n = 12) which is comparable to, but slightly higher than, the value of 0.750 mL/mg wet weight/hr estimated by McCarthy et al. for the uptake of benzo(a)pyrene (BAP, log K_{ow} = 6.5) by *Daphnia* in water containing no HA.[2] It should be noted that these are conditional uptake rate constants because they are based on the total amount of PCB in the water, and not just the freely dissolved concentration. However, as discussed above, the results from the Sep-Pak experiments indicated that in all experiments only a small (and often indeterminate) fraction of the PCB was bound to the DOC.

There is a significant relation between the uptake rate constant and the *Daphnia* wet weights (n = 12, p = 0.032), as shown in Figure 6.3, with smaller *Daphnia* having slightly higher uptake rate constants than larger *Daphnia*. These results are similar to those reported by Landrum, who found that there was a significant increase in K_u values for tetrachlorobiphenyl and BAP as the weight of a benthic invertebrate, *Pontoporeia hoyi,* decreased.[25] Evans and Landrum report K_u values of 0.0535 and 0.0575 mL/mg wet weight/hr for PCB 153 by *Pontoporeia hoyi* and *Mysis relicta*, respectively.[26] While these invertebrates cannot necessarily be compared to *Daphnia*, my average K_u value of 1.71 mL/mg wet weight/hr is more than an order of magnitude higher than their values. However, the average wet weights of *Pontoporeia* and *Mysis* are 8 and 40 times greater than that of *Daphnia* (8.3 and 43 mg, respectively,[26] versus 1 mg for *Daphnia*). Thus, much of the difference between their results and my own could be attributed to the size of the animals rather than their habitat and physiology.

In order to test whether water column DOC has an effect on the uptake of PCB 153 by *D. magna*, a one-way ANOVA was conducted on the data. Since there were no significant differences in the average size of the animals among the three DOC concentrations, a direct comparison could be made between [DOC] and K_u values. The results showed no significant differences among the 3 DOC concentrations (p = 0.973), with average K_u values of 1.73 ± 0.446 (n = 5), 1.65 ± 0.814 (n = 4), and 1.74 ± 0.297 (n = 3) mL/mg wet weight/hr for the SLW, FLW, and 2X-FLW experiments, respectively (Table 6.3). These results assume that K_d is constant and equal to 0.0235/hr for each of the three DOC concentrations. While this assumption may result in a consistent bias in the calculated K_u values, this bias is small. For example, a threefold increase in the K_d value used in Equation 6.4 resulted in less than a 10% increase in the average K_u values calculated.

If the system has reached steady state, the bioconcentration factor (BCF, in mL/mg wet weight) can be measured directly as C_D/C_T. Alternately, it can be determined from K_u/K_d.[26] The BCFs calculated in this manner (Table 6.3) range between 45 and 120 mL/mg wet weight, which corresponds to a dimensionless BCF of 4.5–12 × 10^4 if the wet density of the *Daphnia* is assumed to be 1 g/mL. This BCF is very close to the value of 4.4 × 10^4 reported by Oliver and Niimi for the in situ bioconcentration of PCB 153 by all plankton in Lake Ontario (see their Table 1).[19]

An estimate of BCF can also be made from the empirical relationship developed by Mackay:[18]

$$BCF = 0.048 \, K_{ow} \tag{6.10}$$

where K_{ow} is the octanol-water partition coefficient and the constant, 0.048, reflects the lipid content of the biota (i.e., 4.8% for fish). Data pertaining to the lipid content of pelagic zooplankton are scarce, but Wainman and Lean report seasonal values of about 0.8–1.5% (converted to a wet weight basis) for all zooplankton, including *Daphnia* spp., collected from Anstruther Lake, Ontario.[27] MacDonald and Metcalfe measured slightly lower lipid contents of 1.17, 0.17, and 0.22% for the zooplankton in Lakes Clear, Rice, and Scugog (Ontario), respectively.[28] Assuming a lipid content of 0.2–1.5% and a log K_{ow} value for PCB 153 of 6.9,[29] the predicted BCF from Equation 6.10 would be 1.6–11.9 × 10[4], which is very close to the measured values of 4.5–12 × 10[4]. These results would therefore support the assumption that the dominant concentrating phase in *Daphnia*, as in fish, is lipid, and as a result, bioconcentration occurs via direct partitioning into the lipid fraction.

While lipid levels were ascertained visually in these experiments (see Table 6.3), rigorous statistical analysis of the data was not possible because the lipid index was not calibrated against "true" lipid concentrations. Nonetheless, there does not appear to be a trend in K_u in BCF with increasing lipid level. These results are similar to those reported by Landrum, who found no correlation between lipid content and the uptake rates of BAP and phenanthracene by *P. hoyi*.[25] On the other hand, the variation in the measured K_u values, at a given DOC concentration (Table 6.3), might be a result of the condition (i.e., lipid content) of the *Daphnia*, as has been found by others.[16] Since the lipid index of the *Daphnia* often dropped by 1 unit by the end of the 8-hr experiment, this factor should be considered in all studies involving invertebrates and other biota.

The results published in the literature for experiments conducted on invertebrates using "natural" (i.e., water column) DOC are somewhat mixed. Leversee et al. reported that the removal of DOC from two filtered natural waters resulted in about a 30% increase in the BCF of BAP by *Daphnia*.[1] Similarly, Kukkonen and Oikari[30] and Kukkonen et al.[31] found that the accumulation of dehydroabietic acid and BAP by *Daphnia* were distinctly reduced in natural humic waters, although no reduction in the accumulation of pentachlorophenol was observed.[30] Furthermore, Kukkonen et al. were unable to reconcile the decrease in the bioavailability of BAP with the fraction of the PAH that was bound to the DOC, suggesting that the BAP was, in fact, still available for uptake by the *Daphnia*.[31] Servos and Muir showed that epilimnetic DOC decreased the uptake of dioxin by the amphipod *Crangonyx laurentianus*, but their data suggest that epilimnetic (water column) DOC was less effective in reducing uptake than either HA or interstitial DOC.[4] In fact, Servos et al. found that water column DOC had little effect on the apparent uptake rate of dioxin by rainbow trout (*S. gairdneri*).[8]

In Fawn Lake, it is likely that the water column DOC has a much lower sorptive capacity for PCB than does HA and interstitial DOC and/or that the PCB 153 bound to the DOC is still available for uptake by the *Daphnia*. In these experiments, probably the former is true because given a K_{DOC} value of $\sim 10^4$ mL/g C and a [DOC] of $\sim 10^1$ mg/L, there is still about 90% of the PCB 153 available for uptake by the *Daphnia*. The results from the present study therefore suggest that water column DOC in lakes may be having a negligible effect on the cycling of PCB 153 and perhaps other hydrophobic organic contaminants. Furthermore, both the size (wet weight) and condition (lipid content) of the *Daphnia* are important factors affecting both the magnitude of, and the variability in, the measured BCFs and uptake rate constants. Thus, these variables should be considered in all bioavailability studies.

ACKNOWLEDGMENTS

This work was financed by an OMOE grant to Dr. Harold Harvey at the University of Toronto. I am indebted to Ms. Wei Xu, who provided excellent assistance with all of the uptake experiments, and also to Trent University, for the use of a laboratory and the liquid scintillation counter.

REFERENCES

1. Leversee, G. J., P. F. Landrum, J. P. Geisy, and T. Fannin. "Humic Acids Reduce Bioaccumulation of Some Polycyclic Aromatic Hydrocarbons," *Can. J. Fish. Aquat. Sci.* 40(Suppl. 2):63–69 (1983).
2. McCarthy, J. F., B. D. Jimenez, and T. Barbee. "Effect of Dissolved Humic Material on Accumulation of Polycyclic Hydrocarbons: Structure-Activity Relationships," *Aquat. Toxicol.* 7:15–24 (1985).
3. Landrum, P. F., M. D. Reinhold, S. R. Nihart, and B. J. Eadie. "Predicting the Bioavailability of Organic Xenobiotics to *Pontoporeia hoyi* in the Presence of Humic and Fulvic Materials and Natural Dissolved Organic Matter," *Environ. Toxicol. Chem.* 4:459–467 (1985).
4. Servos, M. R., and D. C. G. Muir. "Effect of Dissolved Organic Matter from Canadian Shield Lakes on the Bioavailability of 1,3,6,8-Tetrachlorobenzo-p-dioxin to the Amphipod *Crangonyx laurentianus*," *Environ. Toxicol. Chem.* 8:141–150 (1989).
5. McCarthy, J. F., and B. D. Jimenez. "Reduction in Bioavailability to Bluegills of Polycyclic Aromatic Hydrocarbons Bound to Dissolved Humic Material," *Environ. Toxicol. Chem.* 4:511–521 (1985).
6. Spacie, A., P. F. Landrum, and G. J. Leversee. "Uptake, Depuration, and Biotransformation of Anthracene and Benzo(a)pyrene in Bluegill Sunfish," *Ecotoxicol. Environ. Safety* 7:330–341 (1983).
7. Black, M. C., and J. F. McCarthy. "Dissolved Organic Macromolecules Reduce the

Uptake of Hydrophobic Organic Contaminants by the Gills of Rainbow Trout (*Salmo gairdneri*)," *Environ. Toxicol. Chem.* 7:593–600 (1988).

8. Servos, M. R., D. C. G. Muir, and G. R. B. Webster. "The Effect of Dissolved Organic Matter on the Bioavailability of Polychlorinated Dibenzo-p-dioxins," *Aquat. Toxicol.* 14:169–184 (1989).

9. Carlberg, G. E., K. Martinsen, A. Kringstad, E. Gjessing, M. Grande, T. Kallqvist, and J. U. Skare. "Influence of Aquatic Humus on the Bioavailability of Chlorinated Micropollutants in Atlantic Salmon," *Arch. Environ. Contamin. Toxicol.* 15:543–548 (1986).

10. Johnson, S., J. Kukkonen, and M. Grande. "Influence of Natural Aquatic Humic Substances on the Bioavailability of Benzo(a)pyrene to Atlantic Salmon," *Sci. Total Environ.* 81/82:691–702 (1989).

11. Landrum, P. F., S. R. Nihart, B. J. Eadie, and L. R. Herche. "Reduction in Bioavailability of Organic Contaminants to the Amphipod *Pontoporeia hoyi* by Dissolved Organic Matter of Sediment Interstitial Waters," *Environ. Toxicol. Chem.* 6:11–20 (1987).

12. Chin, Y.-P. and W. J. Weber, Jr. "Estimating the Effects of Dispersed Organic Polymers on the Sorption of Contaminants by Natural Solids. 1. A Predictive Thermodynamic Humic Substance-Organic Solute Interaction Model," *Environ. Sci. Technol.* 23(6):978–984 (1989).

13. Chiou, C. T., D. E. Kile, T. I. Brinton, R. L. Malcolm, J. A. Leenheer, and P. MacCarthy. "A Comparison of Water Solubility Enhancements of Organic Solutes by Aquatic Humic Materials and Commercial Humic Acids," *Environ. Sci. Technol.* 21:1231–1234 (1987).

14. Evans, H. E. "The Binding of Three PCB Congeners to Dissolved Organic Carbon in Freshwaters," *Chemosphere* 17:2325–2338 (1988).

15. Landrum, P. F., S. R. Nihart, B. J. Eadie, and W. S. Gardner. "Reverse Phase Separation Method for Determining Pollutant Binding to Aldrich Humic Acid and Dissolved Organic Carbon of Natural Waters," *Environ. Sci. Technol.* 18:187–192 (1984).

16. Dauble, D. D., D. C. Klopfer, D. W. Carlile, and R. W. Hanf, Jr. "Usefulness of the Lipid Index for Bioaccumulation Studies with *Daphnia magna*," in *Aquatic Toxicology and Hazard Assessment: Eighth Symposium, ASTM STP 891*, R. C. Bahner and D. J. Hansen, Eds. (Philadelphia, PA: American Society for Testing and Materials, 1985), pp. 350–358.

17. Clayton, J. R., Jr, S. P. Pavlou, and N. F. Breitner. "Polychlorinated Biphenyls in Coastal Marine Zooplankton: Bioaccumulation and Equilibrium Partitioning," *Environ. Sci. Technol.* 11:676–682 (1977).

18. Mackay D. "Correlation of Bioconcentration Factors," *Environ. Sci. Technol.* 16:274–278 (1982).

19. Oliver, B. G., and A. J. Niimi. "Trophodynamic Analysis of Polychlorinated Biphenyl Congeners and Other Chlorinated Hydrocarbons in the Lake Ontario Ecosystem," *Environ. Sci. Technol.* 22:388–397 (1988).

20. "Handbook of Analytical Methods for Environmental Samples," Ontario Ministry of the Environment (1983).

21. Tessier, A. J., and C. E. Goulden. "Estimating Food Limitation in Cladoceran Populations," *Limnol. Oceanogr.* 27:707–717 (1982).

22. Eadie, B. J., N. R. Morehead, and P. F. Landrum. "Three-Phase Partitioning of

Hydrophobic Organic Compounds in Great Lakes Waters," *Chemosphere* 20:161–178 (1990).

23. Evans, H. E., R. D. Evans, and S. M. Lingard. "Factors Affecting the Variation in the Average Molecular Weight of Dissolved Organic Carbon in Freshwaters," *Sci. Total Environ.* 81/82:297–306 (1989).

24. Carlberg, G. E., and K. Martinsen. "Adsorption/Complexation of Organic Micropollutants to Aquatic Humus," *Sci. Total Environ.* 25:245–254 (1982).

25. Landrum, P. F. "Toxicokinetics of Organic Xenobiotics in the Amphipod, *Pontoporeia hoyi:* Role of Physiological and Environmental Variables," *Aquat. Toxicol.* 12:245–271 (1988).

26. Evans, M. S., and P. F. Landrum. "Toxicokinetics of DDE, Benzo(a)pyrene, and 2,4,5,2',4',5'-Hexachlorobiphenyl in *Pontoporeia hoyi* and *Mysis relicta*," *J. Great Lakes Res.* 15:589–600 (1989).

27. Wainman, B. C., and D. R. S. Lean. "Seasonal Trends in Planktonic Lipid Content and Lipid Class," paper presented at Symposium Internationale Linmolgic Conference, Munich, Germany, August 1989.

28. MacDonald, C. R., and C. D. Metcalfe. "A Comparison of PCB Congener Distributions in Two Point-Source Contaminated Lakes and One Uncontaminated Lake in Ontario," *Water Pollut. Res. J. Can.* 24:23–46 (1989).

29. Shiu, W. Y., and D. Mackay. "A Critical Review of Aqueous Solubilities, Vapor Pressures, Henry's Law Constants, and Octanol-Water Partition Coefficients of the Polychlorinated Biphenyls," *J. Phys. Chem. Ref. Data* 5:911–929 (1986).

30. Kukkonen, J., and A. Oikari. "Effects of Aquatic Humus on Accumulation and Acute Toxicity of Some Organic Micropollutants," *Sci. Total Environ.* 62:399–402 (1987).

31. Kukkonen, J., A. Oikari, S. Johnsen, and E. Gjessing. "Effects of Humus Concentrations on Benzo(a)pyrene Accumulation from Water to *Daphnia Magna*: Comparison of Natural Waters and Standard Preparations," *Sci. Total Environ.* 79:197–207 (1989).

32. Reid, R. A., and R. Girard. "Morphometric, Chemical, Physical and Geological Data for Axe, Brandy, Cinder, Fawn, Healey, Leech, Leonard, McKay, Moot, Poker, Red Pine Lakes in the Muskoka-Haliburton Area (1978–1985)," Ontario Ministry of the Environment Data Report DR 87/2.

CHAPTER 7

Binding and Bioavailability of Organic Micropollutants in Natural Waters: Effects of the Quality and the Quantity of Dissolved Organic Material

Jussi Kukkonen, John F. McCarthy, and Aimo Oikari

INTRODUCTION

The dissolved organic material (DOM) pool in natural waters consists of a variety of organic molecules. While some of these molecules have a defined chemical structure, most of the organic material in natural waters has no readily identifiable structure, and the members of this heterogeneous group of organic macromolecules are referred to as *humic substances.* DOM is an important factor in water chemistry and aquatic toxicology because a number of studies have demonstrated that it can bind both metals[1] and hydrophobic organic pollutants.[2-6] The magnitude of the binding, expressed as a partition coefficient, K_p, is related to the hydrophobicity of the contaminant.[5,7] However, the affinity of the organic matter for binding a given contaminant appears to vary among waters from different sources.[3,8,9] The underlying causes of the observed variability in binding affinity of different waters for organic contaminants is not fully understood and hampers attempts to describe and predict the importance of natural organic matter in the transport and fate of organic pollutants in aquatic systems.

The bioavailability of metals and organic pollutants is also affected by dissolved organic matter. DOM reduces the bioavailability of pollutants, and the magnitude of the decrease is related to the extent of the binding between the contaminant and the organic matter.[9-12] Thus, the capability to predict the role of organic macromolecules on the accumulation and toxicity of hydrophobic organic contaminants in aquatic environments is dependent on, and limited by, the poorly understood variability in the binding affinity among natural waters.

One approach to elucidating the source of this variability is to examine relationships between chemical and structural properties of DOM and its capacity to bind organic contaminants. For example, Gauthier et al. have reported for pyrene that the binding coefficients in natural waters correlated with the aromaticity of DOM in the water samples.[13]

It is possible to chemically fractionate DOM and determine if there are underlying similarities in binding affinities of functionally similar subcomponents of the total DOM. Nonionic macroporous sorbents, such as the Amberlite XAD resins, have been used to fractionate DOM into subcomponents based on the hydrophobicity and charge of the molecules.[14]

The objective of this chapter is to integrate our latest studies showing that fractions of DOM isolated using XAD-8 resin differ in their affinity for binding contaminants and to extend these observations to concern the bioavailability of selected model compounds in natural surface waters having a large variation in DOM concentrations.

MATERIALS AND METHODS

The natural water for the XAD-8 fractionation experiment was collected from a stream draining a peat deposit located in Hyde County, North Carolina,[15] natural waters for the benzo(a)pyrene association experiment were collected in North Carolina and Tennessee,[16] and natural waters used in the lake series experiment to study bioavailability of model compounds in different waters were collected in eastern Finland.[17]

Fractionation of DOM

The XAD-8 fractionation of DOM was modified from Leenheer and Huffman.[14] Water samples were filtered through precombusted glass-fiber filters (Whatman GF/C). Samples (150 mL) were acidified (pH $\leq$ 2, concentrated H_2SO_4) and applied to the column of purified XAD-8 resin. The hydrophilic fraction (Hl) of the DOC is defined as that organic matter in the acidified water sample that was not retained by the column. The hydrophobic acid fraction (HbA) is defined as that organic matter eluted when the column was rinsed with 0.1 N NaOH. The hydrophobic neutral fraction (HbN) is defined as that organic matter retained by the XAD-8 and not eluted with base. The HbN fraction was extracted from the resin with methanol. Purifying procedures for different fractions to use them in further experiments are described by Kukkonen et al.[15]

Determination of Partition Coefficients

Equilibrium dialysis[3,5] was used to determine the K_p between model compounds and the fractions of DOM or DOM in the water samples. A filtered (Nuclepore, 0.22 μm) water sample (5 mL) was put into a dialysis bag (Spectra/Por 6, molecular weight cutoff of 1000 daltons) and placed in a glass jar containing an aqueous solution of a radiolabeled compound. Sodium azide (0.002%) was added to inhibit microbial activity. The jar was sealed with a Teflon-lined cap and shaken in the dark at 20°C for 4 days. At least three replicate determinations were made. Solutions inside and outside the dialysis bag were analyzed for ^{14}C activity using scintillation cocktail and a liquid scintillation counter. The outside concentration (C_o) is the freely dissolved organic pollutant, while the difference between the inside and outside concentration (C_p) is the pollutant bound to organic matter in the bag. K_p was calculated as

$$K_p = C_p/(C_o \times DOC) \tag{7.1}$$

where DOC is the concentration of dissolved organic carbon (kg carbon/L).

Accumulation Experiments

Water samples were filtered (Nuclepore, 0.22 μm) and pH adjusted to 6.5 with 0.1 N NaOH and HCl. Aqueous concentrations of ^{14}C-labeled benzo(a)pyrene (BAP), 2,2',5,5'-tetrachlorobiphenyl (2,2',5,5'-TCB), 3,3',4,4'-tetrachlorobiphenyl (3,3',4,4'-TCB), naphthalene (NAPH), and ^{3}H-labeled dehydroabietic acid (DHAA) were 1, 2, 2, 5, and 70 μg/L, respectively—all below the published water solubility limits for each compound.

D. magna were obtained from a culture maintained at the Oak Ridge National Laboratory (Oak Ridge, TN) and were fed a mixture of trout chow, yeast, and *Cerophil* (for the study with the DOM fractions) or at University of Joensuu (Finland) and were fed a culture of *Monoraphidium contortum* (for the study with natural waters). Animals used in these experiments were 6–8 days old and did not have eggs in the brood chamber. Before exposures, daphnids were held for 1 hr in the clean control water to clear their gut contents. Groups of five *D. magna* were transferred to 100-mL glass beakers containing 50 mL of water sample containing one of the radiolabeled contaminants. Four replicate determinations were made for each sample. Beakers were kept in the dark at 20°C. After 24 hr, animals were removed from the water with a widemouthed pipet, collected on filter paper, briefly rinsed in 50 mL of distilled water, and blotted dry; all animals from each beaker were weighed together on a microbalance. The five animals were added to 10 mL of scintillation cocktail and analyzed for radioactivity. The radioactivity remaining in the exposure water was determined. Each experiment included a parallel control experiment using organic-free control water. The results are reported as a 24-hr bioconcentration factor (BCF) calculated as the ratio of the concentration of the pollutant in the animals (nanograms per gram wet weight) and in the water after the experiment (nanograms per milliliter), calculated from the specific activities of the compounds.

The fitting of regression lines shown in the figures as well as all statistical analyses (Student's t-tests, variance analyses, Pearson's correlations) were performed with SAS (Statistical Analysis System).[18]

Table 7.1. Characterization and Comparison of DOM in the Water Samples

Sample	DOC mg C/L	%HI	%HbA	%HbN	%TotHb	ABS$_{270}$	E$_2$/E$_3$	E$_4$/E$_6$	Reference
Hyde County sample	50	22	66	12	78	42.0	4.10	5.50	15
Brook Välioja	38.3	23	75	2	77	37.9	4.47	9.55	17
Brook Liuhapuro	32.2	20	77	3	80	43.4	4.49	12.4	17
Lake Ahvenlampi	20.4	30	63	7	70	29.5	4.71	3.64	17
Lake Louhilampi	18.1	18	61	20	81	32.7	4.78	8.20	17
Lake Makrijärvi	15.1	27	63	10	73	35.9	4.49	2.65	17
Lake Iso-Sormunen	13.5	22	51	27	78	30.6	4.88	3.33	17
Lake Melalampi	9.5	28	59	13	72	35.3	4.90	2.78	17
Lake Piimäjärvi	9.6	25	55	20	75	31.7	5.17	2.56	17
Lake Koitere	7.5	34	51	15	66	38.7	5.62	3.67	17
Lake Höytiäinen	7.5	29	40	31	71	36.9	5.63	4.00	17
Lake Riihilampi	6.8	32	44	24	68	35.1	4.63	2.50	17
Lake Viinijärvi (point 5)	8.4	32	39	28	67	26.4	5.88	5.00	17
Lake Iso-Hietajärvi	6.0	39	41	20	61	18.3	6.36	1.00	17
Lake Tammalammit	5.0	36	46	17	63	22.1	4.34	1.86	17
Lake Valkialampi	4.9	35	45	20	65	18.5	4.46	1.71	17
Lake Viinijärvi (point 1)	4.2	59	28	13	41	12.6	5.46	2.00	17
Lake Likolampi	4.9	48	22	30	52	10.8	4.25	1.50	17
Lake Miilunlampi	2.8	49	37	14	51	17.9	3.76	4.00	17
Lake Kakkisenlampi	2.0	49	38	13	51	22.4	3.29	1.43	17
Lake Kuorinka	3.0	42	19	39	58	13.4	3.79	1.33	
WB	—	51	27	22	49	15.5	na	2.78	16
P1	—	40	28	12	60	27.2	na	1.66	16
P2	—	59	30	11	41	12.1	na	1.53	16
P3	—	56	24	20	44	7.5	na	1.34	16
CH	—	40	40	20	60	27.5	na	2.76	16
H-0	—	40	48	16	60	17.8	na	3.22	16
H-15	—	35	51	14	65	20.0	na	11.1	16
H-30	—	32	26	42	68	2.9	na	1.40	16
H-100	—	31	24	42	69	3.1	na	1.13	16
B-0	—	22	60	17	78	38.0	na	4.32	16
B-50	—	34	36	31	66	9.2	na	1.28	16
ALD (Aldrich HA)	—	30	57	13	70	63.0	na	5.58	16

Notes: %HI = percentage of DOC determined to be hydrophilic.
%HbA = percentage of DOC determined to be hydrophobic acids.
%HbN = percentage of DOC determined to be hydrophobic neutrals (HbN = DOC – HI – HbA).
%TotHb = percentage of DOC determined to be hydrophobic (TotHb = DOC – HI).
ABS$_{270}$ = absorptivity at 270 nm (units of L/mg C × cm × 10^3).
E$_2$/E$_3$ = ratio of absorbances at 250 to 365 nm.
E$_4$/E$_6$ = ratio of absorbances at 465 to 665 nm.
na = not analyzed.

CHARACTERIZATION OF DOM IN NATURAL WATERS

Percentages of hydrophilic (HI), hydrophobic acid (HbA), and hydrophobic neutral (HbN) fractions in experimental waters and some UV-VIS spectroscopic characterizations like ABS$_{270}$ (1000 x absorbance at 270 nm/DOC), E$_2$/E$_3$ (absorbance ratio A250/A365) and E$_4$/E$_6$ (absorbance ratio A465/A665) are reported in Table 7.1. The spectroscopic characterization of isolated DOM fractions is shown in Table 7.2. According to Chen et al., the high E$_4$/E$_6$ ratio

Table 7.2. Spectroscopic Characteristics of Different DOM Fractions in Hyde County Water Sample

Fraction	ABS_{270}	E_2/E_3	E_4/E_6
Hydrophobic acids	59	4.1	7.5
Hydrophobic neutrals	4	4.7	3.4
Hydrophilic compounds	13	5.6	3.1

Source: Kukkonen et al.[15].
Note: Spectra were run at pH 6.0 using samples having DOC concentrations of 10 mg C/L.

can be related to high molecular weight.[19] Schnitzer reported that the E_4/E_6 value for fulvic acids and humic acids extracted from soils are in the range of 7.6 to 11.5 and 3.8 to 5.8, respectively.[20] According to De Haan, fulvic acids from strongly humified and oligotrophic waters are characterized by a relatively low E_2/E_3 ratio (about 4).[21]

The spectroscopic characteristics of the isolated fractions (Table 7.2) suggest that they differ substantially from each other in chemical composition. Differences in absorptivity at 270 nm (ABS_{270}) reflect absorbance of pi-pi* transitions in substituted benzenes and most polyenes and have been related to the aromatic content of isolated soil humic acids.[13] The observed spectral differences suggest that the HbA fraction is enriched in aromatic content, relative to the HbN fraction. The Hl fraction is intermediate between the two other fractions.

Table 7.1 shows the variation in natural waters—from dark-colored brook waters having an extremely large HbA portion to clear water lakes having low DOC concentrations and a small HbA portion. The correlations in the Finnish water series between percentage of HbA and DOC concentration (r = 0.84, p = 0.001), ABS_{270} (r = 0.82, p < 0.001) and hydrogen:carbon atomic ratio (r = -0.81, p < 0.001) and in the U.S. water series between percentage of HbA and ABS_{270} (r = 0.75, p < 0.05) indicate the dominant role of the HbA fraction in the natural waters. These data suggest that the HbA fraction is enriched in aromatic content, as can be expected knowing that the HbA fraction is mainly humic compounds (i.e., fulvic and humic acids). On the other hand, the HbN fraction showed a very low absorptivity at 270 nm (Table 7.2), and the same can be seen in the natural water series. The percentage of HbN fraction and ABS_{270} correlated negatively in the whole data set (r = -0.52, p < 0.05).

BINDING OF CONTAMINANTS BY DOM

Binding of Contaminants to DOM Fractions

The hydrophobic fractions of the Hyde County water sample have the greatest affinity for binding BAP (Figure 7.1).[15] The HbA fraction has a significantly higher K_p (p < 0.05) than the HbN fraction. The Hl fraction has much lower affinity for binding BAP. Amy and Liu have shown similar results for

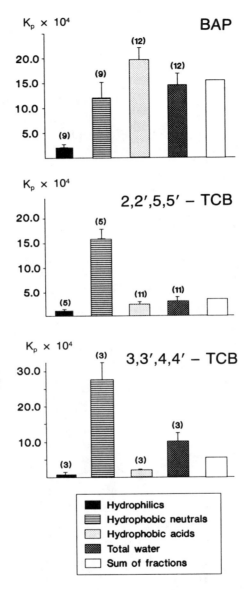

Figure 7.1.   Partition coefficients (K_p) of total (unfractionated) Hyde County water sample and different DOM fractions for BAP, 2,2′,5,5′-TCB, and 3,3′,4,4′-TCB. Bars indicate the mean values ($\pm$ SD), and the number in parentheses is the number of replicates. Data from Kukkonen et al.[15].

phenanthrene in the XAD-8 fractions of DOM.[22] The K_p of the total water appears to reflect the sum of the binding affinities of the individual fractions, with little indication of interactive effects among the fractions. The measured K_p for the total water agrees very well with a cumulative K_p calculated from the sum of the K_p for the individual fractions ($K_{p(i)}$) and the relative contribution (f_i) of the ith XAD fraction to the total DOC:[15]

$$\text{Sum } K_p = (K_{p(HL)} \, f_{HL}) + (K_{p(HBA)} \, f_{HBA}) + (K_{p(HBN)} \, f_{HBN}) \qquad (7.2)$$

The relative binding affinities of the DOC fractions for 2,2′,5,5′-TCB and 3,3′,4,4′-TCB (Figure 7.1) exhibited a different pattern from that observed for BAP.[15] The HbN fraction had the highest affinity for binding TCB. The sum of K_p's of different fractions with TCB also agreed with the measured K_p value in the total water. This different affinity for binding to isolated XAD-8 fractions of DOM was attributed to differences in the electron densities of DOM fractions and model compounds. BAP is an electron-rich compound and will have a tendency to donate its electrons via charge transfer mechanism to electron-deficient compounds like HbA. Conversely, PCBs are electrophiles and may be attracted to the richer electron densities of HbN material. The K_p values for NAPH were much lower (in total water: $K_p = 1150 \pm 476$; in HbA: $K_p = 785 \pm 225$) than for BAP, 2,2′,5,5′-TCB, and 3,3′,4,4′-TCB.

Binding of Contaminants to DOM in Lake Waters

The partition coefficients (K_p) for BAP and 3,3′,4,4′-TCB in different natural waters are shown in Figure 7.2.[17] The K_p values for BAP were similar to those reported for natural DOM samples.[9,23] Also, the K_p values for 3,3′,4,4′-TCB agree well with the published partition coefficients for the same or similar compounds.[4,23] For BAP it was possible to measure the K_p value for every water sample, but for the other model compounds, especially NAPH and DHAA, which have much lower K_p values (~ 300–6000)—that is, not much interaction with DOM—the dialysis method is not sensitive enough to obtain accurate measurements in the water samples with low DOC concentration.[17]

There were strong direct relationships between the K_p values of BAP and hydrophobic acid content of the natural waters ($r = 0.77$, $p < 0.001$, for Finnish waters;[17] $r = 0.74$, $p < 0.01$, for McCarthy et al. data[16]) and a good negative correlation between the K_p values of BAP and the hydrogen:carbon ratio of DOM ($r = 0.76$, $p < 0.001$).[17] The absorptivity at 270 nm (ABS_{270}) gave the best correlation with the K_p values for BAP ($r = 0.87$, $p < 0.001$, from Kukkonen and Oikari;[17] $r = 0.94$, $p < 0.001$, from McCarthy et al.[16]). In Figure 7.3, these data are plotted together. The relationship between ABS_{270} and log K_p values of BAP is similar in these two sets of natural waters. The results of BAP in these two studies also agree well with the results reported by Gauthier et al.,[13] who also showed an excellent correlation between both aromatic content and absorptivity at 270 nm of humic materials extracted from

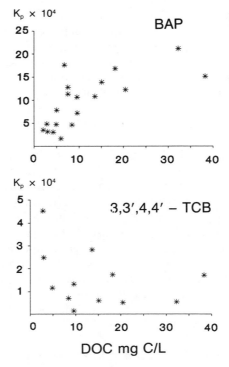

Figure 7.2.   Partition coefficients (K_p) of water samples in lake series from Finland for BAP and 3,3',4,4'-TCB. Each point indicates the mean value of four replicates. Data from Kukkonen and Oikari.[17]

soils and sediments and the partition coefficient for binding of pyrene to these samples. On the other hand, the K_p values for BAP and the percentage of HbN fraction had slight negative correlation (r = -0.53, p < 0.1, from McCarthy et al.;[16] r = -0.40, p < 0.1, from Kukkonen and Oikari[17]), which is in accordance with the results obtained in the study with different fractions.[15] Taken together, these studies suggest that observed differences in affinities of BAP and also some other organic pollutants between different water sources are, at least partly, explained by different percentages of hydrophobic acids and the aromaticity of DOM.

EFFECTS OF DOM ON BIOAVAILABILITY OF ORGANIC CONTAMINANTS

Bioavailability of Contaminants to *D. magna* in DOM Fractions

Accumulation of BAP by *D. magna* in DOM fractions was reduced by increasing the concentration of DOC (Table 7.3). The BCF value for BAP in the organic-free control water was significantly higher than BCFs for all con-

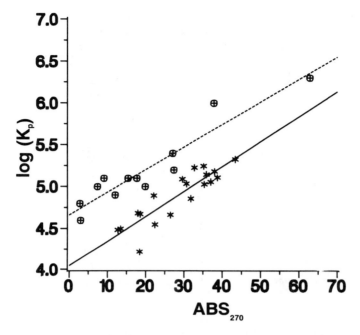

Figure 7.3. The log K_p for binding BAP to different sources of DOM is directly related to the ABS$_{270}$ of the water. *Stars* and the *solid line* are for surface water samples from eastern Finland,[17] and *circles* and the *dashed line* are for surface and groundwater samples from the United States.[16]

centrations of DOM fractions ($p < 0.05$). The HbA fraction had the greatest effect on the bioavailability of BAP, and the HbN and Hl fractions also reduced the bioaccumulation of BAP compared to the control (Table 7.3), but the effect is not as great as for the HbA fraction. Approximately five times more organic carbon from the Hl fraction was required to reduce the BCF to the extent observed for the HbA fraction or the total water. The potency of the HbN fraction is intermediate to the two other fractions.[15]

The HbN fraction was more effective in reducing the accumulation of 2,2',5,5'-TCB than the other carbon sources, although the effect is not significantly different from that for the HbA fraction at the same DOC concentration. The decrease in the BCF due to this fraction was much less than was anticipated on the basis of its affinity for binding 2,2',5,5'-TCB (Figure 7.2). A "biological K_p" for 2,2',5,5'-TCB was back-calculated based on the reduction in BCF with the HbN fraction; this value (approximately 6.4×10^4) was lower than the K_p measured using equilibrium dialysis, but it is still higher than those determined for the other fractions or for the total water.[15]

The bioaccumulation of NAPH in *D. magna* was much less than for the other compounds, and the accumulation data agree with the K_p measurements

Table 7.3. The Bioconcentration Factors for Benzo(a)pyrene, 2,2′,5,5′-Tetra-chlorobiphenyl, and Naphthalene in the Different DOC Fractions

Chemical	Fraction	[DOC]	Observed BCF	Predicted BCF
BAP control		0	5990 ± 679	—
	HbA	1	4792 ± 448	5004
		2	3765 ± 721	4296
		5	3116 ± 334	3017
		15	2151 ± 180	1514
		25	1744 ± 214	1011
	HI	5	5103 ± 535	5408
		10	3565 ± 376	4930
	HbN	5	4430 ± 703	3767
		15	2608 ± 214	2162
22′55′-TCB	control	0	6543 ± 844	—
	HbA	5	6090 ± 713	5834
		10	4669 ± 963	5263
	HI	10	6028 ± 1109	5910
	HbN	10	4164 ± 431	2526
NAPH	control	0	37 ± 4	—
	HbA	5	47 ± 4	37
		10	44 ± 5	36
		25	36 ± 5	35
		50	33 ± 4	34
	HI	10	37 ± 4	36
	HbN		not measured	

Source: Kukkonen et al.[15]
Notes: The numbers are means (± standard deviation) of four replicate accumulation measurements. DOC concentrations are mg C/L. The predicted value of the BCF (Equations 7.3 and 7.4), based on the fraction of the pollutant calculated to be freely dissolved from equilibrium dialysis experiments, is also indicated.

in that NAPH does not appear to have much interaction with dissolved organic material compared to BAP and 2,2′,5,5′-TCB.[15]

Bioavailability of Contaminants to *D. magna* in Natural Waters

Accumulation of model compounds by *D. magna* was reduced by increasing the concentration of DOC also in the natural water series or in the diluted Hyde County water series (Figure 7.4). The relationship between DOC concentration and BCFs is similar in the series of different natural waters from Finland,[17] in diluted concentrations of Hyde County water,[15] and in some water samples or natural humus preparations that are diluted down to different DOC concentrations with control water.[9]

The BCF values for model compounds in the organic-free control water were the same or significantly ($p < 0.05$) higher than BCFs for water samples from Finland,[17] except in the case of NAPH, where three natural waters having low DOM concentration (2–4 mg C/L) revealed significantly ($p < 0.05$) higher BCF values than the control water. The increase of bioaccumulation of NAPH

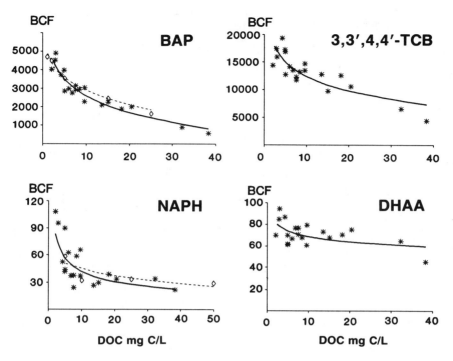

Figure 7.4. The bioconcentration factors (BCFs) of model compounds in natural surface waters from eastern Finland having different DOC concentrations *(stars and the solid line)*[17] and in diluted Hyde County water sample *(diamond and the dashed line)*.[15] Each point indicates the mean value of four replicates, and the lines are regression lines fitted to data points. Note that the control value (no DOM in water) for NAPH is 37.

in the waters having low natural DOC concentration compared to organic-free control water (DOC ≤ 0.3 mg C/L) is an interesting phenomenon, and similar data have been reported earlier; for example, the bioavailability of methyl-cholanthrene to *D. magna* was increased by Aldrich humic acid (concentration, 2 mg DOC/L) in the study by Leversee et al.,[24] but McCarthy et al. showed opposite results in their study with *D. magna*.[10]

The bioavailability of DHAA was reduced by the DOM, even in the less DOM-enriched waters, but the effect of increasing DOM concentration is not as clear as it is for other model compounds used (Figure 7.4).[17] DHAA has a low K_p value,[17] and it is a weak organic acid (pK_a 5.7),[25] which is more than 50% ionized at the experimental pH of 6.5.

The measured BCF values correlated with the percentage of hydrophobic acids, absorptivity at 270 nm, and hydrogen:carbon ratio even in the case of NAPH and DHAA (Table 7.4). This result by Kukkonen and Oikari[17] indicates that in addition to the total DOM concentration, the quality of DOM also affects very clearly the bioavailability of organic xenobiotics. It is impor-

Table 7.4. Statistical Relationships between BCF Values of Model Compounds and Some Chemical Parameters of DOM, Based on Simple Linear Regression Analysis on Pairs of Variables

Dependent Variable	Independent Variable	Slope ($\pm$ SE)	Intercept ($\pm$ SE)	r^2
Log_{10}(BCF of BAP)	DOC	−0.022 (0.001)	3.66 (0.02)	0.94
BCF of BAP	%HbA	−67.4 (7.9)	6139 (407)	0.81
	H/C atomic ratio	2757 (408)	−546 (517)	0.73
	ABS$_{270}$	−93.6 (18.4)	5481 (549)	0.60
Log_{10}(BCF of 3,3′,4,4′-TCB)	DOC	−0.014 (0.001)	4.25 (0.02)	0.86
BCF of 3,3′,4,4′-TCB	%HbA	−190 (29.4)	22214 (1475)	0.70
	ABS$_{270}$	−289 (52.0)	21094 (1516)	0.63
	H/C atomic ratio	7452 (1740)	3954 (2225)	0.50
BCF of Naphthalene	H/C atomic ratio	75.1 (11.7)	−39.4 (14.4)	0.71
	DOC	−54.4 (11.7)	100 (11.5)	0.56
	ABS$_{270}$	−1.69 (0.47)	97.6 (14.0)	0.43
	%HbA	−1.08 (0.31)	103 (15.9)	0.42
Log_{10}(BCF of DHAA)	DOC	−0.004 (0.001)	1.89 (0.02)	0.35
BCF of DHAA	H/C atomic ratio	20.8 (5.56)	45.5 (7.11)	0.44
	%HbA	−0.38 (0.13)	89.4 (6.66)	0.31
	$r^2 < 0.2$ for ABS$_{270}$			

Source: Kukkonen and Oikari.[17]
Notes: The units for the variables are as described in Table 7.1. The regressions between BCFs and DOC are plotted in Figure 7.4.

tant to note that the bioavailability of NAPH and DHAA correlate similarly with the chemical parameters of DOM, as is the case with more lipophilic compounds.

The observed data for bioaccumulation of BAP in different DOM fractions and natural waters were compared to those which would be predicted based on the assumption that BAP bound to the DOM is unavailable for uptake by the organism; that is, bioaccumulation in water containing DOM will be proportional to the fraction of the contaminant that is freely dissolved (f_{free}):

$$\text{predicted BCF in presence of DOM} = \text{control BCF} \times f_{free} \quad (7.3)$$

where f_{free} is calculated from the measured K_p and DOC concentration of each sample:

$$f_{free} = 1/(1 + K_p \times DOC) \quad (7.4)$$

where DOC concentration is expressed as kg carbon/L. The measured BCF values of BAP agreed well with the predicted BCF values for BAP from Equation 7.3 in both experiments with DOM fractions and natural waters (Figure 7.5). The 95% confidence limits for this regression overlaps the 1:1 line, which is predicted by the hypothesis expressed in Equation 7.3 and is consistent with similar results for BAP in *D. magna*,[10] *Pontoporeia hoyi*,[26] and rainbow trout.[11] The study by Kukkonen and Oikari extends these observa-

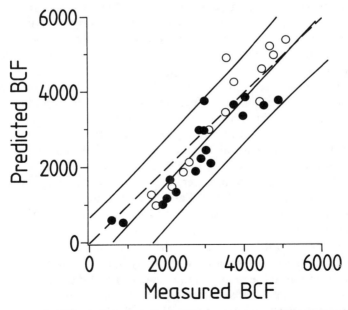

Figure 7.5.   The predicted BCF of BAP (from Equation 7.3) plotted against the measured BCF in the water sample. *Filled-in circles* represent the natural water series from Finland;[17] *open circles*, the experiment with different DOM fractions.[15] The 95% confidence interval *(solid curves)* of the regression line *(solid line)* overlaps the 1:1 line *(dashed line)* predicted by the hypothesis that only the freely dissolved BAP is available for *D. magna*.

tions to a series of natural waters having both quantitatively and qualitatively different DOM content and provides additional confirmation that the effects of natural DOM on bioaccumulation of BAP can be predicted from physico-chemical measurements of K_p's.[17] But we have to keep in mind that this conclusion works well with compounds like BAP, which is highly lipophilic and therefore has a high affinity to the DOM; it appears that a high enough or strong enough interaction between the xenobiotics and DOM is needed before this kind of prediction can be made. Also the best method to measure K_p values may vary from one compound to another. However, Black and McCarthy got similar results for BAP and 2,2',5,5'-tetrachlorobiphenyl by measuring the K_p value of 2,2',5,5'-tetrachlorobiphenyl by a reverse-phase separation method and using Aldrich humic acid,[11] which has a higher affinity to bind xenobiotics than natural DOM.[16]

ENVIRONMENTAL IMPLICATIONS

These reviewed papers have extended previous observations on the role of natural DOM in binding hydrophobic organic compounds and, more importantly, in altering their availability for uptake into biota in different types of natural waters. There is a large degree of variability in the affinity of DOM from different sources of water to bind hydrophobic organic compounds. The total concentration of DOM in a water is not always a good predictor of the capacity of that water for binding organic xenobiotics. It is shown in these papers that the qualitative differences in the nature of organic material from different sources have a large effect on its affinity for binding lipophilic organic xenobiotics. This kind of chemical variability can also explain the results where the K_p values for binding xenobiotics differed by orders of magnitude for DOM from natural waters taken from different locations.[3,8,23,27] These findings may also give us a tool to predict the possible interactions between pollutants and DOM in water, and perhaps even the effects of natural DOM on the transport and bioavailability of contaminants. In the case of BAP, this seems to be quite possible, but for other compounds there is a need for further research.

The total concentration of DOM in the natural waters is one of the main factors controlling the bioavailability of highly lipophilic xenobiotics ($K_{o/w}$ > 10^4), but in addition to the quantity, the quality of DOM (i.e., aromaticity and portion of hydrophobic acids) can also play an important role.

An ecotoxicologically interesting result was the increased bioavailability of NAPH in waters having low DOM concentrations compared to the organic-free control water. It is important to confirm this result with further experiments, and then perhaps also to find some explanations for the results concerning increased toxicity of some organic xenobiotics in natural waters.[12,28]

ACKNOWLEDGMENTS

The works mainly reviewed in this chapter were partly financed by the Academy of Finland/Research Council for Environmental Sciences (project 06/133) and by the Subsurface Science Program, Ecological Research Division, Office of Health and Environmental Research, U.S. Department of Energy, and the Y-12 Plant, Division of Environmental Management, Health, and Safety. The Oak Ridge Y-12 Plant and the Oak Ridge National Laboratory are operated by Marietta Energy Systems, Inc., under contract DE-AC05-84OR21400 with the U.S. Department of Energy.

REFERENCES

1. Alberts, J. J., and J. P. Giesy. "Conditional Stability Constant of Trace Metals and Naturally Occurring Humic Materials: Application in Equilibrium Models and Verification with Field Data," in *Aquatic and Terrestrial Humic Materials*, R. F. Christman and E. T. Gjessing, Eds. (Ann Arbor, MI: Ann Arbor Science, 1983), pp. 333–348.

2. Gjessing, E. T., and L. Berglind. "Adsorption of PAH to Aquatic Humus," *Arch. Hydrobiol.* 92:24–30 (1982).

3. Carter, C. W., and I. H. Suffet. "Binding of DDT to Dissolved Humic Materials," *Environ. Sci. Technol.* 16:735–740 (1982).

4. Hassett, J. P., and E. Milicic. "Determination of Equilibrium and Rate Constants for Binding of a Polychlorinated Biphenyl Congener by Dissolved Humic Substances," *Environ. Sci. Technol.* 19:638–643 (1985).

5. McCarthy, J. F., and B. D. Jimenez. "Interactions between Polycyclic Aromatic Hydrocarbons and Dissolved Humic Material: Binding and Dissociation," *Environ. Sci. Technol.* 19:1072–1076 (1985).

6. Servos, M. R., and D. C. G. Muir. "The Effects of Dissolved Organic Matter from the Canadian Shield Lakes on the Bioavailability of 1,3,6,8-Tetrachlorodibenzo-p-dioxin to the Amphipod *Crangonyx laurentianus*," *Environ. Toxicol. Chem.* 8:141–150 (1989).

7. Chiou, C. T., R. L. Malcolm, T. I. Brinton, and D. E. Kile. "Water Solubility Enhancement of Some Organic Pollutants and Pesticides by Dissolved Humic and Fulvic Acids," *Environ. Sci. Technol.* 20:502–508 (1986).

8. Morehead, N. R., B. J. Eadie, B. Lake, P. F. Landrum, and D. Berner. "The Sorption of PAH onto Dissolved Organic Matter in Lake Michigan Waters," *Chemosphere* 15:403–412 (1986).

9. Kukkonen, J., A. Oikari, S. Johnsen, and E. Gjessing. "Effects of Humus Concentrations on Benzo(a)pyrene Accumulation from Water to *Daphnia magna*: Comparison of Natural Waters and Standard Preparations," *Sci. Total Environ.* 79:197–207 (1989).

10. McCarthy, J. F., B. D. Jimenez, and T. Barbee. "Effect of Dissolved Humic Material on Accumulation of Polycyclic Aromatic Hydrocarbons: Structure-Activity Relationship," *Aquat. Toxicol.* 7:15–24 (1985).

11. Black, M. C., and J. F. McCarthy. "Dissolved Organic Macromolecules Reduce the

Uptake of Hydrophobic Organic Contaminants by the Gills of Rainbow Trout (*Salmo gairdneri*)," *Environ. Toxicol. Chem.* 7:593–600 (1988).

12. Kukkonen, J., and A. Oikari. "Effects of Aquatic Humus on Accumulation and Acute Toxicity of Some Organic Micropollutants," *Sci. Total Environ.* 62:399–402 (1987).

13. Gauthier, T. D., W. R. Seitz, and C. L. Grant. "Effects of Structural and Compositional Variations of Dissolved Humic Materials on Pyrene K_{oc} Values," *Environ. Sci. Technol.* 21:243–248 (1987).

14. Leenheer, J. A., and E. W. D. Huffman. "Analytical Method for Dissolved Organic Carbon Fractionation," Water Resources Investigation, U.S. Geological Survey 79-4 (1979), p. 16.

15. Kukkonen J., J. F. McCarthy, and A. Oikari. "Effects of XAD-8 Fractions of Dissolved Organic Carbon on the Sorption and Bioavailability of Organic Micropollutants," *Arch. Environ. Contam. Toxicol.* 19:551–552 (1990).

16. McCarthy, J. F., L. E. Roberson, and L. W. Burris. "Association of Benzo(a)pyrene with Dissolved Organic Matter: Prediction of K_{dom} from Structural and Chemical Properties of Organic Matter," *Chemosphere* 19:1911–1920 (1989).

17. Kukkonen, J., and A. Oikari. "Bioavailability and Binding of Organic Pollutants in Natural Waters Containing Dissolved Organic Material," *Water Res.* 25:455–463 (1991).

18. Statistical Analysis System. *SAS User's Guide: Statistics,* Version 5 ed. (Statistical Analysis Systems, Cary NC, 1985).

19. Chen, Y., N. Senesi, and M. Schnitzer. "Information Provided on Humic Substances by E_4/E_6 Ratios," *Soil Sci. Soc. Am. J.* 41:352–358 (1977).

20. Schnitzer, M. "Recent Findings on the Characterization of Humic Substances Extracted from Soils from Widely Differing Climatic Zones," in *Proceedings of the Symposium on Soil Organic Matter Studies* (Vienna: International Atomic Energy Agency, 1977), pp. 117–131.

21. De Haan, H. "Use of Ultraviolet Spectroscopy, Gel Filtration, Pyrolysis/Mass Spectroscopy and Numbers of Benzoate-Metabolizing Bacteria in the Study of Humification and Degradation of Aquatic Organic Matter" in *Aquatic and Terrestrial Humic Materials*, R. F. Christman and E. T. Gjessing, Eds. (Ann Arbor, MI: Ann Arbor Science, 1983), pp. 165–182.

22. Amy, G. L., and H. Liu. "PAH Binding to Natural Organic Matter (NOM): A Comparison of NOM Fractions and Analytical Methods," presented Before the Division of Environmental Chemistry, 199th American Chemical Society National Meeting, Boston, April 22–27, 1990.

23. Landrum, P. F., S. R. Nihart, B. J. Eadie, and W. S. Gardner. "Reverse-Phase Separation Method for Determining Pollutant Binding to Aldrich Humic Acid and Dissolved Organic Carbon of Natural Waters," *Environ. Sci. Technol.* 18:187–192 (1984).

24. Leversee, G. J., P. F. Landrum, J. P. Giesy, and T. Fannin. "Humic Acids Reduce Bioaccumulation of Some Polycyclic Aromatic Hydrocarbons," *Can. J. Fish. Aquat. Sci.* 40(Suppl. 2):63–69 (1983).

25. Nyrén, V., and E. Back. "The Ionization Constant, Solubility Product and Solubility of Abietic and Dehydroabietic Acid," *Acta Chem. Scand.* 12:1516–1520 (1958).

26. Landrum, P. F., M. D. Reinhold, S. R. Nihart, and B. J. Eadie. "Predicting the Bioavailability of Organic Xenobiotics to *Pontoporeia hoyi* in the Presence of

Humic and Fulvic Materials and Natural Dissolved Organic Matter," *Environ. Toxicol. Chem.* 4:459–467 (1985).

27. Landrum, P. F., S. R. Nihart, B. J. Eadie, and L. R. Herche. "Reduction in Bioavailability of Organic Contaminants to the Amphipod *Pontoporeia hoyi* by Dissolved Organic Matter of Sediment Interstitial Waters," *Environ. Toxicol. Chem.* 6:11–20 (1987).

28. Virtanen, V., J. Kukkonen, and A. Oikari. "Acute Toxicity of Organic Chemicals to *Daphnia magna* in Humic Waters," University of Joensuu, Faculty of Mathematics and Natural Sciences, Report Series No. 29 (1989), pp. 84–86.

CHAPTER **8**

Solvent-Filled Dialysis Membranes Mimic Bioaccumulation of Pollutants in Aquatic Environments

Anders Södergren

INTRODUCTION

It is generally accepted that the concentration of persistent pollutants in gill-breathing aquatic animals is mainly controlled by equilibrium partitioning; that is, the uptake and depuration of the pollutants is a function of their exchange through the gills and across the body surface before reaching equilibrium levels between the ambient water and the body lipids.[1-3] The levels of the pollutants in organisms belonging to low trophic levels (e.g., plankton, crustacea, shellfish, fish) thus depend primarily on the levels of the pollutant in the water. The uptake of additional quantities through the ingestion of contaminated food does not greatly influence the total concentration attained in the organism. At high trophic levels, however, an age-dependent accumulation is often found.[4,5]

It has previously been shown that passive samplers consisting of solvent-filled membranes, which imitate body lipids, will accumulate organochlorine pollutants in a similar manner to gill-breathing organisms.[6,7] Monitoring of lipophilic, persistent pollutants in aquatic environments with such samplers is therefore an alternative to the determination of the residues accumulated by organisms.[8] To compare uptake patterns of chlorinated and nonchlorinated pollutants, solvent-filled membranes were exposed to polychlorinated biphenyls (PCBs) and polyaromatic hydrocarbons (PAH) in the laboratory and in the field, and their properties during long-term exposure were followed. In addition, the rate of depuration and effects of lipids on the capacity of the membrane to accumulate the pollutants were studied.

MATERIAL AND METHODS

Dialysis membranes (Spectra/Por 3 and 6, cutoff 1000 Da) were filled with about 4 mL of n-hexane and exposed to water in the laboratory or buried in the sediment in the field. The use of membranes with a cutoff of 1000 prevents substances of higher molecular weight from diffusing through their walls, thereby simplifying the cleanup procedure.

The effect of different volumes of solvent in the membranes was followed by varying the amount of hexane from 0.6 to 4.8 mL while keeping the membrane area constant. To study the influence of lipids on the rate of uptake, mixed triglycerides (glyceryl-1,2-myristate-3-palmitate) were added to the solvent of the membranes in proportions of 0.1, 1.0, 5.0, and 10.0%.

The membranes were exposed to a constant level of the substances, which were added to the water in a continuous-flow system. The substances added were creosote, which is used as a wood preservative agent, and Clophen A 50, a mixture of polychlorinated biphenyls (PCBs) with an average chlorination of 50%. The sediment in the field was "naturally" contaminated via effluents from a creosote impregnating site. Among the PAH in the creosote mixture, only fluorene, phenanthrene, and fluoranthene will be discussed here.

Since a relationship is likely to exist between the surface area and the rate of uptake of lipophilic residues, the area of the membranes was held constant at about 1200 mm^2. The membranes were either washed and sonicated in hexane or washed with distilled water before filling to remove the sulfur left from the manufacturing process and the preservatives (usually mixtures of glycerols) that protect the membranes during storage. After being filled with the solvent, the membranes were stored until use in polypropylene bottles filled with distilled water. After exposure the bottles with the membranes were filled with water or sediment from the exposure site before being returned to the laboratory.

Spectra/Por polypropylene closures were used to tie the membrane tubings, and they were protected from being damaged during their exposure in the field by metal holders.[8] The holders were suspended in the water or buried in the sediment.

Before use, a PCB congener (2,2',5,6'-tetrachlorobiphenyl, IUPAC #53) was added to the solvent in the membranes for use as an internal standard. The recovery of the congener served as a check of the functioning of the membrane.[8]

The resistance to microbial degradation was studied by storing two solvent-filled membranes for about 1 year in a suspension of sewage sludge at room temperature. The effect of the solvent on the properties of the membrane was evaluated by comparison with membranes filled with distilled water.

Processing of the samples was simplified since no cleanup of the solvent in the membranes was normally necessary. Depending on the exposure situation, the solvent was evaporated to 1 or 0.25 mL before separation and quantification by gas chromatography. The analytical procedure has previously been described.[6]

In accordance with the definition of the bioconcentration factor (BCF), the capacity of the solvent-filled membranes to accumulate substances was expressed as a membrane concentration factor (MCF = concentration in the membrane/concentration in the water or in the sediment).

RESULTS AND DISCUSSION

The two membranes filled with solvents were resistant to degradation since no solvent was lost after long-term exposure in a sewage sludge mixture (Figure 8.1). The increase in weight of the membranes was mainly a result of adsorption of humic material onto the membrane wall. Damage in the form of shallow cavities was noted, but in no case had holes developed. The results indicate that the solvent partially impregnates the membrane wall and inhibits

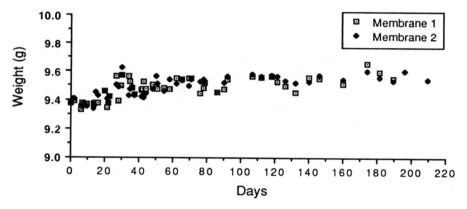

Figure 8.1.   Changes of the content of solvent (hexane) in two dialysis membranes stored in water at about 20°C in the laboratory.

Table 8.1. Uptake of PCBs by Dialysis Membranes (Area 1200 mm^2) Filled with Different Volumes of n-Hexane

Volume (mL)	PCBs (ng/ml)	
	120 hr	12 days
0.6	1.04	284
0.6	1.21	277
0.6	0.88	260
1.2	0.92	272
1.2	0.88	264
1.2	1.32	255
4.8	1.12	264
4.8	1.03	238
4.8	1.10	230

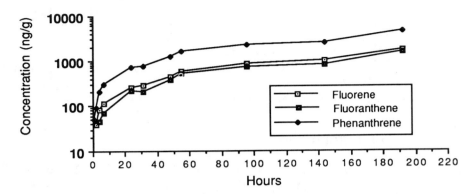

Figure 8.2. Uptake of PAH by solvent-filled dialysis membranes exposed in continuous-flow systems (mean of 4 replicates). The mean concentration of fluorene in the water was 0.13 μg/L (SD 0.06), phenanthrene 0.36 μg/L (SD 0.19), and fluoranthene 0.16 μg/L (0.09) (n = 6).

microorganism growth, presumably by its toxic effects. Membranes thoroughly washed in distilled water and hexane before adding the solvent have been shown to be less affected than membranes washed only in hexane.[8] The solvent-filled membranes may thus be placed for several months in receiving waters, imitating a natural exposure situation of an aquatic organism.

Decreasing the volume of hexane in the membranes by eight times while keeping their area constant resulted in limited changes in their rate of uptake of PCBs (Table 8.1). The amount of solvent in the membrane therefore does not seem to be a crucial factor in determining the functioning of the membrane.

PAH compounds were taken up by membranes buried in sediment or exposed to contaminated water in the laboratory. After 200 hr of exposure in

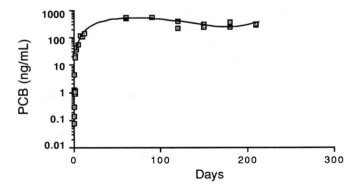

Figure 8.3. Uptake and depuration of PCBs from solvent-filled dialysis membranes. The exposure (7.7 μg/L) was stopped after 12 days and the membranes placed into clean running water. One dot represents one membrane.

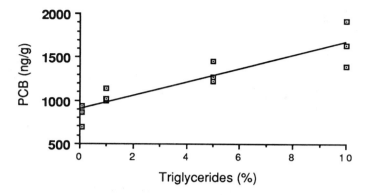

Figure 8.4. Effect of triglycerides added to the solvent-filled dialysis membranes on the uptake of PCBs from water. The membranes were exposed for 12 days. One dot represents one membrane.

the water, the levels in the membranes were still increasing and no steady state was approached, since there existed a significant difference in the uptake of all the compounds at 144 and 192 hr (Student's t-test, $P < 0.005$, Figure 8.2). This is in contrast to the uptake pattern of more lipophilic residues such as PCBs, where an apparent steady state was achieved after about 100–200 hr when exposed in the water[6,7] or in the sediment.[8] At the end of the experiment, fluorene was concentrated in the membranes 231 times, phenanthrene 174 times, and fluoroanthene 225 times relative to their levels in the water. In comparison to the PAH, the MCF of membranes exposed for PCBs in water is higher (about 275).[6] The more lipophilic character of the organochlorine residues compared to the PAH may explain this difference in rate of uptake and accumulation.

The levels of fluorene in membranes kept under identical conditions for 8 days in PAH-contaminated sediment show that it is possible to produce membranes with similar properties to absorb those substances from the interstitial water. The membranes accumulated fluorene (1702 ng/g, SD 156, n = 6) at levels approximately 150 times greater than those in the sediment pore water. The membranes thus seem to absorb the compounds regardless of whether they are exposed to water or buried in sediment. Since no particles can penetrate the membrane, the results show that the compounds taken up are present in a dissolved state in the water and in the sediment pore water.

Once taken up, the PCBs left the solvent-filled membranes slowly (Figure 8.3). After a rapid initial uptake the level stabilized at about 500 ng/mL and decreased only slightly after being placed in clean running water. This is a pattern shared with several aquatic organisms. For example, it has been shown in clearance experiments with various lipophilic, persistent compounds that the rate of uptake by organisms is often fast in comparison to the depuration.[9,10] However, the pattern of elimination seems to be determined by several factors since experimental conditions such as dose and the exposure time have been found to influence the rate of depuration from the organisms. Use of solvent-filled membranes may facilitate clarification of the mechanisms involved since no transformation or degradation of the substances will occur, thus enabling the study of the passive phases in the elimination processes. The solvent-filled membrane can be described kinetically as a homogeneous compartment, which means that uptake and elimination time constants are proportional to the volume of water passing the membrane. These time constants can be broken down into times attributable to water-phase and lipid-phase diffusion flow processes, which can be determined using the solvent-filled membranes.

Addition of triglycerides to the solvent of the membranes changed their capacity to accumulate pollutants (Figure 8.4). Increasing the proportion of triglycerides from 0.1 to 10% doubled the accumulation of the PCB compounds in the membranes but also increased the variability of the results. It is well established that lipids are important in the bioaccumulation process, governing the partitioning of the pollutants between the organism and the water.[9] These results show that triglycerides are of significance in accumulation of lipophilic residues. Since no mechanisms other than diffusion and partitioning are involved when using the membranes, these experiments suggest that the properties of the lipids involved, and hence the partitioning mechanism, are the principal factors determining the rate of uptake and accumulation. The specific details behind these processes may be examined by using the membranes with specific lipids, lipid mixtures, and finally whole body fluids. The individual effects of chosen parameters can be isolated since influences from body functions (degradation, depuration, inhomogeneous distribution between different body fluids, etc.) normally encountered in organisms will not complicate interpretation of the results.

REFERENCES

1. Clayton, J. R., S. P. Pavlou, and F. Breitner. "PCBs in Coastal Marine Zooplankton: Bioaccumulation by Equilibrium Partitioning," *Environ. Sci. Technol.* 11:676–682 (1977).
2. Schneider, R. "Polychlorinated Biphenyls (PCBs) in Cod Tissues from the Western Baltic: Significance of Equilibrium Partitioning and Lipid Composition in the Bioaccumulation of Lipophilic Pollutants in Gill-Breathing Animals," *Meeresforschung* 29:69–79 (1982).
3. Tanabe, S., R. Tatsukawa, and D. J. H. Phillips. "Mussels as Bioindicators of PCB Pollution: A Case Study of Uptake and Release of PCB Isomers and Congeners in Green-Lipped Mussels (*Perna viridis*) in Hong Kong Waters," *Environ. Pollut.* 47:41–62 (1987).
4. Helle, E., H. Hyuvarinen, H. Pyysalo, and K. Wickström. "Levels of Organochlorine Compounds in an Inland Seal Population in Eastern Finland," *Mar. Pollut. Bull.* 14:256–260 (1983).
5. Tanabe, S. "PCB Problems in the Future: Foresight from Current Knowledge," *Environ. Pollut.* 50: 5–28 (1988).

6. Södergren, A. "Solvent-Filled Dialysis Membranes Simulate Uptake of Pollutants by Aquatic Organisms," *Environ. Sci. Technol.* 21:855–859 (1987).
7. Södergren, A., and L. Okla. "Simulation of Interfacial Mechanisms with Dialysis Membranes to Study Uptake and Elimination of Persistent Pollutants in Aquatic Organisms," *Verh. Int. Verein. Limnol.* 23:1633–1638 (1988).
8. Södergren, A. "Monitoring of Persistent Pollutants in Water and Sediment by Solvent-Filled Dialysis Membranes," *Ecotox. Environ. Safety* 19:143–149 (1990).
9. Addison, R. F. "Organochlorine Compounds and Marine Lipids," *Prog. Lipid Res.* 21:47–71 (1982).
10. Opperhuizen, A., and M. S. Schrap. "Relationships between Aqueous Oxygen Concentration and Uptake and Elimination Rates during Bioconcentration of Hydrophobic Chemicals in Fish," *Environ. Tox. Chem.* 6:335–342 (1987).

B. Bioaccumulation

CHAPTER 9

Bioaccumulation of Molecular Markers for Municipal Wastes by *Mytilus edulis*

Paul M. Sherblom and Robert P. Eganhouse

INTRODUCTION

Municipal wastewaters serve as a vehicle for the release of anthropogenic contaminants to the coastal environment. Estimating the wastewater contribution to an organism's tissue burden of specific contaminants (e.g., PAH, PCBs) is often complicated due to alternate potential sources (e.g., industrial waste, stormwater runoff, atmospheric deposition). One means of characterizing the role of municipal wastewaters as a pollutant source to sediment, suspended particles, and biological tissues is through the use of source-specific marker compounds. Two types of such markers that have been used to evaluate waste impacts on sediments and particles are (1) the fecal sterol, coprostanol, and (2) the long-chain linear alkylbenzenes (Figure 9.1).

Coprostanol is produced via microbial hydrogenation of the double bond between carbons 5 and 6 in cholesterol. Hydrogenation at this point can give rise to two possible structures: coprostanol (5β-cholestan-3β-ol) and cholestanol (5α-cholestan-3β-ol). While cholestanol has other sources in the environment and is the thermodynamically favored product, it appears that production by enteric bacteria in higher animals is the dominant source of coprostanol.[1] Coprostanol has been widely used as an indicator of sewage contamination.[1,2] Several authors have also investigated the relationship between organic contaminant and coprostanol concentrations in the marine environment relative to municipal waste inputs.[3-7]

The long-chain linear alkylbenzenes (LABs), a suite of 26 secondary phenylalkanes with alkyl side chains of 10 to 14 carbons, are produced industrially as precursors to the anionic surfactants, linear alkylbenzene sulfonates (LAS). These compounds have been identified in municipal wastes,[8-13] marine sediments,[14-17] and suspended and sinking marine particles.[8,14,18] The presence of LABs in wastewater effluents is thought to result from incomplete sulfonation and carryover in detergents, and/or from desulfonation of LAS.[14]

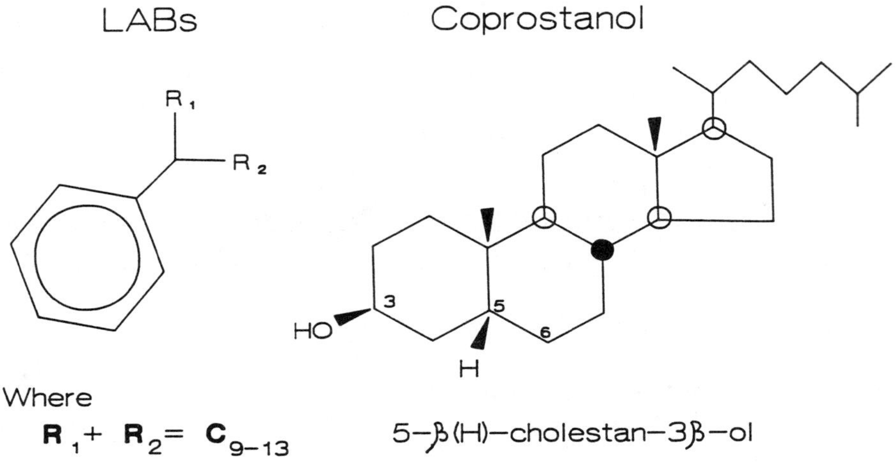

LABs   Coprostanol

Where

$R_1 + R_2 = C_{9-13}$ $5-\beta(H)-cholestan-3\beta-ol$

Figure 9.1. Structures of the municipal waste markers: the long-chain linear alkylbenzenes (LABs) and coprostanol.

The LABs exhibit a range of physicochemical properties spanning those of many hydrophobic organic contaminants (e.g., PAH, PCBs).[19] This enhances their potential utility for mimicking the transport and fate of other hydrophobic organics discharged in municipal wastes.

The marine bivalve, *Mytilus edulis*, has been widely used as a biomonitor of coastal pollution.[22,23] Mussels are well suited to this role because they are essentially stationary, filter large quantities of water, and have a limited ability to metabolize xenobiotics.[24] Bioaccumulation of hydrophobic organic substances is thought to be dominated by partitioning into tissue lipids.[25] Thus, changes in the storage of lipids may be reflected in the tissue burden of hydrophobic contaminants. Whether changes in tissue weight and lipids (related to the organism's reproductive cycle) have effects on the body burden of hydrophobic organics is a matter of discussion.[26,27] Other factors that may affect a comparison of samples across a time series include potential changes in animal size and/or tissue wet weight (nonlipid related).

Both of the molecular markers described above have been identified in organisms.[28-34] Zollo et al. reported the presence of coprostanol in tunicates collected in the Bay of Naples (Italy), but they did not speculate on whether it was biosynthesized or accumulated.[28] Matusik et al. determined the presence of both coprostanol and epicoprostanol (5β-cholestan-3α-ol) in samples of *Mercinaria mercinaria* collected in sewage-contaminated waters.[29] O'Rourke sampled lobsters, clams, and polychaetes from both sewage-impacted and nonimpacted sites.[30] She found coprostanol to be present only in intestinal tissues of organisms collected from contaminated sites. Since mussels are usually analyzed as whole organism composites, the presence of coprostanol might be due to sewage-derived particles lodged in the gut of the organism rather than bioaccumulation.

Werner and Kimerle explored the bioaccumulation and elimination of LABs by fish (*Lepomis macroshirus*) using laboratory exposures.[31] Their results indicated that tissue concentrations were modified by metabolism and/or elimination of the LABs by the fish. However, Albaigés et al. suggest that the presence of LABs in liver samples of fish (*Micromesistius poutassou*) collected off the coast of Spain is indicative of their environmental persistence.[32] Yasuhara and Morita, investigating "volatile" organic components in mussels, report the presence of several alkylbenzenes with alkyl chains of 10 to 13 carbons in length.[33] Murray et al. found the full suite of LABs in mussels collected in Port Phillip Bay (Australia).[34]

The tissue distributions and bioaccumulation rates of the marker compounds need to be evaluated before they can be used to estimate the tissue burdens of other hydrophobic pollutants that may be due to municipal waste discharges. Thus, we chose to monitor the accumulation of coprostanol and the LABs in three tissue pools (digestive gland, gonadal/mantle tissue, and residual tissue) of *Mytilus* exposed to sewage-contaminated waters. The rationale for choosing these three tissues was to isolate potential contributions by ingested particles in the digestive gland, determine if changes in the gonadal lipid content affected tissue concentrations in any of the three tissue pools, and allow the summation of these tissue concentrations in order to compare these data with whole organism composites. We report here preliminary results of a transplant study conducted during the summer of 1988, in which the tissue distributions of these compounds and bioaccumulation rates of the LABs have been determined. The results of the transplant study are compared with time series data of an indigenous population of mussels at the same site.

EXPERIMENTAL

Mussel Deployment and Collection

Mussel specimens were collected from below mean low water at a reference location (Sandwich, MA). This is a nonurban site, and previous analyses of mussels from this population have indicated low levels of anthropogenic organic compounds.[35] Results of the time zero marker analyses, reported below, confirm these organisms to be unimpacted by domestic wastes. The samples were stored over ice and returned to the laboratory. In the lab, mussels were cleaned of epiphytes, and specimens between 3 and 7 cm in length were randomly allocated to 16 polyethylene cages (30 to a cage). The cages were placed in recirculating seawater overnight, and the following day 15 cages were transported (over ice) to a location about 100 m from one of the Nut Island wastewater outfalls (Figure 9.2). Nut Island is one of two municipal wastewater treatment plants discharging into Boston Harbor. The cages were sus-

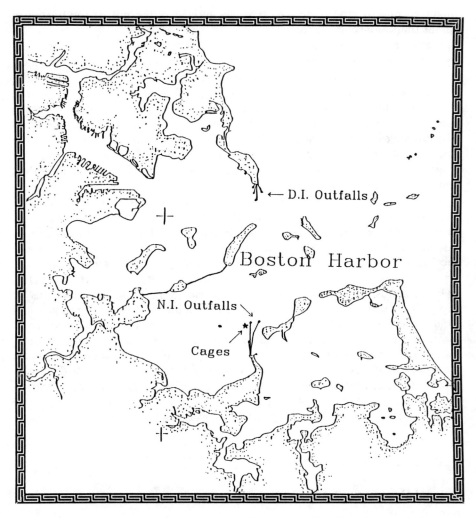

Figure 9.2.   Map of Boston Harbor showing location of the Nut Island wastewater outfalls and the navigational marker where the mussel deployment was located.

pended so that they were always at least a meter below the water surface. At 4-week intervals the organisms were transferred to clean cages due to fouling. At these times the organisms' shells were also cleaned.

Three cages were retrieved on each of the following dates: July 25, August 6, September 2, and September 30, 1988. Native specimens growing on a navigational marker at the site were also collected at these times (Figure 9.2). The mussels were cleaned of epiphytes and stored over ice until dissection. All organisms were dissected within 72 hr of collection. Fifteen organisms were randomly selected from each of the three cages per date. Specific tissue types (digestive gland, gonadal-mantle tissue, residual tissues) from these 15 organisms per cage, were pooled to form three replicate (5 specimens per composite) samples for each tissue type, on each date. The residual tissue was composed of those soft tissues remaining after removal of the digestive gland and gonadal/mantle tissue. It consisted of the foot, gills, muscle, and other tissues. The data for the three tissue pools can be combined to yield a value equivalent to a whole organism composite. During dissection, wet weights of the individual tissues were measured, as was shell length, for each organism.

To define whether the reproductive status of the sampled organisms affected the tissue burden of the molecular markers, quantities of indigenous mussels were collected on the last sampling date (September 30). These were dissected, and the few organisms that represented one or the other extreme reproductive state were composited into samples, which will be referred to as "gonadal-rich" and "gonadal-deplete." Since the goal of this exercise was to focus on the status and tissue burden of the mantle/gonadal tissues, the digestive and residual tissues for these samples were pooled during dissection. Composited tissues were stored frozen ($-10°C$) until analysis could be completed (12 months).

Extraction and Chromatographic Separation

Prior to extraction, the tissue composites (2.5 to 37 g wet weight) were allowed to thaw and transferred in toto to centrifuge bottles containing precombusted anhydrous sodium sulfate, and appropriate recovery surrogates (androstanol, n-nonylbenzene, n-decylbenzene, n-undecylbenzene, n-dodecylbenzene, n-tridecylbenzene, n-tetradecylbenzene) were added. This mixture of tissue, sodium sulfate, and solvent (5–10 mL dichloromethane per gram of wet tissue) was homogenized using a Tekmar Tissumizer. Samples were extracted four times, using the Tissumizer homogenization to facilitate extraction. After each extraction, the mixture was centrifuged (1350 G, 15 min), and the supernatant was decanted and combined with previous extracts of that sample. The extracts were reduced in volume using rotary evaporation. Gravimetric analyses of lipid concentration were performed on aliquots (3 to 7 measurements, 3 to 9 μL each) of the concentrated dichloromethane-lipid extract using a Cahn 29 microbalance. The mean of all measurements for a given extract was used to calculate the total amount of lipid extracted. It should be noted that different extraction methods will result in different lipid yields.[36,37] Thus, the lipid results presented here may not be directly comparable to studies in which different extraction techniques have been used.

An aliquot corresponding to approximately 20 mg lipid was applied to a 1.0 × 30-cm column packed with alumina over silica gel (1:2 v/v, each deactivated 5% with water).[19,38] Four fractions were eluted from this column using hexane (10 mL × 2 fractions), 5% and 30% dichloromethane in hexane (20 mL and 40 mL, combined), and ethyl acetate (40 mL) in succession. The LABs elute with the second fraction, and the sterols in the fourth. The other fractions were not analyzed. Further details of the analytical and separation procedures are reported elsewhere.[19] The sterol fraction was acetylated prior to analysis via gas chromatography using anhydrous pyridine and acetic anhydride.[39] The LAB fraction was concentrated under a stream of dry nitrogen just prior to GC analysis.

Rather than presenting the bioaccumulation results for each of the 26 LABs, the data are given as a summation of all measured LABs. Prior to summing the concentrations of the individual LABs, we evaluated whether they showed any effects of degradation or weathering (i.e., showed variations in isomeric composition). The ratio of internally to externally substituted isomers of the 12 carbon alkyl chain length, which has been suggested to indicate the extent of degradation of the LABs,[17] was determined for all samples. There were no consistent differences in this ratio between tissue pools studied, or over time. This would suggest that degradation was not a cause of differences in LAB concentrations.[19] Summation of the individual LAB isomers provides a convenient means of presenting and comparing the preliminary bioaccumulation results, without an unacceptable loss of information regarding one potential cause of observed differences (i.e., degradation).

Instrumental Analysis

A Varian 6000 gas chromatograph equipped with a hydrogen flame ionization detector and a splitless injector of the design described by Grob[40] was used for quantitation. Analytical separations were performed using 30-m fused silica capillary columns (0.25 mm i.d., film thickness of 0.25 μm). The stationary phases were DB-5 (LABs, J. and W. Scientific) and 50% methyl, 50% phenyl silicone (sterols, Quadrex OV-17 equivalent). The oven temperature was held at 45°C for injection, and the columns were temperature programmed as follows:

- LABs: isothermal at 45°C for 5 min and temperature programmed at 6°C/min to 285°C, with a 30-min hold
- sterols: held at 45°C for 1 min, run up to 255°C at 10°C/min, 2°C/min to 265°C, 1°C/min to 285°C, where it was held for 30 min

Chromatographic data were acquired and integrated using a Nelson Analytical 3000 chromatography data system equipped with a Nelson 763SB intelligent interface. The analytes were quantitated by the internal standard method (n-pentadecylbenzene and cholestane as quantitation standards). The detector response was calibrated daily. Recoveries of surrogates (mean ± 1 standard deviation) were n-nonylbenzene, 70.51% ± 15.52; n-decylbenzene, 91.67% ± 19.54; n-undecylbenzene, 98.53% ± 23.60; n-dodecylbenzene, 97.37% ± 16.56; n-tridecylbenzene, 93.70% ± 15.32; n-tetradecylbenzene, 98.47% ± 29.74; and androstanol, 97.97% ± 13.45. Some of the n-phenylalkanes used had occasional interferences with coeluting peaks. The absence of similar interference with the secondary phenylalkanes in these samples was confirmed using mass spectroscopy. Because of the generally high recoveries, and the

Table 9.1. Mean Shell Lengths and Tissue Wet Weights of the Composited Mussel Samples of This Study

Date	Shell Length (cm)	Mean Tissue Weight (g) ($\pm$ std. dev.)[a]		
		Digest.	Gonadal	Residual
Indigenous organism samples				
3/23/88	6.32 $\pm$ 0.54	8.20	18.95	33.41
5/ 5/88	5.42 $\pm$ 0.62	4.72	10.93	20.70
7/ 8/88	4.23 $\pm$ 0.60	3.00 $\pm$ 0.23	3.77 $\pm$ 0.02	13.03 $\pm$ 0.08
7/25/88	4.88 $\pm$ 0.52	2.64 $\pm$ 0.19	3.58 $\pm$ 0.06	13.54 $\pm$ 1.58
8/ 6/88	5.49 $\pm$ 0.50	4.09 $\pm$ 0.28	6.39 $\pm$ 1.61	21.59 $\pm$ 1.50
9/ 2/88	5.39 $\pm$ 0.44	4.08 $\pm$ 0.42	5.39 $\pm$ 0.26	19.82 $\pm$ 1.22
9/30/88	6.05 $\pm$ 0.51	5.08 $\pm$ 0.05	11.96 $\pm$ 4.45	26.03 $\pm$ 4.00
Transplanted organism samples				
7/ 8/88	6.23 $\pm$ 0.83	5.22 $\pm$ 1.36	10.54 $\pm$ 2.00	24.85 $\pm$ 3.96
7/25/88	6.41 $\pm$ 0.54	5.68 $\pm$ 0.76	12.81 $\pm$ 1.73	27.95 $\pm$ 4.67
8/ 6/88	6.33 $\pm$ 0.44	6.36 $\pm$ 0.59	12.17 $\pm$ 2.36	28.96 $\pm$ 1.79
9/ 2/88	6.44 $\pm$ 0.48	5.33 $\pm$ 0.29	14.19 $\pm$ 4.47	30.20 $\pm$ 2.87
9/30/88	6.25 $\pm$ 0.56	5.77 $\pm$ 0.46	16.50 $\pm$ 3.74	33.07 $\pm$ 3.74

[a]Total composited tissue weights of the three tissue pools, with standard deviation between replicates of tissue pools on a given date.

sporadic interference with some of the surrogates, none of the data presented here have been adjusted for recovery. An estimate of the precision of the analytical procedure was made by analyzing a whole organism composite that had been homogenized using a Vertis Blender. Subsamples of this tissue mixture were taken and extracted using the procedure described above. The total LAB concentrations, determined on a lipid-normalized basis, for three subsamples of this mixture had a coefficient of variation of 12.4%.

RESULTS AND DISCUSSION

Wet and Lipid Weights

Potential biological effects that might affect the measured tissue burdens of the marker compounds were evaluated by monitoring organism size, tissue wet weights, and lipid content over the course of the study. For comparison, data from two indigenous organism samples collected earlier in 1988 are also presented (March 23 and May 5). The shell length data (Table 9.1) indicate that the mean size of the transplanted mussel samples did not change during this study, whereas the size of the indigenous organisms did. These latter samples had a minimum size (4.23 $\pm$ 0.6 cm) at the beginning of the transplant experiment (July 8). Organisms collected subsequently were of larger size, reaching a maximum size (6.05 $\pm$ 0.5 cm) on the September 30 sampling date, when the sizes sampled for the two populations overlapped. The changes in shell size of indigenous organisms may indicate that different age classes of these organisms were collected and analyzed. Differences in tissue burdens between the two populations, and over time for the indigenous population, could result from different periods of exposure to the effluent. This would affect tissue burdens if the compounds were accumulated without elimination (i.e., if tissue concentrations result from cumulative exposure and do not represent equilibrium of the tissues with their environment).

The wet weights for both the indigenous (two replicates except March 23 and May 5) and transplanted (three replicates) composited tissue samples (Table 9.1) roughly follow the changes in shell length. The transplanted organisms appear to show no change, or a slight increase, in the wet weights of the tissue type composites over the course of this study (Table 9.1). Since there are only small variations in the wet weights between times, any differences in the tissue burden of the marker compounds in the transplanted mussels are probably not a result of changes in the size or wet tissue weights of organisms being sampled. However, the changes in size and wet tissue weights for the native mussels taken during this study could possibly affect the concentrations of the marker compounds of these samples for the reasons discussed above.

The concentrations of extractable lipid (milligrams lipid per gram wet weight) determined for each of the mussel tissue pools are presented in Figure 9.3. Fluctuations in lipid concentration (Figure 9.3) of the tissues generally follow those of wet weight and shell size. Lipid content is highest in the digestive gland, with the gonadal/mantle tissues exhibiting slightly higher concentrations than those found in the residual tissues, at most times. The lipid content of the digestive gland in the indigenous population is generally greater than that of the transplanted organisms; the lipid content of the other tissues for these two populations are more similar. One possible explanation of the observed differences in lipid content of the digestive gland could be a physiological response to (assumed) environmental stress for the indigenous population. Another would be diversity between the two mussel populations.

Changes in the reproductive status of a mussel population could be indicated by enrichment of the lipid content of gonadal tissues (reflecting increases in gametogenic tissues). If the whole population undergoes a spawning event, the amount of lipid available for contaminants to partition into, as well as the lipid concentration (mg lipid/g wet weight), should undergo dramatic change. No such changes were observed in the lipid content of the gonadal/mantle tissue or in the other tissue pools sampled from either population (Figure 9.3). This suggests that there was no point in time where a majority of either of these populations were involved in spawning. These results agree with subjective observations of the mussel tissues during dissection, and with histological measurements made of tissues from other mussel populations in Boston Harbor.[41] These mussel populations seem to spawn continuously throughout the summer (i.e., there is always a portion of the population involved in spawning), rather than simultaneously spawning once or only a few times during the summer.[41] This reproductive behavior apparently results in the tissue lipid values remaining fairly constant in these samples during the course of this study.

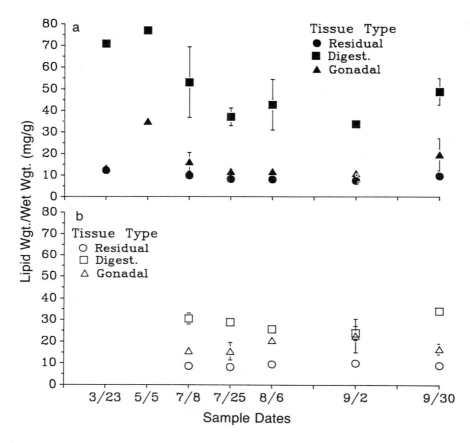

Figure 9.3. Mean (± one standard deviation) lipid concentrations of the tissue pool composites (mg lipid/g wet tissue); *residual* = residual tissues, *digest.* = digestive gland, *gonadal* = gonadal/mantle tissues: *(a)* indigenous organisms, *(b)* transplanted organisms.

Bioaccumulation of Molecular Markers

Tissue concentrations of the molecular markers are reported normalized to lipid weight (Figures 9.4 and 9.5). Coprostanol concentrations in tissues of the indigenous organisms (Figure 9.4a) are quite variable, with no consistent difference between tissue types. The transplanted organisms (Figure 9.4b) show low initial coprostanol concentrations and steady accumulation in the residual and gonadal/mantle tissues. The time zero transplant samples had undetectable amounts of coprostanol in the digestive and residual tissue samples, whereas one of the three gonadal/mantle tissue extracts had a chromatographic peak with the retention characteristics of coprostanol; however, mass spectroscopy could not confirm its identity (other than to indicate a sterol structure).

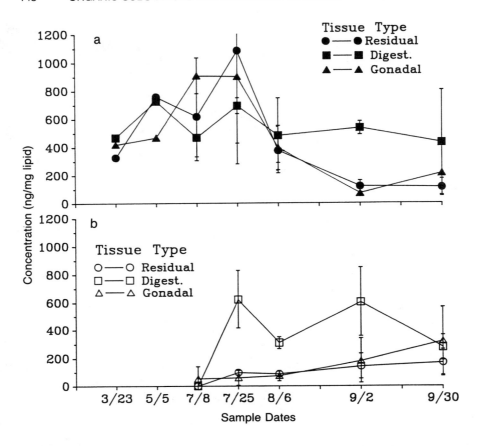

Figure 9.4.   Mean (± one standard deviation) coprostanol concentrations in tissue pools (ng coprostanol/mg lipid); symbols as in Figure 9.3.

Coprostanol concentrations in the transplanted organisms were higher in the digestive gland than in the other tissues through most of the study. In both populations the coprostanol concentrations in the gonadal/mantle tissues and the residual tissues are usually similar. On the last two sample dates of this study, the indigenous sterol distributions seem to be more stable. At these times the gonadal/mantle and residual tissues show similar concentrations between the two populations as well.

Jarzebski and Wenne investigated the tissue distributions of sterols in *Macoma balthica* and suggested that the digestive gland may be a sterol storage site, with mobilization to gonadal tissue during gametogenesis.[42] If this also occurs in *Mytilus*, the scatter in native organism coprostanol tissue concentrations may reflect varying contributions to the composite samples from individuals at different stages of reproductive development. This could indi-

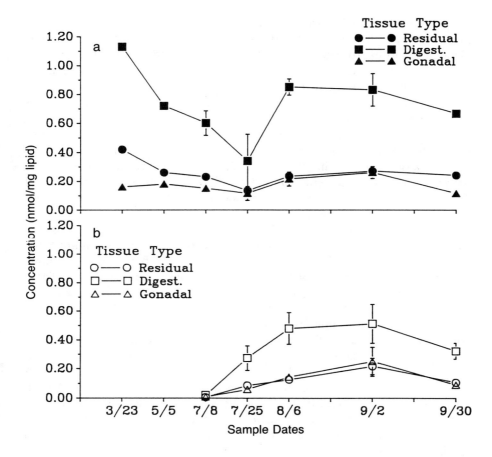

Figure 9.5. Mean (± one standard deviation) of total LAB concentrations in tissue pools (nmol ΣLABs/mg lipid); symbols as in Figure 9.3.

cate that once present in the tissues, coprostanol can be regulated by the organism's normal sterol metabolism.

Tissue distributions of the total LABs (Figure 9.5) are qualitatively similar to those of coprostanol. In both mussel populations the gonadal/mantle and residual tissue pools have similar tissue concentrations. Also, while the transplanted organisms had undetectable concentrations of LABs in all three tissue pools at time zero, by the eighth week the two populations exhibit similar LAB concentrations for residual and gonadal/mantle tissue pools. Total LAB concentrations in the digestive glands are usually higher on a lipid basis than concentrations found in the other tissues. This is consistent with previous reports, which have shown this tissue to be an important storage site for accumulated hydrocarbons.[43-45] For example, Lee et al. reported rapid accumulation of hydrocarbons (alkanes, aromatics) from seawater solutions.[43]

They found these hydrocarbons to be initially taken up by gill tissues, with longer-term accumulation in the digestive gland. Widdows et al. also report higher levels of hydrocarbon accumulation in the digestive gland than by other tissues.[44,45] Further, the digestive gland had higher concentrations of lipids than the other tissues studied.[44]

The elevated concentrations of LABs determined in the digestive glands could reflect contributions of ingested particles, greater partitioning because of the larger lipid pool, or different routes of bioaccumulation for the various tissues. When mussels were exposed to "the water accommodated fraction" of North Sea oil with or without food particles present, organisms exposed to oil with food particles had higher concentrations of aromatic hydrocarbons in all tissues than did organisms exposed to food and oil separately.[44] These differences were most likely due to adsorption of the aromatics to the food particles with subsequent accumulation.[44] This suggests that ingestion of contaminated food particles may be an important route of exposure and bioaccumulation.

The concentrations of the molecular markers in the digestive gland, however, are unlikely to result solely from contributions of sewage-derived particles. Water column particles collected and analyzed during this study had total LAB and coprostanol concentrations in the range of 120 to 595 ng/mg lipid and 670 to 6400 ng/mg lipid, respectively.[19] The digestive gland tissues reached concentrations of 125 to 275 ng/mg lipid (total LABs) and 400 to 700 ng/mg lipid (coprostanol). Using the LAB/lipid concentration to estimate the amount of lipid in the digestive gland that could represent ingested particles indicates that between 20 and 100% of the lipid in this tissue would need to be from ingested particles. Since the lipid content of transplanted mussels digestive gland samples remained fairly constant over the course of this study (Figure 9.3), the elevated LAB concentrations in the digestive gland are unlikely to result solely from the presence of sewage particles.

The attempt to identify native organisms believed to represent extremes of the reproductive cycle, on the last sampling date (September 30), yielded only enough specimens for three samples (two "gonadal-rich" and one "gonadal-deplete"). The concentrations of the molecular markers in these tissue pools (Table 9.2) are compared with other indigenous samples collected on this date. Even though the concentration of lipid in the "deplete" tissues is less than in the other samples, the marker concentrations in the "rich" and "deplete" samples are similar when normalized to lipid weight (Table 9.2). This indicates that while total lipid concentration may affect the mass of an analyte accumulated in these tissues, the lipid-normalized marker concentrations are less dependent on reproductive state. Coprostanol concentrations for these tissues show no relationship with total lipid. The residual plus digestive tissue pools of organisms at the two extremes of reproductive status have similar concentrations, which are higher than those found in the other native organisms sampled on this date. The coprostanol concentration of the gonadal/mantle tissue of the "deplete" sample is roughly the same as that determined for the other

Table 9.2. Values for Lipid Normalized to Wet Weight and the Molecular Marker Concentrations in "Gonadal-Rich" and "Gonadal-Deplete" Tissue Samples

Sample Name	n	Lipid/Wet Weight (mg/g)		Coprostanol (ng/mg)		LABs (nmole/mg)	
		Mean	Std. Dev.	Mean	Std. Dev.	Mean	Std. Dev.
"Gonadal-Rich" (12 weeks)							
Resid./Digest.	2	17.00	0.80	415.87	131.54	0.47	0.08
Gonadal/Mantle	2	19.75	4.74	302.29	58.34	0.22	0.01
"Gonadal-Deplete" (12 weeks)							
Resid./Digest.	1	10.41	—	463.55	—	0.48	—
Gonadal/Mantle	1	8.82	—	209.13	—	0.29	—
Indigenous (12 weeks)							
Resid./Digest.	2	16.08	1.30	257.11	190.97	0.45	0.03
Gonadal/Mantle	2	19.55	7.53	213.03	0.59	0.14	0.05

Note: n indicates the number of samples averaged to give the results listed.

Table 9.3. Results of the ANOVA Analysis of Total LAB Concentration in the Three Tissue Types over Time

Source of Variation	Sum of Squares	DF	Mean Square	F	Significance of F
Total	92.8	35	2.7		
Explained	83.5	11	7.6	19.6	≤0.001
Main effects	80.2	5	16.0	41.4	≤0.001
Time	21.1	3	7.0	18.2	≤0.001
Tissue type[a]	59.0	2	29.5	76.1	≤0.001
1 vs 2 + 3	59.0	1	59.0	171.1	≤0.001
2 vs 3	0.002	1	0.002	0.01	0.93
2-Way interactions					
Time with tissue type	3.3	6	0.6	1.4	0.25
Time with (1 vs 2 + 3)	2.9	3	1.0	2.8	0.06
Time with (2 vs 3)	0.4	3	0.1	0.6	0.65
Residual	9.3	24	0.4		

[a]Tissue types are 1 = digestive gland, 2 = gonadal/mantle tissue, 3 = residual tissues.

native samples, though it is lower than the concentration of the "rich" gonadal/mantle tissues.

Differences between tissue types (gonadal/mantle versus digestive and residual) are also evident for the LABs. The LAB concentration of the residual and digestive tissue pool is roughly twice that of the gonadal/mantle tissues. The effect of tissue type on LAB concentration indicates that different processes may be controlling the contaminant burdens of the various tissues. This data set is inadequate to assess what those processes might be, though they may include route of exposure and elimination.

Bioaccumulation of the LABs

The differences in total LAB concentrations of the three tissue types over time were subjected to analysis of variance (ANOVA). The variables considered were LAB concentration, time, and tissue type, with time being treated as a "fixed effect" (model I ANOVA; time zero samples excluded from this analysis because their zero variance caused a violation of the assumption of homogeneity of variance).[46] The results of the ANOVA analysis are shown in Table 9.3. This table shows the total, explained, and residual variance for this analysis. The explained variance is broken down into that explained by LAB concentration over time, and that explained by tissue type. The variance explained by tissue type is further defined by making comparisons among tissue types. As there are only two degrees of freedom, only two comparisons could be made. Since the LAB concentration in the digestive gland could potentially reflect contributions by particle-associated LABs, it was decided to compare the concentration of this tissue with that of the other two tissue types. This comparison was made by combining the results for the gonadal/mantle and residual tissues and contrasting their tissue burdens with that of the digestive gland. The remaining comparison was then applied to the LAB concentrations of the gonadal/mantle tissue and the residual tissues.

Interaction between the variables would decrease the utility of the ANOVA analysis. The results (Table 9.3) show insignificant interaction between time and tissue type, as well as between time and the gonadal/mantle and residual tissue comparison. The interaction term for the comparison between the digestive gland and the other tissues is only marginally insignificant ($\alpha = 0.056$); a reason for this potential interaction would be that the LAB concentration change over time, in these tissues, is quite different (i.e., the slopes of the tissue concentrations over time are not parallel). This is in contrast to the changes in LAB concentrations over time for the residual and gonadal/mantle tissues, which are very similar.

Since the main effects show insignificant interaction (except as noted), we can utilize the ANOVA analysis to evaluate the LAB bioaccumulation in the tissues over time. The analysis shows that there is a significant time effect for the LAB tissue concentrations, which when evaluated with Figure 9.5, can be considered to be indicative of their bioaccumulation. There is also a significant tissue type effect on the LAB concentration. The comparisons between tissue types shows that there is a significant difference between the LAB concentrations of the digestive gland and the (pooled) data for the other tissues, while there is an insignificant difference in the LAB concentrations of the gonadal/mantle and residual tissues. In summary, there is significant bioaccumulation of the LABs by these tissues over time. The LAB concentrations in the digestive gland are significantly greater than those of the other tissues. The difference between the LAB concentrations of the gonadal/mantle tissue and the residual tissues is insignificant.

Bioaccumulation Rate of the LABs

As noted earlier, it would be useful to estimate the bioaccumulation rate of these compounds prior to using them to indicate the contribution of a municipal wastewater effluent to the tissue burden of other nonspecific pollutants. The accumulation rate of the LABs in mussel tissues over the first 4 weeks of this study (i.e., days 0 to 29) has been estimated. This time period was chosen because there was nearly linear accumulation over this period, suggesting elimination (depuration) could be ignored. The assumption that elimination is negligible allows the bioaccumulation rate to be derived using linear regression of the tissue concentrations versus time. The accumulation rates for the different tissues were calculated using the first-order rate equation:[47]

$$\ln C_2(t) = k_1 t + \ln (C_2(t=0)) \qquad (9.1)$$

where C_2 = tissue concentration (nmol/mg lipid) of total LABs
        t = time (days)
        k_1 = bioaccumulation rate (nmol/mg lipid^{-1}/day)

Table 9.4. Estimated Bioaccumulation Rates of Total LABs in the Transplanted Organisms in Each Tissue Type over the First Four Weeks of the Transplant

$\ln C_2 (t) = k_1 t + \ln (C_2 (0))$	n	R^2
Digestive Gland		
$\ln C_2 (t) = 0.14 (\pm 0.04) - 4.44 (\pm 1.29)$	9	0.69
Residual Tissues		
$\ln C_2 (t) = 0.12 (\pm 0.03) - 5.21 (\pm 0.93)$	9	0.76
Gonadal/Mantle Tissue		
$\ln C_2 (t) = 0.08 (\pm 0.01) - 4.40 (\pm 0.38)$	8	0.89

Note: As in Table 9.2, n refers to the number of data points used to generate the regression line.

The resulting lines for the three tissues are shown in Table 9.4. The slopes (accumulation rate) for the three tissues vary. The digestive gland has the highest rate, and the gonadal/mantle tissue the lowest. The bioaccumulation rates again indicate that the digestive gland is one of the more important tissues for LAB accumulation.

CONCLUSIONS

This work has shown that bioaccumulation of these molecular markers by *Mytilus edulis* is rapid (i.e., 2–4 weeks). Further research should indicate whether these compounds mimic other hydrophobic contaminants with regards to transport, availability, and accumulation.

The data presented show that by the eighth week, the two populations had similar tissue distributions of the molecular markers. The marker concentrations and tissue distributions of the indigenous population indicate that the differences in the size and wet weight of organisms collected had little effect on the tissue burdens observed. The potential that coprostanol tissue concentrations may be regulated by the mussel's normal sterol metabolism complicates the interpretation of tissue data for this compound and may limit its usefulness as a molecular marker.

The digestive gland of *Mytilus* is a lipid-rich tissue, which also seems to function as a storage tissue. The apparent reproductive state of the organisms, and the total amount of (reproductive) lipid available, may have little bearing on tissue concentrations when these are normalized to the tissue lipid concentration (e.g., ng marker/mg lipid). There were significant differences between the LAB concentrations of the digestive gland and the other tissues, even when normalized to lipid content. This may indicate that there are different processes contributing to the contaminant burden of the various tissues for these organisms. These differences could be related to the digestive gland functioning as a storage tissue for the organism.

ACKNOWLEDGMENTS

The authors would like to thank D. Kimball, M. Huerta, L. Bailey, and S. McGroddy for assistance in the field and laboratory. We extend our gratitude to Dr. J. Farrington for providing laboratory space and equipment, and to C. Phinney for the mass spectral analyses. This work benefited from useful discussions with E. Gallagher, A. McElroy, and W. Robinson regarding experimental design and *Mytilus* biology. P. Landrum and two anonymous reviewers made useful comments on a draft of this report.

REFERENCES

1. Walker, R. W., C. K. Wun, and W. Litsky. "Coprostanol as an Indicator of Fecal Pollution," *CRC Critical Reviews in Environmental Control* 10:91–112 (1982).
2. Vivian, C. M. G. "Tracers of Sewage Sludge in the Marine Environment: A Review," *Sci. Total Environ.* 53:5–40 (1986).
3. Boehm, P. D. "Coupling of Organic Pollutants between the Estuary and Continental Shelf and the Sediments and Water Column in the New York Bight Region," *Can. J. Fish. Aquat. Sci.* 40(Suppl. 2):262–276 (1983).
4. Boehm, P. D., W. Steinhauer, and J. Brown. "Organic Pollutant Biogeochemistry Studies, Northeast U.S. Marine Environment. Part 1: The State of Organic Pollutant (PCB, PAH, Coprostanol) Contamination of the Boston Harbor–Massachusetts Bay–Cape Cod Bay system: Sediments and Biota. Part 2: Organic Geochemical Studies in the Hudson Canyon and Gulf of Maine Areas," Final Report, Contract #NA-83-FA-C-00022 NOAA-NMFS (1984).
5. Boehm, P. D., S. Drew, T. Dorsey, J. Yarko, N. Mosesman, A. Jefferies, D. Pilson, and D. Fiest. "Organic Pollutants in New York Bight Suspended Particulates," in *Wastes in the Ocean, Vol. 6: Near-Shore Waste Disposal,* B. Ketchum, J. Capuzzo, W. Burt, I. Duedall, P. Park, and D. Kester, Eds. (New York: John Wiley and Sons, 1985), pp. 251–279.
6. Wade, T. L., G. F. Oertel, and R. C. Brown. "Particulate Hydrocarbon and Coprostanol Concentrations in Shelf Waters Adjacent to Chesapeake Bay," *Can. J. Fish. Aquat. Sci.* 40(Suppl. 2):34–40 (1983).
7. Brown, R. C., and T. L. Wade. "Sedimentary Coprostanol and Hydrocarbon Distribution Adjacent to a Sewage Outfall," *Water Res.* 18:621–632 (1984).
8. Takada, H., and R. Ishiwatari. "Linear Alkylbenzenes in Urban Riverine Environments in Tokyo: Distribution, Source, and Behavior," *Environ. Sci. Technol.* 21:875–883 (1987).
9. Manka, J., M. Rebhun, A. Mandelbaum, and A. Bortinger. "Characterization of Organics in Secondary Effluents," *Environ. Sci. Technol.* 12:1017–1020 (1974).
10. Eganhouse, R. P., and I. R. Kaplan. "Extractable Organic Matter in Municipal Wastewaters. 2. Hydrocarbons: Molecular Characterization," *Environ. Sci. Technol.* 16:541–551 (1982).
11. Burlingame, A. L., B. J. Kimble, E. S. Scott, F. C. Walls, J. W. de Leeuw, B. W. de Lappe, and R. W. Risebrough. "The Molecular Nature and Extreme Complexity of Trace Organic Constituents in Southern California Municipal Wastewater Effluents," in *Identification and Analysis of Organic Pollutants in Water,* L. H. Keith, Ed. (Ann Arbor, MI: Ann Arbor Science, 1976), pp. 557–585.

12. Eganhouse, R. P., and P. M. Sherblom. "Organic Substances Discharged to Boston Harbor," paper presented at the 2nd Annual Symposium of the Massachusetts Bay Marine Studies Consortium, Boston, MA, November 13–14, 1985.

13. Eganhouse, R. P., D. M. Olaguer, B. R. Gould, and C. S. Phinney. "Use of Molecular Markers for the Detection of Municipal Sewage Sludge at Sea," *Mar. Environ. Res.* 25:1–22 (1988)

14. Eganhouse, R. P., D. L. Blumfield, and I. R. Kaplan. "Long-Chain Alkylbenzenes as Molecular Tracers of Domestic Wastes in the Marine Environment," *Environ. Sci. Technol.* 17:523–530 (1983).

15. Ishiwatari, R., H. Takada, S.-J. Yun, and E. Matsumoto. "Alkylbenzene Pollution of Tokyo Bay Sediments," *Nature (London)* 301:599–600 (1983).

16. Eganhouse, R. P., E. C. Ruth, and I. R. Kaplan. "Determination of Long-Chain Alkylbenzenes in Environmental Samples by Argentation Thin-Layer Chromatography/High-Resolution Gas Chromatography and Gas Chromatography/Mass Spectrometry," *Anal. Chem.* 55:2120–2126 (1983).

17. Takada, H., and R. Ishiwatari. "Biodegradation Experiments of Linear Alkylbenzenes (LABs): Isomeric Composition of C_{12} LABs as an Indicator of the Degree of LAB Degradation in the Aquatic Environment," *Environ. Sci. Technol.* 24:86–91 (1990).

18. Crisp, P. T., S. Brenner, M. I. Venkatesan, E. Ruth, and I. R. Kaplan. "Organic Chemical Characterization of Sediment Trap Particulates from San Nicolas, Santa Barbara, Santa Monica and San Pedro Basins, California," *Geochim. Cosmochim. Acta* 43:1791–1801 (1979).

19. Sherblom, P. M. "Factors Affecting the Availability and Accumulation of Long Chain Linear AlkylBenzenes in *Mytilus edulis,*" PhD Dissertation, University of Massachusetts at Boston (1990).

20. Bayona, J. M., J. Albaigés, A. M. Solanas, and M. Grifoll. "Selective Aerobic Degradation of Linear Alkylbenzenes by Pure Microbial Cultures," *Chemosphere* 15:595–598 (1986).

21. Fedorak, P. M., and D. W. S. Westlake. "Fungal Metabolism of n-Alkylbenzenes," *Appl. Environ. Microbiol.* 51:435–437 (1986).

22. Farrington, J. W., E. D. Goldberg, R. W. Risebrough, J. H. Martin, and V. T. Bowen. "U.S. 'Mussel Watch' 1976–1978: An Overview of the Trace-Metal, DDE, PCB, Hydrocarbon, and Artificial Radionuclide Data," *Environ. Sci. Technol.* 17:490–496 (1983).

23. "A Briefing Guide to the National Status and Trends Program for Marine Environmental Quality," Ocean Assessments Division, Office of Oceanography and Marine Assessment, National Ocean Service, National Oceanic and Atmospheric Administration, U.S. Department of Commerce (November 1985).

24. Livingstone, D. R., and S. V. Farrar. "Tissue and Subcellular Distribution of Enzyme Activities of Mixed-Function Oxygenase and Benzo[a]pyrene Metabolism in the Common Mussel *Mytilus edulis* L.," *Sci. Total Environ.* 39:209–235 (1984).

25. Chiou, C. T. "Partition Coefficients of Organic Compounds in Lipid-Water Systems and Correlations with Fish Bioconcentration Factors," *Environ. Sci. Technol.* 19:57–62 (1985).

26. Mix, M. C., S. J. Hemingway, and R. L. Schaffer. "Benzo(a)pyrene Concentrations in Somatic and Gonad Tissues of Bay Mussels, *Mytilus edulis,*" *Bull. Environ. Contam. Toxicol.* 28:46–51 (1982).

27. Risebrough, R. W., B. W. de Lappe, and T. T. Schmidt. "Bioaccumulation Factors

of Chlorinated Hydrocarbons between Mussels and Seawater," *Mar. Pollut. Bull.* 7:225–228 (1976).

28. Zollo, F., E. Finamore, D. Gargiulo, R. Riccio, and L. Minale. "Marine Sterols. Coprostanols and 4α-Methyl Sterols from Mediterranean Tunicates," *Comp. Biochem. Physiol.* 86B:559–560 (1986).

29. Matusik, J. E., G. P. Hoskin, and J. A. Sphon. "Gas Chromatography/Mass Spectrometric Confirmation of Identity of Coprostanol in *Mercinaria mercinaria* (Bivalvia) Taken from Sewage-Polluted Water," *J. Assoc. Off. Anal. Chem.* 71:994–999 (1988).

30. O'Rourke, J. C. "A Survey of Lower Animals for the Presence of Coprostanol," Master's Thesis, University of Massachusetts at Amherst (1980).

31. Werner, A. F., and R. A. Kimerle. "Uptake and Distribution of C_{12} Alkylbenzene in Bluegill (*Lepomis macrochirus*)," *Environ. Toxicol. Chem.* 1:143–146 (1982)

32. Albaigés, J., A. Farran, M. Soler, A. Gallifa, and P. Martin. "Accumulation and Distribution of Biogenic and Pollutant Hydrocarbons, PCBs, and DDT in Tissues of Western Mediterranean Fishes," *Mar. Environ. Res.* 22:1–18 (1987).

33. Yasuhara, A., and M. Morita. "Identification of Volatile Organic Components in Mussel," *Chemosphere* 16:2559–2565 (1987).

34. Murray, A. P., C. F. Gibbs, and P. E. Kavanagh. "Linear Alkyl Benzenes (LABs) in Sediments of Port Phillip Bay (Australia)," *Mar. Environ. Res.* 23:65–76 (1987).

35. Farrington, J. W. Personal communication (1988).

36. de Boer, J. "Chlorobiphenyl in Bound and Non-Bound Lipids of Fishes; Comparison of Different Extraction Methods," *Chemosphere* 17:1803–1810 (1988).

37. Robinson, W. E., and D. K. Ryan. "Bioaccumulation of Metal and Organic Contaminants in the Mussel, *Mytilus edulis,* Transplanted to Boston Harbor, Massachusetts," report submitted to Camp Dresser and McKee, Inc., by the Harold E. Edgerton Research Laboratory, New England Aquarium (1987).

38. Eganhouse, R. P., B. R. Gould, D. M. Olaguer, P. M. Sherblom, and C. S. Phinney. "Analytical Procedures for the Congener-Specific Determination of Chlorobiphenyls in Biological Tissues," Report to the Department of Environ. Qual. Eng. Comm. Massachusetts, U.S. Environmental Protection Agency (1987).

39. Peltzer, E. T., J. B. Alford, and R. B. Gagosian. "Methodology for Sampling and Analysis of Lipids in Aerosols from the Remote Marine Atmosphere," Technical Report WHOI-84-9, Woods Hole Oceanographic Institution (April 1984).

40. Grob, K., and K. Grob, Jr. "Splitless Injection and the Solvent Effect," *J. High Resolut. Chrom. Chrom. Comm.* 1:57–64 (1978).

41. Kimball, D. Personal communication (1988).

42. Jarzebski, A., and R. Wenne. "Seasonal Changes in Content and Composition of Sterols in the Tissues of the Bivalve *Macoma balthica*," *Comp. Biochem. Physiol.* 93B:711–713 (1989).

43. Lee, R. F., R. Sauerheber, and A. A. Benson. "Petroleum Hydrocarbons: Uptake and Discharge by the Marine Mussel *Mytilus edulis*," *Science* 177:344–346 (1972).

44. Widdows, J., T. Bakke, B. L. Bayne, P. Donkin, D. R. Livingstone, D. M. Lowe, M. N. Moore, S. V. Evans, and S. L. Moore. "Responses of *Mytilus edulis* on Exposure to the Water-Accommodated Fraction of North Sea Oil," *Mar. Biol.* 67:15–31 (1982).

45. Widdows, J., S. L. Moore, K. R. Clarke, and P. Donkin. "Uptake, Tissue Distri-

bution and Elimination of [1-^{14}C] Naphthalene in the Mussel *Mytilus edulis*," *Mar. Biol.* 76:109–114 (1983).

46. Sokal, R. R., and F. J. Rohlf. *Biometry* (San Francisco: W. H. Freeman, 1981).
47. Farrington, J. W. "Bioaccumulation of Hydrophobic Organic Pollutant Compounds," in *Ecotoxicology: Problems and Approaches,* S. A. Levin, M. A. Harwell, J. R. Kelly, and K. D. Kimball, Eds. (New York: Springer-Verlag, 1989), pp. 279–313.

CHAPTER 10

Bioaccumulation of p,p'-DDE and PCB 1254 by a Flatfish Bioindicator from Highly Contaminated Marine Sediments of Southern California

David R. Young, Alan J. Mearns, and Richard W. Gossett

INTRODUCTION

Bottom sediments are a major reservoir for residues of the pesticide DDT and polychlorinated biphenyls (PCBs) released into aquatic environments. Fish consumption warnings or fishery closures in areas polluted by these chlorinated hydrocarbons are increasing. Thus, it is important to understand the processes by which such hydrophobic neutral synthetic organic compounds are incorporated into tissues of benthic seafood organisms. The fugacity model of bioaccumulation states that uptake is determined by the chemical fugacity differential between the organism and its environment. For benthic species this model most conveniently is tested by measuring residue concentrations in tissue (C[t]) and in the sediment (C[s]) to which the organism has been exposed. Here we describe such a test conducted through a field study of surficial sediments and a flatfish used successfully as a bioindicator for chlorinated hydrocarbon contamination in the Southern California Bight.

BACKGROUND

Numerous investigations over the last two decades showed that concentrations of DDT and PCB residues in sediments and organisms from the Southern California Bight were among the greatest reported for any coastal marine ecosystems.[1-10] The principal constituents of these residues have been identified, respectively, as p,p'-DDE and a PCB mixture most closely resembling Aroclor 1254.[11-12] Highest values occurred on the Palos Verdes Shelf, which received municipal wastewater discharges from the Joint Water Pollution Control Plant (JWPCP) submarine outfall system of the Los Angeles County Sanitation Districts. Bottom sediments on the shelf also contained relatively high concentrations of organic material and supported large populations of certain benthic/epibenthic organisms, such as the Dover sole (*Microstomus pacificus*). During the 1970s this flatfish, which often is found partially buried in the surficial sediment layer, was severely affected by a fin erosion disease.[13] Distinct gradients of both the incidence of this disease[14] and tissue concentrations of DDTs and PCBs,[15] generally associated with the sediment contamination gradient away from the JWPCP outfall system, suggested that this flatfish was a potentially useful bioindicator of benthic pollution in the Southern California Bight.[16] Therefore, when an extensive survey of bottom sediments was conducted during 1977 along the 60-m isobath of the Southern California coast,[17-18] tissues from Dover sole specimens also were collected and analyzed from a number of sites both on the Palos Verdes Shelf, and from reference zones to the north and south of this highly contaminated area.

PROCEDURES

A synoptic collection of surficial bottom sediments was obtained during summer 1977 with a modified van Veen grab sampler from a water depth of 60 m at numerous stations along the southern California coast.[17-18] The positions (latitude and longitude) of these stations are listed by Word and Mearns.[18] A single grab sample was taken at each station, and the upper 2 cm was subsampled using a clean stainless-steel spatula. Specimens of the Dover sole were collected in bottom trawls conducted along transects near five of the sediment stations on the Palos Verdes Shelf (JWPCP Monitoring Program trawl transects T1–200′ through T5–200′), and near ten stations in the reference zone to the north and south of the shelf (Figure 10.1). In three cases, the trawls were made between sediment stations in the reference zone. Therefore, average values for each pair of sediment samples (from stations 19 and 21; 41 and 45; 45 and 49) were taken as estimates of the surficial sediment concentrations to which flatfish from these trawls were exposed. Generally, six specimens were taken from each station trawl for analysis. The samples of sediment (in precleaned glass bottles with Teflon-lined caps) and flatfish (in plastic bags) were returned to the laboratory and frozen on the day collected, pending processing for analysis. Using procedures described in Word and Mearns,[18] aliquots of the homogenized sediment samples were analyzed for several conventional sediment parameters including total volatile solids (TVS). The methods described by Young et al. were used for the analysis of p,p'-DDE and PCB 1254.[5,11] First, approximately 40 g of wet sediment were oven-dried at 60°C for 24 hr. The sample then was extracted with n-hexane and cleaned up on activated Florisil; one-half of the extract was saponified for PCB analysis. Measurements on these extracts were conducted as described below.

Using a metal scalpel with a carbon-steel blade, the flatfish specimens were dissected while still semifrozen to minimize contamination of the muscle and liver tissue samples by mucous or visceral fluids. Approximately 5–10 g of wet muscle and the entire liver (typically weighing 1–5 g) were taken for DDE and

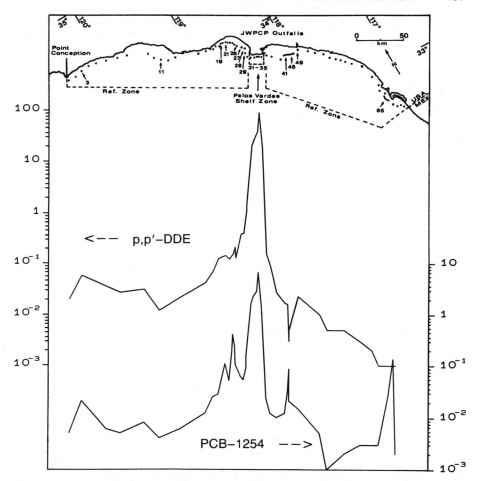

Figure 10.1.   Southern California Bight station locations for the 1977 60-m surficial sediment collections, and corresponding concentrations (mg/kg dry wt.) of *p,p'*-DDE and PCB 1254. Station numbers for sites of Word and Mearns[18] included in this study, and associated reference and Palos Verdes Shelf zones, are indicated.

PCB analysis. In addition, aliquots of these tissue samples obtained from the six specimens collected at two of the Palos Verdes Shelf stations (33 and 34) and at three reference zone stations (41/45, 45/49, and 65) were analyzed for lipid content according to the chloroform/methanol extraction procedure of Bligh and Dyer.[19]

Tissue samples to be analyzed for *p,p'*-DDE and PCB 1254 residues were extracted successively in acetonitrile and *n*-hexane. These extracts then were reduced in volume and cleaned up on activated Florisil. Analysis was conducted by electron capture gas chromatography using packed columns (1.5% OV-17 and 1.95% QF-1 on Gas Chrom Q). Quantitation of *p,p'*-DDE was

Table 10.1. Median Values (and Their Ratios) for Station Concentrations of Sediment Total Organic Carbon, *p,p'*-DDE, and PCB 1254 in the Palos Verdes Shelf (n = 5) and Reference (n = 10) Zones

Zone	TOC (% dry wt.)	p,p'-DDE (μg/g dry wt.)	PCB 1254 (μg/g dry wt.)
Shelf:			
Median	7.6	27	2.3
Range	(4.3–12)	(20–92)	(1.4–6.6)
Reference:			
Median	0.62	0.09	0.06
Range	(0.26–3.7)	(0.001–1.1)	(0.004–0.10)
Ratio of Zone Mds.	12	300	38

Note: Sediment total organic carbon calculated from TVS values using the regression:[22]
% TOC = 0.484 (% TVS − 1.86)

accomplished by direct comparison of its peak height with that of a standard obtained from U.S. EPA. The logarithm (base 10) of the octanol:water partition coefficient (log K_{ow}) for this compound is 5.8.[20] PCB 1254 was quantified against a corresponding Aroclor 1254 standard. The major IUPAC congener in the chromatograph profile chosen for this quantitation has been tentatively identified (by coauthor R. W. Gossett) as congener #110, which has a log K_{ow} of approximately 6.5.[21] All sediment and tissue concentrations were corrected for procedural blank and recovery values.

RESULTS AND DISCUSSION

The distributions of *p,p'*-DDE and PCB 1254 in the 1977 collections of surficial sediment from the 60-m isobath of the Southern California Bight are illustrated in Figure 10.1 and are summarized in Table 10.1. The data indicate that median sediment concentrations of these residues on the Palos Verdes Shelf were 38 to 300 times greater than those in the reference zone. In addition, TVS values quantifying organic content of the sediments ranged from 11 to 27% on the shelf, compared to values below 10% in the reference zone. Thus, for the purposes of this analysis the stations were classified into two groups or zones: a high-contamination shelf zone off the Palos Verdes Peninsula (stations 31–35) and a reference zone containing the other ten stations.

Total organic carbon (TOC) was not measured in these sediment samples. However, Mitchell and Schafer obtained the following regression ($r^2 = 0.986$; $p < 0.001$) between surficial sediment concentrations of TVS and TOC in 1974 samples obtained over a zone extending 16 km from the sludge outfall of Los Angeles City's Hyperion Municipal Wastewater Treatment Plant in Santa Monica Bay:[22]

$$\% \text{ TOC} = 0.484 \ (\% \text{ TVS} - 1.86) \qquad (10.1)$$

Table 10.2. Median Muscle or Liver Tissue Concentrations of p,p'-DDE and PCB 1254 for Dover Sole Specimens from Each Shelf Zone Station and Corresponding Overall Median Values (and Ranges of Station Medians) for the Reference Zone

Sediment Station	Trawl Station	Muscle (μg/g wet wt.)			Liver (μg/g wet wt.)		
		n	p,p'-DDE	PCB 1254	n	p,p'-DDE	PCB 1254
Shelf Zone							
31	T1	2	12	0.51	—	—	—
32	T2	6	16	1.1	6	210	10
33	T3	6	22	1.4	6	240	17
34	T4	6	19	1.2	6	160	12
35	T5	5	8.0	0.21	—	—	—
Median			16	1.1	—	210	12
Reference Zone							
Median			0.24	0.11		0.80	1.5
Range			0.02–2.5	0.01–0.36		0.2–6.7	0.2–5.6
No. Stations			10	10		6	6
Ratio of Zone Mds.			67	10		260	8

Note: Median of individual station median tissue concentrations rounded to two significant figures.

The TVS values used to obtain this regression ranged from 3 to 52%, which encompassed the range (3 to 27%) obtained in the 1977 60-m sediment survey. Thus, this regression equation was used to estimate TOC concentrations from the sediment TVS concentrations.

The sediment concentrations (on a dry weight basis) obtained for the two study zones show that median concentrations of sediment TOC, p,p'-DDE, and PCB 1254 for the shelf zone were higher than those for the reference zone by factors of 12, 300, and 38, respectively (Table 10.1). Further, the percent TOC ranges for the two zones (4.3–12 vs 0.26–3.7) did not overlap, and the lower limit of the ppm DDE range (20) for the shelf zone was 18 times the upper limit of the range (1.1) for the reference zone. Similarly, the lower limit of the ppm PCB range (1.4) for the shelf zone was 14 times the upper limit of the range (0.10) for the reference zone. The fact that the surficial sediments of these two zones were so different in these parameters provided a good opportunity to test, from field data, the utility of the fugacity model of benthos:sediment bioaccumulation for a common marine flatfish of the northeastern Pacific.

In this analysis we have elected to use the median tissue concentration as the measure of central tendency for fish muscle or liver contamination at each station. Therefore, in Table 10.2 we list the median concentration (on a wet weight basis) of p,p'-DDE or PCB 1254 in Dover sole muscle or liver tissue obtained for individual shelf zone stations. Also shown are the reference zone overall median values (and ranges) obtained from the median specimen concentrations of DDE or PCB for each station in this zone. Liver tissue was analyzed in specimens collected at only three of the five shelf zone stations and six of the ten reference zone stations. The ratios of the zone median values indicate that levels of DDE and PCB contamination in the tissues of specimens from the shelf zone were 67 to 260 and 8 to 10 times greater than those in specimens from the reference zone, respectively.

Previous studies had shown that the lipid content of Dover sole specimens collected from the Palos Verdes Shelf was substantially higher than that measured in specimens collected elsewhere off southern California.[13,23] We obtained similar results. Median (wet weight) muscle tissue concentrations of extractable lipid for the shelf and reference zone specimens analyzed (n = 12 and 18, respectively) were 2.36 and 1.34%; corresponding values for liver tissue from all of these specimens were 24.8 and 13.2%. Thus, our best estimate is that muscle and liver tissue for Dover sole specimens collected during 1977 from the Palos Verdes Shelf each contained approximately 80% more extractable lipid than did corresponding specimens from the reference zone.

The very large zonal differences in sediment and tissue concentrations of DDE and PCB first were used to evaluate the least complex form of the fugacity model.[24] This model is a simple partition coefficient commonly termed the *bioaccumulation factor* (BAF):

$$BAF = C_t/C_s \qquad (10.2)$$

where C_t and C_s are a contaminant's concentrations in the specimen tissue and corresponding sediment samples, respectively. In our approach, median wet-tissue-to-dry-sediment ratios for *p,p'*-DDE and PCB 1254 in specimens from each trawl station were calculated by dividing the station median wet weight tissue concentrations by the corresponding dry weight sediment value (Table 10.3). For consistency of units, bioaccumulation factors typically are obtained from the concentration ratios of tissue and sediment each on a dry weight basis. However, percent moisture values for the flatfish tissues analyzed in this study were not available. Further, the fact that criteria for chlorinated hydrocarbon residues in seafood are promulgated on a wet weight basis, while sediment concentrations typically are reported on a dry weight basis, supports the utility of such a mixed-unit index (modified bioaccumulation factor, MBAF) for evaluating conditions leading to contamination of living resources.

The results listed in Table 10.3 suggest that use of the modified bioaccumulation factor may be misleading regarding the relative bioavailability of the contaminants in the two zones. Whereas the ratio of shelf-to-reference zone median concentrations (wet weight basis) for the four tissue-contaminant pairs ranged from 8 to 260 (Table 10.2), the corresponding ratios for the four modified bioaccumulation factors all were less than 1.0, ranging from 0.07 to 0.20. (We note that, assuming the muscle or liver tissue percent water values are similar for specimens from the two zones, the ratios of zone median BAFs also would be similar to those for the MBAFs given in Table 10.3.) Such MBAF (or BAF) values alone might be interpreted as

Table 10.3. Median p,p'-DDE and PCB 1254 Tissue/Sediment Modified Bioaccumulation Factors for Individual Shelf Zone Stations: Ratios of Concentrations in Tissues of Dover Sole Specimens Normalized to Corresponding Surficial Sediment Concentrations and Corresponding Overall Median Values (and Ranges of Station Medians) for the Reference Zone

Sediment Station	Trawl Station	Muscle			Liver		
		n	p,p'-DDE	PCB 1254	n	p,p'-DDE	PCB 1254
Shelf Zone							
31	T1	2	0.55	0.30	—	—	—
32	T2	6	0.57	0.50	6	7.7	4.4
33	T3	6	0.57	0.48	6	6.1	5.9
34	T4	6	0.20	0.18	6	1.8	1.8
35	T5	5	0.40	0.15	—	—	—
Median			0.55	0.30		6.1	4.4
Reference Zone							
Median			2.7	2.0		62	59
Range			0.40–32	0.36–6.1		12–410	9–120
No. Stations			10	10		6	6
Ratio of Zone Mds.			0.20	0.15		0.10	0.07

evidence that p,p'-DDE and PCB 1254 were less available for accumulation by Dover sole specimens from the Palos Verdes Shelf than by specimens from the reference zone.

Therefore, we examined the next level of the fugacity model. Here the approach utilizes a more complex partition coefficient obtained by normalizing C_t to tissue extractable lipid concentration L, and C_s to sediment TOC concentration.[24] The resultant ratio of normalized concentrations is termed the *accumulation factor* (AF):

$$AF = (C_t/L)/(C_s/TOC) \qquad (10.3)$$

These factors were calculated for p,p'-DDE and PCB 1254 concentrations obtained at each trawl station by dividing the station's median concentration for muscle or liver, normalized to the appropriate median lipid concentration value for a given zone and tissue, by the corresponding TOC-normalized sediment concentration (Table 10.4).

This application of the fugacity model of bioaccumulation, incorporating tissue lipid and sediment TOC normalizations, generally yielded good agreement between the degree of contaminant accumulation from bottom sediment (as characterized by station and zone median values) in Dover sole from the two study zones (Table 10.4). Median AF values for p,p'-DDE in muscle tissue of specimens from the shelf and reference zones were 1.7 and 1.8, respectively; corresponding AF values for the liver tissue were 2.0 and 3.4. Similar agreement was observed for PCB 1254. Median AF values for the two zones were 0.96 and 1.3 for muscle tissue, and 1.4 and 2.7 for liver tissue. Thus, despite the very large differences in median levels of sediment and tissue contamination between the two zones, this application of the

Table 10.4. Median Accumulation Factors for *p,p'*-DDE and PCB 1254 in Dover Sole Tissues Obtained for Specimens from Each Shelf Zone Station and Corresponding Overall Median Values (and Ranges of Station Medians) for the Reference Zone

Sediment Station	Trawl Station	Muscle			Liver		
		n	*p,p'*-DDE	PCB 1254	n	*p,p'*-DDE	PCB 1254
Shelf Zone							
31	T1	2	1.7	0.96	—	—	—
32	T2	6	1.8	1.6	6	2.3	1.4
33	T3	6	1.9	1.6	6	2.0	1.9
34	T4	6	1.0	0.96	6	0.86	0.91
35	T5	5	0.74	0.27	—	—	—
Median			1.7	0.96		2.0	1.4
Reference Zone							
Median			1.8	1.3		3.4	2.7
Range			(0.38–14)	(0.24–2.3)		(1.2–19)	(1.0–4.2)
No. Stations			10	10		6	6
Ratio of Zone Mds.			0.94	0.74		0.59	0.52

fugacity model of bioaccumulation yielded results for a given tissue and contaminant that each agreed within a factor of two. These results, based on field data obtained from a relatively small number of specimens (≤ 6) per station and of stations (5–10) per study area, indicate the potential usefulness of the approach in evaluating benthic contamination by major DDT and PCB residues on a regional basis.

In addition to providing comparable results for tissue:sediment ratios over a very large range of exposure, application of this fugacity model to the results of our survey yielded AF values that agree with the value predicted from independent laboratory experiments. McFarland[25] and McFarland and Clarke[26] analyzed results of separate experiments on partitioning of hydrophobic neutral trace organics between (1) sediment organic carbon and water and (2) fish and water. Assuming that octanol was a satisfactory surrogate for the total organic carbon pool to which an organism was exposed, they concluded that, under equilibrium conditions, the partition coefficient that is equivalent to the accumulation factor considered here should have a value of about 1.72. The results of our analysis for *p,p'*-DDE and PCB 1254 presented in Table 10.4 are in good agreement with this prediction. The shelf zone median AF value for these two hydrophobic neutral synthetic organics in flatfish muscle and liver range from 0.96 to 2.0, with a median value of 1.55. If the reference zone median AF values are included, the resultant median value is 1.75, similar to the equilibrium value (1.72) predicted by McFarland and Clarke.[26] Further, the lower (0.96) and upper (3.4) limits of the range of eight zonal median AF values agree with the predicted value within a factor of two.

SUMMARY AND CONCLUSIONS

A simple analysis of field-generated data on two hydrophobic (log $K_{ow} \cong 6$) neutral synthetic organic contaminants of the coastal marine ecosystem off southern California supports the fugacity model of bioaccumulation. Limitations of the study that might compromise the accuracy or precision of the results include estimation of sediment TOC from total volatile solids concentrations and extrapolation of tissue lipid median concentrations for each zone to nonanalyzed specimens. Also, the survey design included relatively few sediment (n = 1) and flatfish (n ≤ 6) samples per station, and relatively few stations per study area (shelf zone: n = 3–5; reference zone: n = 6–10 for liver and muscle tissues, respectively). Further, the variability of sediment exposure experienced by the mobile flatfish specimens trawled near a given sediment station is unknown. Despite these limitations, the accumulation factors obtained for p,p'-DDE and PCB 1254 based on lipid normalization of flatfish muscle and liver tissue concentrations, and TOC normalization of surficial sediment concentrations, produced remarkably consistent results. Ratios of zonal median AFs, based on station median AFs for the two tissues and two contaminants, yielded values ranging from 0.52 to 0.94. These results indicated agreement between shelf and reference zone median AF values that was within a factor of two, despite the large range of sediment and tissue concentrations measured in the two study areas.

Finally, the four median AF values obtained for the shelf zone ranged from about 1.0 to 2.0 (median = 1.6). Corresponding results for the reference zone (where concentrations were lower and resultant uncertainties higher) ranged from 1.3 to 3.4 (median = 2.2). The overall median of these eight values was about 1.8, in good agreement with the value of 1.7 predicted for hydrophobic neutral trace organics from analysis of laboratory partitioning experiments. This provides further support for the reliability of the fugacity model of bioaccumulation, and its potential usefulness in predicting levels of such compounds expected in benthic organisms exposed to contaminated bottom sediments.

ACKNOWLEDGMENTS

We thank the staff of the Southern California Coastal Water Research Project who assisted in study design and collection and analysis of samples, including former Director Willard Bascom, Dr. Jack Word, Theodore Heesen, Harold Stubbs, Michael Moore, Henry Schafer, and Valerie Raco. We also thank Dr. Peter Landrum, U.S. NOAA Great Lakes Environmental Research Laboratory; Dr. Victor McFarland, U.S. Army Engineer Waterways Experiment Station; Charles Bodeen, AScI Corp.; and Dr. Steven Ferraro, Dr. Bruce Boese, Judith Pelletier, Donald Schults, Lynda Wolfe, Jeremy Dvorak, and Summer Young, U.S. EPA Environmental Research Laboratory–Narragansett/Newport, for their assistance. This is ERL-Narragansett's Contribution Number N-144.

REFERENCES

1. Risebrough, R. W. "Chlorinated Hydrocarbons in Marine Ecosystems," in *Chemical Fallout: Current Research on Persistent Pesticides,* M. W. Miller and G. G. Berg, Eds. (Springfield, IL: Charles C. Thomas, 1969), pp. 5–23.
2. Burnett, R. "DDT Residues: Distribution of Concentrations in *Emerita analoga* (Stimpson) along Coastal California," *Science* 174:606–608 (1971).
3. MacGregor, J. W. "Changes in the Amount and Proportions of DDT and Its Metabolites, DDE and DDD, in the Marine Environment of Southern California, 1949–1972," *Fish. Bull.* 72:275–293 (1974).
4. Young, D. R., D. J. McDermott, T. C. Heesen, and T. K. Jan. "Pollutant Inputs and Distributions off Southern California," in *Marine Chemistry in the Coastal Environment,* T. M. Church, Ed. (Washington, DC: American Chemical Society, 1975), pp. 424–439.
5. Young, D. R., D. McDermott-Ehrlich, and T. C. Heesen. "Sediments as Sources of DDT and PCB," *Mar. Poll. Bull.* 8:254–257 (1977).
6. Young, D. R., and T. C. Heesen. "DDT, PCB and Chlorinated Benzenes in the Marine Ecosystem off Southern California," in *Water Chlorination: Environmental Impact and Health Effects,* Vol. 2, R. L. Jolley, H. Gorchev, and D. H. Hamilton, Jr., Eds. (Ann Arbor, MI: Ann Arbor Science, 1978), pp. 267–290.
7. Young, D. R., T. C. Heesen, and R. W. Gossett. "Chlorinated Benzenes in Southern California Municipal Wastewaters and Submarine Discharge Zones," in *Water Chlorination: Environmental Impact and Health Effects,* Vol. 3, R. L. Jolley, W. A. Brungs, and R. B. Cumming, Eds. (Ann Arbor, MI: Ann Arbor Science, 1980), pp. 471–486.
8. Young, D. R. "Chlorinated Hydrocarbon Contaminants in the Southern California and New York Bights," in *Ecological Stress and the New York Bight: Science and Management,* G. F. Mayer, Ed. (Columbia, SC: Estuarine Research Federation, 1982), pp. 263–276.
9. Young, D. R., R. W. Gossett, R. B. Baird, D. A. Brown, P. A. Taylor, and M. J. Miille. "Wastewater Inputs and Marine Bioaccumulation of Priority Pollutant Organics off Southern California," in *Water Chlorination: Environmental Impact and Health Effects,* Vol. 4, R. L. Jolley, W. A. Brungs, J. A. Cotruvo, R. B. Cumming, J. S. Mattice, and V. A. Jacobs, Eds. (Ann Arbor, MI: Ann Arbor Science, 1983), pp. 871–884.
10. Young, D. R., R. W. Gossett, and T. C. Heesen. "Persistence of Chlorinated Hydrocarbon Contamination in a California Marine Ecosystem," in *Oceanic Processes in Marine Pollution: Urban Wastes in Coastal Marine Environments,* Vol. 5, D. A. Wolfe and T. P. O'Connor, Eds. (Malabar, FL: Krieger Publ. Co., 1988), pp. 33–41.
11. Young, D. R., D. J. McDermott, and T. C. Heesen. "DDT in Sediments and Organisms Around Southern California Outfalls," *J. Water Pollut. Control Fed.* 48:1919–1928 (1976).
12. Young, D. R., D. J. McDermott, and T. C. Heesen. "Marine Inputs of Polychlorinated Biphenyls off Southern California," in *Proceedings of the National Con-*

ference on Polychlorinated Biphenyls, F. A. Ayer, Ed. (Washington, DC: U.S. Environmental Protection Agency, 1976), pp. 199–208.

13. Sherwood, M. J. "Fin Erosion, Liver Condition, and Trace Contaminant Exposure in Fishes from Three Coastal Regions," in *Ecological Stress and the New York Bight: Science and Management,* G. F. Mayer, Ed. (Columbia, SC: Estuarine Research Federation, 1982), pp. 359–377.

14. Sherwood, M. J., and A. J. Mearns. "Environmental Significance of Fin Erosion in Southern California Demersal Fishes," *Ann. NY Acad. Sci.* 298:177–189 (1977).

15. McDermott-Ehrlich, D., D. R. Young, and T. C. Heesen. "DDT and PCB in Flatfish Around Southern California Municipal Outfalls," *Chemosphere* 6:453–461 (1978).

16. Mearns, A. J., and D. R. Young. "Characteristics and Effects of Municipal Wastewater Discharges to the Southern California Bight, a Case Study," in *Ocean Disposal of Municipal Wastewater: Impacts on the Coastal Environment,* Vol. 2, E. P. Myers, Ed. (Cambridge, MA: MIT Sea Grant College Program, 1983), pp. 761–819.

17. Word, J. Q., and A. J. Mearns. "The 60-Meter Control Survey," in *Annual Report for the Year 1978,* W. Bascom, Ed. (El Segundo, CA: Southern California Coastal Water Research Project, 1978), pp. 41–56.

18. Word, J. Q., and A. J. Mearns. "60-Meter Control Survey off Southern California," Technical Memorandum 229, Southern California Coastal Water Research Project (1979).

19. Bligh, E. G., and W. J. Dyer. "A Rapid Method of Total Lipid Extraction and Purification," *Can. J. Biochem. Physiol.* 37:911–917 (1959).

20. Veith, G. D., N. M. Austin, and R. T. Morris. "A Rapid Method for Estimating Log P for Organic Chemicals," *Water Res.* 13:43–47 (1979).

21. Hawker, D. W., and D. W. Connell. "Octanol-Water Partition Coefficients of Polychlorinated Biphenyl Congeners," *Environ. Sci. Technol.* 22:382–387 (1988).

22. Mitchell, F. K., and H. A. Schafer. "Effects of Ocean Sludge Disposal," in *Annual Report for the Year Ended 30 June 1975,* W. Bascom, Ed. (El Segundo, CA: Southern California Coastal Water Research Project, 1975), pp. 153–162.

23. Sherwood, M. J., A. J. Mearns, D. R. Young, B. B. McCain, and R. A. Murchelano. "A Comparison of Trace Contaminants in Diseased Fishes from Three Areas," Final Report to U.S. NOAA, MESA New York Bight Project, Grant No. 04-7-022-44002, Southern California Coastal Water Research Project (1980).

24. Ferraro, S. P., H. Lee II, R. J. Ozretich, and D. T. Specht. "Predicting Bioaccumulation Potential: A Test of a Fugacity-Based Model," *Arch. Environ. Contam. Toxicol.* 19:386–394 (1990).

25. McFarland, V. A. "Activity-Based Evaluation of Potential Bioaccumulation from Sediments," in *Dredging and Dredged Material Disposal,* Vol. 1, R. L. Montgomery and J. L Leach, Eds. (New York: American Society of Civil Engineers, 1984), pp. 461–467.

26. McFarland, V. A., and J. U. Clarke. "Testing Bioavailability of Polychlorinated Biphenyls from Sediments Using a Two-Level Approach," in *Proceedings of the Seminar on Water Quality R & D: Successful Bridging between Theory and Application,* R. G. Willey, Ed. (Davis, CA: Hydrologic Engineering Research Center, 1986), pp. 220–229.

PART IV

BIODEGRADATION
A. Anaerobic Dechlorinations

CHAPTER 11

Dechlorinations of Polychlorinated Biphenyls in Sediments of New Bedford Harbor

James L. Lake, Richard J. Pruell, and Frank A. Osterman

INTRODUCTION

The breakdown of polychlorinated biphenyl (PCB) congeners in situ in sediments heavily contaminated with PCBs by processes called *reductive dechlorinations* have been reported.[1-3] These studies characterized several distinct dechlorination patterns, caused by different strains of anaerobic bacteria, which resulted in PCB residues that were altered from the original Aroclor inputs. The upper New Bedford Harbor (NBH), above the Coggeshall St. Bridge (Figure 11.1), is a shallow, approximately 200-acre salt marsh estuary, which received large inputs of Aroclor 1254 (A-1254) and Aroclor 1242 (A-1242) from 1947 to 1970, and possibly Aroclor 1016 (A-1016) from 1970 to 1978, from a capacitor manufacturing plant designated *plant A* in Figure 11.1.[4] Another study found variations in the extent of dechlorination processes in 5- to 7.5-cm and 15- to 17.5-cm sections of cores taken in the northern part of the upper NBH.[5] However, the distributions of PCBs in extracts of sediment core sections taken in the southern part of the upper NBH (Figure 11.1) as part of a pilot dredging study at the Environmental Research Laboratory--Narragansett (ERLN) showed only small alterations relative to mixtures of A-1242 and A-1254. The present study was undertaken to determine the extent of alteration of PCB residues in the sediments of upper NBH resulting from dechlorination processes, and to estimate the rates of these processes.

METHODS

Sediment cores were collected by piston corer in upper and lower NBH during the period July 5–7, 1988, at the locations shown (Figure 11.1). Cores were capped and placed inside sealed plastic bags. The cores were stored on ice shortly after collection and during the transport to the ERLN and then frozen (20°C). From collection to the time they were frozen, cores were held vertically

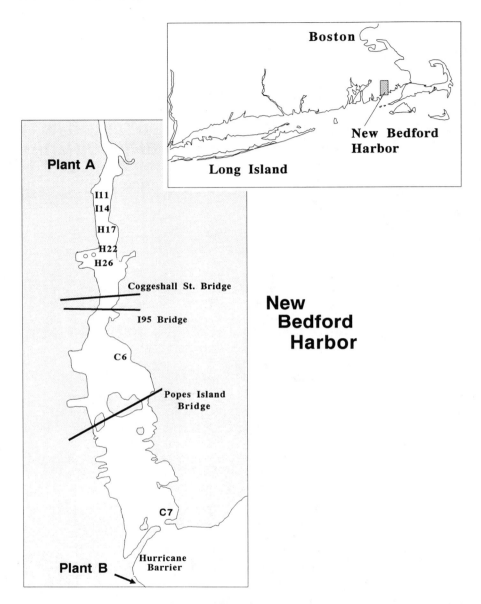

Figure 11.1.   Map showing locations of electrical capacitor plants *A* and *B* and of cores taken in this study. *Small circles* show locations of sediment samples analyzed in pilot dredging study.

to avoid mixing of sediment layers. Samples of core sections were taken from frozen cores using a power drill and a 2.5-cm diameter hole saw to cut plugs from the cores at the desired depths. The hole saw used for sampling was washed in a soap-and-water solution, followed by washing in acetone between cuttings to avoid cross-contamination of samples. Core sections taken for analysis in this study were obtained at 0–2.5, 5–7.5, 15–17.5, 30–32.5, and 45–47.5 cm, but in shorter cores only the top sections could be sampled. The core section samples were extruded into precleaned glass jars, capped, and stored at −20°C until analysis.

Since this was a field study and examined the consequences of processes that were many years in duration, no true experimental control could be incorporated into the study. Our approach was to compare the distribution of PCBs found in sediments of upper NBH with those found in mixtures of Aroclors that contaminated this area. Additional comparisons of PCB distributions were made between NBH sediments and a nondechlorinated anaerobic sediment from Black Rock Harbor, CT.[6] The latter comparisons documented the extent of changes in PCB distributions in NBH relative to those found in anaerobic sediments where no dechlorination had occurred.

Analytical Methods

Core sections were thawed and mixed thoroughly with a stainless-steel spatula, and a weighed aliquot was dried in a dessicator to a constant weight to determine sediment water content. A 1-g aliquot of the wet sediment was extracted with 5 mL of acetone for 30 sec using an ultrasonic probe (Model W-370, Heat Systems, Ultrasonics, Inc). The sample was centrifuged to separate the phases, and the acetone extract was saved. The extraction was repeated, and the extracts combined. Deionized water (5 mL) was added to the combined acetone extracts along with heptane (1 mL). The sample extract was shaken for 30 sec and centrifuged to separate the layers. The heptane extract was removed and reacted with 1 mL concentrated H_2SO_4. The heptane layer was removed, reacted with reduced copper powder to remove elemental sulfur, and then analyzed for PCBs.

Sediment extracts were analyzed for PCBs on a Hewlett-Packard 5890A gas chromatograph (GC) equipped with a splitless injection port, electron capture detector, and a 60-m fused silica column coated with a 0.25-μm coating of DB-5 (J and B Scientific, Inc.). The injector temperature was 270°C, and the detector temperature was maintained at 315°C. The column was held at 150°C for 1 min following injection, then programmed to 290°C at 1°C/min, and held at 290°C for 5 min. The output from the detector was collected on a Perkin Elmer LIMS 3210 computer.

Extracts were diluted prior to GC analysis with measured amounts of heptane containing octachloronaphthalene (OCN). The OCN served as an internal injection standard for peak identification.

The congeners comprising a peak were identified by injections of individual congener standards. For peaks for which standards were not available, identifications were based on retention times from the literature values.[7] The peaks utilized in this study, the corresponding congeners, and the method of identification are shown in Table 11.1.

Aroclor 1016 (A-1016) also was used by the capacitor manufacturing plant. Since A-1242 differs from A-1016 only by a slightly higher abundance of heavier PCB congeners, it is very difficult to differentiate between A-1016 and A-1242 when the higher-molecular-weight range of these mixtures is masked by A-1254. The problem of identifying A-1016 or A-1242 in the presence of A-1254 is even more difficult when dechlorination processes have altered distributions of congeners. To circumvent this problem we have assumed all releases of lower-molecular-weight PCB mixtures by the plant were A-1242. Our justification for this assumption is that A-1016 was substituted for A-1242 because of environmental concerns, and we presume Aroclor releases by the capacitor plant were greatly decreased or eliminated with the beginning of the usage of A-1016. Whether inputs were A-1242 or A-1016 makes little difference to the evaluations of the extent of dechlorinations seen in this study, but the time of the release of the mixture into the environment may affect estimates of dechlorination rates (see subsequent "Results and Discussion").

Quantitation of concentrations was done using external standards of A-1242 and A-1254. Spike and recovery tests of the procedure showed an average recovery of 106.3% (SD 23.7%) for individual peaks present in a mixture of Aroclor standards. Results were not corrected for recovery efficiencies. Triplicate analyses of a homogenate of a highly contaminated sediment using the described procedures showed that the coefficient of variation of the procedure was 7.6% in sediments that had a mean concentration of A-1242 plus A-1254 of 2960 ppm. Blanks were processed with sample sets and showed no contamination that interfered with the analysis of PCBs. All concentrations are on a dry weight basis. Concentrations as ppm (parts per million) refer to μg A-1242 plus A-1254/g sediment.

A computer program was developed to calculate the percentages of A-1242 and A-1254 content of samples from this study. This program used peak P039B as representative of A-1242 and peak P061 as representative of A-1254. These peaks were selected as representative of the Aroclor mixtures because they were found to be the most resistant to changes as a result of dechlorinations in this and another study.[5] Since these peaks are both present in A-1242 and A-1254, the computer program does a series of successive approximations and corrections to determine the percentages of these Aroclors in the residue.

To examine the effectiveness of this technique for estimating the percentages of A-1242 and A-1254 in sediment extracts, mixtures of A-1242 and A-1254 standards were analyzed and predictions of their relative quantities were made using the described technique. The results of these analyses are shown in the notation

$$(a:b - c:d)$$

Table 11.1. Peaks, Corresponding Congeners, and Structures

Peak ID	Tentative Identification of Congener	Structure
P005	10(S),4(S)	26–,2–2
P006	7(S),9(S)	24–,25–
CB006	6(S)	2–3
P008	5(S),8(S)	23–,2–4
CB019	19(L)	2–26
P013	12(S),13(S)	34–,3–4
CB018	18(S)	2–25
P015	15(S),17(L)	4–4,2–24
P016	24(L),27(L)	236–,3–26
P017	16(S),32(L)	2–23,4–26
CB026	26(S)	25–3
CB025	25(L)	24–3
CB031	31(S)	25–4
P024	28(S),50(S)(M)	24–4,2–246
P025	20(S),21(S)(M),53(S),33(S)	23–3,234–,25–26,2–34
P025A	No I.D.	
P026	22(L),51(L)	23–4,24–26
CB045	45(L)	2–236
CB039	39(L)(M)	35–4
P031	52(S),73(L)(M)	25–25,26–35
CB049	49(S)	24–25
P037	44(S),104(S)(M)	23–25,26–246
P038	37(S),42(S),59(L)	3–34,23–24,3–236
CB072	72(S)(M)	25–35
P039A	No I.D.	
P039B	71(L)(M),64(L),	26–34,4–236,2–234
CB040	40(S)	23–23
P044	100(S),67(L)	24–246,25–34
P045	58(L)(M),63(L)	23–35,4–235
P046	74(L),94(L)(M)	4–245,26–235
P047	70(S),61(S)(M),76(L)	25–34,2345–,2–345
P048	66(S),93(S)(M),95(L)	24–34,2–2356,25–236
P049	91(L),98(L)(M),55(L)(M)	24–236,23–246,3–234
P050	56(L)	23–34
P050A	60(S)	4–234
CB089	89(L)(M)(+ others 92,84)	26–234
P053	101(S),90(L)	25–245,24–235
CB099	99(L)	24–245
P055	150(L)(M),112(S)(M),119(S)	236–246,3–2356,34–246

Table 11.1, continued

Peak ID	Tentative Identification of Congener	Structure
P056	83(L),109(L)(M)	23–235,3–2346
P057	152(L)(M),*97(S)*,86(S)(M)	26–2356,23–245,2–2345
P058	*87(S)*,111(L)(M),115(S),81(S)(M)	25–234,35–235,4–2346,4–345
CB085	85(L)	24–234
CB136	136(S)	236–236
P061	77(S),*110(S)*	34–34,34–236
P064	151(S),82(L)	25–2356,23–234
P065	*135(L)*,124(L)(M),144(L)(M)	235–236,24–345,25–2346
P067	*107(L)*,108(L)(M),147(L)(M)	34–235,35–234,24–2356
P069	*149(L)*,106(L)(M),123(L)	245–236,3–2345,24–345
CB118	118(S)	34–245
P037	146(L),161(L)(M)	235–245–35–2346
CB153	153(S)	245–245
CB132	132(L)	234–236
CB105	105(S)	34–234
CB141	141(S)	25–2345
CB179	179(L)	236–2356
CB176	176(L)	236–2346
P082	138(S),163(L)(M)	234–245,34–2356
CB158	158(S)	34–2346
P088	187(S),182(S)(M),159(S)(M)	245–2356,246–2345,35–2345
CB183	183(S)	245–2346
P089	*128(S)*,167(L)	234–234,245–345
CB185	185(S)	25–23456
P093	*174(L)*,181(S)(M)	236–2345,24–23456
CB177	177(L)	234–2356
CB180	180(S)	245–2345
P106	170(S),190(L)	234–2345,34–23456

Table 11.1, continued

Notes: Peak designation as P numbers are used for peaks containing coeluting congeners or where identifications are ambiguous. Identifications listed as tentative because standards for all congeners were not available and other congeners may coelute in the peaks listed. (S) identified with standard; (L) identified by comparison with literature values.[7] Congener (CB) numbering according to Ballschmiter and Zell.[22] Dominant congeners (believed to comprise ≥ 90% of peaks) are in italics. Congeners comprising <0.5% of Aroclors are identified by (M).[7] In structure column, numbers indicate position of chlorine atoms on each ring, and the dash represents separation of the two rings.

where   a = actual percentage A-1242 in standard mixture
         b = actual percentage of A-1254 in standard mixture
         c = predicted percentage of A-1242 from analysis of standard mixture
         d = predicted percentage of A-1254 from analysis of standard mixture

The actual and predicted values showed good agreement (5.6:94.4-7.5:92.5), (27.5:72.5−26.2:73.8), (53.3:46.7−50.5:49.5), (77.4:22.6−74.7:25.3), and (95.6:4.4−93.7:6.3), which indicated the utility of this technique.

The data on the percentage mixture of A-1242 and A-1254 in sample extracts were used with relative concentration data for the peaks in A-1242 and A-1254 standards to reconstruct the original composition of the PCB mixtures that contaminated a specific sediment sample. The heights of peaks calculated to be in these original mixtures are called predicted values and are compared with measured values obtained from analyses of extracts from sediment samples. Comparative abundance plots are used to show the measured abundances (the abundance of congener X extracted from a sediment) relative to the predicted abundance (the abundance of congener X in the Aroclor mixtures which contaminated a specific sediment) and thereby show changes in PCB residues that have occurred since their release into the environment.

RESULTS AND DISCUSSION

The results of sediment analysis showed that PCB concentrations increased from south to north in upper NBH, and the highest concentrations were found nearest the electrical capacitor plant A (Figure 11.1, Table 11.2). In surface core sections (0–2.5 cm) in the upper NBH, PCB concentrations as totals of A-1242 plus A-1254 ranged from 102 ppm to 912 ppm. Surface sections of cores C6 and C7 from lower NBH had lower concentrations, 2.1 and 9.4 ppm. The sediment sample from Black Rock Harbor, CT, contained 21.4 ppm PCBs.

Concentrations in cores from the upper NBH generally increased with depth to the 15- to 17.5-cm section, then decreased in lower core sections. The highest concentration (2960 ppm) was found in the 15- to 17.5-cm section of core I11. Core C7 from lower NBH showed about the same PCB concentra-

Table 11.2. Concentrations and Percentages of Aroclor Mixtures in Sediments

Sample	Depth (cm)	μg A-1242 + A-1254/g(dry)	% A-1242	% A-1254
BRH	Unknown	21.4	42	58
I1101	0–2.9	912	69	32
I1123	5–7.5	2280	71	29
I1167	15–17.5	2960	56	44
I11XX	30–32.5	12	63	37
I11YY	45–47.5	3.2	68	32
I1401	0–2.5	740	72	28
I1423	5–7.5	1200	75	26
I1467	15–17.5	1720	76	24
I14XX	30–32.5	161	52	48
H1701	0–2.5	507	71	29
H1723	5–7.5	660	73	27
H1767	15–17.5	1560	75	25
H17XX	30–32.5	16.6	71	29
H2201	0–2.5	414	75	25
H2223	5–7.5	790	76	24
H2267	15–17.5	753	50	50
H22XX	30–32.5	5.7	56	44
H22YY	45–47.5	1	56	44
H2601	0–2.5	102	61	39
H2623	5–7.5	10	54	46
C601	0–2.5	2.1	39	61
C701	0–2.5	9.4	36	64
C723	5–7.5	7.4	37	63
C767	15–17.5	7.6	39	61
C7XX	30–32.5	7.6	51	49

Note: BRH = sediment from Black Rock Harbor, CT. Other names refer to locations in New Bedford—see map for locations.

tion (9.4–7.4 ppm) in sections from 0–2.5 to 30–32.5 cm. Core C6 and core H26 contained only trace amounts (< 0.2 ppm) of PCB in sections deeper than 0–2.5 cm (C6) and 5–7.5 cm (H26).

In some cores from the upper NBH, the percentage composition of A-1242 and A-1254 changed with depth. Cores I11 and H22 showed a relative increase in the percentage of A-1254 at the 15- to 17.5-cm section. Core I14 showed a similar change at the 30- to 32.5-cm section, but core H17 showed little change in the percentage Aroclor composition with depth. A small relative increase in the A-1254 composition was observed in the 5- to 7.5-cm section of core H26. The increases in percentage composition of A-1254 observed in lower core sections may reflect the history of inputs of Aroclor mixtures to the upper NBH. Although records of PCB purchases by the capacitor plant are incomplete prior to 1963, available records show A-1254 was used prior to 1963, A-1242 was used from 1963 to 1970, and A-1016 was used from 1970 to 1979.[4] The findings that Aroclor mixtures change differently from core to core and the presence of A-1242 and A-1254 at all depths may have resulted from differences in

1. depositional rates
2. percolation rates of PCB mixtures into the sediments
3. mixing of sediments by storms or biota

These results indicate that a historical record of PCB inputs to the upper NBH is not well preserved in some cores and underscores the difficulty in attempting to estimate rates of processes based on sedimentation rates at these locations. Core C7 shows a percentage composition lower in A-1242 and higher in A-1254 than found in the cores from upper NBH. The percentage composition of this core is about 38% A-1242 and 62% A-1254 for the top sections, but changes to 51% A-1242 and 49% A-1254 at the 30- to 32.5-cm section. This NBH core is located just inside the Hurricane Barrier and may have received inputs from other sources, such as capacitor plant B (Figure 11.1).

Substantial changes in the relative distributions of PCB congeners, which appear to be due to reductive dechlorinations, were found in many samples from upper NBH, but samples from lower NBH and BRH showed only small alterations. Comparisons of the relative distributions of PCBs were made using chromatograms of extracts, and using comparisons of the abundances of peaks or congeners in a sample with those present in the original mix of Aroclors that originally contaminated the sediment sample. Comparative abundance plots (CAPs) readily show which peaks are changing relative to the original inputs and are therefore useful to identify peaks that changed as a result of environmental processes. CAPs for a mixture of A-1242 and A-1254 (53:47) standards, core sections H2267 (15–17.5 cm), I1167 (15–17.5 cm), C767 (15–17.5 cm), and BRH sediment are shown (Figures 11.2–11.6). CAPs for the mixture of Aroclor standards showed only small changes between the predicted and measured abundances (Figure 11.2). For the H2267 core section, the bars to the left showed measured abundances below predicted values (less than zero) (Figure 11.3). These bars represent peaks containing congeners that are of relatively low molecular weight and are more volatile and more soluble than most of the other PCBs present. The decreased abundance of these congeners probably resulted from evaporation and/or dissolution of these congeners prior to incorporation of PCBs into consolidated sediment. At higher molecular weights, peaks CB072, P044, P055, CB179, and P088 show measured values that are two or more times greater than the predicted values. These peaks also increase in the sample from BRH and therefore may not be indicative of dechlorination processes. Notable decreases in the relative abundances of peaks P058, CB085, CB132, and CB105 are shown in the CAP for H2267, but similar decreases in the relative abundance of these peaks in the CAPs for BRH or for core section C767 (15–17.5 cm) from lower NBH were not observed. In the most highly dechlorinated sample, I1167 (15–17.5 cm section), the above peaks as well as other peaks (e.g., CB013, P045, P046,

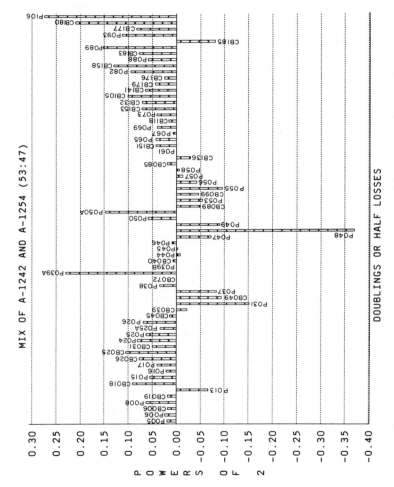

Figure 11.2.   Comparative abundance plot for a 53:47 (weight:weight) mixture of A-1242 and A-1254 standards. Plot was made by determining the original mix of PCBs using peaks P039B and P061, which are representative of A-1242 and A-1254 inputs, respectively, but appear to be resistant to reductive dechlorinations. Measured abundances relative to the predicted starting mix of A-1242 and A-1254 are shown by the length of bars and is expressed to the power of two. Therefore, a value of 2 would indicate the measured abundance of that peak in the sediment was 4 times above the computer prediction of the abundance of that peak in the A-1242 and A-1254 inputs incorporated in the sediment. A value of -2 shows that the abundance of that peak is 0.25 of the computer prediction of the original input.

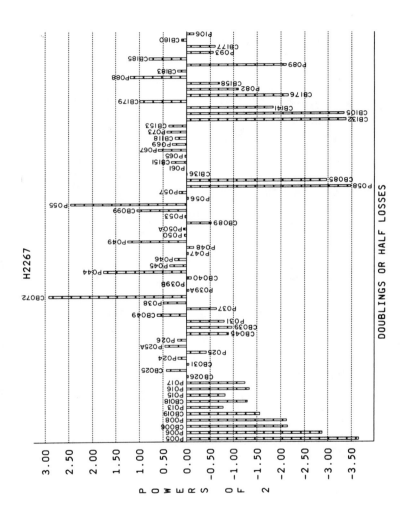

Figure 11.3. Comparative abundance plot for 15- to 17.5-cm section of core H22 (H2267). See Figure 11.2 for details.

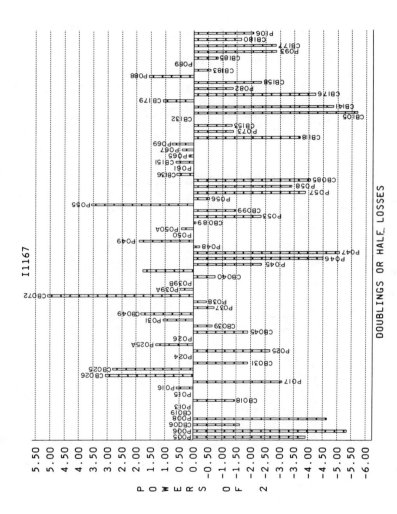

Figure 11.4.   Comparative abundance plot for 15- to 17.5-cm section of core I11 (I1167). See Figure 11.2 for details.

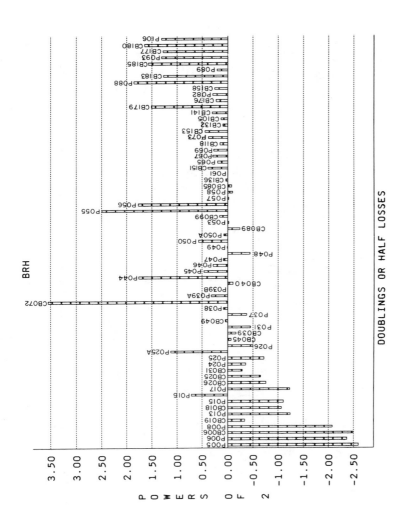

Figure 11.5. Comparative abundance plot for Black Rock Harbor sediment. See Figure 11.2 for details.

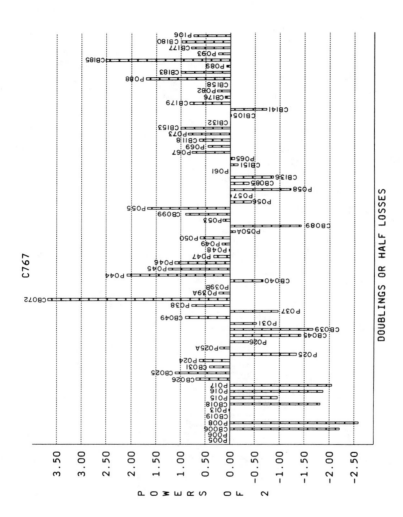

Figure 11.6. Comparative abundance plot for 15 to 17.5-cm section of Core C7 (C767). See Figure 11.2 for details.

P047, P053, CB099, CB153, and CB118) showed considerable decreases, while others (e.g., CB026, CB025) showed increases in relative abundance (Figure 11.4).

In general, the dechlorinations found in upper NBH sediments result in

1. decreases in the relative concentrations of selected higher-molecular-weight congeners, including some potentially toxic mono-*ortho* substituted congeners (e.g., CB105, CB118),[8] and other congeners known for their ability to bioaccumulate (e.g., CB99, CB101, CB153)[9]
2. increases in the relative concentrations of selected lower-molecular-weight congeners

Changes in PCB mixtures as a result of dechlorinations in the upper NBH resulted in PCB distributions that are lower in molecular weight, less bioaccumulatable, and less toxic as measured by capability to induce mixed-function oxidase enzyme systems.[9] These changes appear to be beneficial from an environmental perspective; however, large quantities of partially dechlorinated PCBs remain in upper NBH sediments, and the toxicities of the remaining mixtures are not known.

Plots of the relative abundance of peaks CB025 (structure 24–3), CB105 (structure 34–234), CB118 (structure 34–245), and CB153 (structure 245–245) across sediment samples demonstrate the variability in dechlorinations between locations, core sections, and congeners (Figures 11.7–11.10). These figures show the magnitude of increase or decrease in abundance of a peak measured in a sample relative to the predicted abundance of the peak in the mixture of A-1242 and A-1254 standards calculated as input for the sample.

The plot of the relative abundance of CB025 shows a decrease in the BRH sample, but increases of varying magnitude are observed in samples from upper and lower NBH. The congener comprising this peak (CB025) is a minor component of A-1242 and A-1254, and its increase in samples has been reported as indicative of a reductive dechlorination process.[3] Most of the samples from upper NBH show a factor of four or more increase in relative abundance of this congener. Sample I14XX (30- to 32.5-cm section) and all sections of core H22 show relative increases that are similar to those observed for lower NBH cores C6 and C7. Small increases in relative abundance of CB025 from the 0- to 2.5-cm and the 5- to 7.5-cm sections, to the 15- to 17.5-cm and 30- to 32.9-cm sections, are found in cores I11, and H17, but differences are not pronounced within cores except for the I14 30- to 32.5-cm section. The lower relative abundances of CB025 in I14XX and the H22 core may reflect conditions that are unfavorable to dechlorination or that retard dechlorination rates. The increase in relative abundance observed in C6 and C7 cores may demonstrate the initiation of dechlorination in these samples or may reflect down-bay transport and deposition of partially dechlorinated residues.

The plots of the relative abundance of peak CB105 shows only small changes for BRH, H2223 (5- to 7.5-cm section), and cores C6 and C7; how-

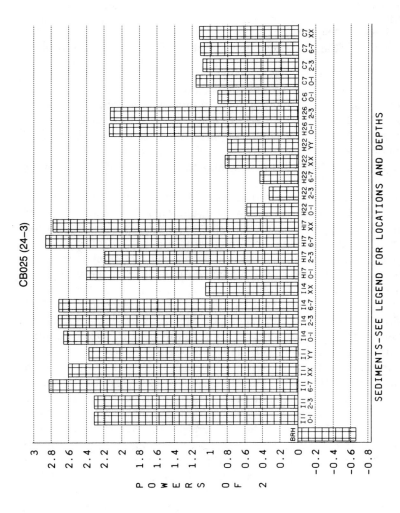

Figure 11.7.   Magnitude of increase or decrease in abundance of peak CB025 (24–3) measured in a sample relative to the predicted abundance of that peak in the mixture of A-1242 and A-1254 standards calculated as input for the sample. Samples are identified as labels for bars, and numbers indicate depth of core sections in inches. Refer to Table 11.2 for section depths in centimeters. BRH sample is at extreme left. Cores from New Bedford Harbor are ordered (left to right) in increasing distance from the outfall of the capacitor plant (see Figure 11.1).

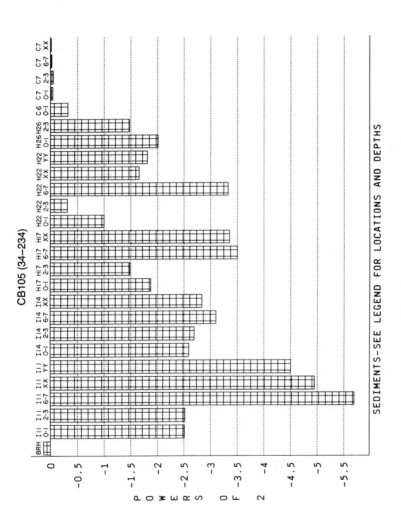

Figure 11.8. Magnitude of increase or decrease in abundance of peak CB105 (34–234) measured in a sample relative to the predicted abundance of that peak in the mixture of A-1242 and A-1254 standards calculated as input for the sample. See Figure 11.7 for details.

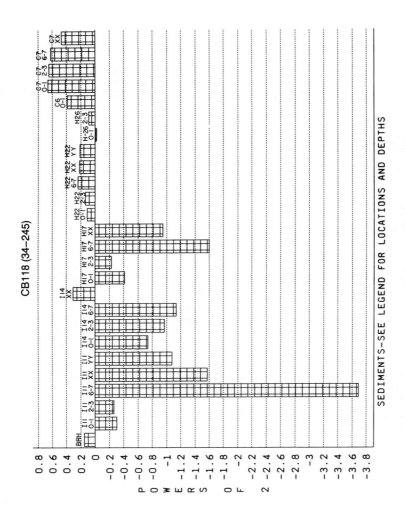

Figure 11.9. Magnitude of increase or decrease in abundance of peak CB118 (34–245) measured in a sample relative to the predicted abundance of that peak in the mixture of A-1242 and A-1254 standards calculated as input for the sample. See Figure 11.7 for details.

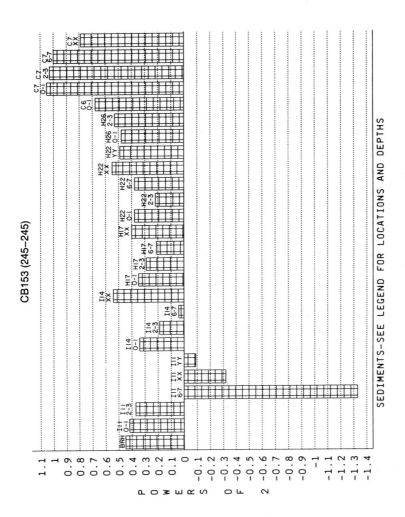

CB153 (245–245)

SEDIMENTS–SEE LEGEND FOR LOCATIONS AND DEPTHS

Figure 11.10.   Magnitude of increase or decrease in abundance of peak CB153 (245–245) measured in a sample relative to the predicted abundance of that peak in the mixture of A-1242 and A-1254 standards calculated as input for the sample. See Figure 11.7 for details.

ever, samples from upper NBH show considerable decreases in abundance of this congener. Lowered relative abundance of CB105 also has been found to be indicative of dechlorination in sediments from the Hudson River.[1] For cores I11, H17, and H22, considerable decreases in relative abundance of CB105 are observed between the top (0–2.5 and 5–7.5 cm) and lower (15–17.5, 30–32.5, and 45–47.5 cm) core sections. These findings show residues are more dechlorinated near the plant and at depth in core sections than in core sections from lower NBH (cores C6 and C7).

Plots of the relative abundance of CB118 showed BRH, H22, H26, and lower NBH (C6 and C7) samples had small increases, but other upper NBH samples, except for I14XX (30- to 32.5-cm section), showed decreases. In upper NBH the greatest decreases were found in the 15- to 17.5-cm sections, and upper core sections (0–2.5 and 5.0–7.5 cm) showed smaller losses. Core section I1167 (15–17.5 cm) showed the greatest loss.

A relative abundance plot of CB153 shows an increase in this congener in all samples except for I1167, I11XX and I11YY (Figure 11.10). The greatest relative decrease was found in sample I1167.

Comparison of the relative abundance plots for these four compounds between the sediment samples shows that the dechlorination processes are not proceeding at equal rates or to equal extents. It appears from these data that the dechlorinations (which are presumably anaerobic microbial processes) may be a stepped series of dechlorinations, with each change in step occurring when the concentration of substrate falls below a suitable level. For example, all sections of core I11 show considerable decreases in relative abundance of CB105 (Figure 11.8), but the decreases for CB118 are much smaller in the 0- to 2.5-cm and 5- to 7.5-cm sections (Figure 11.9). For CB153, only core section I1167 (15–17.5 cm) shows large decreases in relative abundance (Figure 11.10). It appears that the dechlorinating organisms may have depleted the CB105 in sample I1167 (15- to 17.5-cm section), then switched to CB118, and then to CB153. The dechlorinations in other samples are less advanced in the stepwise process.

A more likely explanation for these distributions is that different bacteria are responsible for the dechlorinations. In this hypothesis, as a substrate (e.g., CB105) is completely utilized by one bacterial strain, another organism multiplies to utilize a different substrate (e.g., CB118). This hypothesis is supported by the results of other studies, which indicated that mixtures of bacterial populations or bacterial assemblages were responsible for dechlorinations in sediments from field sites.[10,11] In addition, studies conducted in the laboratory showed changes in growth conditions for bacteria resulted in different distributions of dechlorinated PCBs. The addition of cysteine hydrochloride was found to change the pattern of dechlorination.[12] The addition of biphenyl and maintenance in a N_2 atmosphere for 7 months enhanced degradation of highly chlorinated PCBs in laboratory cultures of PCB-contaminated sediments.[13] Different dechlorination products were found following addition of a trichlorobiphenyl to sediments and heating to 80°C for 30 min compared with maintenance at 24°C.[14] This difference indicates some bacteria may have been killed by the heating, which allowed another bacterial strain to take over the dechlorination process.

Another study of dechlorination in NBH found very little difference in the ratios of A-1242:A-1254 or extent of dechlorination between the upper (5.0–7.5 cm) and lower (15–17.5 cm) sections of individual cores taken in the intertidal zone.[5] They reasoned that the similarities of these core sections indicated the occurrence of an "active vertical transport (mixing) process within the upper estuary sediments." They suggest that this vertical movement may allow all the PCBs now in these sediments to reach the dechlorination zone and be dechlorinated. The present work sampled midchannel sediments in upper NBH and found differences in the proportions of Aroclors 1242 and 1254 and in the patterns and extents of dechlorination between the upper (5.0–7.5 cm) and lower (15–17.5 cm) sections of some cores (Figures 11.7–11.10). These results suggest that for midchannel sediments the vertical movement of PCBs may be more limited than in intertidal sediments. It appears that dechlorination of PCBs in these channel sediments may be limited by physical availability and/or by other factors needed for bacterial growth.

The plots for CB105, CB118, and CB153 (Figures 11.8–11.10) show the differences in the extent of dechlorination between congeners and sites and illuminate the difficulties in determining dechlorination rates. From these plots it is evident that to estimate rates of dechlorination, the congeners being dechlorinated and the sample location must be specified. A further difficulty in estimating rates of dechlorination in upper and lower NBH is that the history of PCB inputs to upper NBH have not been maintained in the sediments.

Although the Aroclor mixtures utilized (and presumably discharged) by the plant changed over the years of manufacture, distinct changes in inputs are not reflected in samples from sediment cores. PCBs were used as impregnation fluids in capacitors from 1947 until 1978. Plant records of PCB purchases are incomplete, but available records show A-1254 was utilized until 1963, when it was replaced with A-1242.[4] In 1971, A-1016 completely replaced A-1242 as an impregnation fluid.[15] Measurements of sediment depositional rates in NBH vary considerably depending on location and have increased substantially from a few millimeters/year to a few centimeters/year since construction of the Hurricane Barrier in 1966.[16] A computer model of upper NBH utilized to predict the distribution and fate of PCBs utilizes a sediment deposition rate of < 1 mm/year.[17] Another report estimates the sediment depositional rate at approximately 3 mm/year.[18] Using these estimates of depositional rates, the depth in the sediment corresponding to the change from A-1254 to A-1242 in 1963 would be (1988 − 1963 = 25 years) between 2.5 and 7.5 cm. As described earlier, depths of the changes from A-1254 to A-1242 varied in the core samples taken in upper NBH (depth to change was > 47.5 cm in core H17), but depths to the change were all in excess of the 2.5–7.5 cm estimated from depositional rates. It appears that the age of a contaminant in a sediment section within upper NBH many not be reliably estimated by using sediment depositional rates.

Although sediment deposition rates cannot be used to age PCB residues in cores from upper NBH, estimates of the average rates of dechlorination from input to time of sampling can be made by assuming the time of input of the Aroclor mixtures. Assuming an input of PCBs in 1963 and first-order kinetics, rate constants and half-lives were calculated for congeners CB031, CB105, CB118, and CB153 using sediment samples that showed smaller (H2267) and larger (I1167) changes as a result of dechlorinations (Table 11.3). For CB031, the rate constants are 0.001 (t^{-1}) and 0.053 (t^{-1}), and the half-lives are 465 years and 13.2 years for H2267 and I1167 samples, respectively. Considerable differences in half-lives were also observed between congeners within the same sample. For example, in sample H2267, CB031 has a half-life of 465 years, but CB105 has a half-life of 7.5 years. These differences emphasize that estimates of dechlorination rates vary greatly depending on the congener and the sample. The calculated rate constants represent averages over the 25-year time period from input to sample collection; other average rate constants and half-lives would be obtained if different input times were specified. The average rate constants do not give specific information regarding the past dechlorination rates. For example, the PCB congeners may have been dechlorinated over a short period of time, followed by years of dormancy. Further, these average rate constants offer no information on present dechlorination rates (if any) or if, and at what rate, these processes will continue in the future.

A variety of factors (e.g., availability of trace metals, nitrogen and minerals, carbon sources, PCB substrate, etc.) impact dechlorination rates in laboratory studies.[19,20] Another laboratory study found that dechlorination progresses under methanogenic, but not under sulfate-reducing conditions.[21] These factors, combined with the patchy distribution of PCBs in sediments of upper NBH, may be responsible for the large range of dechlorination rates estimated in this study.

CONCLUSIONS

1. PCBs in sediments from upper New Bedford Harbor showed considerable compositional alterations relative to predicted starting mixtures of Aroclors 1242 and 1254. These alterations included
   - a relative loss of lower-molecular-weight PCB congeners in all samples, presumably due to dissolution and evaporation prior to incorporation into sediment
   - relative decreases in the content of specific PCB congeners and the build-up of other congeners in some samples by processes that were presumed to be dechlorinations
2. The dechlorination processes varied in extent between samples, with the largest changes observed for samples closest to the outfall from the capacitor plant A in the 15- to 17.5-cm sediment core section. There was a trend toward less dechlo-

Table 11.3. Rate Constants and Half-Lives for Dechlorination of Selected PCB Congeners

Congener	Rate Constants(t^{-1})		Half-Lives (years)	
	H2267	I1167	H2267	I1167
CB031	0.001	0.053	465	13.2
CB105	0.092	0.16	7.5	4.4
CB118	a	0.10	a	6.8
CB153	a	0.04	a	18.8

[a]Peak showed increase in relative abundance; therefore, calculation of rate and half-life were not made.

rinated residues with distance from the capacitor plant A. Samples from lower NBH showed only small evidence of dechlorination, while reference samples from Black Rock Harbor, CT, showed none.

3. Samples with a lower extent of dechlorination showed relative decreases in abundance of specific congeners (e.g., P058, CB085, CB132, CB105). In more extensively dechlorinated samples, relative decreases in abundance of these and other congeners (e.g., CB031, P045, P046, P047, P048, P053, CB099, CB153, and CB118), and increases in abundance of congeners (e.g., CB026, CB025) that resulted from loss of chlorine atoms from more highly chlorinated congeners were observed. The potentially toxic mono-*ortho* congeners appear to be among those congeners most readily dechlorinated in upper NBH. Therefore, these dechlorination processes may have decreased the potential toxicity (as measured by mixed-function oxidase enzyme induction) of the PCB residues. However, large quantities of partially dechlorinated PCBs remain in the sediments of the upper NBH and the toxicities of these remaining mixtures are not known.

4. Considerable differences were observed in the calculated average rate constants for the dechlorinations depending on the sample and the congener.

ACKNOWLEDGMENTS

The authors wish to thank Mr. Michael Carrol, Mr. Forrest Knowles, Mr. Gerard Boudreau, and Mr. Richard Berger of the New England Division of the U.S. Army Corps of Engineers Materials Laboratory in Waltham, MA, for collection of the core samples used in this study.

DISCLAIMER

Mention of product names does not constitute endorsement by the U.S. EPA.

REFERENCES

1. Brown, J. F., Jr., R. E. Wagner, D. L. Bedard, M. J. Brennan, J. C. Carnaham, R. J. May, and T. J. Tofflemire. "PCB Transformations in Upper Hudson Sediments," *Northeast Environ. Sci.* 3:167–179 (1984).
2. Brown, J. F., D. L. Bedard, M. J. Brennan, J. C. Carnaham, H. Feng, and R. E.

Wagner. "Polychlorinated Biphenyl Dechlorinations in Aquatic Sediments," *Science* 236:709–712 (1987).

3. Brown, J. F., Jr., R. E. Wagner, H. Feng, D. L. Bedard, M. J. Brennan, J. C. Carnahan, and R. J. May. "Environmental Dechlorination of PCBs," *Environ. Toxicol. Chem.* 6:579–593 (1987).

4. Monsanto Corporation. Record of PCB purchases for electrical capacitor manufacturing plant in Upper New Bedford Harbor (1985).

5. Brown, J. F., Jr., and R. E. Wagner. "PCB Movement, Dechlorination and Detoxication in the Acushnet Estuary," *Environ. Toxicol. Chem.* 9:1215–1233 (1990).

6. Lake, J., G. Hoffman, and S. Schimmel. "Bioaccumulation of Contaminants from Black Rock Harbor Dredged Material by Mussels and Polychaetes," Technical Report D-85-2, prepared by the U.S. Environmental Protection Agency, Environmental Research Laboratory, Narragansett, RI, for the U.S. Army Engineer Waterways Experiment Station, Vicksburg, MS (1985).

7. Schulz, D. E., G. Petrick, and J. C. Duinker. "Complete Characterization of Polychlorinated Biphenyl Congeners in Commercial Aroclor and Clophen Mixtures by Multidimensional Gas Chromatography–Electron Capture Detection," *Environ. Sci. Technol.* 23:852–859 (1989).

8. Kannan, N., S. Tanabe, and R. Tatsukawa. "Toxic Potential of Non-ortho and Mono-ortho Coplanar PCBs in Commercial PCB Preparations: 2,3,7,8-T$_4$ CDD Toxicity Equivalence Factors Approach," *Bull. Environ. Contam. Toxicol.* 41:267–276 (1988).

9. McFarland, V. A., and J. U. Clarke. "Environmental Occurrence, Abundance, and Potential Toxicity of Polychlorinated Biphenyl Congeners: Considerations for a Congener-Specific Analysis," *Environ. Health Perspect.* 18:225–239 (1989).

10. Bedard, D. L., S. C. Bunnell, and H. M. Van Dort. "Anaerobic Dechlorination of Endogenous PCBs in Woods Pond Sediment," in *Research and Development Program for the Destruction of PCBs,* Ninth Progress Report, General Electric Co. (1990), pp. 43–54.

11. Brown, J. F., Jr. "Differentiation of Anaerobic Microbial Dechlorination Processes," in *Research and Development Program for the Destruction of PCBs,* Ninth Progress Report, General Electric Co. (1990), pp. 87–90.

12. Abramowicz, D. H., M. J. Brennan, and H. Van Dort. "Anaerobic Biodegradation of Polychlorinated Biphenyls," paper presented at American Chemical Society Meeting, Miami, FL, September 10–15, 1989.

13. Rhee, G.-Y., B. Bush, B. Brown, M. P. Kane, and L. Shane. "Anaerobic Biodegradation of Polychlorinated Biphenyls in Hudson River Sediments and Dredged Sediments in Clay Encapsulation," *Water Res.* 23:957–964 (1989).

14. Williams, W. A. "A Systematic Study of Reductive Dechlorination of Trichlorobiphenyls in River Sediments," in *Research and Development Program for the Destruction of PCBs,* Ninth Progress Report, General Electric Co. (1990), pp. 5–14.

15. Weaver, G. "PCB Pollution in the New Bedford, Massachusetts," Massachusetts Coastal Zone Management, Commonwealth of Massachusetts (1982).

16. Summerhayes, C. P., J. P. Ellis, P. Stoffers, S. R. Briggs, and M. G. Fitzgerald. "Fine-Grained Sediment and Industrial Waste Distribution and Disposal in New Bedford Harbor and Western Buzzards Bay, Massachusetts," Woods Hole Oceanographic Institution, WHOI-76-115 (1977).

17. Miller, G. Personal communication, Battelle, Duxbury, MA (1989).

18. Teeter, A. M. "New Bedford Harbor Superfund Project, Acashnet River Estuary Engineering Feasibility Study of Dredging and Dredged Material Disposal Alternatives; Report 2, Sediment and Contaminant Hydraulic Transport Investigations," Technical Report EL-88-15, US Army Engineer Waterways Experiment Station, Vicksburg, MS. (1988).

19. Abramowicz, D. A., M. J. Brennan, and H. M. Van Dort. "Anaerobic and Aerobic Biodegradation of Endogenous PCBs," in *Research and Development Program for the Destruction of PCBs,* Ninth Progress Report, General Electric Co. (1990) pp. 55–69.

20. Niles, L., P. J. Anid, and T. M. Vogel. "Sequential Anaerobic-Aerobic Biodegradation of PCBs," in *Research and Development Program for the Destruction of PCBs,* Ninth Progress Report, General Electric Co. (1990), pp. 71–80.

21. Alder, A. C., M. Häggblom, and L. Y. Young. "Reductive Dechlorination of PCBs in Sediments from the Hudson River and New Bedford Harbor," in *Research and Development Program for the Destruction of PCBs,* Ninth Progress Report, General Electric Co. (1990), pp. 35–42.

22. Ballschmiter, K., and M. Zell. "Analysis of Polychlorinated Biphenyls (PCB) by Glass Capillary Gas Chromatography: Composition of Technical Aroclor- and Clophen-PCB Mixtures," *Fres. Z. Analyt. Chem.* 302:210–31 (1980).

CHAPTER 12

Anaerobic Biotransformation of Halogenated Pesticides in Aquifer Slurries

Joseph M. Suflita, K. Ramanand, and Neal Adrian

INTRODUCTION

There are many physical, chemical, and biological factors that influence the fate of pesticides through soils and surface waters to groundwaters.[1] While these factors interact to mitigate the rate of pesticide migration, there is little doubt that such chemicals do contaminate subterranean aquifers. Not surprisingly, the entry of pesticides to groundwater reserves is associated with the manufacture, use, and disposal of these agricultural chemicals.[2]

Since much of the U.S. population relies on groundwater for drinking purposes, the fate of pesticides in aquifers is an area of intense ecological and toxicological concern. Persistence or dissipation of pesticides will help dictate the level of this concern. The persistence of compounds is, in turn, influenced by the metabolic abilities of the aquifer microbiota. The partial metabolism of pesticidal materials is sometimes of equal concern. Initial biotransformations can lead to the accumulation of intermediates with their own environmental and health impacts.

A variety of redox conditions can exist in aquifers, and the fate of pesticides should be evaluated in the context of the prevailing ecological conditions. Relative to aerobic biodegradation processes, little is known about the biotransformation of pesticides when oxygen is absent from aquifers. Under anaerobic conditions, pesticide metabolism could conceivably be linked to the consumption of other electron acceptors like nitrate, ferric iron, sulfate, or carbon dioxide.

This chapter summarizes several investigations on the predominant transformations of 2,4,5-trichlorophenoxyacetic acid (2,4,5-T), 2,4-dichlorophenoxyacetic acid (2,4-D), and bromacil and presents preliminary findings on the fate of propanil and linuron in anoxic aquifer sediments. We found that aryl reductive dehalogenation reactions represent an important fate process occurring during the breakdown of all of the pesticides examined in this study except linuron. Moreover, reductive dechlorination reactions were catalyzed under methanogenic but not under other redox conditions.

MATERIALS AND METHODS

The anaerobic fate of the pesticides 2,4,5-T, 2,4-D, bromacil, linuron, propanil, and related intermediates was evaluated in slurries obtained from an anoxic aquifer that was contaminated with leachate from a municipal landfill. Spatially distinct sulfate-reducing and methanogenic zones are known to exist within this aquifer.[3]

The samples were collected from the methanogenic zone, and the aquifer slurries were constructed in serum bottles as previously described.[4] Sterile filtered resazurin was added to the groundwater to a final concentration of 0.0002% and served as a redox indicator. Sterile sodium sulfide was added to a final concentration of 1 mM and ensured reducing conditions. The headspace of the bottles was adjusted to N_2/CO_2 (80%/20%) prior to the start of the experiment. Anoxic, filter-sterilized stock solutions of the pesticides were added to the slurries at initial concentrations of 125–500 μM. However, stock solutions of bromacil and linuron were made up in ether and added to sterile serum bottles before addition of sediment or groundwater. After evaporation of the ether, the serum bottles were transferred to an anaerobic glove box. Aquifer sediment and groundwater were then added as described previously.[4] The terminal electron acceptor status was experimentally manipulated by making appropriate amendments of either nitrate or sulfate (20 mM) to stimulate nitrate-reducing and sulfate-reducing conditions, respectively. Slurries that did not receive an exogenous amendment of an electron acceptor were designated the methanogenic incubations. Experiments were performed in at least duplicate and compared with autoclaved or substrate-unamended controls. All incubations were at room temperature in the dark. At intervals, samples were withdrawn by a syringe and stored at –10°C until analysis.

The disappearance of the parent substrates and the accumulation of the intermediate products were monitored on the liquid phase of the aquifer slurries by modifications of previously published HPLC methods.[4,5] The isocratic mobile phases for the various separations consisted of different ratios of 50 mM sodium acetate buffer (pH 4.5) and acetonitrile at a flow rate of 1.2–1.5 mL/min. All compounds were detected by UV absorbance with a variable wavelength detector (Beckman model 165, Beckman Instruments, Inc., Berkeley, CA) operated at 280 or 254 nm. Identification and quantification of the compounds were performed by comparing retention time and integrator responses, respectively, with external standards.

The methane production was detected by gas chromatography.[3] An evaluation of the fate of pesticides, intermediates, and end products was made relative to both autoclaved and substrate-unamended controls. The identity of individual metabolites was minimally based on their chromatographic behavior. However, the identity of the most important intermediates was confirmed by ether extraction and subsequent analysis by GC-MS using a Hewlett-Packard GC 5890 equipped with DB-5 fused silica capillary column and a model 5970 mass selective detector[6] or by LC-MS using a Kratos MS25RF mass spectrometer equipped with a Vestec liquid chromatography ionization interface.[5]

RESULTS AND DISCUSSION

2,4,5-T and 2,4-D

The herbicides 2,4-D and 2,4,5-T (2,4-dichloro- and 2,4,5-trichlorophen-oxyacetic acid, respectively) are often used in combination with each other and are ingredients of many pesticide formulations. These chemicals have a relatively high water solubility, are only slightly retained in soil, can contaminate aquifers, and the trichlorinated derivative tends to resist aerobic microbial destruction.[7]

2,4,5-T and 2,4-D were reductively dehalogenated to lesser halogenated congeners in methanogenic aquifer slurries (Figure 12.1); that is, the *para* or *meta* halide of 2,4,5-T or either chlorine of 2,4-D was replaced by a hydrogen atom. The first detectable metabolite observed during 2,4-D metabolism was 2,4-dichlorophenol, while 2,5-or 2,4-dichlorophenoxyacetate were formed from 2,4,5-T. The latter compounds could then be converted to mono-chlorophenoxyacetate derivatives or to dichlorophenols and eventually to monochlorophenols and to phenol under methanogenic conditions (Figure 12.1).[4,6] No parent substrate transformation was noted in autoclaved controls, and no comparable intermediates could be detected in substrate-unamended controls.

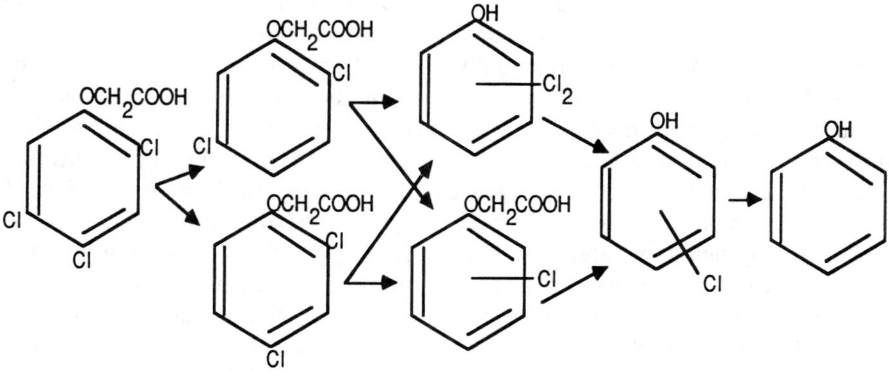

Figure 12.1. Proposed pathway for the anaerobic decomposition of 2,4,5-T and 2,4-D in methanogenic aquifer slurries. Adapted from Gibson and Suflita.[4]

The transient accumulation of the three monochlorophenol isomers but not of phenoxyacetate suggested that the complete removal of all chlorines could not proceed in the presence of an ether-bonded substituent. The ether cleavage always preceded the last halogen removal from the aromatic ring. The pathways for 2,4-D and 2,4,5-T converged on phenol. In the absence of oxygen, the latter compound can be mineralized under a variety of redox conditions.[8-10]

No significant alteration of the parent herbicides was noted in parallel experiments using aquifer slurries sampled from the sulfate-reducing portion of the same aquifer.[4] Several di- and monohalogenated phenolic compounds, which were potential intermediates of the herbicides, acted similarly when they were used as parent substrates. However, such halophenols could only be reductively dehalogenated in methanogenic incubations.[4] The exogenous addition of sulfate to methanogenic aquifer slurries drastically inhibited the dehalogenation of 2,4,5-T.[6]

Bromacil

Bromacil is a moderately to highly mobile herbicide that has been known to persist for up to 2 years after application.[11] It has been shown to leach through soils[11] and is a known contaminant of groundwater supplies.[12] Bromacil is a halogenated nitrogen heterocyclic compound. Heterocyclic compounds are in widespread use and are frequently detected as aquifer contaminants.[13] However, the anaerobic metabolic fate of such materials is poorly understood.[14]

In our studies, liquid chromatographic analysis of methanogenic aquifer slurries amended with bromacil revealed that the parent substrate disappeared from nonsterile samples (Figure 12.2). The loss of the parent substrate was coincident with the appearance of a more polar compound with a shorter HPLC retention time (Figure 12.2). The latter compound was not detected in slurries at the start of the incubation or in substrate-unamended controls. However, trace amounts of a compound which cochromatographed with the bromacil intermediate were detected in autoclaved controls at the end of a 5-month incubation period.[5] Presumably, this reflects the small amount of bromacil that can be abiotically transformed in these incubation systems. No significant degradation of the parent herbicide occurred when the aquifer slurries were incubated under nitrate-reducing or sulfate-reducing conditions.

Based on suggestions in the literature and by analogy to the proposed fate of other nitrogen heterocyclic herbicides, we suspected that bromacil might be hydrolytically dehalogenated.[7,15] Therefore, the presumed metabolite was isolated by HPLC, rechromatographed to verify purity, and subjected to LC-MS analysis.[5] The metabolite resulting from hydrolytic dehalogenation of bromacil should display molecular ion peaks at 199 and 216. However, the thermospray mass spectrum of the metabolite exhibited molecular ion peaks at m/z 183 and 200. Further, unlike the parent substrate, the metabolite molecular ion peak did not exhibit a bromine isotopic abundance pattern. This LC-

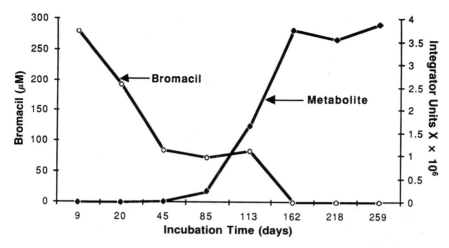

Figure 12.2. The degradation of bromacil and the production of a metabolite in methanogenic aquifer slurries. Adapted from Adrian and Suflita.[5]

MS analysis allowed us to identify the metabolite as 3-sec-butyl-6-methyl-uracil (Figure 12.3). Thus, like the homocyclic halogenated herbicides considered above, bromacil was reductively debrominated, but only under methanogenic conditions. The metabolite was not transformed with further incubation, but studies to clarify the fate of this chemical under other redox conditions have been initiated.

Propanil

Propanil (3,4-dichloropropionanilide) is predominantly used with rice (*Oryza sativa*) and other agricultural crops to control weeds.[16] The metabolic fate of the dihalogenated herbicide has been extensively studied under aerobic conditions.[17,18] Information on the fate of propanil under anaerobic conditions is limited but suggests that propanil may undergo either hydrolysis[16] or reductive dechlorination[19] (Figure 12.4). Propanil can conceivably contaminate groundwater reserves because of its high water solubility. Studies on the anaer-

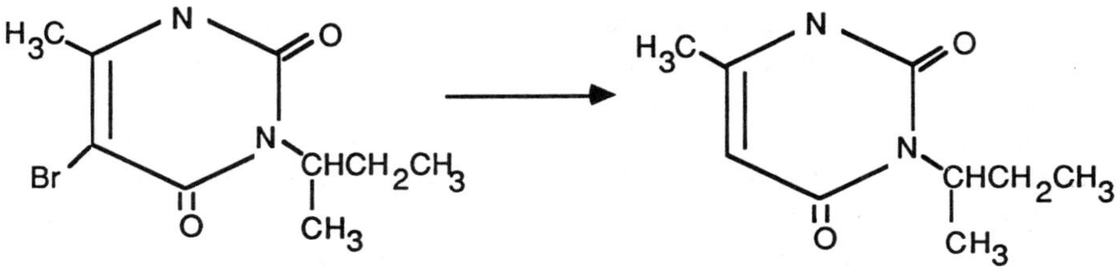

Figure 12.3. The reductive dehalogenation of bromacil to 3-sec-butyl-6-methyl-uracil under methanogenic conditions.

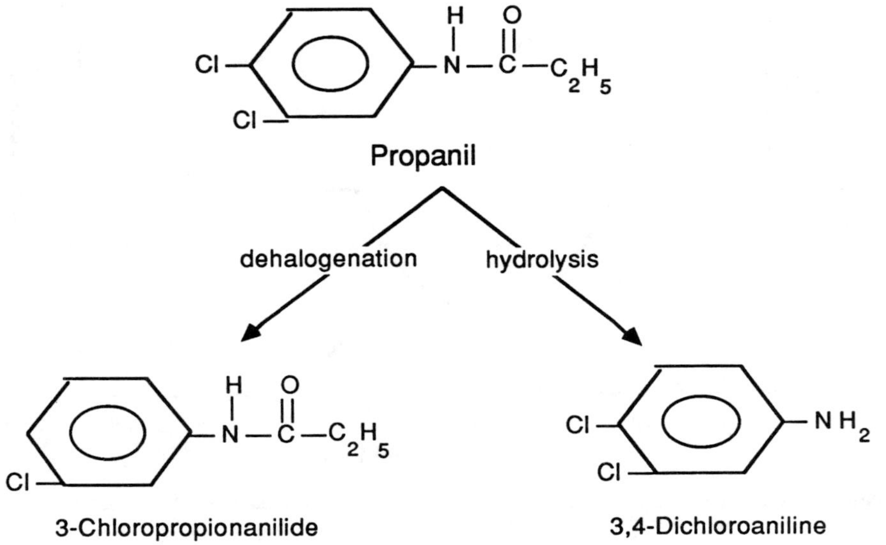

Figure 12.4.   The presumed metabolic fate of propanil in anoxic environments.

obic fate of propanil is restricted to flooded soils and sediments, and no information is available about its behavior in anoxic aquifers. We evaluated the biodegradation of propanil in anoxic aquifer slurries.

The fate of the herbicide was studied in methanogenic, sulfate-reducing, and nitrate-reducing incubations. Propanil was biologically transformed under all three redox conditions in active samples (Figure 12.5); no significant loss of the compound was observed in autoclaved controls (data not shown).

The decomposition of propanil was greater in nitrate-reducing incubations than in other redox conditions. After a lag of about 6 days, 124 μM levels of the parent material were reduced to nondetectable levels by 34 days under nitrate-reducing conditions. During the same period, about 30–35% of the parent compound was still present in corresponding methanogenic or sulfate-reducing incubations (Figure 12.5).

Concomitant with the loss of propanil was the accumulation of another compound in all three types of incubations. This intermediate was more polar and had a shorter retention time than the parent compound when analyzed by HPLC. Chromatographic evidence was used to tentatively identify this compound as 3,4-dichloroaniline. Thus, propanil was hydrolytically cleaved as the primary anaerobic biotransformation reaction to form 3,4-dichloroaniline under all three incubation conditions (Figure 12.5). Similar results were obtained with anaerobic enrichment cultures obtained from a nonflooded soil, but the ecological conditions for the hydrolysis reaction were not delineated.[16] The haloaniline accumulated to near stoichiometric amounts during the early stages of the incubation but did not substantially change with additional time.

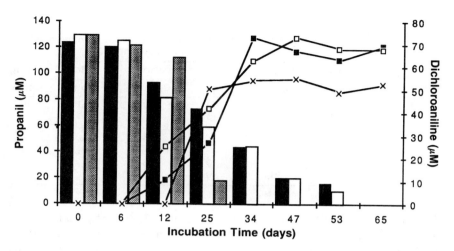

Figure 12.5. The disappearance of propanil *(bars)* and the appearance of 3,4-dichloroaniline *(points)* under methanogenic *(solid black)*, sulfate-reducing *(solid white)*, and nitrate-reducing *(shaded, X)* conditions.

Since propanil continued to disappear after 34 days, it may be that another propanil transformation product was formed but remained undetected in our HPLC analysis. Further work is being directed to clarify this point.

The 3,4-dichloroaniline intermediate was not detected in active aquifer slurries at the start of the incubation or in substrate-unamended controls throughout the period of study. However, after 5 months of incubation, we observed the formation of small amounts of this haloaniline (< 5%) in autoclaved samples, presumably as a result of the abiotic hydrolysis of propanil. The 3,4-dichloroaniline was not significantly altered in either sterile or nonsterile aquifer slurries with continued incubation.

The fate of 3,4-dichloroaniline in sediment slurries obtained from the same anoxic aquifer was examined in previous experiments.[20] Under methanogenic conditions, 3,4-dichloroaniline as well as tri- and tetrachloroanilines were reductively dehalogenated over a 8-month incubation. The same compounds were not transformed in sulfate-reducing incubations. The *para* chlorine was reductively removed from the 3,4-dichloroaniline to result in the accumulation of 3-chloroaniline.[20] The latter compound as well as its isomeric counterparts remained persistent under the test incubation conditions when they were used as parent substrates.[20]

3,4-Dichloroaniline and 3-chloroaniline may result from the anaerobic destruction of propanil as a result of initial amide hydrolysis of the parent herbicide followed (in the case of the monohaloaniline) by a reductive dehalogenation step. Consistent with the above suggestion is the finding of both 3,4-dichloro- and 3-chloroaniline as products of propanil decomposition in rice paddy soil.[16]

Table 12.1. The Disappearance of Linuron from Both Sterile Control and Experimental Aquifer Slurries Incubated under Different Redox Conditions

Incubation Time (days)	Linuron Remaining Under Various Incubation Conditions (% of initial substrate concentration)					
	Methanogenic		Sulfate-Reducing		Nitrate-Reducing	
	Exptl	Control	Exptl	Control	Exptl	Control
19	100	100	100	100	100	100
37	72	—	43	—	96	—
46	59	—	9	—	79	—
56	21	106	1	69	84	58
121	0	98	1	—	85	49
209	0	91	0	86		
306	0	60	0	55		

The addition of sulfate inhibited the dehalogenation of haloanilines in a manner that was comparable to the effect of this anion on the chlorophenols and chlorophenoxyacetates.[20,21] It is not yet known whether the reductive dehalogenation of chloroanilines is possible under nitrate-reducing conditions. The nitrate-dependent biotransformation of 3,4-dichloroaniline and monochloroanilines has been previously shown,[22,23] but the metabolic pathways involved were not elucidated.

Linuron

Substituted urea herbicides including linuron are used extensively for weed control with a wide variety of horticultural and agricultural crops.[24] Sediments of lakes, ponds, irrigation ditches, and other aqueous impoundments are often repositories for many such chemicals added to the environment.[19] There are conflicting reports in the literature concerning the fate of linuron in the environment,[19,25-27] although it is thought that the loss of this compound is predominately through microbiological processes.[27] Since it was previously reported that linuron could be reductively dehalogenated,[19] we undertook a study to clarify the fate of this 3,4-dihalogenated phenylurea herbicide in anoxic aquifer sediments.

We studied the degradation of linuron in aquifer slurries under methanogenic, sulfate-reducing, and nitrate-reducing conditions. Linuron was rapidly degraded under methanogenic and sulfate-reducing conditions, but only slowly transformed under nitrate-reducing conditions. After 56 days of incubation, 80 and 99% of the applied linuron (about 120–150 μM) had disappeared in the methanogenic and sulfate-reducing incubations, respectively (Table 12.1). During the same time frame, only about 15% of the linuron had disappeared in the bottles incubated under nitrate-reducing conditions. After 121-days incubation there was no detectable linuron in the bottles incubated under methanogenic conditions, and only 1% remained in the bottles incubated under sulfate-reducing conditions. However, 85% of the linuron remained in the nitrate-reducing incubations (Table 12.1).

Concomitant with the disappearance of linuron was the appearance of another compound that exhibited a shorter HPLC retention time. A comparison of HPLC and GC retention times of this compound with previously published transformation products tentatively identified the compound as 3-(3,4-dichlorophenyl)-1-methylurea. The compound was derivitized (ethylated) and analyzed by GC-MS.[28] The mass spectrum of the derivitized metabolite contained two predominant peaks at m/z 58 and 86. The mass spectrum of the derivitized transformation product was identical to that of authentic 3-(3,4-dichlorophenyl)-1-methylurea that was similarly derivitized and analyzed. In addition, these two spectra were consistent with the previously published spectral profile of this compound.[28] Therefore, linuron was demethoxylated in the anoxic aquifer sediments (Figure 12.6). After 200 days there was no detectable linuron in the experimental bottles incubated under methanogenic or sulfate-reducing conditions. During this time, there was about 10 and 15% loss of linuron from the methanogenic and sulfate-reducing sterile controls, respectively.

Nevertheless, desmethoxylinuron was easily detected in sterile controls. This transformation product steadily increased with longer incubation times. The formation of this compound may be the result of the slow abiotic destruction of linuron. Stepp et al. have also observed the formation of demethoxylated linuron in sterile controls.[19]

One must cautiously interpret such data since autoclaved controls are almost certainly not as reducing as experimental incubations. It may be that this particular type of transformation is favored under the highly reducing conditions routinely encountered in methanogenic or sulfate-reducing incubation. In our experiments, the desmethoxylinuron reached a maximum when linuron could no longer be detected in experimental incubations. The area of the peak did not substantially change with further incubation, suggesting that

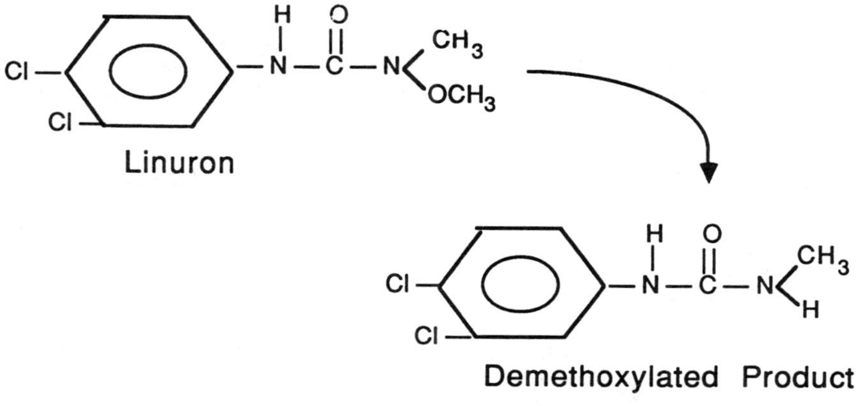

Figure 12.6. The proposed conversion of linuron to desmethoxylinuron in both sterile and nonsterile incubations under anaerobic conditions.

demethoxylated linuron tends to resist further anaerobic destruction. Experiments are planned to address this possibility.

CONCLUSIONS

Under anaerobic conditions, reductive dehalogenation seems to be a predominant process for the removal of halogens from homocyclic or heterocyclic pesticides. Examples of environmental chemicals that are susceptible to such transformations include 2,4-D, 2,4,5-T, and bromacil, as well as a variety of halogenated phenols and anilines that were formed as intermediates during the metabolism of the parent molecules. Methanogenic conditions seem best suited for reductive dehalogenation reactions, but such bioconversions may be possible under other anaerobic conditions. Propanil was hydrolytically cleaved as the primary degradative event under all the test anaerobic incubation conditions, whereas linuron was demethoxylated in both sterile and nonsterile aquifer slurries. This work helps to clarify the fate of polluting organic chemicals that enter or reside in anoxic aquifers.

REFERENCES

1. Creeger, S. M. "Considering Pesticide Potential for Reaching Ground Water in the Registration of Pesticides," in *Evaluation of Pesticides in Ground Water,* W. Y. Garner et al. Ed. (Washington, DC: American Chemical Society, 1986), pp. 548–557.
2. Holden, P. W. *Pesticides and Ground Water Quality: Issues and Problems in Four States* (Washington, DC: National Academy Press, 1986).
3. Beeman, R. E., and J. M. Suflita. "Microbial Ecology of a Shallow Ground Water Aquifer Polluted by Municipal Landfill Leachate," *Microb. Ecol.* 14:39–54 (1987).
4. Gibson, S. A., and J. M. Suflita. "Extrapolation of Biodegradation Results to Groundwater Aquifers: Reductive Dehalogenation of Aromatic Compounds," *Appl. Environ. Microbiol.* 52:681–688 (1986).
5. Adrian, N. R., and J. M. Suflita. "Reductive Dehalogenation of a Nitrogen Heterocyclic Herbicide in Anoxic Aquifer Slurries," *Appl. Environ. Microbiol.* 56:292–294 (1990).
6. Gibson, S. A., and J. M. Suflita. "Anaerobic Biodegradation of 2,4,5-Trichlorophenoxyacetic Acid in Samples from a Methanogenic Aquifer: Stimulation by Short-Chain Organic Acids and Alcohols," *Appl. Environ. Microbiol.* 56:1825–1832 (1990).
7. Kuhn, E. P., and J. M. Suflita. "Microbial Degradation of Nitrogen, Oxygen and Sulfur Heterocyclic Compounds under Anaerobic Conditions: Studies with Aquifer Samples," *Environ. Toxicol. Chem.* 8:1149–1158 (1989).
8. Bak, F., and F. Widdel. "Anaerobic Degradation of Phenol and Phenol Derivatives by *Desulfobacterium phenolicum* sp. nov.," *Arch. Microbiol.* 146:177–180 (1986).

9. Bakker, G. "Anaerobic Degradation of Aromatic Compounds in the Presence of Nitrate," *FEMS Lett.* 1:103–108 (1977).

10. Mikesell, M. D., and S. A. Boyd. "Complete Reductive Dechlorination and Mineralization of Pentachlorophenol by Anaerobic Microorganisms," *Appl. Environ. Microbiol.* 52:861–865 (1986).

11. Hebb, E. A., and W. B. Wheeler. "Bromacil in Lakeland Soil Ground Water," *J. Environ. Qual.* 7:598–601 (1978).

12. Cohen, S. Z., C. Eiden, and M. N. Lorber. "Monitoring Ground Water for Pesticides," *ACS Symp. Ser.* 315:170–196 (1986).

13. Kuhn, E. P., and J. M. Suflita. "Dehalogenation of Pesticides by Anaerobic Microorganisms in Soils and Groundwater—A Review," in *Reactions and Movements of Organic Chemicals in Soils,* B. L. Sawhney and K. Brown, Eds. (Madison, WI: Soil Science Society of America and American Society of Agronomy, 1989), pp. 111–180.

14. Berry, D. F., A. J. Francis, and J.-M. Bollag. "Microbial Metabolism of Homocyclic and Heterocyclic Aromatic Compounds under Anaerobic Conditions," *Microbiol. Rev.* 51:43–59 (1987).

15. Newkome, G. R., and W. W. Paudler. *Contemporary Heterocyclic Chemistry* (New York: John Wiley and Sons, 1982).

16. Pettigrew, C. A., M. J. B. Paynter, and N. D. Camper. "Anaerobic Microbial Degradation of the Herbicide Propanil," *Soil Biol. Biochem.* 17:815–818 (1985).

17. Bartha, R., and D. Pramer. "Pesticide Transformation to Aniline and Azo Compounds in Soil," *Science* 156:1617–1618 (1967).

18. Still, G. G., and R. A. Herrett. "Methylcarbamates, Carbanilates and Acylanilides," in *Herbicides: Chemistry, Degradation and Mode of Action,* P. C. Kearney and D. D. Kaufman, Eds. (New York: Marcel Dekker, 1976), pp. 609–664.

19. Stepp, T. D., N. D. Camper, and M. J. B. Paynter. "Anaerobic Microbial Degradation of Selected 3,4-Dihalogenated Aromatic Compounds," *Pestic. Biochem. Physiol.* 23:256–260 (1985).

20. Kuhn, E. P., and J. M. Suflita. "Sequential Reductive Dehalogenation of Chloroanilines by Microorganisms from a Methanogenic Aquifer," *Environ. Sci. Technol.* 23:848–852 (1989).

21. Kuhn, E. P., G. T. Townsend, and J. M. Suflita. "Reductive Dehalogenation of Chloroanilines in Anaerobic Aquifer Slurries: Effect of Sulfate and Organic Carbon Supplements," *Appl. Environ. Microbiol.* 56:2630–2637 (1990).

22. Bollag, J.-M., and S. Russel. "Aerobic versus Anaerobic Metabolism of Halogenated Anilines by a *Paracoccus* sp.," *Microb. Ecol.* 3:65–73 (1976).

23. Mogilevich, N. F., A. B. Tashirev, and E. A. Romanova. "Conversion of *p*-Chloroaniline by *Escherichia coli* under Anaerobic Conditions," *Mikrobiologiya* 56:205–208 (1987).

24. Caverly, D. J., and R. C. Denney. "Determination of Substituted Ureas and Some Related Herbicide Residues in Soils by Gas Chromatography," *Analyst* 103:368–374 (1978).

25. Engelhardt, G., P. R. Wallnöfer, and R. Plapp. "Identification of N, O-Dimethylhydroxylamine as a Microbial Degradation Product of the Herbicide, Linuron," *Appl. Microbiol.* 23:664–666 (1972).

26. Mapplebeck, L., and C. Waywell. "Detection and Degradation of Linuron in Organic Soils," *Weed Sci.* 31:8–13 (1983).

27. Torstensson, L. "Microbial Degradation of Linuron," in *Weeds and Weed Control*

[Proceedings] (Uppsala, Sweden: Department of Plant Husbandry and Research Information Centre, College of Agriculture, 1977), 18(1):I6-I10.

28. Gunnar, G., T. Popoff, and O. Theander. "Determination of Linuron and Its Metabolites by GLC and HPLC," *J. Chromatogr. Sci.* 16:118–122 (1978).

CHAPTER 13

Reductive Dechlorination of Dichlorophenols in Anaerobic Pond Sediments

Dorothy D. Hale, John E. Rogers, and Juergen Wiegel

INTRODUCTION

A number of aliphatic and aromatic compounds, including xenobiotics, are biodegraded anaerobically.[1-10] Within the past decade, significant progress has been made in understanding the anaerobic biodegradation of organics. Initially, pure or mixed anaerobic cultures of photosynthetic, respiratory, and fermentative microorganisms were investigated.[9,10] More recently the biodegradation of a variety of organic compounds has been studied in samples from several anaerobic sediments, soils, aquifer materials, and sewage sludges under methanogenic conditions.[7-9,11-14]

Chlorinated phenols, which are listed as priority pollutants by the U.S. Environmental Protection Agency,[15] are biodegraded in a number of anaerobic ecosystems.[8,11-14] The initial transformation in the anaerobic biodegradation of chlorophenols is, with few exceptions, reductive dechlorination to phenol. Phenol may then be degraded either through cyclohexanol, cyclohexanone, and adipate to succinate, propionate, and acetate[9,10] or through benzoate and acetate to the end products, carbon dioxide and methane.[16-18]

Much of the early work in our laboratory has concentrated on the degradation pathways of chlorinated phenols. More recently we have directed our studies toward understanding the environmental factors and chemical characteristics that influence the fate of these compounds in anaerobic ecosystems. In this chapter, we present results of experiments designed to examine the effects of environmental parameters on the reductive dechlorination of chlorinated phenols. Research in our laboratory has focused on this reaction because reductive dechlorination is usually the initial step, and possibly the rate-limiting step,[18] in the anaerobic degradation of these compounds.

Table 13.1. Persistence of Dichlorophenols in Anaerobic Sediment Slurries from Five Ponds

Dichlorophenol	Cherokee	Bolton's	Bar H	Sandy Creek	2-Boat
			T_{50} (days)		
2,3–	20 (17)	34 (98)	36	39	29
2,4–	21 (20)	21 (56)	21	21	21
2,5–	33	47	>98	61	>98
2,6–	34 (21)	>98 (224)	>98	>98	>98
3,4–	>84	>84	>84	49	>84
3,5–	35	42	>84	48	21

Note: Numbers represent the time for dechlorination of 50% of a dichlorophenol to a monochlorophenol. Numbers in parentheses represent the T_{50} for a dichlorophenol after its intial addition to sediments from Cherokee and Bolton's Ponds in a second study of microbial dechlorinating activity.[13]

BACKGROUND

To determine the prevalence and specificity of microbial chlorophenol dechlorinating activity in anoxic freshwater sediments, we initially studied the reductive dechlorination of the six dichlorophenols (DCPs) (2,3-, 2,4-, 2,5-, 2,6-, 3,4-, and 3,5-DCP) in sediments from five ponds in the Athens, Georgia, area. Although dechlorination of several isomers was evident in sediments from each of the ponds, a range of from 20 to more than 98 days was required for transformation of 50% of the DCPs to the monochlorophenols (T_{50}, Table 13.1). Sediment microorganisms in Cherokee Pond exhibited the highest dechlorinating activity, as evidenced by T_{50} values for the DCPs of from 20 to 35 days. The 3,4-DCP was an exception with a T_{50} of > 84 days. In contrast, dechlorinating microorganisms in the other four pond sediments were less active toward the DCPs, as reflected in the longer T_{50} values for each of the isomers. In the five sediments, chlorines were removed from the DCPs in the order *ortho* > *meta* > *para*. A similar order of dechlorination was determined for the monochlorophenol products.

The DCP dechlorinating activity present in the most active sediment (Cherokee Pond) and in a less active sediment (Bolton's Pond) were investigated further to examine the extent of the difference in DCP dechlorinating activity of microorganisms in these pond sediments.[13] The dechlorinating activity of the anaerobic sediment microorganisms was examined in sediment slurries repeatedly exposed to 2,3-, 2,4-, or 2,6-DCP. After the final addition of DCP, subsamples of these slurries were individually exposed to each of the six DCP isomers to determine substrate specificity.

Following the initial addition of DCP, a period of adaptation was observed in sediments from both ponds. No significant loss of DCP or production of monochlorophenol occurred during this time. The adaptation periods, ranging from 12 to 14 days in Cherokee sediments and from 35 to 196 days in Bolton's sediments, were similar to those observed in the initial study of five pond sediments. Likewise, T_{50} values for the DCPs in Cherokee sediments were similar to those determined initially (Table 13.1). However, T_{50} values for the three isomers differed two- to threefold from the initial T_{50} values in Bolton's sediments and three- to tenfold between sediments from the two ponds. Adaptation periods were not detectable following a second addition of DCP. Repeated addition of 2,3-, 2,4-, or 2,6-DCP to sediments adapted the indigenous microorganisms to initially remove the *ortho* chlorine without a lag. Adapted Cherokee sediment microbes exhibited faster dechlorination rates and a broader substrate specificity than adapted Bolton's sediment microorganisms (data not shown).

The disparity in DCP dechlorinating activity and substrate specificity of the microorganisms in Cherokee and Bolton's pond sediments exemplifies the difficulty faced in predicting the persistence and fate of some hazardous compounds in similar anoxic environments. The task is further complicated by temporal and spatial variation in sediment characteristics within, as well as between, sites in such environments. In order to address this problem, a study was initiated to monitor selected sediment properties and microbial dechlorinating activities of sediments collected every other month for a year from five sites in Cherokee Pond (Figure 13.1). Experiments were designed to determine correlations between selected sediment properties and rates of dechlorination of 2,4-, 2,5-, and 3,4-DCP. Our objective was to utilize the correlations to predict the persistence in anoxic sediments of chlorophenols with various chlorine substitution patterns.

MATERIALS AND METHODS

Sediment (0–10 cm) and overlying water were collected every other month from May 1988 to May 1989 from selected locations in five sites in Cherokee Pond. The samples were collected in sterile wide mouthed quart Mason jars and Erlenmeyer flasks, respectively, after determination of in situ temperature. The samples were transported to the laboratory and placed into an anaerobic chamber, with an atmosphere 95% N_2:5% H_2. All subsequent manipulations of the sediment and water samples were performed in the chamber. Sediments were sieved and stored as previously described.[13]

Serum bottle microcosm studies were conducted as follows. Slurries of 20 mL (10% dry sediment w/v) were prepared with sediments and site water in 100-mL serum bottles, which were capped with butyl rubber stoppers and crimp sealed. Experiments were initiated by addition of 1 mL of an aqueous stock solution (200 mg/L) of a DCP to the reaction vessels to yield a final concentration of 10 mg/L. Incubation and sampling of serum bottles and high pressure liquid chromatography of slurry extracts have been described previously.[13]

Sediment pH and redox potential (E_h) were determined as follows. Direct pH determinations were made with an Orion Research digital pH/millivolt meter (Model 611) with a combination pH electrode (Orion 910500). The

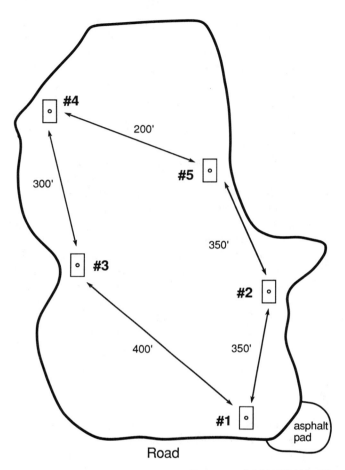

Figure 13.1. Location of the five sediment sampling areas (10 ft x 30 ft) in Cherokee Pond.

electrode was calibrated with pH 4 (potassium biphthalate) and pH 7 (potassium phosphate monobasic-sodium hydroxide) buffers (Fisher Scientific). Redox potential measurements were made for each sediment using a platinum/Ag/AgCl combination electrode (Orion 977800). The redox reference solution was a 0.1 M ferrous ammonium sulfate/0.1 ferric ammonium sulfate in 1.0 M sulfuric acid solution.[19]

Sulfate and nitrate concentrations in water samples were determined with a Dionex 2020i ion chromatograph utilizing an HPIC AS-4 analytical column and electrometer. The standard eluent, run at 1.5 mL/min, was 0.003 M sodium bicarbonate/0.0024 M sodium carbonate. A 0.025 N sulfuric acid solution was used with the continuous flow fiber suppressor. Water samples were injected through a 0.22-μm filter onto a 100-μm loop. A Hewlett-Packard

3390A integrator was used to quantify sulfate and nitrate by comparison to sodium sulfate and potassium nitrate standards, respectively.

Organic carbon analyses were performed on sediment samples ground to a powder with a mortar and pestle after being dried at 105°C and on water samples filtered through glass microfiber filters (Whatman GF/F, 0.7 μm). Persulfate oxidation of the samples followed the protocol for determination of carbon in sediments, soil, and water, as described in the procedures manual of the Oceanography International Corporation, Model 524C carbon analyzer. The carbon dioxide evolved from the samples was quantified by comparison to potassium biphthalate standards using a Horiba PIR-2000 infrared gas analyzer and integrator.

Numbers of 2,4-DCP dechlorinating microorganisms in Cherokee sediments were estimated with a compound-specific most probable number (MPN) assay. Dilutions of 10^{-1} to 10^{-5} were prepared first by serial dilution of 0.5 mL of slurry into 4.5 mL of site water which had been filter-sterilized (0.22 μm) and autoclaved at 121°C and 15 psi for 30 min. Subsequent transfers of 0.5 mL of these dilutions to 4.5-mL volumes of sterile water with 2,4-DCP yielded slurry dilutions with 10 mg/L 2,4-DCP per tube. Triplicate tubes were prepared at each dilution and incubated for 1 month before acetonitrile extracts of slurry dilutions were analyzed by a previously described HPLC protocol.[13] Tubes with a chromatogram having a 2,4-DCP peak area not more than three times the peak area of the 4-chlorophenol were scored positive. The most probable number of sediment dechlorinating microorganisms were estimated from the number of positive tubes in consecutive dilutions with an MS-DOS Turbo Pascal program using the American Society for Microbiology guidelines for MPN determinations.[20]

Analysis of variance, Duncan's multiple range tests, and regression analyses of data were performed using SAS (Release 6.03, SAS Institute, Inc., Cary, NC).

RESULTS AND DISCUSSION

Variability in DCP Dechlorination in Sediments

The time required for reductive dechlorination of 2,4-, 2,5-, and 3,4-DCP to monochlorophenols varied temporally and spatially in Cherokee sediments collected every other month between May 1988 and May 1989. Data for sites 1, 3, and 4 are summarized in Table 13.2. Microorganisms in sediments from these sites exhibited low (site 1), high (site 4), and intermediate (site 3) dechlorinating activity. Anaerobic dechlorinating microorganisms in sediments from sites 2 and 5 exhibited activities similar to those determined in site 3.

No seasonal pattern for dechlorination of the three isomers was evident from the data. With the exception of T_{50} values for the DCPs in July and November 1988 sediments (and in some January 1989 sediments), mean T_{50}

Table 13.2. Persistence of 2,4–, 2,5–, and 3,4–Dichlorophenol in Cherokee Sediment Slurries

Sampling Date	T_{50} (days)								
	Site 1			Site 3			Site 4		
	2,4–	2,5–	3,4–	2,4–	2,5–	3,4–	2,4–	2,5–	3,4–
May	24	26	25	21	20	32	21	22	25
July	192	173	160	88	98	93	12	17	19
September	72	17	29	11	15	20	12	18	20
November	91	155	159	25	92	139	19	14	21
January	10	14	66	7	15	64	10	14	20
March	43	41	50	7	7	6	7	7	9
May	19	16	32	16	21	35	12	9	45

Note: Numbers represent the mean time (n = 3) for dechlorination of 50% of the respective dichlorophenol to a monochlorophenol in three different sediments from the same site.

values for each of the isomers ranged from 6 to 30 days in sediments collected from all sites. Mean T_{50} values for DCPs in sediments from each site except site 4 were elevated in July and November.

Significant differences in the T_{50} values of the three DCPs were observed in sediments from different sites. The mean T_{50} value for each isomer was highest in sediments from site 1, averaging 64, 63, and 74 days for the 2,4-, 2,5-, and 3,4-isomers, respectively. Conversely, the mean T_{50} for each isomer was lowest in sediments from site 4. The 2,4- and 2,5-DCPs were dechlorinated more rapidly (T_{50} = 13 and 14 days, respectively) than 3,4-DCP (T_{50} = 23 days) in sediments from this site. A similar susceptibility to dechlorination was observed for 2,4-, 2,5-, and 3,4-DCP in sediments from site 3, with mean T_{50} values of 25, 38, and 56 days, respectively. Thus, a range of T_{50} values was observed for each isomer in Cherokee sediments from different sites.

In considering the influence of chlorine substitution on DCP dechlorination, a regiospecific pattern was observed for the initial dechlorination of each isomer. As was previously observed in the study of five pond sediments, the 2,4- and 2,5-isomers were reductively dechlorinated to 4- and 3-chlorophenol (CP), respectively, by removal of the *ortho* chlorine, and the 3,4-DCP was dechlorinated at the *para* position to form 3-CP. Dechlorination at the *meta* position of 3,4-DCP was detected only once in the 105 sediment slurries examined, and in this case, 3-CP and 4-CP were produced in approximately equal amounts.

Sediment/Water Characteristics

In order to determine any correlation between the T_{50} values for the DCPs and properties of the sediment-water system, the Cherokee sediment and water samples were analyzed for several physical, chemical, and microbiological characteristics. These included in situ temperature, pH, redox potential (E_h), sediment organic carbon, dissolved organic carbon, nitrate concentration, sulfate concentration, and the number of 2,4-DCP dechlorinating microorga-

Table 13.3. Sediment pH and Sulfate and Nitrate Concentrations (ppm) in Water from Three Sites in Cherokee Pond

Collection Date	Site 1			Site 3			Site 4		
	pH	SO$_4$	NO$_3$	pH	SO$_4$	NO$_3$	pH	SO$_4$	NO$_3$
May	6.4–6.6	0.23	ND[a]	6.3–6.6	0.17	ND	6.4–6.6	0.20	ND
July	6.3–6.7	0.36	ND	6.4–6.7	0.19	ND	6.4–6.5	0.58	ND
Sept.	5.8–6.1	0.77	0.73	6.0–6.1	1.11	0.71	6.0–6.2	0.76	0.72
Nov.	6.5–6.8	0.60	1.47	6.2–6.6	0.62	1.54	6.0–6.2	0.53	1.49
Jan.	5.9–6.0	0.37	ND	6.0–7.0	0.90	ND	6.5	0.08	ND
Mar.	5.8	NW[b]	NW	7.0	NW	NW	6.7	NW	NW
May	4.7–5.4	12.48	ND	5.1–5.7	11.73	ND	5.4–6.6	0.36	ND

Note: pH numbers represent the range of pH determined for three sediments from each site. Reported sulfate and nitrate concentrations are the mean of triplicate determinations of water samples from each of three locations within each site.
[a]Not detectable.
[b]No water column (pond drained).

nisms. Tables 13.3 and 13.4 summarize data on sediment pH, sulfate and nitrate concentration in site water, and number of 2,4-DCP dechlorinating sediment microorganisms of samples from sites 1, 3, and 4.

Some sediment/water characteristics displayed no significant temporal and/ or spatial variation. Sediment temperatures ranged from 10 to 30°C during the sampling year but did not vary from one site to another by more than 0.5°C at any one sampling time. Similarly, water temperatures, which paralleled those of sediments from the same site, varied significantly temporally but not spatially. Mean sediment redox potentials fluctuated during the study period from –125 mV (May 1988) to –4 mV (September 1988). However, spatial variability was limited, as evidenced by the mean E$_h$ range of –32 to –59 mV for sediments from all sites. Sediment redox potentials were highest (+130 mV) in May 1989, when the water column was restored after a 2-month period during which the pond was drained.

Sediment/water characteristics that displayed significant temporal and/or spatial variation were pH, organic carbon content, nitrate and sulfate concentration, and the number of 2,4-DCP dechlorinating microorganisms. The mean pH of sediments from all sites ranged from 5.3 to 7.1 during the study period. Extremely acidic pHs (i.e., 4.7) were reported for May 1989 sediments, which were collected after the water column was restored to the drained pond (Table 13.3). The organic carbon content of Cherokee sediments and water

Table 13.4. Most Probable Number (MPN) of 2,4-Dichlorophenol Dechlorinating Microorganisms in Cherokee Sediments

Sediment Collection Date	MPNs ($\times$ 10^3/g dry sediment weight)		
	Site 1	Site 3	Site 4
September	0.18	0.52	33.00
January	4.60	<2.90	4.60
March	<8.50	19.00	48.00
May	<2.90	48.00	<2.90

varied to a greater extent temporally than spatially (data not shown). During the study year, sediment organic carbon averaged 0.1 to 2.0%. Mean concentrations of total organic carbon (TOC) for sediments from all sites (n = 15) were highest in September 1988 (0.68%), November 1988 (0.92%), and March 1989 (1.1%). However, in sediments from each of the individual sites (n = 3), average TOC was not necessarily elevated at these times. Mean TOC was highest in site 4 sediments (0.89%) and lowest in site 1 sediments (0.48%). Dissolved organic carbon, which was often less than 10 ppm, also varied significantly over time but not with site (data not shown).

The concentration of nitrate and sulfate in site water varied significantly over time and, in some instances, with site (Table 13.3). From September to November 1988, nitrate levels doubled from a mean of 0.72 ppm to a mean of 1.51 ppm. However, nitrate concentrations were not significantly different from site to site. With the exception of September 1988 and May 1989, at every sampling time the average sulfate concentration in water from each site was less than 1 ppm. During the year, sulfate concentrations increased in water samples collected from May through September but generally decreased in water samples collected from September through January. The highest concentrations of sulfate, which occurred in the May water samples from sites 1 (12.48 ppm) and 2 (11.73 ppm), coincided with the restoration of the water column following drainage of the pond. Why a similar peak in sulfate concentration was not observed in water from site 4 is not clear. However, over the study period, the mean sulfate concentration (0.42 ppm) was lowest in water from this site.

The number of 2,4-DCP dechlorinating microorganisms in Cherokee sediments varied temporally and spatially (Table 13.4). At any one sampling time (except January 1989) or site, the number of these organisms in sediments varied from one to two orders of magnitude. MPN values of dechlorinating microorganisms in most sediments increased from September to January and from January to March, and decreased from March to May. Drainage of the pond may have affected MPN values of dechlorinating microorganisms in sediments collected in May.

Correlation of DCP Dechlorination to Sediment/Water Characteristics

A statistical analysis of the data indicated that certain sediment characteristics may be used to predict the T_{50} values of selected DCPs. For each of the isomers, a multiple regression analysis was performed using data from all sites and sampling dates. However, for 2,4-DCP, regression analysis indicated that none of the variables (alone or in combination) accounted for more than approximately 50% of the variation in the T_{50} values. Thus, additional research is needed to identify other sediment characteristics useful in predicting T_{50} values of 2,4-DCP and to determine the reasons that this isomer differs from the others.

Although the number of dechlorinating microorganisms present in the sedi-

Table 13.5. Summary of Stepwise Regression for Dependent Variable T_{50}

Step	Variable Entered	Number In	Partial R^2	Model R^2	F	Prob>F
1	pH	1	0.5375	0.5375	39.5086	0.0001
2	NO_3	2	0.1946	0.7321	23.9701	0.0001
3	SO_4	3	0.0718	0.8039	11.7246	0.0017
4	Eh	4	0.0252	0.8291	4.5726	0.0405
5	CO_2/H_2	5	0.0183	0.8474	3.5931	0.0677
6	TOC	6	0.0154	0.8628	3.2658	0.0811

	DF	Sum of Squares	Mean Square	F	Prob>F
Regression	6	126835.3518	21139.2253	30.41	0.0001
Error	29	20160.9538	695.2053		
Total	35	146996.3056			

Variable	Parameter Estimate	Standard Error	Partial Sum of Squares	F	Prob>F
Intercept	−605.1028	149.7888	11345.2115	16.32	0.0004
pH	115.6724	25.2056	14641.2417	21.06	0.0001
NO_3	105.3080	19.0325	21283.4639	30.61	0.0001
SO_4	−136.4994	30.1955	14206.5686	20.44	0.0001
E_h	0.7187	0.2625	5210.0869	7.49	0.0105
CO_2/H_2	0.0400	0.0184	3300.1914	4.75	0.0376
TOC	− 0.0050	0.0027	2270.3916	3.27	0.0811

ments at the time of 2,4-DCP addition could be not used to predict T_{50} values of this isomer, ongoing experiments in our laboratory indicate that a "threshold" number of actively dechlorinating microorganisms may be necessary before loss of the parent compound is detectable. The adaptation period (i.e., time during which no dechlorination is detectable) of a T_{50} value may thus include an induction-followed-by growth response, as proposed by Linkfield et al. in their study of the adaptation (acclimation) period before dehalogenation of halobenzoates.[21] Recent work by Cole and Tiedje[22] and by DeWeerd and Suflita[23] with the halobenzoate dehalogenating microbe *"Desulfomonile tiedjei"* indicates that the dehalogenating activity of this organism is inducible. Dolfing and Tiedje[24] have also reported a growth yield increase from the reductive dechlorination of 3-chlorobenzoate in a methanogenic coculture with this microorganism. The dechlorinating microorganisms in Cherokee sediments may be similar to this well-characterized organism[25,26] with respect to the inducibility of dechlorinating activity and increased growth from the reaction. If this is the case, a better understanding of the factors governing the induction-followed-by-growth response should improve the prediction of T_{50} values.

Regression analysis of data for both 2,5- and 3,4-DCP indicated that the variables of pH, nitrate and sulfate concentrations, and redox potential accounted for 83% of the variation in their T_{50} values (Table 13.5). Approximately 86% of the variation in T_{50} values of these isomers was explained by using these variables in addition to the ratio of carbon dioxide to hydrogen in the headspace of the test vessels (data not shown) and sediment total organic carbon (TOC). The variables of pH, nitrate, redox potential, and the ratio of carbon dioxide to hydrogen in serum bottle headspaces were positively correlated to T_{50} values; sulfate and TOC were negatively correlated to these values. The negative correlation of sulfate to T_{50} values may result from the enhanced activity in the presence of sulfate of a dechlorinating organism similar to the sulfidogenic *"Desulfomonile tiedjei."* However, this finding contrasts to published results of other researchers on the inhibitory aspects of sulfate on reductive dechlorination.[8,12,27] Thus, further studies should determine the utility of the model in predicting the T_{50} values of DCPs in sediments from other ponds, such as those in the initial study, with different sulfate regimes and sediment/water characteristics.

CONCLUSIONS

The results of the present study indicate that the reductive dechlorination of chlorinated phenols in anaerobic sediments can be correlated to sediment/water properties. In particular, the pH, nitrate and sulfate concentrations, and E_h of sediment-water systems may be used to predict the persistence of selected DCPs, with chlorines removed from the ring in the order *ortho* > *meta* or *para*. The use of these variables has practical implications because they can be determined rapidly with pH, ion selective, and E_h electrodes. Levels of the anions may also be determined by ion chromatography. The data may then be used in regression equations to predict T_{50} values of specified chlorophenols.

ACKNOWLEDGMENTS

We thank William C. Steen for helpful discussions and review of the manuscript and Rudolph Parrish for assistance in selection of sampling locations and statistical analysis of the data. Paul Tratnyek kindly supplied samples of the redox reference solution, and Ralph Peteranderl provided the Turbo Pascal MPN program.

DISCLAIMER

Mention of trade names or commercial products does not constitute endorsement or recommendation for use by the U.S. Environmental Protection Agency.

REFERENCES

1. Davis, J. B., and H. F. Yarbrough. "Anaerobic Oxidation of Hydrocarbons by *Desulfovibrio desulfuricans*," *Chem. Geol.* 1:137–144 (1966).
2. Giger, W., C. Schaffner, and S. G. Wakeham. "Aliphatic and Olefinic Hydrocar-

bons in Recent Sediments of Griefensee, Switzerland," *Geochim. Cosmochim. Acta* 44:119–129 (1980).

3. Kuhn, E. P., P. J. Colberg, J. L. Schnoor, O. Wanner, A. J. B. Alexander, and R. P. Schwarzenbach. "Microbial Transformations of Substituted Benzenes During Infiltration of River Water to Groundwater: Laboratory Column Studies," *Environ. Sci. Technol.* 19:961–968 (1985).

4. Healy, J. B., Jr., and L. Y. Young. "Catechol and Phenol Degradation by a Methanogenic Population of Bacteria," *Appl. Environ. Microbiol.* 35:216–218 (1978).

5. Healy, J. B., Jr., and L. Y. Young. "Anaerobic Biodegradation of Eleven Aromatic Compounds to Methane," *Appl. Environ. Microbiol.* 38:84–89 (1979).

6. Schink, B. "Degradation of Unsaturated Hydrocarbons by Methanogenic Enrichment Cultures," *FEMS Microbiol. Ecol.* 31:69–77 (1985).

7. Kuhn, E. P., and J. M. Suflita. "Dehalogenation of Pesticides by Anaerobic Microorganisms in Soils and Groundwater—A Review," in *Reactions and Movement of Organic Chemicals in Soils,* Soil Science Society of America Special Publication No. 22, B. L. Sawhney and K. Brown, Eds. (Madison, WI: Soil Science Society of America, 1989), pp. 111–180.

8. Gibson, S. A., and J. M. Suflita. "Extrapolation of Biodegradation Results to Groundwater Aquifers: Reductive Dehalogenation of Aromatic Compounds," *Appl. Environ. Microbiol.* 52:681–688 (1986).

9. Young, L. Y. "Anaerobic Degradation of Aromatic Compounds," in *Microbial Degradation of Organic Compounds,* D. T. Gibson, Ed. (New York: Marcel Dekker, 1984), pp. 487–523.

10. Evans, W. C. "Biochemistry of the Bacterial Catabolism of Aromatic Compounds in Anaerobic Environments," *Nature* 270:17–22 (1977).

11. Boyd, S. A., and D. R. Shelton. "Anaerobic Biodegradation of Chlorophenols in Fresh and Acclimated Sludge," *Appl. Environ. Microbiol.* 47:272–277 (1984).

12. Genthner, B. R. S., W. A. Price II, and P. H. Pritchard. "Anaerobic Degradation of Chloroaromatic Compounds in Aquatic Sediments under a Variety of Enrichment Conditions," *Appl. Environ. Microbiol.* 55:1466–1471 (1989).

13. Hale, D. D., J. E. Rogers, and J. Wiegel. "Reductive Dechlorination of Dichlorophenols by Non-Adapted and Adapted Microbial Communities in Pond Sediments," *Micro. Ecol.* 20:185–196 (1990).

14. Suflita, J. M., and G. D. Miller. "Microbial Metabolism of Chlorophenolic Compounds in Ground Water Aquifers," *Environ. Toxicol. Chem.* 4:751–758 (1985).

15. Keith, L. H., and W. A. Telliard. "Priority Pollutants. I. A Perspective View," *Environ. Sci. Technol.* 13:416–423 (1979).

16. Genthner, B. R. S., G. T. Townsend, and P. J. Chapman. "Anaerobic Transformation of Phenol to Benzoate via para-Carboxylation: Use of Fluorinated Analogues to Elucidate the Mechanism of Transformation," *Biochem. Biophys. Res. Commun.* 162:945–951 (1989).

17. Zhang, X., T. V. Morgan, and J. Wiegel. "Conversion of ^{13}C-1 Phenol to ^{13}C-4 Benzoate, an Intermediate Step in the Anaerobic Degradation of Chlorophenols," *FEMS Microbiol. Lett.* 67:63–66 (1990).

18. Zhang, X., and J. Wiegel. "Sequential Anaerobic Degradation of 2,4-Dichlorophenol in Freshwater Sediments," *Appl. Environ. Microbiol.* 56:1119–1127 (1990).

19. Light, T. S. "Standard Solution for Redox Potential Measurements," *Anal. Chem.* 44:1038–1039 (1972).

20. Koch, A. L. "Growth measurement," in *Manual of Methods for General Bacteriology,* R. N. Castilow, Ed. (Washington, DC: American Society for Microbiology, 1981), pp. 182–207.

21. Linkfield, T. G., J. M. Suflita, and J. M. Tiedje. "Characterization of the Acclimation Period before Anaerobic Dehalogenation of Halobenzoates," *Appl. Environ. Microbiol.* 55:2773–2778 (1989).

22. Cole, J. R., and J. Tiedje. "Induction of Anaerobic Dechlorination of Chlorobenzoate in Strain DCB-1," in *Abstr. Annu. Meet. Amer. Soc. Microbiol.* (Washington, D. C.: American Society for Microbiology, 1990), p. 295.

23. DeWeerd, K. A., and J. M. Suflita. "Anaerobic Aryl Reductive Dehalogenation of Halobenzoates by Cell Extracts of *'Desulfomonile tiedjei',*" *Appl. Environ. Microbiol.* 56:2999–3005 (1990).

24. Dolfing, J., and J. M. Tiedje. "Growth Yield Increase Linked to Reductive Dechlorination in a Defined 3-Chlorobenzoate Degrading Methanogenic Coculture," *Arch. Microbiol.* 149:102–105 (1987).

25. Stevens, T. O., T. G. Linkfield, and J. M. Tiedje. "Physiological Characterization of Strain DCB-1, a Unique Dehalogenating Sulfidogenic Bacterium," *Appl. Environ. Microbiol.* 54:2938–2943 (1988).

26. Stevens, T. O., and J. M. Tiedje. "Carbon Dioxide Fixation and Mixotrophic Metabolism by Strain DCB-1, a Dehalogenating Anaerobic Bacterium," *Appl. Environ. Microbiol.* 54:2944–2948 (1988).

27. Kuhn, E. P., G. T. Townsend, and J. M. Suflita. "Effect of Sulfate and Organic Carbon Supplements on Reductive Dehalogenation of Chloroanilines in Anaerobic Aquifer Slurries," *Appl. Environ. Microbiol.* 56:2630–2637 (1990).

B. Cometabolism

CHAPTER 14

The Effects of Groundwater Chemistry on Cometabolism of Chlorinated Solvents by Methanotrophic Bacteria

Anthony V. Palumbo, William Eng, and Gerald W. Strandberg

INTRODUCTION

Degradation of chlorinated alkenes such as trichloroethylene (TCE) by methanotrophic bacteria is a promising technology for the remediation of contaminated groundwater.[1] Ultimately, the success of this approach may be dependent on the influence of groundwater chemistry on degradation rates and extent. TCE can rapidly be reduced to low levels in laboratory cultures growing on defined media.[2] However, if major changes in groundwater chemistry are necessary to achieve substantial TCE degradation, field application of processes (i.e., above ground and in situ treatment) may be limited by cost or logistic problems. For example, the presence of competitive inhibitors may limit the extent of TCE degradation.

Biodegradation of TCE by a variety of mechanisms has been reported.[1,3-10] Some investigators have reported anaerobic degradation of TCE,[8,11] which can apparently produce dichloroethylene (DCE) and vinyl chloride,[12] a known carcinogen, and at contaminated sites TCE is often found in association with DCE. Degradation of TCE to CO_2 by aerobic mixed cultures has also been reported, but the degradation mechanisms have not always been clearly identified.[3,4] TCE degradation by methanotrophs is apparently initiated by the methane monooxygenase (MMO) using a cometabolic process. Normally, methane is oxidized to methanol by MMO.[13] But apparently TCE is also fortuitously oxidized by the monooxygenase. TCE breakdown may begin with epoxidation of the double bond, eventually resulting in formation of carbon dioxide, glyoxylic acid, and dichloroacetic acid, while a small fraction of the carbon from the TCE can be incorporated into the cells.[7] MMO is a fairly nonspecific enzyme and oxidizes methane, ammonia, TCE, and many other compounds.[13] Competitive inhibition may limit the degradation of TCE in the presence of high levels of methane and ammonia; thus, high rates of methane addition to a bioreactor or high levels of ammonia in the groundwater could limit TCE degradation. Another potential effect of groundwater chemistry is modification of the form or specificity of methane monooxygenase. Methane monooxygenase can exist either in free or particulate form depending on culture conditions, and the two forms can exhibit different rates of TCE degradation.[2,9]

The goal of our research is to quantify the potential effects of groundwater chemistry on the biodegradation of TCE by methanotrophs and to define concentrations of methane that need to be added to the system to produce maximum rates of TCE degradation. This includes evaluation of major nutritional requirements (e.g., PO_4) in addition to the focus on competitive inhibition.

MATERIALS AND METHODS

Cultures and Culture Conditions

We examined the degradation of TCE in batch experiments using *Methylosinus trichosporium*, strain OB3b; an isolate (46–1) previously obtained from an Oak Ridge Site;[7] and mixed methylotrophic cultures (JS, S1, DT1, and DT2) isolated from TCE-contaminated sites. *Methylosinus trichosporium* (strain OB3b) was provided by M. E. Lidstrom (California Institute of Technology). The JS mixed culture was isolated from a waste disposal site in Oak Ridge[7] and is currently being used in bioreactor studies of TCE degradation.[14] The DT1 and DT2 mixed cultures are bacteria-amoeba consortia isolated from an Oak Ridge site (R. L. Tyndall, Oak Ridge National Laboratory, personal communication). The S1 consortia was obtained during this study from contaminated groundwater from a Kansas City Department of Energy (DOE) site.[15]

Two types of batch experiments were run with the cultures. In the first type both degradation and growth were observed in 100 mL of sterile mineral salts medium (NATE),[11] prepared in 250 mL culture bottles, and inoculated with 1 mL of starter cultures. The medium contained 50 μg/L $CuSO_4 \cdot 5H_2O$, 10 μg/L $MnSO_4 \cdot H_2O$, 70 μg/L Zn $(NO_3)_2 \cdot 6H_2O$, 10 μg/L $CoCl_2 \cdot H_2O$, 10 μg/L MoO_3, 1 g/L $MgSO_4 \cdot 7H_2O$, 0.2 g/L $CaCl_2$, 1 g/L KNO_3, 0.1 g/L NH_4Cl, 10 mL of 0.27 g/L $FeCl_3$, and 20 mL of 5% potassium phosphate buffer (pH 6.8). Final media pH was adjusted to 6.8. The headspace of each bottle contained 8–8.5% (v/v) methane and in air except as otherwise noted. Each bottle was sealed with a Teflon septum, and to ensure an airtight seal, modeling compound, sandwiched between parafilm, was used to cover the bottle caps. The culture bottles were shaken (inverted, to further guard against gas leakage) on a rotary shaker (fermentation design) at 75 rpm. TCE, oxygen, and methane concentrations in the headspace were followed over time by periodic sampling of 0.5 mL of the headspace with a gas syringe (Hamilton). This design allowed for observation of the growth, methane consumption, and oxygen consumption by the cultures under various conditions. However, because initial populations of bacteria were low, degradation rates were also relatively low.

In the second series of batch experiments, strain OB3b was inoculated at higher cell densities to achieve higher rates of TCE degradation. The bacteria were cultured in 250 mL bottles containing NATE medium and 20% (v/v) methane in the headspace at 22°C for 5 days on a shaker table at 75 rpm. After incubation the cells were concentrated by centrifugation at 2500 rpm for 45 min at 10°C. Harvested cells were then resuspended in a 5 mM phosphate buffer at pH 7.0. Aliquots (12 mL) of the concentrated culture were added to 50-mL vials containing NATE to yield a final concentration of 0.02–0.04 mg/mL of cell protein.

Degradation of TCE was followed in small (50-mL) vials sealed with Teflon-lined septa; three vials were used for each treatment. In most experiments the concentration of one of the components of the media (i.e., ammonia) was varied to generate the different treatments. All vials contained 10% (v/v) methane in the headspace unless otherwise noted and were placed on a shaker table at 75 rpm. A TCE-saturated water solution was added by syringe injection, yielding a nominal initial TCE concentration of 3.0 ppm. At 24-hr intervals over a 3- to 4-day period, bottles from each treatment were sacrificed by addition of 4 mL of hexane to stop the biological activity and extract the remaining TCE. Vials remained on the shaker table for at least 24 hr before GC analysis. Over the range of concentrations tested, the hexane extraction removed > 95% of the TCE added.

Additional experiments were conducted in a bench-scale continuous-flow bioreactor[14] consisting of a 5-cm i.d. × 110-cm long glass column packed with 0.6-cm ceramic berl saddles as a support for the biofilm. The system was a trickle-type packed-bed bioreactor with a gas stream (25 mL/min) containing 4% (v/v) methane and air introduced at the top of the bioreactor. The bioreactor was inoculated with pink-tinted mixed culture (JS) containing methanotrophs. Phospholipid analysis indicated that Type I methanotrophs predominate in the culture (D. C. White, personal communication). With the same mineral salts media used in the batch cultures, 1 mg/L TCE influent concentration, and a 50-min residence time, approximately 50% of the TCE was degraded in a single pass through the bioreactor; further degradation of TCE is evident with liquid recycle.[15]

Analytical Methods

Protein concentration was determined using the Coomassie Blue dye-binding method.[16] A Bio-Rad protein assay kit was adapted for use with a centrifugal fast analyzer (COBA-FARA) and used for the measurements.[17]

TCE concentration in the hexane extract from experiments with the concentrated cell suspensions and in the headspace gas in the other experiments was determined using a Perkin Elmer Sigma 2000 GC with electron capture detector and a 3-ft × 1/8-in. glass column containing 60/80 1% Carbopack B. Other GC operating parameters were

- 100°C oven temperature
- 125°C injector temperature
- 350°C detector temperature
- 30 mL/min of N_2 carrier gas

With these settings TCE retention time was 5.2 min. Analysis of *trans*-1,2-DCE was done using the same gas chromatography parameters as described for TCE analysis except oven temperature was set at 65°C. This gave a DCE retention time of 2.05 min. Liquid *trans*-1,2-DCE standards were used to calibrate the gas chromatograph daily.

In some experiments, ^{14}C-labeled TCE was used to determine TCE degradation rates and breakdown products.[7] After incubation with [1,2-^{14}C] TCE (3.0 mCi/mmol [111 MBq/mmol], Pathfinder Laboratories, St. Louis, MO), the pH of the media was adjusted to 9.5–10, thereby converting all CO_2 gas into carbonate. A subsample of culture was centrifuged, and the pellet was resuspended in NATE to assess the amount of TCE incorporated into cellular material. Remaining TCE was extracted from the supernatant with hexane. Acid was added to convert the carbonate into CO_2, which was trapped in 0.1 N NaOH in a small vial placed in the culture bottle. Subsamples of the water phase and the trapped CO_2 were then counted using a TriCarb 2000CA liquid scintillation analyzer, (Packard, Downers Grove, IL).

Oxygen and methane concentrations in headspace gas were measured with a Perkin Elmer 3920B gas chromatograph equipped with a 6 × 1/8 in. molecular sieve 5A column (Supleco) and a thermal conductivity detector. Both the injector and interface temperature were set at 150°C. Oven temperature (initial and final) was set at 45°C. Retention times were 0.68, 1.3, and 2.3 min for oxygen, nitrogen, and methane, respectively. Oxygen and methane concentrations are reported as percent (v/v) of headspace gas.

Experiments

The effect of ammonia on TCE degradation was examined using concentrated OB3b cells and with a nonconcentrated mixed culture (DT). The experiment with the OB3b cells was conducted in 50-mL vials as described above in NATE media with modified ammonium chloride concentrations of 0 to 1.0 mg/L, and TCE degradation was followed by GC techniques. Growth of the DT culture was followed in the 250-mL bottles as previously described, and the fate of TCE was followed using radiolabel techniques at concentrations of 0.1 and 2.5 mg/L of ammonia chloride. In the experiment with the DT culture, initial methane and oxygen were 8 and 18% of headspace gas, respectively.

The effect of phosphorus concentration on growth and TCE degradation was determined in an experiment where five concentrations of phosphorus (1.4, 3.2, 6.2, 25, 100 µg/mL) were used. A total of 29.6 µg (final concentration = 0.29 μg/mL) of TCE was added to each bottle. Nonconcentrated cells of strain 46-1 were used in these experiments.

The growth of the JS mixed culture was examined at various methane levels after adding NATE elements (to make up 10% of the final volume) to the site water (90% of final volume). Methane levels were 1.2, 3.5, 5.5, 7.5, and 9.7% (v/v) of headspace. Initial oxygen levels were 18% (v/v) of headspace for all treatments. Initial concentration of TCE in the incubation water was about 4.7 mg/L.

In a second experiment using site groundwater, the proportion of groundwater was varied by the addition of NATE nutrients and distilled water to yield final concentrations of site water of 22.5, 45, 67.5, and 90%. The purpose of this experiment was to determine the effect of TCE concentration and micronutrient conditions on the growth and TCE degradation. We determined that the site groundwater initially contained 12.3 mg/L and 4.7 mg/L TCE, and the concentrations in the treatments varied in proportion to the amount of site water added. Initial methane and oxygen concentrations were 8 and 18% (v/v) of headspace gas, respectively.

The presence of the DCE in the site water prompted us to examine the degradation of TCE in the presence of *trans*-1,2 DCE. A comparison of the ability of the DT2 and JS consortia to degrade TCE (0.3 mg/L) with 0, 30, and 63 mg/L of *trans*-1,2-DCE added to the bottles was conducted to determine if DCE inhibited TCE degradation. Initial methane and oxygen concentrations were 8 and 18% (v/v) of headspace gas, respectively. TCE degradation was followed using both radiolabel and GC techniques, and degradation was followed using GC analysis.

The effects of methane (0 to 20% v/v), ammonia (0, 2.5, and 10 mg/L), and copper (0.2 and 1.0 mg/L) concentrations on TCE degradation were examined in the fixed-film, packed-bed bioreactor system. TCE degradation was compared among the different treatments by analysis of the offgas.

Data Analysis

Analysis of variance (ANOVA) with Duncan's multiple range test was used to test for significant treatment differences in total TCE transformation and the transformation to breakdown products in experiments using the radiolabeled TCE. Other data were analyzed using Lotus 1-2-3 (Lotus Corporation)

RESULTS AND DISCUSSION

Growth of Cultures Exposed to Site Water

Although at all concentrations of site water the JS consortia eventually consumed the same amount of methane and oxygen, consortia growing in the higher concentrations of the site water consumed the methane and oxygen at a slower rate, indicating a decreased growth rate (Figure 14.1a). The unsterilized treatment without any inoculum contained 25% site water and also displayed methane and oxygen consumption, indicating the presence of methane-utilizing organisms in the site water. The rate of methane and oxygen consumption, however, was not as rapid as in the treatment containing 25% site water with added JS mixed culture (Figure 14.1).

Although an enrichment (S1) from the site water was used in subsequent

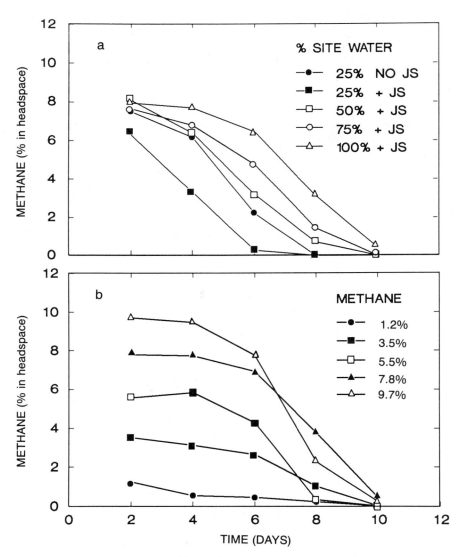

Figure 14.1. Methane utilization by the JS consortia growing in site water: *(a)* with varying percentages of site water; *(b)* with varying initial methane concentrations.

experiments and was demonstrated to degrade TCE, no evidence for degradation of TCE was observed in these experiments with site water with the added JS culture. The lack of significant TCE degradation despite the evidence for growth of the methanotrophs (utilization of methane) indicates that there was inhibition of the TCE degradation in the site water.

In the second experiment, examining the effect of methane on the growth of methane-utilizing consortia exposed to the site water, the methane was substantially depleted in all treatments after 10 days (Figure 14.1b). As in other experiments, oxygen consumption was significantly correlated with the amount of methane consumed (r^2 = 0.995, N = 5), and there was no evidence for TCE degradation.

Much of the impetus for the following work came from the observation that in the water from the DOE Kansas City site we could demonstrate growth of methane-utilizing bacteria (Figure 14.1), but there was no evidence for TCE degradation in the site water.

Biodegradation of TCE in the Presence of *trans*-1,2-DCE

The results of the DCE experiments indicated that DCE could have had an effect on the TCE degradation rates in the site water. Both the DT2 and JS consortia transformed significantly (F = 19.88; d.f. = 2, 13) greater amounts of TCE at lower *trans*-1,2-DCE concentrations (Figure 14.2). The decrease in the extent of degradation of the TCE was statistically significant (95% level) and was proportional to the concentration of *trans*-1,2-DCE added; the correlation coefficient (r) for the relationship between the percent degradation of TCE, measured using the radiolabel data, and the *trans*-1,2-DCE concentration was -0.92 (n = 6) for the DT2 cultures and –0.94 (n = 6) for the JS cultures. The DT2 culture was significantly (F = 12.54; d.f. = 1, 11) more efficient at degrading the TCE, transforming a mean of 22.27% of the added TCE compared to a mean of 12.38% transformation by the JS mixed culture. The GC data gave similar results for total TCE conversion (data not shown). Both consortia converted a high percentage of the TCE to CO_2, and there was no significant difference (F = 1.73; d.f. = 1, 11) between the consortia in the proportion of the transformed TCE that was converted to CO_2 (mean = 50.5%).

DCE degradation in the bioreactor was more efficient than the TCE degradation.[14] In a single pass the bioreactor removed ~ 50% of a 1 ppm solution of TCE but reduced a 1 ppm solution of *trans*-1,2-DCE to below the limit of detection. At these equal concentrations of TCE and DCE there was no obvious effect of *trans*-1,2-DCE on TCE degradation.[14] DCE degradation by methane-utilizing cultures is well documented.[9,18] However, demonstration of the competitive inhibition between TCE and DCE degradation is less well documented but could be important due to their co-occurrence. The kinetics of the inhibition are currently the subject of more detailed study in our laboratory. Because the laboratory doing the analysis at the site reported that the

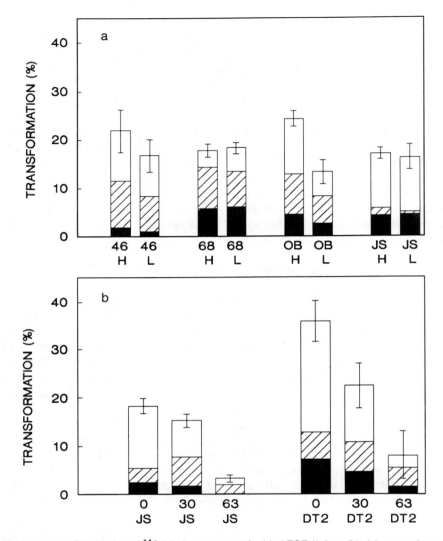

Figure 14.2.   Distribution of ^{14}C label as percent of added TCE (0.3 mg/L): *(a)* comparison of distribution by the 46–1, 68–1, and OB3b cultures, and the JS consortia; *(b)* comparison of JS and DT2 consortia with 0, 30, and 63 mg/L added *trans*-1,2-DCE. The amount incorporated into cell material is given by the *solid bars* on the bottom, into water soluble products is given by the *cross-hatched bars* in the center, and into CO_2 is given by the *open bars* on the top. The range for the total transformation is given by the error bars.

DCE present was in the *trans* form, *trans*-1,2-DCE was used in these experiments. However, the laboratory is now reporting that the DCE is present in the *cis* form. This should not affect the conclusions since other experiments have indicated that the *cis* form may have a more pronounced effect on the TCE degradation rate (Eng, unpublished data).

Effects of Ammonia, Methane, and Phosphorus on TCE Degradation

In the batch experiments high concentrations of added ammonium chloride appeared to inhibit TCE degradation by OB3b. Cultures incubated in the presence of 0.05 mg/L ammonium chloride had higher initial rates (1.35 μg TCE/hr/mg protein) of TCE degradation than cultures without ammonium or with higher concentrations of ammonium (Figure 14.3). In an experiment conducted with a mixed culture with nonconcentrated cells, increasing the ammonia concentration from 0.1 to 2.5 mg/L resulted in a 50% decrease in amount of ^{14}C TCE degraded during the growth of the bacteria. The proportion of $^{14}CO_2$, water-soluble products, and cell-bound ^{14}C did not vary at different ammonia concentrations. In the absence of methane, degradation was not detected ($< 3\%$) regardless of ammonium concentrations (Figure 14.4).

Methane was similarly demonstrated to reduce TCE degradation in both pure and mixed culture studies. In experiments with 0, 2, 10, and 20% (v/v) methane in the headspace of the vials, maximum degradation (>3.0 μg TCE/ hr/mg protein) by the concentrated OB3b cultures was observed in the treatments with only 10% (v/v) methane in the headspace. In the absence of

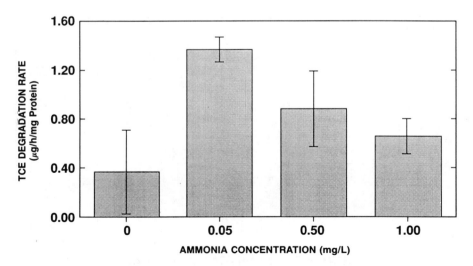

Figure 14.3. TCE degradation rate (μg/hr/mg protein) by OB3b with increasing concentrations of ammonium chloride. Data are given as calculated slope $\pm$ SE.

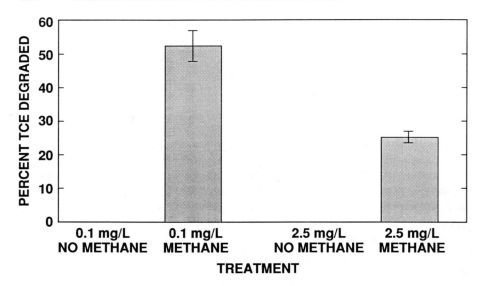

Figure 14.4. TCE degradation (%) by mixed culture DT1 at 0.1 and 5.5 mg/L ammonium chloride with and without methane.

methane in the headspace, degradation was substantially lower (0.40 μg TCE/ hr/mg protein). The rate of TCE degradation progressively declined at a concentration of 20% (v/v) methane in the headspace (Figure 14.5). In the mixed culture experiments the effect of methane on TCE degradation rate was apparent at relatively high levels of methane. We found that 29% of the added TCE

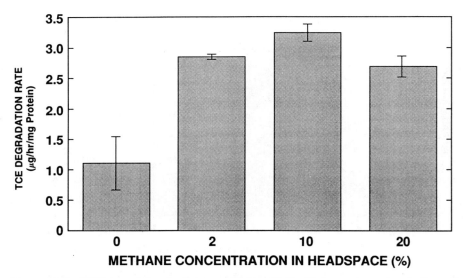

Figure 14.5. TCE degradation (μg/hr/mg protein) by OB3b with increasing concentrations of methane.

was transformed by strain 46-1 with 10% added methane (10% to CO_2), and only 16% of the TCE was transformed with 16.7% methane (6% to CO_2). The decrease in degradation was probably due to competitive inhibition.

Methane concentrations at or above 4% (v/v) supported methanotrophic growth, and TCE and *trans*-1,2-DCE degradation in the bioreactor. A methane concentration of 2% was not sufficient to support the predominance of the methanotrophic population. Over time a yellow-pigmented, non-TCE-degrading species developed rapidly at 2% methane. In shorter experiments, cutoff of the methane supply resulted in a slight decrease in degradation over 4 hr, followed by a rapid decrease and a complete halt in TCE degradation by 14-16 hr. A resumption in the methane supply resulted in resumption of TCE degradation within 1-2 hr. Methane concentrations of 10% could not be shown to significantly reduce the extent of TCE degradation. However, the sensitivity of TCE degradation rates in a bioreactor to methane has been shown by Leahy et al.[6]

There is considerable evidence for ammonia oxidation by methanotrophs, and MMO is implicated in some of these studies.[13] The presence of ammonia can reduce the growth rate of methanotrophs,[11] presumably by competitive inhibition of methane uptake.[19] Thus, it is likely that the effect on TCE degradation rates is also competitive interactions since both TCE and methane are competing for sites on the MMO.

Variations in phosphorus content in the range tested affected the growth rate of the organism but not the rate of TCE degradation. The methane and oxygen consumption data indicate that the variations in phosphorus content slightly affected the growth rate of the organism (Figure 14.6), with higher levels of phosphorus leading to higher growth rates. However the rate or extent of TCE degradation was not significantly affected (data not shown). Thus, the concentrations of phosphorus in the media can be significantly reduced from those present in the original formulation of the NATE media, which contains phosphorus as a pH buffer as well as a nutrient. Since pH can be an important parameter in TCE degradation,[9] some buffering of pH may be needed.

Changes in media composition in the bioreactor did not result in changes in the extent of TCE degradation similar to those observed in the batch experiments. The effect of ammonia was not seen in an experiment where concentrations of ammonia chloride of 0, 2.5, and 10 mg/L were used. However, peak TCE degradation was seen in the batch experiments at a concentration only slightly greater than 0 (0.05 and 0.1 mg/L) ammonia chloride. Thus, concentrations between 0 and 2.5 mg/L may yield different results. Also, changes in copper and manganese concentration and the addition of 0.1 mM EDTA all had no effect on the TCE degradation rate. The general lack of effects in the bioreactor could be due to the design of the bioreactor masking effects that are evident in the batch systems. For example, the higher biomass may lead to copper limitation at higher copper levels than in the batch cultures. More work

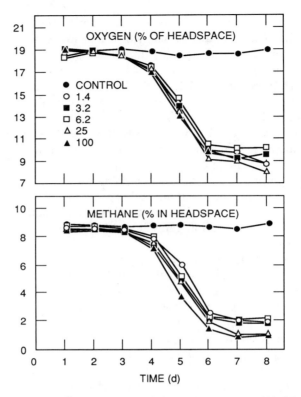

Figure 14.6. Methane and oxygen consumption by strain 46–1 at 1.4 (O), 3.2 (■), 6.2 (□), 25 (x), and 100 (▲) μg/mL of phosphorus and the control (●).

needs to be done examining the effects of factors that change TCE degradation rates in batch cultures in bioreactor systems.

Other experiments have indicated that manganese concentrations may influence degradation rates.[15] Manganese is a cofactor of some oxygenase enzymes,[4] and alterations of its concentration may affect the specificity of the methane monooxygenase. However, there may be a more subtle effect involved. In the defined media the presence of chelators results in changes in the concentration of the free form of all the trace metals when the total concentration of one of them is varied. Thus, in order to isolate effects to changes in the activities of one trace metal, experiments must be designed in which the activity of only one component varies. Thus, defining the specific trace metals involved in controlling the TCE degradation rate will be a complex undertaking. The influence of trace metals on TCE degradation could be due to shifting of methane monooxygenase between the soluble and the particulate form, as has been shown to occur under conditions of copper limitation.[2,9]

SUMMARY

Our results indicate that constituents of the medium have a significant effect on TCE degradation by methanotrophs. Depending on the initial composition, substantial modifications in the chemical composition of groundwater may be required to achieve rapid rates of TCE degradation in aboveground bioreactors. Ammonia concentration has been shown to be an important factor in these studies. In batch cultures ammonia clearly limits TCE degradation by both pure and mixed cultures. However, in bioreactors the effect is not clear and warrants further study. Phosphorus concentrations can clearly be substantially reduced from those present in the NATE without reducing degradation rate.

The lack of evident degradation of TCE in the Kansas City site samples may have been due in part to the presence of DCE in the site water. This phenomenon would probably be less important in bioreactors where the active microbial biomass would be much higher. Recent experiments have shown that DCE and TCE do degrade simultaneously and appear to be competitive inhibitors.[20] Ammonia has never been analyzed for at the site, but conditions are reducing so ammonia may have had an effect on decreasing the TCE degradation in the site water.

ACKNOWLEDGMENTS

We wish to thank Steve Herbes, Terry Donaldson, and other members of the staff of Oak Ridge National Laboratory, for providing critical reviews of the manuscript. This research was sponsored by the U.S. Department of Energy under contract DE-AC05–84OR21400 with Martin Marietta Energy Systems, Inc. Publication no. 3715 of the Environmental Sciences Division, Oak Ridge National Laboratory.

REFERENCES

1. Wilson, J. T., and B. H. Wilson. "Biotransformation of Trichloroethylene in Soil," *Appl. Environ. Microbiol.* 49:242–243 (1985).
2. Tsien, H.-C., G. A. Brusseau, R. S. Hanson, and L. P. Wackett. "Biodegradation of Trichloroethylene by *Methylosinus trichosporium* OB3b," *Appl. Environ. Microbiol.* 55:3155–3161 (1989).
3. Fliermans, C. B., T. J. Phelps, D. Ringelberg, A. T. Mikell, and D. C. White. "Mineralization of Trichloroethylene by Heterotrophic Enrichment Cultures," *Appl. Environ. Microbiol.* 54:1709–1714 (1988).
4. Fogel, M. M., A. R. Taddeo, and S. Fogel. "Biodegradation of Chlorinated Ethenes by a Methane-Utilizing Mixed Culture," *Appl. Environ. Microbiol.* 51:720–724 (1986).
5. Jansen, D. B., G. Grobben, and B. Witholt. "Toxicity of Aliphatic Hydrocarbons and Degradation by Methanotrophic Cultures," in *Proceedings of the 4th European Congress on Biotechnology,* Vol. 3, M. Neijssel, R. R. Van der Meer, and K.

C. A. M. Luyben, Ed. (Amsterdam: Elsevier Science Publishing, 1987), pp. 515–518.

6. Leahy, M. C., M. Findlay, and S. Fogel. "Biodegradation of Chlorinated Aliphatics by a Methanotrophic Consortium in a Biological Reactor," in *Biotreatment: The Use of Microorganisms in the Treatment of Hazardous Materials and Hazardous Wastes. Proceedings of the 2nd National Conference* (Silver Spring, MD: Hazardous Materials Control Institute, 1989).

7. Little, C. D., A. V. Palumbo, S. E. Herbes, M. E. Lindstrom, R. L. Tyndall, and P. J. Gilmer. "Trichloroethylene Biodegradation by Pure Cultures of a Methane-Oxidizing Bacterium," *Appl. Environ. Microbiol.* 54:951–956 (1988).

8. Kleopfer, R. D., D. M. Easley, B. B. Haas, Jr., T. G. Deihl, D. Jackson, and C. J. Wurrey. "Anaerobic Degradation of Trichloroethylene in Soil," *Environ. Sci. Technol.* 19:277–280 (1985).

9. Oldenhuis, R., R. L. J. M. Vink, D. B. Janssen, and B. Witholt. "Degradation of Chlorinated Aliphatic Hydrocarbons by *Methylosinus trichosporium* OB3b Expressing Soluble Methane Monooxygenase," *Appl. Environ. Microbiol.* 55:2819–2826 (1989).

10. Nelson, M. J. K., S. O. Montgomery, W. R. Mahaffy, and P. H. Pritchard. "Biodegradation of Trichloroethylene and Involvement of an Aromatic Biodegradative Pathway," *Appl. Environ. Microbiol.* 53:949–954 (1986).

11. Whittenbury, R., K. C. Phillips, and J. F. Wilkinson. "Enrichment Isolation and Some Properties of Methane-Utilizing Bacteria," *J. Gen. Microbiol.* 61:205–218 (1970).

12. Vogel, T. M., and P. McCarty. "Biotransformation of Tetrachloroethylene to Trichloroethylene, Dichloroethylene, Vinyl Chloride, and Carbon Dioxide under Methanogenic Conditions," *Appl. Environ. Microbiol.* 49:1080–1083 (1985).

13. Bédard, C., and R. Knowles. "Physiology, Biochemistry, and Specific Inhibitors of CH_4, NH_4^+, and CO Oxidation by Methanotrophs and Nitrifiers," *Microbiol. Reviews* 53:68–84 (1989).

14. Strandberg, G. W., T. L. Donaldson, and L. L. Farr. "Degradation of Trichloroethylene and *trans*-1,2-Dichloroethylene by a Methanotrophic Consortium in a Fixed-Film, Packed-Bed Bioreactor," *Environ. Sci. Technol.* 23:1422–1425 (1989).

15. Garland, S. B., II, A. V. Palumbo, W. Eng, C. D. Little, G. W. Strandberg, T. L. Donaldson, and L. L. Bolla. "The Use of Methanotrophic Bacteria for the Treatment of Groundwater Contaminated with Trichloroethylene at the Bendix Kansas City Plant," ORNL/TM-11084, Oak Ridge National Laboratory, Oak Ridge, TN (1989).

16. Bradford, M. M. "A Rapid and Sensitive Method for the Quantitation of Microgram Quantities of Protein Utilizing the Principle of Protein-Dye Binding," *Analyt. Biochem.* 72:248–254 (1976).

17. Jiminez, B. Personal communication (1989).

18. Moore, A. T., A. Vira, and S. Fogel. "Biodegradation of *trans*-1,2-Dichloroethylene by Methane-Utilizing Bacteria in an Aquifer Simulator," *Environ. Sci. Technol.* 23:403–406 (1989).

19. Ferenci, T., T. Strom, and J. R. Quayle. "Oxidation of Carbon Monoxide and Methane by *Pseudomonas methanica*," *J. Gen. Microbiol.* 91:79–91 (1975).

20. Eng, W. "Biodegradation Kinetics of Chlorinated Ethylenes by *Methylosinus trichosporium* (OB3b)," MS Thesis, University of Tennessee, Knoxville, TN (1990).

CHAPTER 15

Anaerobic Degradation of Aromatic Hydrocarbons and Aerobic Degradation of Trichloroethylene by Subsurface Microorganisms

Dunja Grbic-Galic, Susan M. Henry, E. Michael Godsy, Elizabeth Edwards, and Kevin P. Mayer

INTRODUCTION

Homocyclic and heterocyclic aromatic hydrocarbons, which are constituents of petroleum, oil derivatives, and pesticide mixtures (e.g., creosote), and chlorinated aliphatic hydrocarbons, which are extensively used as solvents, are frequent subsurface contaminants.[1] Some of these compounds are known or suspected carcinogens; many of them are toxic. Their fate and transport in the subsurface environment will depend on their own physical and chemical characteristics and those of the environment and will be influenced by physical, chemical, and microbiological environmental processes. Among these, microbiological processes can change the pollutants and influence their fate the most profoundly. In numerous cases, microorganisms will cause complete degradation (mineralization) of the pollutant molecules, provided the environment is conducive to microbial growth and metabolism.

Homocyclic aromatic hydrocarbons are completely degraded by microorganisms under aerobic conditions, in the presence of molecular oxygen as a reactant and an electron acceptor for microbial respiration.[2] Homoaromatics are fairly reduced molecules and therefore prone to oxidative transformations. They are also quite stable resonant structures, but microbial oxygenases, which introduce atoms of oxygen into the aromatic molecule, are powerful enough catalysts to exert this transformation under physiological conditions. Aerobic microbial degradation of aromatic hydrocarbons is well understood, and aerobic microbial processes are widely used for *in situ* treatment of petroleum-contaminated groundwater aquifers.[1] However, microbial activity quickly depletes oxygen, and frequently the rate of oxygen consumption exceeds the rate at which oxygen can be introduced into a contaminated subsurface habitat. As a result, anaerobic conditions develop. These phenomena stress the importance of understanding the possibilities of anaerobic microbial transformation of aromatic hydrocarbons.

Heterocyclic aromatic hydrocarbons, which contain nitrogen or sulfur in their ring structure, are less stable than homoaromatics; therefore, they can be microbially oxidized not only using molecular oxygen but also using water as an oxygen source.[3] In some cases, it has been shown that the early oxidation products from these compounds are the same under aerobic and anaerobic conditions.[4-6] It would be logical to expect that these compounds will be easier to deal with anaerobically than their homocyclic counterparts.

Chlorinated aliphatic hydrocarbons (C_1 or C_2) with more than two chlorines per molecule are highly oxidized chemicals that are more prone to reductive than to oxidative transformations.[7] Under anaerobic conditions, these compounds are sequentially reduced to less chlorinated products: for example, tetrachloroethylene (PCE) and trichloroethylene (TCE) yield 1,2-dichloroethylene isomers (DCE) and vinyl chloride (VC);[8,9] carbon tetrachloride (CT) is frequently dehalogenated to chloroform (CF).[10] These processes naturally occur in contaminated groundwater aquifers.[11] Such transformations are not desirable, however, because the products can be more carcinogenic (e.g., VC) or toxic (e.g., CF) than the parent compounds. From this standpoint, it is necessary to understand the conditions that are conducive to, and the prerequisites for, aerobic transformation of halogenated solvents. As was first discovered by Wilson and Wilson in 1985,[12] some chlorinated solvents, such as TCE, can indeed be transformed not only anaerobically but also aerobically.

In the last several years, a lot of the work in the laboratories within the Environmental Engineering and Science Program at Stanford University has been devoted to studies of anaerobic transformation of homocyclic and heterocyclic aromatic hydrocarbons under methanogenic conditions and of aerobic transformation of TCE by methanotrophic populations and communities. Some of this work, specifically using groundwater aquifer microcosms, enrichments, and pure cultures, will be summarized in this chapter.

ANAEROBIC MICROBIAL TRANSFORMATION OF AROMATIC HYDROCARBONS

Background

The first experimental results indicating anaerobic microbial oxidation of homocyclic monoaromatic hydrocarbons were published in 1980.[13] The authors observed formation of small amounts of $^{14}CO_2$ and $^{14}CH_4$ from ^{14}C-labeled toluene and benzene in methanogenic microcosms derived from salt-marsh and estuarine sediments contaminated by petroleum. However, it took several more years before a conclusive proof of anaerobic oxidation of these compounds was obtained.[14,15] By using ^{14}C-labeled toluene and benzene, $H_2^{18}O$, and anaerobic sludge-derived methanogenic consortia, it was shown that the initial transformation step involved oxidation of the aromatic hydrocarbon substrate by oxygen from water (hydroxylation).[14] In toluene, which is an alkylated compound, the oxidation occurs on the methyl group forming an alcohol or on the ring forming a cresol.[15] Further transformation steps overlap with previously established pathways for oxygenated aromatic compounds (alcohols, aldehydes, and acids).[16,17] It is most likely that transition metal complexes in microbial enzymes catalyze oxidative substitution of aromatic hydrocarbons in a similar way as do strong metal oxidants—such as Co(III) fluoroacetate in fluoroacetic acid—that are involved in abiotic reactions of this type, as previously demonstrated.[18,19] Recently, data have become available that show that polynuclear aromatic hydrocarbons are also biodegradable anaerobically, with nitrate as an electron acceptor (soil microcosms),[20,21] as well as under methanogenic conditions (sludge-derived consortia).[22]

In 1983, Schwarzenbach et al. first observed selective removal of toluene and xylenes relative to other components of landfill leachate in the anaerobic zone of a contaminated groundwater aquifer.[23] Their observations were quickly followed by almost identical findings for a different groundwater aquifer by Reinhard et al.[24] These were the first indications that groundwater microorganisms might be capable of transforming homocyclic aromatic hydrocarbons under anaerobic conditions. Furthermore, because no increase in the concentration of reduced alicyclic rings was observed in those aquifers, there was a possibility that the transformation was starting with an oxidation rather than a reduction as typical for oxygenated aromatic compounds. In 1985, Kuhn et al. presented evidence that the three xylene isomers were degraded by denitrifying bacteria in laboratory microcosms filled with subsurface sediments.[25] More detailed studies of toluene and *m*-xylene degradation under denitrifying conditions followed,[26] and the denitrifying pathway for toluene mineralization was soon delineated;[27] this pathway was very close to the methanogenic toluene-degrading pathway previously proposed by Grbic-Galic and Vogel for anaerobic sludge-derived consortia.[15] Parallel with this work, Wilson et al.[25] found that methanogenic aquifer microcosms, derived from a landfill leachate-contaminated groundwater aquifer, degraded benzene, toluene, ethylbenzene, and *o*-xylene; ^{14}C-labeled toluene was mineralized to [14]CO_2.[28] In a subsequent paper, *m*-xylene was added to this list;[29] the microcosms were derived from an aviation gasoline–contaminated aquifer. Other publications followed, presenting benzene degradation by aquifer microorganisms under denitrifying conditions,[30] toluene and *p*-xylene transformation with sulfate possibly acting as an electron acceptor,[31] and the first finding of toluene degradation by groundwater bacteria with Fe(III) as an electron acceptor by Lovley et al. in 1989.[32] The most recent discovery is a pure culture of a denitrifier (*Pseudomonas* sp.), originally derived from a groundwater aquifer, which mineralizes toluene and *m*-xylene.[33]

The information on anaerobic degradation of heterocyclic aromatic hydrocarbons containing nitrogen in their structure, such as indole, quinoline, and isoquinoline, is quite extensive. These hydrocarbons have been demonstrated to degrade under denitrifying,[34] methanogenic,[4,34,35] and sulfate-reducing conditions,[36] and the mechanism for the initial oxydation was shown to be identical to that for homocyclic aromatic hydrocarbons, namely, incorporation of oxygen from water into the aromatic substrate.[37] Furthermore, methanogenic aquifer microorganisms were shown to partially transform these compounds[5] or to completely mineralize them[6,38] in laboratory microcosms containing aquifer material contaminated by creosote. Benzothiophene, a sulfur heterocycle, is also degraded by such microcosms.[39]

In this chapter, we summarize the most recent results of our studies on anaerobic degradation (under methanogenic conditions) of toluene and o-xylene and of indene, naphthalene, indole, quinoline, isoquinoline, and benzothiophene by groundwater aquifer–derived microcosms and suspended microbial enrichments.

Materials and Methods

The aquifer material for these studies was derived from a creosote-contaminated groundwater aquifer in Pensacola, FL, at an abandoned wood-preserving plant;[40] it was collected using the continuous-flight auger method.[41] The samples were obtained from a depth of 5–6 m at a site 30 m downgradient from the contamination source. The groundwater at the sampling spot was devoid of dissolved oxygen, was approximately 60–70% saturated with respect to methane, and contained significant amounts of hydrogen sulfide as well as sufficient nitrogen and phosphorus concentrations for microbial activity.[38] Features of the site, aseptic and anaerobic sampling and sample transfer procedures, and the characterization of the aquifer sand have been described elsewhere.[6,38,39]

Toluene (Puresolv TM, scintillation grade) was purchased from Packard Instrument Co. (Downers Grove, IL); p-xylene and m-xylene (Baker TM grade) were obtained from J. T. Baker Co. (Phillipsburg, NJ). Benzene (99 + % pure), ethylbenzene (99 + % pure), o-xylene (98.2% pure, HPLC grade), naphthalene (99 + % pure, scintillation grade), heterocyclic aromatic hydrocarbons (indole, quinoline, isoquinoline, benzothiophene), oxygenated aromatic compounds (phenol, p-cresol), and all other chemicals used in these studies were obtained from Aldrich Chemical Co., Inc. (Milwaukee, WI). ^{14}C-methyl-labeled toluene (purity greater than 98%; specific activity 4.9 mCi/mmol), and ^{14}C-methyl-labeled o-xylene (purity greater than 98%) were purchased from Sigma Chemical Co. (St. Louis, MO).

The microcosms for the study of homocyclic aromatic hydrocarbon degradation were set up in 250-mL serum bottles sealed with Teflon-coated Mininert valves (Alltech Assoc.). The bottles contained 150 g of aquifer solids, 100 mL of prereduced defined mineral medium with vitamins, and 50 mL of headspace (30% CO_2 and 70% N_2). The medium was modified after Owen et al.[42] by

Table 15.1. Aromatic Substrates Added to Saturated Methanogenic Microcosms with Pensacola, Florida, Aquifer Solids and the Initial Degradation Results (260 Days of Static Incubation at 35°C)

Aromatic Compounds Added and Concentrations (mg/L)	Fate of Aromatic Substrates
Group 1 *Benzene (12)* *Naphthalene* (4)	No degradation of *aromatic hydrocarbons* during 260 days of incubation.
Group 2 *Benzene (12)* *Naphthalene* (4) Phenol (50)	Phenol completely degraded in 80 days of incubation. No degradation of *aromatic hydrocarbons* during 260 days of incubation.
Group 3 *Toluene* (4) *Ethylbenzene* (4) o-*Xylene* (4) p-*Xylene* (4)	*Toluene* completely degraded in 120 days of incubation. o-*Xylene* completely degraded in 255 days of incubation. No degradation of *ethylbenzene* or p-*xylene* during 260 days of incubation.
Group 4 *Toluene* (4) *Ethylbenzene* (4) o-*Xylene* (4) p-*Xylene (4)* p-Cresol (5)	p-Cresol completely degraded in 80 days of incubation. *Toluene* completely degraded in 100 days of incubation. o-*Xylene* completely degraded in 200 days of incubation. o-*Xylene* degradation starts after the first spike of *toluene* has been completely degraded; the two processes continue in parallel thereafter. No degradation of *ethylbenzene* or p-*xylene* during 260 days of incubation.

Note: Aromatic hydrocarbons are italicized; additional aromatic substrates are not.

reducing concentrations of all inorganic nutrients approximately one order of magnitude; adding zinc, selenium, and aluminum; and using amorphous ferrous sulfide as a reducing agent instead of a combination of sodium sulfide and ferrous chloride. The serum bottles containing the medium were autoclaved prior to microcosm preparation; vitamin solution and the buffering sodium bicarbonate solution were added after autoclaving and were sterilized by filtration through 0.2-μm pore-size microbiological filters. The microcosms were prepared and then incubated at 35°C in an anaerobic glovebox. Eight different combinations of aromatic hydrocarbons, with or without oxygenated aromatic compounds (phenol, p-cresol) as accessory substrates, were added as carbon and energy sources for microorganisms. Four groups of microcosms received mixtures of aromatic hydrocarbons (two to four components), with or without oxygenated aromatic compounds, in which each component was present at a concentration of at least 40 mg/L; these microcosms showed no microbial activity toward aromatic hydrocarbons. The other four groups received one order of magnitude lower concentrations of substrates; these four combinations are outlined in Table 15.1. No electron acceptors (except for CO_2) were added to the microcosms, thus creating conditions which should be conducive to fermentation and methanogenesis (after all the natural electron acceptors from the aquifer solids have been depleted). For each combination of the substrates, duplicate active microcosms and one autoclaved biological control (containing all the microcosm constituents) were established and monitored. The degradation of aromatic hydrocarbons, over time, was measured by sampling headspace (for aromatic hydrocarbon analysis) and liquid phase (for polar aromatics analysis) and analyzing the samples of Hewlett-Packard Series II Model 5890A gas chromatograph (Hewlett-Packard, Avondale, PA) with an HNU Model PI 52-02A photoionization detector (HNU Systems, Inc., Newton, MA) and a 30-m × 0.53-mm DB-624 megabore fused silica capillary column with 3-μm film thickness (Durabond, J and W, Inc., Rancho Cordova, CA).

Suspended mixed cultures degrading toluene and o-xylene were enriched from the active microcosms by transferring 20 mL of the liquid and approximately 10 g of the solid portion of the microcosms into 180-mL of defined anaerobic mineral media with toluene, o-xylene, or a combination of these substrates (4 mg/L each). After the degradation of the aromatic substrates had gone to completion, the cultures were refed 5 mg/L of each of the substrates, and upon completion of degradation of this secondary spike were transferred again (30 mL, after vigorous shaking) into 170 mL of fresh media with 5 mg/L of the respective substrates (single or in binary mixture). ^{14}C-labeled toluene and xylene were recently spiked to the suspended cultures in order to determine the mass balance of toluene and xylene degradation; the initial concentration of the label was 1000 dpm/mL for each compound. The ^{14}C activities in the headspace and the culture fluid were measured using Tri-Carb liquid scintillation system (No. 4530; Packard Instrument Co.), according to the procedure described by Grbic-Galic and Vogel.[15]

Microcosms for studies of methanogenic transformation of polynuclear, heterocyclic (indole, quinoline, isoquinoline, and benzothiophene), and homocyclic aromatic hydrocarbons (indene, naphthalene) were prepared in 500-mL serum bottles with approximately 400 g of aquifer solids and 250 mL of prereduced defined mineral medium as described by Godsy and Grbic-Galic.[39] Single hydrocarbons were added to the microcosms as sole organic carbon and energy sources in the concentration of 10–40 mg/L. Sorption of the examined compounds to aquifer solids had been found to be negligible.[6] Duplicate microcosms, autoclaved biological controls, and live controls unamended with aromatic hydrocarbons were monitored in parallel using daily sampling and analysis procedures. Gas chromatography (GC), mass spectrometry (GC-MS), and high-performance liquid chromatography (HPLC) techniques, used to monitor the disappearance of substrates, formation and transformation of intermediates, and production of final products, are described elsewhere.[6,38,39] In addition to the small microcosms, a large anaerobic microcosm containing approximately 4 kg of aquifer material and 2.5 L of contaminated groundwater from the site was set up in a 4-L hermetically sealed glass bottle equipped with gas- and liquid-sampling ports and a U-tube manometer.[6] The water in this microcosm was amended with amorphous ferrous sulfide as a reducing agent. The microcosm was used to follow the fate of some of the hydrocarbons listed above when present in a mixture (a simulation of the situation in the field). Gas production and composition, substrate transformation, and intermediate formation and degradation were monitored at 7-day intervals by using GC, HPLC, and GC-MS.[6] All the microcosms were incubated in an anaerobic chamber at 22°C.

Results and Discussion

Methanogenic Degradation of Homocyclic Aromatic Hydrocarbons[43]

As indicated in Table 15.1, methanogenic microcosms derived from the Pensacola aquifer underwent a long acclimation period before the onset of aromatic hydrocarbon degradation. Once the activity was enriched, 4–5 mg/L of toluene or *o*-xylene were degraded in approximately 2 weeks; initially, however, about 100–120 days were required for complete degradation of toluene, and 200–250 days for *o*-xylene. The initial lag period may be due to small populations originally present on the aquifer solids, especially when the microcosm size is so small, and to slow growth rates typical of anaerobic microbial communities. It may also be due to the absence of the required enzymatic activity, to the necessity of induction or a genetic event that would trigger the right type of catalysis, or to various other reasons.[44] We are currently experimenting with the fresh, unacclimated aquifer material from the same source in an attempt to find out whether the addition of higher concentrations of toluene (10 mg/L) or high concentrations of accessory carbon sources (100 mg/L *p*-cresol, 150 mg/L acetate) would accelerate the buildup of the aromatic-degrading community and decrease the initial lag.

The results in Table 15.1 suggest that the addition of *p*-cresol accelerates the onset of degradation of toluene and *o*-xylene. *p*-Cresol had been shown previously to be an early intermediate in degradation of toluene by anaerobic sludge-derived methanogenic consortia;[14,15] it is conceivable that this compound plays the same role in groundwater-derived methanogenic microcosms (Table 15.2). Our current work, which includes enrichment and isolation of pure cultures from toluene- and *o*-xylene-degrading microcosms, will hopefully elucidate the *p*-cresol effect.

Toluene and *o*-xylene were the only aromatic hydrocarbons degraded by these consortia; benzene, ethylbenzene, other xylene isomers, and naphthalene were not. The available literature on anaerobic degradation of aromatic hydrocarbons by aquifer microorganisms generally indicates that alkylated aromatic hydrocarbons are more easily degraded than the unsubstituted ones. There are also indications that the activity is site specific and that the compounds that are degraded in one aquifer will not necessarily be degraded under similar conditions in another aquifer. The microbial activity of this type is not ubiquitous. If the process application (*in situ* treatment) is considered, the first step with each specific site should be laboratory investigations of the indige-

Table 15.2. Homocyclic and Heterocyclic Aromatic Hydrocarbons Examined in This Study and Some of the Products of Their Methanogenic Degradation

Aromatic Hydrocarbons	Earliest Oxidation Intermediates Detected	Final Products
Toluene	p-Cresol[a]	CO$_2$, CH$_4$
o-Xylene		CO$_2$, CH$_4$
Indene		CO$_2$, CH$_4$
Naphthalene	2-Ethylphenol[a] Benzofuran[a]	CO$_2$, CH$_4$

Table 15.2, continued

Aromatic Hydrocarbons	Earliest Oxidation Intermediates Detected	Final Products
Indole	Oxindole	CO_2, CH_4
Quinoline	Quinolinone	CO_2, CH_4
Isoquinoline	Isoquinolinone	CO_2, CH_4
Benzothiophene	p-Hydroxysulfonic acid	CO_2, CH_4
	Phenylacetic acid	CO_2, CH_4
	Thiophene-2-ol	

[a]Intermediates not found in this study but indirectly implied (p-cresol from toluene) and detected in sludge-derived methanogenic consortia metabolizing the same aromatic hydrocarbon substrates.[14,15,22]

nous microorganisms and their capabilities under simulated aquifer conditions.

It is interesting to note that the examined microbial communities showed high specificity for only one (o-) of the three xylene isomers. Wilson et al., in contrast, observed degradation of both o-and m-xylenes by methanogenic microcosms derived from another contaminated groundwater aquifer.[29] The composition of microflora from these two sites is obviously different; groundwater chemistry and availability of specific nutrients might be among the numerous possible causes that could determine the makeup of the microbial communities.

Suspended, stable, mixed methanogenic cultures (consortia) were enriched from the active microcosms and tested for their capability to degrade toluene and o-xylene as sole organic carbon and energy sources. The results of these preliminary experiments are shown in Figures 15.1 and 15.2. One of the cultures was fed only toluene, another only o-xylene, and the third a mixture of these two compounds. In the microcosms, toluene was degraded first and o-xylene (a more complex substrate) second; in the acclimated suspended cultures the degradation of both compounds occurred simultaneously. Furthermore, the binary mixture does not seem to affect the degradation of either of the two compounds—the rates of removal of toluene and o-xylene as sole substrates are the same as the rates for the respective compounds in the mixture. Methane production occurs in all of the suspended cultures, with the amount of methane produced approaching very closely the stoichiometrically expected values. Isolation of pure cultures from the suspended consortia, which is under way, will help understand the community structure and answer

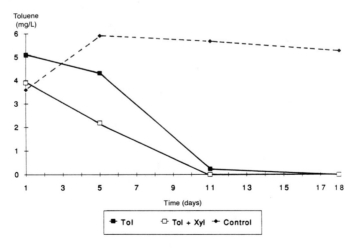

Figure 15.1. Toluene degradation by suspended mixed methanogenic cultures containing toluene or a mixture of toluene and xylene as carbon and energy sources. The chemical control contains both toluene and xylene. *Tol* = toluene; *Tol + Xyl* = toluene plus xylene.

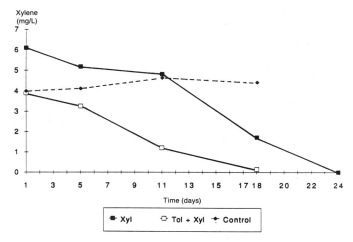

Figure 15.2. Xylene degradation by suspended mixed methanogenic cultures containing xylene or a mixture of toluene and xylene as carbon and energy sources. The chemical control contains both toluene and xylene. *Xyl* = xylene; *Tol + Xyl* = toluene plus xylene.

the question of whether the toluene and *o*-xylene degradation are catalyzed by the same group of microorganisms or by two different groups working simultaneously. We have also just started the use of ^{14}C-labeled toluene and *o*-xylene; this will enable us to perform accurate mass balances.

Methanogenic Degradation of Homocyclic and Heterocyclic Polynuclear Aromatic Hydrocarbons[6,38,39,45]

Transformation of indole (initial concentration 40 mg/L) in small microcosms fed this heterocycle as the sole organic carbon and energy source, started without a lag, and was completed in 25 days. The formation of oxindole, the earliest intermediate of indole oxidation (Table 15.2), started on day 6 and by day 16 reached the expected stoichiometric maximum, indicating complete conversion of indole. Oxindole persisted for a month, but afterwards was completely mineralized to CO_2 and CH_4 (day 53). Quinoline (initial concentration 20 mg/L) as sole substrate was oxidized after a lag period of 20 days; the degradation was completed in 55 days after the beginning of the incubation period. Isoquinoline was oxidized completely in 60 days; this period included 35 days of the initial lag. Quinolinone and isoquinolinone, the early transformation intermediates of quinoline and isoquinoline, respectively (see Table 15.2), were formed in stoichiometric amounts from their parent compounds; they persisted until quinoline and isoquinoline were completely removed and then were degraded, ultimately to carbon dioxide and methane. Additional transformation intermediates detected by HPLC and GC-MS in quinoline-degrading microcosms included 2,3-dimethylpyridine, aniline, benzoic acid, phenol, 1,9-nonanediol, nonanoic acid, and octanoic acid.[38,45] These intermediates indicate that the degradation of quinoline is initiated through introduction of an oxygen function (hydroxy group), most likely from water, and that subsequent degradation steps include side chain transformations and ring cleavage reactions typical of anaerobic degradation of oxygenated aromatic compounds.[16,17] Compounds like 2,3-dimethylpyridine suggest that not only the heterocyclic but also the homocyclic ring of quinoline may be the site of the initial oxidative attack. Similar results were obtained with benzothiophene, a sulfur heterocycle (10 mg/L initial concentration), whose degradation was started after a 12-day lag and was completed by day 24. We were not able to detect the earliest intermediate of benzothiophene transformation, but a whole series of oxidized mononuclear aromatic intermediates, both homocyclic and heterocyclic, were identified in the culture fluid: p-hydroxysulfonic acid, thiophene-2-ol, phenylacetic acid (see Table 15.2), 2-hydroxyphenylacetic acid, 2-oxophenylacetic acid, benzyl alcohol, benzoic acid, and phenol.[39,45] In addition to the aromatic intermediates, alicyclic compounds (cyclohexyl alcohol, cyclohexanecarbocylic acid) and aliphatics (2-methyl-2-hexanol, 3-hexenol, 2-methyl-1,2-propanediol, thiopropionic acid, hexanoic acid, 2-hexenoic acid) were also detected. All these intermediates were transient and completely disappeared by the end of the fourth week of incubation, when the substrate was ultimately converted to stoichiometric amounts of CO_2 and CH_4.

It is interesting to note that the early oxidation intermediates of nitrogen heterocycles (oxindole, quinolinone, isoquinolinone) persisted for a long time in the laboratory microcosms (and in the field, see the following), whereas the early oxidation intermediate of benzothiophene was further transformed so fast that we could not even detect it in the culture fluid. These results suggest that the nitrogen heterocycles are probably initially transformed by microorganisms different from those that transform sulfur heterocycles. The results also suggest that the populations that are responsible for degradation of oxidized nitrogen heterocycles are possibly present in very low numbers in the aquifer material and need to build up before the transformation of these compounds can be observed experimentally. This phenomenon is currently under investigation.

Indene and naphthalene, fed as individual substrates to the smaller microcosms, were completely degraded in from 1 (naphthalene) to 2 months (indene) with stoichiometric production of carbon dioxide and methane.[22] No intermediates were detected. It is interesting to note that microcosms of an even smaller size (150 g of aquifer solids, 100 mL of medium) used in a separate experiment, as well as the microcosms described previously in the section on toluene and o-xylene degradation (also containing only 150 g of aquifer solids and 100 mL of medium), did not degrade naphthalene in 10 months of incubation. The same was observed with benzothiophene. These results emphasize the impact of the small microbial numbers present in the subsurface and of the heterogeneity in microbial distribution within an aquifer. Smaller microcosms may easily be devoid of microorganisms that are crucial for the success of certain transformation processes.

The results from the largest microcosm tested (4 kg of aquifer solids, 2.5 L of contaminated groundwater) indicate that quinoline and isoquinoline are completely removed during the first 40 days of incubation; quinolinone and isoquinolinone take 150 and 180 days, respectively, but are also completely degraded to CO_2 and CH_4. Quinoline and isoquinoline degradation occurs simultaneously with the degradation of some of the other components in the contaminated groundwater−benzoic acid and volatile fatty acids. Quinoline and isoquinoline degradation precedes the degradation of phenol and cresols (sequential degradation in a complex mixture).[6] Acetic acid seems to be an intermediate in the methanogenic degradation of all of these compounds; it peaks shortly after benzoic acid and volatile fatty acids are eliminated and then peaks again concurrently with the removal of quinolinone, isoquinolinone, and cresols.[6] These findings can be conveniently compared with the observations from the field (Figure 15.3) because the groundwater velocity at the depth of 5–6 m is about 1 m/day and the distance traveled downgradient from the contamination source equals approximately the residence time in the large microcosm. The microcosm results simulate very closely the results of field measurements: quinoline and isoquinoline decrease disproportionately downgradient when compared to the conservative tracer (3,5-dimethylphenol)[38] and are completely removed within the first 50 m downgradient from the source, whereas their early oxidation intermediates, quinolinone and isoquinolinone, persist for about 200 m before they are eliminated. Furthermore, acetic acid, suggested to be an important intermediate in the laboratory methanogenic microcosms, temporarily increases also during the downgradient movement in the aquifer as creosote constituents are being degraded (not shown in the figure).[6] Figure 15.4 shows the behavior of homocyclic polynuclear aromatic hydrocarbons (PAH)−indene, naphthalene, 1-methylnaphthalene, 2-methylnaphthalene, and acenaphthene. Although the laboratory experiments indicated successful degradation of both indene and naphthalene to carbon dioxide and methane, field observations suggested efficient selective transformation of indene only, while the other PAH compounds remained persistent within the 200 m of the test zone. The difference between the laboratory and field results for PAH compounds (except for indene) does not necessarily mean that these compounds are not biodegradable in the field, but probably that they are not degraded during downgradient travel in this particular section of the aquifer.

Conclusions

The indigenous methanogenic communities from the Pensacola, Florida, groundwater aquifer (creosote contaminated) are capable of degrading two simple monoaromatic hydrocarbons−toluene and o-xylene−in laboratory microcosms and suspended cultures. Once the microbial cultures are adapted

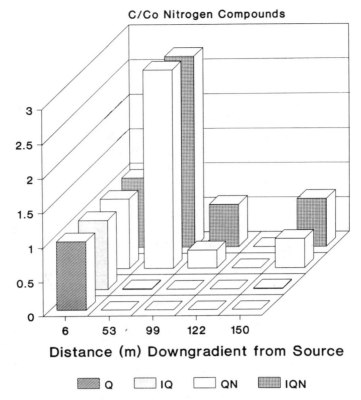

Figure 15.3.   Concentration of nitrogen heterocyclic compounds relative to the concentration of the conservative tracer (3,5-dimethylphenol), downgradient from the contamination source. *Q* = quinoline; *IQ* = isoquinoline; *QN* = quinolinone; *IQN* = isoquinolinone.

to the aromatic hydrocarbon substrates, the degradation occurs quickly (complete conversion to CO_2 and CH_4 in less than 2 weeks). Other compounds degraded include some constituents of the water-soluble fraction of creosote (indene, naphthalene, indole, quinoline, isoquinoline, and benzothiophene); the degradation of some of these compounds has been observed and measured also in the field. The fact that the number of compounds degraded increases with the microcosm size, stresses the importance of sufficiently abundant and diverse biomass in biodegradation of these contaminants under methanogenic conditions. This is important to keep in mind when designing possible *in situ* treatment; nutrient addition to encourage microbial growth might prove helpful.

According to the results of laboratory experiments with some of the compounds (indole, quinoline, isoquinoline, and benzothiophene), the initial transformation step is oxidative, and the oxygen for this reaction is probably

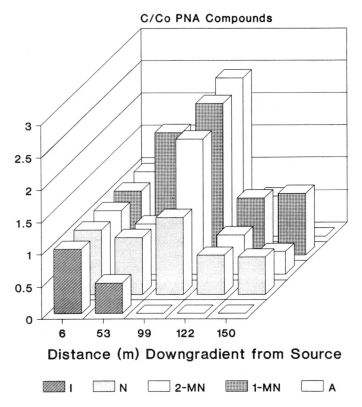

C/Co PNA Compounds

Distance (m) Downgradient from Source

| ▨ I | ▢ N | ▢ 2-MN | ▨ 1-MN | ▢ A |

Figure 15.4. Concentration of homocyclic PAH relative to the concentration of the conservative tracer, downgradient from the contamination source. *I* = indene; *N* = naphthalene; *2MN* = 2-methylnaphthalene; *1MN* = 1-methylnaphthalene; *A* = acenaphthene.

derived from water. A conclusive proof of this possibility was provided by Pereira et al. using $H_2^{18}O$ in sludge microcosms transforming quinoline.[37] After the initial oxidation, the transformation pathways overlap with the pathways previously suggested for oxygenated aromatic compounds. In general, the overall pathways for polynuclear heterocyclic compound transformation seem to be similar to the degradation routes for mononuclear homocyclic aromatic hydrocarbons under methanogenic conditions.[14,15]

AEROBIC MICROBIAL TRANSFORMATION OF TRICHLOROETHYLENE

Background

In 1985, Wilson and Wilson suggested that methanotrophic communities from soil might be responsible for aerobic degradation of trichloroethylene (TCE).[12] This finding resulted in an explosion of research on the topic, and soon results were published that indicated that mixed cultures consisting of methanotrophs and heterotrophs—which were quite common in soil, sediments, and the subsurface—could completely mineralize this compound to carbon dioxide, chloride, and water.[46-50] The first step of TCE transformation by methanotrophs is most likely an epoxidation to TCE-epoxide, catalyzed by methane monooxygenase (an enzyme with a very broad substrate specificity), as first proposed by Henry and Grbic-Galic.[47] The epoxide is extremely unstable in aqueous solution and breaks down into various products that can be degraded by heterotrophs. Several researchers have succeeded in isolating pure cultures of methanotrophs that transform TCE,[51,52,53] or in detecting and analyzing the activity in known methanotrophic strains.[54,55] In addition to methanotrophs, other bacteria are capable of fortuitous transformation of this compound, such as ethylene oxidizers,[52,65] propane oxidizers[56] and pseudomonads that grow on aromatic compounds.[57-60]

The investigations at Stanford University of TCE transformation by methanotrophs started in the form of parallel efforts in the field and in the laboratory. The field experiment (Moffett Field Naval Air Station, Mountain View, CA) concentrated on stimulation of growth of the indigenous methanotrophic communities by injecting methane and oxygen into the aquifer; the resulting activity toward TCE and other halogenated aliphatics was then observed.[61] In the laboratory, detailed studies were undertaken in microcosm systems and with suspended mixed and pure methanotrophic cultures in order to learn about the relevant microorganisms and about the prerequisites and optimal conditions for the TCE transformation process. Some of these laboratory studies are described in the following.

Materials and Methods

Microcosms Containing Aquifer Solids[62-64]

The aquifer solids were obtained from a pristine part of the Moffett Naval Air Station site from a depth of 5–7 m, using a hollow-stem auger drilling rig.[63] The solids consisted of a fine to coarse sand, gravel, and minor clay. The inner portion of the core was aseptically removed with a sterilized metal pipe, and the <2-mm size fraction used to pack six glass columns (40 × 2 cm). The columns were saturated with air-stripped and filter-sterilized groundwater from the site; the same water was used for all the subsequent exchanges.[62] Each of the columns received 50 μg/L of ^{14}C-labeled TCE. Four of the columns received dissolved methane; two did not (controls). Two of the methane-fed columns (5 mg/L dissolved methane) and one of the two control columns were amended with 22 mg/L of dissolved oxygen (the water had been saturated with O_2 by bubbling pure oxygen through it for an hour before use), while the other two methane-fed columns (saturated methane solution) and the remaining control received hydrogen peroxide (85 mg/L) instead of oxygen. The 22 mg/L of dissolved oxygen in the O_2-amended columns were sufficient to maintain aerobic conditions even after all the methane was depleted. All the columns (incubated at 22°C) were operated as sequential batch reactors at the exchange intervals of 3 days to 2 weeks. The maintenance of the columns and exchanges and the establishment of a breakthrough curve using bromide, dissolved oxygen, and dissolved methane as tracers have been described elsewhere.[62,63] The effluent was analyzed for methane concentration (by GC), dissolved oxygen (by dissolved oxygen probe), ^{14}C-labeled TCE and other ^{14}C-labeled compounds (by GC and scintillation counting), and hydrogen peroxide (by peroxide test strips, EM Science, and titration with ceric sulfate).[62-64]

Additional experiments were performed in 35-mL batch microcosms that were periodically sacrificed for measurements.[64] The microcosms were completely filled, without headspace, and contained 1.5 g of well-mixed aquifer solids from the columns, 2 mL column effluent, and a mineral medium with 4.5 mg/L of dissolved methane, 24 mg/L of dissolved oxygen, and 50 μg/L of TCE. At each measuring interval, triplicate microcosms were sacrificed. Each of them was analyzed for methane, dissolved oxygen, ^{14}C-labeled TCE, and $^{14}CO_2$. Batch microcosms were used to study the interaction between the concentration of methane present and TCE degradation and the influence of formate and methanol addition on the TCE transformation under no-growth conditions.

Suspended Mixed and Pure Cultures[65]

Mixed cultures consisting of methanotrophic and heterotrophic bacteria were enriched from aquifer solids or groundwater from the Moffett Field site. Continuously stirred reactors containing 1 L of defined mineral medium[65] under a continuous flow of 25% methane in air were inoculated with approximately 1 g of aquifer solids or 20 mL of groundwater. The reactors were then incubated at room temperature. Stable enrichments were obtained by five to ten sequential transfers to new reactors and were confirmed by microscopic and macroscopic observations (consistent micromorphology and macromorphology). A pure methanotrophic culture was obtained from one of the stable enrichments by streaking dilutions of the mixed culture on agarose plates with defined mineral medium and incubating the plates in an atmosphere of approximately 25% methane in air. Culture purity was proven by growth in defined mineral medium with methane as the sole organic carbon and energy source, by the absence of growth on multicarbon substrates, and by scanning and transmission electron microscopy.[52,65]

Three stable suspended mixed cultures and the pure culture were tested for their capabilities to transform TCE by transferring actively growing cultures from the reactors (in which they were incubated under a continuous stream of approximately 35% methane in air) to shake flasks. The bottles of degradation studies were incubated upside-down on a shaker at 21°C. In addition to the defined mineral medium cited above, Whittenbury mineral medium[66] was used for some of the experiments. The effects of CH_4, O_2, and TCE concentrations, reducing power availability, and mineral medium formulation on TCE transformation were studied. The techniques used in these experiments are extensively described elsewhere,[52,53,65,67-71] and include cell biomass determination on a dry-weight basis; staining with sudan black B for lipid storage granules;[72] radiotracer experiments with ^{14}C-labeled TCE; sampling of culture headspace for unlabeled TCE and analysis on a Tracor GC Model MT-220 DPFFN (Tracor, Austin, TX), equipped with an electron capture detector (method developed by Criddle[10]); gas partitioning for analysis of CO_2, O_2 and CH_4 in the headspace; evaluation of acid intermediates on a Dionex ion chromatograph Series 4000i (Dionex Corporation, Sunnyvale, CA); and detection of carbon monoxide as a TCE transformation product on a Trace Analytical RGD2 reduction gas detector (Trace Analytical, Menlo Park, CA).

The maximum TCE transformation rate coefficient k (d[-1]), the half-saturation constant K_s (mg/L), and second-order rate coefficient k/K_s (L/mg-day) were determined using Monod kinetics for substrate degradation, $-dS/dt = kXS/(K_S + S)$, where S equals TCE concentration (mg/L); X, biomass concentration (mg/L); and K_s, half-saturation coefficient for TCE (mg/L). Except where noted, no methane was added, and it was assumed that the biomass concentration, X, was constant during the duration of the experiments. The correlation coefficient for the fit of the data to the model was greater than 0.95.[65] The mass of TCE was converted to aqueous concentration using a dimensionless Henry's constant of 0.33 at 21°C.

Results and Discussion

Microcosms Containing Aquifer Solids[62,64]

After 3 months of feeding methane and oxygen (in which period an active methanotrophic community was successfully established), the columns were amended with TCE. The added TCE was strongly sorbed to the aquifer solids so that only half of ^{14}C-labeled TCE could be recovered in the effluent after the treatment period.[62] After nearly 1 year of operation, the stabilized communities in the columns degraded 15 to 20% of TCE to [14]CO_2; no activity toward TCE was observed in the control column, which was fed no methane. These results agree very well with the results from the field,[61] where 20% removal of TCE was the maximum value observed; sorption seems to be the major limiting factor. No transformation products other than CO_2 were observed in the column effluent.

The addition of hydrogen peroxide as an oxygen source decreased the methane consumption. Whereas oxygen-amended columns consumed 98% of the added methane in the 3-day exchange period, the hydrogen peroxide–amended ones consumed only 87%. However, more oxygen was utilized by bacteria in the H_2O_2-amended columns than in the oxygen-amended columns, indicating that hydrogen peroxide had a negative impact on the methanotrophs, possibly enabling the heterotrophs to outcompete the methanotrophs for the available oxygen. The high oxygen concentrations generated by H_2O_2, rather than the H_2O_2 itself, could have been the agent that caused the inhibition of the methanotrophic activity. In the experiments with suspended microbial cultures, high oxygen inhibited TCE transformation (see the following section).[65] No TCE-degradation experiments were performed in the H_2O_2-amended columns.

Batch microcosm results indicated temporal separation of methane utilization and TCE transformation. This suggests a possible competition between methane and TCE for the active sites on the same enzyme (see the following section) and the continuation of the enzyme activity in the absence of the growth substrate, probably due to utilization of reducing power from the internal bacterial storages, as suggested by Henry et al.[52] The addition of formate (an energy source for methanotrophs) and, to a lesser degree, methanol (Figure 15.5) increased the amount of TCE converted to CO_2 in the absence of methane, emphasizing the importance of an accessory energy (reducing power) source for TCE degradation by methanotrophic communities.

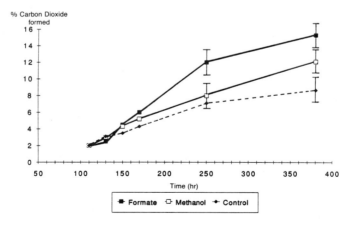

Figure 15.5. The effect of formate and methanol addition on TCE transformation by batch microcosms in the absence of methane. Each data point represents the mean of measurements on triplicate microcosms. Bars represent one standard deviation. Modified after Lanzarone et al.[763]

Suspended Mixed and Pure Cultures[47,52,53,65,67-71]

Three micromorphologically and macromorphologically different methane-grown mixed cultures were enriched from the Moffett Field groundwater aquifer: culture MM1 from aquifer solids; culture MM3 from groundwater; and culture MM2 from the effluent of a TCE-degrading, methane-enriched column packed with the aquifer solids.[63] All of them consisted of various gram-negative bacteria; MM2 also contained a fungus (yeast). MM1 and MM3 contained only type II methanotrophs; MM2 contained both types I and II. The methanotrophs in mixed cultures MM1 and MM3 had lipid storage granules; methanotrophs in the mixed culture MM2 did not.[52,53,65,69] A pure culture of a type I methanotroph was isolated from MM2 and characterized as a *Methylomonas* sp. strain MM2.[53] The pure culture grew well on methane and methanol but did not grow on multicarbon substrates; it lacked lipid storage granules.

MM1, MM2, MM3, and *Methylomonas* sp. strain MM2 all transformed TCE in the presence of methane as well as in its absence (no-growth conditions). Rates varied from 2.3 L/mg-day to 0.003 L/mg-day (second-order rate coefficient k/K_s), depending on culture characteristics, growth, and incubation conditions. Coefficient K_s (mg/L), which can be interpreted to represent the affinity of the enzyme for TCE, varied with culture and growth conditions, ranging from 0.2 to 1.3 mg/L.[65,70] When sufficient reducing power was available, 100% of the TCE was transformed. Acetylene inhibited TCE oxidation and methane oxidation. Methane competitively inhibited TCE oxidation. The main product in the mixed cultures was CO_2 (mineralization); a significant portion of carbon from ^{14}C-labeled TCE was associated with the biomass, and a smaller fraction (5-10%) remained in nonvolatile aqueous products. In the pure culture, 70-80% of the TCE carbon remained in nonvolatile aqueous intermediates, 10-20% was associated with the biomass, and the rest was converted to CO_2.[65] Three unidentified acids were present in the aqueous intermediate fraction. Standard coelution on the ion chromatograph confirmed that these acids were not monochloroacetate, dichloroacetate, trichloroacetate, or glyoxylate. Both formate and carbon monoxide were found to be transformation intermediates, and both were oxidized by the pure culture.[71]

Mixed cultures MM1 and MM2 and the pure culture *Methylomonas* sp. strain MM2 were tested for their capability to transform TCE with no, low, and high concentrations of methane present (0, 0.45, and 4.5 mg/L initial aqueous concentration). The high concentration of methane slowed down TCE transformation, as would be expected because of the phenomenon of competitive inhibition. However, MM2 and the pure culture exhibited significantly slower rates of TCE transformation in the absence of methane. This corresponds to their lack of lipid storage granules.[69] Lipid inclusions-containing MM1, in contrast, transformed TCE equally well, both in the presence and absence of methane. The methane monooxygenase system, which is responsible for the TCE oxidation, requires a source of reducing power to reduce the residual atom from the oxygen molecule to water.[73] Lipid storage granules (an internal source of reducing power) should facilitate the transformation process in the absence of the growth substrate.[65,69] In another experiment, the cultures that contained lipid inclusions (MM1 and MM3) remained active toward TCE for a longer time under starvation conditions than did the culture that lacked lipid granules (MM2).[69] The addition of formate (an auxiliary reducing power source) to methane-starved *Methylomonas* MM2 cells increased the TCE transformation rate and enabled the microorganism to sustain the TCE transformation longer than in the absence of formate.[69]

Oxygen is required by methanotrophs both for respiration and for the oxidative function of the methane monooxygenase. Many methanotrophs, however, have been described as microaerophilic and grow best at oxygen tensions below atmospheric. High oxygen concentrations at 50% of headspace were inhibitory, reducing TCE transformation by approximately 20% in all the cultures tested. Oxygen at 35% was not inhibitory. When cultures were incubated under near-anoxic conditions ($< 1\% \ O_2$), very little methane or TCE was oxidized. When oxygen was depleted, TCE transformation stopped.[65] High concentrations of TCE were toxic to the cultures. At TCE concentrations up to 10 mg/L, all the methane present was utilized, and all the TCE transformed by mixed cultures. At 44 mg/L of TCE, no methane was utilized and only 20% of the TCE was transformed.[65] There were indications that the TCE oxidation itself was toxic to the pure culture. The *Methylomonas* sp. strain MM2 cells that oxidized TCE maintained at a concentration equal to or not greater than 6 mg/L were significantly impaired in their capability to oxidize methane in a subsequent experiment.[67]

Carbon monoxide, a TCE transformation product which was oxidized by *Methylomonas* sp. strain MM2, had a significant inhibitory effect on TCE oxidation. This was due, at least in part, to the competitive inhibition exerted by carbon monoxide.[71]

The mineral medium for microbial growth influenced the TCE transformation rate significantly. Growth in Whittenbury mineral medium,[66] which contained EDTA (a metal chelator) and FeEDTA, resulted in a three-fold (*Methylomonas* sp. strain MM2) to 15-fold (MM1) increase in the rate of TCE transformation.[53,65] Omission of EDTA from the Whittenbury mineral medium resulted in an order-of-magnitude decrease in rates of TCE transformation. EDTA may be affecting the availability of a required metal, or sequestering an inhibitory one.

Conclusions

Different mixed methanotrophic/heterotrophic cultures transforming TCE were isolated from the Moffett Field aquifer when different selection procedures were used. This indicates a great heterogeneity of microbial communities in the subsurface. The site was not initially contaminated with TCE; the capabilities of the indigenous methanotrophs to tackle this compound are due not to adaptation but to the broad substrate specificities of their methane monooxygenases. Methanotrophs are crucial both as members of the food chain and as catalysts in the degradation of TCE. They support heterotrophs with their metabolic by-products, and by oxidizing TCE they promote the formation of TCE transformation intermediates that can be mineralized by the heterotrophs.

In process applications, methanotrophs may be exposed to methane depletion either accidentally or intentionally as a part of the process design. Formate addition would provide a source of reducing power during such periods of starvation and might serve to both increase TCE transformation rates and prolong TCE transformation in the absence of methane. In the field experiment, addition of formate resulted in increased removal of TCE during periods of methane depletion.[61] Methanotrophs with storage polymers such as lipid inclusions contain an endogenous reserve of reducing power and may survive starvation and transform TCE during starvation for longer periods than those that lack storage polymers. Such methanotrophs may be well suited for process applications in which methane depletion occurs. It may be desirable to seed reactors with lipid inclusions–containing methanotrophs and to promote the growth of such methanotrophs in field applications.

The aquifer methanotrophs used in these studies were sensitive to hydrogen peroxide exposure and to high concentrations of oxygen. The potential for inhibition should be taken into consideration if H_2O_2 or pure oxygen is used in methanotrophic treatment applications. The pronounced influence of the growth medium formulation on TCE transformation rates indicates that the groundwater chemistry will be very important in successful *in situ* treatment; this phenomenon, as well as the phenomena of TCE oxidation toxicity and inhibition of TCE transformation by the degradation product carbon monoxide, should be considered in the design of process applications.

ACKNOWLEDGMENTS

This work has been funded by grants from the U.S. Air Force Office of Scientific Research (AFOSR 88-0351), U.S. Environmental Protection Agency (EPA CR 815721-01-0 and EPA R 815738-01-0-OCS), and U.S. Department of Interior (DOI 14-08-0001A-1357), all awarded to D. Grbic-Galic, and by the U.S. Environmental Protection Agency grant EPA CR-812220-01-0, awarded to P. V. Robertson which D. Grbic-Galic was a coprincipal investigator. The views and conclusions contained in this chapter are those of the authors and should not be interpreted as necessarily representing the official policies or endorsements, either expressed or implied, of the Air Force Office of Scientific Research, the U.S. EPA, or the U.S. government.

REFERENCES

1. Lee, M. D., J. M. Thomas, R. C. Borden, P. B. Bedient, C. H. Ward, and J. T. Wilson. "Biorestoration of Aquifers Contaminated with Organic Compounds," *CRC Crit. Rev. Environ. Control* 18(1):29–89 (1988).
2. Gibson, D. T., and V. Subramanian. "Microbial Degradation of Aromatic Hydrocarbons," in *Microbial Degradation of Organic Compounds*, D. T. Gibson, Ed. (New York: Marcel Dekker, 1984), pp. 181–252.
3. Chapman, P. J. "Degradation Mechanisms" in *Proceedings of the Workshop: "Microbial Degradation of Pollutants in Marine Environments,"* P. H. Pritchard, Ed., U.S. EPA Report-600/9-79-012 (1979), pp. 28–66.
4. Bennett, J. L., D. M. Updegraff, W. E. Pereira, and C. E. Rostad. "Isolation and Identification of Four Species of Quinoline-Degrading Pseudomonads from a Creosote-Contaminated Site at Pensacola, Florida," *Microbios Letters* 29:147–154 (1985).
5. Pereira, W. C., C. E. Rostad, D. M. Updegraff, and J. L. Bennett. "Fate and Movement of Azaarenes and Their Anaerobic Biotransformation Products in an Aquifer Contaminated by Wood-Treatment Chemicals," *J. Environ. Toxicol. Chem.* 6:163–176 (1987).
6. Godsy, E. M., D. F. Goerlitz, and D. Grbic-Galic. "Transport and Degradation of Water-Soluble Creosote-Derived Compounds," in *Intermedia Pollutant Transport: Modeling and Field Measurements*, D. T. Allen, Y. Cohen, and I. R. Kaplan, Eds. (New York: Plenum Press, 1989), pp. 213–236.
7. Vogel, T. M., C. S. Criddle, and P. L. McCarty. "Transformations of Halogenated Aliphatic Compounds," *Environ. Sci. Technol.* 21(8):722–736 (1987).
8. Vogel, T. M., and P. L. McCarty. "Biotransformation of Tetrachloroethylene to Trichloroethylene, Dichloroethylene, Vinyl Chloride, and Carbon Dioxide under Methanogenic Conditions," *Appl. Environ. Microbiol.* 49:1080–1083 (1985).
9. Barrio-Lage, G., F. Z. Parsons, R. S. Nassar, and P. A. Lorenzo. "Sequential Dehalogenation of Chlorinated Ethenes," *Environ. Sci. Technol.* 20:96–99 (1986).
10. Criddle, C. S. "Reductive Dehalogenation in Microbial and Electrolytic Model Systems," PhD Thesis, Stanford University, Stanford, CA (1989).
11. Bouwer, E. J., B. E. Rittmann, and P. L. McCarty. "Anaerobic Degradation of Halogenated 1- and 2-Carbon Organic Compounds," *Environ. Sci. Technol.* 15:596–599 (1981).
12. Wilson, J. T., and B. H. Wilson. "Biotransformation of Trichloroethylene in Soil," *Appl. Environ. Microbiol.* 29:242–243 (1985).
13. Ward, D. M., R. M. Atlas, P. D. Boehm, and J. A. Calder. "Microbial Biodegradation and Chemical Evolution of Oil from the Amoco Spill," *AMBIO, J. Human Environ. Res. Manag., Royal Swedish Acad. Sci.* 9:277–283 (1980).
14. Vogel, T. M., and D. Grbic-Galic. "Incorporation of Oxygen from Water into Toluene and Benzene During Anaerobic Fermentative Transformation," *Appl. Environ. Microbiol.* 52:200–202 (1986).
15. Grbic-Galic, D., and T. M. Vogel. "Transformation of Toluene and Benzene by Mixed Methanogenic Cultures," *Appl. Environ. Microbiol.* 53:254–260 (1987).
16. Healy, J. B., Jr., L. Y. Young, and M. Reinhard. "Methanogenic Decomposition of Ferulic Acid, a Model Lignin Derivative," *Appl. Environ. Microbiol.* 39:436–444 (1980).

17. Grbic-Galic, D. "Anaerobic Degradation of Coniferyl Alcohol by Methanogenic Consortia," *Appl. Environ. Microbiol.* 46:1442–1446 (1983).
18. Kochi, J. K., R. T. Tang, and T. Bernath. "Mechanisms of Aromatic Substitution. Role of Cation-Radicals in the Oxidative Substitution of Arenes by Cobalt(III)," *J. Am. Chem. Soc.* 95:7114–7123 (1973).
19. Fukuzumi, S., and J. K, Kochi. "Electrophilic Aromatic Substitution: Charge-Transfer Excited States and the Nature of the Activated Complex," *J. Am. Chem. Soc.* 103:7240–7252 (1981).
20. Mihelcic, J. R., and R. G. Luthy. "Degradation of Polycyclic Aromatic Hydrocarbon Compounds under Various Redox Conditions in Soil-Water Systems," *Appl. Environ. Microbiol.* 54:1182–1187 (1988).
21. Mihelcic, J. R., and R. G. Luthy. "Microbial Degradation of Acenaphthene and Naphthalene under Denitrification Conditions in Soil-Water Systems," *Appl. Environ. Microbiol.* 54:1188–1198 (1988).
22. Grbic-Galic, D. "Microbial Degradation of Homocyclic and Heterocyclic Aromatic Hydrocarbons under Anaerobic Conditions," *Dev. Industr. Microbiol.* 30:237–253 (1979).
23. Schwarzenbach, R. P., W. Giger, E. Hoehn, and J. K. Schneider. "Behavior of Organic Compounds During Infiltration of River Water to Ground Water: Field Studies," *Environ. Sci. Technol.* 17:472–479 (1983).
24. Reinhard, M., N. L. Goodman, and J. F. Barker. "Occurrence and Distribution of Organic Chemicals in Two Landfill Leachate Plumes," *Environ. Sci. Technol.* 18:953–961 (1984).
25. Kuhn, E. P., P. J. Colberg, J. R. Schnoor, O. Wanner, A. J. B. Zehnder, and R. P. Schwarzenbach. "Microbial Transformations of Substituted Benzenes During Infiltration of River Water to Ground Water: Laboratory Column Studies," *Environ. Sci. Technol.* 19:961–968 (1985).
26. Zeyer, J., E. P. Kuhn, and R. P. Schwarzenbach. "Rapid Microbial Mineralization of Toluene and 1,3-Dimethylbenzene in the Absence of Molecular Oxygen," *Appl. Environ. Microbiol.* 52:944–947 (1986).
27. Kuhn, E. P., J. Zeyer, P. Eicher, and R. P. Schwarzenbach. "Anaerobic Degradation of Alkylated Benzenes in Denitrifying Laboratory Aquifer Columns," *Appl. Environ. Microbiol.* 54:490–496 (1988).
28. Wilson, B. H., G. B. Smith, and J. F. Rees. "Biotransformations of Selected Alkylbenzenes and Halogenated Aliphatic Hydrocarbons in Methanogenic Aquifer Material: A Microcosm Study," *Environ. Sci. Technol.* 20:997–1002 (1986).
29. Wilson, B. H., B. Bledsoe, and D. Kampbell. "Biological Processes Occurring at an Aviation Gasoline Spill Site," in *Chemical Quality of Water and the Hydrologic Cycle*, R. C. Averett and D. M. McKnight, Eds. (Chelsea, MI: Lewis Publishers, 1987), pp. 125–137.
30. Major, D. W., C. I. Mayfield, and J. F. Barker. "Biotransformation of Benzene by Denitrification in Aquifer Sand," *Ground Water* 26(1):8–14 (1988).
31. Reinhard, M., F. Haag, and P. L. McCarty. "Selective Degradation of Toluene and *p*-Xylene in an Anaerobic Microcosm," in *International Symposium on Processes Governing the Movement and Fate of Contaminants in the Subsurface Environment: Paper Abstracts* (San Francisco: International Association on Water Pollution Research and Control; and Stanford, CA: Western Regional Hazardous Substance Research Center, 1989), p. A5.
32. Lovley, D. R., M. J. Baedecker, D. J. Lonergan, I. M. Cozzarelli, E. J. P. Phil-

lips, and D. I. Siegel. "Oxidation of Aromatic Contaminants Coupled to Microbial Iron Reduction," *Nature* 339:297–300 (1989).

33. Zeyer, J., P. Eicher, J. Dolfing, and R. P. Schwarzenbach. "Anaerobic Degradation of Aromatic Hydrocarbons," in *Advances in Applied Biotechnology Series, Volume 4: Biotechnology and Biodegradation*, D. Kamely, A. Chakrabarty, and G. S. Omenn, Eds. (Houston: Gulf Publishing Co., 1990), pp. 33–40.

34. Madsen, E. L., A. J. Francis, and J.-M. Bollag. "Environmental Factors Affecting Indole Metabolism under Anaerobic Conditions," *Appl. Environ. Microbiol.* 54:74–78 (1988).

35. Berry, D. L., E. L. Madsen, and J.-M. Bollag. "Conversion of Indole to Oxindole under Methanogenic Conditions," *Appl. Environ. Microbiol.* 53:80–182 (1987).

36. Bak, F., and F. Widdel. "Anaerobic Degradation of Indolic Compounds by Sulfate-Reducing Enrichment Cultures, and Description of *Desulfobacterium indolicum* gen. nov. sp. nov.," *Arch. Microbiol.* 146:170–176 (1986).

37. Pereira, W. E., C. E. Rostad, T. J. Leiker, D. M. Updegraff, and J. L. Bennett. "Microbial Hydroxylation of Quinoline in Contaminated Ground Water: Evidence for Incorporation of the Oxygen Atom of Water," *Appl. Environ. Microbiol.* 54:827–829 (1988).

38. Godsy, E. M., D. F. Goerlitz, and D. Grbic-Galic. "Anaerobic Biodegradation of Creosote Contaminants in Natural and Simulated Ground Water Ecosystems," in *U.S. Geological Survey Toxic Waste—Ground Water Contamination Program: Proceedings of the Third Technical Meeting*, B. J. Franks, Ed., U.S. Geological Survey Open-File Report 87–109 (1987), pp. A17–A19.

39. Godsy, E. M., and D. Grbic-Galic. "Biodegradation Pathways for Benzothiophene in Methanogenic Microcosms," in *U.S. Geological Survey Toxic Substances Hydrology Program—Proceedings of the Technical Meeting*, G. E. Mallard and S. E. Ragone, Eds., U.S. Geological Survey Water-Resources Investigation Report 88-4220 (1989), pp. 559–564.

40. Mattraw, H. C., Jr., and B. J. Franks. "Description of Hazardous Waste Research at a Creosote Works, Pensacola, Florida," in *Movement and Fate of Creosote Waste in Ground Water, Pensacola, Florida: U.S. Geological Survey Toxic Waste-Ground Water Contamination Program*, H. C. Mattraw, Jr., and B. E. Franks, Eds., U.S. Geological Survey Water Supply Paper 2285 (1984), pp. 1–12.

41. Schalf, M. R., J. F. McNabb, W. J. Dunlap, R. L. Crosby, and J. S. Fryberger. *Manual of Ground Water Sampling Procedures: NWWA/EPA Series* (Worthington, OH: National Water Well Association, 1981), p. 93.

42. Owen, W. F., D. C. Stuckey, J. B. Healy, Jr., L. Y. Young, and P. L. McCarty. "Bioassay for Monitoring Biochemical Methane Potential and Anaerobic Toxicity," *Water Research* 13:485–492 (1979).

43. Edwards, E., and D. Grbic-Galic. "Anaerobic Biodegradation of Homocyclic Aromatic Compounds," in *Abstr. Annu. Meet. Amer. Soc. Microbiol.* (Washington, DC: American Society for Microbiology, 1990).

44. Linkfield, T. H., J. M. Suflita, and J. M. Tiedje. "Characterization of the Acclimation Period before Anaerobic Dehalogenation of Halobenzoates," *Appl. Environ. Microbiol.* 55:2273–2278 (1989).

45. Grbic-Galic, D. "Anaerobic Microbial Transformation of Nonoxygenated Aromatic and Alicyclic Compounds in Soil, Subsurface, and Freshwater Sediments," in *Soil Biochemistry, Vol. 6*, J.-M. Bollag and G. Stotzky, Eds. (New York: Marcel Dekker, 1990), pp. 117–189.

46. Fogel, M. M., A. R. Taddeo, and S. Fogel. "Biodegradation of Chlorinated Ethenes by a Methane-Utilizing Mixed Culture," *Appl. Environ. Microbiol.* 51:720–724 (1986).

47. Henry, S. M., and D. Grbic-Galic. "Aerobic Degradation of Trichloroethylene (TCE) by Methylotrophs Isolated from a Contaminated Aquifer," in *Abstr. Annu. Meet. Amer. Soc. Microbiol.* (Washington, DC: American Society for Microbiology, 1986), p. 294.

48. Henson, J. M., M. V. Yates, J. W. Cochran, and D. L. Shackleford. "Microbial Removal of Halogenated Methanes, Ethanes, and Ethylenes in an Aerobic Soil Exposed to Methane," *FEMS Microbial. Ecol.* 53:193–201 (1988).

49. Henson, J. M., M. V. Yates, and J. W. Cochran. "Metabolism of Chlorinated Methanes, Ethanes,and Ethylenes by a Mixed Bacterial Culture Growing on Methane," *J. Industr. Microbiol.* 4:29–35 (1989).

50. Strand, S. E., M. D. Bjelland, and H. D. Stensel. "Kinetics of Chlorinated Hydrocarbon Degradation by Suspended Cultures of Methane-Oxidizing Bacteria," *Res. J. WPCF* 62(2):124–129 (1990).

51. Little, C. D., A. V. Palumbo, S. E. Herbes, M. E. Lidstrom, R. L. Tyndall, and P. J. Gilmer. "Trichloroethylene Biodegradation by a MethaneOxidizing Bacterium," *Appl. Environ. Microbiol.* 54:951–956 (1988).

52. Henry, S. M., F. Thomas, and D. Grbic-Galic. "Electron Microscopy Studies of TCE-Degrading Ground-Water Bacteria," in *Abstracts of the 9th Annual Meeting of the Society for Environmental Toxicology and Chemistry* (Washington, DC: Society for Environmental Toxicology and Chemistry, 1988), p. 74.

53. Henry, S. M., and D. Grbic-Galic. "Effect of Mineral Media on Trichloroethylene Oxidation by Aquifer Methanotrophs," *J. Microbial Ecol.* 20:106–137 (1990).

54. Oldenhuis, R., R. L. J. M. Vink, D. B. Janssen, and B. Witholt. "Degradation of Chlorinated Aliphatic Hydrocarbons by *Methylosinus trichosporium* OB3b Expressing Soluble Methane Monooxygenase," *Appl. Environ. Microbiol.* 55:2819–2826 (1989).

55. Tsien, H.-C., G. A. Brusseau, R. S. Hanson, and L. P. Wackett. "Biodegradation of Trichloroethylene by *Methylosinus trichosporium* OB3b," *Appl. Environ. Microbiol.* 55:3155–3161 (1989).

56. Wackett, L. P., G. A. Brusseau, S. R. Householder, and R. S. Hanson. "Survey of Microbial Oxygenases: Trichloroethylene Degradation by Propane-Oxidizing Bacteria," *Appl. Environ. Microbiol.* 55:2960–2964 (1989).

57. Nelson, M. J. K., S. O. Montgomery, E. J. O'Neill, and P. H. Pritchard. "Aerobic Metabolism of Trichloroethylene by a Bacterial Isolate," *Appl. Environ. Microbiol.* 52:383–384 (1986).

58. Nelson, M. J. K., S. O. Montgomery, W. R. Mahaffey, and P. H. Pritchard. "Biodegradation of Trichloroethylene and Involvement of an Aromatic Biodegradative Pathway," *Appl. Environ. Microbiol.* 53:949–954 (1987).

59. Nelson, M. J. K., S. O. Montgomery, and P. H. Pritchard. "Trichloroethylene Metabolism by Microorganisms That Degrade Aromatic Compounds," *Appl. Environ. Microbiol.* 54:604–606 (1988).

60. Wackett, L. P., and D. T. Gibson. "Degradation of Trichloroethylene by Toluene Dioxygenase in Whole-Cell Studies with *Pseudomonas putida* F1," *Appl. Environ. Microbiol.* 54:1703–1708 (1988).

61. Semprini, L., G. Hopkins, and P. V. Roberts. "Results of Biostimulation and Biotransformation Experiments," in *In-Situ Aquifer Restoration of Chlorinated*

Aliphatics by Methanotrophic Bacteria, P. V. Roberts, L. Semprini, G. D. Hopkins, D. Grbic-Galic, P. L. McCarty, M. Reinhard, C. V. Chrysikopoulos, M. E. Dolan, F. Haag, T. C. Harmon, S. M. Henry, R. A. Johns, N. A. Lanzarone, D. M. Mackay, K. P. Mayer, and R. E. Roat, Eds., U.S. Environmental Protection Agency, Robert S. Kerr Environmental Research Laboratory, EPA Report-600/2-89/033 (1989), pp. 65–90.

62. Mayer, K. P., D. Grbic-Galic, L. Semprini, and P. L. McCarty. "Degradation of Trichloroethylene by Methanotrophic Bacteria in a Laboratory Column of Saturated Aquifer Material," *Water Sci. Technol.* 20(11/12):175–178 (1988).

63. Lanzarone, N. A., K. P. Mayer, M. E. Dolan, D. Grbic-Galic, and P. L. McCarty. "Batch Exchange Soil Column Studies of Biotransformation by Methanotrophic Bacteria," in *In-Situ Aquifer Restoration of Chlorinated Aliphatics by Methanotrophic Bacteria*, P. V. Roberts, L. Semprini, G. D. Hopkins, D. Grbic-Galic, P. L. McCarty, M. Reinhard, C. V. Chrysikopoulos, M. E. Dolan, F. Haag, T. C. Harmon, S. M. Henry, R. A. Johns, N. A. Lanzarone, D. M. Mackay, K. P. Mayer, and R. E. Roat, Eds., U.S. Environmental Protection Agency, Robert S. Kerr Environmental Research Laboratory, EPA Report-600/2-89/033 (1989), pp. 126–146.

64. Mayer, K. P., and D. Grbic-Galic. "TCE Degradation by Methanotrophic Bacterial Communities in Aquifer-Simulating Microcosms," in *International Symposium on Processes Governing the Movement and Fate of Contaminants in the Subsurface Environment: Paper Abstracts* (San Francisco: International Association on Water Pollution Research and Control; and Stanford, CA: Western Region Hazardous Substance Research Center, 1989), p. A18.

65. Henry, S. M., and D. Grbic-Galic. "TCE Transformation by Mixed and Pure Ground Water Cultures," in *In-Situ Aquifer Restoration of Chlorinated Aliphatics by Methanotrophic Bacteria*, P. V. Roberts, L. Semprini, G. D. Hopkins, D. Grbic-Galic, P. L. McCarty, M. Reinhard, C. V. Chrysikopoulos, M. E. Dolan, F. Haag, T. C. Harmon, S. M. Henry, R. A. Johns, N. A. Lanzarone, D. M. Mackay, K. P. Mayer, and R. E. Roat, U.S. Environmental Protection Agency, Robert S. Kerr Environmental Research Laboratory, EPA Report 600/2-89/033 (1989), pp. 109–125.

66. Whittenbury, R., K. C. Phillips, and J. F. Wilkinson. "Enrichment, Isolation, and Some Properties of Methane-Utilizing Bacteria," *J. Gen. Microbiol.* 24:225–233 (1970).

67. Henry, S. M. "Treatment of Alkyl Halide Contamination by Methane Oxidizers: Defining the Best Methanotroph," in *Abstracts of Technical Papers Presented at the 62nd Annual WPCF Conference* (San Francisco: Water Pollution Control Federation, 1989), p. 27.

68. Henry, S. M., and D. Grbic-Galic. "Variables Affecting Aerobic TCE Transformation by Methane-Degrading Mixed Cultures," in *Abstracts of the 8th Annual Meeting of the Society for Environmental Toxicology and Chemistry* (Washington, DC: Society for Environmental Toxicology and Chemistry, 1987), p. 207.

69. Henry, S. M., and D. Grbic-Galic. "Effects of Availability of Reducing Power on TCE Transformation by Methanotrophs," in *International Symposium on Processes Governing the Movement and Fate of Contaminants in the Subsurface Environment: Paper Abstracts* (San Francisco: International Association on Water Pollution Research and Control; and Stanford, CA: Western Region Hazardous Substance Research Center, 1989), p. A4.

70. Henry, S. M., A. A. Dispirito, M. E. Lidstrom, and D. Grbic-Galic. "Effects of Mineral Medium on Trichloroethylene Oxidation and Involvement of a Particulate Methane Monooxygenase," in *Abstr. Annu. Meet. Amer. Soc. Microbiol.* (Washington, DC: American Society for Microbiology, 1989), p. 256.

71. Henry, S. M., C. S. Criddle, and D. Grbic-Galic. "Inhibition of Trichloroethylene Oxidation by the Putative Degradation Intermediate Carbon Monoxide," in *Abstracts of the 10th Annual Meeting of the Society for Environmental Toxicology and Chemistry* (Washington, DC: Society for Environmental Toxicology and Chemistry, 1989), p. 70.

72. Norris, J. R., and H. Swain. "Staining Bacteria," in *Methods in Microbiology, Vol. 5A*, J. R. Norris and D. W. Ribbons, Eds. (London: Academic Press, 1971), pp. 105–133.

73. Hou, C. T., "Microbiology and Biochemistry of Methylotrophic Bacteria," in *Methylotrophs: Microbiology, Biochemistry, and Genetics*, C. T. Hou, Ed. (Boca Raton, FL: CRC Press, 1984), pp. 1–53.

CHAPTER 16

Biodegradation of Organic Contaminants in Sediments: Overview and Examples with Polycyclic Aromatic Hydrocarbons

Carl E. Cerniglia

INTRODUCTION

The ability of microorganisms to degrade potentially hazardous organic chemicals has been recognized for many years. In fact, xenobiotic chemicals are potential energy sources for indigenous microorganisms and could be important in the natural cycling of carbon in nature. It has become axiomatic that xenobiotics are susceptible to biodegradation if their chemical structures are similar to those found in naturally occurring compounds. Bacteria and fungi constantly exposed to a structurally diverse range of chemicals have evolved the enzymatic apparatus to degrade a wide variety of organic compounds. Unfortunately, many xenobiotics have structural features never found in naturally occurring compounds and are therefore not readily susceptible to microbial attack.

Polycyclic aromatic hydrocarbons (PAHs) are a major class of environmental contaminants originating from both petrogenic and pyrogenic sources.[1-8] Many PAHs are cytotoxic, mutagenic, and carcinogenic to both lower and higher eukaryotic organisms (Figure 16.1).[2,9-12] Due to their hydrophobic nature, most PAHs in aquatic ecosystems rapidly become associated with particles and are deposited in sediments. A variety of processes, including volatilization, sedimentation, chemical oxidation, photodecomposition, and microbial degradation, are important mechanisms for environmental loss of PAH (Figure 16.2). Microbial degradation of PAH can have a significant effect on the PAH distribution in sediment, especially near the sediment-water interface.[13-16]

There is considerable interest in the use of microorganisms to decontaminate PAH-polluted environments.[17] Successful bioremediation is dependent upon the availability of microorganisms that possess the catabolic enzymes needed to degrade PAH. Mono- and dioxygenases are two groups of enzymes that are

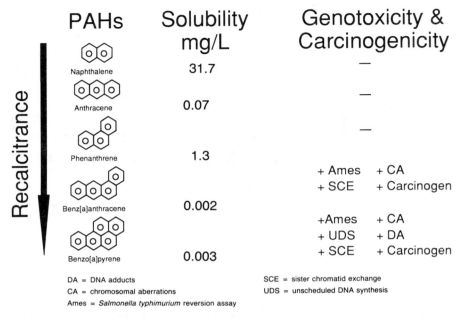

Figure 16.1.   The structures and chemical and toxicological characteristics of polycyclic aromatic hydrocarbons.

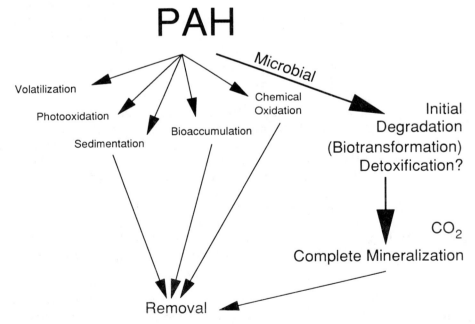

Figure 16.2.   Schematic representation of the environmental fate of polycyclic aromatic hydrocarbons.

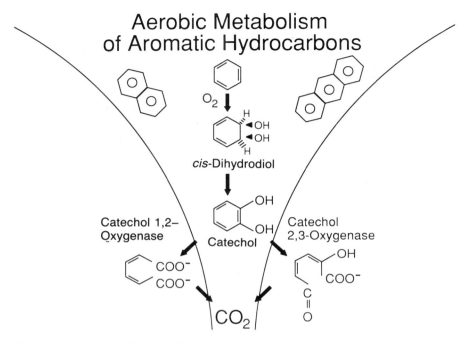

Aerobic Metabolism
of Aromatic Hydrocarbons

cis-Dihydrodiol

Catechol 1,2–
Oxygenase

Catechol

Catechol
2,3-Oxygenase

CO_2

Figure 16.3.   Major pathways of bacterial oxidation of polycyclic aromatic hydrocarbons.

important to the microbial catabolism of PAH. Dioxygenases incorporate both atoms of the oxygen molecule into the PAH. This dioxygenase reaction is the major mechanism for the initial oxidative attack on PAH by bacteria, which leads to the formation of dihydrodiols that are in the *cis* configuration.[15] Enzymatic fission of the aromatic ring is also catalyzed by dioxygenases (Figure 16.3). In contrast to bacteria, fungi oxidize PAH via a cytochrome P-450 monooxygenase by incorporating one atom of the oxygen molecule into the PAH and the other into water.[18-23] Metabolic pathways and enzymatic mechanisms for the microbial metabolism of PAHs containing two or three aromatic rings have been well studied.[15] However, there are very few studies on the microbial degradation and detoxification of higher-molecular-weight PAHs. Our current knowledge on the microbial degradation of PAH is summarized below:

1. Biodegradation of lower-molecular-weight PAHs by a wide variety of micro-organisms has been demonstrated, and the biochemical pathways have been investigated.[15]
2. There is limited information on the microbial utilization of PAHs containing four or more aromatic rings; however, cometabolism of high-molecular-weight PAHs by bacteria has been demonstrated.[24-32]
3. Biodegradation of unsubstituted PAHs always involves the incorporation of molecular oxygen catalyzed by monooxygenase(s) or dioxygenase(s).[15] How-

ever, there is also increasing interest and speculation concerning anaerobic decomposition of PAH.[33,34]

4. Many of the genes coding for bacterial degradation of PAH are plasmid associated.[35,36]

5. Fungi hydroxylate PAH as a prelude to detoxification, whereas bacteria oxidize PAH as a prelude to ring fission and assimilation.[15,18-23]

6. Fungal metabolism of PAH is highly regio- and stereoselective.[19,22]

7. White-rot fungi have the ability to cleave the aromatic rings of PAH.[37]

8. Microbial degradation of PAH can occur under denitrifying conditions.[33,34]

9. Lower-molecular-weight PAHs, such as naphthalene and phenanthrene, are degraded rapidly in sediments, whereas higher-molecular-weight PAHs, such as benz(a)anthracene or benzo(a)pyrene, are quite resistant to microbial attack.[13,38,39]

10. Environmental factors can have a significant effect on PAH biodegradation.[40]

11. There are higher biodegradation rates for PAH in PAH-contaminated sediments than in pristine sediments.[38,39,41]

12. Procaryotic pathways for naphthalene metabolism predominate in sediments from freshwater and estuarine sediments.[41]

Recent investigations in my laboratory on the biodegradation of PAH has led to the isolation of a *Mycobacterium* sp. that is able to extensively degrade PAHs containing up to five fused aromatic rings.[25,27] The ultimate usefulness of the *Mycobacterium* in the bioremediation of PAH-contaminated sediments depends upon its survival and function in diverse ecosystems.[26] The versatility of the PAH-degrading *Mycobacterium* and its potential for use in the biodegradation of PAH-contaminated sediments will be reported.

MATERIALS AND METHODS

Isolation of the Polycyclic Aromatic Hydrocarbon Degrading Bacterium

The bacterium was isolated from a 500-mL microcosm containing 20 g of sediment, 180 mL of estuarine water, and 100 μg of pyrene.[25,27] The sediment was obtained from a drainage pond chronically exposed to petrogenic chemicals. After incubation of the microcosm for 25 days under aerobic conditions, the sediment samples were serially diluted and screened for the presence of PAH-degrading microorganisms.[25,27]

The screening medium consisted of mineral saits medium (44) containing (per liter): NaCl, 0.3 g; $(NH_4)_2SO_4$, 0.6 g; KNO_3, 0.6 g; KH_2PO_4, 0.25 g; K_2HPO_4, 0.75 g; $MgSO_4 \cdot 7H_2O$, 0.15 g; LiCl, 20 μg; $CuSO_4 \cdot 5H_2O$, 80 μg; $ZnSO_4 \cdot 7H_2O$, 100 μg; $Al_2(SO_4)_3 \cdot 16H_2O$, 100 μg; $NiCl \cdot 6H_2O$, 100 μg; $CoSO_4 \cdot 7H_2O$, 100 μg; KBr, 30 μg; KI, 30 μg; $MnCl_2 \cdot 4H_2O$, 600 μg; $SnCl_2 \cdot 2H_2O$, 40 μg; $FeSO_4 \cdot 7H_2O$, 300 μg: agar, 20 g; and distilled H_2O, 1000 mL.

The surfaces of the agar plates were sprayed with a 2% (wt/vol) solution of a PAH dissolved in acetone: hexane (1:1, vol/vol) and dried overnight at 35°C to volatilize the carrier solvents. This treatment resulted in a visible and uniform surface coat of the PAH on the agar. Inocula (100 μL) from the 10^{-1}, 10^{-2}, 10^{-3}, and 10^{-4} dilutions of microcosm sediments were gently spread with sterile glass rods onto the agar surface; the plates were inverted and incubated for 3 weeks at 24°C in sealed plastic bags to conserve moisture.

When colonies surrounded by clear zones (Figure 16.4) due to polycyclic aromatic hydrocarbon uptake and utilization were observed (after 2 to 3 weeks), they were subcultured into fresh mineral salts medium containing 250 μg/L each of peptone, yeast extract, and soluble starch, and 0.5 μg/mL of a PAH dissolved in dimethylformamide. After three successive transfers, a bacterium was isolated that was able to degrade pyrene, a PAH containing four aromatic rings.

Growth of Organism and Culture Conditions

The *Mycobacterium* sp. was grown in 125-mL Erlenmeyer flasks containing 30 mL of basal salts medium (19) supplemented with 250 μg/mL each of peptone, yeast extract, and soluble starch and 0.5 μg/mL of pyrene dissolved

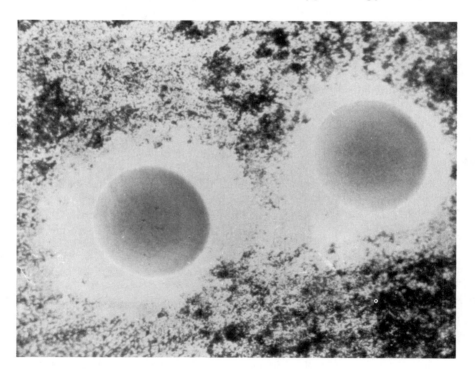

Figure 16.4. Photograph of *Mycobacterium* sp. colonies on MBS agar containing low levels of nutrients and coated with pyrene. The clear zones around the bacterial colonies indicate pyrene utilization.

in dimethylformamide. The cultures were incubated in the dark at 24°C for 72 hr on a rotary shaker operating at 150 rpm. Cells in the midlogarithmic phase of growth were harvested by centrifugation at 8000 G for 20 min at 4°C. The harvested cells were resuspended in sterile 0.1 M *tris*(hydroxymethyl)aminomethane buffer (pH 7.5) at a concentration of 3×10^6 cells/mL and used as inoculum for studies of PAH biodegradation.

Biodegradation Experiments

Biodegradation of PAH by the *Mycobacterium* sp. was monitored in a flow-through microcosm test system.[42-44] This system enables simultaneous monitoring of mineralization (complete degradation to CO_2) and the recovery of volatile metabolites, nonvolatile metabolites, and residual PAH. Microcosms in this test system consisted of 500-mL glass minitanks containing 100 mL of minimal basal salts medium, 0.92 μCi of ^{14}C-labeled PAH, and 50 μg of unlabeled PAH. The PAHs used and their sources were [1,4,5,8-^{14}C]naphthalene (5.10 mCi/mmol), Amersham/Searle Corporation, Arlington Heights, IL; [9-^{14}C]phenanthrene (19.3 mCi/mmol), Amersham/Searle; [3-^{14}C]fluoranthene (54.8 mCi/mmol), Chemsyn Science Laboratories, Lenexa, KS; [4-^{14}C]pyrene (30.0 mCi/mmol), Midwest Research Institute, Kansas City, MO; 3-[6-^{14}C]-methylcholanthrene (13.4 mCi/mmol), New England Nuclear Corporation, Boston, MA; and 6-nitro[5,6,11,12-^{14}C]chrysene (57.4 mCi/mmol), Chemsyn Science Laboratories.

Each microcosm was inoculated with 1.5×10^4 cells/mL, mixed twice weekly, incubated at 24°C for 14 days, and continuously purged with compressed air. The gaseous effluent from each microcosm was directed through a volatile organic trapping column containing 7 cm of polyurethane foam and 500 mg of Tenax GC (Alltech Associates, Inc., Deerfield, IL) and a $^{14}CO_2$ trapping column (50 mL of monoethanolamine:ethylene glycol, 7:3 vol/vol). Mineralization was measured at various intervals by adding duplicate 1-mL aliquots from the $^{14}CO_2$ trapping column to scintillation vials containing 15 mL of a 1:1 mixture of Fluoralloy and methanol (Beckman Instruments Co., Fullerton, CA). Autoclaved inoculated microcosms, and microcosms lacking the *Mycobacterium* sp., were included to detect abiotic PAH degradation.

RESULTS AND DISCUSSION

There are four major objectives in my research program concerning PAH biodegradation:

1. to determine the relationships between chemical structure and PAH degradation by measuring mineralization rates in microcosms, getting good mass balance accountability of undegraded PAH and of volatile and nonvolatile metabolites
2. to isolate microorganisms from environmental sites chronically exposed to

PAHs, which have the ability to degrade PAHs containing four or more aromatic rings

3. to elucidate biochemical pathways and reaction mechanisms for PAH degradation in environmental samples

4. to determine if PAH-degrading bacteria would be useful in the biological decontamination and detoxification of PAH-polluted sites

It is clear from previous investigations that it is relatively easy to isolate microorganisms, using classical enrichment and plating techniques, which can utilize lower-molecular-weight PAHs containing two or three rings. The focus of research in my laboratory is to isolate microorganisms that degrade the higher-molecular-weight PAHs. A summary of our recent investigations is reported below.

Enrichment of PAH-Degrading Bacterium

A pyrene-degrading bacterium was isolated by direct enrichment from sediment samples taken from an oil field near Port Aransas, TX (Figure 16.4). By repeated streaking and isolation, we obtained an isolate, strain Pyr-1, which was identified as a *Mycobacterium* sp. on the basis of the following morphological and biochemical properties:[45] It formed gram-positive, acid-fast rods (1.4 μm in length and 0.7 μm in width). The 15 biochemical tests, mole percent G + C analysis of 66%, and the characterization of the mycolic acids with a carbon chain length of C_{58} to C_{64} were consistent with the assignment of this organism to the genus *Mycobacterium*.

Utilization of PAH by Mycobacterium

The *Mycobacterium* utilized naphthalene, phenanthrene, fluoranthene, pyrene, 3-methylcholanthrene, 1-nitropyrene, and 6-nitrochrysene when grown in mineral salts medium supplemented with low levels of peptone, yeast extract, and soluble starch.[25] This bacterium was unable to utilize these PAHs as the sole source of carbon and energy. Pyrene-induced *Mycobacterium* cultures readily degraded naphthalene (59.5%), phenanthrene (50.9%), fluoranthene (89.7%), pyrene (63.0%), 1-nitropyrene (12.3%), 3-methylcholanthrene (1.6%), and 6-nitrochrysene (2.0%) to CO_2 within 48 hr of incubation (Figure 16.5). Pathways for the initial degradation of pyrene, naphthalene, fluoranthene, and 1-nitropyrene are shown in Figures 16.6–16.9.

The *Mycobacterium* sp. initially oxidized pyrene to form both pyrene *cis*- and *trans*-4,5-dihydrodiols.[28] Oxygen-18 incorporation experiments showed that both atoms of the *cis*-pyrene dihydrodiol were derived from molecular oxygen, but only one atom of molecular oxygen was incorporated into the *trans*-pyrene dihydrodiol (Figure 16.6). 4-Phenanthroic acid, 4-hydroxyperinaphthenone, and cinnamic acid were identified as ring fission products.[28] The *Mycobacterium* sp. initially oxidized naphthalene in the 1,2-positions to form naphthalene-1,2-dihydrodiols. Similar to pyrene oxidation, both the naphthalene *cis*- and *trans*-1,2-dihydrodiols were isolated in a ratio of

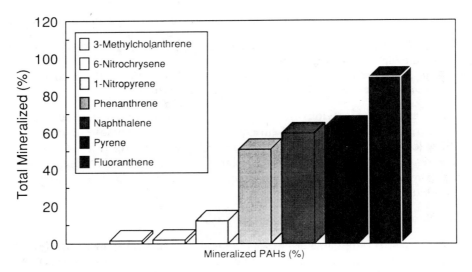

Figure 16.5. Mineralization of 3-methylcholanthrene, 6-nitrochrysene, 1-nitropyrene, phenanthrene, naphthalene, pyrene, and fluoranthene by the *Mycobacterium* sp.

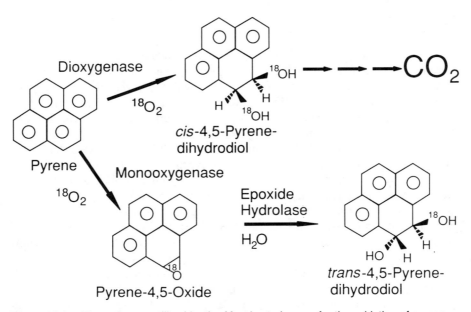

Figure 16.6. The pathways utilized by the *Mycobacterium* sp. for the oxidation of pyrene.

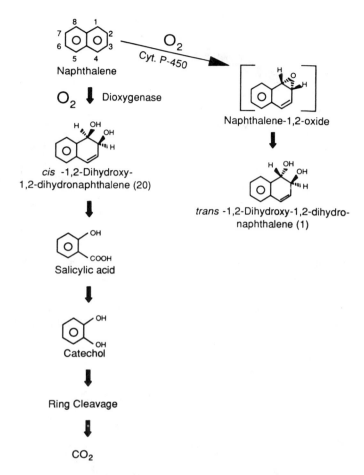

Figure 16.7. The pathways utilized by the *Mycobacterium* sp. for the oxidation of naphthalene.

20:1. The naphthalene *cis*-1,2-dihydrodiols are further metabolized to salicylate and catechol by the classical bacterial oxidation of naphthalene pathway (Figure 16.7). The *Mycobacterium* sp. extensively degrades fluoranthene to CO_2 (Figure 16.8). However, a ring cleavage metabolite was isolated and identified as 9-fluorenone-1-carboxylic acid. 1-Nitropyrene is degraded very slowly by the *Mycobacterium* sp., and little mineralization occurs, which indicates that the nitro-substituent may sterically block initial enzymatic attack and ring cleavage enzymes since pyrene is rapidly degraded. However, 1-nitropyrene *cis*-4,5-and 9,10-dihydrodiols were isolated and characterized (Figure 16.9).

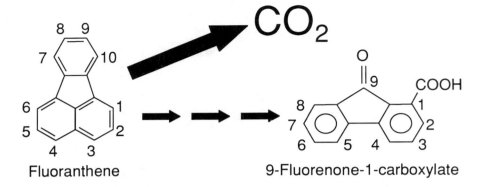

Fluoranthene   9-Fluorenone-1-carboxylate

Figure 16.8. The pathways utilized by the *Mycobacterium* sp. for the oxidation of fluoranthene.

Microcosm Studies to Evaluate the PAH-Degrading Capacity and Survival of the Mycobacterium When Added to Pristine Sediments

Figure 16.10 indicates that 2-methylnaphthalene and phenanthrene were mineralized to 10 and 14%, respectively, after 28 days in microcosms contain-

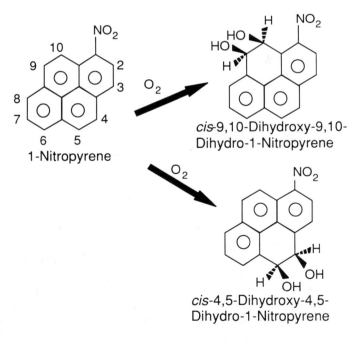

1-Nitropyrene

cis-9,10-Dihydroxy-9,10-
Dihydro-1-Nitropyrene

cis-4,5-Dihydroxy-4,5-
Dihydro-1-Nitropyrene

Figure 16.9. The pathways utilized by the *Mycobacterium* sp. for the oxidation of 1-nitropyrene.

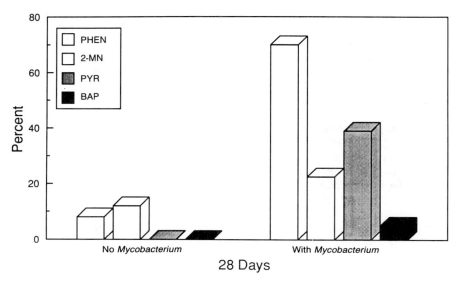

Figure 16.10. Mineralization of phenanthrene *(PHEN)*, 2-methylnaphthalene *(2-MN)*, pyrene *(PYR)*, and benzo(a)pyrene *(BAP)* in microcosms from De Gray Reservoir sediments and water, with and without *Mycobacterium* inoculation.

ing sediment and water from De Gray Reservoir, Arkadelphia, AR. De Gray Reservoir is a pristine lake, which receives relatively little chemical inputs, and has a low PAH-degrading microbial population.[26,38,41] When similar microcosms were inoculated with the *Mycobacterium* sp. (1.5 × 10[5] cells/g of moist sediment), mineralization of 2-methylnaphthalene and phenanthrene increased to 26 and 71%, respectively. In addition, pyrene and benzo(a)pyrene degradation were observed, whereas previously we did not see degradation of high-molecular-weight PAHs in De Gray Reservoir sediments lacking the *Mycobacterium*. Therefore, the *Mycobacterium* sp. competed with indigenous microflora and enhanced mineralization of PAHs.[26]

Our research indicates that the *Mycobacterium* sp. isolated from an oil-contaminated estuarine site is very versatile and can mineralize low- and high-molecular-weight PAHs. The process is cooxidation, since low levels of organic nutrients are necessary to initiate growth and metabolism of the PAHs. The mechanism of oxidation is unique, since the *Mycobacterium* has both mono- and dioxygenases to catalyze the initial attack on the PAH.

In conclusion, when one discusses the use of microorganisms in the remediation of hazardous wastes, such as PAH, some bioremediation issues that should be addressed are the following:

1. a complete understanding of the chemical, toxicological and ecological characterization of the site
2. more data on the fate, metabolism, and kinetics of high-molecular-weight PAH biodegradation at the site

3. determination of biochemistry and mechanisms of many of the high-molecular-weight PAH degradative pathways
4. determination of conditions that will ensure the survival of the biological detoxification system
5. effective transportation of the biological detoxification system to the site
6. development of procedures for employing immobilized cells to decontaminate PAH-contaminated soils
7. determination of whether bioremediation is a cost-effective means of cleanup of PAH-contaminated wastes
8. getting the PAH-degrading microorganisms (large biomass) there and making them grow and function
9. understanding the fate of plasmid DNA or recombinant strains in wastewater or sediments
10. optimizing a PAH-degrading microbial system for environmental use
11. basic research on coupling aerobic and anaerobic biodegradation systems
12. research on specific bacteria used at a site, such as salt-tolerant or chemical-tolerant bacteria

REFERENCES

1. Hites, R. A., R. E. Laflamme, and J. G. Windsor. "Polycyclic Aromatic Hydrocarbons in Marine/Aquatic Sediments: Their Ubiquity," in *Petroleum in the Marine Environment,* Advances in Chemistry Series, L. Petrakis and F. T. Weiss, Eds. (Washington, DC: American Chemical Society, 1980), pp. 289–311.
2. "Polynuclear Aromatic Compounds. Part 1, Chemical, Environmental and Experimental Data," in *IARC Monographs on the Evaluation of the Carcinogenic Risk of Chemicals to Humans* (Lyon, France: World Health Organization, 1983), pp. 95–451.
3. Jacob, J., W. Karcher, J. J. Belliardo, and P. J. Wagstaffe. "Polycyclic Aromatic Hydrocarbons of Environmental and Occupational Importance," *Fres. Z. Anal. Chem.* 323:1–10 (1986).
4. Johnson, A. C., and D. Larsen. "The Distribution of Polycyclic Aromatic Hydrocarbons in the Surficial Sediments of Penobscot Bay (Maine, USA) in Relation to Possible Sources and to Other Sites Worldwide," *Mar. Environ. Res.* 15:1–16 (1984).
5. Jones, K. C., J. A. Stratford, K. S. Waterhouse, and N. B. Vogt. "Organic Contaminants in Welsh Soils: Polynuclear Aromatic Hydrocarbons," *Environ. Sci. Technol.* 23:540–550 (1989).
6. Means, J. C., S. G. Ward, J. J. Hassett, and W. L. Banwart. "Sorption of Polynuclear Aromatic Hydrocarbons by Sediments and Soils," *Environ. Sci. Technol.* 14:1524–1528 (1980).
7. Morehead, N. R., B. J. Eadie, B. Lake, P. D. Landrum, and D. Berner. "The Sorption of PAH onto Dissolved Organic Matter in Lake Michigan Waters," *Chemosphere* 15:403–412 (1986).
8. *Polycyclic Aromatic Hydrocarbons: Evaluation of Sources and Effects* (Washington, DC: National Academy Press, 1983).
9. Dipple, A., R. C. Moschel, and C. A. H. Bigger. "Polynuclear Aromatic Carcino-

gens," in *Chemical Carcinogens,* 2nd ed., C. E. Searle, Ed. (Washington, DC: American Chemical Society, 1984), pp. 41–163.

10. Keith, L. H., and W. A. Telliard. "Priority Pollutants. I. A Perspective View," *Environ. Sci. Technol.* 13:416–423 (1979).

11. Martelmans, K., S. Haworth, T. Lawlor, W. Speck, B. Tainer, and E. Zeiger. "Salmonella Mutagenicity Tests. II. Results from the Testing of 270 Chemicals," *Environ. Mutagen.* 8(Suppl. 7):1–119 (1986).

12. Miller, E. C., and J. A. Miller. "Searches for Ultimate Chemical Carcinogens and Their Reactions with Cellular Macromolecules," *Cancer* 47:2327–2345 (1981).

13. Bauer, J. E., and D. G. Capone. "Degradation and Mineralization of the Polycyclic Aromatic Hydrocarbons Anthracene and Naphthalene in Intertidal Marine Sediments," *Appl. Environ. Microbiol.* 50:81–90 (1985).

14. Bauer, J. E., and D. G. Capone. "Effects of Co-Occurring Aromatic Hydrocarbons on the Degradation of Individual Polycyclic Aromatic Hydrocarbons in Marine Sediment Slurries," *Appl. Environ. Microbiol.* 54:1649–1655 (1988).

15. Cerniglia, C. E., and M. A. Heitkamp. "Microbial Degradation of Polycyclic Aromatic Hydrocarbons in the Aquatic Environment," in *Metabolism of Polycyclic Aromatic Hydrocarbons in the Aquatic Environment,* U. Varanasi, Ed. (Boca Raton, FL: CRC Press, 1989).

16. Lewis, D. L., R. E. Hodson, and L. F. Freeman. "Effects of Microbial Community Interactions on Transformation Rates of Xenobiotic Chemicals," *Appl. Environ. Microbiol.* 48:561–565 (1984).

17. Nicholas, R. B. "Biotechnology in Hazardous Waste Disposal: An Unfulfilled Promise," *ASM News* 53:138–142 (1987).

18. Cerniglia, C. E., W. L. Campbell, J. P. Freeman, and F. E. Evans. "Identification of a Novel Metabolite in Phenanthrene Metabolism by the Fungus *Cunninghamella elegans,*" *Appl. Environ. Microbiol.* 55:2275–2279 (1989).

19. Cerniglia, C. E., W. L. Campbell, P. P. Fu, J. P. Freeman, and F. E. Evans. "Stereoselective Fungal Metabolism of Methylated Anthracenes," *Appl. Environ. Microbiol.* 56:661–668 (1990).

20. Cerniglia, C. E., J. P. Freeman, G. L. White, R. F. Heflich, and D. W. Miller. "Fungal Metabolism and Detoxification of the Nitropolycyclic Aromatic Hydrocarbon 1-Nitropyrene," *Appl. Environ. Microbiol.* 50:649–655 (1985).

21. Cerniglia, C. E., D. W. Kelly, J. P. Freeman, and D. W. Miller. "Microbial Metabolism of Pyrene," *Chem. Biol. Interact.* 57:203–216 (1986).

22. Cerniglia, C. E., D. W. Miller, S. K. Yang, and J. P. Freeman. "Effects of Fluoro Substituents on the Fungal Metabolism of 1-Fluoronaphthalene," *Appl. Environ. Microbiol.* 48:294–300 (1984).

23. Cerniglia, C. E., G. L. White, and R. H. Heflich. "Fungal Metabolism and Detoxification of Polycyclic Aromatic Hydrocarbons," *Arch. Microbiol.* 50:649–655 (1985).

24. Barnsley, E. A. "The Bacterial Degradation of Fluoranthene and Benzo[a]pyrene," *Can. J. Microbiol.* 21:1004–1008 (1975).

25. Heitkamp, M. A., and C. E. Cerniglia. "Mineralization of Polycyclic Aromatic Hydrocarbons by a Bacterium Isolated from Sediment below an Oil Field," *Appl. Environ. Microbiol.* 54:1612–1614 (1988).

26. Heitkamp, M. A., and C. E. Cerniglia. "Polycyclic Aromatic Hydrocarbon Degradation by a *Mycobacterium* sp. in Microcosms Containing Sediment and Water from a Pristine Ecosystem," *Appl. Environ. Microbiol.* 55:1968–1973 (1989).

27. Heitkamp, M. A., W. Franklin, and C. E. Cerniglia. "Microbial Metabolism of Polycyclic Aromatic Hydrocarbons: Isolation and Characterization of a Pyrene Degrading Bacterium," *Appl. Environ. Microbiol.* 54:2549–2555 (1988).
28. Heitkamp, M. A., J. P. Freeman, D. W. Miller, and C. E. Cerniglia. "Pyrene Degradation by a *Mycobacterium* sp.: Identification of Ring Oxidation and Ring Fission Products," *Appl. Environ. Microbiol.* 54:2556–2565 (1988).
29. Kelley, I., and C. E. Cerniglia. "The Metabolism of Fluoranthene by a Species of *Mycobacterium*," *J. Ind. Microbiol.* (in press).
30. Mahaffey, W. R., D. T. Gibson, and C. E. Cerniglia. "Bacterial Oxidation of Chemical Carcinogens: Formation of Polycyclic Aromatic Acids from Benz[a]anthracene," *Appl. Environ. Microbiol.* 54:2415–2423 (1988).
31. Mueller, J. G., P. J. Chapman, B. O. Blattmann, and P. H. Pritchard. "Isolation and Characterization of a Fluoranthene-Utilizing Strain of *Pseudomonas paucimobilis*," *Appl. Environ. Microbiol.* 56:1079–1086 (1990).
32. Mueller, J. G., P. J. Chapman, and P. H. Pritchard. "Action of a Fluoranthene-Utilizing Bacterial Community on Polycyclic Aromatic Hydrocarbon Components of Creosote," *Appl. Environ. Microbiol.* 55:3085–3090 (1989).
33. Mihelcic, J. R., and R. G. Luthy. "Degradation of Polycyclic Aromatic Hydrocarbon Compounds under Various Redox Conditions in Soil-Water Systems," *Appl. Environ. Microbiol.* 54:1182–1187 (1988).
34. Mihelcic, J. R., and R. G. Luthy. "Microbial Degradation of Acenaphthene and Naphthalene under Denitrification Conditions in Soil-Water Systems," *Appl. Environ. Microbiol.* 54:1188–1198 (1988).
35. Burlage, R. S., S. W. Hooper, and G. S. Sayler. "The TOL (pWWO) Catabolic Plasmid," *Appl. Environ. Microbiol.* 55:1323–1328 (1989).
36. Williams, P. A. "Genetics of Biodegradation," in *Microbial Degradation of Xenobiotics and Recalcitrant Compounds,* T. Leisinger, R. Hutter, A. M. Cook, and J. Nuesch, Eds. (New York: Academic Press, 1981), pp. 97–130.
37. Bumpus, J. A. "Biodegradation of Polycyclic Aromatic Hydrocarbons by *Phanerochaete chrysosporium*," *Appl. Environ. Microbiol.* 55:154–158 (1988).
38. Heitkamp, M. A., and C. E. Cerniglia. "Effects of Chemical Structure and Exposure on the Microbial Degradation of Polycyclic Aromatic Hydrocarbons in Freshwater and Estuarine Ecosystems," *Environ. Toxicol. Chem.* 6:535–546 (1987).
39. Herbes, S. E., and L. R. Schwall. "Microbial Transformation of Polycyclic Aromatic Hydrocarbons in Pristine and Petroleum Contaminated Sediments," *Appl. Environ. Microbiol.* 35:306–316 (1978).
40. Shiaris, M. P. "Seasonal Biotransformation of Naphthalene, Phenanthrene and Benzo[a]pyrene in Surficial Estuarine Sediments," *Appl. Environ. Microbiol.* 55:1391–1399 (1989).
41. Heitkamp, M. A., J. P. Freeman, and C. E. Cerniglia. "Naphthalene Biodegradation in Environmental Microcosms: Estimates of Degradation Rates and Characterization of Metabolites," *Appl. Environ. Microbiol.* 53:129–136 (1987).
42. Heitkamp, M. A., and C. E. Cerniglia. "Microbial Degradation of *t*-Butylphenyl Diphenyl Phosphate: A Comparative Microcosm Study among Five Diverse Ecosystems," *Toxic. Assess.* 1:103–122 (1986).
43. Huckins, J. N., J. D. Petty, and M. A. Heitkamp. "Modular Containers for Microcosm and Process Model Studies on the Fate and Effects of Aquatic Contaminants," *Chemosphere* 13:1329–1341 (1984).
44. Johnson, B. T., M. A. Heitkamp, and J. R. Jones. "Environmental and Chemical

Factors Influencing the Biodegradation of Phthalic Acid Esters in Freshwater Sediments," *Environ. Pollut.* Ser. B, 8:101–118 (1984).

45. Skerman, V. B. D. *A Guide to the Identification of the Genera of Bacteria,* 2nd ed. (Baltimore, MD: Williams and Wilkins, 1967).

CHAPTER 17

The Use of Chemical Diffusing Substrata to Monitor the Response of Periphyton to Synthetic Organic Chemicals

Scott D. Schermerhorn, Gina Abbate, and Roy M. Ventullo

INTRODUCTION

The role of naturally occurring bacterial communities in the removal of chemicals from aquatic systems is being addressed.[1-4] Of special interest are those communities of bacteria that attach to a substratum and form a complex community with algae and fungi, often referred to as *periphyton*.[5-7] Periphyton can be found attached to rock, cobble, and other stationary surfaces in most flowing water systems. Because of the close physical proximity of the heterotrophic and autotrophic components, efficient cycling of CO_2, O_2, carbon, and nutrients may occur between trophic levels.[6-8] It has also been suggested that the heterotrophic components within periphyton communities play a major role in the biodegradation of allochthonous organic input.[2,9]

Laboratory studies are often used to measure rates of biodegradation, which are then used to estimate degradation in the environment. It is often difficult to extrapolate results obtained in laboratory systems to project the fate of chemicals in the environment, where conditions may be, and often are, different from those in the laboratory. The effects of many parameters need to be considered: temperature, nutrient concentration, chemical structure and concentration, as well as the acclimation of the microbial community to biodegrade the compound of interest. Chemical fate models need accurate information about biodegradation in situ to more closely predict the fate of both natural and xenobiotic chemicals in aquatic systems.[10,11]

In situ bioassay systems that have used point-source manipulation of inorganic nutrients have been successful in influencing communities in lotic and benthic environments.[12,13] Until recently, only inorganic manipulation of the autotrophic component of the periphyton community through point-source diffusion has been reported.[12-15] The advantages of point-source diffusion through substrata are the following:

1. Concentrations of material diffusing outward can be measured and controlled while the community is in its ever changing natural environment.
2. The substrata can provide relatively high chemical concentrations to the periphyton communities while adding little to the large volume of the stream.
3. Treatments using this technique can be replicated and placed in a variety of different areas within an aquatic system.

Periphyton growth on such substrata should be influenced by the release of material (inorganic or organic), and the results of this influence can be examined both quantitatively and qualitatively with regard to biomass, bacterial and algal numbers, primary and secondary production, and biodegradative ability.

Since it has been suggested that acclimation to chemicals is an important process regulating biodegradation rates,[3,10,16] our goals were

1. to develop a bioassay system in which a diffusing substratum would serve as a point source of synthetic organic chemical release
2. to use such a system to measure periphyton response to constant chemical exposure in situ
3. to characterize acclimation periods and biodegradation kinetics of synthetic organic chemicals by the periphyton communities

MATERIALS AND METHODS

Sample Site

Periphyton communities were obtained by incubating the bioassay system in the East Fork of the Little Miami River, east of Cincinnati, Ohio. Periphyton communities were allowed to colonize and develop for 3 weeks.

Organic Chemicals

Six organic chemicals were examined in this study: linear alkylbenzene sulfonate (LAS), nitrilotriacetic acid (NTA), linear primary alcohol ethoxylate (LAE), 4-nitrophenol (PNP), Monotallowtrimethylammonium chloride (MTTMAC), and a detergent builder, succinate tartrates (ST). All chemicals were obtained from the Procter and Gamble Company (Cincinnati, OH), with the exception of 4-nitrophenol (Aldrich, Milwaukee, WI). Radiolabeled materials (^{14}C) used for the mineralization studies were obtained from Procter and Gamble and were shown to be greater than 98% radiochemically pure by HPLC and/or TLC analysis.

Organic Chemical Diffusion Studies

The six organic chemicals were individually added to solutions of 20% molten agar to obtain final concentrations of either 20 or 200 mM. Trace amounts of radiolabeled chemical were added to each solution in a ratio that allowed for the detection of 1% release. The solutions were then mixed well, poured into ceramic saucers, and allowed to solidify. The tops of the saucers were sealed with Plexiglas and silicone sealant. The diffusing ceramic substrata were then placed in glass bowls filled with distilled water, which was continually stirred. Water from the glass bowls was removed daily, assayed for radioactivity by liquid scintillation spectrometry, and replaced with the same volume of fresh distilled water for a minimum of 21 days.

Inorganic Diffusion Studies

Nitrate and phosphate, as $NaNO_3$ and K_2HPO_4, were individually added to solutions of 20% molten agar to achieve final concentrations of 500, 50, or 20 mM. The solutions were poured into ceramic substrata, allowed to solidify, and sealed as described above. The substrata were then placed in 18 megohm ultrapure water (Millipore Corporation), which was continually stirred. Water was removed daily and assayed for NO_3^- and PO_4^- ions by ion chromatography (Dionex Corporation). A Series 2000 ion chromatograph with an HPIC/AS4 strong-anion exchange column was used with 0.25 mM carbonate eluent at a flow of 2 mL/min, and 0.025 N H_2SO_4 served as the regenerant. Anions were quantified by peak area using an SP 4620 integrator. Calibration was by Dionex standard 5-anion solution (Dionex Corporation).

Exposure Studies

Clay ceramic saucers with a known surface area (141.5 cm²) were filled with agar solutions containing various concentrations of LAS, LAE, and ST, and were attached to a 4-ft × 4-ft sheet of Plexiglas. In a second experiment involving low concentrations of LAS, inorganic nitrate (500 mM) and phosphate (20 mM) were also added. The Plexiglas was then suspended under a rack of PVC pipe and polyfloats and placed in the river. The ceramic substrata were positioned within the photic zone of the stream at a depth of 18 in. below water surface. This system was modeled after other floating in situ assay systems.[14,17,18] Periphyton communities were allowed to develop for at least 21 days on the ceramic substrata placed in the East fork of the Little Miami River. The substrata were recovered, and a portion of the periphyton communities (10 cm²) was carefully scraped into 125-mL flasks and equipped with CO_2 traps. Samples were spiked with appropriate ^{14}C substrate (5–8 µCi, 50 µg/L), and the $^{14}CO_2$ released due to mineralization/respiration of the test compound was trapped with 0.75 N KOH and counted by liquid scintillation spectrometry.[1,16] Data were expressed as the cumulative percentage of the radiolabeled compounds recovered as $^{14}CO_2$.

Biodegradation Parameters

Mineralization curves were fitted to a first-order production equation:[1,16]

$$y = a(1 - e^{(-k(t-c))})$$

where y = percent of initial ^{14}C added recovered as $^{14}CO_2$
          t = time in days
          a = the extent of degradation (asymptote of CO_2 produced)
          k = the first-order rate constant
          c = the lag time before the onset of mineralization

This equation provides the kinetic parameters of the first-order rate constant, mineralization extent, mineralization half-life (ln $2/k$), and lag-time. All parameter estimates (a, k, c) were obtained by least-squares analysis by using iterative techniques and a nonlinear computer program (Statpro, Penton Software).

Structural Characteristics

Periphyton communities were also analyzed for structural components. Protein and carbohydrate concentrations were determined spectrophotometrically on homogenized communities.[19,20] Dry weights, as well as total numbers of bacteria, determined by direct fluorescence microscopy, were also performed.[21]

Statistical Analyses

Statistical analyses were performed by nonparametric techniques using a computer program (Statpro, Penton Software). Nonparametric statistical analyses were used because of the limited number of true replicates ($N = 2$ to 5 individual replicates) and the lack of a normal distribution on which to base parametric assumptions. Variance was determined by Kruskal-Wallis (nonparametric ANOVA) and Mann-Whitney U tests performed on all true replicates. Significance levels were determined based upon tables compiled by Rohlf and Sokal.[22]

RESULTS

Diffusion Studies

All organic compounds tested diffused out of the ceramic substrata at a measurable rate. These laboratory studies indicate that the rate of release for the chemicals was on the order of micrograms per day (Figure 17.1). LAS diffused at a mean rate of 1.5 $\mu g/cm^2/day$ from an internal concentration of 200 mM. The 200-mM solutions of LAE, NTA, and ST were released at a mean rate of 365 $\mu g/cm^2/day$, 34.6 $\mu g/cm^2/day$, and 113 $\mu g/cm^2/day$, respectively. MTTMAC was released at a mean rate of 58.3 $\mu g/cm^2/day$. Release rates for PNP were 5 $\mu g/cm^2/day$ and 1 $\mu g/cm^2/day$ for the two concentrations examined. LAE (a nonionic water-soluble compound), NTA (a low-

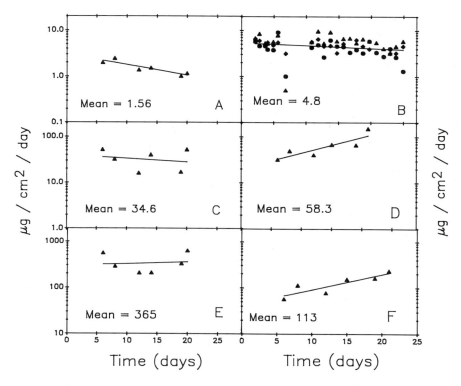

Figure 17.1. Diffusion of various synthetic organic chemicals through ceramic substrata (n = 3): *(A)* LAS, *(B)* PNP, *(C)* NTA, *(D)* MTTMAC, *(E)* LAE, and *(F)* ST. Internal concentration for all chemicals was 200 mM. All data points shown are mean values (n = 3) of replicate substrata except *B*, which illustrates the reproducibility of the diffusion rates through replicate substrata (▲, ●, ◆).

molecular-weight but charged compound), and MTTMAC (a quaternary ammonium compound) all diffused more readily than LAS (a negatively charged hydrophobic compound) and PNP (a substituted phenol). The results indicate that these chemicals are available to the communities on the outside surface, and the amount released is proportional to the amount added to the dish. It appears that hydrophobicity, molecular structure, and charge regulate diffusion rates.

The diffusion of inorganic chemicals was also measured. As expected, release rates for NO_3 and PO_4 demonstrated dependence on internal concentration. Mean release rates for NO_3 and PO_4, over a 30-day period from an internal concentration of 500 mM, were 40 and 1200 $\mu g/cm^2/day$, respectively. The release of PO_4 was undetectable from internal concentrations of 20 mM. Release rates of NO_3 and PO_4 declined over time and were within the range of previously reported values.[12-15,18] We also detected the release of SO_4 at a rate of 33 $\mu g/cm^2/day$. Since no sulfate salts were added, the likely source was the ceramic substrata and/or the agar. These sources provided SO_4 to the communities from all substrata, including unamended controls.

Exposure Studies

Having established that these various organic compounds were released and available to the outer surface of the ceramic substrata at predictable concentrations, we employed an in situ bioassay system to measure the effect of chemical exposure on periphyton communities. The periphyton was exposed to various concentrations of unlabeled chemicals for 21 days. Exposure of the community resulted in shorter lag times and a greater extent of mineralization than seen in the unexposed controls (Figures 17.2 and 17.3). For unexposed communities, the mean lag-time for LAS was 10 hr, the maximum percentage mineralized was 38%, and the half-life was 76 hr. Those communities previously exposed to LAS degraded the chemical faster (half-life, 40 hr) and to a greater extent (60–70% CO_2) with no appreciable lag period evident (Figure 17.2).

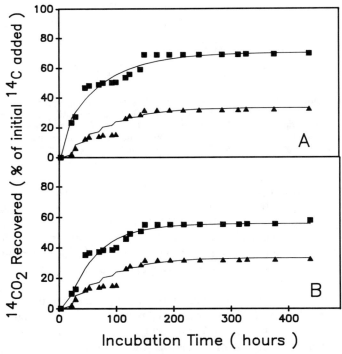

Figure 17.2. Percent of radiolabeled LAS recovered as $^{14}CO_2$ in representative periphyton communities exposed to *(A)* less than 0.1 μg LAS/cm²/day (▲, control; ■, exposed) and *(B)* 1.56 μg LAS/cm²/day (▲, control; ■, exposed). Data points plotted around first-order mineralization curve as predicted by nonlinear regression.

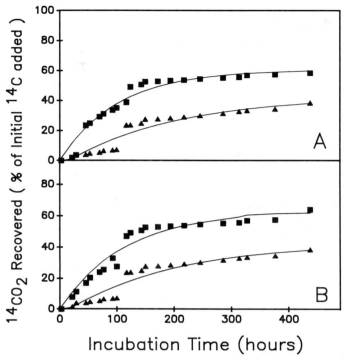

Figure 17.3. Percent of radiolabeled ST recovered as $^{14}CO_2$ in representative periphyton communities exposed to *(A)* 113 μg ST/cm^2/day (▲, control; ■, exposed) and *(B)* 1.13 μg ST/cm^2/day (▲, control; ■, exposed). Data points plotted around first-order mineralization curve as predicted by nonlinear regression.

The mineralization of succinate tartrates yielded similar results. In general, the unexposed communities showed longer lag times and half-lives when compared to those communities that were exposed. Lag time was reduced by 10 hr in those communities that were exposed to ST. The extent of mineralization ranged from 48–55% in all communities. Communities that were exposed to 11 μg/cm^2/day mineralized more, and had a shorter half-life (67 hr), than the unexposed communities (Table 17.1).

LAE degradation by periphyton communities was rapid and extensive. However, exposure to the chemical had little effect on the kinetics of mineralization (Table 17.1). The mean half-life for periphyton communities, both exposed and unexposed to LAE, was 2 days, and approximately 80% was mineralized (Figure 17.4). Previous studies on the biodegradation of LAE have also reported rapid and extensive mineralization of the compound.[23]

To determine if chronic exposure of the periphyton to lower concentrations of a chemical would elicit similar responses in biodegradation kinetics, a second experiment was carried out using linear alkylbenzene sulfonate released at concentrations of ng/cm^2/day. Those communities that were exposed to

Table 17.1. Biodegradation Kinetic Parameters for Periphyton Exposed to Various Synthetic Organic Chemicals

Chemical Exposure (μg/cm^2/day)		Mean Rate Constant (day^{-1})	Mean Lag Time (day^{-1})	Mean Half-Life days	Mean $^{14}CO_2$ Evolved (% of ^{14}C added)
LAE	0.0	0.35 $\pm$ 0.07	0.14 $\pm$ 0.14	2.0	79
	360	0.33 $\pm$ 0.07	0.00	2.1	77
ST	0.0	0.22 $\pm$ 0.12	0.62 $\pm$ 0.33	3.1	40
	11	0.25 $\pm$ 0.02	0.28 $\pm$ 0.07	2.8	55
	113	0.17 $\pm$ 0.09	0.19 $\pm$ 0.19	4.0	50
LAS	0.0	0.22 $\pm$ 0.05	0.37 $\pm$ 0.07	3.2	38
	0.15	0.42 $\pm$ 0.03[a]	0.05 $\pm$ 0.06[a]	1.6[a]	68
	156	0.40[a] $\pm$ 0.01[a]	0.28 $\pm$ 0.04[b]	1.7[a]	60

Note: Mean values (n = 2 to 3) $\pm$ standard deviation.
[a]Significantly different from unexposed control at $p < 0.05$ level.
[b]Significantly different from control at $p < 0.10$ level.

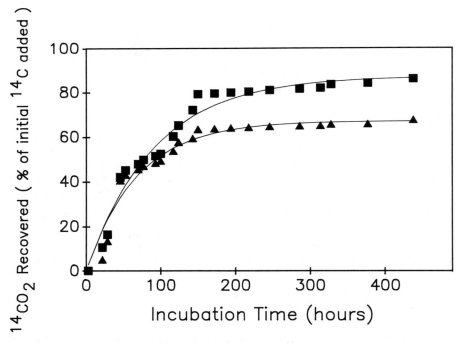

Figure 17.4. Percent of radiolabeled LAE recovered as $^{14}CO_2$ in representative periphyton communities exposed to 365 μg LAE/cm^2/day (▲, control; ■, exposed). Data points plotted around first-order mineralization curve as predicted by nonlinear regression.

Table 17.2. Kinetic Parameters for Periphyton Communities Exposed to Linear Alkylbenzene Sulfonate

LAS Exposure (ng/cm²/day)	Rate Constant (day⁻¹)	Lag Time (day ⁻¹)	Half-Life (days)	¹⁴CO₂ Evolved (% of ¹⁴C added)
0.0	0.14 ± 0.04	0.41 ± 0.07	5.4	50 ± 16
0.15	0.22 ± 0.04	0.40 ± 0.05	3.6	72 ± 4
15	0.20 ± 0.02[a]	0.30 ± 0.04[a]	3.4[a]	82 ± 1
15[b]	0.22 ± 0.02[a]	0.26 ± 0.03[a]	3.2[a]	63 ± 6
150	0.21 ± 0.02[a]	0.29 ± 0.03[a]	3.2[a]	77 ± 10

Note: Mean values (n = 3 to 5) $\pm$ standard deviation.
[a]Significantly different from the unexposed controls at $p < 0.05$ level.
[b]Exposed to 40 μg NO_3/cm²/day.

15–150 ng LAS/cm²/day differed significantly in rate constant, lag time, and half-life from the unexposed controls (Table 17.2). The same communities did not differ statistically with regard to bacterial numbers or dry weight (Table 17.3). Periphyton communities exposed to less than 1 ng/cm²/day exhibited no differences from the unexposed controls. The communities that were exposed to 15 ng LAS/cm²/day in combination with 40 μg NO_3/cm²/day also showed significant differences in rate constants and half-lives when compared to the unexposed controls, but not from those communities exposed to LAS alone.

DISCUSSION

The diffusion rates of organic chemicals through the ceramic substrata were constant, showing only slight decline over an extended time period. As has been demonstrated for inorganic nutrients, the diffusion of organic material was linear, and the amount of chemical influencing the periphyton community could be estimated. Organic chemical release rates did not appear to decline over time as precipitously as reported for inorganic ions.[12,14,17] This may have been due to the characteristics of the organic compounds tested. The organic chemicals are larger molecules and perhaps more interactive with the ceramic and/or the agar than inorganic ions. It is evident, however, that the internal

Table 17.3. Structural Characteristics of Periphyton Communities Exposed to Linear Alkylbenzenes Sulfonate

LAS Exposure (ng/cm²/day)	Dry Weight (mg/cm²)	Bacteria ($\times$ 10⁷ cells/cm²)	Protein (μg/cm²)	Carbohydrate (μg/cm²)
0.0	15.5 ± 2.8	5.31 ± 1.54	588 ± 142	617 ± 181
0.15	16.0 ± 2.7	3.69 ± 1.29	927 ± 529	517 ± 238
15	10.7 ± 1.8	4.95 ± 0.94	588 ± 378	336 ± 254
15[a]	12.1 ± 5.0	6.55 ± 1.54	183 ± 214	259 ± 55[b]
150	9.3 ± 2.8	5.00 ± 0.86	216 ± 72[b]	296 ± 136[b]

Note: Mean values (n = 3 to 5) $\pm$ standard deviation.
[a]Exposed to 40 μg NO_3/cm²/day.
[b]Significantly different from the unexposed controls at $p < 0.01$ level.

chemical concentration can be set far enough over the threshold concentration needed to influence the community (discussed below) as to make the decline in chemical release over time negligible.

The nature of the chemical tested influenced the release rate (Figure 17.1). When the internal concentrations of the chemicals were equal (200 mM), the differences in release rates were likely dependent on molecular structure, molecular weight, hydrophobicity, and charge. The compounds with the highest (LAE) and the lowest (LAS) release rates are similar in molecular weight. The differences in the rate of release can be attributed to the nonionic and hydrophilic nature of LAE. These properties resulted in a less sorptive molecule compared to LAS, which is negatively charged with a hydrophobic alkyl chain.

It has been shown that the prior exposure of bacterial communities to synthetic organic chemicals reduces the lag time before mineralization.[1,2,4,9,24] This study confirms results obtained by other investigators. In addition to shortened lag times, increases in the mineralization rate constants were also observed (Tables 17.1 and 17.2). Explanations for such differences are being explored. Several hypotheses have been offered to explain lag times:

1. the time for microbial populations to grow to a sufficient size to affect the removal of the compound
2. induction or derepression of enzymes necessary for degradation
3. genetic change, i.e., mutation, gene exchange, or rearrangement
4. diauxie patterns of preferential substrate usage

Other work has suggested that an increased number of organisms is responsible for the greater activity.[25-27] Additional explanations that have been suggested include the absence of essential inorganic nutrients, transient inhibitory conditions, predation by protozoa, and the nature of the chemical.[3,9] In our study, physical and chemical parameters were maintained at natural conditions with only the presence of the chemical varied, thereby eliminating other environmental factors as an influence on the acclimation time before mineralization. The release of chemicals in this study was low, on the order of $\mu g/cm^2/$ day, and was likely below the threshold for bacterial growth as a sole substrate.[26,28] We postulate that the cells were induced by the presence of the trace concentrations of the chemical but grew on photosynthate in the periphyton matrix and/or autochthonous dissolved organic carbon in the water column of the stream.

Initial rates of chemical release may influence the types of pioneering organisms that adhere and colonize the substrata. The ceramic substrata tested also provided a selective surface for populations that were resistant to any toxic effects of the compound being released. Further, communities chronically exposed to chemicals may be specialized in the use of that compound for energy and carbon requirements. Such specific heterotrophic assemblages in the community may outcompete other components of the periphyton for nutrients or adherence sites, or use extracellular secretions that may result in a low species diversity.

Rate constants and half-lives varied between the two experiments involving LAS (Tables 17.1 and 17.2). Such variability may be attributed, in part, to seasonal differences. Rate constants were higher and half-lives shorter in those samples colonized in late summer than in those colonized in winter (mid-December). Inorganic NO_3 did not stimulate LAS biodegradation, probably due to the already high concentration of NO_3 found in the water column ($\sim$ 7 mg/L). Inorganic PO_4 likewise had no effect and can be assumed not to have influenced the periphyton communities since the internal concentration used resulted in no detectable release in laboratory diffusion studies (above). Since bacterial density, as well as biomass estimates of protein, carbohydrate, and dry weights, were similar for all exposed and unexposed communities (Table 17.3), our results indicate that some type of acclimated population was present on all substrata that released chemical compound. It is not known if specific degraders capable of mineralizing the diffusing compound were the first to colonize these substrata and reproduced, or if the initial colonizers underwent some type of genetic regulation/deregulation.

Communities exposed to succinate tartrates also demonstrated similar trends of shorter half-lives and lag times, supporting the notion that the heterotrophic component of the epilithic community was influenced by the presence of the chemical. As has been previously demonstrated, LAE is a readily degradable compound, and populations need not acclimate to it in order for biodegradation to occur.[23] Since acclimation by periphyton to some chemicals occurs, rate data must incorporate acclimation time for modeling chemical fate in aquatic systems.[2,3,10,11] Only by determining the lag time for active degradation can estimations of bioremoval be used to enhance the predictability of chemical fate modeling.

The ceramic substrata incubated in situ can serve as a reliable point source of material to study periphyton response to organic and inorganic amendment. Such a system allows acclimation to occur in situ and has potential for use in a variety of studies, including the response to nutrient stimulation,[13,14,18] exploration of diauxie, and toxicity assessments. Such a system can also be used to determine biodegradation kinetics of other synthetic organic compounds in situ without exposing the environment to high concentrations of chemical. In addition to aquatic settings, ceramic substrata may be useful as a point source of chemicals in sediments.

CONCLUSIONS

Several conclusions can be drawn from this study:

1. Organic compounds of various structure and charge diffuse through ceramic substrata.

2. Periphyton communities grown on such diffusing substrata are influenced by the material released.
3. In response to chemical diffusion, first-order biodegradation rates and the extent of mineralization are increased.
4. Lag time preceding mineralization is decreased by the preexposure of communities to those compounds.
5. The in situ bioassay system which capitalizes on point-source diffusion is a useful system to study the response of periphyton communities to synthetic organic chemicals.

ACKNOWLEDGMENTS

This study was funded in part by the Procter and Gamble Company, a grant-in-aid of research awarded by Sigma Xi, and the University of Dayton Research Council. The authors wish to thank Dan Davidson for technical field assistance.

REFERENCES

1. Larson, R. J., and R. M. Ventullo. "Kinetics of Biodegradation of Nitrilotriacetic Acid (NTA) in an Estuarine Environment," *Ecotoxicol. Environ. Safety* 12:166–179 (1986).
2. Lassiter, R. R., R. S. Parrish, and L. A. Burns. "Decomposition by Planktonic and Attached Microorganisms Improves Chemical Fate Models," *Environ. Toxicol. Chem.* 5:29–39 (1986).
3. Linkfield, T. G., J. Suflita., and J. M. Tiedje. "Characterization of the Acclimation Period before Anaerobic Dehalogenation of Halobenzoates," *Appl. Environ. Microbiol.* 55:2773–2778 (1989).
4. Spain, J. C., P. H. Pritchard, and A. W. Bourquin. "Effects of Adaption on Biodegradation Rates in Sediment/Water Cores from Estuarine and Freshwater Environments," *Appl. Environ. Microbiol.* 40:726–734 (1980).
5. Cole, J. J. "Interactions between Bacteria and Algae in Aquatic Ecosystems," *Ann. Rev. Ecol. Syst.* 13:291–314 (1982).
6. Costerton, W. J., K. J. Cheng, G. G. Geesey, T. L. Ladd, J. C. Nickel, M. Dasgupta, and T. J. Marrie. "Bacterial Biofilms in Nature and Disease," *Ann. Rev. Microbiol.* 41:435–464 (1987).
7. Haack, T. K., and G. A. McFeters. "Microbial Dynamics of an Epilithic Mat Community in a High Alpine Stream," *Appl. Environ. Microbiol.* 43:702–707 (1982).
8. Haack, T. K., and G. A. McFeters. "Nutritional Relationships among Microorganisms in an Epilithic Biofilm Community," *Microb. Ecol.* 8:115–126 (1982).
9. Wiggins, B. A., S. H. Jones, and M. Alexander. "Explanations for the Acclimation Period Preceding the Mineralization of Organic Chemicals in Aquatic Environments," *Appl. Environ. Microbiol.* 53:791–796 (1987).
10. Rittman, B. E., and P. L. McCarty. "Model of Steady State Biofilm Kinetics," *Biotechnol. Bioeng.* 22:2343–2357 (1980).

11. Rittman, B. E., and P. L. McCarty. "Evaluation of Steady State Biofilm Kinetics," *Biotechnol. Bioeng.* 22:2359–2373 (1980).

12. Fairchild, G. W., and R. L. Lowe. "Artificial Substrates Which Release Nutrients: Effects on Periphyton and Invertebrate Succession," *Hydrobiologia* 114:29–37 (1984).

13. Fairchild, G. W., R. L. Lowe, and W. B. Richardson. "Algal Periphyton Growth on Nutrient Diffusing Substrates: An In Situ Bioassay," *Ecol.* 66:465–472 (1985).

14. Lowe, R. L., S. W. Golladay, and J. R. Webster. "Periphyton Response to Nutrient Manipulation in Streams Draining Clearcut and Forested Watersheds," *J. N. Am. Benthol. Soc.* 5:221–229 (1986).

15. Munn, M. D., L. L. Osborne, and M. J. Wiley. "Factors Influencing Periphyton Growth in Agricultural Streams of Central Illinois," *Hydrobiologia* 174:89–97 (1989).

16. Larson, R. J. "Kinetic and Ecological Approaches for Predicting Biodegradation Rate of Xenobiotic Organic Chemicals in Natural Ecosystems," *Current Perspectives in Microbial Ecology.* M. J. Klug and C. A. Reddy, Eds. (Washington, DC: American Society for Microbiology, 1984), pp. 677–686.

17. Peterson, B. J., J. E. Hobbie, T. L. Corliss, and K. Kriet. "A Continuous Flow Periphyton Bioassay: Tests of Nutrient Limitation in a Tundra Stream," *Limnol. Oceanogr.* 28:583–591 (1983).

18. Pringle, C. A., and J. A. Bowers. "An In Situ Substratum Fertilization Technique: Diatom Colonization on Nutrient-Enriched, Sand Substrata," *Can. J. Fish. Aquat. Sci.* 41:1247–1251 (1984).

19. Bradford, M. "A Rapid and Sensitive Method for the Quantitation of Microgram Quantities of Protein Utilizing the Principles of Protein Dye Binding," *Anal. Biochem.* 72:248–254 (1976).

20. Strickland, J., and T. Parsons. *A Practical Handbook of Seawater Analysis* (Ottawa: Canada Alger Press Ltd., 1977), pp. 231–234.

21. Hobbie, J., R. Daley, and S. Jasper. "Use of Nuclepore Filters for Counting Bacteria by Fluorescence Microscopy," *Appl. Environ. Microbiol.* 33:1225 (1977).

22. Rohlf, F., and R. Sokal. *Statistical Tables,* 2nd ed. (San Francisco, CA: W. H. Freeman and Co., 1981).

23. Larson, R. J., and I. M. Games. "Biodegradation of Linear Alcohol Ethoxylates in Natural Waters," *Environ. Sci. Technol.* 15:1488–1493 (1981).

24. Shimp, R. J. "Adaptation to Quaternary Ammonium Surfactant in Aquatic Sediment Microcosms," *Environ. Toxicol. Chem.* 8:201–208 (1989).

25. Spain, J. C., and P. A. Van Veld. "Adaptation of Natural Microbial Communities to Degradation of Xenobiotic Compounds: Effects of Concentration, Exposure Time, Inoculum, and Chemical Structure," *Appl. Environ. Microbiol.* 45:428–435 (1983).

26. Van der Kooij, D. A., A. Visser, and W. A. M. Hijnen. "Growth of *Aeromonas hydrophilia* at Low Concentrations of Substrates Added to Tap Water," *Appl. Environ. Microbiol.* 39:1198–1204 (1980).

27. Ventullo, R. M., and R. L. Larson. "Adaptation of Aquatic Microbial Communities to Quaternary Ammonium Compounds," *Appl. Environ. Microbiol.* 51:356–361 (1986).

28. Shehata, T. E., and A. G. Marr. "Effect of Nutrient Concentration on the Growth of *Escherichia coli.*" *J. Bacteriol.* 107:210–216 (1971).

C. Genetic Engineering and Molecular Techniques

Molecular Analysis of Biodegradative Bacterial Populations: Application of Bioluminescence Technology

Gary S. Sayler, J. M. Henry King, Robert Burlage, and Frank Larimer

INTRODUCTION

Subsurface soil contamination and groundwater pollution problems have stimulated considerable attention concerning the potential for in situ bioremediation as an efficient and cost-effective treatment technology. This attention is directed toward utilizing the degradative capacity of bacteria to eliminate specific contaminants from the subsurface environment. Yet, it has been only in the past decade that the occurrence of relatively diverse and viable microbial populations in shallow aquifers[1,2] and deep subsurface materials[3,4] has been demonstrated and fully appreciated.

The potential for in situ bioremediation of subsurface contamination is limited, in a practical sense, to two general approaches: (1) stimulation of degradative activity of indigenous bacterial populations and (2) introduction of nonindigenous microorganisms with known degradative potential.

The first approach assumes that the necessary genetic information encoding specific biodegradative pathways or cometabolic degradation (such as methanotrophic oxidation of trichloroethylene) exists within the subsurface microbial community. The second approach assumes that the necessary genetic information can be introduced and maintained in the subsurface microbial community sufficiently long to accomplish the remediation objectives. In this regard, subsurface bioremediation is no different than other bioremediation practices or biological waste treatment. However, due to the occluded and often remote nature of the contaminants in this environment, the application of reliable engineering strategies for the remediation process and monitoring of the biological activity is difficult. Consequently, methods to enhance the population density and metabolic activity of degradative organisms (whether indigenous or not) are confined to the addition of nutrients and electron acceptors, control of hydraulic flow rates, and optimizing partial pressure of gaseous components (such as O_2 and CH_4) in the system.

The success of such bioremediation efforts ultimately is determined by the genetic capacity for biodegradation. Relatively little work has been done to evaluate the occurrence of known genetic systems mediating biodegradation or to apply molecular biological techniques to evaluate the genetic information or gene products associated with biodegradation in subsurface environments. An objective of this chapter is to summarize current molecular information on the occurrence of bacterial plasmids and specific degradative (catabolic) genes in subsurface microbial communities. A second objective is to demonstrate the development and use of biomolecular techniques such as bioluminescent reporter technology to measure activity of degradative genes in subsurface materials.

PLASMIDS IN SUBSURFACE BACTERIA

Plasmids are extrachromosomal genetic elements existing as closed circular double-stranded DNA molecules. They are relatively small, 0.1–1.0% the size of the bacterial chromosome, but may contain all the genes necessary for complete catabolism of some pollutants, such as toluene, naphthalene, and chlorobiphenyl. While degradative genes are not unique to plasmids, a wide variety of bacterial species maintain plasmids encoding a diversity of degradative activities.[5] In some polluted environments the frequency of bacteria carrying plasmids may approach 50% and is positively correlated with pollution.[6-8]

Three studies have examined the distribution of plasmids in subsurface bacteria: one in shallow aquifers[8] and two in deep subsurface sediments[9,10] (Table 18.1). In these studies, bacterial populations were prevalent in most samples at densities above 1×10^4/g and up to 1×10^8/g, even in deep subsurface core materials. Plasmids were abundant in nearly all sample materials and were found at a significantly higher frequency (by a factor of two) in deep subsurface materials than in shallow aquifer material. It was also noted that the plasmids of many of the deep subsurface bacteria were quite large, often exceeding 400 kb (kilobase pairs), while plasmids from shallow aquifers rarely exceeded 100 kb in size. This may be partly attributed to differences in plasmid isolation techniques.[9] In general, most catabolic plasmids are larger than 50 kb, and the conclusion can be drawn that many of these plasmids are large enough to contain catabolic function.

The presence of DNA sequences related to the toluene catabolic plasmid TOL (117 kb) was examined in all three studies,[8-10] using different forms of DNA hybridization detection. No TOL-related sequences were found in the bacterial populations from shallow aquifers;[8,10] however, seven bacterial isolates were recovered from the deep subsurface that had sequence homology to TOL,[9] four of which appeared to be plasmid associated. Jimenez also detected

Table 18.1. Comparative Plasmid Distributions in Subsurface Bacterial Populations

Sample Type	(n)	Contamination	Depth (m)	Bacterial Density $g^{-1} \times 10^4$	Plasmid Frequency %	Toluene[a] Plasmid	References
Shallow Aquifer	(6)	none	4–6	.5–9.1	3.2	–	Ogunseitan et al.[8]
	(5)	contaminated	7–8.5	5–9.5	17.5	–	
Deep Subsurface	(50)	none	0.2–260	<.001–10,000	37.8	+	Fredrickson et al.[9]
Deep Subsurface	(8)	none	21–420	.1–1,000	nd	+	Jimenez[10]

[a]Presence of DNA homologous to TOL plasmid DNA as determined by either colony, southern, or blot hybridization with TOL plasmid DNA. (nd, not determined) (n, number of samples).

TOL sequences in total DNA extracts from the same deep subsurface materials.[10]

The TOL plasmid has been introduced successfully into shallow aquifer microbial communities under laboratory simulation.[11] A strain of *Pseudomonas putida* harboring the TOL plasmid and an antibiotic resistance plasmid RP4 (60 kb) was maintained up to 8 weeks in aquifer material at cell densities of approximately 1×10^4/g.[11] Using DNA hybridization procedures, cells harboring both of these plasmids could be readily discriminated from the indigenous bacteria in the sample.[11] Similar DNA hybridization techniques were useful for monitoring the population density of indigenous bacterial strains in the aquifer samples.[11,12] In addition, a newly described species, *Pseudomonas geomorphus,* indigenous to the shallow aquifer environment was found to accept and maintain the RP4 plasmid as a result of conjugative matings with *E. coli* strain RC709.[13]

These data provide clear evidence that some subsurface environments may have the genetic potential to degrade environmental contaminants. Furthermore, it is possible to introduce specific degradative genetic information into subsurface bacterial communities and monitor its persistence over extended periods of time using modern molecular techniques. However, there is little evidence to suggest that these plasmids or organisms are active under in situ conditions conducive to bioremediation.

BIOLUMINESCENT REPORTER PLASMIDS

Recently, it has been demonstrated that the genes responsible for bioluminescent light emission from certain marine bacteria can be linked directly to degradative genes on plasmids to act as light-emitting "reporters" of degradative gene activity.[14,15] This new bioluminescent reporter can act as a biosensor to measure both the exposure of a bacteria to a specific chemical and the induction of activity of degradative genes.

This new reporter technology was demonstrated using the naphthalene degradative genes of the naphthalene catabolic plasmid NAH7[16] found in some *P. putida* strains. The NAH7 plasmid is evolutionarily closely related in structure and function to the TOL plasmid. On the NAH7 plasmid, the *nah* catabolic genes occupy a relatively small portion of the 83-kb plasmid (Figure 18.1). The *nah* genes are organized in two regulated clusters, or operons. The first operon, which encodes enzymes of the upper pathway, is responsible for the dioxygenase (*nahA*) mediated oxidation of naphthalene to a *cis*-naphthalene dihydrodiol intermediate and eventually to salicylate, the product of *nahF*. The upper pathway operon is composed of a promoter region where the RNA polymerase binds and begins transcription of the *nahA-F* genes to mRNA. The second, or lower pathway, operon is responsible for the oxidation of salicylate, initiated by *nahG*, to central intermediates in the tricarboxylic acid cycle.

Separating the two operons is the regulatory gene *nahR*, which regulates the

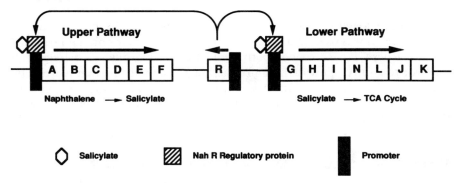

Figure 18.1. Structure and organization of naphthalene catabolic genes of the NAH7 plasmid.

expression of both pathways. In the absence of naphthalene, the protein product of *nahR* binds near the promoter regions for both the upper and lower pathways and does not allow efficient RNA polymerase binding and transcription.[17] In the presence of naphthalene, a small amount of the metabolite salicylate accumulates and binds to the *nahR* gene product, presumably changing its conformational form and allowing the RNA polymerase to transcribe the genes.[16] This salicylate induction results in a high level of gene expression (transcription) and eventual synthesis of the catabolic enzymes.

Two genetic engineering strategies were used to develop bioluminescent reporter plasmids that would respond to naphthalene exposure or salicylate induction with concomitant production of visible light. These strategies are described in Figure 18.2. In both genetic engineering approaches a promoter-

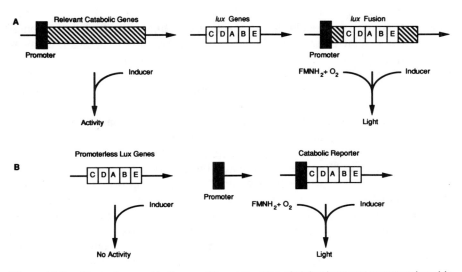

Figure 18.2. Strategies used in the genetic construction of bioluminescent reporter plasmids.

less *lux* gene cassette,[18] derived from the *lux* genes of the marine bacteria *Vibrio fischeri*, was used as the source of structural genes for bioluminescence. The *lux* genes CDABE encode both the luciferase that oxidizes a long-chain aldehyde to a fatty acid with light production and a reductase that recycles the fatty acid to the aldehyde. In these *lux* cassettes the genes are inactive until they are placed under control of a promoter of either *nah* or *sal* operons of the NAH7 plasmid.

SENSING AND QUANTIFICATION OF BIOLUMINESCENCE

An on-line remote sensing detection system was developed to accurately quantify bioluminescence. The sensing system consists of a commercial photomultiplier digital display unit (Oriel, Model 7070) with a photomultiplier tube (model 77340) connected to a flexible liquid light pipe and collimating beam probe.[14,15] Light output (at 490 nm) is converted into amperes from a photoelectric-induced effect. Sampling frequency and data acquisition are controlled by an IBM PS/2 personal computer using custom software. In comparison to conventional bioluminescence assays, such as autoradiography and scintillation counting, the photomultiplier detection system is rapid, sensitive, and permits both on-line and in situ determinations of bioluminescence.

GENETIC CONSTRUCTION OF REPORTER STRAINS

Two reporter strains were constructed for this study, both of which utilize the *lux* genes of *Vibrio fischeri*. In the first strain, the promoter for the upper pathway of the naphthalene plasmid NAH7 was cloned into the pUC18 plasmid using standard molecular genetic techniques (Figure 18.3). Taking advantage of convenient restriction sites in this construction, the promoter was subcloned on a 2.3-kilobase fragment and inserted into the promoterless *lux* plasmid vector, pUCD615. The resulting plasmid, pUTK9, forms a transcriptional fusion between the *nah* promoter and the *lux* structural genes. This fusion plasmid was introduced into *Pseudomonas putida* strain PB2440, which also contained an intact NAH7 plasmid. NAH7 was necessary to provide the *nahR* regulatory gene, and for the ability to grow on naphthalene. This bioluminescence reporter strain has been designated RB1351.

The second reporter strain was created by transposon mutagenesis of a *P. fluorescens* strain 5R, using the promoterless *lux* transposon Tn4431 (Figure 18.4). Strain 5R is an environmental isolate from a manufactured gas plant (MGP) soil and possesses a NAH7 homologous plasmid, pKA1. Tn4431 was introduced into this strain by conjugation with *E. coli* HB101, which contains the transposon on a transmissible plasmid, pUCD623 (Figure 18.4). The resulting transconjugant 5RL, containing the *lux* recombinant plasmid pUTK21, was selected for the tetracycline resistance marker also on the

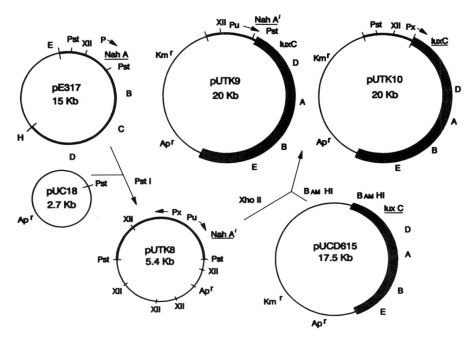

Figure 18.3. Subcloning of the *nah* promoter and construction of pUTK9 and pUTK10. A PstI fragment from pE317 was cloned into the PstI site of pUC18, creating pUTK8. An XhoII fragment of pUTK8 was cloned into the *lux* vector pUCD615 at the BamHI site to create both pUTK9 and pUTK10. P_u, *nah* upper pathway promoter; P_x, promoter in reverse orientation; *XII*, XhoII; *E*, EcoRI; *Ap'*, ampicillin resistance; *Km'*, kanamycin resistance. Arrows show direction of transcription. From Burlage et al.[14]

Tn4431 and the ability to grow on naphthalene. The transposon was shown to have inserted into the *nahG*, as demonstrated by gene probing with appropriate sequences and by the accumulation of salicylate when supplied with naphthalene. Salicylate hydroxylase is the product of the *nahG* gene, and an interruption in this gene prevents the further degradation of salicylate. In order to avoid the accumulation of salicylate, which is the inducer molecular for both the upper and lower pathways, the recombinant plasmid pUTK21 was moved to another environmental *P. fluorescens* strain that was able to degrade salicylate but not naphthalene. The resulting strain, HK44, is able to completely mineralize naphthalene and exhibits the same bioluminescent characteristics as strain 5RL.

LIGHT EMISSION AFTER NAPHTHALENE INDUCTION

In order to determine whether the *lux* constructions described above are responsive to induction by naphthalene, the following experiment was per-

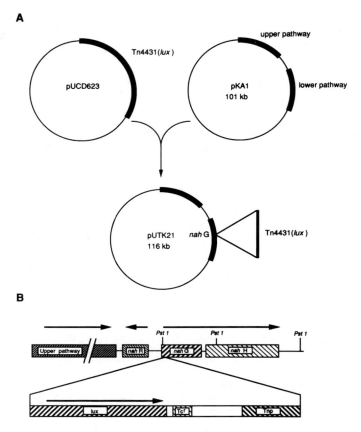

Figure 18.4. Construction of bioluminescent reporter plasmid pUTK21 *(A)* and proposed location of lux transposon *(B)*. From King et al.[15]

formed. Colonies of RB1351 were grown on rich agar medium with antibiotic selection. The colonies were exposed to naphthalene vapor by placing naphthalene crystals on the lid of the plates. Figure 18.5 demonstrates the light output of this strain before and after induction. Light induction is fairly rapid (less than 10 min for maximum response) and very stable for many hours under these conditions. The approximately 20-fold increase in light output compares favorably with the results of other investigators who have studied the expression of the upper pathway operon of NAH7. In the original NAH7 host strain, naphthalene induction results in a 20-fold increase in specific mRNA quantity.[19] Results with the HK44 strain are comparable in both magnitude and response. Control experiments using strains without the *nahR* regulatory gene or without the *nah-lux* fusion would not emit light under any conditions, demonstrating the stringent control of this system (data not shown).

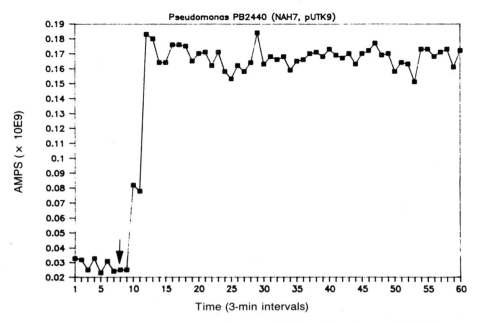

Figure 18.5. Response of RB1351 colonies to naphthalene. *Pseudomonas* RB1351 was grown to mature colonies on LB agar medium. Naphthalene was supplied as vapor from crystals placed on the lid of an inverted plate at time point 8 *(arrow)*. From Burlage et al.[14]

NAPHTHALENE DEGRADATION IS CORRELATED WITH LIGHT PRODUCTION

In order for this strain to qualify as a reporter of genetic expression, it was necessary to correlate the signal (light production) with the relevant phenotype (in this case, naphthalene utilization). This was accomplished with a series of mineralization experiments in which a ^{14}C-labeled naphthalene was added to a culture of RB1351 and then periodically examined for by-products of catabolism. Figure 18.6 shows the course of the catabolic reactions over a period of 3 hr, including the light output during this time. A minimal salts medium was used when naphthalene was the sole carbon and energy source. Under these conditions the growth rate was very slow, and the viable count was unchanged throughout the experiment. As shown in the figure, the degradation of naphthalene proceeds quickly after addition to the culture medium. Light generation also responds rapidly, demonstrating that the promoters controlling light expression and naphthalene degradation are regulated in an identical manner. Subsequent experiments using other media demonstrated that naphthalene utilization was always accompanied by light production, so the responses are correlated.

It was expected that addition of naphthalene to a growing culture in a liquid medium would also result in a rapid bioluminescent response, similar to that

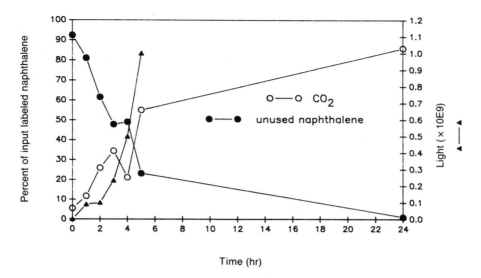

Figure 18.6. Mineralization assay with RB1351. Duplicate vials were incubated with ^{14}C-naphthalene in Basal Salts medium. Fractions of ^{14}C in CO_2 and in unused naphthalene are indicated. Light output was measured immediately before fraction analysis. Cell concentration remained at 3×10^7 throughout the experiment. From Burlage et al.[14]

seen with the colonies described above (Figure 18.5). This was not true. In rich medium, naphthalene crystals were added when the culture was in an exponential rate of growth (log phase). Light generation was approximately 4 hr, until the culture had entered a slower rate of growth, and did not become stable until a further 6 hr had elapsed. Mineralization experiments demonstrated that significant naphthalene utilization was not observed during the exponential phase of growth, but increased substantially during the slower rate of growth.[14] This was an unexpected result and suggests that either a catabolite repression is involved in regulation of this operon, or that the operon is growth-rate regulated. This work shows the potential of the *lux* system for describing genetic expression in a unique and useful manner. Further experiments to define this effect are in progress in this laboratory. The results of these experiments will undoubtedly offer greater insight into the ways in which degradative strains may be utilized for the destruction of contaminants in a bioreactor setup.

DYNAMIC SENSING OF NAPHTHALENE DEGRADATION AND LIGHT OUTPUT

A continuous culture system was employed to determine the dynamic response nature of the bioluminescent reporter strains to periodic naphthalene exposure. The experimental system has been previously described[20] and consists of a 1-L reactor supplied with a dual nutrient feed supply either saturated with naphthalene or containing no naphthalene. An on-line offgas sampling system was used to determine the naphthalene concentration in the gas phase, and the liquid naphthalene concentration in the reactor was calculated using Henry's law.[21] The response of strain HK44 to square wave perturbations in naphthalene exposure with a frequency of 4 hr is shown in Figure 18.7. A 15-min lag was observed in the bioluminescent response to changes in naphthalene exposure. Bioluminescence increased linearly at a rate of 0.39 μamps/hr during the 2-hr naphthalene exposure period, followed by a near-linear reduction in light output during the 2-hr period with no naphthalene. During the naphthalene exposure phase of the feed cycle, the liquid naphthalene concentration in the chemostat increased to a steady-state concentration of between 0.4–0.5 mg/L, and the naphthalene degradation rate remained almost constant. When naphthalene addition to the reactor was ceased, the reactor liquid naphthalene concentration decreased exponentially to 0.1 mg/L. Interestingly,

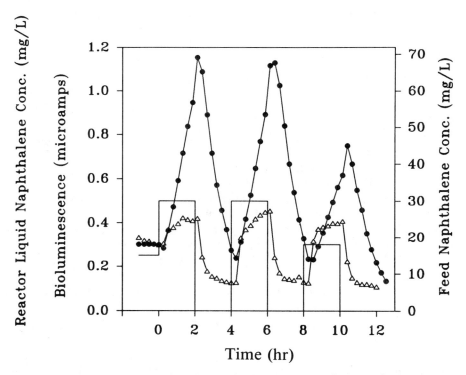

Figure 18.7. Dynamic response of strain HK44 in continuous culture to 4 hr square-wave perturbations in naphthalene. Chemostat operating conditions were as follows: temperature, 25°C; dilution rate, 0.4 hr^{-1}; dual feed system containing a minimal salts medium supplemented with sodium succinate (100 mg/L), yeast extract (100 mg/L), tetracycline (14 mg/L), and naphthalene (to one feed supply only, 30 mg/L). ●, bioluminescence; _____, naphthalene feed concentration; △, reactor liquid naphthalene concentration. From King et al.[15]

in the third perturbation cycle when the feed naphthalene concentration was reduced from 30 to 18 mg, both the rate of increase in bioluminescence (0.26 μamps/hr) and the peak bioluminescence attained were reduced. These data suggest that the rate of increase in bioluminescence may be proportional to the naphthalene degradation rate. By using square wave perturbations ranging in periodicity from 0.5 to 16 hr, bioluminescence was shown to be related to naphthalene exposure. During prolonged continuous naphthalene exposure under steady-state conditions, the level of bioluminescence remained constant.

IN SITU SIMULATIONS

An important application of the bioluminescent reporter technology is for in situ analysis of microbial biodegradative activity. In comparison to conventional activity assays, bioluminescent assays are noninvasive, nondestructive, rapid, and population specific. We have already demonstrated bioluminescence sensing in a chemostat, which may be considered analogous to a waste treatment reactor. However, an alternative application for the technology is for monitoring activity in situ in soils or groundwaters. Remote sensing of bioluminescence in such complex matrices is inherently more problematical than it is in liquid culture systems. Quenching of light by the opaque matrix, particulate interference, and the development of biofilms might all be expected to affect sensitivity and light monitoring. To demonstrate the utility of the bioluminescent reporter technology in such complex matrices, experiments were conducted using stirred batch soil slurries of contaminated and uncontaminated soils. Slurries were prepared by the addition of 10 mL of uninduced HK44 cells (10^9 cells/mL) in phosphate buffered saline to 10 g of soil. The slurries were stirred to provide aeration, and bioluminescence was monitored by placing the liquid light pipe probe into the slurry. Two soil types were used: an uncontaminated Etowah soil obtained from East Tennessee and a soil from an MGP site contaminated with naphthalene (1240 mg/kg) and other polycyclic aromatic hydrocarbons (total PAH concentration, 3227 mg/kg). As expected, no bioluminescence was observed in the uncontaminated Etowah soil used as a control (Figure 18.8). However, bioluminescence indicative of naphthalene exposure and degradation was detected in the MGP soil naturally contaminated with PAH, and when exogenous naphthalene (10 mg) was added to the Etowah control soil (Figure 18.8). Light production in the MGP soil is significant, since it was induced by endogenous naphthalene and this illustrates a further use of such reporter strains, namely, as an assay for the bioavailability of contaminants in environmental matrices.

Additional experiments would be required to correlate the bioluminescence levels reported in Figure 18.8 with actual biodegradative activity levels. In this respect it would be necessary, for example, to conduct various calibration experiments using constitutive light-producing strains in the different soils to

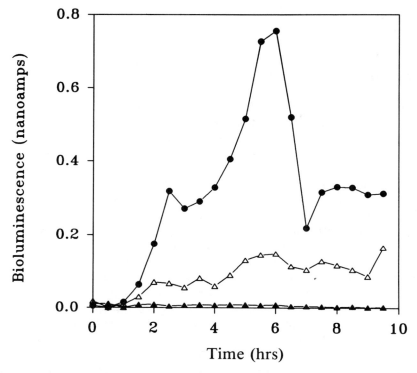

Figure 18.8.   Detection of bioluminescence in stirred batch soil slurries inoculated with uninduced cells of strain HK44. The slurry consisted of 10 g soil and 10 mL of cell suspension (10^9 cells/mL). Etowah soil (uncontaminated), ▲; Etowah soil amended with 10 mg naphthalene, △; MGP soil, ●. From King et al.[15]

determine the relative light-quenching effects of the respective soil matrices. Then from the results of pure culture chemostat studies, it should be possible to convert the in situ response data into actual activity levels. However, the results reported here can be used as a qualitative indicator of activity, and it is possible to hypothesize about the differences observed in the bioluminescent responses of strain HK44 in the two soil types. The rate of increase in light production was greater in the MGP soil than in the Etowah soil amended with exogenous naphthalene, possibly indicating a higher initial biodegradative activity in the former. A number of factors could explain the subsequent transient peak in activity in the MGP soil—for example, exhaustion of bioavailable naphthalene (the inducer of bioluminescence) or a decrease in the survival of the introduced reporter strain. It was hoped that the latter effect could be minimized by using strain HK44, which was originally isolated from an MGP soil. Although it was not performed in these studies, the survival of the bioluminescent reporter strain could be followed by DNA hybridization procedures. In the Etowah soil amended with naphthalene, bioluminescence—

and hence naphthalene biodegradation activity — remained relatively constant for up to 16 hr.

CONCLUSIONS

The successful use of microbial biodegradation processes for in situ remediation of subsurface contamination will require further development of strategies to control the structure and activities of microbial communities. These controls can be used to modulate the activities of indigenous subsurface microorganisms, if they exhibit the genetic potential or physiological capacity for contaminant degradation. Although degradative capacity exists in some surface environments, it may be necessary to enhance such populations or to add nonindigenous organisms to the environment. Based on simulations in the laboratory, bacteria containing degradative (catabolic) plasmids can be introduced and maintained in subsurface materials. Additionally, plasmids may also be introduced to indigenous subsurface microorganisms to deliver catabolic genes into the microbial community.

Regardless of the genetic capacity of subsurface microbial communities for biodegradation, there are still questions concerning maintenance of the functional activity of the organisms in the environment. These questions concern the need to deliver sufficient carbon and energy sources as well as electron acceptors to maintain biochemical activity. There is also the need to develop reliable methods to measure the catabolic activity and response of the degradative organisms to environmental manipulation in remediation practice.

The applications of genetic engineering techniques to develop reporters of biological activity may contribute to the analysis of functional activity in the environment. The development of bioluminescent reporters for catabolic activity in naphthalene degradation is an example of such applications of genetic engineering methods. The *lux* reporter strains developed for sensing degradation have been shown to be stable in batch and continuous culture simulations of environmental treatment. Using remote light sensing techniques, light emission from as few as 10^6 organisms per gram of soil can be detected during naphthalene degradation. The threshold of light detection with current light measuring systems is as low as 10^3 bioluminescent bacteria. It has been demonstrated that light emission is directly correlated with naphthalene degradation. The induction of the light response of the reporter strains is also rapid, occurring in as little as 15 min after exposure to naphthalene. Since light emission is a process that is coupled to intracellular accumulation of naphthalene and biochemical induction of naphthalene degradative genes as well as the *lux* genes, light production is also a direct measure of bioavailability of naphthalene and possibly of other related compounds in environmental matrices. Preliminary evidence has recently been obtained showing that phenanthrene also induces a bioluminescent response (unpublished results).

This exposure to, and bioavailability of, indigenous naphthalene contaminants in MGP soils was clearly demonstrated by addition of the reporter strains to the naturally contaminated soils and the induction of light by this very specific bioassay method.

It is anticipated that such reporter strain technology will find significant use in establishing environmental regimes most conducive to microbial degradative activity, hence bioremediation. In addition, the reporter strain technology may also provide a practical measure of the presence of and exposure to specific chemical contaminants in the subsurface environment. In this regard, the technology will likely have joint use in contributing to optimization of remediation practices as well as environmental toxicological applications in exposure assessment.

ACKNOWLEDGMENTS

This investigation was supported by the U.S. Air Force, Contract #F49620-89-C-0023; U.S. Geological Survey, Office of Water Research, Grant #14-08-0001-G1482; Gas Research Institute, Contract #5087-253-1490; Electric Power Research Institute, Contract #RP-3015-1; and the University of Tennessee, Waste Management Research and Education Institute.

REFERENCES

1. Hirsch, P., and E. Rades-Rohkohl. "Microbial Diversity in a Groundwater Aquifer in Northern Germany," *Dev. Ind. Microbiol.* 24:183–200 (1983).
2. Balkwill, D. L., and W. C. Ghiorse. "Characterization of Subsurface Bacteria Associated with Two Shallow Aquifers in Oklahoma," *Appl. Environ. Microbiol.* 50:580–588 (1985).
3. Chapelle, F. H., J. L. Zelibor, Jr., D. J. Grimes, and L. L. Knobel. "Bacteria in Deep Coastal Plains Sediments in Maryland: A Possible Source of CO_2 to Groundwater," *Water Resour. Res.* 23:1625–1632 (1987).
4. Fliermans, C. B., and D. L. Balkwill. "Microbial Life in Deep Terrestrial Subsurfaces," *Biosci.* 39:370–377 (1989).
5. Sayler, G. S., S. W. Hooper, A. C. Layton, and J. M. Henry King. "Catabolic Plasmids of Environmental and Ecological Significance," *Microbiol. Ecol.* 19:1–20 (1990).
6. Hada, H. S., and R. K. Sizemore. "Incidence of Plasmids in Marine *Vibrio* spp. Isolated from an Oil Field in the Northwestern Gulf of Mexico," *Appl. Environ. Microbiol.* 41:199–202 (1981).
7. Burton, N. F., M. J. Day, and A. T. Bull. "Distribution of Bacterial Plasmids in Clean and Polluted Sites in a South Wales River," *Appl. Environ. Micobiol.* 44:1026–1029 (1982).
8. Ogunseitan, O. A., E. T. Tedford, D. Pacia, K. M. Sirotkin, and G. S. Sayler. "Distribution of Plasmids in Groundwater Bacteria," *J. Ind. Microbiol.* 1:311–317 (1987).
9. Fredrickson, J. K., R. J. Hicks, S. W. Li, and F. J. Brockman. "Plasmid Incidence

in Bacteria from Deep Subsurface Sediments," *Appl. Environ. Microbiol.* 54:2916–2923 (1988).

10. Jimenez, L. E. "Molecular Analysis of Deep Subsurface Bacteria," Westinghouse Savannah River Company Report WSRC RP-1039 (1989).

11. Jain, R. K., G. S. Sayler, J. T. Wilson, L. Houston, and D. Pacia. "Maintenance and Stability of Introduced Genotypes in Groundwater Aquifer Material," *Appl. Environ. Microbiol.* 53:996–1002 (1987).

12. Sayler, G. S., D. Harris, C. Pettigrew, D. Pacia, A. Breen, and K. M. Sirotkin. "Evaluating the Maintenance and Effects of Genetically Engineered Microorganisms," *Dev. Ind. Microbiol.* 27:135–149 (1987).

13. Breen, A., D. A. Stahl, B. Flesher, and G. S. Sayler. "Characterization of *Pseudomonas geomorphus:* A Novel Groundwater Bacterium," *Microbiol. Ecol.* 18:221–233 (1989).

14. Burlage, R. S., G. S. Sayler, and F. Larimer. "Bioluminescent Monitoring of Naphthalene Catabolism Using *nah-lux* Transcriptional Fusions," *J. Bacteriol.* 172:4749–4757 (1990).

15. King, J. M. H., P. M. DiGrazia, B. Applegate, R. Burlage, J. Sanseverino, P. Dunbar, F. Larimer, and G. S. Sayler. "Rapid Sensitive Bioluminescent Reporter Technology for Naphthalene Exposure and Biodegradation," *Science* 249:778–781 (1990).

16. Yen, K.-M., and C. M. Serdar. "Genetics of Naphthalene Catabolism in Pseudomonands," *CRC Critical Reviews in Microbiology* 15:247–267 (1988).

17. Schell, M. A., and E. F. Poser. "Demonstration, Characterization, and Mutational Analysis of NahR Protein Binding to *nah* and *sal* Promoters," *J. Bacteriol.* 171:837–846 (1989).

18. Rogowsky, P. M., T. J. Close, J. A. Chimera, J. J. Shaw, and C. I. Kado. "Regulation of the *vir* Genes of *Agrobacterium tumefaciens* Plasmid pTiC58," *J. Bacteriol.* 169:5101–5112 (1987).

19. Schell, M. A. "Transcriptional Control of the *nah* and *sal* Hydrocarbon-Degradation Operons by the *nahR* Gene Product," *Gene* 36:301–309 (1985).

20. DiGrazia, P. M., J. M. H. King, B. L. Hilton, J. W. Blackburn, P. R. Bienkowski, B. A. Applegate, and G. S. Sayler. "Dynamic Systems Analysis of Naphthalene Biodegradation in a Continuous Soil Slurry Reactor," *Appl. Environ. Microbiol.* (submitted).

21. Truong, K. N., and J. W. Blackburn. "The Stripping of Organic Chemicals in Biological Treatment Processes," *Environ. Prog.* 3:143–152 (1984).

List of Authors

Gina Abbate, Department of Biology, University of Dayton, 300 College Park Drive, Dayton, Ohio 45469–2320

Neal Adrian, The University of Oklahoma, Department of Botany and Microbiology, 770 Van Vleet Oval, Norman, Oklahoma 73019–0245

Robert Burlage, Center for Environmental Biotechnology, Department of Microbiology and the Graduate Program in Ecology, The University of Tennessee, Knoxville, Tennessee 37932

Carl E. Cerniglia, Microbiology Division, National Center for Toxicological Research, Food and Drug Administration, Jefferson, Arkansas 72079

Rita R. Colwell, University of Maryland, Center of Marine Biotechnology, 600 East Lombard Street, Baltimore, Maryland 21202

Miriam Diamond, Institute for Environmental Studies, University of Toronto, Toronto, Ontario M5S 1A4

Elizabeth Edwards, Stanford University, Department of Civil Engineering, Stanford, California 94305–4020

Robert P. Eganhouse, Southern California Coastal Water Research Project, 646 W. Pacific Coast Highway, Long Beach, California 90806

William Eng, Department of Microbiology, University of Tennessee, Knoxville, Tennessee 37996

Hayla E. Evans, Roda Environmental Research, P.O. Box 447, Lakefield, Ontario K0L 2H0

E. Michael Godsy, Stanford University, Department of Civil Engineering, Stanford, California 94305–4020

Richard W. Gossett, Southern California Coastal Water Research Project, 646 W. Pacific Coast Highway, Long Beach, California 90806

Dunja Grbic-Galic, Stanford University, Department of Civil Engineering, Stanford, California 94305–4020

Dorothy D. Hale, Technology Applications, Inc., Environmental Research Laboratory, USEPA, Athens, GA 30613–0801 and Department of Microbiology, University of Georgia, Athens, Georgia 30602

Susan M. Henry, Environmental Sciences Division, Lawrence Livermore National Laboratory, P.O. Box 5507, L-453, Livermore, California 94550

J. M. Henry King, Center for Environmental Biotechnology, Department of Microbiology and the Graduate Program in Ecology, The University of Tennessee, Knoxville, Tennessee 37932

Ivor T. Knight, Department of Biology, James Madison University, Harrisonburg, Virginia 22807

Jussi Kukkonen, University of Joensuu, Department of Biology, P.O.Box 111, SF-80101 Joensuu, Finland

James L. Lake, U.S. Environmental Protection Agency, Environmental Research Laboratory-Narragansett, 27 Tarzwell Drive, Narragansett, Rhode Island 02882

Peter F. Landrum, Great Lakes Research Laboratory, National Oceanographic and Atmospheric Administration, Ann Arbor, Michigan 48105

Frank Larimer, Biology Division, Oak Ridge National Laboratory, Oak Ridge, Tennessee 37831

Henry Lee II, Pacific Ecosystem Branch, Environmental Research Laboratory-Narragansett, U.S. Environmental Protection Agency, Marine Science Center, Newport, Oregon 97365

Donald Mackay, Institute for Environmental Studies, University of Toronto, Toronto, Ontario M5S 1A4

Kevin P. Mayer, U.S. Environmental Protection Agency, Region IX, 75 Hawthorne Street, H-6-4, San Francisco, California 94105

John F. McCarthy, Environmental Sciences Division, Oak Ridge National Laboratory, Building 1505, M.S. 6036, P.O. Box 2008, Oak Ridge, Tennessee 37831–6036

Alan J. Mearns, U.S. National Oceanic and Atmospheric Administration, Ocean Assessments Division-Pacific Office, 7600 Sand Point Way N.E., Seattle, Washington 98115

Aimo Oikari, University of Joensuu, Department of Biology, P.O.Box 111, SF-80101 Joensuu, Finland

Frank A. Osterman, U.S. Environmental Protection Agency, Environmental Research Laboratory-Narragansett, 27 Tarzwell Drive, Narragansett, Rhode Island 02882

Anthony V. Palumbo, Environmental Sciences Division, Oak Ridge National Laboratory, P. O. Box 2008, Oak Ridge, Tennessee 37831

James R. Pratt, School of Forest Resources and Graduate Program in Ecology, Penn State University, University Park, Pennsylvania 16802

Richard J. Pruell, U.S. Environmental Protection Agency, Environmental Research Laboratory-Narragansett, 27 Tarzwell Drive, Narragansett, Rhode Island 02882

K. Ramanand, The University of Oklahoma, Department of Botany and Microbiology, 770 Van Vleet Oval, Norman, Oklahoma 73019-0245

John E. Rogers, Environmental Research Laboratory, USEPA, Athens, GA, 30613-0801, and Department of Microbiology, University of Georgia, Athens, Georgia 30602

Gary S. Sayler, Center for Environmental Biotechnology, Department of Microbiology and the Graduate Program in Ecology, The University of Tennessee, Knoxville, Tennessee 37932

Scott D. Schermerhorn, Department of Biology, University of Dayton, 300 College Park Drive, Dayton, Ohio 45469-2320

Paul M. Sherblom, Mote Marine Laboratory, 1600 Thompson Parkway, Sarasota, FL 34236 (NOTE: Work reported in Chapter 9 was performed when Paul Sherblom was associated with the Environmental Sciences Program, University of Massachusetts at Boston, Boston, MA 02125)

A. Södergren, Department of Ecology, Chemical Ecology/Ecotoxicology, Lund University, S-223 62 Lund, Sweden

Warren Stiver, Institute for Environmental Studies, University of Toronto, Toronto, Ontario M5S 1A4

Gerald W. Strandberg, Chemical Technology Division, Oak Ridge National Laboratory, P. O. Box 2008, Oak Ridge, Tennessee 37831-6227

Joseph M. Suflita, The University of Oklahoma, Department of Botany and Microbiology, 770 Van Vleet Oval, Norman, Oklahoma 73019-0245

Roy M. Ventullo, Department of Biology, University of Dayton, 300 College Park Drive, Dayton, Ohio 45469-2320

Juergen Wiegel, Department of Microbiology, University of Georgia, Athens, Georgia 30602

David R. Young, U.S. Environmental Protection Agency, Environmental Research Laboratory-Narragansett, Pacific Ecosystems Branch, Hatfield Marine Science Center, Newport, Oregon 97365

Index

Absorbance ratio, 114
Acclimation, 12, 283, 293
Accumulation. *See* Bioaccumulation
Acenaphthlene, 251
Acetate, 211
Acetic acid, 251
Acetylene, 258
Acid volatile sulfides (AVS), 85
Acute end points, 6
Acute responses, 26
Adipate, 211
Advection, 57
Aerobic biodegradation, 8, 12, 199
Aerobic dechlorination, 10
Aerobic microbial biotransformation, 254–260
Age-dependent bioaccumulation, 129
Age of ingested sediment, 88
Algae, 283. *See also* Periphyton
Alicyclic compounds, 250. *See also* specific types
Aliphatics, 211, 239, 240, 250. *See also* specific types
Alkaline phosphotase, 34
Alkanes, 149. *See also* specific types
Alkenes, 225. *See also* specific types
Alkylbenzenes. *See* Long-chain linear alkylbenzenes (LABs)
Alkylbenzene sulfonates, 12
 linear. *See* Linear alkylbenzene sulfonates (LAS)
Aluminum, 242
Amberlite XAD resins, 112
Amino acids, 87–88. *See also* specific types
Ammonia, 11, 225, 228, 229, 233–236
Ammonia chloride, 235
Ammonia monooxygenae (AMO), 11
Ammonia oxidizers, 11
AMO. *See* Ammonia monooxygenase
Anaerobic biodegradation, 8, 10, 211, 225, 242

Anaerobic biotransformation, 199–208, 240–253
Anaerobic dechlorinations, 8, 9–10
Anaerobic pond sediments, 211–220
Analysis of variance (ANOVA), 100, 152, 153, 229, 286
Aniline, 250
Animal cultures, 97
ANOVA. *See* Analysis of variance
Anthracene, 95
Aquifer slurries, 199–208
Aquifer solids, 254–255, 256–257
Aroclor 1016, 173, 176
Aroclor 1242, 173, 176, 178, 180, 193
Aroclor 1254, 159, 162, 173, 176, 178, 180, 182, 187, 193
Aromatic compounds, 211, 241, 242, 243. *See also* Aromatic hydrocarbons; specific types
Aromatic hydrocarbons, 149. *See also* Aromatic compounds; specific types
 anaerobic microbial transformation of, 240–253
 biodegradation of, 239, 243, 245
 biotransformation of, 240, 240–253
 heterocyclic, 239, 240, 241, 242
 homocyclic, 239, 240, 241, 242, 244
 oxidation of, 241
 polycyclic. *See* Polycyclic aromatic hydrocarbons (PAHs)
Aromaticity of DOM, 112, 118, 124
Assays, 65–68. *See also* Bioassays; specific types
Assimilation, 74, 86, 88–90
Atrazine, 33–35
AVS. *See* Acid volatile sulfides

Bacteria, 283, 286, 289. *See also* Periphyton; specific types
 acclimation of, 12
 biodegradation of, 69

319